ACT OF FAITH

America's longest running criminal conspiracy
perpetrated against children

Stephen Rubino

DORRANCE
PUBLISHING CO
EST. 1920
PITTSBURGH, PENNSYLVANIA 15238

Dorrance Publishing Co
585 Alpha Drive
Suite 103
Pittsburgh, PA 15238
Visit our website at *www.dorrancebookstore.com*

ISBN: 978-1-6393-7138-9
eISBN: 978-1-6393-7949-1

"We know now that the abuse crisis in the Church is systemic, that it occurs across cultural boundaries, that its principal hallmark is a cover-up enabled by clerical and hierarchical cultures that had, over centuries, become enclaves of privilege and secrecy, a world that saw itself as ontologically different from the rest of humanity and beyond accountability."

~ *National Catholic Reporter* Editorial Staff,
Published May 3, 2019

Dedication

To Helen, our family warrior who provided
the love, grit, and inspiration for me to carry on
for the last thirty-eight years.

....

And to the clients who have passed.
Your memory will be with me forever.

....

And to the memory of Barbara Blaine,
a former client turned colleague and cherished friend.

Contents

PROLOGUE...ix

PART ONE: GENESIS...1
Chapter One: The Wake-Up Call...**3**
Chapter Two: The Abyss...**49**
Chapter Three: A Bit of History...**123**
Chapter Four: A House of Cards...**163**
Chapter Five: I'm Done with Secrets...**207**

PART TWO: REVELATION...235
Chapter Six: The Black Box...**237**
Chapter Seven: You Need to Kill It...**281**
Chapter Eight: Running into The Darkness...**327**

PART THREE: DELIVERANCE...387
Chapter Nine: Trust No One...**389**
Chapter Ten: It's Always About the Money...**447**

EPILOGUE...583
ACKNOWLEDGMENTS...589
AUTHOR'S NOTES...595

Prologue

In 2016, I was finally able to assemble in one place thousands of notes, names and cryptic phrases written on calendars, journals, and other bits of ephemera that I had carted around with me for decades. I confess that it was a bit disconcerting to see thirty-five years of legal practice stuffed into six bankers boxes, stacked in two cardboard pillars on the corner of my desk. With virtually no game plan, I began to fill a working flip chart of topics, events, people, rectangles, squares, circles, lines, and arrows. It was a confounding experience to decipher the Rubik's cube of scribbles I had written on the fly at airports, train stations and Pop Warner football games. I needed to see the unfiltered arc of history that had engaged me since 1985, free from the traditional demands of the attorney client relationship. I concluded that there was no way I could write this book without doing serious violence to the attorney-client privilege and the understandable desire of the abuse survivors to once and for all be free from any further inquiry or examination. Yet there was a numbing sameness in the horror of the stories the survivors and their families recounted to me that needed to be told, away from private mediation sessions, depositions or in open court.

Later that year, I was watching *Spotlight,* the 2016 Oscar winner for Best Picture, in a friend's home in Vero Beach, Florida. I knew many of the characters portrayed in the movie, and it was clear to me that it was a top shelf drama in the genre of *All the President's*

Men. It was also at that moment that I realized I had to move forward with *Act of Faith*. Despite the drama of journalists ripping the scab off of an institutional coverup protecting sexual offenders in the Archdiocese of Boston, another equally compelling story needed to be told. That story would shine light onto the lives of survivors, their families and the constellation of personalities and events that form the DNA of the longest, and some would argue, largest, criminal conspiracy in American history. In the words of one survivor, "This happened to me! It was not a goddamn moral failing, it was a crime against a kid!"

There is no *unringing* the bell of the sexual abuse of a child. The impact is life-long, with survivors attempting to manage the maddening randomness of the reoccurring memories and circumstances of their abuse.

One survivor in particular articulated the problem. "It's like I put all that shit in a black box and put in on the top shelf in my closet. As long as the box stays shut, I'm okay. My problem is I never know when the black box will open and ruin my day."

With some minor exceptions, historical fiction is just that. The writer's imagination and experience are infiltrated by real events, people and places that form the ambience of what it was like to be there and live through the cyclone of emotional chaos. *Act of Faith* is an homage to the survivor community and their families. In a sense, it is a love letter to the human spirit of resilience and coping, as there is little "recovery" within our collective understanding of the word. In the end, the Mark Twain adage resonates. "Truth is indeed stranger than fiction."

PART ONE
GENESIS

CHAPTER ONE

The Wake-Up Call

FEBRUARY 6, 1959, PULLED IN A RIP CURRENT
Giovanni Natale slid his hand to his side pocket and gently tapped the roll of quarters tucked into his work trousers. The celebrated master stone carver glanced at his pocket watch and at precisely 12:30 P.M. strode into the carver's shed. Giovanni's default visage was a stern countenance. The compact man, standing barely over five feet with a weather-worn ruddy complexion, wore a meticulously groomed moustache and a shock of thick, white hair barely marshalled by his traditional flat cap. Giovanni held the respect of every man on the team for no other reason than his raw talent and production.

The nondescript shed was positioned directly behind the exterior wall of the north apse of the nearly finished National Shrine of the Immaculate Conception. The cramped wooden structure was filled with work benches, large perimeter windows and dust-laden drawings. An antediluvian woodstove that had avoided the scrap yard stood in the middle of the room, belching a fine layer of soot over the roof joists that doubled as shelves. Empty bottles of wine and champagne that had celebrated each milestone in the construction project were displayed on the joists.

For the next nine months, the Shrine would be the center of the stone carving universe. The clutch of talented artisans who

3

immigrated to the United States in the 1920s from Western Europe had come in search of a better life and found work as ornamental stone carvers during the heyday of government and church construction projects in the District of Columbia.

As the door closed behind Giovanni, the chairs of seventeen men groaned against the unfinished oak floor as they stood in unison. The men dutifully waited for Giovanni to take his chair. Giovanni caught a glimpse of a faint smile on Joseph Natale's face, the master's first-born son and lead apprentice.

It was the weekly layout meeting where the master carver would translate the original sculptor's vision and architectural renderings for all of the religious iconography that would adorn both the interior and exterior of the Shrine into actual work assignments for the following week. Giovanni had written each man's name and work assignment on a blue sheet of paper. A space was left for the men to sign and hand back the following week. The first blue sheet in the stack was his. It was titled "Master and J. Natale, final carving/polish J. Angel tympanum - south face." The Annunciation tympanum, the large semi-circular decorative carving over the main door that depicted the sacred biblical event, would be Giovanni's last major work.

As he handed out each sheet, a slow roll of grousing and grunts filtered back to the front of the room.

Giovanni turned to his son and snarled. "Are those questions I hear about next week's work?"

Joseph spoke at once. "No, Master, just a concern about the prediction of rain for next week," Joseph said to hoots of laughter, breaking the tension.

"Excellent. Then if there are no actual questions, enjoy the rest of your lunch and let's stay on schedule. The dedication date of this magnificent Shrine has not changed, nor will it. Like your beautiful work, November 20, 1959 is in stone. *Capisci!"*

4

ACT OF FAITH

Giovanni strode down the pedestrian walkway that separated Catholic University's campus from the Shrine with nervous anticipation. Tucking the blueprints from the layout meeting under his arm, he walked south from the north apse toward Michigan Avenue. He wanted to take a final look at the scaffold he and Joseph would be working on the following week and make sure the tympanum had been installed above the main door with the necessary wooden safety frame firmly attached.

As Giovanni walked, he caressed the roll of quarters in his pocket. His mind drifted off to Viggiu, Italy, his boyhood home, and to the woman he had loved for as long as he could remember. He pulled out of the blueprint roll a colored photograph of the plaster cast of John Angel's masterpiece and began his climb to the top of the scaffold.

Giovanni had learned everything he knew about the ancient art from his father in Italy, but his anger for the grand master still burned white hot. There were few, if any, other people in the world who could replicate Angel's masterpiece in stone, and even fewer who possessed the talent to create an original work of art. Giovanni knew that his talent would have been better served as a sculptor of original works, but he had been pushed into the family marriage caste and into the life of a stone carver by tradition and the unyielding demands of his father. While he had gained worldwide recognition as a carver, the title "artist" had eluded Giovanni. Now at the close of his rewarding career, Giovanni was pulled in a rip current between the goodness and talent of his family, and a desire to rekindle the fire of his youth.

A cold breeze whistled through the plastic sheeting covering his workspace. Once on top, he turned his back on the draped carving and surveyed the grand entrance to the Shrine below him, bordered by Michigan Avenue and a host of Catholic seminary and university buildings. He exhaled forcefully, feeling somewhat vindicated in what he had accomplished.

Leaving time to descend the scaffold and get to the payphone in the Shrine cafeteria, Giovanni removed a flat carpenter's pencil lodged under his hat to check the scale of the carving against the photograph. Gently removing the drape to reveal the sculpture, his canvas work jacket bunched at the elbow from the girth of his forearms.

As he studied the carving, he blinked as nerve endings began to fire in his scalp. There was something terribly wrong. What looked acceptable up close would flatten and look horrible below in the eyes, veil and hair of Mary, the main character in the sculpture.

Giovanni let loose a torrent of Italian curses as he processed his mistake. The brass stops on the *maccinetta di punta*, the pointing machine used by all stone carvers to measure exactly how deep to cut into the stone to create the image, had loosened, making the points too shallow. It was a common mistake made by novices doing their first work with the *maccinetta di punta*.

The Master was now forced to confront a life of deceit. Giovanni quickly looked at his work calendar to see when he did his points on the faces depicted in the tympanum. He knew the answer before he actually got to the page in his pocket diary. It had to have been on a Friday. His carefully curated persona was now fully exposed as he stared at the entry for Friday, December 5, 1958.

Giovanni's mood soured. For the last decade, the first and fourth Friday of every month were the days he would feed a roll of quarters plus eight more into the cafeteria's closeted payphone for a joyful three-minute international call to Italy to speak to Josephine Gentilli, not his wife of forty years and not the mother of his three children, but the woman he had yearned for ever since he left Italy.

FEBRUARY 10, 1959, WASHINGTON, D.C.
Oblivious to the shuffling of the Washington Post paperboy and the bitter cold, an overweight feral cat loitered in front of Joseph and Lucy Natale's home. The Natale household, a small two-story

duplex at the corner of 14th and Shepherd Streets, was situated in the Brookland enclave of the city's northeast quadrant, just below the Franciscan Monastery. Joseph and Lucy shared their home with their two children and Lucy's unmarried sister Rosemary. The neighborhood was also known as "Little Rome" due to the dozens of Catholic institutions clustered in this section of the city. Being this close to the lifeblood of the Catholic Church, Lucy could not have picked a better place to live and raise her family.

It was just 4:45 A.M., early even for Joseph, when the noise from the kitchen pried him from a deep sleep.

Out of habit, Joseph reached for his wife, Lucy, but she was gone. Lying in bed and barely awake, the familiar cadence of kitchen work took over Joseph's brain.

The pleasant scent of *Medaglia D'Oro* brewing from the espresso pot mingled with the aroma of root vegetables and herbs sautéing on the stovetop. Joseph's last vestige of sleep gave way to the rhythmic chopping of the chef's knife on the tavola echoing down the hallway.

"Lucy! What the hell are you doing out there?" Joseph shouted.

"It's time to get up, Joe. We have things to do for tonight," Lucy said, unfazed by Joseph's grumpiness.

Lucy Natale was clear-eyed as to the task that lay ahead of her. A multi-course Italian holiday feast was an exercise in detail and sequence, demanding both precise timing and patience. Lucy was dressed for the day's work in a pair of high-waisted garden slacks and a denim shirt knotted at her waist, accentuating her taller than average height. Her thick, shoulder length chestnut hair was pulled back off her face in a ponytail, framing a flawless complexion.

"I know we're having company tonight, but Christ, Lucy, why are you up so early?" Joseph hollered.

"So, tell me you're staying home from work today to cook and I'll come back to bed."

Joseph knew when to keep his mouth shut. Lucy's version of company translated to twenty-five relatives and friends crammed into the front three rooms of the small home. The occasion was *"Martedi Grasso"* or "Fat Tuesday," or, in the annual irreverent toast by the patriarch of the family, Giovanni Natale, "The last decent meal until Easter."

From his bed, Joseph noticed that frost had formed at the corner of his bedroom window. It would be another cold day outside with his father on the scaffold as they carved the Annunciation tympanum at the National Shrine.

Joseph rolled onto his side and pushed his shoulders off the bed, throwing his legs and feet to the floor.

Halfway there, he thought.

Years of carving hard stone and climbing scaffolds had taken their toll on his thirty-eight-year-old body. Joseph remembered his father telling him, "When you lay your head down on your pillow at night, die to the day. Then, when you wake up, you will be refreshed, reborn and filled with inspiration." Neither Joseph's mind nor his body offered much room for inspiration this morning.

He sat on the side of the bed for a moment, taking inventory of the pains in his joints. Slowly, like every other day, he pushed himself off the bed.

Joseph shuffled down the dimly lit hallway, squinting at the light coming from the kitchen.

"Momma, what are you doing here this time of day?" Joseph asked as he lumbered into the kitchen, still trying to get his bearings.

Anna, Joseph's mother who lived next door in the attached duplex, was quick with a retort. "Joseph, really, what does it look like I'm doing? Why don't you carve a statue of me, standing next to the stove frying chicken cutlets? That's what I do —I cook. Fifty years I cook. You and your *grosso culpo* father, you should carve a statue of me!"

"So, Momma, where would we put such a statue from the big shot Master Carver Giovanni Natale? Next to the crucifix?" Joseph chortled.

"Don't start with me this early, Joseph." Anna slapped the counter with her wooden spatula. "Go help Lucy. Make yourself useful! We have the whole family coming tonight!"

Joseph slowly flexed his fingers, eyeing the hot water filling Lucy's large kettle in the sink. Pushing it aside, Joseph held his hands under the running water and waited for his fingers to come to life.

"Let me get a cup of coffee, and I'll get the lunches ready for the kids."

Of course, Joseph knew full well that the next day was Ash Wednesday, the first day of Lent. Lucy was in her element, preparing a grand meal in the heart of the house for the family to enjoy and to mark the beginning of a sacred religious season.

Joseph poured a double shot of espresso from the stove pot and stepped out onto the back porch for a cigarette and silence.

The long inhale from the morning's first Camel settled him. The smoke held in the air. A shadowy, seductive veil surrounded his head, then slowly dissipated into the darkness. The cold air gripped Joseph's body as he pushed his face into the coffee steam for the warmth and the comforting aroma. He chuckled to himself that, at least for the moment, working with his father was easier than dealing with his family life. He took a long drag from his cigarette, finished his coffee and re-entered the arena.

"So, I guess watching *Rawhide* with Frannie is out for tonight?"

"What!" Lucy shrieked.

"Lucy, tonight is Tuesday. Frannie and I watch *Rawhide*, you know, the cowboy show with Clint Eastwood, every Tuesday night at seven-thirty."

Anna started to laugh as she kept her eyes firmly fixed on the tomato paste and garlic sautéing in a huge cast iron skillet that nearly covered the entire stove top.

9

"Momma!" Lucy turned to Anna with fire in her eyes. Turning back to Joseph, Lucy saw his massive arms outstretched and a huge grin on his face. He swallowed her up in an embrace.

"*Ah la mia bellisima!*" He pulled her closer to him and whispered, "My sweet, beautiful wife, tonight we have a party, and tomorrow—Lent—just like Pop always says, we'll suffer like dogs."

Lucy squirmed under his grasp as he planted a big kiss on her lips while reaching for the softness of her backside and a playful squeeze.

"Stop it, Joseph, we're in the kitchen," Lucy said, embarrassed.

"Okay, okay. That's enough, Joseph," Anna snapped. "Get the lunches ready; you're acting *stupido*."

Ignoring the comment, Joseph set about the ritual of crafting a hand tooled chicken cutlet sandwich. It was not a burden. He actually enjoyed making his children their lunches. It was a way he could briefly connect to their lives and still maintain the pace of his carving at the Shrine and meet the daily demands of his own father. He did not want the next generation brought up by a father who had little time for anything other than work. Before he started, he jotted out a note for both lunch bags. "*Today, learn something new, laugh and do something for someone else. All my Love, Poppa.*"

Using the same care he typically reserved for his stone carving, Joseph cut the warm chicken on the bias, leaving uniform one-inch strips, which he gently laid into each roll.

"C'mon, Joseph, get on with it so we can get everything ready for tonight. It's a sandwich. Don't make a project!" Anna howled.

"No, Momma, it's a work of art that looks like a sandwich."

Joseph paused to admire his handiwork. He did agree with Lucy on at least one point. Good food creates good memories.

"Joseph, you going to eat this morning?" Anna asked as she sweated several chopped onions for the tomato gravy.

"No, Momma, I made extra and will eat something later at break."

"That's not breakfast. You need to eat something now."

"I'll be fine. Besides, Poppa called last night and he wants to walk to work today."

"So, let him walk. He must want something," Anna said coldly, cutting Elizabeth's sandwich in quarters.

"Momma, please, it's too early for this," Lucy said.

Giovanni's love affair was with his work and classical music, not with Anna, his children or the rest of the family. While they looked like the quintessential Italian family, and by all accounts were very successful, there was always a distance between Giovanni and everyone else.

Francis, Joseph, and Lucy's only son, was the one exception to this rule. Every night, Giovanni would come over and sit with Francis while he practiced his piano. With his eyes closed and not saying a word, Giovanni would smile and slowly sway his hand to the melodies floating from the keyboard. At the end he would smile, kiss Francis, pronounce, "That sounds *molto bene* Francisco," and leave.

It was a bitter reality that hung silently over the household; Giovanni's family took second position to his world class carving talent. Every week he turned over most of his pay to Anna, didn't seem to have a mistress or gamble or drink to excess, except for two glasses of his homemade grappa on Sunday nights. He was always physically present for family events and celebrations but was never quite there emotionally. Inexplicably, he could go from being a petulant, demanding taskmaster to Joseph at work, to a caring, supportive mentor to Francis as he practiced the piano.

Out of four siblings, Joseph was the only one who followed his father into the ancient craft of stone carving. Joseph's entire adult life had been spent under his father's hyper-critical eye. Exceptional artistic execution would get a simple "not bad." Marginal work or worse, a mistake, would yield an explosive, withering rebuke.

Joseph's enduring childhood image of his father was Giovanni sitting in his chair after dinner, listening to orchestral scores, his eyes closed and waving his hand like a conductor, before turning to his sketchpad and the next day's work. He would fall asleep with his pencil in hand and his pad on his lap.

Joseph walked out on the porch and saw his father was already waiting for him at the bottom of the steps. The two men headed for Michigan Avenue for the thirty-minute walk to the Shrine.

"What's up, Pop? You could have picked a better day to walk you know," Joseph said as he closed his coat against the wind.

"What's wrong? So, it's a little cold; you'll be outside all day. You're not going to freeze. Besides, you got some extra around the belt."

"I know I'll be outside all day, that's the point, Pop. I'm all ears."

MOMMA, WE DON'T HAVE TIME
Still half asleep, Elizabeth pulled her blanket behind her as she padded into the kitchen.

"Good morning, Grandmom. Morning, Mommy, smells really good in here."

Anna smiled and rushed to her granddaughter, giving her a kiss while holding both of her cheeks. "You hungry? Let me fix you something. What do you say?"

"No, I'll just have some cereal," Elizabeth said through the tousled hair covering her face, the blanket wrapped tightly around her slender frame.

"Here, drink some juice. How about some pancakes and syrup and a little fried pancetta?"

"Hmm that sounds good."

"Momma, we don't have time. Let's just do the cereal for the kids, it's too much," Lucy said.

"Get your brother up, Lizzie, and we'll get you both fed and off to school, one, two, three," Anna said, ignoring Lucy.

"Frannie! Grandmom says to get up, she's making breakfast," Elizabeth yelled from the table.

Lucy bit her tongue. She hated when Anna ignored her in her own house as if she were in charge of her children. The fact that two strong women were vying to impress their wills in one 150 square feet of kitchen space, all over what the children would eat for breakfast, was the price Lucy had to pay for having her in-laws next door. On many prior occasions, this battle of wills would end up with an argument about how Anna spoiled the kids and undermined Lucy, culminating in a day or two speaking hiatus between the women.

However, this morning was different. Lucy was aware of how much she needed Anna now and for the next forty-five days until Easter, just like the other times when Lucy's work at the church would take her away from the house. For Anna, church never trumped family.

"Francis, where are you? It's time to eat!" Lucy was startled by the sound of her harshness toward her son, realizing it was more directed at Anna.

Francis bolted into the kitchen half dressed. "I'm here, Momma, don't be mad."

"Honey, I'm not mad. It's just Grandmom, and I have a lot of work to do before tonight's party, that's all. C'mon, sit down and eat."

Anna was gifted in the kitchen, and after decades of cooking six to seven days a week she had developed a creative efficiency matching that of a Michelin starred chef. For Anna, food was a gift of love, to be eaten and understood as a metaphor for life. Humble ingredients mixed together formed an alchemy of sophisticated taste, flavor and texture, always served with her signature catchphrase, "Eat this, it's good for you."

For Anna, and now Lucy, food had become more than a means to sustain the body. It relayed the daily message that "All that matters in life you can learn at the table." Meals were not formal affairs; they were intimate gatherings that subliminally reinforced

13

that the gathering is the point and that as individuals we do matter, and that sharing what we do best is good for one's soul and the souls of others. For Anna, the art of cooking was, at some level, an emotional balm that recast an otherwise loveless marriage into something she could live with.

How better to honor the family unit than to work with passion to create a legacy of love and consistency above station and titles? This was the food culture that Anna Natale lived by. The hollowness of her marriage would at times blunt her enthusiasm, but time and time again she returned to the course for no other reason save the love she saw in the eyes of her grandchildren.

A pancake breakfast was not just a box of Bisquick to which she added milk. It was box batter indulged with a tablespoon of honey, vanilla extract, and scents of cinnamon and nutmeg, grilled on a well cured black skillet, greased with an end piece of prosciutto from Parma. All of this she finished off with a dollop of sweet butter, real wood-fired maple syrup from Vermont and a sprinkling of powdered sugar infused with lemon zest. Even Lucy had to marvel as she joined her children and Anna for an impromptu gourmet feast on a school day morning.

"C'mon, kids, go ahead and eat. Grandmom made you a beautiful breakfast."

Anna reached for their arms from her corner of the table and smiled. "Lucy, do you want me to save the last two for Rosemary?"

"I don't know, I guess. She was out last night so she's probably hung over."

"Was she out with a man?"

"I don't know, Momma, I wasn't with her," Lucy said as she stood up to leave the kitchen. "Call me when the kids come down from washing up," she added as she poured a cup of espresso and excused herself. On the way out she silently reached for the half empty pack of Camels Joseph left for her in the kitchen drawer.

"They're not good for you. You'll get wrinkles around your lips," Anna said as she gathered the dishes from the table.

"I know, Mom, I know." Exasperated, Lucy stepped onto the back porch for a moment of peace. The nicotine instantly helped quiet her thoughts. She glanced at the cup Joseph had left on the rail earlier that morning. Running her finger around the lip of the cup, she thought of the first day she met Joseph on the beach in Ocean City, Maryland. So many things had changed since their carefree days of dating. Lucy married Joseph, but she also married Joseph's family.

With that, reality took hold. She uttered a quick Hail Mary and felt soothed by her unflinching belief that the Mother of God would be at her side for the rest of the day. She had a dinner to cook for twenty-five people with barely ten hours to go. She squeezed a rind of lemon into her coffee, gave it a swirl and slammed down the double shot in one gulp.

Lucy came through the door as her children entered the kitchen. She gathered their lunchboxes on the kitchen table and took out her notepad for the day.

"Okay, let's go through the list."

It was a ritual the children knew by rote.

"You say your morning prayers? Brush your teeth? Have your homework? Frannie, do you have your music book?"

Every question was answered with a well-practiced nod.

"And Francis, before you start your chores this afternoon, you need at least thirty minutes practice on the piano. And remember, tomorrow is Ash Wednesday. You both need to tell me what you will give up before you get your ashes in the morning."

"What did you give up when you were my age, Momma?" Elizabeth asked.

"Lots of things."

"Like what?" Elizabeth pressed.

"Like candy or favorite foods and sometimes I did things that were hard or things I didn't want to do. Like my mother said to me, it was a way to honor Jesus when he went into the desert for forty days of fasting. It's all about sacrifice, Elizabeth. It's like what Francis is going to do between now and Easter."

"What are you doing for Lent, Frannie?" Elizabeth asked.

Lucy answered for him. "Francis is going to memorize the entire Latin Mass for both the altar server and the priest. He'll know both parts," Lucy said proudly.

"Okay, then, that's what I want to do too, Momma. We'll do it together. Me and Frannie."

Francis burst out laughing. "Lizzie, you can't do that, girls can't be altar servers."

"Is that true, Momma?" Elizabeth asked.

"Yes. Only boys are permitted to serve Mass, Elizabeth."

"Why?" Elizabeth was stunned by being excluded solely on the basis of her sex. "Because that's part of God's plan for us. It's like a plan for boys to think about becoming a priest. It's a tradition in the Church. Isn't that right, Frannie?"

Francis left the kitchen to grab his coat, trying to escape the questioning.

"Frannie, are you going to be a priest?" Elizabeth said, loud enough to be heard down the hallway.

Francis walked back into the kitchen. "No, I'm not going to be a priest!"

Lucy struggled to maintain her composure as she forcefully retied the knot in her denim shirt. "Francis, never say never. But for now, you promised Monsignor Ryan you would learn the Mass in Latin, am I right?"

"I know," Francis said. "So, how about if I give up piano practice for Lent, Momma?"

Francis immediately saw his mother's mood darken as a frown formed on her face.

"Would Monsignor Ryan think that was funny, Francis?"

"Monsignor doesn't think anything is funny," Elizabeth said, finishing her last sip of orange juice and taking her glass to the sink.

"Elizabeth, I was not talking to you."

"I know, but he doesn't... And why do we have to give up anything for Lent? Is Poppa giving up anything for Lent?"

Anna's eyebrows arched as she let out a quiet moan, her eyes fixed squarely on the sauté pan of base ingredients for her tomato gravy.

Lucy had had enough. She snapped her kitchen towel on the table, startling her children. "What in the world has gotten into the both of you? We'll talk about this when you get home but understand, this is going to be just like every other Lenten season. We sacrifice as a family for forty-six days because we are honoring Jesus who fasted in the desert for forty days and who died for us on the cross. Do you both understand me?"

"Yes, Mother," Elizabeth replied meekly.

"Francis?"

"Yes, Momma."

"Now pull yourselves together. Get your lunches and *get going,* or you'll be late for school. And Elizabeth, don't go repeating that nonsense about not giving up something for Lent. You'll get in more trouble than you're already in."

Lucy watched her children march to the front of the house and down the steps, overwhelmed by how difficult the morning had already been.

Anna turned the stove off, taking a seat at the kitchen table. "They're just kids, Lucy. Don't let them upset you."

"I know they're kids, Mom, but they know better."

IT'S TIME TO RETIRE

A light breeze cut into Joseph's chest as he walked with his father. He buttoned his coat up to his neck and thrust his hands into his pockets to keep warm.

17

Giovanni did not speak for a whole block. A heavily patinaed leather tool pouch slung over his shoulder rattled and thumped at his hip as he walked.

With each step, Joseph became more aggravated.

"I just went around the bend with my wife at five o'clock this morning. So, like I said, Pop, what's on your mind?"

"You know the points I made on the Annunciation?"

"Sure, on Mr. Angel's tympanum over the south facing main door? That's what we're starting today, right?" Joseph asked.

"Yes. I made some mistakes around Mary's eyes. The points are too shallow, and I need to do them over. The shadow from the eyebrow, her hair, everything will be all wrong if we polish now."

"So what? Better they are too shallow than too deep. We'll do them over and I'll check your measurements, no big deal. Put new marks on it, drill down to the right depth and the shadow will turn out perfect. So, what's up with Grandpa's tool bag? I haven't seen that for twenty years."

"I want to use his violino to do the finish on the drapery, the hair of the angel and Mary's eyes."

"What the hell for? That makes no sense. Pop, once the new points are set, we'll use the air drill. It'll take forever to finish the hair and drapery with a hand drill. Besides, if we take a week to do the finishing on the eyes with a hand drill, we'll be way behind your goddamn schedule."

Seething, Giovanni gritted his teeth. "Joseph, this violino has finished more carvings than you and I have started. Now all of a sudden you too good to run your grandfather's hand drill?"

"No, of course not. But Jesus, Pop, I was thirteen when I stopped hand running the violino for you. What's the point? We need to get this finished. Do you want me to finish for you?"

"No, goddammit, it's mine to finish."

Joseph felt his anger starting to rise. He had always been in his father's shadow and believed his own talent had been overlooked because the entire shop viewed him as Giovanni's apprentice.

"This is my last."

"Last what, Pop? What in the hell are you talking about?"

"I'm going to retire and turn over the Shrine to a new Master to get everything completed for the opening, but I want to finish the Annunciation before I tell anyone."

"All because you made a few goddamn pointing mistakes? Everyone has to do their points over at one time or another."

"It was the mistake of a novice, not a master. The Annunciation has to be right." Giovanni grunted.

"That's the most ridiculous thing I've ever heard. You're the Master Carver for the National Shrine of the Immaculate Conception and we're only eight months away from opening."

"Yeah, yeah, but I'm old and my hands have left me."

"What the hell do you mean your hands have left you? Christ, Pop, your goddamn hands are at the end of your arms, you old fool."

Giovanni had slowed over the last few years, but even at sixty years of age he was in top form as a stone carver. Joseph expected an explosion from his father and a flurry of Italian curses for calling his father a fool, but the master struck an uncharacteristic tone with his apprentice.

"It's my fingers, Joseph. By mid-morning, whether I'm using hand tools or the air drill, they start to go numb. By lunchtime, I just can't feel the tips of my fingers. I cannot carve. My mind knows what to do but the fingers don't work right. If I cannot keep up with everyone in the shop, it's time for me to stop."

Joseph remembered holding his own stiff hands under the hot water at the sink earlier that morning. Even so, it was hard for Joseph to feel any empathy for the man who had emotionally abused him for the last thirty years. The moment passed, and the issue now was pure business. Joseph decided to probe his father's decision.

"Okay, Pop, you're sixty, and you don't think you can carve anymore. You say it's time to retire. I get that, but what the hell are you going to do? You can't listen to classical music all day and come over at night and listen to Frannie play the piano."

"I'm not."

"So, what are you going to do? You damn well can't stay home all day. Momma and you would kill each other in the first week."

"I'm not."

"Pop, you keep saying I'm not, so why don't you stay at least until the Shrine opens in November? We'll do the work together, like we're doing now."

Giovanni looked down at the crosswalk and frowned as they walked up 12th Street to the light.

"What do you say, Pop?"

"I'm the master. You're the apprentice."

"You've made that perfectly clear over the years, Pop."

"So what, Joseph? So fucking what!" Giovanni said, raising his voice again. "So what if I make that clear? The years you have spent at my side have made you better – yes?"

"Yeah, I think so."

"You think so or you know so?" Giovanni bellowed, ignoring the curious glances of the other pedestrians in the crosswalk.

Joseph hated this dynamic. They had nothing in common save the work ahead of them. Joseph was in no mood to argue now. He had a full day ahead of him and *Martedi Grasso* that evening.

"You're right, Pop; you made me a better carver," Joseph said, having gone through this routine before.

"No, you're wrong, like always. You're wrong, Joseph. You made yourself a better carver!"

Joseph was stunned and stopped walking. It was the first genuine compliment his father had paid him in over twenty years.

"What's the matter? Cat got your tongue? C'mon, keep walking or we'll be late. Everybody thinks I name Angelo as master when it's time for me to leave." Giovanni tugged on Joseph's sleeve to move him out of the crosswalk.

"Well, aren't you?"

"No. Keep walking, Joseph. Angelo is a great carver, but all he really wants is the title. Angelo's number one is Angelo. The work should be number one, everything else should be number two. How you say *lecare il culo a qualcuno* in English?"

Joseph started to laugh. "You mean Angelo's a brown noser."

"Yes, brown noser. Angelo is a *grande* brown noser. Angelo thinks I'm old and *stupido* and I don't see what he wants. I talked to the Rector, and he said it's my decision. I told him I want you as next Master Carver for the Shrine. Besides, after all these years how could the Shrine be dedicated without a Natale as the Master Carver?"

Joseph could barely believe his ears. He never thought this day would come. "What about the rest of the shop?"

"I talked to everyone, except Angelo. Between you and him, they picked you. So, I picked you, and the Rector agrees."

"Do you think Angelo will stay? He's a great carver, I would hate to lose him before the opening."

"After I leave, Angelo will be your problem. He'll be pissed off for a few days, but in the end, I think he stay. Being a master means more than being a great carver."

"So, what's next for you?"

"I'm going to finish the Annunciation, I just told you that."

"No, Pop, I meant after you retire."

"I think I'll go back home to Italy. I miss the countryside, the olive harvest, the wine making, the square and the people—all of it. I'll go to the quarry and visit the old-timers. I'll have plenty to do. That's where I want to die."

"Momma will have a fit. She'll never go back to Italy."

"I know she won't. I'm not going to ask her," Giovanni said coldly.

"Pop, you've been married for forty years; you can't just up and leave and go back to Italy. You can never go back. Things change, people die, it's never the same."

"She wasn't my choice."

"Who wasn't your choice?" Joseph asked.

"There was a girl I loved in Viggiu. Your grandfather arranged the marriage between your mother and me. That was it, no questions. That's the way it was back then. Sure, over the years, I've come to care for her…"

"Pop, that's such a load of horseshit. You care for Mom, Pop? That's it? You care for her? After all these years, that's the best you got?"

"I was in love with someone else. I was the one who broke her heart. I was the one who shamed her. I was the one who broke my promise. So, I go back to Viggiu and keep my promise."

"Pop, enough. This is crazy talk. How do you know she's even alive?"

"She's alive. I talked to her last Friday. I called her on the pay phone in the cafeteria."

"Christ, you're serious. What's her name?" Joseph asked, stopping at the corner of 10th and Michigan Avenue.

"Josephine Gentilli. She still lives in Viggiu with her two cats. She never married because of me."

"Wait a minute. You're going to leave your family and your whole life here, to set up house with a sixty-something-year-old woman with two fucking cats that you had some mad teenage crush on? Christ, Pop, you hate cats."

"Joseph, you have no right to talk to me like that."

"I have every right, Pop. You may not like it, but I have every right."

"Maybe, maybe not. We've got work to do now. I'm done talking and you stay silent about all of this until I tell your mother."

The two men walked along the quad between Catholic University's Mullen Library and the east facade of the Shrine.

"When? When do you intend to do all of this?" Joseph asked.

"Couple of months, maybe three."

Joseph felt like his head was about to explode. In the span of thirty minutes, he had been told that he was going to become the Master Carver at the Shrine and that his father was going to blow up the family over some long-lost love. He ticked back over his life's milestones and marveled at how celebrations always seemed to come hand in glove with sorrow. Lucy's passion for the institution of marriage and family was tempered by the omnipresent Catholic orthodoxy. Francis' stillborn twin was never far from Lucy's thoughts. Joseph's own career and love of stone carving was shackled by a maniacal taskmaster seemingly bent on destroying his artistic expression. Today was no different.

Both men checked in with the foreman and proceeded to the foot of the scaffold on the south-facing tympanum.

"Joseph, put all this behind you. It's time to go to work. When you are the master, you leave everything at home. I made a horrible mistake. Now I have to fix it. Nothing comes to this job except your effort to carve like the great masters that went before you. Do you understand?"

"Yeah, Pop, I got it."

Joseph hitched the safety rope to his father and followed him up the scaffold. His grandfather's tool bag clanked against each rung until he reached the top.

"So, we're really going to do this?" Joseph hollered up to his father.

"What?"

"Do the finish detail on a twenty-foot section of relief sculpture with Grandpop's violino?"

"You're not the master yet, Joseph," Giovanni shouted as he tossed down the two ends of the violino string. He looped the midpoint of the string over the free rolling wooden gear on the drill shaft.

Joseph stared at the cord; each end knotted with an ancient, three-inch dowel of walnut. It took him back to when he started at his father's side in Viggiu.

"You remember how to do this? My hand moves on the stone, your pull on the string moves with me. I move, you move. Slow and steady. *Capisce?*"

"I remember, Pop. Let's get going," Joseph said as he pulled his wool cap over his ears.

WE SUFFER LIKE DOGS

It was nearly three o'clock when Lucy began putting the finishing touches on three trays of antipasto. Anna scoured several pots to make room on the stove top. Company would start to arrive in just two hours.

"Momma, I hear the kids; they're right on time. Hello! I hear you – we're in the kitchen. Both of you, grab a tea towel and dry the pots for Grandmom. How was school – good? How was your day, Francis?"

"It was great, Momma. I met our new music teacher. He's going to be the new Music Director at the Shrine and teach at St. Francis and at Campus School. He liked how I played and said he wanted to work with me—maybe even teach me how to play the organ. He said I play beyond my years. I think that means he liked it."

"That's great, Frannie. It does mean he likes your playing. What's his name?"

"I don't know. I don't remember."

"What do you mean you don't remember?" Lucy said as she went to Francis' side to help dry the pots.

"It's Father something."

"So, he's a priest?" Lucy asked.

"Yes. He said he was staying at St. Francis' rectory with Monsignor Ryan."

"Oh, my God. Is his name Father Dolan?"

"Yes, that's it—Father Andy Dolan. He told us to call him Father Andy. How did you know?"

"I met him last month at the Sodality meeting. Monsignor Ryan introduced him, and he's been saying the eleven o'clock Sunday Mass, and guess what?"

"What?"

"Last week I invited Monsignor Ryan and the new priest over for *Martedi Grasso* and they're coming. Maybe you could play something with Father Dolan for everybody tonight."

"Lucy, have you told Joseph priests are coming tonight?" Anna asked as she scoured the last of the pots.

"No, Momma, you know how he gets."

"I know how he gets, that's why I asked," Anna deadpanned.

"I'll handle it."

"Fine, just handle it when I'm not around."

"What do you mean, Momma? How does Poppa get?" Francis asked, eyeing the covered tray of fresh *sfogliatella* pastries on the counter.

"Never mind, Francis. Now off to the parlor and get your piano practice finished. Elizabeth, did you have a good day too?"

"It was okay," Elizabeth said as she flopped into a kitchen chair. "You know, Momma, school is school."

At home Elizabeth was a whirlwind of activity, outgoing, boisterous and very comfortable in her own skin. But outside the home she was a fragile, easily wounded eleven-year-old girl who desperately tried to fit in. Elizabeth hated her curly hair and dark complexion and would beg Lucy every summer to let her color her hair a lighter shade of brown to be more like the other girls at school.

Lucy knew well the power of pre-teenage cliques and struggled to translate the nuances of immigrant assimilation for her children. Italian, for the most part, was abandoned as the language of choice in front of the children. Women, especially Italian women, had to deal with many moth-eaten, sexist stereotypes both inside and outside of the home. It was a complicated dance that took patience and timing, neither of which were Lucy or her daughter's strong suits.

Juxtaposed with Elizabeth's volcanic emotional independence was the detritus of the male dominated Italian social order. It was crushing for Lucy to watch Elizabeth attempt to navigate the palpable ethnic and gender discrimination of the day.

Elizabeth was tall like her mother and naturally gifted with athleticism and speed. She excelled at every sport but was averse to playing on any team reserved only for girls. Not having a physical outlet, she discovered running, where the only competition was between herself and the clock. Running became her safety net. It represented to Elizabeth a level playing field, where there was no pressure to fit in, only to excel against the clock.

Noticing a sadness in Elizabeth's demeanor, Lucy pulled a chair out from the kitchen table and sat next to her. "Elizabeth, what's the matter, honey?"

"It's nothing, Momma."

"Well, it's obviously something," Lucy said as she put her arm around Elizabeth. "So, tell me, what happened today?"

Elizabeth leaned against her mother as Lucy pulled the hair off her daughter's face.

"So, what's wrong?"

"You know Mrs. McGinty?"

"Yes, she's the rectory secretary and she's on the P.T.A."

"Yeah, I guess. Well, anyway, she was a judge at our science fair, and she asked me my name and whether this was my own work."

"And what did you say?"

"I told her my name and said it was all my work."

"Did you have a tone?"

"No, what do you mean?"

"Like the tone you have right now. You know exactly what I mean."

"No, Mother, I didn't have a tone."

"Okay, so then what happened?" Lucy asked, thinking this was just some overwrought preteen drama.

"She said, 'Oh, I must be confused.' Then she said it was very good work for a girl. Then she asked me again if it was my work, and I said yes. Then she asked me if Elizabeth was my middle name because she thought I looked more like a 'Maria,' but to keep up the good work anyway."

"Jesus, Mary, and Joseph, what an Irish *stronzo*," Anna blurted out.

"Momma, please, Lizzie knows more than a few words in Italian," Lucy said.

"Well, she's an asshole, Momma."

"Elizabeth Anne Natale! I know your grandmother just used that word but in my presence you do not curse. It's a sin and I don't appreciate that language, even coming from your grandmother. Now tell me what happened next, without cursing."

"I started to cry, and I just stared at her until she left. Then Sister came over and asked what happened, but I didn't tell her," Elizabeth said as her lip started to quiver.

"Why not?" Lucy coaxed.

"I dunno, Momma, I just didn't want to talk to her," Elizabeth sobbed.

Lucy tried hard to not let her anger get the best of her. She cradled her daughter's face in her hands. "Listen to me, honey, did you get a grade on your project?"

"Sister Angela gave me an A."

"No, Sister did not *give* you an A, you earned that A. That old, starched biddy was just being ignorant. Just ignore her. You did what you were supposed to do, and your teacher thought your effort deserved an A. That's all that matters."

Lucy wished at that very moment that Mrs. McGinty was right in front of her. On any other day Lucy would not have left this alone, but now was not the time to concentrate on Elizabeth and her difficulties with school. Besides, Lucy had bigger fish to fry on the school front for both of her children. Lucy held Elizabeth on her lap until her heaving settled.

"Okay, no more talk of Mrs. McGinty. She's a poop and you got the best of her by getting an A on your project."

"Is that a curse, Momma?" asked Elizabeth.

The tension in the tiny kitchen was split as both women burst into laughter.

"Maybe a little one," Lucy said as she kissed Elizabeth on her cheek.

"Come here, child. Give me a hug," Anna said, swallowing Elizabeth up in her apron. "Eat some *sfogliatella*, your Momma and I made them fresh this morning. I'll make you a chocolate milk. You'll feel better."

Anna moved right behind Elizabeth's ear and whispered, "*Stronzo.*"

Elizabeth giggled and nodded in agreement.

"Lucy, I hear Joseph coming up the steps. I'm going next door to wash up and change," Anna said. "Lizzie, go and get Francis and bring up twenty-five folding chairs from the basement and put them in the living room. Be careful on the steps. Go on now, *andiamo*! Lucy, you tell Joseph about the priests while I'm across the way."

"I told you I'll handle it; he'll be fine."

"We'll see," Anna said, hanging her apron on the porch.

Lucy waited at the kitchen table, formulating her plan. A moment later, she heard Joseph clamoring up the back steps.

"Hey, Lu, come to the back door and bring a towel," he yelled.

Lucy grabbed a large drying towel from the hook and went to the door. "What on earth happened to you? You look like a ghost; you're covered in dust."

"Well, your father-in-law has a weed up his backside and decided that he had to start the finish work on the tympanum with Grandpop's violino."

"I don't understand. Why are you doing that?"

"Lu, you got an hour? Because that's what it would take to explain the bullshit that went down today."

"We don't have an hour, Joseph, and stop cursing in the house. Go back on the porch, we just mopped the kitchen and I don't want that dust all over the floor."

Lucy rushed down the hall to get a robe for Joseph to change into so she could throw his clothes right into the washer.

"Here, put this robe on and take your clothes off."

"Lucy Natale, you surprise me. Outside on the porch, with the kids running around?"

"Very funny, Joe. You know, sometimes you can be a real pain in the ass," Lucy said as she turned to walk back into the kitchen.

"I know but you can be so cute when you're pissed off." Joseph peeked into the dining room. "Good God, look at this spread. You and Momma do all of this since this morning?"

"Yes, from antipasto to homemade desserts."

"Incredible, just incredible. Pop is right. After looking at this spread, we'll suffer like dogs after tonight."

"Joe, I forgot to mention that I invited Monsignor Ryan and the new priest Father Dolan just to stop by," Lucy said as she carefully adjusted the saran wrap over the antipasto platters.

"Jesus, Lucy, why did you do that? Those guys aren't going to just stop by. What you really mean is they're going to stop by, look at all this food, stay for dinner and drink more than they should. I don't get it, Lucy, this is family. Why do you want those priests around? Nobody likes to be on tiptoes when it's just us. And really, you forgot to mention? That's pretty lame for as long as we've been married."

"Well, it might be a bit lame."

"A bit?"

"If you and your brothers and uncles feel uncomfortable around the parish priest it's probably because you're talking about something you shouldn't be. I expect both you and Pop to behave tonight. Besides it looks like the Shrine's new Music Director is teaching music at St. Francis and he really liked how well Frannie plays and wants to work with him."

"So, how many priests are coming?"

"Just Monsignor and the new priest, Father Dolan. He's the new music teacher. You know, he was the priest that said eleven o'clock Mass last Sunday."

"*That's* the guy who's coming to our house for dinner?" Joseph demanded.

"Yeah, Father Dolan, he lives at the rectory with Monsignor Ryan. Why, what's the problem?"

"Well, Lu, let me give you a bulletin. He's a poof."

"He's a what?"

"A poof."

"What's that? I've never heard that word."

"Lu, for Christ's sake, you really do need to get out more. He's a homosexual."

"What do you mean? I mean, how do you know, and don't use that word in this house!"

"You invited him into our house."

"You're being ridiculous, Joseph, and you need to be careful with what you say."

"What? I need to be careful talking to you?"

"Of course not, but if anyone hears that…"

"Hears what?"

"Speaking ill of a priest, you could be excommunicated. Besides, how could you possibly know that?"

"You remember last week, Mario got sick and asked me to pitch in with the collection?"

"Yes, and…?"

"And I had to count the money and turn it over to Father Dolan. Well, he talks really swishy, like he has a rod up his ass. And he wears those shirts where you put those thing-a-ma-bobs in the cuffs."

"Good lord, Joseph, you mean cuff links? And you're saying *I* need to get out more?"

"Yes, and he also paints his nails with that clear shiny stuff you use."

"Joseph, you're being ignorant," Lucy said as Anna walked through the front door.

"Joseph, what are you being ignorant about now?" Anna asked.

"Momma, please, don't encourage him."

"Momma, how many priests have you seen that wear French cuffs and paint their nails?" Joseph asked.

"More than a few, why?" Anna quipped.

"Momma, that wasn't helpful. Let's just drop the whole thing. Joseph, go clean up and you mind your manners tonight. Monsignor and Father Dolan are guests in your home. Treat them as guests. I have to go clean up and change. By the way, your daughter informed me this morning that in her opinion we shouldn't give anything up for Lent. Any idea where she could have gotten such a notion?"

"Nope, but that's an interesting idea. Do you think we should try it this year?"

"I don't think that's funny at all, Joseph. You really want to start with me on the importance of Lent to this family the day before Ash Wednesday?"

"Right, I'll go get cleaned up and help the kids with the chairs."

YOU LOOK LIKE A MILLION BUCKS

Lucy was exhausted and angry. She lingered at the kitchen sink, eyeing her reflection in the window.

My God, she thought. *I look more like the scullery maid than the hostess.* She slipped out of the kitchen to her bedroom to change.

"Momma, is Rosemary home yet?" Lucy yelled from her bedroom.

"I just saw her car pull up," Anna answered.

"When she gets in, ask her to come to my room."

Lucy stared at herself in the vanity mirror next to her dresser and saw glimpses of the young girl on the Ocean City boardwalk, but with her hair pulled back in a tight ponytail, her face looked sad and haggard.

Rosemary knocked and opened her sister's bedroom door.

"What's up, Luce?"

"Can you help me with something?"

"Sure."

"Come in. Close the door. Look at me. Tell me what you see."

"What?" Rosemary said, confused. "Lu, we got a whole house full of people coming over, there's no time for this."

"Don't worry about the company. Tell me what you see."

"You want the truth?"

"I know what the truth is. I want to hear you say it."

Rosemary put her purse and keys on the bed and kicked off her shoes. "Okay, to start with, you're a mess. You look exhausted, you've been on your feet all day, your nails look like they belong to a truck driver, you don't have any makeup on, and you are starting to get crow's feet around your lips from smoking. You have perfect skin that women would die for and you're letting yourself go."

"Goddamn, Rosemary. You're my sister!" Lucy said, making the sign of the cross.

"Well, you said you wanted the truth. Come to think of it, I don't think I've ever heard you curse."

"Yeah, well there's a first time for everything. You make me sound like I look like one of the bag ladies in the Safeway parking lot. And another thing… I can't stand when Anna is right."

"What do you mean?"

"Oh, she catches me sneaking cigarettes and always has a comment about wrinkles."

"That's what old grandmas do, they comment."

"Will you help me with my hair?"

"Sure, but you need more than a hairstyle, Luce. Go wash your face and get out of those ratty clothes."

Rosemary went to Lucy's closet looking for something that said hostess and not kitchen maid. Rosemary flipped through every piece of clothing hanging in Lucy's closet. "No, not this... definitely not this. Jesus, Lu, where do you get your clothes from, the Goodwill? I'm sorry, that was mean. Remember those black velvet v-notched cigarette pants we bought at Garfinkel's two years ago that you never wore? Do you still have them?"

"Well, I have them, but I could never wear them tonight with the priests here and everything," Lucy said.

"Don't kid yourself; they love to look. Do they fit?"

"How do you know the priests like to look?"

"They're men, aren't they? If they're not looking at women, they're trolling for poofs on Capitol Hill. And one other thing... this celibacy stuff is all smoke and mirrors."

"My God, Joseph just used that word fifteen minutes ago. Am I the only adult in this house that didn't know what it meant?"

"What word?"

"Poof!"

"It doesn't matter, Lucy. Do the pants fit?"

"I think they still fit, but they're so tight."

"That's the point, Lucy. You have long legs and a cute butt. Now what about that white blouse we bought? It had a Queen Anne's neckline. Where's that?"

"It's up on the shelf, but it's too much."

"Too much what?"

33

"You know…"

"No, I don't know."

"Too much cleavage," Lucy said.

"Now listen. You're the hostess. You have to stop being a slave to everything else in your life and take care of yourself a little better. You have the best legs in the family, and you have great boobs. Women would die for your figure, and you don't pay any attention to yourself. Now let's get you ready for this party."

Taller than her sister, Rosemary did not share Lucy's utilitarian taste in clothes. Fashion for Rosemary was the antithesis to what was generally accepted for professional women at the time. Partial to high-waisted, tailored pantsuits with wide cuffs in the style of Kate Hepburn, she bristled at the notion that women needed to dress a certain way to be validated for their work. Rosemary, with her cropped salt and pepper hair and emerald green eyes, stepped to the beat of a different drummer and she wanted everyone to know. Cigarettes and whiskey mixed frequently with a salty vocabulary in order to make a point with her male colleagues on Capitol Hill.

Lucy stripped down to her underwear and put the pants and blouse on.

"Now come over here to the mirror," Rosemary said.

Lucy started to blush, and her eyes filled with tears.

"C'mon, Lucy, why are you crying? You look fabulous. Just sit still and let me fix your hair and makeup- and stop with the tears. I can't put makeup on with tears."

Rosemary untied Lucy's ponytail and brushed out her hair. The natural curl fell perfectly at her shoulder. She closed her eyes and leaned back into her sister.

"You used to brush my hair out like this when we were little."

"Yeah, and you were a pain in the ass always telling me how to do it," Rosemary said, laughing.

"I'm your older sister. Who else would I boss around?"

The scalloped blouse revealed just a hint of the fullness of Lucy's breasts. The ever-present tiny gold cross around her neck was the perfect complement.

"Do you have any lipstick and rouge?"

"Why do I need rouge on my face? It's red enough," Lucy said as Rosemary pinched her on the cheek. "Ow, that hurts. The rouge is in the top drawer of my dresser."

"Lipstick?"

"Right here," Lucy said as she slid open the center drawer of her vanity.

Rosemary brushed a little concealer under her sister's eyes and rubbed a hint of rouge on her cheeks as Lucy looked on.

"Okey dokey, you're starting to look like a hostess."

"You don't think I look like a tart?"

"Tarts can't do what you do, sweetie."

"What do you mean?"

"What I mean is you take care of the kids, your husband and your in-laws, you even take care of me. You spend countless hours doing volunteer work at the church. You cook like a first-rate chef, you clean, and you have to put up with Anna's bullshit."

"That's not fair, Rosemary. That's just her way; you know, old school. Plus, she adores the kids."

"But listen to me, Lucy. Somehow you got it in your head that you are the keeper of the family's souls. You do all of this stuff for other people every damn day, then you wake up and do it all over again. Jesus, I don't want to sound like Anna, but am I right?"

"Yes, but…"

"Yes, but nothing. Do you think anyone else in the family would go to this effort to celebrate the day before the Lenten season? What about Mary or Celeste? How about your cousin Connie?"

"No, but it's important. I don't understand why Joe, you, Anna, for all I know my own children are not as…"

"As what?"

"As committed to the Catholic faith."

"You mean as committed to the Catholic faith as you are."

"Well, yes, that's exactly what I mean. After all we're talking about our own eternal salvation."

"Oh, I see, I thought we were fixing you up for a party," Rosemary said as she pulled the stopper from a nearly full bottle of Chanel No. 5 and dabbed it on the back of Lucy's neck.

Lucy smiled at her sister. "So, tell me the truth. You don't worry about your soul?"

"Lucy, I don't want to hurt your feelings, but honestly I give my soul very little thought. I try to live a good life, I love the people who love me, I work hard, try to have some fun and that's about all the time I have. I just think everything else will take care of itself."

"Well, you do believe in God, don't you?"

"Do you believe in God?"

"Of course I do. You don't?"

"Does it matter?"

"Of course it matters, Rosemary."

"Then you have faith, and maybe one day I'll have faith."

"I can hardly believe my ears, Rosemary."

"Lucy, let me tell you a story. I had a date…"

"With a guy?"

"Now who is being mean?"

"I'm sorry, Rose, that was uncalled for. I just want you to meet a nice guy you can settle down with. Go ahead, tell me your story."

"Well, I was out with this guy—gosh, maybe a year ago, and he was a religious history professor at one of the Ivy League schools, I think it was Yale. We got into this discussion about religion."

"I can hardly believe you went out on a date with a guy and were talking about God," Lucy said, laughing.

"No, wait… there's more. So, he asked me, 'How old do you think the world is?' meaning like the earth."

"What did you say?"

"I laughed. I told him I had no idea."

"What did he say?"

"He proceeded to tell me that the earth is about four and a half billion years old. Then he asked me how long I thought humans have been walking around?"

"What did you say?"

"Had no idea," Rosemary giggled.

"You said this was a date? Like a real date?"

"Oh, yeah, this was over dinner at Costin's."

"Well, at least you got a good steak out of it. C'mon, Rose, where is this going?"

"I'll tell you. He said there's scientific evidence that humans have been around for five million years. So, if we've only been walking around for five million years and the earth is four and a half billion years old, where was God during all that time?"

"That's ridiculous," Lucy huffed. "What did you say?"

"I was like, 'what?' I don't think I said anything. Then he said —I'll never forget this— he said, 'Rosemary, religion came to the planet because no one could understand thunder and lightning.'"

"Did you tell him he was talking stupid?"

"No, I didn't."

"Why, for heaven's sake?"

"Because, Lucy, it actually made me think. What if all this God stuff was made up?"

"You sound like Joe. It's not made up and it's not God stuff, and one more thing, you should go to confession – tomorrow."

"It doesn't matter who I sound like, it's how I feel. Now let's finish you up and get you ready for the party. Put your lipstick on and I'll look for a belt and scarf."

"I have a red and white polka dot scarf behind the door."

"Perfect!"

"And grab that patent leather belt on Joe's tie rack. I think that will work."

"Now we're talking. You have any flats?"

"Just the ones I got for this outfit."

"Well, get them out, Lucy; you have a house full of guests to tend to."

Lucy looked at herself in the mirror. Then she looked at Rosemary in the mirror.

"What do you think, Ro?"

"You're the hostess, what do you think?"

Lucy felt the blood rushing to her face. She liked what she saw. "I think the hostess is ready for a dinner party, even if you are a lost soul."

Rosemary put her arms around Lucy and kissed her on the cheek. "I think you look like a million bucks. Don't worry about me or my soul. I'll be fine. And start using that Chanel Joe gave you last Christmas or I'm going to take it."

"Oh, my gosh, I think I hear people already coming in," Lucy said.

"Then it's time for your grand entrance," smiled Rosemary.

Lucy took a deep breath and walked out of the bedroom to greet her guests. She could hear more than a dozen voices talking over each other as a plume of cigarette smoke stabbed the air in the hallway to the kitchen. Francis loaded the record turntable with an eclectic mix of Mozart, Gershwin and rock and roll, and the party was on.

A TOAST TO THE DOGS

"Lu, more people at the door, can you get it? I have my hands full with the drinks," Joseph called from the living room.

Lucy worked her way back to the front door. She could feel Joseph's eyes on her the whole way as she walked past his makeshift bar.

"Looking pretty snazzy, Mrs. Natale."

"Behave yourself, Joseph," she whispered back as she pushed through the crowd to the front door. "Come in, Monsignor, we're so glad you could make it. And Father Dolan, welcome to our home."

"Lucy, I wouldn't miss this event with your family," Ryan said.

Monsignor Cletus Ryan and Father Andrew Dolan presented as a contrast in styles. Ryan, paternal looking with longish red hair, had an air of congeniality to go along with his quick Irish wit. A student of Church history and philosophy, Ryan was a dyed-in-the-wool company man whose allegiance was to Catholic orthodoxy and the hierarchical governance of the Church. Ryan loved to socialize and was not shy about his fondness for sour mash whiskeys. He had come from working class stock in Newark, New Jersey, his father a conductor on the B&O Railroad, his mother a public schoolteacher. He was the youngest of three brothers and thus an ideal candidate for the priesthood in an Irish family.

"Thanks for having me, Mrs. Natale," Father Dolan said.

"Please, it's Lucy. Mrs. Natale is in the kitchen with my father-in-law Giovanni."

"Ah, I see. Well, in this case, it's beauty before age," Dolan said with a wry smile.

The younger priest looked nothing like the older pastor from St. Francis de Sales. Lanky, with a wide brow and high cheekbones, Dolan was impeccably groomed, sporting a finely tailored set of black clerics. His matching double-breasted cashmere topcoat was accessorized with a white silk scarf. A shock of thick blonde hair cascaded out from under his black beret. Dolan's first love was music. In the priesthood, Dolan found a convenient environment where he could fit in and develop his musical talent.

Joseph moved from behind wife. "Father Dolan, let me introduce myself."

"I'm sorry Joseph, I didn't see you," Lucy said. "Father Dolan, this is my husband, Joseph Natale."

Joseph, still annoyed, quickly thrust his hand out to the priest to see what was on the other side. It was soft, like a woman's manicured hand, just as he had expected.

"Father, would you like some wine? White, perhaps, or a soft drink?"

"No thank you, Mr. Natale. I'll wait for dinner."

Joseph glanced at Dolan's hands. "Hey Father, those are some really nice cuff links, where'd you get them?"

"Oh, do you collect cuff links?"

"No, I'm a stone carver at the Shrine. We don't have much use for French cuffs."

Lucy knew what Joseph was up to and quickly moved the priests toward the living room. "Let me fix you and Monsignor a drink while you get something to eat. All the food is in the dining room. How about a Manhattan, beer, red wine... whatever you like."

"Manhattan, Lucy, that sounds great."

"Father Dolan, what will you have?"

"If you have a beer that would be great."

"Joseph, could you get those, please?"

"Sure thing."

Lucy walked Monsignor Ryan into the dining room. "Monsignor, would you bless the food before everyone starts eating and I'll get everyone's attention. Don't forget to mention Anna and then my father-in-law will do his toast. I hope you're not offended, it's a little off color, but he does it every year and the kids get a kick out of it," Lucy whispered to Monsignor.

"Not to worry, Lucy. We're glad to be here with your family."

Lucy walked to the center of the living room to get everyone's attention.

"Everyone, hello! Kids, c'mon. Pop, Momma, could you come into the dining room and bring everyone in? Monsignor's going to give the blessing. Frannie, turn the record player off for just a minute."

"Okay, Momma."

"Go ahead, Monsignor."

Ryan moved to the head of the dining room table and waited for everyone to settle.

"Well, first of all, Lucy and Joseph, I would like to thank you for sharing this wonderful meal to celebrate the beginning of our most solemn observance in the liturgical calendar. It is a period of prayer and penance, a period of sacrifice and reflection. We do these acts, some small and some big, to acknowledge that Jesus did indeed die on the cross for our sins and ascended to heaven to take his rightful place, next to God the Father. So, Father Dolan, would you please offer the blessing?"

"Of course. Everyone, please, join hands," Dolan continued as several of the younger children crawled under the table. Dolan spread his arms and faced the entire assembly, intoning a traditional Catholic blessing. At the conclusion, Dolan turned to Giovanni. "I am told by Monsignor Ryan that you have a toast prepared?"

"I do, Father, thank you. It's good to see everyone here, and on time for a change."

Anna stood there expressionless, the only one who didn't laugh. Giovanni had a curious knack for making most people laugh when he insulted them. Everyone knew that his bedtime was 8:30 P.M., and on more than one occasion, he had asked people to leave because a celebration had lasted past the appointed hour. This had been a source of many heated arguments in both houses, so it came as quite a shock to both Anna and Lucy when Giovanni modified his annual 'toast to the dogs.'

"I know you think I'm going to give my normal toast," Giovanni continued as the children giggled in anticipation. "But tonight is a little different and a little special. I'm going to work for another two or three months, and then retire. A new Master Carver will be announced. The new Master Carver for the Shrine will be..." Giovanni paused for dramatic effect. "My son, Joseph Natale!"

The room burst into cheers for Joseph while Anna blanched, frozen by the news that her life was about to change.

"Joseph was picked by the carvers in the shop, the Rector and most importantly, by me. Now I want everyone to raise their glasses and salute my wife Anna and my daughter-in-law Lucy for such a fine meal. Tonight, just this one time, if you stay past eight-thirty, if it's okay," Giovanni said, wagging his finger at the family. "So, now my toast. Tonight, we have a party, the last decent meal until Easter." The younger children crowded around his feet. Then, in his most dramatic, jowl-shaking growl, he delivered his famous line. "Tomorrow, until Easter, we suffer like dogs," Giovanni said, letting out a piercing wolf howl to the delight of everyone.

This year Giovanni's toast shocked Lucy on many levels. Her husband was going to be the Master Carver at the Shrine, Giovanni had given his wife an unprecedented public compliment, and Monsignor Ryan and Father Dolan had belly laughed at Giovanni's toast to the "dogs."

She walked behind Joseph, lightly kissed him on the neck, and whispered, "Congratulations! I guess you did have some news today. I'm so happy for you; this is what you always wanted. Did you know it was coming or were you surprised?"

"Shocked is more like it, but you haven't heard the half of it."

"What do you mean?"

"I'll tell you later."

"Is it bad?"

"Lucy, I actually don't know how to answer that."

Lucy pivoted away from Joseph to attend to her guests in what had become a very familiar routine. The children were outside playing tag or screaming in the dark basement while playing hide-and-go-seek. Francis was playing duets on the piano with Father Dolan and Joseph was circulating the rooms emptying ashtrays and refilling drinks. The men had congregated on the front porch to smoke cigars, drink grappa, and repeat the same stories they had told for the last twenty years.

The women did what they always did. Anna sat with her sister at the kitchen table, speaking mostly in Italian and giving instructions to the other women as to where things should be put away. The dishes got washed and dried, the leftovers got wrapped and sent to various homes, and through a blue haze of cigarette smoke the gaggle talked over each other, oftentimes erupting into shrieks of laughter.

"Momma, I can't thank you enough for all your help. I could not have been ready without you."

Anna pulled at Lucy's shoulder and kissed her on the cheek. "It's what we do, Lu, year after year."

"How well I know, Momma; how well I know."

"By the way, you look pretty tonight."

"Thank you, Momma, that's really sweet." Lucy was struck by the old woman's thoughtfulness and sincerity. "I was a little worried it was too…"

"Too what? Too saucy with the priests around?"

"Yes, exactly, but I was tired of looking like the maid."

Anna got up from the table. "Think about it this way, my dear, where would Italian cooking be without red pepper? Besides, for the next forty days, all they will have to look at in the pews will be the old-timers like me with big cabooses and boobs down to their waists."

"Momma, I think you're beautiful."

"Yeah, and I think you're going blind," Anna replied as both women laughed and embraced.

"So, what do you think about Pop retiring?"

"I think I have a headache. I'm going to bed. When I wake up, if God spares, it'll have been a bad dream. Lu, just tell Pop I was on my feet all day, if he even asks," Anna said as she grabbed her coat and left.

"Wow, I think Anna's really upset. What are you going to do with Gio around twenty-four hours a day?" Rosemary asked as she poured a good amount of anisette into her espresso.

"Send him to work with you to stuff envelopes," Lucy said laughing.

"Not a chance of that, big sister. On that note, I'm off to bed. I have an early morning. And seriously, Lu, spectacular dinner."

"Thanks, honey, and thanks for the makeover. Don't forget your ashes tomorrow. Maybe after our conversation you should double up."

"I'm not sure a double brand of black soot on my forehead will go with my outfit tomorrow. I think I have a better idea; you should get your ashes in that outfit; you'll be the talk of the parish."

Lucy blushed and waved her up the stairs. "You're incorrigible. Go to bed, Ro!"

I'M NOT SLEEPY EITHER

"Okay, okay, I gave you an extra hour," Giovanni announced at nine-thirty. "Everyone should go home because tomorrow's a workday. The furniture and chairs can wait until tomorrow." Giovanni grabbed his coat and walked to Joseph and Lucy, kissing them both on the cheek. "I'll see you tomorrow."

Michael, Joseph's brother, and Mary offered to drive the slightly inebriated priests back to the parish and by nine forty-five the house was quiet.

"Joe, could you open a couple of windows to get the smoke out?" Lucy asked. "Those cigars stink."

"It's pretty chilly."

"The air feels good, just for a little bit."

Joseph opened the front window and the kitchen window to get some circulation.

"Do you have any cigarettes left in the drawer?"

"Yes."

"Get me one and I'll get my coat."

"Do you want some grappa?"

"Good Lord no, but if you have any of Pop's rye left I'll take a shot of that."

The couple settled into canvas chairs on the small back porch with their nightcaps.

"Here's to you, Lu; great night."

"And here's to you, Joseph, on your promotion to Master Carver. Bottoms up!" Lucy felt the warmth of the whiskey filling her chest.

"You know, Lu, that Dolan fellow, I don't like him. I don't like the way he spends all his time hanging around the kids, playing piano and those stupid card tricks. I even overheard him asking Lizzie about school. Don't you think that's weird? At least Ryan was out on the porch doing shots with my brothers."

"Yeah, and you got him drunk. Father Dolan was just being polite. He's a young priest trying to fit in at the parish. He's not going to get drunk in front of his Monsignor. What are you trying to say?"

"What I'm trying to say is that it's not normal for a grown man at a party with a houseful of adults to want to spend time hanging around the kids the whole time. It's not normal."

"You just don't like him because you think he's, what did you call him?"

"A poof. You tell me, Miss Catholic USA, if he is a homosexual how does that happen in the priesthood? Can you answer that?"

"Joe, please, no more tonight. Between you and Rosemary I can't take anymore tonight. Just trust me on this. I will keep an eye on the kids around Father Dolan, but honestly, I think you're overreacting. Not everybody knows the quarterback of the Redskins and does shots with the boys out on the porch. Joseph, I talked to Rosemary tonight so let me ask you…"

"Ask whatever you want, honey," Joseph said.

"How is it possible that you don't have more time for God?"

"But I do, I go to church every day. I go to the Shrine and sometimes I go to the Cathedral."

"Joseph, be serious. I'm worried about your soul."

"My soul is fine, Lu. I married you, didn't I?"

"I give up. So, what's the rest of the story with today and your father?"

"What story?" Joseph asked, distracted by Lucy's outfit.

"You said I didn't know the half of it at dinner and you would tell me later. It's later. So, what happened?"

"I thought we were talking about Dolan, Rosemary and my soul."

"We're done talking about Father Dolan and Rosemary. She basically said she has no time for God, and I'm really done talking about your soul. I love you both but really, I can't get my head around all of this. So, what's the rest of the story?"

"Well, I'm not so sure we should be done talking about Dolan, but to make a long story short, the reason Pop is quitting is that his hands go numb after an hour or two because of the vibration of the air tools. I've heard about that happening before. That's why he wants to finish the tympanum with Grandpop's violino, there's no vibration. It'll take at least two months to finish. I actually started to feel sorry for the old S.O.B."

"Geez, that's pretty harsh, Joe. So, why don't you just finish it for him?"

"I told him that and he started screaming at me. He has it in his mind that this is his last work. He wants to go out his way, on his own terms."

"Momma's worried, she's thinking it's a bad dream."

"Well, Lu, it is a bad dream. Pop wants to go back to Italy and live out his years with a woman he said he was in love with until he was forced to marry Momma."

"Good God. You're not talking about Josephine Gentilli, are you?"

"How did you know her name?"

"You know, men are so stupid. Momma knew about Josephine from the beginning."

"So, why did she marry Pop and have all of us kids?"

"Because that's the way it was back then, it was all arranged by their fathers. I really think that after she started having all of your brothers and sisters, she thought Pop would come around and forget about Josephine and settle into his new life in the States. What did you say to him?"

"I got pissed off. Told him he was an old fool and that he was going to blow up the family over some long-lost teenage love."

"How'd that go?"

"Not good, he told me I had no right to talk to him like that and to basically shut up and keep quiet about it."

"You know, Josephine never married."

"Jesus, Lu, you know the whole story!"

"Momma told me last year. She still hears from her friends in Viggiu. Joe, do you really think he'll do it?"

Joseph looked directly into Lucy's eyes, her face softly lit by the streetlight in the alley.

"Lu, at this moment, to be honest, I don't know what to think. You want another shot?" Joseph asked with a twinkle in his eye.

"You trying to take advantage of me?"

"Absolutely, you look gorgeous tonight," Joseph said as he leaned over, kissing Lucy's hand.

"If I have another shot, you'll have to carry me to bed. Besides, I was tired of looking like an old rag."

Joseph lightly kissed her on the lips. "I like carrying you to bed. And Lu, you've never looked like an old rag."

Lucy flicked a cigarette out of the pack of Camels. "No more shots, but I will have one more cigarette, then I have to put a lid on today. There's a lot going on tomorrow at church. I know you're really busy at work, but could you run the kids up to St. Francis to get their ashes before you leave for work? It opens at six-thirty, and I'll make sure they're ready to go when you are."

Joseph's first impulse was to say no, but today had been hard enough without going to bed with hurt feelings or an argument. Lucy took a long drag from her cigarette.

"Sure. I can take them."

"Thanks, that's a big help. You coming to bed?"

"No, I'm going to sit out for a while. I'm not sleepy."

Lucy slipped out of her coat and stood up to face Joseph. She leaned over and nuzzled against Joseph's ear, whispering, "Well, Joseph Natale, the new Master Carver at the Shrine, I'm not very sleepy either."

CHAPTER TWO

The Abyss

LENT, FEBRUARY 27, 1959

Giovanni sat at the kitchen table sipping an after-dinner glass of his grappa while he thumbed through the headlines of the Evening Star newspaper. Anna stood at the sink staring out the kitchen window. Her hands hovered over the dinner dishes as hot water and soap suds flooded the bowl.

Word had come to Anna from friends in her hometown that Josephine Gentilli, Giovanni's first love, was having her entire apartment repainted. It had been three weeks since *Martedi Grasso* and nothing more had been said about Giovanni's retirement.

She ticked off the decades of memories in her mind as she methodically moved the dishes through the soapy water, through the rinse and then to the drying rack. The births of their children, their grandchildren, the countless family celebrations and the summers in Ocean City all collided with anger, pride and embarrassment.

"Do you have something you want to tell me?" she asked, still staring out the kitchen window.

"No. Why, am I supposed to?"

"Gio, when will you leave the Shrine?" She continued with the dishes, still looking out the window above the sink.

"Not sure. I'll know when it's time. Probably when the lead architect and sculptor sign off on the Annunciation."

Anna had had enough. "Are you going to embarrass me and just leave for Italy and Josephine, or do you want a divorce?"

Giovanni slammed the newspaper down on the table. "What are you talking about, Anna? Who said anything about Josephine?"

"Gio, don't insult me. Viggiu isn't that far away. People talk."

"You mean people gossip. Listen to me, I've never been unfaithful to you, I've never dishonored you. I did what both our fathers asked of me and of you!"

"Gio, you make it sound like I had a choice," Anna snapped. "After forty years you at least owe me some answers."

"I do owe you some answers. When I have some answers, I'll tell you. Let's just leave it at that."

"No! Let's not just leave it at that!" Anna yelled, dropping a dish in the flooded sink.

Surprised, Giovanni got up and pulled out the opposite kitchen chair. "Dry your hands. Forget about the dishes. Come over here and sit."

Anna took her apron off and threw it on the counter, settling into the chair across from Giovanni. Her face started to flush.

"You remember what you said when we got married?"

"Yes, and I should have never said it."

"What did you say, Anna?" Giovanni said, leaning across the table and looking directly at her.

"I said I knew you loved Josephine."

"And? What else did you say, Anna?"

"I said we'll give it a try and if it doesn't work, we'll part as friends."

"Those were your words, Anna, not mine. Now, no more tonight. We'll talk again, okay? I'm going next door to listen to Frannie practice."

"You listen to me, old man. If you leave, we will not be friends."

"Yeah, yeah," Giovanni muttered as he grabbed his jacket and headed for the back porch.

"Hello, anybody home?"

Lucy glanced at the clock, somewhat deflated. Her husband and children had just sat down for a quiet Lenten dinner. She had gone out of her way to set the table with the family china and make Frannie's favorite dessert.

Tomorrow was the oral exam for the altar boys who were memorizing the Latin responses, and Lucy wanted Francis to get the highest score. That would mean he would be both the first altar server and have his pick of the scheduled Masses. She decided it wasn't worth an argument.

"Pop, we're in the dining room, we're just sitting down. Pull up a chair. Frannie, make room for your grandfather."

"No, no, I just finished dinner. You eat, I'll wait in the living room. Frannie, you going to play tonight?"

"Yes, Grandpop."

"By the way, Joseph, did you tell Lucy what you did today?" Giovanni smiled at Lucy across the table. "Joseph was the master and Giovanni was the apprentice."

"What do you mean, Joseph?" Lucy said, momentarily forgetting her angst over her dinner plans going awry.

"Pop pulled the cord on Grandpop's violino while I did the carving for the shadowing on the drape of the Annunciation."

"I would have liked to have had a picture of that," Lucy chuckled.

"And what?" Giovanni said, taunting Joseph. "What else happened?"

"And it turned out perfect."

"Hear that, Lucy? Perfect!" Giovanni thundered, stomping his foot under the table.

"Yes, Pop, it was a beautiful thing." Joseph smiled, removing the tinfoil covering the main dish on the table.

"What's that pink stuff, Momma?"

"Elizabeth, please, it's not pink stuff, they're salmon cakes. Take two and wait for the peas and potatoes to come around."

"Do we have any pasta or peanut butter and jelly?"

"No. I prepared salmon for tonight's dinner."

"Lizzie, just put some ketchup on them, ketchup works for stuff like this," Francis said.

"Lizzie, Francis, now listen up. Your mother took the time to make you dinner. There's salad, some of Catania's fresh bread and some provolone and olives on the table. It is Lent. Lent is important to your mother, so that makes Lent important to all of us. Now we're all going to eat the dinner your mother prepared. Elizabeth, you can put ketchup on the salmon cakes if you like, but there's no pasta, and there's no peanut butter. Are we all clear?"

"Yes, Poppa," said Francis.

"Elizabeth?"

"Yes, Poppa."

"Thank you, Joseph. That was nice of you to say," Lucy smiled.

Joseph winked at Lucy, and for just a moment they seemed to be on the same page when it came to religion.

Giovanni settled into the chair next to the piano. He took out his sketchpad to plan the next day's work for the shadow line on the last two panels of the Annunciation's drapery. Giovanni covered his face with his hands and slipped into his mind's eye, envisioning where the setting sun would hit the last two panels of drapery. For twenty minutes, he worried that the last two would not have any contrast in the late afternoon sunlight because of the fullness of the previous fold in the stone.

"Joseph, I have the solution. Francisco! Are you coming?"

"Hold on, Pop. We're clearing the table."

"Go ahead, Joseph, talk to your father and Frannie, start your piano practice. Twenty minutes tonight, then you and Lizzie can finish up any trouble spots on your responses, then to bed. You need a good night's sleep. Elizabeth and I will clear the table and clean up."

"So, what's the solution you've come up with, Pop?" Joseph asked as he took his place across from the piano.

"Come here and look at this sketch. Remember when I was standing below you around three this afternoon, you know the way the sun hit the drapery?"

"Yeah, and the shadow got lost in the next fold, I remember."

"What if you scale down the right side of the fold just a little? Look here, see this shading on the right side of the fold?"

"Yep, I see it."

"And decrease the depth of the next crease in the fold a little more each time until the end?"

"So, you get a decreasing depth of field moving from left to right as the sun sets. Like a horizontal cascade of light washing over the folds in the drapery."

"Exactly!"

"Bravo, Pop. That's a pretty damn good idea. So, do you think you can manage that with your hands? Because we can't redo the points now."

"It's for a younger man. I'll run the drill and follow, like today."

Elizabeth stood in the middle of the kitchen with her arms folded across her chest. "Momma, Frannie should help too, it's not fair."

"Elizabeth, grab those dishes and put them in the sink. I want to show you something."

Elizabeth was not at all happy, and it showed as she stomped across the kitchen. "Momma, it's just not fair. We do the dishes and clean up, and Frannie goes and plays piano for Poppa and Grandpop. It makes me so mad! What? Why are you looking at me like that?"

"Like what, Elizabeth?"

"Like, why are you smiling at me?"

"Honey, come here and sit down."

Elizabeth sat down and stared at the floor.

"I know you're angry and it's okay. I just want to share something with you instead of just getting mad back at you and sending you to bed."

Elizabeth's eyes started to fill with tears.

"You don't have to get this upset. Look around, what do you see?" Lucy said warmly.

"I see I'm in the kitchen getting ready to do the dishes...again."

"No, look around and tell me what you see?"

"Momma! I'm in the kitchen. That's what I see."

"Well, honey, that's not what I see. I see the heart of our home, where we spend most of our time. Where Grandmom and I fix your meals, where we talk and catch up, where you tell me about your day and eat cookies and milk after school, and where I fix up your cuts and bruises. Women work in the kitchen. It's where we worry about our children, plan our day and where we keep things running smoothly in the house for our family. It's not glamorous and trust me, there are days when I wish I had someone taking care of me, but when I see our family together it makes it all worthwhile. When you get older, you'll understand."

"Momma, when I get married and have kids, my husband will do dishes and split the work in the house, half and half. I may not even have any dishes."

"Really now? No dishes," Lucy laughed. "And where do you think you'll find such a husband that doesn't want dishes in the house?"

"I don't know but I will, I promise."

"Well, he probably won't be Italian."

"Well, maybe I won't get married at all and be like Aunt Rosemary. I'll work, like a lawyer or a doctor or something."

"Lizzie, when the time comes just understand, whatever you do it'll be your choice, and you have to be prepared to live with your decision, right or wrong. It's getting late. C'mon, I'll wash you dry, and we'll be finished in a jiffy. Then you can go listen to Frannie while Grandpop falls asleep."

No dishes, Lucy thought. *Where does she come up with that kind of thinking?*

Francis was hard at work playing scales to warm up his fingers. After five minutes he began to slow as he told his father of his introduction to the composer Niccolo Paganini by Father Dolan.

At *Martedi Grasso*, Father Dolan had told Lucy and Joseph that he believed Francis had a rare and transcendent talent. Joseph was woefully uninformed about music, but he loved listening to his son play. Despite being concerned about the time Francis was spending with Dolan, Joseph could tell his son was not only progressing but did indeed have a gift at the keyboard.

Francis stared past the sheet music, his hands poised just above the keys. The first notes reverberated off the soundboard of the piano and Giovanni closed his eyes.

"He plays like a grown man, Joseph, listen to him."

Settling effortlessly into the rhythm of the composition, Francis entered into his private world. His awareness of his surroundings faded, replaced by the give and take of touch, timing, and pressure on the piano keys. Francis softly played through the first third of the piece, and with each musical phrase he seemed to suspend and manipulate time for anyone within earshot. Everyone in the room began to feel their emotions heighten as the music transported them into a deepened state of awareness.

Lucy watched intently as her son's body wavered in the space between self-consciousness and inspiration, as his music allowed him to soar above the constraints of teenage inhibition. Pangs of guilt surfaced as she recalled the pressure that she had brought to bear on Francis in the last month. Without speaking a single word, Francis transported himself and his listeners into both the past and what lay ahead. For Francis music was life. He knew he was different, much different than his friends. What troubled Francis was that he did not know why he was so different.

The angst laden relationship between Joseph and his father now seemed trivial to Joseph as he listened to his son. The boy's presence and ability to express himself at the keyboard replaced the words that rarely came to Francis in conversation. Joseph watched his son behind the piano and saw nothing timid or unsure. The obvious talent of his son softened Joseph's heartache that he would be the last Natale stone carver. It was evident; music would be his path.

It was unlike anything Joseph had seen or heard before. The music of his young son allowed him to wade through the melancholy of the last year spent working with Giovanni. He sat in his chair, struck by the fact that he had just experienced pain, joy, hope and inspiration all in the same three minutes. Two somber chords in the key of D flat major, the last slightly softer than the first, ended the piece.

"That music was just beautiful, just beautiful," Joseph said.

"Thanks, Poppa."

Giovanni finished the last of his grappa and Joseph followed him to the front porch.

"See what I mean, Joseph? Frannie has something special, and you need to figure out how to get him better instruction and get him away from that goddamned priest before he has him playing church music the rest of his life. I've listened to a lot of music in my time, and he could go far."

"I know, Pop, I just got to figure it out. But between Lucy, the church shit, and the money better instruction would cost..."

"Listen, if it's just money, I can help."

"It's not just the money. I'll figure it out. You okay to get back?" Joseph said, putting his hand on his father's arm.

"What the hell's the matter with you? It's thirty feet away. I'm retiring, I'm not dying," Giovanni said. "I'll be fine; you just get ready for tomorrow. No mistakes. *Capisce?*"

"I got it, Pop. You know, if you take up with that woman you're gonna miss all this."

"Her name is Josephine and I'll have my memories."

"The kids will have their memories, too, when you leave."

"Ah they're young. They'll get over it. Besides, they can come and visit me in Italy."

"Pop, you really need to think about this before you walk away from everything."

Giovanni knew his son was right. "I'm done thinking tonight. You just be ready to go tomorrow."

TEST DAY - ST. FRANCIS DE SALES PARISH HALL

Sixteen boys had been chosen for the altar server training. This oral exam, coupled with the final walk through just before Easter, would determine the pecking order for each Mass and which servers would get the first pick of the coveted envelopes filled with money from weddings and funerals.

Monsignor Ryan opened the meeting.

"Gentlemen, take a seat at one of the desks and let's get started. First, there are to be no papers, pencils or your study guides available during the test. If anyone has anything with them bring it up now and give it to Father Dolan."

The tension in the room seemed to mount as one by one each boy deposited their materials with Father Dolan. Francis thought of the panna cotta and Oreos the night before, thinking he should have studied more.

"So, from this moment on, anyone caught with test materials in their possession will be expelled from these proceedings and your parents will be notified. Are we clear?"

"Yes, Monsignor," the boys snapped to attention and answered in one voice.

"Now, for this test to be totally unbiased both Father Dolan and I will wait outside for the results and the oral exam will be administered by Sister Mary Bridget."

Audible gasps and whispers filtered through the assembled boys. Sister Mary Bridget was legendary at St. Francis de Sales, but not in a good way.

"Okay, gentlemen, settle down. I know what you're thinking, but for Father Dolan and me to find out if you guys really know the Mass, you have to perform under pressure. You're at the altar celebrating with the priest, which is the central act of our divine worship. It's where Jesus becomes present through the bread and wine that is on the altar at Mass. Transubstantiation: it's at the core of our Catholic beliefs, the Body and Blood of Christ who died for our sins." Monsignor Ryan turned to the student nearest the door. "Mr. Cullen, go into the hallway and ask Sister Mary Bridget if she would join us."

"Yes, Monsignor."

Francis felt his pulse quicken as Sister Mary Bridget walked into the room. Her presence was like a malevolent energy field, amplified by the torso length wooden rosary beads clacking in the folds of her habit. She had a menacing air. Her brow was tightly contorted by the white coif below her veil, forming a permanent scowl across her face.

Then there was the ruler, the ever-present, foot long steel ruler she carried in her right hand. On good days, when a student made a mistake in math class, she would tell the child how stupid they were and slap the white scapular that covered her floor length black tunic with the steel ruler until her face started to turn purple. Sister Mary Bridget's favorite saying was, "I'm so sorry, you're just off-the-boat-stupid today." If she didn't like a certain student, and she hardly liked anyone, they would get a flick of the flat part of the ruler on their calf or thigh and be left with a two-inch welt to explain when they got home. Francis hated everything about her.

"Gentlemen, please welcome Sister Mary Bridget."

"Good afternoon, Sister Mary Bridget," the boys stammered.

Francis looked straight ahead as Sister Mary Bridget nodded ominously to Monsignor Ryan and Father Dolan.

"I'll leave you to it, Sister. We'll be outside in the hall. If you would please report your results to me, then Father Dolan and I will meet with the boys and let them know where they stand."

"Very well, Monsignor. If there's nothing else, please allow me to proceed."

Francis could feel the sweat starting to form in his hairline.

"I hope you don't think all of you will pass this test today because you will not. So, let's see how quickly I can find out who the stupid people are in this room so I can get back to my vespers. If you answer questions correctly, you stay in your seat. If you answer incorrectly, you leave your seat and go to the back of the room and wait in absolute silence. You'll get one additional question when we're finished, and if you make another mistake, you're out and go to the bottom of Monsignor's list for servers." Sister Mary Bridget slammed the table with the ruler, making all the boys jump in their seats. "Am I clear?" she screamed, her words piercing the air like darts.

"Yes, Sister."

"Yes, Sister what?"

"Yes, Sister Mary Bridget," the boys answered back.

"Mr. Cullen, is the Gloria said during a Mass for the Dead?"

"Yes, Sister Mary Bridget."

"That is incorrect. Go to the back of the room, you stupid boy."

"Mr. Green, is the Gloria said during Advent?"

"No, Sister."

"That's correct, stay in your seat." Sister Mary Bridget strode between the rows, slapping her open palm with the ruler, intent on finding her next victim. "Mr. Green, is the Gloria said on Christmas day?"

"No, Sister."

"That's incorrect. The last Sunday of Advent is the last Sunday before Christmas. Advent is over. Go to the back of the room with the other stupid boy. I'll say this one time so listen carefully. *Júdica me, Deus, et discérne causam meam de gente non sancta: ab hómine iníquo, et dolóso érue me.* Mr. Farrell, what is the first line of the response?"

"*Quia tu es, Deus, fortitúdo mea.*"

"Correct, stay in your seat. Mr. Cotter, what is the second line?"

"*Quare me repulísti...*"

"Correct, stay in your seat. Mr. O'Neill, what is the last line?"

"*Salutáre vultus mei, et Deus meus.*"

"You stupid boy!" Sister Mary Bridget went to full throttle, menacing the class as she flailed at her scapular. "Who is the salvation of my countenance and my God? Are you kidding me? Mr. O'Neill, go to the back of the room with the other stupid boys. Mr. Natale, what is the last line?"

"*Et quare tristis incédo, dum afflígit me inimícus?*"

"Is that a question at the end?"

"Yes, Sister."

"What does it mean?"

"And why do I go sorrowful whilst the enemy afflicteth me?"

Sister Mary Bridget fixed a withering gaze toward Francis as she approached him. "Correct, Mr. Natale. You think you're pretty smart, don't you? Let me ask you, when the priest says *Munda cor meum ac lábia mea, omnípotens Deus* during the Creed, what is the next line?"

"Sister, the next line is *qui lábia Isaíæ Prophétæ cálculo mundásti igníto.*"

"What does it mean?"

"Who didst cleanse the lips of the prophet Isaias with a burning coal? But the priest does not say that during the Creed, it's right before he reads the Gospel."

Sister Mary Bridget exploded. "How dare you sass me during this sacred test! Leave the room and wait in the hall until I report this to the Monsignor. Leave at once!" she screamed.

"But, Sister, I wasn't..."

"Do not speak another word or I promise you the son of God will strike you down unless I do it first. Now leave!"

Francis, flushed and shocked by Sister Mary Bridget's attack, left his seat and went out into the hallway where he started to cry. He saw Dolan and Monsignor Ryan at the end of the hall and he knew they had seen him crying.

Father Dolan walked past him and held his index finger to his lips, gently tapping Francis on the shoulder. He smiled at Francis, whispering, "Relax, it'll be okay." Dolan was amazed and excited that time and time again these opportunities presented themselves. It was as if it *was* God's will.

Francis put his head down staring at the brown terrazzo floor and could only think of what his mother was going to do when she found out he had been kicked out of the test.

Dolan knocked as he entered the room. "Excuse me, Sister Mary Bridget, but may I have a word?"

"Father, I'm right in the middle of testing, and I have Vespers starting in twenty minutes."

"Sister, Monsignor Ryan would like to speak to you out in the hall."

"Very well," she said curtly. Sister Mary Bridget flung open the door and stomped down the hallway to Monsignor Ryan, her full-length habit chafing loudly against her body. "Monsignor Ryan, I'm right in the middle of administering your test for the altar boys. I'm not even sure you want most of them, pretty much stupid boys off the boat. And that Natale boy, he's just a smart aleck from Little Rome. Do you know what I mean?"

"Actually, Sister, I don't know what you mean. I know the Natale boy. He comes from a good family. He has been working very hard on the Mass liturgy and the responses; I believe he has even memorized the celebrant's portion of the Mass. What did he do to get kicked out of the test?"

"He sassed me in front of the rest of the boys. If I had some soap, I would have washed his mouth out right there on the spot."

"Really? That's not what I heard, Sister Mary Bridget."

"What do you mean, Monsignor Ryan? Were you eavesdropping on me?"

"No, I would say I was exercising my authority as the Pastor in charge of both the parish and school of St. Francis de Sales where your teaching order, the Sisters of Sacred Heart, serve at the pleasure of his Eminence, John Cardinal Cushing. Now, back to your original question, what I mean, Sister, is a thirteen-year-old caught you in a very unfair, one could say trick question, and you lost your temper. And no, I was not eavesdropping on you, I could have heard you standing outside on Rhode Island Avenue."

Sister Mary Bridget, her face blossoming into a crimson red, clenched her rosary beads in her fist.

"So, Sister Mary Bridget, here's my suggestion. Father Dolan will handle the balance of the test, and you can go to your Vespers, and there will be no need for me to contact your Mother Superior in Ohio."

"I'll take my leave, Monsignor Ryan," she said, turning her back on him.

"Sister Mary Bridget, do not ever turn your back on me."

The nun stopped and whirled around. "Of course, Monsignor. My apologies."

"Oh, one other thing, Sister, I don't ever want to hear about or see you with that ruler while you are teaching on this property. Are we clear, Sister Mary Bridget?"

"Perfectly, Monsignor Ryan."

"Is there anything else, Sister Mary Bridget?"

"Nothing else. I'll look forward to working in this venerable parish known for its Christian spirit and adherence to Catholic dogma and of course the vows its faithful servants have made."

"Your point, Sister?"

"My point, Monsignor, is that frequently our novitiates assist housekeeping in the cleaning of the rectory, and we offer that work for the good of the Church and to ensure scandal is not visited on the faithful. That is my point. Good evening, Monsignor, Father Dolan." Sister Mary Bridget spun in place, her habit wrapping tightly around her body as she glided down the hallway.

"Quite a put-down, Monsignor, that was impressive," Father Dolan said.

"You are an idiot. Is that what you think, Father Dolan, a put-down? Sister Mary Bridget is neither afraid of me nor intimidated, so in the future I would bear that in mind. And the part about the scandal to the faithful – well let me put it this way – there is precious little privacy in a rectory. She just took a shot across your bow. Do you understand what I'm saying?"

"I do, Monsignor."

"My suggestion to you is to make sure I have six altar boys who know what the hell they're doing for Easter services and then concentrate on your duties at the Shrine. I didn't ask for you to be in this parish. You're here because the Archbishop needed to find a place for you to, how should we say, to give you a fresh start in the priesthood. And we needed Sunday Mass coverage when Father Sadowsky retired. Now get the Natale boy back in the room and make your decision on the rest."

EASTER SUNDAY MORNING, MARCH 29, 1959

St. Francis de Sales parish was located at 2019 Rhode Island Avenue in the District of Columbia. Boasting the longest continuous congregation in Washington, D.C., it had become a favorite of the Cardinal Archbishop who would frequently come and offer Mass.

Lucy watched from her closet as Joseph struggled with the top button of his shirt and his tie. Every time he would try to snug his knotted tie to his collar the top button would come undone.

"Here, put this new one on. Should be fine," she said.

Joseph untied his tie and changed into his new shirt. It felt good on his body. "Is this the same size?"

"Same size, Joseph."

The shirt was a size larger, but Lucy was going to wait for a quieter time to talk to Joseph about his last visit to Dr. Irey. It seemed he wanted Joseph to lose some weight as he noted some higher-than-normal blood pressure readings and had enlisted Lucy's help to manage Joseph's diet better. Gio had warned her that Joseph was touchy about his weight after he had asked Joseph why he was so out of breath climbing the scaffold at work. Easter Sunday morning, with a big family brunch scheduled for the afternoon, was not the time to have that discussion.

Nervousness caused Lucy to shiver under her spring coat as the car rumbled up 14th Street past the Franciscan Monastery. Staring out the window, her mind raced with memories of the past.

"What's the matter?" Joseph asked.

"It's nothing, just reminiscing about how fast the years have gone by."

"You know what they say, Lucy...*Time waits for no one.*"

"I'm really happy that we will receive communion as a family today. I just wanted you to know that. You know, we've come a long way from that day I first saw you on the beach in Ocean City."

"Is there something else bothering you?"

"No, not really, I was just thinking about the kids. I know you're disappointed with Frannie not having any interest in stone carving..."

"That's not true. Sure, I thought about it, but he does have a calling, and he should pursue it."

"You mean the priesthood?"

"The priesthood? Hell, no, not the priesthood! I was talking about his music and the piano. Christ, Lucy, he's thirteen years old, why are you thinking he wants to be a priest? Did he say something?"

"No, he didn't, I just thought..."

"Now listen. I'm not fooling with you. This is serious. You got to stop this priest stuff. You remember just before we got married and you talked about the nuns and how they thought you had a vocation?"

"I know I know..."

"Let me finish. You said no. You made a decision that you wanted to get married and raise a family. This isn't about you or your regrets, Lucy. I promised you I wouldn't interfere with how you raised the kids as Catholics, but I didn't sign on to you pressuring Frannie to become a priest. Francis has to choose his own life. I wanted him to be a carver. He has no interest in that. Do you realize that I will be the last Natale carver ever? I have to live with that disappointment. You know the Catholic faith isn't as important to me as it is to you..."

"It's not important to you at all," Lucy said as she started to cry.

"That's not true, you remember the other night at dinner? Religion is important to me because it's important to you. I'm just not a card carrying Catholic like that guy on T.V., Billy whatshisname? Jesus, Lucy, why are you crying now?" Joseph said as he turned the corner of Monroe Street and South Dakota Avenue. "We're almost there. You okay?"

"Yes, I'm fine. You know, Joe, I really do envy you."

"Why is that?"

"It's just you seem to have everything figured out. I mean life is so simple for you. You have your family, you have your work, and if you're not thinking about having sex, it's about baseball or food."

"Don't forget the Redskins."

"See what I mean? That's why I envy you. You have life all figured out."

As they walked from the car, Joseph reached for her hand and kissed her on the cheek as they got to the front door of the church.

Before the official ceremony began, the church was filled with the rhythmic chant of the choir from the Franciscan monastery. As soon as they crossed the threshold of the church, the powerful aroma of frankincense and myrrh permeated the air. It was a scene that Lucy had dreamt about.

Francis stood erect next to Monsignor Ryan, looking older than his years with his hair slicked back tight against his head and his white starched surplice lying perfectly over a new floor-length black cassock.

"Man, the boy looks good, Luce. You should be very proud," Joseph whispered from behind Lucy.

Lucy squeezed Joseph's hand as they took their seats on the aisle of the pew nearest to the vestibule. "We should both be proud, Joseph."

As the organ sounded to announce the beginning of the Mass, Lucy and Joseph turned and faced Monsignor Ryan as he entered the church. Lucy's heart almost burst with pride as she watched Francis leading the procession into the packed church carrying the cross of Jesus down the center aisle.

Monsignor Ryan greeted parishioners as he processed down the center aisle. Spotting Lucy perched at the end of the pew, he leaned over and whispered, "Francis knows the Mass better than some of my young priests. You should be very proud. Drop by the rectory mid-morning tomorrow. I have something for you."

Tears welled in Lucy's eyes and her face flushed watching her son take his position next to Monsignor Ryan on the altar. She clutched her rosary to her chest. She had never felt closer to God than at that moment. Notwithstanding her comments to Joseph, her goal of Francis becoming a priest was beginning to take shape. Easter Sunday, 1959 was a watershed moment in the life of Lucy Natale. *A job well done*, she thought. *With bigger and better things to come.*

THE NEGOTIATION - ST. FRANCIS DE SALES RECTORY, MARCH 30, 1959

Springtime in Washington was Lucy's favorite season. Cherry trees were beginning to blossom on Rhode Island Avenue between South Dakota Avenue and 20th Street. Lucy had gone to the church early, as it was her week to help arrange the altar decorations and disperse the dozens of Easter lilies left from Easter Mass around the nave, the baptismal front and the Shrine to Mary. It was just past 10:30 A.M. as she walked from the church to the parish rectory a half block away. She rang the doorbell and entered the waiting room.

"Oh, Mrs. McGinty, good morning, how are you? Lovely Easter service yesterday, wasn't it?"

"It was, indeed, Mrs. Natale. Is there something I can do for you?"

"Monsignor asked me to stop by and…"

"That's odd. I don't see anything on his appointment calendar," Mrs. McGinty sniffed.

"I was hoping to run into you today. I understand you met my daughter."

"No, I don't believe I know your daughter."

"Oh. That's funny. I think you met her at the science fair you were judging last month and were very impressed with her work. You said she reminded you of your niece, Maria. You must remember."

"I don't have a niece named Maria."

"Oh, maybe I misunderstood what my daughter Elizabeth told me about the science fair."

Mrs. McGinty's imperious veneer began to crumble as Lucy noticed a slight tremor in her hand.

"Are you alright, Mrs. McGinty? Can I get you some water?"

"I'm fine. Excuse me, I'll see if Monsignor Ryan is available."

Lucy took a seat in the waiting room, satisfied that she had made her point. The double doors of Monsignor Ryan's office slid open. The look on Lucy's face revealed her surprise at seeing Ryan dressed in a tan turtleneck and black slacks.

"Lucy, please come into my office. This is my day off so excuse my appearance, but I wanted to talk to you as soon as I heard the news." Ryan ushered Lucy into his office and closed the door. "By the way, what did you say to Mrs. McGinty?"

"Just some girl talk. Why do you ask?"

"Because she looked like she had just seen a ghost when she told me you were here."

"Maybe you're working her too hard."

"I doubt that. Mrs. McGinty tries to make everyone believe she runs the place, but to be honest she's a bit on the nosey side for my taste."

"I wouldn't know. But in any event, Monsignor, what's the news? You have me curious."

"Of course. Well, the news is Father Dolan had a meeting last night with the current Rector at the Shrine, and they're planning a youth concert in November when the Shrine opens, and it was suggested by the Rector that Francis enter the competition to perform at the concert. Father Dolan believes that if Francis continues his music studies with him when he is teaching at Campus School, he'll have an excellent chance of winning a spot on the program."

"My goodness, that is news. But as you know, Frannie isn't enrolled at Campus School."

"Well, there's more. Are you familiar with Campus School?"

"I am, Monsignor; I'm actually very familiar with the school. I've read some of Thomas Shield's writings on progressive education and was very impressed. But as you know, we can barely afford the tuition here at St. Francis."

"Well, Lucy, there may well be a way around that. There aren't enough deserving students from the ranks of the professors to fill the school, so it was decided by Cardinal Cushing and the provost at Catholic University to open the enrollment to qualified Archdiocesan children. Francis certainly fits the bill. If he were at Campus, he could continue his instruction with Father Dolan..."

"What about Elizabeth?" Lucy said, taking a seat across from Ryan's desk.

"I'm sorry, I forgot about Elizabeth. Father Dolan didn't mention Elizabeth."

"Thank you for the offer, Monsignor, it's very kind of you to think of Francis, but my children must stay together. Neither Joseph nor I have any desire for them to be separated."

"What if two slots were made available to your family and the tuition were the same as St. Francis? Would that change your mind?"

"Monsignor, I know it's not the same. My brother-in-law works there maintaining the University grounds and has his kids there, and I believe it's almost $500 per student. That's $1,000 a year for grammar school, and we simply don't have that kind of money," Lucy said, exasperated.

"Did I not hear at *Martedi Grasso* that Joseph was the new Master Carver at the Shrine?"

"Yes."

"And your father-in-law is the current Master Carver?"

"Yes."

"There's a scholarship fund for deserving students that could pay the difference between the tuitions. With Giovanni and Joseph's work on the Shrine, I would happily make that recommendation. I mean after all, the Shrine is on the campus of Catholic University."

"I don't want to speak to Joseph about this unless I know you can do this. I apologize for being so forward."

"No need to worry about that, Lucy. I'll let you know tomorrow, just so we're clear. If this does happen, Campus is a lot closer to your house than St. Francis and St. Anthony's parish is even closer so it would be my hope that you would remain a part of our parish family."

"Monsignor, I would never leave this parish. We're here because we feel at home. This parish is our family and where Joseph and I got married, and where Francis served his first Mass."

"Excellent. We have an understanding then."

"We do. I'll wait to hear from you, Monsignor. Thank you for thinking of us," Lucy said, standing up and grabbing her purse.

"By the way, Lucy, Campus School altar boys will be serving Mass at the Shrine to cover all the Masses planned for the church."

"So you're saying my son would serve Mass at the Shrine?"

"Yes, if Francis is enrolled in Campus School he would be on the list."

"My word, Monsignor, that is quite something. I'll wait to hear from you," Lucy stammered.

THE BEGINNING

Francis raced to the bus stop at South Dakota and Rhode Island Avenue for the twenty-minute ride to the Sacred Music Director's Office in the Crypt Church in the basement of the Shrine. During the 1920s, the stone foundation of the Shrine evolved into a low vaulted church in its own right. For nearly three decades, as the Crypt Church meandered through the Great Depression and World War II, it was frequented by thousands of pilgrims and moneyed patrons, despite the on again off again construction.

Francis looked for his father to wave to as he raced from the bus stop, but no one was on the scaffold in front of the Annunciation tympanum. Francis ran up the steps to the east terrace and then down the steps to the Crypt Church and into the waiting room of the Sacred Music Director's Office.

Father Dolan looked up from his desk. "You're late, Mr. Natale."

"I'm sorry, Father, the bus from school is a three-block walk."

"That's an excuse, Francis. If you want me to continue to work with you, without paying anything for these lessons, you make sure you're on time. Do you understand what I'm telling you?"

"I'm sorry, Father, I won't be late again."

"Okay, warm up and clear your mind, and I'll get today's sheet music ready. Your father picks you up at five sharp and we have work to do."

Francis was surprised at how angry Father Dolan got for only being five minutes late. He sat on the stool staring at the keys and slowly pieced together a chord progression from a blues lick he had listened to on the radio the night before.

"What's that?" Father Dolan demanded.

"I'm sorry, Father, I heard it last night. I'll warm up with the regular stuff."

"You heard it last night? Where?"

"It was on the radio, WMAL Jazz Tonight I think is the name. It comes on at eight, so I get to listen a little before bed."

"Where did you get the money to buy sheet music for rock and roll piano music? I'm sure you didn't get it from your parents."

"I don't have sheet music. I just heard it. I saw the notes in my head."

"You're playing that by ear? I don't believe you."

"It's true. Really, Father, I'm not lying."

Dolan slid onto the stool inches from Francis and put his arm around his shoulder. Francis stopped playing his warmup, distracted by a pungent mix of cigarette smoke and English Leather cologne.

"Why did you stop?"

"I don't know, I just thought you were really mad at me when I came in late."

"I'm sorry, Frannie, I just have a lot on my mind with the opening just five months away. Do you forgive me?" Dolan asked as he pulled Francis even closer. "I mean it, Francis, I'm truly sorry for upsetting you."

"It's okay, Father," Francis said as he tried to subtly put some separation between himself and Dolan.

"Let's get back to you seeing notes of music in your head. You said you like rock and roll."

"I do, Father, I think it's fun, and I get excited when I hear it. I just want to play it."

"You know some in the Church would think that playing that is sinful."

"Do you think it's sinful, Father?"

"Actually, Francis, I don't, but because some people would question why a priest is playing honky-tonk and rock and roll music on the piano, I keep it a secret and only play when I go out of town. Do you have secrets, Frannie?"

"I don't know, not really. Maybe some."

Dolan smiled at his young student. "Listen to this lick I'm going to play. You said you could see the notes, pretend you are back in your room listening to the radio."

Dolan was a classically trained musician. He had played at Carnegie Hall and had taken the Silver Medal at the American Protégé International Piano and Strings Competition but shortly after his recital he entered the seminary at the urging of his mother. There he found little competition for his talent, which translated to being quickly noticed by the bishops. But more importantly, in the seminary he had found a refuge, a place where his life actually worked for him.

"You ready?" Dolan asked, watching Francis intently.

Francis closed his eyes and laid his hands on his thighs.

"Yes, Father."

"Here I go!" Dolan said.

The piano exploded into a driving bass line of a Boogie Woogie riff that combined some Jerry Lee Lewis high octane rock and roll with some of Pine Top Smith's classic 1928 hit record. Dolan played for about forty-five seconds and suddenly stopped.

"What did you hear, Francis?"

"Well, I heard it, but I saw the notes in my head."

"So, you're saying you can quote the lick you just heard or saw 'in your head,' as you say?"

"Yes," Francis said firmly.

"Before you play, tell me what you see?"

"It's like a warm-up for both hands working together. E-flat, D, C, B-flat, G and then you do it over again up and down, down and up, and at the end some other rock and roll stuff."

"Show me."

Dolan got up and let Francis sit in the center of the bench. Francis closed his eyes and for a second nodded his head to capture the beat, then launched his body at the keyboard. Dolan watched as Francis mimicked the lick perfectly. When Francis was nearing the end, he looked up at Dolan staring at him and then improvised using some bars from Pine Top Boogie and Stormy Weather.

"I added a couple of things at the end. Did you like them?"

"I love them. And I love the way you play. Let me ask you, do you know any Chopin?"

"Not really, I like to play Mozart. His stuff makes me feel really good. My grandfather plays him on the phonograph all the time."

"So, you don't know any Chopin?"

"Maybe somewhere I've heard something, but I haven't played his stuff."

"Francis, music is not stuff. It's a measure, a bar, a chord; it's a triplet or a half note, a symphony, an opera, a melody, a concerto, a variation or a composition. It's not called stuff. Are we clear about that?"

"Yes, Father."

Dolan played the first three minutes of Chopin's Fantaisie – Impromptu in C-Sharp. It was a standard competition piece that any potential prodigy would need in his repertoire.

"What about all those notes? Do you see all of those notes as well?"

"I do. I mean at the beginning there are a lot of notes," Francis laughed. "But I think I got most of them. Do you want me to play it?"

"I do, if you can."

Dolan was confident that Francis would lose the melody after a minute or so as the tempo changed dramatically at the twentieth measure. Chopin had written in a complicated cross rhythm, with the left hand playing triplets and the right hand playing sixteenth notes, then suddenly switched to slower more sophisticated phrasing, allowing the beginning melody to reappear. The twentieth measure came and went with Francis nailing both the entry and exit points of the down and up-tempo changes of the *allegro agitato*.

Dolan smirked. He realized the boy's raw talent far surpassed his own, which made Francis even more desirable. In a year, maybe two, Francis would not be as malleable or as available for time alone with Dolan. The window of opportunity would shortly close.

The heavy wooden door to the makeshift studio creaked open.

"Excuse me, Father Dolan, I don't mean to interrupt."

"Francis, stand up. That's the Rector, Monsignor Flynn," Dolan hissed.

"Is this the young man you were telling me about, Father?"

"Yes, Monsignor Flynn, this is Francis Natale. His father is soon to be the Master Carver for the Shrine."

"I'm aware of who the boy's father is. I hired him, Father Dolan."

"Of course, Monsignor, I'm sorry."

"Pleased to meet you, Francis," Monsignor Flynn said. "Father Dolan has spoken very highly of your talent on the piano and your family. Was that you playing as I walked in?"

"Yes, Monsignor."

"It was beautiful, just beautiful. Are you going to compete for the solo performance at the opening of the Shrine in November?"

"I'm not sure. I haven't talked to my parents."

"I'll leave you with your charge, Father Dolan. By the way, did I hear some crazy saloon type piano music just a little bit ago?"

"Well, sometimes Francis warms up with some rock and roll music to get the fingers nice and limber."

"Is that a fact? Do you think any of the great composers of the eighteenth or nineteenth centuries warmed up with rock and roll?"

"I suspect not, Monsignor Flynn."

"Perhaps you could find a more suitable warm-up exercise for your student."

"Of course, Monsignor. Absolutely."

"Good day, Father. Francis, it was a pleasure to meet you. Say hello to your father."

"I will, Monsignor Flynn."

Dolan waited until he heard both the music room and outer office door close before he spoke. With his reading glasses pulled to the tip of his nose and using his most affected Irish brogue, he turned to Francis. "Perhaps you could find a more suitable warm-up exercise for your student."

Francis howled in laughter, nearly falling off his piano stool. "You were playing it first, Father!"

"I know, and you kept my secret. That tells me a lot about you."

"Well, no one likes a tattletale."

"You're right; no one does like a tattletale. You love music, Francis?"

"I do, Father, I really do. I love everything about it. It's like it's in me and has got to come out."

"You have a gift, Francis. I would say you have a gift from God, but with every gift there comes responsibility."

"What do you mean, Father?"

"You know, Francis, as God's earthly representative a priest has a very special relationship with God. Do you believe that?"

"I do, Father."

"So, I'm sitting here next to you as God's representative. Tell me, why do you believe this, Francis?"

"I don't know. I heard Momma say it. Sister Mary Luke said it in religion class when we were learning about the Mass, you said it, Sister Mary Bridget said it…"

"And as a result of all that instruction you believe this to be true in your heart. So, in a way, if I tell you something it's like God telling you something. Is that right, Francis?"

"Yes, Father."

"So, let me tell you why that's so important. First, because if you believe that my word is the word of God, it makes you special in the eyes of God. Can you imagine, Francis, in the eyes of God? I am guiding your growth as a musician as God's representative on earth. Do you believe that?"

"I do, Father."

"He has singled you out for this special relationship with me. He has chosen you to have the world hear your music. God has also chosen you to share a priest's special love. How does that make you feel, Francis?"

"Good."

"Good, Francis? It doesn't make you feel special?"

"It does, Father. It does make me feel special."

"Now the trick is, in order for God to continue to think you're special he will give us tests."

"Like in school?"

"No, tests from God will be in our thoughts and actions and at times may not make sense to you when you're doing them. Because you have been chosen, there will be lots of people who won't understand."

"Like who?" Francis said.

"Like your parents, your family, your friends. That is why what we do here when it's just you and me must remain private and not shared with anyone. It's just between you, God, and me. No one else will understand. Francis Natale, do you promise God that our time together will be private?"

"I do, Father."

"Do you swear before God, Francis?"

"Yes, Father, I do."

"What's your favorite piece of music to play?"

"I really like the Paganini stuff we were working on last week. No wait, not stuff... I mean the Variation on a Theme for the 18th Movement that was written for the piano by Rachmaninoff."

"Alright, Francis, you are listening, that's excellent. You start, and I'll get us some refreshment."

Francis played the piece flawlessly while Dolan put two Coca-Colas on a tray with an assortment of candy and cookies.

"You changed the tempo a bit. That's not how you've played it before."

"I know, it's just I feel really good right now."

"That feeling is from God, Francis, remember that."

"Wow, is that Coke for me?"

"Well, one's for you, the other one's for me," Dolan said, handing a Coke to Francis and sliding onto the bench next to him.

"And the Baby Ruth? Can I have one of those too?"

"Absolutely. You did well today, Francis."

"Momma would never let me have candy before dinner."

"Do you remember what I told you about secrets and keeping things that happen in this studio private? Do you remember your oath to God?" Dolan asked as he placed his hand on Francis' knee.

"I do, Father."

"Excellent, drink up. I want you in the waiting room at five sharp. Your father is never late."

At precisely 5:00 P.M., the door to the office of Sacred Music opened and Joseph walked in. As Joseph removed his cap, a fine layer of limestone dust flaked onto his thick eyebrows.

"I'm sorry for the dust, Father Dolan, I was running late."

"Poppa, you look like a ghost," Francis laughed.

"Francis, that's the face of an artisan in the service of God." Dolan turned to Joseph. "The Rector speaks very highly of you and your father's work. And of course, your son, my word! His talent is something to behold."

Joseph was uneasy with the compliment from the priest. "Thank you, Father, but Lucy is waiting dinner. I would love to talk more, but we have to hurry to catch the 5:10 bus."

"Of course. Francis, good work today, and keep our lessons in mind when you practice."

"I will, Father."

Joseph and Francis stood at the top of the east entrance of the Shrine.

"Poppa, do you want to walk?"

"No, then we'll really be late. Momma is waiting dinner and she wants to talk to you and Elizabeth."

"Are we in trouble?"

"No, I don't think so. Are you in trouble?"

"No, I don't think so, but Elizabeth is always in trouble for something. You sure you don't want to walk?"

"I'm sure. Why do you want to walk so bad?"

"Because it's going to stink in the bus with all those people. It always stinks this time of day."

"Those are working people, Francis. You come from working people. Mind your manners and get on the bus."

Eight minutes later the bus stopped a block and a half from the house. Joseph looked at his watch and relaxed, he would walk through the kitchen door at five-thirty, right on time.

"Boy, that smells good. What's for dinner?" Joseph asked.

"Pot roast, potatoes, vegetables, salad and fresh biscuits. And your mother made us an apple pie," Lucy said.

"*Fantastico*! Let me get this dust off and wash my hands."

Francis turned to his mother. "Poppa says you want to talk to Lizzie and me. Are we in trouble?"

"Certainly not, this is good news," Lucy said as she covered the roast to rest.

"So, what is it, Momma?"

"There will be plenty of time after dinner. Get your sister and tell her to wash up. Dinner is on the table in five minutes. And Francis, change your shirt, you're a little gamey for the dinner table."

Francis turned and looked at his father. "Poppa! I told you the bus stunk!"

"It's good for you to be around working folks, that's who we are. Now mind your mother before you get a strap," Joseph said as Francis scampered to his room.

"Joseph, was that really necessary?"

"Frannie's getting soft, with all the piano and altar boy stuff. He didn't want to ride the bus because of the smell."

"So, you think it's some right of male passage to ride in a stinky bus? You're starting to sound like your father."

"Never mind who I sound like, no son of mine is going to grow up soft."

Lucy knew exactly when to avoid a potential argument over Joseph's view of masculinity. Any more discussion about the bus ride home would be pointless.

"I know what you're saying, Joseph. Now help me set the table for this beautiful dinner I made for you."

Lucy waited until dinner was almost over. She knew intuitively that news of change was better tolerated on a full stomach. She put her fork down and got everyone's attention. "Now listen to this, because both of you did so well in school this year, Monsignor Ryan offered us two spots for you and Lizzie to go to Campus School. You will be with all of your cousins until you start high school. What do you think?"

"I don't want to switch schools, Momma. I'll miss my friends."

"Lizzie, you have three of your cousins there, and you can see your friends every day after school. Campus is only a ten-minute walk from here, and you'll make new friends. Francis, they have a beautiful music room and get this, they have a Steinway baby grand piano that you can use for your piano practice. You can take your lessons there or at Father Dolan's office like today. It's a wonderful opportunity for both of you."

"Does Sister Mary Bridget teach there?" Frannie asked.

"Not at all. It's a different order of nuns, the Sisters of Notre Dame. They also teach at the Notre Dame high school next to Gonzaga where hopefully you will both go to high school if God spares."

"Lizzie, you'll have Sister Mary Bridget next year for math if you don't switch. You know she carries that steel ruler around like an ax."

"That's enough, Frannie."

"I know but…"

"Then it's settled?" Lucy asked, anxious for consensus.

"It's not going to cost any more than St. Francis?" Joseph asked.

"Nope, same price."

"You know Bunker Hill is a two-minute walk from the house and they could go to public school for free, and I could finish the basement and get you that window air conditioner you've been yammering about."

Joseph saw Lucy's ice blue eyes grow to a fixed stare from across the table. He had crossed a line and knew that his only course was a full retreat.

"Listen, kids, I was just kidding with your mother. She knows what's best for your education, and Campus School is a great opportunity for both of you. So, it's settled. Finish this year at St. Francis and then off to Campus School to finish grammar school."

"So, public school is out?" asked Elizabeth.

Lucy tried to close the conversation. "It's out, Elizabeth. No daughter of mine is going to public school when we have this kind of opportunity staring us in the face. Now who wants pie?"

"I'm not hungry. May I be excused?" Elizabeth asked.

"Are you sure you don't want a piece of Grandmom's apple pie?"

"Yes."

"Alright, clear your dishes and put them in the sink and you can go outside and play a little before it gets dark."

Frannie hurried out the back door after Elizabeth, the screen slamming behind him. Lucy stood up and looked straight into Joseph's eyes.

"Don't say it, Lucy. I know what you're thinking."

"Joseph Peter Natale, you have no idea what I'm thinking at this very second."

"I know, I know, you're mad."

"I'm way past mad, Joseph, I'm at the point where I truly wonder why I chose to raise our children in the Catholic faith with you as their father. Do you really mean to say that a public school education is better than our children going to Campus School?"

"C'mon, Lucy…"

"Joseph, I'm serious. Don't say another word, or we're both going to end up saying something that we'll regret. I'm going out for a walk."

"I'll come along, and I'll help you with the dishes when we get back."

"No. You're not invited. If you want to do something, do the dishes and clean up the kitchen and make sure the kids are ready for school tomorrow."

"Jesus, Lucy, how long are you gonna be gone?"

Lucy hung her apron on the hook and grabbed her purse. "I'm not sure," she said as she closed the back-porch door behind her.

JUNE 15, 1959

Summer weather had arrived in Washington, but it was still the middle of June. There had already been eight ninety-degree plus days, and the official first day of summer was still a week away. It was nearly dark, and an early pod of lightning bugs danced at the edge of Lucy's azalea bushes in the backyard. She took a mental inventory of her children's voices playing on the front steps and heard someone rummaging around in the refrigerator.

"Joseph, is that you?"

"Yeah. You want something?" Joseph asked Lucy.

"No, I'm fine, I have a glass of wine. Come out here, I want to talk to you."

Joseph pulled a cold long neck Pabst Blue Ribbon out of the refrigerator, opened it with a church key hanging next to the door and went out to join Lucy on the porch. She took a long drag on her cigarette and pushed her head back to clear the smoke.

"I'm sorry for staying mad at you for so long."

"It's okay. I was wrong for the comment about public school, so I just decided to leave it alone until you came to your senses."

"What's that supposed to mean?"

It took days for Lucy to cool off. In her eyes, Joseph had placed her in an impossible position in front her children. He had broken their agreement. Whether he meant it or not didn't matter to her.

"It doesn't mean anything, Lucy."

"That's the point, Joseph. It means everything to me. It doesn't have anything to do with my coming to my senses. You divided us in front of the kids on whether a Catholic education, a progressive Catholic education to boot, was just as good as what is offered at the public schools. Do you understand or even care that the only ones that were given this opportunity were the children of college professors? That's why the school was built in the first place. It's a top-of-the-line experimental school. They really only wanted Frannie. I had to convince Monsignor Ryan that it had to be both kids and at the same price that we're paying now. You just don't get it; to suggest that I would prefer a window air conditioner and a finished basement over a Catholic education for our children is almost more than I could bear."

"I don't know what to say."

"I don't want you to say anything. What I want you to do is honor the agreement you made with me before we got married. Did you not agree that we would raise our kids in the Catholic Church?"

"I did."

"So, I don't want you to say anything, and I don't want you to undermine me in front of the kids. What I want you to do is keep your promise. That's all I'm asking."

Joseph thought about his courtship with Lucy and wondered why he persisted in trying to distance his kids from an unforgiving orthodoxy and its confounding rituals, rules and regulations. No meat on Fridays, stand here, kneel there, Jesus rising from the dead, Moses parting the Red Sea. *Pure goddamn foolishness*, he thought. He wondered if any of it really mattered. But it was not hurting his children, so why should he make his life miserable by aggravating Lucy?

83

His hunch, a hunch he could not act on or even get his head around, brought his thoughts full circle. He was a stone carver, pure and simple. He was not religious and never would be. He hedged his bets on eternal salvation by living an honorable life as a stone carver, husband, and father. He had to trust that Lucy would make the right decisions for their children and leave it at that. If they were like him, they would figure it out anyway—that most of Catholicism was voodoo.

"Well, are you going to say anything?"

"You said not to say anything."

"Don't be a smart-ass."

"Didn't I write the deposit check out for the tuition at Campus School?"

"You did, but I had to ask you three times about it."

"That's because you wanted to pay the bill a month early for God sakes." Joseph turned back to Lucy. "We done?"

"If you say you're done, then we're done, Joseph."

NO STRINGS AND NO PARENTS

The summer of 1959 unfolded into a routine. Brutal heat and humidity persisted throughout the entire summer with August being the worst.

The bright spot for the summer was the annual family vacation to Ocean City, Maryland the week before school started. Joseph and his two brothers rented three houses side by side on 12th Street and the Boardwalk, and Giovanni and Anna stayed a night or two at each house. To say this year's trip was a welcome relief was an understatement. The beach was wide at 12th Street and both Joseph and Lucy spent the days playing in the water with their children, nieces and nephews. Joseph would rent a raft for each child while Lucy and her sisters-in-law would shuttle back and forth between the beach and the house with an endless variety of sandwiches, drinks and snacks.

At night, the kids roamed the boardwalk, using their savings for rides, Thrasher's French fries with malt vinegar and Fisher's caramel popcorn while the parents simply took a break from everything that filled their lives back home. Late afternoon ocean breezes wrapped around a second-floor deck where hearts, gin rummy, cold beer and Manhattans filled the void left by the relentless grind of the other fifty-one weeks of the year. Lucy even lightened up her dinner routine with barbecued hot dogs and hamburgers on a Friday night with, as Joseph would confide to Rosemary, some "cockamamie" dispensation from Monsignor Ryan. It was a time that everyone looked forward to, and it went by much too fast.

The last night was always special; an al fresco, sit down feast. Giovanni would give each grandchild a crisp ten-dollar bill, and tell them that they could spend it on anything the boardwalk had to offer. "No strings, and no parents," he would say to the children's cheers and laughter. Anna, Lucy and Mary cooked a massive amount of spaghetti and clams, jumbo lump crab cakes with hot sauce, lemon wedges or homemade tartar sauce, corn on the cob and fried flatbread served on six narrow card tables on the walkway between two of the houses. Three families, twenty-five people in all, sat in the open-air eating, laughing and drinking until the mosquitoes from the bay side of the island ran everyone inside or up onto the boardwalk. From the street, they looked like a gaggle of ravenous hobos, but to the Natale family, this was the essence of life.

Lucy was cleaning up with the other women, but Joseph was eager to get out of the house and up to the Boardwalk. "Lucy, you ready? It's almost eight-thirty and the kids will be back at eleven," he said.

"Be right there. You have the cups?"

"All ready, just waiting on you."

For Joseph and Lucy, their last night at the beach was always special for another reason. They would fill two plastic cups with vodka and orange juice and sneak onto the oceanfront deck at the Beach Plaza Hotel. It was an elaborate, silly scheme that they both delighted in. Joseph would enter through the basement with the two cups and walk as if he were late to meet a hotel guest in the lobby. Lucy would come onto the deck from the boardwalk and grab two rockers in the corner facing the ocean. "Miraculously," Joseph would spot his quarry on the outdoor veranda walking past the hostess. The silly ruse, which worked every time, would conclude when Lucy would impatiently signal to Joseph, and they would settle into their corner rockers with a view of the boardwalk and a warm ocean breeze blowing on their faces.

"You look sexy when you're misbehaving. What would Monsignor Ryan say?"

"I hardly think Monsignor Ryan has any room to talk."

"Lucy Natale, are you holding out on me?"

"He's a man, isn't he?"

Lucy harkened back to Rosemary's comment about celibacy being smoke and mirrors. It did seem odd to her that God would want a grown man to relinquish the love, companionship and sexual intimacy with his chosen partner in order to effectively serve the faithful. *I mean really, what's the point?* she thought. *Especially since men are always thinking about having sex.*

"Honest to God, Lucy, I'll never figure you out."

"Isn't that the point of a long and happy marriage? I keep you in a state of constant wonderment. That's my job."

Joseph laughed and leaned back in his rocker. "See where all those beach chairs are stacked, just past 11th Street?"

"Yes, why?"

"That's the exact spot I saw you for the first time. You remember?" Joseph prodded. "The racy bathing suit, lipstick, bobbed hair, the whole nine yards."

"Yeah, and you were strutting around like a bronzed peacock carrying that cooler across the beach."

"Got you to notice, didn't I?"

"I have to say you caught my eye. A lot has changed since then, Joseph."

"Yeah, but for the better."

"Mostly," Lucy said.

Joseph leaned in and brushed the hair off her face.

"Don't even think about it, Joseph. You're not getting lucky tonight. The walls are way too thin."

Joseph smiled. "You don't know what I was thinking, Lucy."

"Joseph, how long have we been married? I know exactly what you were thinking. By the way, Pop reminded me of something when he gave the kids their money. Have you been giving Francis money? I found a ten-dollar bill in his pants that went through the washer."

"Well, did you ask him where he got it?"

"I did, he said he got it from Father Dolan for filing sheet music in folders and then labeling them."

"Dammit, Lucy, this is what I was talking about. Our son is doing odd jobs for a priest and we don't even know a thing about it."

Joseph, expecting an argument, was surprised by Lucy's response.

"You're right, Joseph. Tuesday, when you go back to work, come straight home. I'll go and meet Francis at five, and I'll talk to both of them at the same time."

"You sure? I can handle Father Dolan."

"I'm sure he knows what you think of him. It would be better coming from me."

SEPTEMBER 7, 1959,
OFFICE OF THE SACRED MUSIC DIRECTOR
Lucy knocked on the door and entered the waiting room, taking the

seat closest to the music room door. While she could hear her son playing, she also wanted to see where Francis was spending so much of his time. Curiosity got the best of her. She knocked on the studio door and waited for an answer.

"Yes, what is it?" Dolan replied impatiently.

She opened the door and saw Francis at the piano with Father Dolan standing behind him.

"Momma, what are you doing here?"

"It's Tuesday, Francis, I was picking up the bread at Catania's so I told your father I would pick you up."

Dolan was quick to inventory the threat. "Mrs. Natale, my apologies. It's so good to see you. I was actually going to call you later tonight. If I had known you were coming, I would have invited you to hear the whole lesson. Francis has made some pretty incredible strides with his music."

"That's very nice of you to say, Father, but what was it that you wanted to speak to me about?"

"Well, I haven't told Francis, but Monsignor Flynn wants Francis to perform at the youth concert."

"Really! Did you hear that, Momma?" Francis asked.

"I was told there would be a competition, how is it that Francis was selected? I mean it's wonderful news, don't get me wrong, it's just I'm a little confused."

"We had planned on a competition, but as you know this is Monsignor Flynn's office. He has listened to Francis play almost every day he has come here. It was his decision of course. I agreed, but Francis was chosen to perform based on his ability. That assumes you have no objection."

"It would be an honor, but Father, may I have a minute to talk to you in private?"

"Of course, Mrs. Natale. Francis, wait outside for your mother and close the door behind you. Excellent work today."

"Thank you, Father. So, I come back tomorrow since Monday was a holiday?" Francis asked.

"Tomorrow, 3:45 sharp."

Francis left the room and waited next to the closed door, trying to overhear what his mother and Father Dolan were talking about.

"We're very grateful for the amount of time you have spent with Francis. We could never have afforded the cost of this level of instruction, and please don't misunderstand, but a couple of weeks ago I was doing Francis' wash and I found a ten-dollar bill in his pants. He said you had given it to him for helping file sheet music."

"Is that a problem, Mrs. Natale?"

"Well, yes and no. It's wonderful Francis is helping out around the office, but $10 is quite a lot of money, and both my husband and I would have preferred to know about it before you asked Francis. Joseph is very set in his ways and…well, we'll just leave it at that."

"Please, Mrs. Natale. Again, my apologies. Of course you're right. If Francis works here in the future, I will surely call ahead."

"And the money, Father…$10 is way too much under the circumstances."

"I completely understand, Mrs. Natale. As a matter of fact, I was going to call you tonight about another matter."

"Another matter? What's that, Father?"

"Monsignor Flynn thought that it might prove very inspirational for Francis to visit the Moller organ factory in Hagerstown, Maryland with the Shrine's organist. Of course, I would also accompany them if you allowed Francis to go. The Moller firm has won the bid to install the pipe organ in the Upper Church, and it would be a nice little reward for Francis. And, to be honest, Monsignor Flynn thinks Francis might be a natural on the organ."

"Oh, Father Dolan, I'm not sure about that. Francis and Elizabeth had their first day at Campus School today, and I expect the workload will be quite a bit different than at St. Francis. With the amount of time piano takes up I don't want him to fall behind in his schoolwork."

"Of course this would be an excused absence and if he missed any work, he would have the time to catch up. Why don't you talk to your husband and let me know?"

"When is this trip to Hagerstown scheduled for?"

"Next Thursday."

"Okay, Father. Let me talk to Joseph and I'll get back to you. You said you would be going along with the organist as well?"

"Of course. If you permit Francis to go."

"Very well. I must be going. Thank you, Father, for everything you're doing for Francis. I just want you to know how grateful we are."

"Mrs. Natale, a talent like Francis doesn't come around very often. He plays most pieces by ear. That is very unusual for someone his age, or any age for that matter. It's a talent that needs to be nurtured and explored to see how far it will take him. I would also say, and please forgive me, he has the temperament to be a priest. I went to Julliard. I remember when my parents said I had to choose between my vocation and my music. That was not true as you can see. It's just something to think about."

"Have you talked to Francis about this?"

"No. Vocational discernment is a process and Francis is still too young, but his music may very well lead him down that path."

"My word. That's quite a lot to think about. Thank you again but I must go, or I'll be late for dinner. I'll talk to Joseph and let you know."

"Of course. And Mrs. Natale, I wouldn't speak to Francis about my comment about the priesthood. Better for him to come to those issues on his own."

"I understand. Good day, Father."

Dolan realized that Lucy Natale was not to be trifled with. But her blind spot, which Dolan instantly recognized, was her ritualistic reverence to the role of priests in Catholic orthodoxy. That would be his pathway to Francis.

DINNER, SEPTEMBER 7, 1959

Lucy looked at her watch as she rushed into the house. "Joseph, we're home! Where are you?"

"Out back," Joseph said, taking a long swig from his beer. I'm reading the paper. Dinner wasn't ready, so I came out back for a smoke and a beer. Where the hell have you been, Lucy?"

"Oh, my God, you're like a spoiled child. Your mother put dinner in the warmer oven. It's all ready and the salad is in the fridge. I told you I was going to pick up Frannie and talk to Father Dolan."

"I know, but it's almost six."

"We walked home."

"Why, too stinky for the prince?" Joseph huffed.

"Joseph, don't be an ass. Besides, it was my idea and I wanted to talk to Frannie." Lucy poked her head back into the kitchen. "Frannie, Elizabeth, wash up; dinner will be on the table in ten minutes."

"What's for dinner?" Joseph asked curtly.

Lucy wished she had eaten the other end of the loaf of bread. "Well, I don't know; it's past five-thirty. Are you still hungry?"

"Now who's being an ass? Did you talk to Dolan?"

"I did, and he apologized for not letting us know."

"Is that it?"

"No, there's more, but I'll let Frannie tell you. Now wash up and cut the bread and pour some wine, unless of course you've lost your appetite."

"So, what's for dinner?"

"It's a surprise," Lucy said tartly as she left Joseph on the porch. "Frannie, get the salad and lemon wedges out of the fridge. Elizabeth, put the bread on the table."

Joseph poured two glasses of wine as Lucy removed a tray of baked ziti and a platter of fried chicken cutlets from the warmer oven.

"That looks delicious."

"Your mother made it for us," said Lucy as Joseph looked at the bread tray. "I was going to eat the other end, but your son saved it for you."

"Okay, Lucy, you made your point."

The family settled around the dinner table and Elizabeth said grace. As was their custom, the news of the day was shared.

"Okay, Lizzie, you're first."

"Why am I always first?"

"Because you're the youngest, dopey. We'll change it when you're the oldest."

"That's not funny, Frannie, I'm not stupid. I'll never be the oldest."

"Kids, come on, tell your mother and me about your day. I have news myself."

"Well, I like Sister Mary Allison. She's not like Sister Mary Bridget at all. She laughs a lot, and she loves candy. They have a science fair in the spring. I knew some of the other girls from this summer, so I ate lunch with them. We played kickball during recess."

"Was there any school?"

"Let her finish, Joseph."

"What else? Oh, I forgot. Me, Mary, Pat Wilkins, and Angela Murray, we have to get all the missals at the seats for the children for first Friday Mass. We take turns, and I'm the first one to do that, because I had the longest straw. What else? Oh, and I get dismissed forty-five minutes early to do this. It was good; I liked it. Oh, and we have to pick up the clean surplices for first Mass and the bottles of the wine and water at the convent and bring them over to the sacristy."

"You mean the cruets," Francis interrupted.

"Shut up, Frannie."

"Like I said, not much school. Did you get any homework?"

"Oh, Poppa, it was the first day, Sister said we would get homework for the weekend."

"What about you, Frannie?"

"Well, Poppa, school was like regular. I went to piano practice and boy did I get surprised." Francis grew animated. "You know Monsignor Flynn?"

"Of course I do, he's my boss."

"Well, they were going to have a competition for the soloist for the youth concert when they dedicate the Upper Church, but they want me to play! Can you believe it? I'm going to play on T.V.!"

"Oh, Frannie, can I have your autograph?" Elizabeth said in mock delight.

"Shut up, Lizzie, you're just jealous."

"Okay, that's twice. Now both of you stop using that type of language in this house," Lucy said in a tone both children recognized as trouble.

"Ha, ha, ha," Elizabeth persisted, trying to get the last word.

"Lizzie, that's enough."

"Frannie, be sure to go tell Grandpop after dinner. That's really a big accomplishment. You worked very hard, so good for you and I'm very proud of you," Joseph said.

"And Joseph, what's your news?" Lucy interjected.

"They set the actual dates for the opening of the Upper Church at the Shrine. It's now going to be a three-day event starting on November 20. So, for us, it's non-stop work until the dedication. So, I guess that qualifies as news."

"It sure does, then you'll finally hold the title of Master Carver of the Shrine of the Immaculate Conception," Lucy said with pride.

"Thanks, Lucy. Okay, what's your news?"

"Well, my news is that I talked to Father Dolan about the ten-dollar bill I found. Now, Francis, pay attention, he agrees that if you're going to work, he will talk to us first and let us know and that it was too much money for filing sheet music."

"Geez, why did you say that was too much, Momma?" Francis said.

"Be quiet, Frannie. It's too much money, no discussion on that. But Father Dolan also asked our permission if you could go to the Moller organ factory in Hagerstown when he and Monsignor Flynn do their monthly inspection for the Upper Church organ. Wait, there is more, you may be allowed to play it."

"Wow! I can't believe it. Poppa, can I go?" Francis pleaded urgently.

"Let me talk to your mother."

"Poppa, Father Dolan said some of the pipes are thirty feet high and if a pane of glass were right next to it, it would break, no kidding. Please, Poppa, can I go?"

"I think it'll be fine, Joseph. It was Monsignor Flynn's idea, and the Shrine's organist will be there as well. It's a nice reward for all of Frannie's work. They're coming back the same day, and Father Dolan said if Frannie misses any schoolwork the nuns will give him time to make it up."

Joseph hesitated and looked at Lucy. A faint smile of approval crossed her face. Lucy could not shake her exhilaration as she replayed Father Dolan's phrase – *the temperament of a priest.*

"Please, Poppa, can I go?"

"Okay, you can go, but just a day trip. When is it?"

"Next Thursday."

Francis jumped out of his chair and ran around the table to hug his father.

"Kids, clear the table and put the dishes in the sink, then go next door and thank your grandmother for dinner. Frannie, tell Father Dolan when you see him tomorrow that you can go, and I'll call him myself to confirm that it's okay with your father and me for you to go."

Elizabeth scraped and rinsed the dishes while Francis cleared the rest of the table.

"Hurry up with that, I want to tell Grandpop about the youth concert," Frannie said.

"Hold your horses. It's not like you're Elvis or anything. We're not done with the dishes," Elizabeth said.

"I heard that, Elizabeth! Stop fighting with your brother and do your chores," Lucy called from the dining room.

Joseph waited until he heard the back door slam. "Lucy, I don't think this is a good idea."

"Joseph, sooner or later you're going to have to recognize your son is different. He has a gift. People are going to notice, and while we will always do the right thing by him, we have to accept that we're really just along for the ride. Cancelling the competition was your boss' idea for heaven's sake. He works in the same office where they have the music studio. He's heard Frannie play. That's why he cancelled the competition."

"I know, but it's just that there's so much priest stuff in our lives: Father Dolan, Monsignor Ryan, now Flynn..."

"Just think how proud you'll be when your son is on national T.V. playing the piano. Joseph, trust me on this, I laid out our ground rules with Father Dolan. Frannie's not the problem. You want something to worry about, worry about Lizzie."

"What's wrong with Lizzie?" Joseph asked, alarmed.

"With all this attention Francis is getting, I can see it in her eyes. I saw it tonight at the table."

"What did you see?"

"She's feeling left out. I know you'll be really busy in the next two months, but you have to find a way to spend more time with her. She needs to know how special you think she is."

"I tell her that."

"Telling her that is not enough. She has to feel it. You have to show her. Just spend time with her. That's all I'm asking."

AN ACT OF FAITH

The next day, Francis made the walk from Campus School to the Shrine in just fifteen minutes. There was a shortcut that the neighborhood boys showed him where he could jump the fence behind Varnum Street and walk straight down the railroad tracks behind Catholic University's football field to the back of the Shrine. Francis got to the studio early and started his warmup, using some of the rock and roll he had played when Monsignor Flynn caught him. Suddenly, the door flew open, and there was Father Dolan. His face was cherry red, and he was angry.

"What are you doing?"

"I was just warming up, Father."

"Didn't Monsignor tell you not to play rock and roll in this office?"

"Yes, Father."

"And what about our discussion about what goes on here remains private?" Dolan hissed.

"I didn't talk to anybody."

"Really? What about the $10? You didn't tell me that your mother found the money I gave you, which, my friend, as you well know was out of the collection box at St. Francis." Dolan drew within inches of Francis's face. "Then you didn't tell me you made up some goofy story about filing sheet music. What if your mother hadn't told me what you had told her, you stupid little shit? What then?"

"I'm sorry, Father."

"You're sorry? Sorry doesn't cut it, Francis. This whole relationship can be over in a snap. The lessons, the money, the soda and candy, the trip to Moller, the youth concert, all of it. I can make it go away; all I have to do is say the word. Is that what you want?"

"No."

"No what?"

"No, Father, that's not what I want." Francis wilted and tried to catch his breath between sobs.

"Francis, come sit next to me."

Still tearful, Francis complied. Dolan reached for a handkerchief from his pocket.

"Here, take it and wipe your face. Go to the washroom and blow your nose and let's get started."

Francis left and was back within a few minutes.

Dolan unlocked the bottom drawer of his desk, removed a black folio with a manila folder inside and brought it back to the piano bench. "You settled?"

"Yes, Father."

"Now listen to me. You're special. I know I can be impatient, but you have a gift from God when you sit at the keyboard. Now pull yourself together. I want to talk to you before we start. Here, sit next to me. You know, God's love for you is special, so when I correct you it's because I love you both in the spiritual sense and in the physical sense. Take for example the day you were born. When you came into this world you didn't have any clothes on, did you?"

Francis nervously laughed at the suggestion. "Of course not, Father, I was a baby."

"You were I'm sure, a beautiful naked baby, a naked body in God's image. The same is true for little girls when they are born. So, have you ever seen a naked woman?"

"Gee, Father, what kind of question is that?"

Dolan saw the look of concern on Francis' face.

"Oh, Francis, don't be worried, you're not going to get in any trouble. I just need to be sure since you're one of the special boys chosen to share love with a priest, that your education in this area is proceeding along. Here, let me show you something." Dolan pulled two magazines out of his folio.

"Father, what are you doing with those?" Francis stammered, stunned at the sight of Father Dolan holding issues of *Playboy* and *Male Pix*.

"It's okay, Francis, go ahead and look at them."

"What if someone walks in?"

"Don't worry, Francis, I locked the door, and we would hear them come into the foyer before anyone came into the studio."

"You sure?"

"Yes, of course. This is all part of God's plan."

Francis started to gingerly flip through the pages of the March 1959 issue of *Playboy*. "Wow, look at that," he said, his eyes glued to the centerfold playmate.

As soon as Francis heard his own words, a wave of confusion and embarrassment swept over him. He had heard about *Playboy* from a boy at school who found it under his father's bed, but he never dreamed he would be looking at his first issue with his music teacher, who happened to be a priest.

"Do you like looking at pictures of naked women? It's okay if you get excited. God understands; it is entirely natural. He put us together so that you'll understand that love can be beautiful for those chosen by God to share their love with a priest."

Francis stared down at the page not knowing what to say. Pausing at the Audrey Dalton centerfold, he began to feel the blood rushing to his face. He thought of all the times he confessed his "impure thoughts," realizing for the first time that this was what he had been talking about in the confessional.

"Well, Francis, do you like it?"

"Yeah, I like it, but it doesn't feel right, you being a priest and all that...I don't know, it's just really weird."

"Well, Francis, it might be unusual to you, but do you accept that this is part of God's plan?"

"If you say so, Father."

"I do say so. And another thing, do you remember what you promised God about our time together?"

"Yes, Father."

"What do you remember, Francis?"

"That it is secret, that it's just between you and me."

"And God, Francis, don't forget God. God is the master of this plan. So, it'll be our secret."

"Father, I can't tell anyone about this?"

"Not even your parents, Francis?"

"Especially my parents, Father."

"That's exactly what I wanted to hear. Just between you, me and God. Now, what about this one?"

"That's gross, Father!" Francis said as Dolan laid an issue of *Male Pix* in front of him. "Those are naked guys in there with their weenies all hanging out."

"Now wait a minute, Francis. We're both males; you're not saying we're gross, are you? If you saw me naked you wouldn't say I was gross, would you?"

Francis was at a loss for words. His undershirt started to stick to him as tiny beads of sweat rose on his back. He didn't know what to say and continued to stare at the keyboard. Dolan's voice grew low and hoarse as he pulled Francis to him in a one-sided embrace. He kissed Francis lightly on the neck and whispered, "God loves you, Francis."

Francis could hear his heart beating. His ears grew hot, and an awful scent of wintergreen breath mints mixed with cigarette smoke and lingered, searing into his brain what would become a lifelong memory.

"Father, I'm feeling kind of dizzy."

"It's okay, Francis" Dolan whispered. "God knows this is all new for you. Just give it some time, and you will understand. You'll come to love both boys and girls, just like me. Just like God wants you to, it's all a part of God's plan for you. It's a gift Francis, just like your musical talent."

"But, Father, isn't looking at these pictures a sin?"

"Absolutely not. You're with me, and we're beginning to find out how we can love each other as part of God's plan. Do you understand me, Francis?"

"I guess, Father."

"Give it some time, Francis. Process this like you process hearing music for the first time. You believe in God, don't you?"

"Of course I do, Father."

"And when I turn the host and the wine into the body and blood of Christ during the Mass, your faith allows you to believe that fact with every fiber in your soul. Isn't that right, Francis? What is that called?"

"Transubstantiation, Father."

"Excellent, Francis, excellent! So, our loving each other as part of God's plan is an act of faith. Isn't that also right, Francis?"

"Yes, Father." Francis kept staring at the keyboard and realized his eyes were going out of focus. Images of Dolan kissing him and Audrey Dalton's naked body flashed in front of him, and he suddenly felt sick.

"Okay, we only have twenty minutes left. Let's do some work on a Mozart piece, you remember the Sonata for Two Pianos in D? We played it last week. Did you know Mozart was a devout Catholic? It was rumored he wanted to be a priest, but his father disapproved. Francis, what are you doing?"

Francis took his hands off the keyboard. "If you don't mind, Father, I feel a little sick."

"What's wrong, Francis?"

"I don't know, I just don't feel that good. First I'm hot then I'm cold."

"Okay, Francis, just this one time." Dolan grew close to Francis again and looked him straight in the eye. "Look at me!"

Francis turned his head and faced Dolan.

"If you are to get the things in life that you want, you'll have to work hard and listen to all of my instruction. Don't forget that

Francis. Your whole life will change when you stop listening to me. God has put you and me on a journey. It's his plan, Francis. It's not your plan, it's God's plan. That's what you take with you when you leave here today. Remember every word I say to you because the day you stop listening to me is the day bad things will start to happen to you. Are we clear, young man?"

"Yes, Father."

By the time he left the office, most of the blood had drained from Francis' face. He needed air, outside air, to get his bearings. He jogged across the parking lot and around Mullen Library, heading for the railroad tracks that bypassed the Michigan Avenue bridge. He started to run, wondering who had seen him coming out of his music lesson with Dolan. What would they think? Would there be some way his parents would know he had just looked at dirty pictures with a priest?

Francis worried he would be called queer, but he wanted to play in the youth concert. He struggled with the fact that he liked looking at the pictures of naked women and the extra money but felt a need to unburden himself in confession. What if Lizzie found out and told her friends at school? Equal measures of shame, guilt, paranoia, lust and enjoyment fueled the kaleidoscope of emotions pounding in his gut.

He reached the front door of his house and tried to calm himself before facing his mother. Francis retrieved the Evening Star newspaper from the mailbox. Dolan's voice replayed in his head. "This is God's plan."

Keep saying it, Francis said to himself as he opened the door and walked into the house.

"I'm home, Momma."

"In the kitchen, Frannie. Dinner's almost ready. Go ahead and wash up. How was your day?"

"It was cool. Father Dolan told me that Mozart was a Catholic and that he wrote a lot of music for the Church. I like playing his stuff."

"Okay, go wash up. We have lamb stew tonight."

In the bathroom, Francis scrubbed his face and hands with soap and a washcloth. Then he started the process all over. He rinsed his face, then watched the white lather turn to gray water as it swirled into the drain, keeping safe the secrets of his new life.

BREAKING THE ICE - THURSDAY, SEPTEMBER 23, 1959

Elizabeth stood next to her bed in her underwear. "Momma, why did you lay out this dress for school? It's a church dress and the girls will make fun."

"Just put it on and come to breakfast and your father will explain."

Joseph was already at the table. Both his children were going to have big days and he had asked Giovanni to cover for him at work so he could have breakfast with his family.

"Go ahead, Joseph, tell Elizabeth why she's dressed in her church clothes."

"Okay, well today's a big day for you, Elizabeth," Joseph said.

Elizabeth rolled her eyes. "I know, Frannie's going to Hagerstown to see a bunch of pipes."

"No, Miss Smarty-Pants, it's a big day for you too."

"I wasn't invited, Poppa."

"Elizabeth, you're being rude to your father, now stop," Lucy said.

"I'm sorry, Poppa."

"Lizzie, you're not going to school this morning. You're coming to work with me."

"Why?"

"Well, the artist and carver signature cornerstones are being laid into the wall of the Children's Chapel in the Crypt Church. The Archbishop is going to bless it, and they want a picture of a boy and girl with him. You're the girl, and your picture is going to be in the Catholic Standard with the Archbishop."

Elizabeth looked up from her plate and smiled from ear to ear. "Really, Poppa?"

"Yes, really."

"Frannie, have you ever had your picture in the Catholic Standard?"

Francis smiled at his sister. "No, Lizzie, you'll be the first."

"Hear that, Momma, I'll be the first," Elizabeth giggled.

"Okay, eat up. You don't want to be late. Francis, keep your coat and tie on when you're at the Moller factory and Lizzie, I'll see you at the Chapel. After the pictures, you can change into your school dress in the ladies room at the Shrine, and I'll drop you to school for the afternoon."

"Or I could stay with you, and we could take the bus downtown to go shopping at Woodies."

"Nice try, Lizzie," Joseph laughed. "Okay, let's go or we'll be late."

Joseph brought Francis to the Sacred Music Office at the Shrine and kissed him goodbye. "Be a good boy. I'll see you tonight. You know I'm very proud of you and I love you."

Francis was shocked when he heard those words. He had never heard them from his father. "I love you too," he stammered back.

Francis took a deep breath and opened the door to the Sacred Music Office.

Dolan was in the waiting room with his coat on. "You ready? You have to go to the bathroom?"

"No. Where's Monsignor Flynn?" Francis asked.

"Monsignor has to stay because the Archbishop is going to dedicate the Children's Chapel. I hear your sister's going to be there at the dedication with your father."

"So, we're going up alone?" Francis asked, alarmed.

"Why, is that a problem, Francis?"

"No, Father, it's just…"

"Just what?" Dolan demanded.

103

"Nothing, Father, I'm ready."

"Okay, that's what I want to hear. Don't worry, our organist is already up there. He's waiting for us. You have something ready to play if you're asked?"

"Do they have pianos at organ factories?"

"Sometimes they do when they want to hear a melody, but I'm sure you'll get an opportunity to play the organ. Let's go out the back door, my car's in the lot."

The parking lot for staff was on the west side of the Shrine.

"Where's your car, Father?"

"It's the '59 Dodge Royal," Dolan said proudly.

"The one with the white fins? That's your car?" Francis asked, shocked.

"Yes, do you like it?"

"I love it, are you kidding? That car is so cool."

"It has swivel seats and a record player in the dash, so it's way cool," Dolan chuckled.

"Do you have any rock and roll records, Father?"

"No, they don't make those records for this player, but I do have some Tony Bennett, and I have Beethoven's 5th Symphony. When we get off Rockville Pike and onto Route 40, we can put that on the player. It won't skip so much on a better road."

The ride north out of the city was uneventful. Rockville Pike headed towards Frederick, Maryland, and Route 40, the National Turnpike. Thirty minutes north of the city the landscape changed, revealing lush rolling hills and farms that Francis had never seen before.

Dolan pulled over at a scenic overlook just before the traffic picked up going into Frederick.

"Want to hear some music?" Dolan asked as he opened the Highway Hi-Fi and started Beethoven's 5th Symphony.

"Sure, that would be great."

"Listen to that, Francis. Stunning music, wouldn't you agree?"

Francis hesitated, noticing the same black folio that Dolan had taken the *Playboy* out of lying on the seat between them.

"I see you looking at the folio, Francis. Do you want to look at the magazines again?"

"I don't know, you think it's okay?"

"Of course. You're with me, and we're the only car in the lot."

Francis pulled the *Playboy* out of the folio and turned to the pictures of Audrey Dalton and June St. Claire. He went back and forth between the pages.

"You like that don't you, Francis?"

Francis' face started to flush as he struggled for words.

"Go ahead, you can say it."

"You sure it's not a sin?"

"Nope, not with me."

"I do like it, Father."

"Well, Francis, I can see that," Dolan laughed, eyeing Francis' crotch.

"I like the way they look."

"You mean you like looking at naked women with their boobies hanging out."

Embarrassed, Francis closed the magazine and stared out the window. In his mind he heard his father telling him he loved him and to be a good boy.

"Do you know where we are?"

"Not really."

"Right below us, thousands of men died fighting the Battle of Monocacy during the Civil War. Have you learned much about the Civil War?"

"It was about slavery, I know that."

"Right, men trying to own other men and women. Only God has the right to make a plan for a man's life. Wouldn't you agree with that, Francis?"

"Yes, Father."

"You hungry? I made us some meatloaf sandwiches and there's some cold Coke in the cooler."

"I'm starving."

Dolan and Francis talked about what they heard in Beethoven's Symphony, trying to figure out what inspired his music as they ate their sandwiches. Francis relaxed as Dolan gave him a short Civil War lesson on how Lt. General Jubal Early was delayed by a day in his march to Washington by the forces of Major General Lew Wallace.

"Seems like a funny place to listen to Beethoven knowing that so many men died just below us protecting the retreat line to Washington. Wouldn't you agree, Francis?"

Francis kept looking out the window toward the river.

"What's the matter?" Dolan raised the center armrest and slid towards Francis.

Francis moved a little closer to the window.

Dolan pulled Francis to him and grabbed his hand. "Feel how hard this is?" Dolan guided Francis' hand to his penis. Yours does the same thing when you look at those pictures doesn't it, Francis?"

Francis started to cry.

"Stop it right now. Relax, there's nothing wrong here, just relax."

Dolan got the *Playboy* out, opened it to the naked pictures of June St. Claire and handed it to Francis. "Look at her Francis, she's gorgeous."

Francis stared at the pictures as Dolan pinned him in place with his hand, rubbing the boy's growing penis.

"Go ahead and take it out. I'll show you what to do. Just keep looking at the pictures."

Francis was frozen in his seat. Dolan unzipped his fly and pushed his underwear aside.

"Oh, God… oh, Father, I'm…."

Within seconds, Dolan caught the ejaculate in a white handkerchief.

"What's that?" Francis shrieked.

Dolan let out a big belly laugh. "That's your seed, my boy, that's your seed and make damn sure you keep it away from any girlfriends."

"I don't have a girlfriend."

"Good and you don't need one. Now it's my turn."

"What do you mean?"

Francis jumped in his seat when he saw Dolan's erect penis. "I can't, Father. I can't."

"Oh, yes, you can, do it just like I did yours. It's God's plan, Francis. You're with a priest, and this is our special love. Now do it."

Francis' hand shook as he gingerly approached Dolan.

"Go ahead, it doesn't bite."

Francis hesitated.

"Oh, for God's sake." Dolan grabbed Francis' hand and wrapped it around his penis and with a few furious strokes it was over.

Francis started to cry again.

"Listen to me, you little shit. I got you out of school for a full day, took you for a ride in my brand-new car and made you lunch. If I don't see a little more cooperation and respect, I'm going to tell your parents that I found this *Playboy* in your book bag. If you think you're crying now, wait until that happens. Who do you think your mother will believe, an agent of God or a little shit like you? Is that what you want?"

"No, Father," Francis said as he wiped his tears away on his sleeve.

"That's better. Now get yourself together. I have work to do, and I told these people at Moller I was bringing a brilliant young pianist with me so you could see a massive pipe organ in person. Now, are we on the same goddamned page of music, Francis?"

"Yes, Father."

AREN'T THEY BEAUTIFUL, MOMMA?

Joseph and Elizabeth stood on the east terrace, a broad receiving area that divided the entrance to the Upper Church and the lower Crypt Church.

"You excited to meet the Archbishop?"

"I guess. I think I like being out of school and getting my picture taken with you for the newspaper even better."

Joseph chuckled. "Me, too, but for sure, don't tell Momma that when she gets here. And make sure you're polite to the Archbishop."

"Don't worry, Poppa, I know what to do."

Sunlight began to peek through the trees that bordered the green in front of the Mullen Library and McMahon Hall. The slightest hint of fall color formed a perfect frame around the stone reliefs that rose above them on the east façade. Elizabeth turned around and looked up as the shadows made the stone come alive on the sculpture above the steps in the Crypt.

"Did you do all of these?"

"Do what?" Joseph asked.

"All of these statues and the stuff over the arches."

"No, I had a lot of help from your grandfather and other carvers."

"Which one did you do?"

"Well, I worked on almost all of them at one time or another."

"What about this one?" Elizabeth asked as she looked up and fixated on the faces of two Native Americans.

"Do you like that one?"

"I do, I like that one a lot."

"I like that one, too. It's called *I Will Give Glory O Lord O King*."

"I like the faces of the Indians. I wish I could touch them. I want to touch the ones that you did."

Joseph's body surged with unvarnished pride as he realized that his daughter had connected to his artistry.

"Well, I can't get you up that high, but the plaster cast that we took all of our measurements from is still in our shop. You can touch that."

"Can we go now?"

"Lizzie, I just saw Momma pull into the visitor parking lot. We'll go later."

"Yoo-hoo, Joseph! What are you doing up there?" Lucy said as she climbed the steps to the east terrace.

"Just taking in the sights. Lizzie wanted to see some of the carvings we did for the east tympanums."

"I certainly hope you're not making the Archbishop wait."

"Aren't they beautiful, Momma? Look at the two Indians around the corner."

Lucy pulled as comb from her purse and ran it through the back of Elizabeth's hair.

"Momma! Stop."

"Stand still and be quiet. Let me finish. I'm sure the carvings are beautiful, but let's get inside so we're not late. We can look at them later," Lucy said as they started down the basement steps to the Crypt Church.

"I think I want to carve stone when I grow up," Elizabeth said.

Lucy stopped dead in her tracks and turned around to face Joseph. "Now see what you started," she said as they headed down the steps.

ETERNAL SALVATION – DROPPING THE HAMMER

Depending on traffic, the drive from Hagerstown, Maryland was between three and four hours. It had been a long day and Francis said very little on the way back, sitting as close as he possibly could to the door. He tried to ignore any thought of the parking lot incident earlier in the day, focusing rather on the excitement of exploring a new instrument.

It was just before 6:00 P.M. when Dolan and Francis headed down North Capitol Street, made a left and headed toward the

Natale home. Rush hour traffic was still heavy as they stopped at the red light in front of the Shrine.

Dolan broke the silence. "Francis, you did very well today. What you did with the curator, having never before played organ was… well, it was remarkable. Now, as to the other stuff."

"I know, Father, it's our secret. It's part of God's plan."

Dolan's tone grew grave. "It's more than that, Francis."

"What do you mean, Father?"

"What I mean, Francis, is if you speak of our time together when we are expressing our love for each other, you will lose eternal salvation. That is our goal in life, that when we die we will go to heaven to live in everlasting happiness. If you break your promise of secrecy about God's plan, you will lose eternal salvation and you will be cast into the fires of hell. Forever. Do you know how long forever is, Francis?"

"No."

"It's so long that you will know nothing else but the fire on your flesh as you burn alone with no one to rescue you. So, do you clearly understand, Francis?"

Francis' voice started to shake. "I do, Father. I won't speak to anyone about God's plan."

"Do you love me, Francis?"

Francis immediately thought of his father and hesitated.

"Well?"

"I do, Father."

"You do what, Francis?"

"I love you, Father."

"Good boy. Now, get your happy face on and I'll walk you to the door."

"Do you think that's a good idea?" Francis asked with a worried look.

"Of course it is. The only thing that happened today is that you got closer to God. Now let's go."

For the first time, Francis felt he had two lives he was living. He paused on the porch, willing himself to believe that somehow this was all part of God's plan.

He took a deep breath and opened the door.

"Momma, we're home."

CAMPUS SCHOOL, THURSDAY, OCTOBER 1, 1959

A few minutes before nine o'clock, thirty-five children began to crowd the entrance door to Sister Mary Allison's classroom. Four enormous tilt-in casement windows flooded the classroom with warm early fall sunlight.

All of the children were familiar with the "ready and rest" drill. They scurried to the cloakroom to hang up their coats and deposit their lunches.

"One minute left," Sister Allison said, raising her voice.

The children rushed to their desks, placing their books in the compartments underneath their seats and took out their pencils, placing them on the desks.

"Twenty seconds!"

One by one, each child folded their hands neatly in front of them, placing them on top of their desks.

Sister Mary Allison addressed her seventh-grade class. "Children, please pay attention. I do not hear silence! For every minute you make me wait I take two minutes off your recess."

The class went dead silent.

"Excellent. Now, today is the Thursday before first Friday. What happens at nine-fifteen? What is it that we all do today?"

Mary Pat Bailey's hand shot up so hard Elizabeth thought it might pop out of her shoulder socket. "We go to confession to prepare our souls to receive the Lord."

"Excellent, Mary Pat. Girls, you'll go first when we get to chapel. Boys, you will wait in the first two pews in front of the altar. No wandering around and no talking. You're in God's house. Now, Mass starts tomorrow at 8:00 A.M. sharp. If you're late that means you're tardy, and if you're tardy you stay after school. After Mass, we all come back to the lunchroom where your mothers will have milk, donuts and some fruit for you. So, do we all know what we're doing?"

"Yes, Sister," the class answered in unison.

"Miss Natale, do you have any other responsibilities today?"

"Yes, Sister, at two o'clock I get a hall pass and I meet Sister Rosalind at the convent. She gives me the cleaned surplices for the altar boys. Then I put out the bottles, I mean the cruets, so Father Dolan can fill them with water and wine and place all the missals in the pews."

"Anything else?"

"Oh, I forgot, I hang the surplices next to the cassocks in the closet, and then I match the name on the cassock with the name on the surplice."

"Excellent, Elizabeth. All right, everyone stand and file out single file. Remember, we walk in silence so you can prepare for confession with an honest examination of your conscience."

Elizabeth sat in the pew waiting for her turn in the confessional box. Sister Mary Allison was keeping a careful watch on the boys, giving Elizabeth a chance to whisper to her best friend sitting next to her.

"Angela, do you have any sins to confess?"

"No, I just make ones up," Angela giggled.

"What do you mean? Making things up is lying."

"Shhh! Sister will hear us. Just tell him you used a bad word, were disrespectful to your parents or took some change without asking. Whatever you do, stay away from the impure thoughts stuff. If you confess to having impure thoughts you have to talk more to the priest, and Father Dolan is creepy. You want to get out of there with three Hail Mary's, three Our Fathers and an Act of Contrition. Elizabeth, do you have any real sins to confess?"

"Don't be stupid, Angela, of course I don't."

Elizabeth stood dutifully in line just out of earshot while Angela was in the chamber, waiting for the red light to turn green and the door to open for her turn. She examined the confessional carefully and realized it was made of beautiful wood with hand carved corners like the corners her father carved in stone. It reminded her of a fairy tale where little elves would try to figure out which door on the wall held the secret treasure. The problem for Elizabeth was that the real structure had no elves, it smelled old and musty and she had no sins to confess.

Angela exited the confessional smiling, holding three fingers at her side. Elizabeth walked past her, gingerly opened the door and knelt, waiting for the door to close behind her. As she took her position on the kneeler, she heard faint mumbling. It was Father Dolan talking to another girl in the class on the other side of the confessional. Elizabeth wondered whether the priest was hearing real sins or made-up ones. Without any warning, a small gauze covered door slid open revealing the partial silhouette of Father Dolan.

"In the name of the Father, Son, and Holy Ghost, Amen. Bless me, Father, for I have sinned, it has been two weeks since my last confession," Elizabeth said.

"Go on."

"I sassed my parents, and I took some of my father's change out of his pocket without telling him."

"Anything else?"

"I got my brother to do some of my math homework and I turned it in as mine, and I used a curse word one time."

"What was it?"

"Do I have to say it?"

"Yes, you do, child."

"Can I spell it, instead of saying it?"

"Yes."

"S-H-I-T."

"Anything else?"

"No, Father."

"Your voice sounds familiar; do I know you child?"

"Yes, I am Elizabeth."

"Elizabeth Natale?"

"Yes, Father."

"I understand it's your turn to help with the altar preparation for First Friday?"

"Yes, Father."

"Very well. Elizabeth, please be sure to be on time. I have some important instruction for you."

"Yes, Father."

"Our Lord Jesus Christ, who has left power to his Church to absolve all sinners who truly repent and believe in him, of his great mercy forgives you all your offenses. By his authority committed to me, say three Hail Mary's, three Our Fathers and make a good Act of Contrition. I therefore absolve you from all your sins. In the Name of the Father, and of the Son, and of the Holy Spirit, Amen. Go in peace."

Elizabeth left the confessional and flashed the same three fingers to Angela. Throughout the day Elizabeth kept close tabs on the clock.

At 1:50 P.M., Sister Allison called her name.

"Elizabeth, it's time for you to go attend to your assignment. Get your things out of the cloakroom and be at the back door of the convent to pick up the surplices. Don't dawdle. Father Dolan is extremely punctual."

"Yes, Sister."

At exactly 2:00 P.M., Elizabeth knocked on the back door of the sacristy.

"Come in. Ah, Elizabeth, it's so good to see you again," Dolan said as he opened the door.

"Hi, Father."

"Did you bring the surplices?"

"Yes, and the wine bottles."

"They're cruets, Elizabeth. Okay, go and hang them up in the altar boy closet and bring the cruets to me. Did Sister Rosalind tell you that the cruets had been washed?"

"Yes, Father."

"Excellent. When you're finished with that come back to the vestment room. I want to talk to you."

Elizabeth quickly dispatched her tasks and met Dolan back in the priest vestment room. She had never been in the vestment room. She looked around and marveled at the ornate counter, extra wide drawers and full-length mirrors.

"Wow. It's really neat in here. What are all the mirrors for, Father?"

"They're to make sure that before you go out onto the altar everything's in place. Come here, child, I want to talk to you," Dolan said, settling into a straight-backed chair in the corner of the room. "Come, come closer and sit in my lap,"

"Is that okay, Father? Sister Mary Allison said to get my work done and leave as soon as I was finished."

Dolan was able to reach her arm from his chair and slowly guided Elizabeth to sit on his lap.

"There. Comfortable?"

"I guess, Father. You sure this is okay?"

"Elizabeth, do you believe in God?"

"Oh, yes, Father, why?"

"Because if you believe in God, you also must believe that when a priest says something is okay, it is okay. Do you believe that?"

"Yes, Father."

"So, come sit with me and tell me what has Francis shared with you about our time together."

"He said you were a hard piano teacher, but that you knew your stuff."

"Anything else? This is like a test, Elizabeth, but it's a test straight from God. If you pass this test, he will show you his mercy."

"Am I in trouble, Father?" Elizabeth asked, looking at the floor.

"No, of course not, Elizabeth. I just want to know what Francis has shared with you."

"Well, there were two things."

Dolan clenched his teeth, his torso stiffening in his chair. "And what were those two things, Elizabeth?"

"Francis said you let him play some gigantic organ and that you gave him candy during piano practice. He said the organ was really cool."

"Anything else?"

"No. That's it, Father. So, do I pass the test?"

"You're halfway there. Now listen carefully, Elizabeth. Some children are chosen by God to spend special time with a priest."

"Was Francis chosen?"

"He was, Elizabeth. God chose him. And guess what, God has chosen you as well. But I'm not sure you can keep a secret as well as Francis can."

"Father, I can keep a secret better than Francis."

"Is that so? Why do you say that Elizabeth?"

"Because."

"Because why, Elizabeth?"

"If I told you, it wouldn't be a secret anymore."

"That's true, Elizabeth, but I'm a priest. I'm God's earthly representative, and he knows everything."

"Can you get God to tell you my secret?"

"I can if I ask, but one of your tests today is for you to tell me," Dolan said, amused.

"Okay, I heard my parents talking that my Grandpop is going to leave and go back to Italy and leave Grandmom behind."

"That's your secret?" Dolan asked, relieved.

"Yes, did God not know that?"

"Of course he did, I was just surprised that you held that secret for so long. I'm very proud of you. So, do you want to be one of God's chosen special girls?"

"I do, Father. Then I'll have something special like Frannie," Elizabeth said, squirming in Father Dolan's lap.

"That's right, Elizabeth, but the same rules apply to you as they do to Frannie. If you break your promise and tell anyone, even Francis, about this special love, this special bond you will have with your priest, you will lose the opportunity for eternal salvation. That means you'll never be with your family in heaven. You will burn in hell with the rest of the ugly sinners that have turned their backs on God. Do you understand, Elizabeth? Is this something that you believe you can do?"

Elizabeth's eyes grew wide. "It is, Father," she said firmly.

"Do you promise before God, Elizabeth?"

"I promise, Father," Elizabeth said, sliding off his lap.

Dolan got up and adjusted his chair directly in front of the full-length mirror. "Turn around, Elizabeth. Face the mirror and place your hands on the side of the frame."

Elizabeth saw her reflection and watched her hands disappear as she grabbed the sides of the mirror. She could feel Dolan's breath on her neck directly behind her.

"Now close your eyes, Elizabeth, and keep them closed. Feel the power of the Lord Jesus Christ on your body. Are they closed, Elizabeth?"

"Yes, Father, they're closed. Is this going to hurt?"

"No, Elizabeth. God's plan for you is to feel this wonderful gift."

Dolan reached under Elizabeth's dress and placed his hands just beneath her underwear waiting for her to move or open her eyes. "Good, Elizabeth, you're doing great. Keep your eyes closed."

Elizabeth shuddered as Dolan slipped two fingers underneath her underpants and into her vagina.

"Your eyes still closed?"

"Yes, Father, but it's starting to hurt."

"You're doing great, Elizabeth. God is granting you a very special love that very few girls will ever experience. Do you believe that Elizabeth, with your whole heart and soul?"

"I do, Father, I believe it."

"Excellent, my child. Remember, Elizabeth, you're doing this for God."

Francis was more than halfway home when he realized his mother had told him to wait for Elizabeth and walk her home. He was sure if he told his mother he had forgotten he would get into trouble, so he turned around. The clock on the National Bank building read three o'clock as Francis made his way back to the corner of 10th Street and Shepherd Avenue. He wondered why he hadn't run into Elizabeth as he backtracked.

Francis got to the back door of the sacristy in the alley behind Aquinas Hall and waited for Elizabeth. After a few minutes, he decided to make sure she was still there before he left to go home and face the wrath of his mother for forgetting Elizabeth. Francis opened the door and listened. He realized that he was not supposed to be in the sacristy unless he had been assigned that day, but a sudden noise coming from the hall got the best of his curiosity. Peeking around the corner, he could see the vestment room door ajar. He slowly inched toward the door.

Francis was shocked when he saw Elizabeth's reflection in the full-length mirror. He took a quick breath of air in through his nose, emitting an audible gasp. His sister's yellow dress was over her waist and her underpants were down around her ankles, her face grimacing and her eyes tightly shut. He heard Dolan groan and Francis' brain froze. He had heard that same groan in his car on the way to Hagerstown two weeks before.

Dolan was lodged on Elizabeth's backside. "Keep your eyes closed, Elizabeth," he gasped.

"What's that warm stuff on my butt, Father?"

"It's called ejaculation, child. It's all part of God's plan. Keep your eyes closed and hold still. I'll wipe it off."

Francis quickly backed up and hid in the closet that stored the surpluses and cassocks for the altar boys. His heart was beating so fast his body was shaking. A minute or so later he heard Father Dolan speaking in a muffled voice. He heard the vestment door squeak open and the outside door to the alley open and close, then silence. Minutes passed but they seemed like hours. He was on his knees and was starting to get a cramp in his leg, so he shifted position under the long robes. He heard heavy steps enter the room and walk to the closet. The door flung open, and Dolan was on him yanking him out of his hiding spot.

"What are you doing here, Francis?"

"Nothing, Father, I thought I forgot a book."

"You're lying! What did you see that made you hide in a closet?" Dolan grabbed both of Francis' arms and shook him. "What did you see?" Dolan shouted as he placed his lips to Francis' ear. "Tell me, Francis, or this will be the end for you!"

Francis was frozen. He could not speak.

"Okay, Francis, I'm going to tell you what you saw. You saw your sister being chosen as one of God's angels to share a special love with her priest. That's what you saw. And just like you, she promised to keep that secret with God and me. Just like you did. And Elizabeth knows if she breaks her promise to God, she will forfeit any chance she could have of everlasting happiness in heaven with her family. Just like you did, Francis. Take a deep breath."

Francis stood there motionless.

"Do it!" Dolan raged.

Francis began to let air come into his chest.

"Keep breathing. Everything's fine. Do you want to achieve eternal salvation and keep your family safe, Francis?"

"Yes, Father."

"Yes, Father, what? Repeat what I just said," Dolan hissed.

"Yes, Father I want to achieve eternal salvation and keep my family safe."

"Good. So, while you're here, make yourself useful. Help me prepare the altar for Mass tomorrow morning."

When the altar was ready, Dolan moved behind Francis and turned him around by the shoulders.

"You will be silent about what you saw. God has plans for Elizabeth and you will be abandoned by your family and cast into the fires of hell if you get in the way of God's plan." Grabbing him by both arms and pulling him within inches of his face, Father Dolan said, "Do you understand, Francis?"

"Yes, Father."

"And will you remain silent for the rest of your life?"

"Yes, Father."

Dolan held Francis tight in his arms and kissed him passionately on the lips. "Now go home, Francis, and do as I say. God loves you."

"Yes, Father."

Francis walked home, unable to process what had just happened. His cheeks were red from crying and he had rubbed his lips raw with the sleeve of his jacket. Francis knew he needed a believable story to tell his mother. He grabbed a small branch from a tree, closed his eyes and walloped himself, enough to draw blood from his cheek and lip. He figured a trip over a curb and a fall would answer any questions.

Elizabeth was already home when Francis arrived.

"What in the world happened to you?" Lucy asked.

Francis started crying. "I forgot to wait for Elizabeth. I was almost home so I ran back, but then I tripped on a curb and fell right on my face and my nose is killing me. When I got back to Aquinas Hall, all the doors were locked up, so I came home. I looked for her, Momma, I did. I'm really sorry, Momma."

"Oh, Francis, don't be upset. Elizabeth walked home by Providence Hospital. That's why you didn't see her. It was a mistake, that's all. You remembered to go back, that's all that matters. I'm just worried about your nose."

"Frannie, I've been home for a half hour. You didn't see me at Aquinas Hall?" Elizabeth said, munching on an after-school snack at the kitchen table.

"No, why?" Francis asked.

"Does your nose hurt too much to play ball tag before dinner?"

"You want to play ball tag now?" Francis asked, incredulous.

"Yeah, but if your nose is broken or something we don't have to play."

"I don't want to play, Lizzie," Francis said, waiting for something to happen.

"Lizzie, if you're not going to play help me set the table," Lucy said.

Francis tried to process why everything seemed so surreally normal. Elizabeth was helping his mother set the table for dinner. Grandmom was at the stove tending to a pot of tomato gravy and potato gnocchi, one of Poppa's favorite meals. He waited for Elizabeth to say something, but nothing was mentioned. Francis left the kitchen to go to his room, stopping at the top of the stairs so he could eavesdrop. Nothing.

Dinner proceeded as normal. Dishes were cleared, homework started and finished, and baths were drawn. His mother and father came into his room to say goodnight as they always did, kissed him and left.

"You're going to have quite a shiner in the morning, but you'll be okay in a few days," Joseph said as he closed the door.

Francis lay in bed until he saw the shadow from the hall light go off. The house was silent. He crept out of bed and cracked the door to listen. Surely Elizabeth would say something now.

Nothing.

CHAPTER THREE

A Bit of History

SOME ACTS OF AN IMPRUDENT NATURE

Monsignor Cletus Ryan was a planner. He viewed everything in his life, including his pastoral work at St. Francis, through the lens of his own career advancement. Ryan was well aware that a sexually charged sub-culture was firmly imbedded in the Church hierarchy. Sexual acting out with children and adults had been a common occurrence within the "celibate" priesthood since the thirteenth century. Every upwardly mobile Bishop in the world had to navigate the secrecy of the hierarchy, and Ryan's handling of Dolan's situation now looked to be a disaster.

Dolan's presence in his parish was a test, and to date Ryan's emotions had clouded his judgment. His written request to see the Archbishop on a personnel matter needed to be pitch perfect in tone.

As Ryan struggled for the right words in his draft, his attention was drawn to the sealed manila folder lying in his open briefcase on the floor. His conversation with Monsignor Flynn relating to Andrew Dolan had not gone well, so before his inquiry filtered back to the sycophants that inhabited the chancery, he needed to request a private audience with the Archbishop. Troubled, deep in thought and sipping several ounces of Jack Daniels, he was interrupted by a furious knock on his office door.

"Mrs. McGinty, would you please stop that racket and come in?"

"Archbishop Guilfoyle is on the phone," she said breathlessly, looking as if she were about to faint.

"Mrs. McGinty, you need to get a hold of yourself," Ryan barked as she stood there waiting for him to pick up the phone. "Tell the Archbishop I'm upstairs and I'll take it in my room."

Mrs. McGinty, deflated, was clearly annoyed by Ryan having frustrated her less than subtle attempt to eavesdrop.

"As you wish, Monsignor," she said in a snit.

Ryan grabbed his briefcase and bolted up the wooden staircase to his private quarters. He thought the call was either going to be bad news or *really* bad news, as the Archbishop had never called him on the phone before. He stared at the blinking plastic hold button on his phone in the anteroom of his private quarters, took a deep breath, pushed the button and picked the receiver up off the cradle.

"Good morning, Your Excellency. I'm sorry to have kept you waiting. I was on my way to my private quarters when you called."

"Ah, Cletus, not to worry, it's so good to hear your voice. It's been too long."

"The pleasure is mine, Excellency."

"Cletus, what is your schedule today?" Guilfoyle asked.

"Today?" Ryan stammered, shocked that his call from the Archbishop of Washington had become urgent. He kicked himself for raising the issue of Father Dolan with Monsignor Flynn.

"Unless of course you're too busy today, then we can put it off."

"Of course not, Your Excellency, I am at your disposal. When would you like to see me? I could be at the chancery in thirty to forty-five minutes depending on traffic."

"Actually, Cletus, instead of the chancery come to my home. I know it's a little further out, but it will give us some privacy that otherwise is not afforded at the chancery. Do you know where I live?"

"Yes, off Nebraska Avenue on Warren Street. I was there for your barbeque last August."

"Indeed, Cletus. I will look for you within the hour. Just knock on the front door and come in."

"Your Excellency, is there anything I should bring with me to prepare for our meeting?"

"Just yourself, Monsignor."

Ryan was filled with anxiety as he quickly changed into his best clerics and ran some liquid Kiwi bootblack over his shoes. He knew he was in trouble. The question was how much trouble. All the Archbishop's sweetness on the phone was pure bullshit from a man used to getting his own way. Cletus had been a fool to go to Flynn about Dolan's predilections and it was obvious now that Flynn had talked to the Archbishop. While Ryan had his suspicions about Dolan, particularly after Sister Mary Bridget's less than obscure comment, he just didn't like the guy. His so-called "imprudence" was just a bullshit cover-up. To Ryan, Dolan was one of many petulant, arrogant jackasses coming out of seminary and, in this case, using his talent as a musician to cover for his predatory activities with kids.

A one-on-one meeting with the Archbishop at his private residence was the consequence for Ryan's not keeping his mouth shut and rocking the boat.

Mrs. McGinty, armed with the black three ringed binder she used for the parish schedule, was at the foot of the stairs dutifully waiting for Ryan to reappear.

"Is there anything you would like me to do, Monsignor?"

"Yes, give my apologies to any scheduled appointments I may miss today. I have an important meeting with the Archbishop that just came up. I'll be back later."

"I didn't have that on your schedule, Monsignor."

"Of course you didn't, Mrs. McGinty. Like I said, it just came up."

Flummoxed, Mrs. McGinty held her ground at the bottom of the steps. "When is later, Monsignor?" she asked forcefully.

Exasperated, Ryan stopped just before the landing. "My dear Mrs. McGinty, I know you're trying to be helpful, but please do try to temper your curiosity for things that don't concern you. Later means later. For the exact time, you'll be able to note that when you see me again. Good day, Mrs. McGinty."

It was a crisp bluebird sky October morning. The ride to the Archbishop's residence settled Ryan.

What's the worst that could happen? Ryan pondered. Perhaps a simple rebuke for not coming to the Archbishop in the first place. After all, it was the Archbishop who had arranged for Father Dolan's transfer from Los Angeles to St. Francis de Sales, and Guilfoyle had chosen Ryan to supervise a smooth transition for the talented priest who was dealing with "some acts of an imprudent nature."

"Who the fuck talks like that?" Ryan wondered aloud to himself in the car. He checked his watch. Fifty-six minutes had passed since he had hung up the phone. He parked his car in the single car driveway of the Archbishop's home.

At 4110 Warren Street, housing the Archbishop and his priest secretary, was an elegant Georgian Revival executed with a colonial twist. Built in 1942 and framed by well-manicured gardens and multi-leveled terraces, the three-story home was clad in quarried Pennsylvania fieldstone and traditionally shuttered with six over six double hung windows. A multi-colored flagstone walkway led to the front door, which was adorned with an oversized fall welcome wreath. Ryan knocked twice and entered the home, closing the door behind him.

"I'm in here, Cletus."

Ryan followed the voice down a long hallway and entered the Archbishop's library. Guilfoyle walked around his ornate desk to greet Ryan and to offer his ring. Ryan knew instantly that this was no informal visit with the Archbishop as he bowed at the waist and kissed Guilfoyle's ring.

Guilfoyle, dressed in black slacks and a red flannel shirt, was portly, with soft boyish facial features. Wisps of thinning, sandy blond hair hanging down to his shirt collar were offset by brilliant blue eyes, making the Irish boarding house orphan who rose to the rank of "Archbishop of America's Archdiocese" in Washington, D.C., a visual anomaly.

"Pardon my casual attire, Cletus, this is how I dress when I'm home."

"No apologies necessary, Your Excellency."

"So, are things well, Cletus?"

"They are, Your Grace. The parish is active with excellent Mass attendance. So, things are going well. I do have to admit that I'm more than a bit curious as to why you wanted to see me so urgently."

"Well, Monsignor, it's complicated. I was writing you last Friday to inform you that I wanted you to serve on the College of Consultors and to accept the role of Vice Chancellor for the Archdiocese. As you know, Cletus, the College of Consultors is reserved for my most senior priests and ones who understand the political aspects of the Church."

"With respect, Your Excellency, of course I'm flattered that you're considering these assignments for me. However, I didn't receive any letter from you."

"That's because it's right here on my desk."

"I see. So, I assume you now have some reservations?"

"You would be correct, Monsignor, I do."

"And, Your Excellency, would those reservations be centered on my conversation with Monsignor Flynn regarding Father Dolan?"

"Yes, they would. That's why I like you, Cletus, you get right to the nub of the matter."

Ryan looked away. He knew he had disappointed the head of his archdiocese. He also knew that his career was at that moment in extreme jeopardy.

"Why did you not come to me directly with your concerns about Father Dolan?"

"To be honest, Your Excellency, I went to Monsignor Flynn because the opening of this Shrine is on his shoulders. Dolan is a priest living in my rectory and with all that you're burdened with at the moment I wanted to handle the situation myself. When Father Dolan came to me you said that he had a bit of a history around some imprudent activities. But you said that was in the past and he had recovered."

"That's correct, Cletus, and that is what I believed," Guilfoyle said defensively.

Ryan continued. "I didn't ask you what it was and agreed to keep an eye on his spiritual maturation as a priest. I now have a sense as to what the issue may be. You're right, I should have come to you first. It was a mistake in judgment, Excellency."

"A mistake in judgment likely to happen again, Cletus?"

"Never to happen again, Your Excellency."

"I see. Well, I suppose you're wondering why you're here, alone in my home?"

"Like I said, I'm more than a little curious, Archbishop."

"Well, I assume, Monsignor Ryan, that if I offer these two appointments to you, you will accept and do the work I ask of you in the name of our faithful Catholic community."

"I would be honored and of course I would accept these positions as your obedient cleric."

"Excellent. So, let's talk. Of course, you know that I'm working furiously to meet the financial goals of the Shrine's Building Committee. We're scheduled to open the doors on November 20. What is that—a month and a half away?"

"It will be a great day, Your Grace."

"It will be a great day if we meet our fundraising goals, Cletus. Thousands of Marion devotees are counting on us to make this Shrine to Mary Immaculate a reality, a concrete testimony to our Catholic presence in society, a statement in stone of our beliefs, a place to worship and a place to give homage to the Mother of God. We're reaching our goals, but we're not there yet. Do you know, Cletus, how we're going to get there?"

"I'm sorry, Archbishop, I work in a parish tending to souls in need and those who may not even know they are in need."

"So, let me ask you, Monsignor Ryan, how many children are in your parish school?"

Ryan was blindsided by the question and felt totally exposed in front of his Archbishop, who surmised instantly that he had caught Ryan flat-footed.

"It's not my intention to embarrass you, Cletus, but if I'm to look to you for leadership in the Archdiocese and ultimately recommend you go onto bishop's track, you need to strategically process the information that's in front of you. It will be the nickels and dimes of Catholic school children and their love of Mary Immaculate that will put us over the top, not the patrons that want to use money to hedge their own mortality with God. Don't get me wrong, they of course help, and I'll be damned if I'm not going to take their money, but it will be the children that make this America's Church for generations to come."

Guilfoyle settled into an overstuffed chair in his library and motioned for Ryan to sit down. He was one of the Church's great strategic thinkers and was an expert in getting Catholics to part with their money. In 1949, in the United States, there were 4.4 million children under Catholic instruction. Guilfoyle built his plan around the children and the children he believed were the Church's future. He called it "the three P's." Get the kids in the *pews*, get their *pennies* and they will grow up to be *patrons* of Holy Mother Church.

"Cletus, did you know that in 1958 there were nearly eight million children under Catholic instruction? Or 7,750,377, to be exact. That's a 76 percent increase in the children of God in one decade! If I had a dollar from each one of those children, I could fund fifteen of the interior chapels and all the exterior iconography in one shot."

Ryan, squirming in his chair, forced down the reflux that was bubbling in his chest.

"So, Cletus, not to put too sharp a point on this discussion," Guilfoyle said, pointing his finger at Ryan, "of those nearly eight million school children I mentioned, you've been entrusted with 470 souls at St. Francis de Sales Grammar School."

Ryan sat there pale and bewildered, having just been taken to the ecclesiastical woodshed by his Archbishop. The worldview of the emerging vitality of Catholic America had escaped him entirely. While he had been tending to the souls of St. Francis de Sales, he had been content to let inertia care for the continued growth of the Catholic population.

What a small-minded statement to make to your Archbishop, he thought.

"Come out back with me. It's a beautiful day. You'll feel better about all of this when we're done."

The backyard of the Archbishop's residence was an expansive, perfectly groomed, cross-cut lawn surrounded by a medley of mature sugar maples, white oaks and persimmon trees. A warm autumn sun framed the stunning border of vibrant color, making it a serene oasis in an otherwise bustling section of the city. In the rear of the yard was a flagstone terrace with several lounge chairs surrounded by boxwoods. In the center stood a statue of the Blessed Virgin. To the left and right of the statue were two ironwood kneelers inlaid with the crest of the Archdiocese.

"Come sit, Cletus, in the fresh air. Tell me your concerns about Father Dolan. What do you know?"

"I'm not sure I know anything, Your Grace. It's a feeling I have when I've observed him."

"Could you be more specific, Cletus?"

"He's almost childlike when he's around the children. I first noticed it at the home of one of my parishioners for a family get-together the evening before Ash Wednesday."

"What did you notice?"

"Except for when I introduced him to all the adults, he spent the entire time with the children at the party, playing silly songs on the piano with their son. Based on the circumstances... I mean after all, Archbishop, it wasn't a kid's party. We were invited there as guests by Mrs. Natale to celebrate and pay respects to the upcoming Lenten season. It just made me uncomfortable."

"I see. Tell me, Cletus, is this the same Natale boy that Father Dolan is giving music instruction to?"

"Yes, I believe he has been asked to play on the last day of the opening of the Shrine at the children's concert."

"Then we're talking about the same boy. I understand he's somewhat of a virtuoso, according to Monsignor Flynn."

"Well, I wouldn't know about that, Archbishop, but I've heard him play and his talent does appear to be well beyond his years."

"Is there anything else that concerns you, Cletus?"

Ryan hesitated and stared at the statue of Mary Immaculate in the yard. He knew he was being cross-examined by Guilfoyle but had still not been given any specifics as to why Dolan had been transferred from Los Angeles.

"Cletus, is there something else?"

"There is but I'm not sure I should tell you."

"You are not sure you should tell your bishop something that may affect the entire Archdiocese? Need I remind you of your special obligation to obey your Ordinary? Vows that you took on the day of your ordination to the priesthood?"

"Archbishop, I'm totally aware of my obligations in this matter. My hesitation is around involving you in something that I did."

"You did? We're talking about Father Dolan. What on earth did you do?"

"I went into Father Dolan's quarters, his private quarters."

"Is he aware that his privacy has been violated?" Guilfoyle demanded.

"I suspect he will be when he realizes some things in his room are missing."

"Good God, Monsignor, you stole from another priest?"

"Not exactly, Archbishop, I would rather think I was protecting the reputation of my parish, the oldest parish in the Archdiocese, the same one that you entrusted to me."

"Don't be coy, Cletus, it doesn't become you."

"I apologize, Your Grace. I removed from Father Dolan's desk a certain amount of pornography, Your Excellency."

Guilfoyle grew grave and took a seat in one of the wrought iron chairs on the flagstone terrace. "You mean magazines?"

"Yes, magazines and…"

"And what?" Guilfoyle bellowed, losing his patience.

"And some Polaroid pictures, Your Excellency. They're pictures of young people, Your Excellency."

Jolted by the new information, Guilfoyle became alarmed. "And do you have them?"

"Yes, I put them in the trunk of my car."

"Does anyone else know you have them?"

"No. The house was empty when I went into Father's room."

"Come pray with me, Monsignor." The Archbishop got up from his lounge chair and both men knelt on the ironwood kneelers in front of Mary Immaculate, intoning the prayer, "Hail Mary, full of grace."

After the prayer, Guilfoyle directed Ryan to retrieve the photographs from his car and to meet him in the library. As Ryan walked to his car, he realized that the entire episode was out of control, and he had no one to blame but himself. He cursed the day he laid eyes on Andrew Dolan. When Ryan returned, Guilfoyle was seated behind his desk looking out onto the expanse of the backyard.

"Lay the envelope on my desk and take a seat, Cletus," Guilfoyle said without turning around. "Monsignor, what do you know about the Secret of the Holy Office?"

"Archbishop, I know it's the highest level of secrecy ordered by the Holy Father. There was a discussion about it in moral theology when I was in seminary."

"Monsignor, let me ask you, do you believe secrecy serves a useful purpose for the greater good of the Church?"

"I do, Archbishop, in most cases."

Guilfoyle's desk chair heaved under his weight as he turned to face Ryan. "Ah, in most cases you say. And in what cases do you suppose, Monsignor, that the Secret of the Holy Office should not apply?"

"Are you asking me for my opinion, Archbishop?"

"Yes, indeed I am, Monsignor."

"I believe men like Dolan are dangerous. They're vipers on the ground, lying in wait for any opportunity to seduce little boys and girls into an ungodly state of sin. I think they should be referred to the Holy See for involuntary laicization."

"I see. Returning these priests immediately to the lay state?"

"There should be no other viable alternative for men who have so far removed themselves from the sacred ideals of the priesthood."

"And, Monsignor, are you suggesting that cases like these should be subject to the Holy Office?"

"I'm not so sure, Your Excellency."

"Do you agree that when I was consecrated to this office by His Holiness the Pope that I was made responsible to God for the welfare of our priestly community and our community of faithful believers?"

"I do."

"And with all your training, Cletus, do you accept that a bishop's first duty is the protection of the whole as opposed to the few?"

Ryan nodded.

"Do you accept that any scandal, particularly one involving sexual contact with a minor by a priest that becomes notorious within the community of the faithful, is to be avoided at all costs? Do you accept that proposition as a priest incardinated to this Archdiocese?"

"I do, Archbishop, but as a priest I do worry about the children."

"Does your priestly worry about the children extend beyond your duty to the community?"

"I'm not sure I understand your question, Archbishop."

"Does your worry suggest to you a course of action to discuss these matters with the child's parents, or to report the incident to the authorities or to perhaps announce your revelations in the weekly parish bulletin?" Guilfoyle asked sarcastically. "Tell me, Monsignor Ryan, how would your worry about the children be manifested?"

"I don't know, Archbishop. I think I would come to you for guidance."

"Is that what you want from me, Cletus, guidance?"

"I do, Your Grace."

Guilfoyle stood up from his chair and walked toward Ryan. Ryan instinctively stood and the two men faced each other.

"Monsignor Cletus Robert Ryan, are you prepared to swear your allegiance to the Secret of the Holy Office?"

"I am, Your Excellency."

"Please kneel and take my hand and touch the episcopal ring of this office."

Ryan went down on both knees and gently grasped his bishop's hand, touching the crest of the episcopal ring with his thumb.

"By the power invested in me by His Holiness Pope Pius XII as Archbishop, and as Assistant to the Pontifical Throne, do you,

Cletus Robert Ryan, permanently and forever give your solemn oath never to reveal any fact or confidence that would do harm in any degree to Holy Mother Church or to any of its faithful adherents?"

"I do, Archbishop." Ryan's face flushed with excitement and dread, realizing that he had passed the point of no return.

"Excellent, Monsignor. Now let's get to work." Guilfoyle walked past Ryan over to a hinged wall painting of Madonna of the Streets, revealing a small wall safe. After several tries, the tumblers lined up and the door thumped open. Guilfoyle removed a plain envelope and placed it on his desk next to the cache of photographs.

"Archbishop Curran, before he passed away, left me this envelope and a key to the Secret Archive of the Archdiocese. This envelope was in there; it is to be diligently stored as strictly confidential, revealed only to those who are in a position requiring this information. Your new appointments satisfy that requirement. I'll do the same for my successor when the time comes. Now tell me what you know about the Papal Decree issued in 1922 called *Crimen Sollicitationis*?"

"Well, I understand the title to mean the canon law crime of solicitation in the confessional, but as far as the context here, I've never heard of such a decree."

Guilfoyle removed the cover page of the document, revealing the unmistakable seal of the Pope. "This envelope contains the norms that the Holy Father has instructed the bishops of the world to follow in adjudicating grave sexual offenses committed by clerics not only by solicitation in the confessional but all sexual crimes committed against children. All the procedures are laid out here, step by step. There are no opinions here, no exceptions, no worries and no equivocations. The investigations, deliberations and judgments are to be done under the permanent seal of the Secret of the Holy Office. This is my sworn obligation. Do you understand?"

"I do, Archbishop, I completely understand. But did you say that these norms were issued in 1922?"

"I did indeed." Guilfoyle turned to the manila folder Ryan had retrieved from the car. "Have you looked at the photographs?"

"Unfortunately, yes."

"Do you know any of the children?"

"No, but I recognize the location of some of the photos."

"You mean you know where they were taken?" Guilfoyle asked, somewhat surprised.

"Yes, two of the pictures were of girls. They had their backs to the camera and their skirts pushed up with their bare bottoms showing. They were taken in the vesting room at Aquinas Hall."

"Jesus, Mary and Joseph!" Guilfoyle fumed.

"The other was of a boy's penis, and it appeared he was in Father Dolan's car when the picture was taken. The interior of the car is quite unmistakable. I don't know any names, but I suspect the boy is Francis Natale."

"Not the boy Monsignor Flynn has been telling me about? Christ, Cletus, the boy's father was just named the Master Carver at the Shrine. I mean how would you know looking at a picture of a kid's penis?"

"Well, I don't know for sure, but I've seen them interact. It's ridiculous the amount of time he's spending with him. It cannot be all piano practice. Plus, Francis is my head altar boy, and I was supposed to go with Father Dolan more or less as a chaperone when he took the boy to visit the Moller Organ facility."

"Ah yes, Cletus, the Moller Company, they are building the organ for the Shrine. It was donated by the Military Vicariate, a magnificent gift from our brother chaplains."

"Well, in any event, Archbishop, at the last moment I had a conflict and, long story short, Francis went up to Hagerstown alone with Father Dolan. I never mentioned it to the parents, and I assume the boy didn't either because I never heard anything about it. Since that trip I have seen a change in the boy." Ryan tried to gauge

Guilfoyle's facial expression. "If you pardon me, Archbishop, you don't seem surprised by all of this."

"Of course it's shocking, Monsignor, but I'm not surprised. He had some of these same issues arise in Los Angeles. That's why I wanted your steady hand to guide him through his recovery, along with the fact that Flynn had been whining for a top shelf Sacred Music Director for the opening. Father Fitzgerald wrote me there was a risk he would act out again, but damnit, Cletus, Father Dolan promised me he would not!"

"With respect, Archbishop, had I known more of his exact history I would have been better able to serve you."

"Perhaps, Monsignor."

"Who, may I ask, is Father Fitzgerald?"

"He is the medical director for one of the Paraclete Houses in New Mexico that treats troubled priests."

"Did you say Paraclete Houses?"

"Yes, Monsignor, the Servants of the Paraclete in Jemez Springs is just one of several Catholic inpatient treatment facilities that provides this kind of work for bishops."

"My God, Archbishop, I had no idea."

"Of course you didn't. Now you know," Guilfoyle said with little emotion as he opened the folder and looked at each one of the photographs.

Ryan would recall much later that Guilfoyle's facial expression never changed. It was as if he were reading an editorial in the Washington Post.

"I feel as if I have failed you, Your Grace."

"You haven't failed me, Cletus, you've given me the unique opportunity to manage this sordid mess under the Holy Father's norms for the protection of the faithful. You would only fail me by breaking your silence on what has transpired here. As you can imagine, it is for your protection as well."

Guilfoyle placed all the photographs back into the manila folder and then placed the entire folder into a larger sealed envelope marked "Contents under the Secret of the Holy Office," and returned both the Papal Decree and the photographs into his safe.

"Now, Cletus, go back to your rectory in high spirits. You're now a member of the College of Consultors and a Vice Chancellor to the Archdiocese. I'll take care of all of this and if I need you, I will personally call you. Do not discuss this with anyone, including your own spiritual advisor. Are we clear?"

"Yes, Your Excellency. Should I prepare for you to relieve Father Dolan of his parish duties?"

"Now, Cletus, think about what you just said. In six weeks, the world's news media plus all three television networks will descend upon us for the opening of America's Church. We have three full days of liturgical celebrations and events. We have a youth concert and Father Dolan is the Sacred Music Director for the entire affair. What, precisely, would you suggest I do at this time? What, Cletus? Please tell me!"

"My apologies, Archbishop. That was impertinent and a stupid thing to ask based on our current circumstances. I was just…"

"You were just what?"

"I was just thinking of St. Luke."

"Of course you were, Monsignor. Chapter 17, Verse 2: 'It would be better for him that a millstone be hanged around his neck than offend one of these little ones.' Is that what you were thinking about, Cletus?"

"Yes, Archbishop, precisely."

"Well, St. Luke didn't have our job, Cletus, now did he? You know what they say…"

"What would that be, Archbishop?"

"If our job were easy everyone would be doing it. Cletus, I want you to take a day off and clear your head. To deny people their faith by introducing scandal you deny Christ, Cletus, just as St. Peter did. That, as you know, can have profound consequences."

"I understand your point, Archbishop. If there's nothing else, I'll take my leave."

"No, Cletus, I think we're done for now. Congratulations on your two new appointments. I'll make the announcement in the Catholic Standard. Go in peace and let the perpetual light of Christ shine upon you."

"Thank you, Your Excellency."

Ryan drove back to the rectory. His meeting had unnerved him, but he was not buying the crock of shit the Archbishop was selling. The devastation of a child was somehow, according to the Archbishop, not enough to justify a sex scandal being visited upon the Catholic faithful. But the abuse of a child was not an act of God, it was a child of evil emanating from the twisted mind of a despicable priest who broke his vow of chastity.

How could the purging of that cancer be scandalous to the faithful? he wondered. *Why can't the Archbishop see that obedience to the mandate of silence is the wrong approach to the welfare of the faithful?*

It didn't matter anymore. Ryan's lust for career advancement eclipsed any concern he had for the children. He had been co-opted into an ongoing criminal conspiracy. As a future bishop, his choice now was clear. Ryan would walk this journey in lockstep with the Archbishop, confident that a two-thousand-year-old Church could weather any storm. His role would be what he promised his bishop it would be on the day of his ordination—perpetual obedience.

Ryan pulled his car into the rear parking lot of the rectory.

"Jesus Christ, she's still here," Ryan muttered, seeing Mrs. McGinty's turquoise '56 Nash Metropolitan still in the lot.

Mrs. McGinty was waiting for him at the threshold of the rectory vestibule, three-ring notebook in hand, despite his having been gone for the last six hours.

"Monsignor Ryan, there were three appointments you missed that I made excuses for and rescheduled for Friday."

"Mrs. McGinty, please write up a memo for me as to who the individuals are and their phone numbers. I know it's late so you can leave it on my desk, and I'll tend to it after I get a bite to eat."

"But, Monsignor, I already rescheduled these appointments."

"Yes, I understand, but Friday may not be convenient."

"But Monsignor…"

"Mrs. McGinty, please, there is a novena tonight at the parish and I'm doing the benediction, and I need to get washed up and get to the church. I'll see you in the morning." Ryan closed the conversation, leaving for his private quarters.

He closed the door to his apartment, wishing he could simply take a hot shower and go to bed. A hot washcloth felt good on his face, temporarily shielding him from the grit of his new mission. A knock at the door jolted him back to full alert.

"Yes, what is it?" Ryan called out.

"It's Andrew, Monsignor, may I have a minute?"

"Of course, Father, I'll be right there," Ryan said, grabbing a towel and tossing it around his neck. He opened the door to see Dolan, visibly upset.

"Monsignor, I had some personal papers in my desk that now are missing, and I…"

"And you what, Father?"

"I'm not sure how to proceed. I mean I don't want to accuse anyone…"

"Any accusation that an individual would remove personal papers from a priest's private quarters would be very serious indeed. Perhaps you simply misplaced them. Did you check in your office at the Shrine? What exactly would I be looking for in case they turn up?" Ryan asked, casually drying his face with the towel.

"Never mind, Monsignor, I'm very sorry to have troubled you. I'll retrace my steps; I'm sure they'll turn up. It was just some letters from my parents and their will. You know, things that have sentimental value."

"Of course, Father. I'll say a prayer to St. Anthony, he usually comes through for all things worth finding."

"Thank you, Monsignor."

"Is there anything else, Father?"

"No, thank you for your concern. Actually, Monsignor, there is one more thing. That comment made by Sister Mary Bridget the night we had the testing for the altar boys, do you remember what she said?"

"That would be hard to forget, Father."

"Do you think she's capable of some sort of prank or mischief?"

"Lord only knows what Sister Mary Bridget is capable of, but if she were so inclined, I believe she would direct her wrath toward me."

"Right. I'm sorry to have disturbed. I'll see you at the novena, Monsignor."

Ryan closed the door, flopped into his recliner and opened a beer, exhausted by playing cat and mouse with a sexual predator and the Archbishop that was protecting him.

THE HOME OF GIOVANNI NATALE THE NEXT DAY

Giovanni added two pieces of seasoned oak to the Rumford fireplace, hoping to take the morning chill out of the living room. Gathering his notebook and a fresh cup of coffee, he settled into his chair to re-read the letter he planned to give to Anna. While it was clear to him that she would never understand his motives for leaving at this late stage in their life, Giovanni believed a record should be created that would at least offer an explanation for his decision.

He looked around the room and began to realize he was going to miss it. When the family bought the house, Giovanni gutted the living room and installed a herringbone teak floor and quarter sawn cherry paneling, covering the ceiling with newly invented acoustic fabric. In the corner, sitting on a room sized Serapi Persian carpet, was a Zenith Chippendale phonograph player with a Trans-Oceanic AM and FM radio receiver. Two bow armed Morris chairs designed by Gustave Stickley and matching ottomans sat in front of the fireplace and a small inlaid side table doubled as Giovanni's desk. On it sat one of his prized possessions, an original table lamp from New York's Tiffany Studios, given to him when he was named Master Carver at the Shrine. The leaded glass shade cast red, green and amber hues of light from the floral design, creating the perfect mood for him to listen to his music and create the sketches that would document his body of work. He was about to leave it all behind to keep his promise to Josephine. Behind him, he could hear Anna coming down the steps from her bedroom.

"You're all dressed, Anna, where are you going so early?"

"I'm taking the bus downtown to Catania's. Connie made some fresh *sfogliatella*. I want to get some for Frannie and Elizabeth for tonight when they're just out of the oven."

"I got up early and made some coffee, I thought we could talk."

"About what?"

"Awhile back you told me you deserved some answers and I want to give them to you. And I want to give you a letter I wrote for you."

"Just like that, Gio? At six o'clock in the morning you want to give me some answers, and you wrote a letter. Are you still leaving for Italy?"

"Yes, I bought my ticket yesterday. I leave November first."

"Then there's nothing to talk about," Anna said coldly. "Maybe you should give your letter to your grandchildren and your son so they can understand that their grandfather is a selfish *jadrool*. You want to talk, Gio, go talk to your grandchildren, and find out what's wrong next door."

"What do you mean, something wrong?"

"If I knew, I certainly wouldn't be talking to you about it. Your lunch is in the refrigerator." Anna grabbed her coat and stormed out of the kitchen, headed for the bus stop.

Giovanni tucked his letter into his notebook and gathered his coat and lunch. He decided he would go next door and wait for Joseph to go to work with him. Walking out the back, he crossed over the alley to his son's back porch.

"Hello, the house," Gio yelled from the back steps.

"Come on in, Pop, the door is open," Lucy yelled back.

Giovanni entered through the kitchen, carrying his lunch pail and his notebook in a canvas briefcase.

"Good morning, Lucy, is Joseph ready for work?"

"Yes, he's coming down now. You want a cup of coffee?"

"No, I'm good, I just want to catch a ride with Joe."

Giovanni settled into the front seat as Joseph pulled the car out of the back alley and headed up 14th Street toward the Shrine.

"I told your mother I'm leaving November 1."

"I'm guessing it didn't go well. I saw her stomping past the house to the bus stop. Where the hell was she going at 6:15 in the morning?"

"She said she was going to Catania's but she's probably going down to talk to Gianna and the rest of the hens."

"Christ, Pop, can you blame her? You're leaving her high and dry."

"No, I'm not leaving her high and dry. I'm leaving her everything: the house, everything in it, and most of the money. You know the house is paid for, Joseph, is your house paid for?"

"Pop, this isn't about me or my house. You're the one who has created all of this uproar."

"I'm not riding in with you to talk about any of that. It's done."

"Right. Whatever you say, Pop," Joseph said angrily as he turned left on Michigan Avenue heading toward the Shrine.

143

"Your mother said there's something wrong with the kids."

"What do you mean? What did she say?" Joseph asked, looking directly at his father.

"Well, she actually said there's something wrong in the house."

Joseph felt a knot building in his stomach. He had felt a change in the house with the kids, but it was nothing he could put his finger on. Lucy had assumed it was the pressure of the run-up to the concert and Elizabeth feeling jealous of all the attention Frannie was getting. Joseph felt that there was more but other than his instinct there was nothing he could point to, so he had tried to let it go and concentrate on work.

"Do you want me to talk to them?"

"No, I don't, Pop," Joseph said forcefully. "We haven't told the kids anything about you leaving. I'll have my hands full with that nightmare, and with you leaving three weeks before we open, I don't need anything else on my plate. I'll talk to Francis to see if I can find out anything."

I DON'T WANT ANY OF YOUR HELP
Thursday morning, Lucy kissed Francis and Elizabeth and gave each of them their lunch and some milk money. Francis had overheard Elizabeth telling their mother that she wouldn't be home until a little before four because she had Mass duty.

After two blocks of silence Francis decided to talk to his sister.

"You look sad, Lizzie, what's the matter?"

"Why do you care?"

"I just thought you looked down in the dumps, that's all."

"Well, I'm not, so stop asking me questions."

"I heard you tell Momma you have Mass duty today. See, jerk-face, that's not a question," Francis mocked.

"What about it?"

"Well, it's not a first Friday."

"Yeah, well tell that to Father Dolan. The rest of the girls have Mass duty for first Friday for the kids. But now Father Dolan has some stupid Mass he says for the Sisters every Friday, and he chose me to prepare the altar."

"Okay, do you want some help? I can come over before piano practice."

"No. Just leave me alone, Francis. I don't want any of your help. And don't wait for me, I can walk home alone. I'm eleven you know."

They returned to silence as they crossed Michigan Avenue and turned up Varnum Street. Francis counted 432 square blocks in the sidewalk as he formulated a plan to confront Father Dolan.

PIANO PRACTICE - OFFICE OF THE SACRED MUSIC DIRECTOR

Francis walked across the green from the Mullen Library toward the east terrace of the Shrine. He was two half-flights down the steps of the Crypt Church when he heard someone calling out his name through the heavy wooden doors.

"Francis, wait just a moment," a sharp voice called out.

Surprised, Francis turned around and saw the long-withered visage of Monsignor Flynn.

"Hello, Monsignor Flynn."

Flynn didn't acknowledge the greeting. "Father Dolan called and said he would be fifteen minutes late and that you were to warm up with…wait I wrote it down," Flynn said as he pulled out a scrawled note from his pocket. "Chopin's Etude Opus 10 Number 1, do you know what that means?"

"I do, Monsignor," Francis said flatly.

"Very well, Francis, the door is open. And keep up your practice schedule, we're only six weeks from the opening."

"Yes, Monsignor, I will."

Francis had no intention of warming up with Chopin. He walked through the office into the studio and turned on the lights.

He gently let his fingers glide over the black lacquered maple rim of the Steinway case that housed the instrument he had decided would be Elizabeth's salvation.

Francis had memorized the full fourteen-minute piano roll from George Gershwin's 1925 Rhapsody in Blue. For the next fourteen minutes, time traveled for Francis. He allowed himself to get lost in his thoughts about the love and hate he had for Dolan, trying to make some sense out of what he was about to do. As he struck the iconic notes of the opening he closed his eyes, letting his fingers find the notes that would free his sister from a monster and his accomplice. Music offered him solace but it came with a price. Nearing the end, Francis paused and listened. Dolan was right on time. Francis continued playing as the studio door flung open.

"Mr. Natale, what in the world do you think you're doing? That's not Chopin's warmup as I directed!"

Keeping his eyes closed, Francis sped through the last three variations, emphasizing the powerful B flat chord at the end. He looked up and smiled.

"I know, Father, did you like it?"

"Don't be cute, Francis, I'm in no mood. Finish your warmup with Chopin's Etude Opus 10 Number 1 as I instructed you. Monsignor Flynn told me he gave you my message." Dolan was yelling now. "Did he not give you my message, Francis?"

"Yes, Father, he gave me your message. I didn't feel like warming up with that. I like Gershwin's music better for a warmup."

"Oh, I see, the compliant student has now become the petulant artist."

"I don't know what petulant means, Father."

"It means you're being a real asshole so why don't we cut the bullshit and get back to work."

"Did you see my sister today?" Francis asked as he closed his eyes, trying to control the shaking in his voice.

"Of course I saw her. She did her work at Aquinas Hall. I've been seeing her every Thursday, Francis, remember?"

"No, I meant did you see her like the day you found me in the closet?" Francis asked, keeping his head down and staring at the keys on the piano.

Dolan leaned over and spoke directly into Francis' ear. "That, young man, is none of your business. It's between God and your sister and me. How dare you question me on such a sacred topic? What are you trying to say, Francis? Let's get to it."

"I want you to leave Elizabeth alone."

"Hey, Francis, let me give you a bulletin, you're not in charge. I'm in charge. I'm doing God's will."

"I don't think that's God's will."

"Oh, now I see, you think that it's okay for you to look at pictures of naked women and jack-off with a priest? Made you feel pretty damn good now didn't it, Francis?"

Francis didn't know what to say. Guilt and anger flooded his brain. Finally, the words he never thought he would speak came tumbling out. "I'll do it."

"Do what, Francis, what the hell are you talking about?"

"I'll do it. You know, in that picture you showed me."

"What picture?"

"You know, the picture of those two guys doing that stuff with their weenies."

"Oh, the chivalrous knight wants to protect his sister. So, now you want to make a deal. Am I hearing you right?"

"Yes. If you leave Elizabeth alone."

"And if I agree, Francis, you'll do what I say and be silent about it?"

"Yes."

"Yes *what*, Francis? I want to hear you say it."

"I'll do what you say, Father, and be silent about it."

"Do you promise before God and the lives of all those you hold dear, Francis?"

"I do, Father," Francis said, wiping away his tears.

"Get to work on your warmup and I better hear Chopin. I want you to repeat it five times. Do you remember it, Francis?"

"I remember it," Francis said derisively.

"Watch your tone, Francis, this isn't a game," Dolan said as he pulled up a chair and sat directly behind Francis.

Even with his small hands Francis had mastered the entire movement in a matter of a dozen or so practice sessions. The second and fourth finger pivots, flexible shifting with the middle finger and the thumb tucked neatly under the arch of his hand, allowed Francis to move effortlessly through the ascending and descending octaves. By the beginning of the third sequence Francis was channeling his talent to escape the jumble of debilitating emotions. Resignation and dread collided violently with memories of sexual gratification that seemed wildly out of place with everything he knew. At the conclusion of the fifth sequence, Francis turned around and faced Dolan, who was still seated.

A smug look came over Francis' face. "What's next, Father?"

"What's next, Francis, is you're going to make good on your promise."

"What…you mean here? Father, I can't," Francis said, frightened.

"No, not here, you dumb shit. I have a place in mind. Get your books and follow me. If we run into someone on the way tell them that we're going to the sacristy."

Francis prayed that someone would be in the memorial hall or at least in the back of the Crypt Church. Dolan led the way to the sacristy. Hope turned to fear as Francis realized they were alone. Just before the main door on the right there was a staircase up to the ground floor in the event of an emergency. Across from the landing was a hallway that led to a darkened empty space awaiting the stone, marble and mosaic adornments of a devotional chapel to Our Lady of Ta' Pinu, Patroness of Malta. Dolan grabbed Francis' hand and pulled him into the darkened space.

"Now, Francis, it's time for you to cement your deal with God and me." Dolan unzipped his trousers. "Now get on your knees and don't make a sound."

THE NATALE HOME LATER THAT EVENING

"Great dinner, Lucy."

"Thanks, Joe, Momma gave me a new recipe for meatballs with just veal and pork, no beef. Did you like them?"

"They were delicious, but there was no beef in them?"

"Nope and they were baked and not fried."

"I don't believe you."

"Swear to God, not an ounce of beef and they were baked. Besides, Dr. Irey wants you on a heart healthy diet, so I decided we'll take little steps and get your blood pressure down," Lucy said as she organized the dishes and silverware on the drying rack.

"Christ, Lucy, you sound like a nun," Joseph said mocking his wife. "My blood pressure's fine, Luce."

"No, it's not, Joseph. I was with you on your last visit, remember?"

"Here, let me help you finish drying. There's something I want to talk to you about."

"Must be serious if you want to help me finish the dishes. Get me a cigarette and a small shot of Pop's rye and I'll finish here and meet you out back."

Joseph poured a two-ounce shot of rye for Lucy and a two-ounce shot of grappa for himself, grabbed two cigarettes and his heavy work coat and settled into a chair out on the back porch.

"It's chilly," Lucy said, wrapping herself in Joseph's work coat.

Joseph lit both cigarettes and gave one to Lucy.

"So, what's the problem, Joe?"

"I'm not quite sure. Pop told me this morning he had booked his ticket for November 1."

"I know. Momma came over this morning and cried for an hour. I just don't know what to say to her. I know she doesn't want to be alone, but your father has been such a shit for all these years. To leave her and then rub that woman in her face… I swear, Joseph, if you ever did anything like that to me, I'd slit your throat."

Joseph choked as he gasped for air to clear the grappa from his throat. "Jesus, Lu, that's a bit harsh."

"Well, maybe, maybe not," Lucy said arching her eyebrow. "So, what's up?"

"When Pop left this morning, he said I needed to talk to the kids and that there was something wrong in the house. Truth be told, Lucy, I've felt it. I mean, did you see them tonight? Hardly anything was said during dinner. Christ sakes, they didn't even fight like they usually do. Pop said Momma said there's something wrong in the house."

"Come on, Joe." Lucy inhaled deeply on the Camel. "We've been through this before. I'm sure Frannie's just a bundle of nerves getting ready for the concert. I know Father Dolan's really working him hard and I think Lizzie's jealous of all the attention. She told me the other day she thought she would do better in school at Bunker Hill."

"She did? What did you say?"

"I told her she was being ridiculous and that she was staying right where she was. So, I know that made her angry."

"Maybe she just doesn't like it," Joseph offered meekly, not wanting to tread on a sore subject.

"We've been there as well, Joseph, so I would ask you not to bring it up with her. I'll tell you what, you talk to Frannie this weekend and I'll try to talk to Lizzie. Father Dolan has to go somewhere so there's no piano practice except what he does here."

ACT OF FAITH

SATURDAY MORNING, OCTOBER 10, 1959,
AT THE NATALE HOME

Saturday was a day full of work for Lucy. Clothes needed to be washed and hung out, shopping for the upcoming week's meals needed to be done, Sunday dinner needed to be planned, and the Bible studied for Mass. But Saturday night brought a merciful respite. Joseph would go out for Chinese take-out and at seven-thirty, everyone in the house would settle in to watch an hour of Perry Mason's crime solving genius.

Frannie was still in his pajamas watching the morning cartoons.

"Frannie, is your sister up?" Lucy asked.

"I don't think so, Momma."

"Turn the T.V. off at nine-thirty. I have cooked oatmeal warming on the stove and some cut up fruit or you can have some cereal. I want you both up and dressed before I leave and after breakfast, I want you to—"

"I know, Momma, practice my piano," Francis interrupted, preoccupied by the silliness of Laurel and Hardy.

"Hey! I'm serious, Francis. Now go and wake your sister."

Francis snapped out of his daze. "Can I watch till the end of the movie, Momma?"

"Yes, I'm going next door to get Grandmom then we're going shopping. So, before I leave, I want you both up and dressed."

Lucy gathered her list and grocery cart and parked it at the bottom of the steps to her mother-in-law's house. For the next thirty minutes over coffee and fresh biscotti, Lucy and Anna compared notes on recipes and composed a working grocery list for the week.

"You ready, Mom?" Lucy asked.

"All set," Anna answered.

"I'll meet you out front. I'm just going to run over and check on the kids before we leave."

Lucy went in through the back door and entered the kitchen. It was just as she had left it. The T.V. was still on but Francis and Elizabeth were not downstairs. Furious, she turned to go upstairs when she saw Francis sitting on the top step.

"What on earth are you doing and where's Elizabeth?"

"She won't get up, Momma. She's crying about something, but she told me to get out."

Lucy walked up the stairs, past Francis on the landing, and knocked on Elizabeth's door.

"Frannie, I told you to leave me alone," Elizabeth screeched through the door.

"Lizzie, it's Momma," Lucy said as she walked into her daughter's bedroom. "Frannie, go next door and tell Grandmom I'll be a few minutes. Now, Lizzie, what's going on?" Lucy asked as she slid into the bed next to her daughter.

"Nothing, I just don't want to get up."

"Really? It's almost nine and it's Saturday, the sun is shining…"

"I told you, Momma, it's nothing, I just want to stay in my room," Elizabeth said with her back to her mother, facing the wall.

"Lizzie, c'mon turn over, let me see you." Lucy gently pulled at Elizabeth's shoulder and took a handkerchief from her purse. "Now what's wrong?"

"Sister told me that I was being replaced for Thursday Mass duty with another girl in the class because I forgot the cruets at the convent and the girls called me stupid and made fun of me. I hate it there; I just hate it and I don't want to go back."

"Did you forget them?"

"No, Momma, they weren't there. The only thing I saw was the surplices, so I brought them over."

"When did all this happen?"

"Yesterday," Elizabeth said, still sobbing.

"Why didn't you say anything at dinner last night?"

"Why should I? You're just going to make me stay at Campus. I hate it there."

Lucy ignored the wave of guilt that came over her as a passing emotion, refusing to let her daughter's hurt feelings get in the way of her Catholic education. "I know you're upset, honey, and if you want to spend the day in your bedroom it's okay, but you're staying at Campus. This is where you'll get the best education. If things don't always go your way, you'll have to rise above it. And trust me, Lizzie, things don't always go the way we want. I'll be here for you, and I'll talk to Sister if you want."

"I said no, Momma." Elizabeth turned away from Lucy.

"Suit yourself, Elizabeth," Lucy said as she kissed the back of her head.

Francis was just outside the door and heard everything. He knew exactly what had happened and he wished God would strike Dolan dead in his tracks so all of this would be over.

Lucy stepped over Francis and hurried down the steps to meet Anna.

"Francis, get going on your piano practice," she said as she slammed the front door. "Mom, I'm sorry to keep you waiting. Lizzie had something happen at school and she's very upset. It could be her hormones, but she's giving me a run for my money."

"What was it?" Anna asked as they walked to the bus stop.

"I'm not really sure. It had something to do with not bringing the cruets over from the convent for Mass yesterday. And she hates school. Joseph's going to talk to Francis this afternoon. Maybe we'll find out what's really going on."

"You mean with the kids?" Anna asked.

"No, with Lizzie."

"Oh."

"What does that mean, Momma?"

"It doesn't mean anything. I don't know, just seems things are different with the kids. Maybe they know something about the S.O.B. leaving. Kids have big ears you know. When are you going to tell the kids about Gio?"

"I don't know, Momma, I was hoping he would change his mind."

"I wouldn't count on that," Anna said dryly.

They boarded the bus at Michigan Avenue and 14th Street for a short ride just past the district line into Maryland. Ten minutes later, with very little conversation along the way, the bus dropped them off at the parking lot of the Giant food store in Mount Rainer.

"I don't know, Mom. Ever since I moved them to Campus it's been one thing after another. I can't think about that now. Let's split up, you get all the vegetables and I'll go look at the meats. Then we'll take the bus downtown to Catania's, get the bread and have some lunch with Connie. How's that sound?"

"Good. We'll both get through all this *stonzate*," Anna said warmly, giving Lucy a kiss on the cheek.

Joseph got home promptly at twelve and went right for the refrigerator. He opened it and smiled at what he saw. There on a plate were two pork sandwiches layered with broccoli rabe and provolone cheese. He poured himself a glass of chianti.

"Hey, Frannie, what's that you're playing?"

"Why, do you like it?"

"Well, it's different, for sure."

"So, you don't like it?"

"No, no, I didn't say that, it just sounds a little dark, kinda angry."

"It's supposed to be, Poppa. It's called Suggestion Diabolical or Diabolique. It's by a composer named Prokofiev."

"Is he Russian?"

"Yes, Poppa, he's Russian," Francis said, annoyed.

"Don't get snarly, Frannie. For my taste I like the other Russian guy you played, he's a little easier on the ear. How long you been at it?"

"A little over an hour. I'm done now. I have some more to do, but I was going to do it later."

"You had lunch? Mom left two pork sandwiches in the fridge."

"I'm not hungry, Poppa."

"Well, you gotta eat."

"I'll have something later, I'm really not hungry."

"Okay, last chance because I'm gonna eat them both."

"That's okay, if I get hungry Momma said there's some leftover stew."

"Where's Lizzie?"

"She went over to Mary Pat's house. She left a phone number, it's on the table."

"Hey, there's a college football game on television today on NBC. I saw it in the paper today. It starts at twelve-thirty, it's going to be a doozy, Michigan State and Iowa. Do you want to watch it with me?"

"Maybe later. I'm going out to the garage. I bent some spokes on my bike and I'm going to straighten them."

"Why don't you wait, and I'll help you after the game? Then when we finish you can get back to your piano practice."

"That's okay, I can do it." Francis got up and avoided any eye contact with his father as he went out the back porch to the garage. He was filled with rage and wanted to lash out but didn't know how. He wanted to tell his father about Dolan but was terrified of the consequences.

Joseph settled in front of the T.V. with his lunch and realized he had lost his appetite and was in no mood to watch football. He wrapped the other sandwich for Francis and went out back to the garage.

"Hey buddy, how's it going?"

Francis had two needle nose pliers and was working to straighten the spokes.

"Going good. Have three more to do."

"You want me to hold the wheel?"

"Sure, that would help."

Joseph watched his son's face intently as he concentrated on the repair. He remembered when he used to rock Francis to sleep on his chest when he was an infant, and he was saddened by the realization that they had grown so far apart.

"I thought you were going to watch the game," Francis said matter-of-factly.

"I read it wrong in the paper. We get Princeton-Penn. The real football game is Michigan-Iowa, but apparently only the Midwest gets to see that. Anyway, I came out here to tell you about a surprise and ask you a question. What do you want to hear first?"

"The surprise," Francis said, looking up from his wheel and smiling.

Joseph pulled out a white envelope from his breast pocket.

"What is it?" Francis asked.

"Go ahead open it up and see for yourself."

Francis peeled open the sealed envelope, revealing the four tickets to the Redskins-Steeler game the following week.

"Is the eighteenth a Sunday?"

"Of course it is. The 'skins always play on Sunday," Joseph said curtly. "Why, is there a problem?"

"I think I have the first rehearsal for the concert that day and I have to be there."

Francis saw the look of disgust on his father's face, which made him feel even more isolated.

Joseph was ready to explode but didn't raise his voice. "Well, let me talk to Father Dolan and see if he can rearrange the time just this once."

"No, Poppa, I don't want you to talk to Father Dolan," Francis said defiantly.

Francis never saw the backhand that struck him flush on his cheek as he fell backward over an orange crate he was using for a seat. Joseph was over him in an instant and pulled him up by the shirt as Francis tried to cover his face.

"Don't hit me, Poppa!"

Joseph pulled the boy to within inches of his face. "Now listen, you little prima donna..."

Francis went limp in Joseph's grasp and started to cry uncontrollably. Joseph roiled with guilt as he pulled Francis to a chair and held him in his lap.

"I'm sorry, Frannie. I lost my temper. C'mon, stop crying and let's get to the bottom of what's going on. Talk to me, Frannie, I'm begging you."

Francis heaved for several more minutes as Joseph tried to calm him, hoping that Lucy would not come home and see what a mess he had made.

"Now listen, I'm really sorry. I should have never hit you. That was wrong, I'm ashamed and I apologize. I mean it. I was wrong. Now let's talk this out. Are you worried about the concert, something at school, what's bothering you?"

"Everything's fine, Poppa, really."

"I don't believe you, Francis. You're not acting like everything's fine. You go off like a firecracker when I mention I'll talk to Father Dolan. It can't be that bad, Frannie. Just tell me what's going on, you're with me. It's safe, there's nothing to worry about. Is Dolan putting too much pressure on you for the concert? Is that it?"

Francis broke free from his father and screamed at him, "We're not safe!"

"What are you talking about, Francis?" Joseph said, feeling his heart beating faster. Fighting to stay even toned, he said, "We're not leaving here until you tell me why we are not safe in our own house. I'm not giving up on you, Frannie. I'll stay right here until hell freezes over. Just tell me, whatever it is, and we'll deal with it. You said we're not safe. Why are we not safe?"

"Father Andy...." As soon as Francis heard himself say "Father Andy," he began to shake uncontrollably.

"What? What about Father Andy?" Joseph demanded.

"He told me bad things would happen to us if I broke my promise."

"What promise? What kind of bad things? What are you talking about, Frannie?" Joseph got down on one knee, close to Francis' face.

Francis cracked. "I saw Father Andy doing something bad to Elizabeth in Aquinas Hall." He could not bear to tell his father about his own abuse.

"Wait a minute, slow down. What did you just say? What do you mean something bad?"

"He had her pants down and he was like hunched over behind her," Francis said, choking through his words. Francis wanted to unburden himself. "I went back over to Aquinas Hall because I forgot Momma wanted me to walk Elizabeth home and I saw it. I saw what Father Dolan was doing to Elizabeth and he had his pants down. I hid in the closet, but Father Dolan caught me and told me if I told anyone God would punish me and I would burn in hell forever and bad things would happen to the family."

Joseph gasped for air as he fell to the floor, pulling Francis into his lap. He held him tightly and wiped the tears off his face. Joseph rocked his son for several minutes as his anger churned to the surface. "That no good motherfucker. Is there anything else, Francis?"

"No, Poppa, I'm sorry I didn't tell you. I thought Lizzie would tell you."

"Does she know you saw her?"

"No."

"Okay let's go."

"Where?" Francis said, alarmed.

"You are going to tell Monsignor Ryan what you just told me. I'll be right there next to you. Now get in the car, Francis."

"Poppa, please, let's talk to Momma first. Please, I don't want to talk about it with Monsignor Ryan!"

"Is what you told me the truth, Francis? Did you see with your own eyes what that son-of-bitch did with Elizabeth?" Joseph thundered.

"I did Poppa, but…"

"Then do as I say and get in the goddamn car."

It was a short ride to the rectory on Rhode Island Avenue from the Natale home. Nothing was said but Francis could see beads of sweat forming on Joseph's forehead and rage building in his face. Crossing Rhode Island Avenue and making a quick left turn, Joseph sped up the alley to the parking lot in the back of the priest's rectory. Francis was convinced that the end was near. God would strike him dead as soon as his father told Monsignor Ryan what had happened.

"Come with me, Francis." Joseph grabbed his son and pulled him out of the car. "I want you to tell Monsignor Ryan exactly what you just told me."

"Poppa, please, don't. You're hurting my hand!"

Joseph loosened his grip.

"Poppa let's go home. Let's talk to Momma," Francis pleaded.

"Is what you told me the truth?" Joseph thundered.

"Yes."

"Then we'll tell Monsignor Ryan. He's a good man, he will know what to do."

Joseph knocked on the front door and walked into the rectory without waiting for someone to answer.

"Excuse me, Francis Natale, what is going on here and who is this with you?" Mrs. McGinty said indignantly.

"Mrs. McGinty, this is my…"

"Francis, do not say another word. My name is Joseph Natale. Mrs. McGinty, I'm Francis' father and I want to speak to Monsignor immediately."

"Well, I'm very sorry, Mr. Natale, but that's quite impossible. Monsignor Ryan doesn't have any appointments scheduled this afternoon and he doesn't have any visitation hours on Sunday. So, what day next week works for you? I'll consult Monsignor's calendar and confirm your appointment."

"Trust me, Mrs. McGinty, Monsignor will want to talk to me right now. I know he's here; his car is out in the back lot. So, do whatever you have to do, but get him down here right now because I'm not leaving," Joseph bellowed.

Francis felt his father lose his grip on his hand as he slumped into a chair in the waiting room.

"Frannie, get me a glass of water from the cooler," Joseph said as the right side of his face started to contort.

"Mr. Natale, are you alright?" Mrs. McGinty said, alarmed by what she saw.

"Francis, hurry," Joseph said hoarsely.

"Here, Poppa. Poppa, what's wrong? Your face is all red and crooked!"

Joseph grabbed his chest and choked for air, vomiting the water he had just drunk. Joseph stood up. "I can't breathe, Frannie." His eyes rolled to the back of his head, and he collapsed, hitting the floor with a loud thud.

"Poppa!" Francis screamed. "Call somebody for help! Mrs. McGinty!"

"Monsignor Ryan, Father Dolan, help me!" Mrs. McGinty screamed up to the second floor.

Francis went to his father and rolled him over on his side. Joseph's lip oozed blood from the fall and an awful sound came from his throat, then there was silence.

"Poppa, wake up!" Francis cried as he shook his father's body.

Monsignor Ryan and Father Dolan hurtled down the steps. Ryan pushed Francis aside and rolled Joseph's body on his back, wiping the blood from his mouth, and started chest compressions.

"Francis, call your mother, use the phone in the office. Hurry! Mrs. McGinty, call the police and rescue squad, do it!" Ryan ordered, shaking Mrs. McGinty out of her shock.

Looking at Joseph, Ryan knew the exercise was fruitless. Joseph was unresponsive, his eyes closed, his face having lost all its color. Ryan tried to find a pulse in Joseph's neck, then put his head to Joseph's chest to listen for any heartbeat. Joseph's torso was rigid, suggesting he was dead before he hit the floor. Ryan began to whisper over Joseph's body.

"My gracious Lord God, I entreat you to forgive any sin this man, Joseph Natale, has on his soul as you receive him into your Kingdom. I ask this in the name of the Father, Son and Holy Spirit. Amen." Ryan got up on one knee.

"Don't stop, Monsignor, you have to save him!" Francis screamed.

"Francis, your father is with the Lord. Did you call your mother?"

"There was no answer," Francis said as he fell to his knees, sobbing.

"Monsignor, can I do anything?" Dolan asked.

Ryan met Dolan's eyes in a cold stare from across the room.

"I suspect, Father Dolan, that you have done quite enough already. Mrs. McGinty, get a blanket from the upstairs hallway closet and cover Mr. Natale and stay with him until the ambulance and Mrs. Natale get here. As soon as they arrive, come and get me. I'll call the Archbishop from my office."

"Monsignor, are you sure it's okay for me to go upstairs?" Mrs. McGinty said with an air of formality.

"Mrs. McGinty, will you just get the goddamn blanket and do what I ask you?" Ryan snapped.

"Of course, Monsignor, I wasn't thinking. I'm sorry."

Dolan quickly leaned over Francis, who had his head buried in his father's chest, and whispered in his ear. "This is God's punishment, Francis, for breaking your promise. If anyone asks, you came here with your father to talk to the Monsignor about entering minor seminary. Am I clear?"

Without moving his head from his father's chest, Francis nodded in agreement.

Dolan grabbed Francis' hand. "Come with me, child, and we'll say a prayer as your father's soul enters God's Kingdom."

Francis knew by the evil in Dolan's face that he needed to keep silent. His mother would be there in a few minutes and the possibility of losing both parents was too much to bear.

CHAPTER FOUR
A House of Cards

THERE'S NOTHING YOU WANT TO TALK TO ME ABOUT?
Francis stood motionless by the passenger side door of Monsignor
Ryan's car. Images of being in Father Dolan's front seat at the
Monocacy battlefield overlook flashed in front of his eyes.

"Francis, get in, we must hurry." Ryan rushed to where Francis
was standing.

Francis, frozen in place, jumped when Ryan put his hand on his
shoulder. "No. I can't leave Poppa."

"Francis, your father is with the Lord. We must find your mother
and tell her. Now, please, get in." Ryan opened the car door and
pushed Francis into the car.

Francis looked out the windshield and realized that he was on
the exact same route that he had taken with his father less than an
hour ago. This was God's punishment; it was real just like Father
Dolan said it would be.

"Francis, listen to me. I know what you just witnessed was
horrible but why did you and your father come to the rectory
in the first place?" Ryan waited for the boy to answer, but
Francis continued to stare out the window. "Francis, did you
hear me? There will be questions. Your mother will want to
know what happened."

"Poppa died," Francis said as anger crept into his tone. "That's what happened."

"I understand, Francis, but why did you come to the rectory on a Saturday afternoon?"

Francis was silent.

"Francis, I'm speaking to you!" Ryan barked.

"Poppa was coming to see you."

"Me? About what?" Ryan asked.

"About the seminary. I was in our garage fixing my bike spokes, and I kinda just mentioned that I was interested in the minor seminary, and he got really mad and said he wanted to talk to you."

"Since when have you been interested in minor seminary? You've never spoken to me about any of this," Ryan fired back in rapid succession, trying to unravel the story as to why a father and son would arrive unannounced at his rectory on a Saturday afternoon.

"Father Dolan and I had been talking about it."

Ryan was livid, caught in the middle of criminal conspiracy to cover-up sexual crimes against children. It was absolute horseshit that Francis Natale had any desire to become a priest. Ryan felt completely out of control as Dolan seemed to be one step ahead of him. He was not going to get through to Francis by force. He had to take another tack.

"Francis, I don't believe you. What did your father want to talk to me about?" Ryan asked calmly.

"Me going to minor seminary, Monsignor. It's the truth.

"Francis, if there's more to this story, now's the time for you to speak up."

"I told you, Monsignor, it was about minor seminary."

"It's a long road you're on, Francis. Are you certain there's nothing you want to talk to me about before we go inside?"

"I'm sure," Francis whispered. Before Ryan could get the car in park, Francis opened the door and bolted up the front steps. "Momma!"

"I'm on the back porch, Frannie. Where's Elizabeth?"

"Momma! Come here!"

Instinctively, Lucy knew that something was wrong. She dropped her packages and rushed to the front door. Monsignor Ryan's ashen face confirmed her fears.

"Lucy, sit down, would you," Ryan said.

Lucy began to disassociate herself from the crushing news of Joseph's death. Her wails of grief frightened Ryan and Francis. Lucy fell to her knees, gasping for air. "Start over. Tell me exactly what happened," she demanded.

Ryan's stomach was churning. This was unlike any death notification he had ever given. What he told Lucy was a blatant lie, cementing his complicity in a breach of trust so vile he could hardly believe that this was the price for career advancement.

"I was actually upstairs when it happened. Mrs. McGinty was there but apparently Francis told Joseph he was interested in pursuing a vocation to the priesthood at minor seminary. Joseph was upset and wanted to talk to me, and he drove to the rectory with Francis. Lucy, I did everything I could to revive him. I'm not sure he was conscious, but I gave him the Last Rites. I am so sorry."

Francis covered his face and sobbed.

Lucy needed to get to her husband. "Francis, hand me the phone," Lucy ordered as she struggled to compose herself. She dialed Anna's number next door and choked out the news. "Hello, Momma, where's Gio?"

"He's in the front room listening to the radio, why?"

"Come over right now, Monsignor Ryan is here. There's been an accident."

Anna dropped the phone, missing the cradle. "Gio, come with me next door. Lucy said there was an accident."

Giovanni had only heard that tone in Anna's voice once before. He jumped out of his chair and rushed into his son's house without waiting for Anna.

"What's wrong, Lucy?" Giovanni asked, walking through the door.

"Mr. Natale, your son had a heart attack," Ryan said as Anna gasped and grabbed for her husband.

Giovanni tried to catch his breath. "Is he okay?"

"He's dead, Pop," Lucy said.

"Dear God in heaven!" Anna shrieked as she doubled over, sliding into Joseph's chair in the parlor. For several seconds the only sound in the room was labored breathing.

Lucy got on her knees in front of Anna. "Anna, listen to me, I have to go to the hospital. I want to see Joe before anybody touches him," Lucy sobbed.

"Lucy, please, let me drive you," Ryan said.

Lucy noticed Giovanni's hands shaking as they drove the six blocks to Providence Hospital. "Pop, try to take it easy. I need you," Lucy said, trying to calm him.

"I don't understand how this could happen. I just spoke to him this morning," Giovanni said, his voice trailing off.

"Were you with my son when he died?" Gio asked Ryan.

"Yes, Mr. Natale. As soon as I heard the commotion down in my office, I rushed downstairs and tried to revive him. I did everything I could."

"Francis saw all of this?" Lucy asked, hoping he was spared watching his father die in front of him.

"He was with Joseph when he passed, Lucy." Ryan's voice started to shake.

"My God, my poor baby."

"Why was my son in your office?" Giovanni asked.

"Lucy, would you prefer to tell your father-in-law?" Ryan asked.

"Gio, Francis told Joseph something about the priesthood and Joseph got angry and went over to the rectory," Lucy said.

"Is that true, Monsignor?"

"I never talked to him, Mr. Natale. Francis told me that information on the way to the house. Apparently, Joseph died right after he got to the rectory. Do you know any other reason why Joseph would want to see me, Mr. Natale?"

"No, I don't, Monsignor, that's why I asked you. My son gets upset and dies. It makes no sense. My boy is dead. I am alive. This is not how it's supposed to go."

Ryan was getting uncomfortable.

"Who talked to my grandson about the priesthood, Monsignor Ryan?" Gio asked in a firm voice.

"I believe it was Father Dolan, Mr. Natale."

Giovanni grunted and turned around in his seat to look directly at Lucy. "The priest that Joseph didn't like. Did you hear that, Lucy?"

Lucy could see in his eyes the very same resentment of the Church she had seen in Joseph's eyes countless times before.

WHERE IS EVERYONE?

Elizabeth bounded through the back door into the house.

"Where is everyone?"

"We're out front," Anna called.

Elizabeth walked into the front of the house where Rosemary and Anna were sitting on the couch and Francis was slumped in a chair.

"Why are you crying, Frannie? What did you do?"

"Francis didn't do anything, Lizzie," Rosemary said. "Come here and sit with us on the couch. We have to tell you something."

Elizabeth settled into the couch, keeping her eyes squarely on her brother. "What? What's wrong, Grandmom?"

Anna reached for Elizabeth and put her arms around her. "Your Poppa had an accident and died this afternoon."

Elizabeth pushed herself away from Anna and stood in the middle of the room. "That's not true, Grandmom! Why would you say something like that? Frannie, is this true? Poppa's dead?" Elizabeth shouted angrily.

"It's true, Lizzie. I saw it. Poppa asked me for some water, and he just fell over," Francis cried.

"You saw it where?" Elizabeth demanded.

"Poppa and I were at St. Francis," Francis responded tearfully.

"But what happened?" Elizabeth screamed.

"Nothing! He just fell over, Lizzie, and then he was gone!"

"Poppa was always with *you* and now he's dead. I hate you, Frannie. I hate you. I don't ever want to speak to you again!" Elizabeth screamed at her brother.

Rosemary got up and tried to hold Elizabeth as she started to flail about, but she broke free and ran upstairs to her room.

"Elizabeth, wait. Please, let's talk about this," Rosemary called as she followed her up the stairs.

"Rose, let her cry it out," Anna said. She went to Francis, still slumped in Joseph's button tufted Queen Anne chair, and sat in front of him on the ottoman. "Now listen to your grandmother. Have I ever said anything that wasn't true? C'mon, Francis, look at me," she said as she gently tugged on his chin. "Have I ever lied to you?"

"No, Grandmom," Francis said as Anna clasped his face and rubbed Francis' cheeks with her thumbs, wiping his tears away.

"Elizabeth doesn't hate you."

"She does, Grandmom. If I had kept my mouth shut, Poppa would still be here. Poppa's dead because of me."

"Oh, my God, Francis, that's so not true," Rosemary interjected. "You have to get that right out of your head, right now. Your father could have had a heart attack at any time. It could have been when he was working or driving a car. You didn't do anything wrong. You have to believe that."

Francis got up out of the chair and walked to the piano. "Well, I don't, Aunt Rose," he said as he sat on the stool staring at the keyboard. He placed his hands just above the keys and closed his eyes. All he could see was his father's face as he struck the first notes of Rachmaninoff's Variation 18, a Rhapsody on Themes. Francis moved toward the end of the piece, recapping the soft melody that runs throughout. Elizabeth's bedroom door flew open, slamming into the wall, startling everyone on the first floor.

"Frannie, you can play all you want but it won't bring Poppa back!" Elizabeth screamed from the top of the landing as her door thundered shut. Francis flinched as the house went deathly quiet. Taking a slow deep breath, he started the piece again. Francis realized he had no choice but to keep Dolan's secret. A slurry of confusion and shame mixed with anger. He needed a place to hide, and music was his only safe space.

"Let him play, Rose," Anna said as she walked into the kitchen, tears streaming down her face. "Rose, come help me in the kitchen. There will be people coming shortly and we have to have something for them."

"Oh, Anna, you don't want me in the kitchen. Besides, this is no time for you to be worried about food."

Anna grabbed a knife and stared at a block of hard cheese on the tavola.

Rosemary slid behind her and put her arms around Anna's waist, putting her hands over the knife. Rosemary held Anna as her body shuddered with grief at the loss of her first-born son.

"C'mon, Anna, you sit out front with Francis. They should be home soon. I'll take care of all this in the kitchen," Rosemary said as she guided the older woman to a chair. "Here, put your feet up and I'll bring you a glass of wine."

Through the afternoon and early evening, word of Joseph's death spread quickly through the parish and the tight knit community around Shepherd Street. Connie Formica brought bread and desserts from Catania's and organized a half dozen other friends and family members to bring covered dishes. Mike Vitaglio from Uncle Mike's Pizza on Monroe Street delivered six large pizzas and a huge mixed garden salad with a note of condolence written on a plain brown bag signed by all the kitchen staff. Over the next hour, the Natale house filled with family, friends and several of Joseph's co-workers from the Shrine, each bringing food, wine or both. Rosemary organized all the food buffet style on the dining room table and placed napkins, dishes and silverware on the side table so people could help themselves.

Monsignor Ryan waited with Giovanni and Lucy until the forms had been signed at the hospital for an autopsy and arrangements had been made for George Pumphrey to pick up Joseph's body to prepare it for burial. The hospital nurses and orderlies closed the curtain and waited at a discrete distance from Joseph's gurney to give Lucy some privacy to say her goodbyes.

"Pop, do you want some time with Joe?" Lucy asked.

"No, I'll wait for you outside. I have his face turning the violino in my head. He's laughing, saying to me, *I can't believe we're doing this.* That's what I'll remember."

Lucy asked for a pair of scissors from the attendant at the door of the hospital morgue. Entering, she was struck by how cold it was in the room. Lucy approached Joseph's body, lightly moving her hand over his covered torso. A nurse had folded the sheet neatly at Joseph's shoulder, revealing his head. A folding chair was placed at the side of the gurney. Lucy ran a finger over the bruise on his lip, wiped his mouth and smoothed his hair.

"My hard-headed warrior," she said, patting his face. She slumped in the chair next to Joseph's body and held his hand to her lips. Rage, guilt and a shaken belief in God caused Lucy to hyperventilate as she wailed alone in a cold room. She felt abandoned by her core beliefs. "Dear God in heaven, how could you do this to me?" she screamed.

Lucy stared at her husband on the gurney and kissed him on the lips, cutting two locks of his hair for Francis and Elizabeth. A sudden wave of exhaustion seeped into her body. The overwhelming guilt she felt over causing Joseph's outrage about Francis entering minor seminary would have to wait. It was time to go.

Monsignor Ryan and Giovanni were standing in the hall.

"I overheard you, Lucy. God did not take Joseph from you," Ryan said.

Lucy walked to within inches of Ryan's face. "Monsignor, do not talk to me about God right now. I really need to get home to my children."

"Of course, Lucy. Whatever you need," Ryan said, unwilling to tangle with Lucy's fury.

Both Lucy and Gio were shocked when they saw cars double parked on both sides of the street heading to their house a few blocks up from the corner of Shepherd and 14th Street.

"Lucy, I think a lot of people have heard of Joseph's passing," Ryan said.

"Oh, my God. I should have come home sooner."

"I'm sure Anna has everything under control. It'll be fine," Gio assured her.

"Monsignor, will you at least come in and get a bite to eat? I'm sure there's plenty of food, knowing my mother-in-law."

"Thank you, Lucy, but I really must get back. I haven't been able to talk to the Archbishop, and he needs to be advised. We can plan the services tomorrow. Do you think you'll have visitation for one night or two?"

Hearing that, Lucy burst into tears. "Joe and I never even talked about what he wanted. I don't even have a place to bury him," she sobbed, slumping into the corner of the back seat.

Giovanni got out of the car and opened the rear passenger door. "Hey, hey... Lucy, it's okay, we'll figure it out. Thirty years ago, Anna made me buy six plots at Mt. Olivet, so where Joe will be buried is settled. I'll talk to the guys at the shop about his stone. So, we're good. Now wipe your face, you don't want everyone in the house seeing you like this. You have a hanky?"

"Of course I do. Every woman my age carries a hanky," she said, managing a smile as she pulled her compact mirror and embroidered handkerchief from her purse. "My God, Gio, I look like Maggie from the Bowery." Lucy peered into the tiny mirror.

"You want me to throw everybody out?" Giovanni asked.

"Of course not. Just give me a second to fix my face. I'm sorry, Monsignor."

"No worries, Lucy; take your time," Ryan said.

Giovanni walked around to the driver's side and thrust his hand through the open window. "I appreciate you staying with us, Monsignor," he said as he shook hands with the priest. "That was kind of you."

"Under the circumstances, it was the least I could do. I'll call on Lucy tomorrow. Good night, Mr. Natale. And good night, Lucy. Call me if there's anything you need." Then, resting his hand lightly on her shoulder, Ryan added, "I'll see you sometime tomorrow."

Lucy took Giovanni's arm as they walked up the steps to the front porch.

"The priest had soft hands, Lucy. Not much work in those hands."

"Christ, Pop, that's something Joseph would say."

Giovanni opened the door to a house full of people. "I know," he said, kissing the back of Lucy's hand.

Lucy wove her way through the subdued crowd, enduring an amalgam of hugs, tears and awkward conversations. She opened the back door to let some fresh air into the house to exhaust the haze of smoke as she looked for her children.

"Ro, thanks so much for pitching in," Lucy said, giving her sister a long, tearful embrace. Rosemary could feel Lucy's body shaking as she held on to her. Lucy was not letting go as both sisters sobbed.

"Here, Luce, sit down. What can I get you?"

"Nothing, my head is pounding. I can't even think about food right now. Ask Joe to-" Lucy stopped mid-sentence. "I can't believe it, Rose, he's really gone. I was going to ask Joe to get me some rye. I'm trying to remember if I kissed him goodbye this morning and I can't. I can't remember," Lucy said, panic rising in her voice.

"Lucy, you're torturing yourself. You kiss him goodbye every morning, I'm sure you did this morning."

"Then why can't I remember it, goddammit?" Lucy said, banging both fists on the counter.

Giovanni poured two fingers of rye into a small glass. "Here. Sip on this, Lucy, it'll settle you down a bit."

"I don't want to settle down, Pop," Lucy said, slapping the table. "I just lost my husband." Lucy got up from her chair and whispered in Giovanni's ear, "And in three weeks you're leaving for Italy, you selfish son-of-a-bitch."

"Goddammit, Lucy, I just lost my son today," Giovanni roared. "You may not think I loved him, but I loved him very much."

Lucy was frozen in shock at the words that had come out of her mouth. She rushed to Giovanni, throwing both of her arms around him. "My God I'm sorry, Pop. Please forgive me. I didn't mean what I said, I'm just pissed off. I'm sorry for taking it out on you."

"I loved my son, Lucy."

"Do you still love me?" Lucy asked as she folded into his arms.

"Most days," Giovanni said, a faint smile crossing his face.

"Whew, I'm glad that got settled," Rosemary said, trying to break the tension. "I thought we were about to have one of those crazy Italian wake brouhahas you read about in the papers."

"We still have time, anything's possible with this family," Giovanni quietly muttered to Rosemary.

"Where are the kids, Ro?" Lucy asked as she felt the warmth of the whiskey in her chest.

"They're upstairs. Frannie played the piano nonstop for two hours, same thing over and over. Then just got up and went upstairs to his room a few minutes ago. Didn't say anything. Elizabeth has been up in her room since you left. She's really mad at Frannie. Seems she has in her head that Frannie is somehow responsible."

"I'll go talk to them," Lucy said, getting up from the kitchen table.

"Let me talk to Elizabeth, Lucy. I want to show her something Joe was using yesterday to carve some boss stones," Giovanni said.

Giovanni walked upstairs to Elizabeth's bedroom and knocked two times on the door.

"Go away. I don't want to talk to anybody. Just leave me alone."

"It's Grandpop, Lizzie, can I come in?"

Gio heard her get off the bed and walk to the door.

"Did Momma send you up here? Because I don't want to talk to anyone," Elizabeth said through the door.

"Lizzie, open the door. Please, I want to show you something. And no, your Momma didn't send me up here."

Giovanni saw the doorknob turn and he took a half a step back into the hallway.

Elizabeth opened the door a few inches. Her face was flushed and swollen from crying.

"You said you wanted to show me something. What is it?" Elizabeth said sharply.

"I do. It's something that has been in the family a long time. It was your great grandfather's and your Pop used it to carve his signature boss stones."

"What's a boss stone?"

"Well, the big ones usually go on ceilings at a point where all the panels come together. It's like a very ornate flower or decoration."

"Like an angel on top of a Christmas tree?"

"Something like that. When a carver like me or your Poppa wants to leave his mark, he can either carve his name in the stone or leave a tiny carved boss stone at the bottom of the piece. You remember the picture of you in the Catholic Standard with your Pop?"

"Yes."

"He said you really liked the one above the east terrace."

"The one with the Indian girl?"

"Yes, that's it. It's called *I Will Give Glory O Lord O King*. The Indian girl is Pocahontas and the man carrying the cross flag is Captain John Smith, the explorer."

"Poppa said he worked on that a lot. He brought me over to your workshop after the picture was taken to see the plaster mold he used from the artist."

"Here's what I want to show you, Lizzie," Giovanni said tenderly as he knelt by the edge of her bed. He pulled out of his pocket a slender roll of oilcloth and unwrapped it, revealing a four-inch point chisel with a rosewood handle that fit perfectly into the palm of his hand.

"My father used this tool and passed it on to me. I used it and gave it to your father. Your Poppa used this to make the braids for Pocahontas. Here, take it and put it in your hand. Your Poppa used this just yesterday. I want you to have it to keep. If I need it, I'll come and ask to borrow it."

Elizabeth looked up and smiled at Giovanni.

"You'll let me use it, right?" Giovanni teased.

Elizabeth looked at her grandfather and nodded.

"Your Pop told me how disappointed you were when you could not put your hand on the Indian girl in the sculpture. If we go tonight, you can do that. Your Pop was up on the scaffold all week cleaning up some of the detail on all the overhead tympanums. On Friday he was working on the one you wanted to touch, and the scaffold is there right now. On Monday it'll be taken down and moved. So, it's now or never, Lizzie."

"You mean I can actually touch it?"

"Yes, you can if we go tonight."

"Okay, let's go," Elizabeth said eagerly, forgetting for a moment why she was going.

"Do you have some coveralls?"

"I do."

"Good, I'll go downstairs and tell your mother."

Lucy was on her way upstairs as Giovanni left Elizabeth's room.

"How's she doing?" Lucy asked.

"Come on downstairs and I'll tell you what's going on." Giovanni followed Lucy down the stairs and into the kitchen, noticing that there seemed to be even more people in Joseph's home than before he had talked to Elizabeth.

"You want me to start throwing people out? This is getting out of hand," Giovanni said as he entered the kitchen.

"Mind your manners, old man," Anna snarled.

I LEFT YOU SEVERAL MESSAGES

Ryan pulled into the parking lot behind the rectory and realized the lot was empty. That meant the house was empty and he could enjoy his Jack Daniels and cigar in peace on his second-floor balcony. He came in from the back porch without turning on a light to avoid any memory of what had happened in his office eight hours ago. He climbed the staircase to his quarters but couldn't escape the image of Joseph's lifeless body sprawled out in front of Mrs. McGinty's desk.

As he approached the entrance to his suite, he saw several pink message slips hanging neatly in the wooden file slot built onto his door. He unclipped them from the wooden clothespin and glanced at them. They were all from Archbishop Guilfoyle. He went to his liquor cabinet and got a bottle of Jack Daniels and a Montecristo Number 3 from his small humidor.

Ryan debated whether to even call. He had an excuse; he could still be with the Natale family, and no one knew he was home. But guilt, duty and his thirst for career advancement overcame his desire to escape into the distilled Tennessee sour mash. Ryan picked up the phone and dialed the Archbishop's residence. Guilfoyle picked up on the first ring.

"This is the Archbishop."

"Good evening, Archbishop, this is Monsignor Ryan returning your call."

"I left you several messages, Monsignor."

"I have them here in my hand, Archbishop. I was with the Natale family at the hospital, and I just returned home. I hope I'm not calling too late."

"Of course not, Cletus. This is a very unusual set of circumstances. I called the rectory and Mrs. McGinty filled me in."

"I'm sure she did, Archbishop."

"In any event, I'd like to discuss this with you in person. Can you come over?"

"I have a ten-thirty Mass at the parish tomorrow, so I could probably get there around noon."

"I'm sorry, Cletus, I was not clear. I know it's late, but I would like to speak with you this evening. You're welcome to stay over if that helps."

"I'll be fine but thank you for the offer, Archbishop. Let me get myself back together and I'll drive up."

"I'm sorry, Cletus, to pull you back out, but I have Mass tomorrow at the Cathedral and a luncheon for the wives of enlisted Naval personnel down at the Navy Yard."

"Of course, Archbishop. I'll see you shortly." Ryan waited until he heard the Archbishop click off and slammed the phone down, sending his plastic ashtray crashing to the floor.

After the day's events, Ryan was in no mood for playing a game of semantic cat and mouse with his Archbishop. What he really wanted was for some of his more colorful congregants whom he saw mostly at funerals to mend Father Dolan's ways by kicking the shit out of him or perhaps worse.

Ryan pushed aside the Jack Daniels and his violent fantasy. In order for his career to stay on track, he needed to suppress his anger to a level where he could have a controlled conversation with his Archbishop.

Traffic was light for such a beautiful weekend evening as he traversed Rock Creek Park to the residence of the Archbishop. Ryan strode up the long walkway to the front door and knocked. To Ryan's surprise, the Archbishop opened the door dressed in his pajamas, robe and slippers.

"I'm sorry, Cletus, I should have told you to come as you were," Guilfoyle said, realizing that his informal appearance surprised Ryan.

"Thank you, Your Grace, it wasn't a bother. How can I help?"

"Come, let's talk in my library. I want to know what the family knows. May I offer you some Jack Daniels?"

"That would be excellent. To be honest, Your Grace, I'm not sure the family knows anything," Ryan said as he reached for the generous pour of whiskey the Archbishop placed on his desk.

"Under the circumstances, Cletus, that's a fairly bizarre attitude to take. I talked to Mrs. McGinty and she said there was some big blow up between you and Mr. Natale."

Ryan realized that he might have stepped over the line. "I apologize, Archbishop, I didn't mean to sound callous. I'm just very frustrated with the whole situation. Mrs. McGinty is an idiot and a busybody. So, it wouldn't surprise me if there's some confabulation in her report. I hardly knew Mr. Natale and never spoke to him about anything today. My suspicion is that the boy told his father about Dolan or somehow he found out and that's why he was so angry, demanding to see me unannounced at the rectory."

"What about Mrs. Natale? Do you think she knows anything?"

"Well, I was with her and her father-in-law all afternoon and then at the hospital. I think one of them would have said something if Francis had told them, especially Joseph's father. He's a tough old bird, plus I think he would kill Dolan with his bare hands if he knew anything about it."

"About what, Cletus? Maybe there's nothing to tell."

"Are you serious? What do you mean by that, Archbishop?" Ryan exploded.

"Based on the whiskey and the circumstances of the day I will ignore your tone, but I understand that Mr. Natale was coming to your rectory unannounced because the boy was considering the minor seminary and the father objected."

"Mrs. McGinty told you that?"

"She did."

"So, with respect, Your Excellency," Ryan said sarcastically, "where do you suppose she got that information? Because she certainly didn't get it from me or the boy. I didn't find out about the seminary story until Francis told me in the car after we left the rectory."

"Monsignor, I'm sure Mrs. McGinty got that specific information from Father Dolan. And for all we know that's the truth. So, to be precise, neither you nor I know anything untoward happened to the Natale boy. All we know is that Mr. Natale was upset, and the boy says it was because his father objected to him entering minor

179

seminary. That's what we know, Monsignor Ryan. Isn't that the nub of the matter?"

"And the pictures I gave you, Archbishop?"

"You mean the personal property of a priest that you removed from his private living quarters? Is that what you're referring to?"

"Yes."

"Oh, those... well, let's just say we'll deal with those if they ever see the light of day, shall we? If the boy makes an accusation, we'll deal with it. We have options, but until that time you need to keep your eye on the facts and not suppositions, no matter how well informed you believe them to be."

"I understand, Archbishop."

"I want to believe that Cletus, I truly do. I want you to understand what's at stake here for the good of the Church, our Archdiocese and our Marian devotion."

"I do understand what's at stake. I also see a family devastated by the sudden death of a loved one."

"I appreciate that, Cletus, but the pain of the few cannot rule the spiritual welfare of the many. Let's just for the moment assume all your suspicions are correct about Father Dolan. What exactly would you have me do right now? Please share your wisdom, Monsignor."

"I see your point," Ryan said.

"These are the conundrums that fill moral philosophy books. But in the real world, Cletus, there's no choice whatsoever. In fact, your future as a brother bishop and guardian of the faithful depends on this commitment. Are we clear on that specific point?"

"Crystal clear, Archbishop."

"Excellent. Clarity always helps the mood. When will you speak to Mrs. Natale next?"

"I suspect tomorrow after ten-thirty Mass. I know she wants to speak to me about arrangements for the Funeral Mass."

"Have there been any announcements?"

"No, that wouldn't happen until Monday in any event."

"I would like you to tell her that I would be honored to con-celebrate her husband's Funeral Mass with you at the Crypt Church where Joseph labored for so many years. He was the newly named Master Carver, his father was Master Carver here for the last twenty years, so it would be the only fitting place to say his Funeral Mass. Of course, if you or Mrs. Natale would prefer a parish service I wouldn't object. After all, we're not a parish at the Shrine and I'll have to issue an exception from the executive committee."

"How could she refuse, Archbishop? I'll ask her tomorrow and of course I would be honored to con-celebrate Joseph's Funeral Mass with you."

"He was a baptized Catholic was he not?"

"He was, Archbishop. A fallen away skeptic but a Catholic nevertheless."

"Then it's settled. Once she has agreed I will notify Monsignor Flynn so he can make the necessary preparations. One other thing, Monsignor… maintaining control over this potentially volatile situation is paramount. When you speak to Mrs. Natale, suggest to her that I will permit a short eulogy to her husband. It's somewhat unusual under the Order of Christian Funerals. But under the circumstances, with what we're trying to accomplish, it may prove beneficial for us to bend the rules a bit. Do you understand what I'm saying?"

"I do, Archbishop."

"Make sure it's short, and I don't want anyone speaking from the pulpit. Tell her I'll introduce the person designated and they can face the congregation where the first pew meets the sanctuary. Are we clear?"

"I understand completely, Your Grace," Ryan said as he drained the last of the Jack Daniels from his glass.

"You look tired, Cletus. Go home and get some rest. Are you sure you're fine to drive?"

"Oh, Archbishop, I'm fine. The drive back will relax me. It's been a trying day."

"I'm sure. Let me walk you out."

At the door, Guilfoyle offered his ring. Ryan hesitated for just a second, then went down on one knee, knowing that kissing Guilfoyle's ring would cement his future.

"You're a good man, Cletus. Few are called into the service of protecting the majesty of Holy Mother Church," he said as Ryan bowed and then embraced the Archbishop. "May the blessing of God Almighty descend upon you during this sacred endeavor. Good night, Cletus, and stay in touch."

"Thank you, Archbishop. Good night."

I LIKE WALKING WITH YOU WHEN IT'S DARK

Giovanni and Elizabeth left from the back porch and headed west up the alley. After a quick ten minute walk the unlikely duo had crossed the darkened quad in front of the Mullen Library and were facing a wall of scaffolding on the east side of the nearly finished Shrine.

"Now listen, young lady. This isn't your mother talking. You see that security guard? He's a friend, well sort of a friend. He's going to want to know why I'm here this time of night. I'm going to tell him I'm going to walk my granddaughter up that scaffold in the corner so she can put her hands on a piece of sculpture her daddy worked on yesterday and who happened to suddenly die this afternoon. He's going to pitch a fit and then he's going to let us go up. You won't say a word and when we're down you'll thank him. His name is O'Reiley. Mr. O'Reiley. Now I want you to stand right under this light post and don't move until I come and get you. You understand what I'm saying to you, Elizabeth?"

"Yes, Grandpop," Elizabeth said, wide eyed.

"Did you bring your Poppa's chisel like I told you?"

"Yes, Grandpop, I have it in my pocket."

"Okay. Wait right here."

Fred O'Reiley was writing a ticket for a car parked in the Assistant Rector's parking spot when he looked up and saw Giovanni.

"Gi, what the hell are you doing here this time of day? Hey, I heard about your boy. I'm really sorry. You doing okay?"

"No, not really, Freddy. It's been a tough day."

"So, why aren't you home with your family?"

"You see that girl under the lamppost?"

"Yeah, who is she?"

"I need a favor. That's my son's daughter, my granddaughter. I want you to take a little stroll across the quad. Then I can walk her up that scaffold behind you so she can lay her hands on the sculpture her father finished up yesterday. Five minutes, ten minutes max. She's having a hard time with all this so it would help her a lot."

"You want to do fucking what? Are you crazy? That's forty feet in the air. Flynn would fire my fat ass and your granddaughter could fall. Then what, Gi? I can't. I can't let you do it. If anybody finds out, I'll lose my job."

Giovanni got within inches of O'Reiley's face. "Listen to me, you Irish fuck. I asked you nice. Now I'm not asking. So, here's the deal: You can get the beating of your fucking life in about thirty seconds, or you can loan me your flashlight so I can get her up there to touch some stone her daddy worked on yesterday. Ten minutes. We're up and out in ten minutes. So, what's it gonna be?"

"You didn't even bring a goddamn flashlight," O'Reiley said.

"Why? I knew you had one," Giovanni said, holding his hand out.

"Here, take it, you shit-face wop."

"Now you're talking, you Irish prick." Giovanni smiled and grabbed one of Fred's fleshy jowls and pinched it. "You want a kiss?"

"Get the fuck away from me, Natale. Ten minutes. I mean it, Gi, or I'll call the cops."

Giovanni turned to Elizabeth. "Lizzie, come on. We have to hurry."

Giovanni followed as Elizabeth bounded up the east steps to the base of the scaffold that rested above the entrance to the Crypt Church.

"It looks higher from down here, Grandpop," Elizabeth said nervously.

"Just do exactly what I tell you and you'll be fine. There's a platform at the top so you'll be safe. On the way up, you'll go first, and I'll put the light on exactly the spot I want you to step. On the way down, I'll go first, and I'll put your foot right on the spot I want you to step. Now if you don't think you can do this we'll turn around and go home."

"I can do it."

"Okay, here we go."

Elizabeth got the hang of weaving over and under each wooden bent of the rising scaffold and in three or four minutes they were standing in front of Pocahontas and John Smith giving thanks to the Lord.

"Wow it's bigger than I thought being this close," Elizabeth said as she ran her fingers over the braids. "She's so pretty, Grandpop." Elizabeth spread her arms, rubbing the faces of all the figures. She put her hands to her nose, smelling the limestone dust.

"Get out the tool I gave you and unwrap it," Giovanni snapped.

Elizabeth carefully unwrapped the chisel and held it to her chest.

"Now look at the bottom here, right in the corner. Do you see it?"

"I see it, Grandpop. It looks like a little button or a mushroom."

"It's called a miniature boss stone. Your Poppa carved it when it was first installed. Let me have the tool." Giovanni crouched down and deftly hand bored seven tiny pilot holes around the base of the small stone protrusion.

"Okay, put this back in the oil cloth and put it in your pocket." Giovanni handed her the tool. From his pocket he pulled the exact same tool but instead of a point chisel this one had a flat cutting edge. "Now be careful, it's sharp. Hold it just like I showed you when we were in your bedroom. It's the same type of tool but has a different edge. Now lie down and put the edge right where I tell you. Come on, hurry up, we're running out of time."

Elizabeth got down on her stomach to be at eye level with the base of the stone. Giovanni guided the tip of the chisel and set it squarely on the middle pilot hole. "Now it's right where it's supposed to be. Do you have a good grip on it?"

"I do."

"Okay, hold it steady with your right hand and with your left tap the back of the tool with the fat part of your palm. Real gentle."

Elizabeth did exactly as she was told. She grasped the chisel in her hand, put the tip at the base of the boss stone and gave it a tap.

"Now one more time, just like the first. Then one more time and just nudge it lightly," Giovanni instructed.

On the third tap the boss stone cleaved cleanly from its base, falling into Giovanni's hand.

"Okay, good work. Put it in your pocket and when you thank Mr. O'Reiley don't say a word about the boss stone."

"I got it, Grandpop," Elizabeth said excitedly.

"Hey, you two. Ten minutes are up, come on down," O'Reiley yelled from the base of the scaffold.

"On our way, Freddy."

Once on the ground, Elizabeth walked directly to O'Reiley. "Thank you, Mr. O'Reiley, for letting us go up there."

"Not a word about this, Miss Natale. Okay?"

"Okay."

"I'm sorry about your Pop."

"Thanks, Mr. O'Reiley."

Giovanni held Elizabeth's hand as they walked back to the house.

"When we get to the house, tell your Momma and Grandmom I went to bed."

"Don't you want to come in, Grandpop?"

"No. It's been a long, awful day and I want to go to sleep. You should, too. Tomorrow will be different around here, but it will be tomorrow, and we'll figure it out."

Elizabeth reached out for Giovanni's hand and pulled on his coat to kiss him. "Thanks, Grandpop, for getting me Poppa's stone," she said, clutching it to her heart. "I like walking with you when it's dark."

"I do too, Lizzie. You're a good partner."

"Okay. I'll see you tomorrow, Grandpop."

"I'll be here, now go inside and go to bed."

Through the lace curtains a streetlight bathed the inside of the house in an iridescent hue. Giovanni went immediately to his phonograph and put on the last ten minutes of the finale of La Traviata. Nothing could shake him from the belief that Joseph's death was his fault, God's punishment for a life of deceit and betrayal. No amount of finely executed sacred art would save him.

Settling into a chair with a tumbler of grappa, he wept thinking of his time as a young boy. The day he set foot on the ship to America was the marker that his time had passed. He was a fool to think he could go back.

PICK A SIDE

Elizabeth walked into the kitchen from the back porch and was surprised to see so many people still in the house.

"Thank God you're home. I was starting to worry. Where's your grandfather?" Lucy asked, giving Elizabeth a long embrace.

"He just left. He said he wanted to go to bed."

"Have you been with him all of this time? It's been dark for over an hour. Where did you go?"

"Yes, Grandpop took me over to where Poppa was working yesterday."

Lucy squeezed Elizabeth a little harder and kissed her on the forehead. "You okay, honey? Do you want to talk?"

"No. Momma, can I go to my room, I really don't want to be around all these people," Elizabeth said.

"Sure, we'll talk in the morning."

As Elizabeth climbed the stairs, the conversation of over a dozen relatives speaking in both Italian and English faded. Passing the bathroom, she stopped, turned on the light and looked in. On the shelf, just below the mirror, was her father's shaving brush, its bristles sticking up out of the cup in full bloom. Next to the shaving cup was a white porcelain bottle of Old Spice. Elizabeth walked over and pulled out the tiny grey stopper and put her nose to the opening. That was it. That was the scent her mind was looking for when she was on the scaffold. That was her Poppa's smell. Elizabeth took the boss stone from her overalls and sprinkled the Old Spice on the stone, letting it dry in her hand, and turned off the light.

Walking past Francis' room, she saw a light coming from under the door.

"Are you awake, Frannie?" Elizabeth called, putting her lips to the door frame.

"I thought you were never going to talk to me again."

"I changed my mind. Will you just open the door?"

Francis thumped off his bed and unlatched the door, returning to his bed but leaving the door closed.

"Can I come in?"

"If you want," he said as Elizabeth opened the door and peered into the room.

"What do you want, Elizabeth, to tell me Poppa dying was all my fault?" Francis said curtly.

"I'm sorry about what I said to you. I was mad at you."

"Yeah, and what about the part that Poppa was always with me? That's not true, Elizabeth. I'm mad just as much as you with Poppa dying and all."

Elizabeth sat on the end of Francis' bed and started to cry. "Frannie, I said I was sorry."

Francis did not say anything and turned over on his side as Elizabeth got up to leave.

"Where did you go?" Francis asked with his back still turned to Elizabeth.

"I was with Grandpop. We walked to the Shrine and then we climbed up on a platform where Poppa had been working yesterday."

"You did not," Francis said, angrily turning to face his sister.

"We did, Frannie, honest. I can prove it."

"How? You're just making it up, Lizzie."

"Look." Elizabeth took the stone and oil cloth pouch out of her overalls.

"What's all that?" Francis demanded.

"Listen, Frannie, don't be stupid. Grandpop took me up to where Poppa was working. He showed me this stone thing that Poppa used to sign some of the stuff he was working on. We cut the stone off with a couple of taps on the back with the tool."

Francis stared at the chisel and boss stone lying on his bed. "For real, Lizzie?"

"Yes, for real. Pick it up, Frannie, and smell it."

Francis edged his hand toward the stone.

"Go ahead, Frannie, it won't bite. Pick it up and smell it."

Francis picked up the stone and held it to his nose. "It smells like Poppa," Francis said, startled.

"Grandpop said it was carved out of limestone and you can soak it and whatever you soak it in the smell will stay on the stone. He used some other word that I forget but it's like a hard sponge. Anyway, I put some of Poppa's Old Spice on it so we can remember him."

"You mean so you can remember Poppa."

"Do you want the stone?" Elizabeth said, getting frustrated.

"Grandpop gave the stone to you."

"Frannie, why are you so stupid sometimes? You weren't there with us. How could Grandpop give you one?"

"Do you think there are more?"

"I don't know, probably. We can ask him tomorrow. If Grandpop can't get us one more, we can share the tool and the stone and then trade back and forth. I can keep the chisel and you can keep the stone or the other way around. What do you think, Frannie?"

"That's a good idea, Lizzie."

"Which one do you want to keep tonight?" Elizabeth asked.

Francis reached for the stone, put it to his nose and inhaled deeply. "I'll keep the chisel," Francis said, smiling.

Elizabeth picked up the stone, put it in her pocket and walked to the bedroom door.

"Lizzie, I'll see you in the morning. And thanks for Poppa's chisel."

"It's okay," Elizabeth said, standing at the door with her back to Francis. "Can I stay?"

"Where?" Francis said.

"Here, can I stay here tonight?"

"You mean here in my room the whole night, like go to sleep here?" Francis said incredulously.

"Yes, I don't smell or anything," Elizabeth said indignantly. "I'm afraid to go to sleep by myself."

Francis got off his bed and walked to the door where Elizabeth was standing, grabbing two belts hanging from the hooks on the back of his bedroom door. He put both belts together and laid them on his bed vertically down the middle.

"Pick a side and stay on your side. Just tonight, Lizzie, okay?"

"Just tonight," Elizabeth smiled.

"You promise, Lizzie?"

"I promise."

WE ALL HAVE HISTORY, MONSIGNOR

Monsignor Ryan stumbled into the rectory kitchen, hung over and with a headache that pounded the base of his neck so deeply that he could feel his pulse. He kicked himself for pulling the weekend cook out of the parish budget. Now he had to fend for himself. He scanned the contents of the refrigerator but everything in it turned his stomach.

Glancing at his watch, he chugged two tumblers of water from the kitchen spigot, trying to dilute the half-life of nearly a full fifth of Jack Daniels from the night before. He had two hours to pull himself together before ten-thirty Mass. He filled a kettle of water to make hot lemon water to settle his stomach and searched the cupboard for some plain crackers. Ryan was still standing over the stove waiting for the kettle to come to a boil when Dolan appeared in the kitchen.

"My word, Monsignor, you look like you had a very hard night," Dolan said cheerily.

"Don't be an asshole, Father. And I suppose you had a lovely evening last night?"

"Well, I admit, Monsignor, the Natale business was a bit unsettling, but life must go on."

"A bit unsettling? Is that what you said, Father, a bit unsettling?" Ryan snapped as adrenaline began to mix with his blood alcohol.

"Well, of course it was a tragedy for the family, but I suspect Mr. Natale was a walking time bomb. He would have died sooner or later. The boy said his mother was worried about his heart." Dolan took a seat at the kitchen table.

"A man fucking died in our rectory because of you!" Ryan shouted across the table.

"Did he now?" Dolan said arrogantly. "I thought he died because he got upset that his son was going to join our ranks and he wanted to talk to you."

"Spare me your bullshit, Father. And this business about minor seminary, I suppose that was all the boy's idea?"

"Well, of course I spent a little time with him discussing the pros and cons of an early discernment of a priestly vocation, but by and large it was all his idea."

"You prick. I'm not naive, I saw you talking to Francis when his father was dead on the floor. I saw the look on your face. I saw the terror in the boy's eyes."

"Monsignor, is there a purpose to this conversation or, should I say, accusation? What exactly do you want from me?"

"The truth would be nice. Why don't you start with the truth about your 'troubled history' as the Archbishop so delicately put it?"

"You know something, Monsignor? This reminds me of a game we used to play just after I entered seminary. You know what it was called?"

"No, Father Dolan, please enlighten me?"

"It was a rather crude game but the gist of it was, 'I'll show you mine if you show me yours.'"

"You're a pig," Ryan spat.

"Am I now? So, let's play a game. Monsignor, you tell me about your weekly sojourns to the strip joints in downtown Baltimore and I'll tell you mine."

Ryan lunged across the kitchen table and caught Dolan square in the chest, driving him to the floor. Ryan had Dolan pinned on his back with his fist raised to bash his skull into the kitchen floor when, just as quickly as it happened, Ryan rolled off him.

"I'm sorry, Father, I lost my head."

"You lost your head! You old fuck, you could have killed me! Now you listen to me," Dolan said as he scrambled to his feet. "We all have history. You have history, I have history… Jesus Christ, the Archbishop has history."

"What the hell is that supposed to mean?" Ryan said, still trying to catch his breath.

"Take your head out of your ass, old man. Did you ever wonder about the bevy of young seminarians around him all the time and the way he fawns all over them? I saw you at the barbeque last summer, are you blind?"

"At least I don't have pictures of my *troubled history*."

"Okay, so now it's finally all out on the table. I knew it wasn't Sister Mary Bridget, I knew it was you sneaking around in my room. Where are they? I want them back."

"I don't have them."

"So, you got rid of them, did you? You think I'm gullible enough to believe that shit?"

"I don't care what you believe, Father. I'm telling you; I don't have them."

"So, where are they?"

"I gave them to the Archbishop."

Dolan flinched, taking a deep breath. "I see." Dolan stood in front of Ryan and, without saying a word, nodded his head slightly as if he were processing some invisible equation on a blackboard.

"Good, then they're safe. Like I said, Monsignor, we all have history, even your beloved Archbishop. So, let's just leave it at that and forget all this unpleasantness. You realize, you sanctimonious shit, that all this is a house of cards. You blow the whistle on me and it all comes down on everyone, including you, Monsignor Ryan. If you will excuse me, I need to prepare for ten-thirty Mass."

LET THEM SLEEP

Rosemary poured herself another cup of coffee and lit a cigarette. It unnerved her to be alone in the kitchen, as the familiar Sunday

192

morning rhythm and smells of the house were overtaken by the rituals of mourning. The kids were still asleep, Lucy was up in her room and Anna and Giovanni were still next door. She did not know what she should be doing. Obviously, this week would be different. Finally, she heard someone coming down the stairs.

"Hey, Rose, why are you all dressed?" asked Lucy.

"Well, you're all dressed," Rosemary responded.

"Yes, honey, but I'm going to church. Where on earth are you going in your Sunday best?"

"I thought I'd go with you."

"Really? You want to go to church? Maybe there's hope for your soul after all."

"Well, let's not get carried away. I really don't want to go to church, but I want to be with you."

"That's sweet, Ro, but let's keep that between us. I'm sure Monsignor Ryan will be happy to see you."

"Where are the kids, Lucy?"

"They're still sleeping."

"Do you want me to go wake them?"

"No. Let them sleep. I would think losing their father counts as a good excuse for missing Sunday Mass. Besides, I think they were up late because they're both curled up in Francis' bed like when they were little. Let me leave a note for them." Lucy walked down her front steps and got into Rosemary's car as her cheery façade began to crumble.

"So, we're going to St. Francis?" Rosemary asked.

"No."

"Oh, so then we're going to St. Anthony's?"

"No," Lucy said flatly.

"Okay, this isn't a mystery dinner, Luce. What church are we going to?"

"I changed my mind; I'm not going to any church. God does not want to see me today. I'm angry, Rose, angrier than I've ever been in my life. I lost my husband yesterday and I'm fucking angry," she said as she slapped the dashboard with her fists. "I'm pissed off at God and I don't care." Lucy burst into tears. "Go, Rose, just drive up the hill."

"Listen to me, Lucy. I didn't get the religion gene like you did, but I know one thing…"

"Yeah, Ro? What the hell do you know?"

"God didn't take Joseph. He didn't just wake up and say, 'Lucy, today I'm going to fuck you up and take your husband away and turn your life upside down.' Joseph died because he had a bad heart."

Lucy looked out the window as the car climbed Monastery Hill on 14th Street, seething about what really had her angrier than she had ever been.

"Ro, you know what I'm really pissed about?" Lucy asked as she wiped her face.

"That could cover a lot of ground today. What in particular are you pissed about?"

"I'll tell you. It's the number two."

"What?" Rosemary said.

"The world is built around two. Couples like Jack and Jill, ham and eggs, Ozzie and Harriet, mac and cheese, Ward and June, Ralph and Alice. Christ, they even marched into fucking Noah's Ark two by two…"

"Oh, that two. Well, big sister, I can tell you all about that two. Don't forget Tom and Jerry," Rosemary said, laughing.

"Ro, come on I'm being serious. Think about it…"

"I think about it all the time, Lucy," Rosemary said.

"Well, I haven't. I've never had to," Lucy said quietly. "Yesterday I became a widow with two children."

Rosemary pulled into the Hot Shoppe drive-in on Rhode Island Avenue and, for the next two hours, the two sisters reminisced, drank coffee, and ate sticky buns, trying to make sense of the new life that lay ahead.

I MISSED YOU AT CHURCH

Lucy knocked on the front door of the rectory precisely at twelve-thirty, praying that she would not have to see Mrs. McGinty.

Monsignor Ryan was waiting in the vestibule. "Hello Lucy, Rosemary. Were you able to get any rest last night?"

"Not much, Monsignor, but thank you for asking."

"Lucy, I'm sorry, I should have thought about this last night. Would you prefer to meet in the Parish Hall since Joseph was here yesterday? Again, I'm so sorry I didn't think of this earlier."

"That's quite all right, Monsignor. I wanted to come here. It's where my husband passed. I actually want to be here. Could you show me where he was?"

"Lucy, please, don't do this," Rosemary pleaded. "We can go over to the hall like Monsignor said."

"I'll be fine, Rose. Show me, Monsignor. Show me where Joe collapsed."

"It was right here, Lucy, right in front of Mrs. McGinty's desk."

"Where was his head, Monsignor?"

"Lucy, this is really creepy," Rosemary said.

"Then leave, Rose," Lucy said icily. "Show me, Monsignor, where was Joe's head?"

Ryan pointed to a spot on the carpet. "His head was right here, Lucy."

Lucy bent down, touched two fingers to her lips and placed them on the spot. Getting up, she made the sign of the cross. "Now we can talk about Joe's funeral."

"Come, let's sit in my conference room. I actually have some news for you from the Archbishop."

"From the Archbishop? What on earth could that possibly be, Monsignor?" Rosemary asked as she took a seat at the conference table.

"Well, as you know, I had to notify the chancery of Joseph's passing here at the rectory. The Archbishop felt the loss personally, as Joe and your father-in-law worked so hard for so many years on the Shrine's sacred art and on the push to open November 20. In any event, he wanted me to convey to your family that it would be his honor to con-celebrate Joe's Funeral Mass at the Crypt Church with Monsignor Flynn and me. The Archbishop has already talked to Monsignor Flynn, so if that is what you would like, the Archbishop would be honored to accommodate your wishes."

"I don't know what to say. This is so unexpected," Lucy said.

Rosemary turned in her seat to face Lucy. "Say yes, Lucy. Joseph deserves this tribute."

"Rose, please, let me think. Monsignor, our family is in no shape to pay the honorarium for such a blessing as that. I mean, the Crypt Church with the Archbishop, that's just too much." "No one's asking, Lucy. No one's expecting anything from your family. The Shrine is not a parish. It operates under the collective wisdom of the Nation's Bishops under the guidance of Archbishop Guilfoyle. This is his call. This Mass is the Archbishop's way of honoring the Master Carver of the Shrine and his family for his work and sacrifice to make our opening possible."

"Monsignor, you know our family. You know more than most that Joseph was not, how should I say it, a model Catholic."

"Lucy Piera Natale, it's not nice to speak harshly of the dead," Rosemary snapped.

"And tell me, Lucy, what is a model Catholic?" Ryan said, trying to elevate the conversation away from a disagreement between sisters. "Every one of us has chinks in our armor. We all stumble from time to time. What's important is that we let God into our life to get back up. Joseph was a good man. He supported and loved his wife and family, he raised his children in the faith, he was faithful in his marriage vows, he worked hard, and he died as he lived. He apparently wanted to give me his blunt opinion of Francis' vocation in the same uncompromising way he carved stone into beautiful masterpieces. Did he go to Mass every Sunday? No, but did he live an exemplary life? Absolutely he did. By the way, I missed you at Church this morning," Ryan said with a smirk.

Lucy decided she was going to ignore the crack about not going to Mass. What Ryan said about Joseph was true but the Archbishop presiding at his Mass seemed over the top. Something made her uneasy, but she simply could not put her finger on it. Lucy looked at Ryan directly in the eye.

"Then I say yes, Monsignor. Our family would be honored for the Archbishop to preside at Joseph's Funeral Mass."

"Excellent. One last item, Lucy... while it's out of the ordinary, the Archbishop will permit a very short eulogy to be spoken from just in front of the first pew by a family member. Something short, and I must see it first, if of course that's something you would like to do. It speaks very highly of Joseph that the Archbishop would permit this. Typically, it's done at the wake."

"I don't know what to say, Monsignor. Please thank the Archbishop when you see him."

"You can thank him yourself when you see him," Ryan said.

"Ro, we should go. Peter and Louis are going over to the house with the girls, but I don't want to leave the kids by themselves for too long. Monsignor, thank you again for all you have done."

"Anytime, Lucy. Try to have a good rest of the day. I'll inform the Archbishop of all the details. I'll talk to you tomorrow."

Lucy did not speak the whole way home. Rosemary pulled her car into the alley, trying to avoid any neighbors wishing to pay their respects.

"What's the matter, Lucy? You haven't said a word since we left. Is there something wrong with the arrangements?"

"Archbishop Guilfoyle doesn't even know Joe. He met him once for a picture. There's something not right. I lived with the guy all my adult life and believe me he was no saint. He was irreverent and completely disinterested in the Church, but we had a deal; the Catholic education and training of the kids were my responsibility and he deferred to me. We had plenty of fights, and that's what's bothering me. He would have come to me first when Frannie told him about the priesthood. I just can't imagine he would go to the rectory with Frannie without talking to me first. Now the Archbishop of Washington wants to say the Funeral Mass for my husband. It just doesn't make any sense to me."

"What are you saying, Lucy?"

"Rose, honestly I don't know what I'm saying. Something's telling me there's more to the story."

For the next hour around the dining table, Giovanni, Anna, Lucy and Rosemary planned out the details for the next three days through the burial at Mt. Olivet. Grief and shock molted into a long to-do list that for the moment masked the unspeakable misery of losing a precious loved one before his time. The only loose ends at the conclusion of the family meeting were who would do the eulogy and whether Francis wanted to play at the viewing or the Funeral Mass or both. Still reeling from the shock of losing their oldest brother, both Louis and Peter demurred, as did Mary and Cecilia.

"Gi, who do you think should give the eulogy?" Anna asked.

"Maybe the priest if he wants to talk about Joe?"

"Absolutely not!" Lucy shouted. "Joe would not like that at all."

"Pop, do you think you could do it?"

"Me? No, I would make a mess of it."

"He would, Lucy," Anna said. "Something would tick him off and he would start hollering, or he would stumble on his words. Trust me, there would be something that would get under his skin, and he would make a mess of my son's funeral in front of the Archbishop and the family."

"You know, Anna, I'm sitting right here."

"Giovanni, you tell your daughter-in-law I'm wrong and I'll shut up."

Giovanni hesitated.

"Go ahead, Gi, tell her the truth."

"She's right, Lucy. I don't think I could do it."

"Don't anyone look at me," said Rosemary as she pushed her chair away from the kitchen table and poured herself another scotch.

"Then I'll do it," Lucy said.

"That's ridiculous, Lucy. You're the widow," Anna said.

"Just let the priest do it," Gio huffed, tiring of the conversation.

"I said no, Pop, and that's final."

Elizabeth walked in from the front room of the house carrying the dictionary her parents had given her and Francis when they started Campus School.

"I'll do it, Momma. I looked it up in our dictionary. Look, it's right here." Elizabeth flopped the book onto the kitchen table. "Eulogy. 1. A speech or writing in praise of a person 2. High praise or ..."

"Commendation. The word is commendation, Lizzie. And sweetie, you're a dear to offer but it's really something adults do. Besides, we'll be saying goodbye to Poppa and it'll be very sad."

"I don't have to say goodbye."

"Elizabeth, this is all hard enough. There's no need to be disrespectful to your father's memory."

"I'm not, Momma. I have Poppa right in my pocket," Elizabeth said, reaching into her pocket. Elizabeth placed the boss stone on the table. "Pick it up, Momma, it smells like Poppa."

"Elizabeth, where did you get this?" Lucy said, realizing that Joseph had given her a stone exactly like the one on the table that was in her jewelry box.

Elizabeth turned to Giovanni.

"Well, Lizzie, the cat's out the bag now. You might as well tell her."

A surge of energy and pride pulsed through Elizabeth as she described her exploits with her grandfather, making certain to censor out the curse words by saying "Then Grandpop used a bad word," but leaving in the part when "Grandpop was going to give the old fat Irish guy the beating of his life if he didn't let us climb up top."

"Up top where?" Lucy asked in a state of shock.

"We climbed up the scaffold to where Poppa was working," Elizabeth said as Lucy took a deep breath and tried to contain her emotions.

"Elizabeth, you could have left that out," Giovanni said quietly.

"So let me get this straight," Lucy said gritting her teeth. "You took my daughter out for a so-called walk after dark, then you threatened the guard at the Shrine with the beating of his life, had Elizabeth climb up some rickety-ass scaffold, then proceeded to vandalize a piece of sacred art to get Joe's signature stone."

"Yes, but I had a flashlight and the scaffold is not rickety-ass. I never would have put Elizabeth in any kind of danger," Giovanni offered meekly.

"Really now?" Lucy screamed as she slapped the table with her open hand making everyone jump in their chairs. Lucy marched over to the cabinet where Joseph hid the rye, downed a full shot glass and slammed the empty glass on the counter. "You know what I think, old man?" Lucy said as Giovanni looked at the floor with his hands clasped in his lap. "I think you're outrageous, you're arrogant and you're reckless, but I love what you did for my daughter and your son Joe would have laughed his ass off if he heard that story." Lucy's body started to heave with deep sobs from her belly as Anna, Rosemary and Elizabeth rushed to her side.

"Lucy, Anna and I have everything covered here. Go upstairs and get some rest. All of this will be here tomorrow," Rosemary said.

"Momma, can I start to write something for Poppa's Mass?"

"Of course, you can, but I'm not making any promises. I'll want to read it first and Monsignor Ryan must approve it. So, if it becomes too hard for you, I'll ask Monsignor Ryan to do Poppa's eulogy. Okay?"

"Okay, but I think you'll like it when it's done."

I THINK IT'S TIME WE PART WAYS

Francis arrived for music practice with Dolan at exactly three-thirty Monday afternoon. Dolan was in the anteroom filing sheet music in the open file boxes.

"I didn't expect you today, Francis, with everything that happened over the weekend."

Francis felt a sudden surge of anger but did not respond.

"So, are you here to work?" Dolan asked dryly.

"My mother says it's best I stay on a schedule as much as possible."

"She's a smart woman," Dolan said. "Get going and start warming up. Something intricate, perhaps some of Chopin's Number 10."

"Yes, Father." Francis settled into the studio and placed his father's rosewood chisel on the small shelf next to the music rack, starting in on Chopin's Ballade Number 1 in G minor. Francis stared at the rosewood tipped tool as the sadness of the first several measures gave way to fiery chords and dynamic finger sprints reflecting his grief, anger and much darker homicidal fantasy.

"That's not Chopin's Etude Number 10, Francis, and what on earth is that nasty thing doing on my piano?" Dolan reached for Joseph's chisel.

"Don't touch that, Father!" Francis lashed out, surprising even himself by his tone. "It was my father's, and my grandfather gave it to me and my sister."

"I see. Like I said a second ago, you're not warming up with Number 10."

"You said Chopin. It's Chopin's Ballade Number 1."

"I know what it is, Francis," Dolan said. "You know something, Francis? I've been trying to decide when to have this conversation and now seems like the perfect time. Francis, I think it's time we part ways. We'll get through your father's funeral and then finish up with the concert for the Upper Church opening next month, but after that you'll need to find another instructor. I've tried to guide you; I've tried to show you the intricacies of growing up and how God shows his love. But you broke your promise to me and to God and you've been punished. And now, son, there's a trust issue between us. You're the only one responsible, Francis. If you hadn't broken your word your father would be alive today. You need to learn from this, Francis. I'll simply tell your mother I'm holding you back. Another music instructor will pick you up with your talent, but we're done after November 20. Besides, I believe I'll be moving to New York to take over for the retiring Music Director at St. Patrick's Cathedral. I can only give you advice, Francis. The more you talk about our time together the more you'll be punished. More tragedy will be visited on your life and the lives of the people who love you. It is God's will. Do you understand what I'm saying, Francis?"

"Yes, Father."

"And one other thing, Francis. I've noticed flashes of anger in you. Anger is a very dangerous emotion that can create a host of unexpected consequences. I would hate to have to expose you as a homosexual."

"I'm not a homosexual."

"Funny, Francis, you would have fooled me. The pictures of you in my car suggest otherwise," Dolan said in a sadistic guttural laugh. "And, please, Francis," Dolan cackled, "let us not forget our times in the stairwell by the sacristy, they were fantastic."

Francis was devastated. Maybe he was a homosexual. Part of him recognized he was being manipulated but he still did not speak up.

Why do I let him have his way with me? Francis thought, disgusted with himself.

"Do you want me to use this piano until the concert?"

"I don't give a shit what you do, Francis. Just make sure you're ready for the concert. I'll give you the set sheet for the youth concert rehearsals next Monday."

Knowing he was no match for Dolan, Francis reached for the chisel, placing it back into the oilcloth and left for home.

I'LL REMEMBER THE GLASS AS HALF FULL

To say that most of the family and hundreds of friends were surprised that the Archbishop of Washington celebrated Joseph's Funeral Mass would be an understatement. Many of the worshippers had watched the Shrine rise from its tortured on again off again beginnings. The Shrine, destined to be an architectural force in the city and celebrated as a stunning jewel of Marian devotion, was nearing completion. Joseph had been part of a decades long mission carving multiple statues, engravings and multi-dimensional reliefs. Having the Archbishop officiate the Mass was a stunning honor bestowed by the Archdiocese on the family of the Shrine's Master Carver just weeks before its dedication.

Lucy had asked Rosemary to type an extra copy of the eulogy that she kept in her purse, just in case anything happened to Elizabeth's copy. After Ryan approved the eulogy, Lucy read it through one more time. While it was heartbreaking, she realized that Elizabeth seemed to have a much better awareness of what was really important in life than she did. Lucy wasn't sure whether that should make her happy for her daughter or depressed that her own religiosity had overshadowed the simple joys of family life.

Her children seemed to be much more present in the moment than she had ever been. As Lucy sat at her husband's Funeral Mass, she wondered whether Joe, with his incessant irreverence, had embedded in their children a much deeper understanding of life.

Archbishop Guilfoyle intoned the traditional prayer of the faithful, with the congregation responding in unison. *"Lord, hear our prayer."*

As the entreaties droned on, Lucy became distracted as she stared at Elizabeth's eulogy. Her trance was broken when she heard Joseph's name echoing off the vaulted ceiling in the Crypt Church.

"We pray for those who mourn Joseph's death especially his parents Giovanni and Anna, his beloved wife Lucy, his loving children Francis and Elizabeth and his brothers and sisters Louis and Peter and Mary and Cecilia; that you may find strength and consolation in the hope that we have through the resurrection of Jesus from the dead. We pray to the Lord.

Lord, hear our prayer."

Archbishop Guilfoyle looked up from his missal. "Please be seated," he said as he waited for the congregation to settle into their pews.

"Thank you. As the spiritual shepherd of the Archdiocese of Washington, I, along with the Pastor of St. Francis de Sales Church, Monsignor Cletus Ryan, am honored to be here with you this morning to celebrate the life of our dearly departed brother Joseph. His daughter Elizabeth will now say a few words in remembrance of her father."

Giving her mother a kiss, Elizabeth stood and stepped in front of the first pew to face the congregation.

"If you need to stop, I can finish this for you," Lucy whispered to Elizabeth.

"I can do it, Momma," Elizabeth said as she unfolded the eulogy Rosemary had typed for her.

"When I looked up the word eulogy in our dictionary at the house it said it was a speech in praise of a person. So, when I think of Poppa it was easy to write down his praise. Poppa is everywhere. All you have to do is look around. Grandpop showed me all the stone and saints and other people that Poppa carved here in this church and upstairs in the big church, so that is praise."

Giovanni put his hand on Lucy's shoulder and started to cry.

"My favorite one is the Indian girl giving thanks to the Lord and last Saturday night my Grandpop took me up there so I could touch it. When you leave and walk up the stairs, turn around and look up. It's right there. So, all of that is praise, too.

"Poppa was always home for Sunday dinner and sometimes helped Momma clean up the dishes and he did everything around the house that needed to be fixed. Every year we would go to Ocean City, and we had Poppa all to ourselves. We would play in the ocean and Poppa and Uncle Peter would get me and Frannie on their shoulders and we would play King of the World until one of us would fall into the water and at night Poppa would sneak me and Frannie money to go on the rides, but he told us not to tell Momma, but I guess it's okay to tell her now. Poppa always laughed when he was in Ocean City.

"My Poppa loved Momma. The reason we know that is because all the time Poppa would tease Momma about why she didn't like sports and that would make her laugh and then they would go out on the back porch and talk. Best of all, Poppa would come in at night and give Frannie and me a kiss goodnight. So, I think all that is praise for Poppa.

"When I was talking to Sister Mary Allison when she was helping me with Poppa's eulogy, she showed me a glass of water and then she asked me if it was half empty or half full. I thought it was a trick question," Elizabeth said as a murmur of laughter filtered through the assembly. "So, I said I don't know, and she said that was the right answer. She said I could remember Poppa and think about the time we won't have with him in the future, or I could remember my Poppa and think about the time we did have with him in the past. So, when I remember Sister's glass of water,

I'll remember Poppa and I'll remember the glass as half full. The End. Thank you."

Clear-eyed, she stood in front of the Archbishop as applause reverberated through the church. Francis was paralyzed by the thought of everyone in the church finding out what he had done to his family. He looked at Elizabeth, expressionless. He knew that they were both beginning a trip on an uncharted landscape, where the ugliness of the past would be locked up in a black box, put away for some other time, or perhaps forever.

CHAPTER FIVE

I'm Done with Secrets

WHY ARE WE GOING THIS WAY?
Francis exited the Crypt Church through the center aisle, hand in hand with Lucy and Elizabeth. A wave of nausea flooded over him as he walked past the Sacred Music Office. Climbing the staircase to the east terrace and the awaiting procession, the crisp fall air helped dissipate the revulsion and guilt he felt as he recalled the ugly memories of his time with Father Dolan.

All of this is my fault, Francis thought. *Everything that has happened is because I broke my silence, broke my promise to God.*

Lucy put her arms around both of her children as they walked. "Frannie are you okay? You look pale," Lucy said.

"I'm okay Momma, I just want this to be over so we can go home."

Giovanni and Anna were close behind, followed by Rosemary and Joseph's brothers and sisters. The family, a traditional study in black, waited for the funeral director to organize the motorcade from Michigan Avenue to the cemetery.

Many of Joseph's mourners came up to Elizabeth to tell her how well she did delivering the eulogy, but the compliments only seemed to reinforce a numbing sensation in her body. Nothing really seemed to matter. She felt totally detached from the family's embrace, isolated by the secret that she believed she could never share. She was angry that God had chosen her for Dolan's attention, and now Poppa was gone.

The sun reflected off the chromed embellishments on the 1959 Cadillac hearse as the motorcade assembled at the east terrace of the Shrine. Cars were lined up from the north exit of the Shrine parking lot across the campus of Catholic University, stretching past McMahon Hall, down the chicane between the gymnasium and the Schools of Nursing and ending at the Brookland Avenue entrance to the east side of the campus. Giovanni and Anna, along with Lucy and the children, settled into the first car directly behind the hearse for the slow ride to Mt. Olivet Cemetery.

"Look, Anna. Look behind us. I can't believe the line of cars," Giovanni marveled.

"Joe touched a lot of people," Lucy said, dazed as she leaned back in her seat. As the procession plodded down Michigan Avenue, Francis realized they were heading toward their house on Shepherd Street.

"Why are we going this way to the cemetery, Momma?" Francis asked.

Gio spoke up first. "It's an Italian custom, Francis. We take your Poppa past your house and any neighbors who can't go to the funeral can wave goodbye. Your Poppa's friends from work will be there on the front steps of your house."

The procession proceeded to the corner of Taylor and 14th Street; another right turn would take it directly past Joseph and Lucy's house.

"Open the window, Frannie, so your mother can hear."

Francis rolled down the rear window on Lucy's side and pulled his jacket collar up against the cold air. The hearse approached the family home and paused for several seconds as it came to the corner of Shepherd and 14th Street.

All of the carvers who worked at the Shrine were lined up in their best church clothes at the curb. Their bicep muscles pushed against the fabric of their suits as they stood at attention waiting for the hearse. Each man held a square-topped steel hammer and a pitching tool. Then Lucy heard it—the carver's dirge. In a precise cadence, one after the other, each carver struck his pitching tool three times. The high-pitched report caused Lucy and Anna to flinch. As the last man struck his pitching tool the procession slowly got underway.

Lucy let her head fall back into the seat.

"Lucy, I didn't mean to upset you, but the men wanted to say their goodbye as carvers."

"You didn't, Pop, it was beautiful what they did. It's just so damn sad it makes me want to throw up."

"I know, Lucy, your husband and our son passed before his time."

Anna was shocked. In all the years that they had been married Giovanni had never uttered those words. It was either "my son" or "your son."

"You've never said that before," Anna said.

"I know, but I'm saying it now," Giovanni said impassively.

Lucy let the import of that conversation pass as she directed her attention to the ritual of burying her husband. It took nearly another half an hour for the end of the motorcade to get to the entrance of the cemetery.

The funeral procession came to a crawl. The gravel driveway leading to the burial plot rutted and crunched under the weight of the hearse, abruptly ending the family's escape from their grief.

Cold air rushed into the limousine as a solemn attendant opened the door. The family trudged along a path made for them between dozens of graves and mature ash trees. The freshly cut grass and fallen leaves, still damp from the morning dew, stuck to their shoes.

The family took their places in the six white chairs facing Joseph's casket, which rested under a green canopy.

Monsignor Ryan carefully opened his breviary to the Rite of Final Committal. In a strong baritone voice, Ryan began the formal prayer. After several minutes of entreaties, he addressed the entire group of mourners.

"Before we go our separate ways, let us take leave of our brother Joseph. May our farewell express our affection for him; may it ease our sadness and strengthen our hope. One day we shall joyfully greet him again when the love of Christ, which conquers all things, destroys even death itself."

Ryan moved to a small wooden table next to the grave and handed the aspergillum, the cylindrical implement with a bulbous end that contained Holy Water, to Lucy.

"Elizabeth and Francis, come with me. I'll sprinkle Poppa's casket with Holy Water with this wand, then you do the same. Then hand it to Grandpop."

Francis held his mother's arm as she began to shake in front of the casket. She jerked the aspergillum once toward her husband's coffin. The Holy Water dotted the top of Joseph's polished mahogany casket with glistening white orbs that seemed frozen in place. Lucy passed the wand to Francis who did the same, handing the implement off to Elizabeth who let it drop to her side. Giovanni and Anna slid in behind her and slowly raised her arm.

"Go ahead, Lizzie. Just like when we were up with Pocahontas. I'll help you," Giovanni said.

Elizabeth gave one violent shake and collapsed in her grandfather's arms.

Monsignor Ryan retrieved the aspergillum from Anna and began the final prayer at Joseph's grave.

Ryan closed his breviary and addressed the group. "This concludes the service. The family has asked me to thank each and every one of you for coming and invite you to a luncheon at A. V.

Ristorante, which is located at 607 New York Avenue, to celebrate Joseph's life."

Lucy asked Anna to take Elizabeth and Francis to the limousine. As soon as they were on their way, Lucy went directly to Monsignor Ryan and hugged him tightly. "Thank you, and the Archbishop, from the bottom of our hearts. It was a beautiful service. Joe would have been so proud. We'll be forever indebted to you." Lucy stepped back and grasped both of Ryan's hands. "Will I see you at A.V's?"

"Unfortunately not, I have some meetings that I must attend to," Ryan said.

"Then maybe dinner at the house one Sunday?"

"That would be lovely, Lucy, thank you."

"When things settle down, I'll call you and we can set a date, maybe after the opening and before Christmas."

"That would be perfect, Lucy, thank you again." Ryan walked to his car, riveted by the warmth of her skin and the scent of her hair.

ALL THE WAY

Many of Joseph's friends grabbed handfuls of earth from the open grave and dropped them carefully on his casket. Some left flowers picked from the bunches that were taken from the Crypt, while Giovanni and several of the Shrine carvers brought limestone dust from the statutory ornamentation to send Joseph on his journey to the next life.

Slowly, the cars left in small groups to gather at A.V. Ristorante's for the traditional comfort food and camaraderie.

A.V.'s place was a Washington staple, where the political elite and the wealthy shared space with the common man. The dark red walls and low lighting aligned perfectly with the aroma of garlic and oregano and countless autographed pictures of celebrities and Washington's power elite.

Lucy surveyed the surreal scene. A crowd of revelers gorged themselves on mountains of food while Frank Sinatra's '57 hit *All the Way* blared on a continuous loop.

Joseph was dead. She was alive. Their children had lost their father and she was now a single parent living next door to her dead husband's parents. Lucy tried to suppress her anger to fit into the role of widowed mother. The party atmosphere contrasted harshly with the raw emotion of a family in shock and mourning. Her sadness overwhelmed any notion of celebrating Joe's life and she realized that tomorrow would mark the beginning of a new reality for her. Watching the gaiety, she wondered who would be there for her in the coming weeks and months.

Lucy turned to Rosemary and whispered, "I can't take much more of this."

"I know, Lucy, but you can't leave now. What if I get you a drink?"

Glancing at the wristwatch Joseph had given her the previous Christmas, Lucy ground a half-smoked cigarette into the ashtray on the table.

"My God, Rose, have you seen the kids? I forgot all about them. I haven't seen them in over an hour."

"I just talked to them a few minutes ago. They're out in the lobby and they want to go home."

"Would you be a dear and take them home? I'll follow in a half hour or so. That will give me a good excuse. Enough partying."

Rosemary had parked her car in the side lot, so she was able to get the kids out through the bar without a lot of fanfare and goodbyes. Elizabeth and Francis climbed into the car without saying a word.

"You guys are awfully quiet," Rosemary said, trying to get a read on the emotional temperature of both children.

"What's to talk about?" Elizabeth said curtly.

"No need to bite my head off, Lizzie," Rosemary said.

"I'm sorry, Aunt Rose. I just hate it."

"Hate what, Lizzie?" Rosemary asked.

"I hate everything."

"Do you hate me?"

"You know what I mean, Aunt Rose. I don't hate you, but I do hate God!"

"You better stop talking like that, Lizzie," Francis said.

"Yeah, says who, Frannie? You and Momma? What's going to happen, Frannie," Elizabeth taunted her brother. "Tell me, Frannie, what's going to happen?" Elizabeth screamed in the car. Tell me, Francis, what's really going to happen? Can you bring Poppa back, Frannie? Can you?" Elizabeth demanded, starting to lose control.

Francis just looked at his sister.

"Right, Frannie, you can't, so just shut up."

Rosemary pulled her car to the curb in front of the house. As soon as the car was in park, Elizabeth jumped out and ran to her bedroom, slamming every door in her wake.

"Frannie, she'll cool off in a day or two."

"Maybe. But Aunt Rose, I really don't care what she does. She's right, I can't bring Poppa back." Francis walked into the house and started playing the piano.

Rosemary was stunned. Lucy was going to have her hands full. Rosemary went to the kitchen and poured a tumbler full of ice water and scotch. Soothed by the sound of Francis playing Rachmaninoff's 18th Variation on a Theme, she settled into Joseph's chair, realizing that she might not be missing much. Being a single woman, financially independent with no kids or husband seemed pretty damn good at that moment.

SO WHAT'S IT GOING TO BE, GIOVANNI?

Anna rendered the fat from the speck in a black skillet with three large brown eggs.

"Are you eating breakfast?" Anna called out to Giovanni who was sketching in his notebook in the front room.

"You cooking?"

"What, did you hire a cook for me? Of course I'm cooking."

"Then I'll have some," Giovanni grunted.

"It's on the table, Gio, and turn down your opera. It's too early in the morning for sopranos." Anna slid Gio's plate on the table and turned back to the stove to pour herself a cup of coffee.

Giovanni dropped the newspaper on the table, staring at a large piece of grilled Italian bread covered by warmed slices of speck and three sunny side up eggs flecked with black pepper and flakes of cayenne.

"Since when don't you like sopranos?" Giovanni asked seriously.

"I don't want to talk about sopranos, Gio."

"So, what do you want to talk about?" Giovanni asked, cutting into the bread and speck.

"Joseph died on October 10. You told me you were leaving soon. When's soon? So, what's it going to be, Giovanni?"

"I'm staying on at the Shrine for a while longer."

"Don't mock me, old man. I'm not talking about that. I'm talking about Josephine Gentilli."

"I know who you're talking about," Giovanni said.

Anna reached into her apron pocket and tossed a wax sealed envelope on the table with her name on the front.

"What's this?" Giovanni asked.

"What's it look like, Gio?"

"Well, it looks like a letter for you," he said, picking it up and turning it over to check for a return address.

"It's from Josephine," Anna said tersely.

"How the hell do you know that?"

"Connie gave it to me the night of Joseph's wake."

"The spy you mean. So, you know that Josephine came over last month?" Giovanni asked, placing both his knife and fork on his plate.

"Of course I do, and Connie's not a spy, she's a friend," Anna said defensively.

"A friendly spy then," Giovanni said, not willing to let it go. "So, you don't know what Josephine said to me?"

"All I know is that she was in the parking lot at my son's wake, didn't talk to anyone but you, then sent me a letter that was given to me by Connie. That's what I know, Giovanni."

"So, goddammit, just read the letter why don't you!" he shouted, pushing his plate away.

"No!" said Anna as she slapped her open palm on the table, causing the silverware to jump off the plate and fall to the floor. "I want you to read it out loud."

"Fine, I'll read the goddamn letter!" Giovanni shouted as he picked up the letter and broke the seal. "Why is it so important that I read a letter addressed to you?"

"Because I'm done with secrets, Gio. I'm done with the fog of being in limbo. I deserve much, much better, and I'll tell you one more thing... I don't deserve after forty years of marriage to be a third wheel."

Giovanni rubbed the letter between his thumb and index finger, admiring Josephine's elegant handwriting on the buttery sheets of embossed Florentine writing paper. He cleared his throat as he stared at Josephine's words on the paper.

"Dear Anna:

While I know we have never met, in a curious way I feel I have known you for years. With that, it is my hope that you will accept my sincere condolences upon the passing of your son Joseph. I am aware that Giovanni shared with you our plans for him to come to Italy and live with me upon his retirement."

"*Stronzo*," Anna muttered, loud enough for Giovanni to hear. "Shut up, woman, if you want me to finish this letter."

> "*I write this to make you aware of several other things that you may not know. Giovanni and I met when we were fifteen years old. We were madly in love and wanted to marry as soon as we were able, but our fathers arranged our marriages to other people. Giovanni went along with the arrangement. I did not, much to my father's upset. I have had a very full and enriching life, just one that I did not expect. I should also tell you that Giovanni and I never shared a bed, even when we objected to our father's decree on hearing that our marriage was not going to happen. I have watched from afar as your family grew and Giovanni's career progressed. I found an odd sense of satisfaction in those events in that I loved him first. My honor as a woman is mine alone to protect.*"

"Her honor, Giovanni? What about my shame?" Anna interrupted.

Giovanni ignored the comment.

> "*I have come to realize that Giovanni does love you and his family in America. I informed him at Joseph's wake that I would no longer entertain any thought of our being together.*"

Anna leaned her head back in the chair and closed her eyes.

> "*On Joseph's passing, Giovanni informed me that his children, grandchildren, Joseph's wife and of course you should not be burdened with a selfish legacy of ill-fated*

love. I fully agreed with that sentiment. As it relates to me, Giovanni believed his planned actions to be a question of honor as he promised he would come back to me. I have relieved him of that promise. I thought it was very important to deliver that message in person because, as I suspect you know, your husband can be stubborn to a fault. Speaking for myself, I can honestly say I have no regrets. Anna, all I can ask of you is that you find a way in your heart to love the father of your son, may his soul rest in peace.

Respectfully, Josephine Gentilli,
Viggiu, Italy October 13, 1959."

Giovanni reached for his handkerchief to dry his eyes. "Now what?" he asked.

"Now what? Now I'm going to put my coat on and walk up the hill to the Monastery and say a rosary," Anna said wistfully. "I could have been friends with Josephine. I made room for your clothes in my closet. If you're staying, move your clothes into the closet. If you're not, I'd like you to leave today."

"And if I stay, what then, Anna?"

"I guess we're back to what you said forty years ago, Gio. We'll give it a try and see what happens," Anna said as she picked up Josephine's letter from the table.

HERE'S THE PLAY LIST
Francis got to the Sacred Music Office on time, but he could hear that someone else was playing in the studio, so he took a seat in the anteroom and waited. School had become a challenge since Dolan's abuse had begun and the only thing that held his interest was music and his upcoming appearance at the youth concert. As he was

looking through his sheet music the door suddenly opened, and Father Dolan appeared.

"It'll be a few minutes, Francis."

Before Francis could say anything, Dolan closed the door, locking the deadbolt into place. Francis had heard that ominous sound before.

Ten minutes later, Dolan reappeared with a young boy. Francis noticed the boy's face was flushed, much like his was the first time Dolan showed him the pictures in the black folio.

"Okay, run along. I'll see you next week. Remember the instructions I gave you. Okay, Francis, you can go in and practice. I'll be in and out and I'll try not to be a distraction. Here's the play list for the concert. It's show time in a week, young man, so I want perfect execution. I'll have final rehearsal at 4:00 P.M. on the nineteenth. You got all that?"

"I'll be ready."

"You better be ready," Dolan said harshly.

"Who was that kid? He wasn't very good," Francis stated.

"That's why he was here. He wants to get better, Francis. Not everyone is blessed with your talent."

"Is that all?" Francis asked.

"What's that supposed to mean, Francis?"

"Nothing, Father."

"No, no, you started this, Francis. What did you mean by *is that all?*"

"Are you showing him God's love? That's what I meant, Father. Like you showed me God's love? Are you giving him the same instruction you gave me?" Francis taunted.

Dolan rushed over to Francis, stopping within inches of his face. "Listen, you little shit, you had your chance. It was perfect, but you broke your promise and you, my boy, you were punished severely. Oh, wait a second, wait just a second," Dolan said, letting out a sadistic laugh. "I get it, you're jealous!"

"I'm not," Francis protested, squirming on the piano bench.

"Yes, you are, Francis; you're blushing. You miss it, don't you?"

Francis stared at the keyboard and gritted his teeth. "I want to be your student."

"Say that a little louder, Francis, I didn't quite get that," Dolan said sarcastically.

"I want to be your student," Francis said on the verge of tears.

"What else, Francis, what else do you miss?"

Francis sat on the bench not saying a word.

"I see," Dolan, said. "So, you were wrong in breaking your promise to be silent?"

"I was wrong, Father."

"And you want to get back in my good graces I suppose?"

"I do, Father."

"Well, Francis, I'm just not sure I can trust you."

"You can, Father, I promise on my father's grave."

"That's really admirable, Francis, but your father's gone. Now if you said you promise on Elizabeth that might make a difference. You of course remember the agreement you made with regard to your sister?"

"Yes. I do."

"So, are you saying that we can pick up where we left off, Francis?"

"Yes, Father."

Dolan went to his briefcase and removed his black folio. "You may want to look at this before you come. I want you to practice for twenty minutes and bring the folio to me where we met last time. Do you remember where it was?"

"Yes."

"I'm done playing around with you, Francis. Do you understand me?"

"Yes, Father." Francis was ashamed of his own sexual bargaining and repulsed by what he was prepared to do to maintain his status as Dolan's prized student. His father would be alive if he had kept his mouth shut. Now he had to make a deal with the devil to survive and keep Elizabeth and the rest of his family safe.

"Yes, Father what, Francis?"

"Yes, Father Dolan."

"Good, and Francis, be careful with that folio. It would be hard to explain how you got it. In case you're wondering, no one would believe you got it from a priest. By the way, don't get too excited before you come and meet me. You wouldn't want Monsignor Flynn to walk in with you sitting at the piano with a boner," Dolan said, laughing. "I'll see you in twenty minutes. Don't be late."

TAKE CARE OF IT, FATHER

Dolan glanced at the phone as he readied the music selections for the three-day opening of the Shrine. Annoyed that the Archbishop had not provided him additional support at the parish, he dialed Monsignor Ryan's number. Dolan put his feet up on his desk. This was going to be a phone call he would enjoy.

"Good afternoon, Vicar General's office. Cecilia speaking."

"Good afternoon, Cecilia. This is Father Andrew Dolan at the Sacred Music Office at the Shrine. Is Monsignor Ryan available?"

"Let me check, Father. Are you getting excited for next week?"

"Oh, yes, it'll be a momentous day in the history of the Archdiocese."

"Okay, Father, please hold on and I'll get Monsignor Ryan's attention."

"Dolan, Ryan here, what is it," Ryan grumbled into the phone.

"I'm sorry to bother you at the chancery, Monsignor, but we have six altar boys from the parish who will be on the altar for next week. The Archbishop has directed that everyone will receive communion, so he has requested that the boys avail themselves of the sacrament of confession tomorrow afternoon."

"So, take care of it, Father, you're the curate."

"Well, that's just it, Monsignor. Archbishop Guilfoyle wants me to meet with all the network television liaison folks to brief them on the liturgy that they'll be witnessing during the broadcast. The only time everyone is available is of course tomorrow when confessions will be ongoing."

"How convenient, Father," Ryan said, piqued at Dolan's barely veiled arrogance.

"Of course you know I would never have called you had we been fully staffed at the parish."

"Believe me, Father, I am well acquainted with our deficits at the parish."

"I understand, Monsignor. Nevertheless, may I report back that you will cover confessions for the boys?"

"You may," said Ryan as he slammed the phone into the cradle.

NOVEMBER 16, 1959

The next morning, Francis woke up with a knot in his stomach. Throughout the school day, he watched the clock. At 1:55 P.M., the announcement came from Sister Mary Carolyn.

"Will the six young men chosen to participate in next week's opening of the Shrine report to the vestibule at Aquinas Hall. Monsignor Ryan will hear your confession."

Francis felt his scalp tingling with unrelenting tension. He was overwhelmed by shame and guilt. He needed to unburden himself.

But what words can I use? he thought. He was sexually involved with a priest. He liked the attention, he got sexually aroused and at the same time he hated everything about Dolan, but he kept coming back.

Why? he thought, clenching his fists. He liked to look at dirty magazines, he lied to his parents and when he told Joseph what had happened to Elizabeth, God struck his father down in front of his own eyes. How could he even play a note with Father Dolan on the altar next week? Francis fell behind the other boys, making sure he was last.

Finally, it was his turn. The dark, lacquered cherry confessional loomed in front of him. The finely turned spindles on the corners framed an intricately carved door that seemed like something out of a horror movie. Before he moved, he glanced to the top of the confessional to be sure both sides had green lights and he was alone. As he entered the stall closest to the wall, he knelt and listened for the kneeler switch to roll over, turning the green light to red. As the sliding gauze-covered window in the middle compartment slowly slid open, Francis knew he was in trouble. Inside, the priest's torso was slouched into the built-in seat, his purple stole around his neck. Francis began to panic. It was Monsignor Ryan.

"Are you the last," Ryan said calmly.

"Yes, Monsignor."

"Is it your honest intent to confess your sins before Almighty God?"

"Yes, it is, Monsignor."

"Please continue, my son."

"In the Name of the Father, the Son and the Holy Spirit, amen. Bless me, Father, for I have sinned, it has been two weeks since my last confession." Francis started to stumble over his words.

"Go on."

Francis could not speak. Ryan waited for his penitent to speak.

"Are you still there?"

"Yes," Francis said.

"Is this Francis?"

"Yes."

"I thought I recognized your voice. What's wrong?"

"I'm afraid."

"Afraid of what, my son? You are in the merciful arms of your Savior," Ryan soothed.

"I'm afraid to tell you about my sins and I'm afraid if I tell you someone else will die."

"Are you talking about your father?"

"Yes, Monsignor," Francis said, his voice starting to crack.

"It's alright, child, there's no sin that cannot be reached by God's mercy."

"I don't believe that, Monsignor."

"I see. What exactly are you afraid of?"

"If I tell you my sins then I will lose my mother!"

"How could you possibly lose your mother, Francis?"

"That's how Poppa died. I broke my promise to God." Francis heard his words and realized there was no going back now. "When I told Poppa he died in your office."

"When you told your Poppa what?" Ryan asked.

"That I saw Father Dolan with his pants down humping on Elizabeth."

"Francis, there was no promise to God. Your father died because he had a bad heart."

"That's not true. He died because I told," Francis insisted.

"Francis, do you believe that God knows everything?"

"Yes."

"Good, that's a start. Do you know the word inviolable?"

"No."

"Well, it means that if anything I hear in this sacrament of confession is repeated, I will no longer be a priest; that I will immediately be excommunicated from the Church of our Lord and Savior. That's how private our conversation is. Have you ever heard that before?"

"No."

"Do you believe I would ever lie to you if it meant I would no longer be a priest in the eyes of God?"

"No, I don't think you would do that."

"So, Francis, if you believe that, understand that by confessing your sins you're not talking to me as a man. You're talking to God directly through me. I am God's earthly representative. Since God already knows everything, there are no secrets between you and Him. When you confess your sins to me, God knows that by your participation in this sacred process you are truly sorry and that is the reason why God will bestow upon you His forgiveness. Do you understand that, Francis?"

"I think so."

"So, why don't you start from the beginning."

"I can't, Monsignor."

"That's fine, you don't have to say anything you don't want to, but just so we're clear, if you don't make an honest confession you cannot receive the Eucharist. Correct?"

"Yes, Monsignor."

"And if you cannot receive communion, you cannot be on the altar with the Archbishop at the Mass for the Shrine's opening. Correct?"

"Yes. I understand, Monsignor."

"It may even put your performance at the youth concert in jeopardy. Do any of these facts help you with your decision to go forward?"

"Nothing I say to you can ever be repeated?" Francis asked.

"Not a single word to anyone on this earth, with God as my witness, Francis."

Francis took in a deep breath and exhaled fully. "Okay, I'll tell you what happened."

Cletus Ryan sat back and absorbed one blow after another. In all his years as a priest, never had he heard of this level of depravity and vile manipulation of another person, let alone a boy. He knew that priests sexually acting out with children was not a new phenomenon for the Church. It was an issue that in years past had been handled discreetly with little or no scandal created.

This was different. This was explosive. Dolan was a manipulative, sadistic predator with prior history of being a sexual offender. Ryan's gut churned as sweat poured off his body. What he said next could change the course of the entire Archdiocese at a time when the world's eyes were focused on Marian devotion and the soaring edifice to be dedicated in less than a week. It could also dramatically change his career trajectory if he could not convince Francis that he, too, was at fault and had sinned.

"Is there anything else, Francis," Ryan stammered as he tried to clear his throat.

"No, Monsignor, I told you everything."

"Who else have you told, Francis?"

"Just you and Poppa."

"Have you discussed what happened to you with your sister or anyone else in your family?"

"No."

"Do you intend to discuss this with anyone after you leave here today?"

"I don't want to."

"That's good, Francis."

"Do you feel you seduced Father Dolan?"

"What does that mean?"

"It means did you encourage him to have physical contact with you?"

"No, Monsignor, I was afraid when it happened."

"Did Father Dolan force you to do anything?"

"No, I wouldn't say he forced me."

"Did you resist his advances?"

"I kinda looked out the window. I remember I started to cry; I remember that."

"Did you ever tell him to stop?"

"No, but Father said it was a special love from God and I wanted him to be my music teacher."

"God does not love his children that way, Francis. You and Father Dolan turned your face away from God when you were engaged in such activity. Do you understand that you bear some of the responsibility for your actions with Father Dolan, that you succumbed to the temptation of viewing vile images of the male and female form? Is that the reason why you felt the need to confess your sins?"

"Yes, Monsignor."

"Do you accept the responsibility for your actions?"

"Yes, Monsignor."

"And before God, Francis, can you now say you're sorry for your sins?"

"I'm sorry, Monsignor. So, God didn't punish me by striking down Poppa?"

"Our God is a loving God, Francis, what you thought was a punishment was simply a loss of your own making."

"I didn't kill my Poppa, Monsignor," Francis said defiantly.

"No, you didn't, Francis. But you didn't tell him about your own actions, only what you observed with Father Dolan and your sister."

"I was afraid to."

"Your father had a weakened heart. It was the upset created by you in telling him about Elizabeth that caused the event. Being accountable for your actions is not to be confused with a so-called punishment from God."

"So, I'm responsible for Poppa dying."

"In part, Francis. You do bear some of the responsibility and by the Grace of God He is prepared to forgive you for your actions. Do you understand, Francis, that part of the responsibility you owe for your actions is to the Church and your family?"

"What do you mean, Monsignor?"

"What do you think would happen if the parish knew about you and Father Dolan? What do you think would happen to your mother if word got out in the community? What would everyone think? What if it became known that part of the reason your father died was because you told your father about Elizabeth's abuse, but you didn't tell him that you were sexually involved with a priest? Do you think she would appreciate that? Do you think Elizabeth would feel you were helping her?"

"Elizabeth hates me."

"If you keep your silence and ask for God's forgiveness, Elizabeth will come to love you, Francis. When you told me in the car that your Poppa was angry because of your interest in the priesthood, that wasn't true was it?"

"No, not when I told you."

"So, now you do have an interest in the priesthood," Ryan persisted.

"Yes, I think I do."

"Francis, think on that some more and when you're ready come talk to me. Okay?"

"Yes, Monsignor."

"I don't want you to have any further physical contact with Father Dolan. Is that agreed? Say three Hail Mary's and three Our Father's and make a good Act of Contrition."

"Yes, Monsignor."

"Wait here, I'll leave first. When I open your door you can leave. Go in peace, my child, and put all of this behind you. You have a big week next week."

"Yes, Monsignor."

"God, the Father of Mercies, through the death and resurrection of his Son, has reconciled the world to himself and sent the Holy Spirit among us for the forgiveness of sins; through the ministry of the Church may God give you pardon and peace, and I absolve you from your sins in the name of the Father, and of the Son, and of the Holy Spirit. Amen."

Francis left the confessional more confused than ever. He had been absolved of all of his sins, the abuse by Father Dolan was over. But there was no absolution that could ease the weight of his and Elizabeth's abuse and his responsibility for his father's death. He was left with a secret that he could never tell.

HAVE YOU READ THE REPORTS?

The Vicar General's office at the chancery had a direct passageway to the Archbishop's office. The Archbishop had an annoying habit when he wanted to smoke of walking into Ryan's office and taking a seat, lighting his cigar and puffing away. It was perhaps the most annoying habit of the Archbishop, causing incessant comment from Mrs. McGinty on the smell still lingering on his clothes upon his return to his residence at St. Francis de Sales. The promised appointment of a new pastor had not occurred, so Ryan was doing double duty at the chancery and at St. Francis. With the possibility of Dolan being transferred, Ryan's patience with the Archbishop was running thin.

"Cletus, have you read the reports from New Mexico on Dolan's last visit there?"

"I have, Archbishop. They're pretty demoralizing, if the involuntary laicization is off the table."

"Well, it certainly is off the table from the Vatican's perspective at this juncture. You can't just kick a priest out of the priesthood. I assume there has been no awareness of the Natale incidents made known to you?"

"Other than what I do know, no nothing more."

"Excellent, let's hope it stays that way. I've met with Dolan and I have given him a fraternal correction. He seemed genuinely remorseful, as they all do when confronted with such behavior, and

228

agreed that a change in scenery may be in order. He comes from a good Irish family so with the proper representations, New York may take him off our hands. I've had some preliminary conversations with Cardinal Riordan."

"What do you mean representations, Archbishop?"

"Misguided affection without remorse can be troublesome for a bishop, but we should strive to give Father Dolan every opportunity to be a good priest. We'll need to focus his personnel file on his great accomplishments with regard to the opening of the Shrine."

"So, you're actually going to recommend him?"

"Of course I am."

Ryan was amazed at the semantic gymnastics Guilfoyle went through to talk about a sexual predator. He understood he was a willing participant in the movement of Dolan to another parish. He was also acutely aware that no fraternal correction would stop a predator from gaining access to children.

Guilfoyle got up from his desk and turned his back on Ryan. "With a fraternal correction and guidance, a change in scenery may prove to be the right ingredient for Father Dolan to find success. I certainly cannot forward the reports to New York. You agree with that, Monsignor, do you not?"

"Don't you think they would be entitled to them if they're considering taking him into the Archdiocese?" Ryan asked.

"Under some circumstances, yes, but without Dolan's consent and Cardinal Riordan requesting them, they must remain confidential. You will learn, Cletus, that bishops helping bishops is the rule not the exception."

"I saw the reports," Ryan said.

"Indeed you did, Cletus. You reviewed them as Vicar General of this Archdiocese and under my express authority, guided by our Holy Father's rescript of *Crimens Solicitations*. Cletus, I'm trying to bring you along on the handling of these types of sensitive matters, but frankly you seem resistant to my methods and reasoning. Are you resistant, Cletus? Have I misjudged your commitment to the longevity of our glorious priesthood?"

"I can tell you, Your Grace, with great authority that having been given the opportunity to perhaps influence a positive outcome of this unfortunate situation, I believe I have contributed greatly to the outcome that you desire. Of course, there are no guarantees in life that circumstances beyond our control won't cause scandal to the faithful."

"I can also say with great authority you are being somewhat opaque, Cletus."

"It's because I must, under our joint obligation as priests, protect certain communications as inviolable."

"Ah, I see. You've heard the boy's confession. Good show, Cletus, good show. Perhaps in the near future you would act as my confessor if circumstances require," Guilfoyle countered, taking the opportunity to blow a huge cloud of cigar smoke into Ryan's face.

"It would be my high honor, of course within the proscriptions of my priestly office, Your Grace."

"I understand, Cletus, just don't take your eye off the ball. What's on your calendar for Monday?"

"Well, with it only being five days out from the twentieth and having a curate who's one-hundred percent engaged in the Shrine's opening it's only me at the parish. And of course, I have my duties here at the chancery. So, with respect, Archbishop, my plate's rather full."

"I'll make some calls and get you coverage for Monday. You're going to New York with me. I've been able to secure four center orchestra tickets to the opening of the Sound of Music with Mary Martin."

"Good Lord, Bishop, how on earth were you able to get those?"

"Friends in the labor unions. Let's leave it at that, Cletus."

Ryan could barely contain his excitement. "I can't believe you have tickets. I just love Mary Martin, I saw her in South Pacific and she's just marvelous. I can't thank you enough for including me."

"Well, now you have a front row Broadway seat. I figured with everything else that has happened you could use a break."

"That's very kind of you, Archbishop."

"You said you had four tickets. Who else is going?"

"It's still a business trip, Cletus. You will meet me at Union Station at ten-thirty Monday morning. Our train leaves at eleven. A car will pick us up at one forty-five at Penn Station and we'll go straight to the Palace and meet with Cardinal Riordan and your counterpart in New York. We'll take care of this Dolan business, have a great pre-theater dinner at Frankie & Johnnie's and it's a five-minute walk to the Lunt-Fontanne for the show. It'll be a grand evening and we'll take care of a little problem. Two birds with one stone—I always love when that happens."

"Shall I bring formal attire?"

"No. Cardinal Riordan likes to go out in simple clerics when he goes to Broadway. He saves the red hat and robes for when he needs to raise money," Guilfoyle said, laughing.

"What's my role, Archbishop, for this meeting with the Cardinal?"

"To be blunt, Cletus, you have no role. I'll do the talking. You're there to simply support the Archdiocese and me. This meeting is about one thing, Cletus, one bishop helping his brother bishop. It's as simple as that."

"I understand, Archbishop. Do you intend to travel with the pictures and the reports from New Mexico?"

Ryan saw the Archbishop's face fill with anger.

"I only meant that to do so may not be wise under the circumstances. They do present a security risk to your office and of course the Archdiocese."

"Oh. My apologies, Monsignor, I thought for a second you were about to suggest that we actually bring those items to New York."

"Certainly not, Your Grace. I understand our mission."

"Then it's set. I'll see you Monday morning at Union Station, ten-thirty sharp. Come through the center arch in front. I'll be just inside the door in the main waiting room."

"I'll be there."

"You know, Cletus, there will be three auxiliary bishops retiring between New York and Washington during the next two years. When the Papal Nuncio calls for recommendations, your name will be on those lists that go to the Holy Father. I wanted you to know that before we went to New York."

"You're very kind to share that with me, Your Grace. If it's God's will, I can only pray I'll be up to the task."

"You will be, Cletus. That's precisely why you are here today."

IS THERE SCANDAL?

Cletus Ryan found the Monday morning madhouse at Union Station unnerving. The Capital City transportation hub shuttled thousands of commuters onto the rails connecting cities up and down the East Coast. Commuters and sightseers mixed with titans of business and government to form serpentine queues at various platforms.

On any other day, Ryan would find the wide expanse of the Main Terminal waiting room an architectural marvel but today was a day for him to be wholly focused on his career track.

"Here I am," Guilfoyle yelled, finally getting Ryan's attention. "I'm glad you're on time. We're on track eight. Do you have everything?"

"All set!"

The northeast corridor from Washington to New York traversed the Pullman train yards, tenement houses, small businesses and factories; a post war jumble of mixed uses and poor zoning providing a preview of the coming urban blight.

232

Twelve hours later, Ryan sat alone in a decadently styled bedroom at Cardinal Riordan's Manhattan residence trying to process the blur of events. The Powerhouse, as insiders knew it, occupied the corner of 51st and Madison Avenue, a seat of significant power in the belly of midtown. The posh residence was an elegant, perfectly executed Gothic Revival mansion.

Sipping dry martinis in Cardinal Riordan's private dining room, the two leaders of over six million Catholics obliquely discussed the risks and benefits of managing a talented and twisted sexual predator over porterhouse steaks, baked potatoes and wedges of iceberg lettuce dripping with freshly churned Roquefort dressing.

Cardinal Timothy Riordan, a short, rotund man with a cherubic face, piercing green eyes and thick fingers, was no one's fool.

"Is there scandal, Bishop Guilfoyle?" he asked in a calm tone.

"I think not, Your Grace. I believe it has been managed."

"Has the matter of his personnel file been addressed, Bishop Guilfoyle?" Riordan asked.

"Of course, Your Grace. Your personnel board will find everything in order. I will of course transfer the contents of the Secret Archive if you desire that."

"That will not be necessary, Bishop Guilfoyle. Based on Father Dolan's accomplishments and your recommendation, I believe we have an arrangement that can work. May I assume that if I have a similar circumstance arise in the future, that I can call on you?" Riordan asked.

"Absolutely, Your Grace. it would be my honor to assist the Archdiocese of New York in any way possible."

"Then it's settled. We will wait an appropriate amount of time from the opening of the Shrine and then we will initiate Dolan's transfer. After a reasonable period of good behavior, I will initiate proceeding to incardinate him into the Archdiocese. I will post him in the western part of the state to minimize any potential further lapses in judgement."

What stunned Ryan most was the cold detachment both the Cardinal and Archbishop displayed in their tortured wordsmithing of Dolan's "lack of maturity in his past assignments." Misinterpreted affection and fraternal corrections were callously substituted for sexual assault and cover-up. As they waited for Cardinal Riordan's private secretary to confirm that he had arranged a backstage meet and greet with Ms. Martin after the show, Ryan wondered whether he would ever get used to sacrificing the safety of potentially thousands of children for the sake of reputation.

For the assembled princes of the Church, it was a simple transaction. The giving and receiving of favors was the sole purpose of the meeting. The suppression of scandal was paramount; nothing else mattered to either prelate.

Ryan's rush of adrenaline over a successful outcome surrounding the Dolan issue was fueled by several post-show bottles of vintage Haut Brion. His excitement, however, was short-lived.

The next morning found him nursing a numbing headache with a glass of Alka-Seltzer and a bottle of aspirin. He struggled to write down everything that happened. Recalling Francis' confession, Ryan winced as he reprised his role in the conspiracy. He smiled when he thought of Mary Martin. She might not have been so happy to meet the Cardinal of the Archdiocese of New York and the Archbishop of Washington if she had known they were orchestrating a sinister cover-up of crimes against children.

Ryan saw his future as trying to outrun a metastasizing cancer. Only through the grace of God would the Church's secrets be kept from the light of day.

PART TWO
REVELATION

CHAPTER SIX

The Black Box

MANHATTAN'S UPPER EAST SIDE, 1994

Elizabeth's bedroom was dark. She pulled the drapes open on a floor to ceiling window, revealing the night world of the Upper East Side of Manhattan. Slowly walking side to side, Elizabeth carefully made her bed, making sure the bedspread fell exactly one inch from the floor on all sides.

The ambient light from the city guided her to the walk-in closet in her bedroom. There she retrieved a tailored, black wool Armani pants suit, underwear, stockings, heels, a white silk blouse, an Hèrmes scarf and a single strand of pearls. She carefully arranged each item along the side of the bed in the order she would put them on. Moving to her armoire, Elizabeth removed her running shoes, compression no-show socks, tights, a singlet, a headband and a Nike windbreaker. On the opposite side of her bed, she repeated the process, laying each item out on her bed in the precise order she would put them on.

Today was a big day for her. At 9:15, the executive committee of McCabe, Willis & Houghton would gather for its annual partnership meeting to determine if she would become only the second woman to be offered an equity partnership in the law firm's history.

During the last week, Elizabeth had felt a movement in the darkness that kept her past locked away. The secrets of her

237

childhood, often accompanied by shame, rage and guilt, came on her like physical blows jolting her consciousness. A mix of alcohol, valium, mania and brutal workout regimens allowed her to keep the darkness at bay and function in the professional world. To the outside world she was driven, relentless and highly successful. Only Elizabeth knew the truth. It was a facade to keep the black box of memories tucked neatly away in the deepest recesses of her mind.

Standing naked in front of a full-length mirror, Elizabeth carefully studied her body in the shadows of the predawn light. The firmness of well-developed muscles contoured her form. At forty-six she had the body of a thirty-year-old woman, feminine with a hard sinewy exterior shell. She was an enigma in the law firm with few friends. But for her productivity, she would have been let go years ago.

Closing her eyes, she carefully stretched all of the major muscle groups to prepare herself for the next ninety minutes of punishment. Looking at her feet, knuckled and calloused after decades of running, she bent down and picked up two twenty-pound rubber coated dumbbells. Beads of sweat began to form on her body as she went through four sets of overhead presses.

Quickly dressing into her running clothes, Elizabeth opened her briefcase to check her daily planner. Her secretary had clipped a pink phone message from her brother Francis to the cover. He wanted to meet in New York for lunch. Francis had made a name for himself as a recording artist, adjunct professor at Julliard and a beloved parish priest in the Archdiocese of Washington. He had zero interest in Church politics or career advancement, content to donate his music royalties to local charities serving the homeless and AIDS population in Washington.

Riding the elevator down to the street level, Elizabeth stared at the message for a moment then crumpled it up in a ball, tossing it into the waste basket on the curb. She had no intention of seeing her brother.

ACT OF FAITH

LENOX HILL TO 51st AND LEXINGTON ON THE 6 TRAIN

Alistair Shamus McCabe was the consummate study in bespoke
Savile Row finery. From his Grieves and Hawke charcoal pinstripe
suit to his brilliantly polished black Balmoral custom made cap-toe
shoes, McCabe's look epitomized the de rigueur of chairman and
managing partner of an elite New York City law firm.

McCabe, Willis & Houghton was one of the oldest, and by far
the most profitable, merger and acquisition firms in the city. As its
mergers and acquisitions practice grew in reputation, so did its
litigation department. The "M & A" work acted as a natural feeder
for multi-million-dollar regulatory matters, antitrust defense and
corporate disputes.

McCabe litigators, led by Robert Willis, were formidable. Their
aggressive approach to deal making and acquisitions was
complemented by the top shelf competence of their trial lawyers.
McCabe made a point of hiring only the best law graduates, keeping
only those who were willing to go through years of skill-based
training in the nuances of corporate expansion, regulatory matters,
brand protection and trial techniques.

Graduating at the top of his class at Harvard in 1963, Robert
Willis, with his long white hair tied in a neat ponytail, cultivated a
genial attitude toward all people and places, except for when he was
in a courtroom. There, he was a ruthless mercenary who seemed to
thrive at the jugular of any adversary that dared lock horns with
one of the firm's corporate clients.

In the legal community he was known as "the prince of fucking
darkness." The nickname was given to him by one of his early
adversaries. The moniker fit and the legend grew, given Willis'
penchant for wearing black three-piece suits, white silk ties and
black alligator cowboy boots.

Alistair McCabe took one last look in the mirror, adjusted his bow
tie tight to his collar and secured his grandfather's pocket watch into

his waistcoat. Meticulously groomed, clean shaven with high cheekbones, an elegant patrician peered back at him. He liked what he saw. The walk from his Lenox Hill brownstone to the 44th floor of 345 Park Avenue took nineteen minutes including the eight-minute ride on the MTA 6 Train south to Lexington and 51st Street. As he strolled off the elevator into the lobby vestibule, he noticed through the glass wall water element the shrouded image of his two other partners. Together they formed the equity committee of the firm.

Managing this eclectic stew of testosterone-laden brilliance fell upon its chairman, Alistair Shamus McCabe, and Robert Willis, who was also the firm's managing partner. They were two strong egos under the same circus tent. McCabe protected his territory with his majority ownership of stock and his uncanny ability to draw M & A clients to the firm, while Willis counted on the loyalty of his staff and his clients who willingly paid outrageous fees for being represented by the best trial lawyer in the city.

From the moment one stepped through the oversized glass doors, everything about the firm was geared to impress and intimidate. McCabe had hand-picked the quarter-sawn wide plank flooring of Brazilian tiger wood. The rich reddish brown of the heartwood was a stunning complement to the lighter hued sapwood, producing a surreal, undulating wave of mottled textures. The floor was laid on a sleeper grid to create a deep tonal resonance and bizarre sense of self-consciousness in clients as they walked the twenty steps to the reception desk and over three matching oversized Seirafin Persian rugs.

Leather club furniture and comfortable couches were complemented by an entire gallery of Thos. Moser handcrafted armchairs, side tables and benches. Floor to ceiling bookcases housed vast sections of National Reporter volumes. Black and white limited series prints from famous photographers depicting Americana in its inexorable march through the twentieth century adorned the walls.

The requisite number of Baccarat crystal figurines and vases dotted the map tables, along with coffee table books celebrating the Arts, Science and Architecture. Copies of the day's New York Law Journal were on every side table to remind each visitor that this was indeed a law firm. A not-so-subtle copy of Sun Tzu's *The Art of War*, along with reprints of the firm's successes, sat in a cherry paneled nook along the side wall of each private lavatory in the men's room. Nothing was left to chance or misinterpretation.

The annual equity committee meetings, a source of great annoyance to McCabe, were for the most part nothing more than window dressing for the firm's rank and file.

Despite his elegant and refined exterior, which exuded the mien of an aristocratic consensus builder, Al McCabe's governing philosophy for the firm was more akin to a turn of the century street boss from Hell's Kitchen. His operational preference was to keep everyone in place with the tried-and-true currency of contentment: money.

As the firm grew both in revenues and prestige, the malcontents who wanted to eat everything that they killed found it difficult to walk away. The skyrocketing salaries and obscene perquisites the M & A practice brought to the firm, along with free in-house dining and paid social memberships throughout the city, were a juggernaut that not only fed McCabe's ego but also allowed him to maintain control over his lawyers.

"Gentlemen, top of the morning to you," McCabe bellowed, trying to take them off guard. "Robert, I can't tell you what a delight it is to chair the annual slicing up of the pie."

"Cut the crap, Al, we rarely vote to share the pie," Willis retorted.

"What's the matter, Bob? I'm just trying to save you money. I… excuse me, Bob," McCabe said, catching himself, "I meant to say if we name a partner everyone's equity is diluted."

"Jesus, Al, you say that every year."

"Yes, I do, Robert, I do say that every year. I say that because our revenues, and by the way, your profits, have increased by an average of 14 percent over the previous years when we didn't admit a new equity partner. So, what's that tell you, Bob?"

Peter Appleton was the firm's CFO and had the quintessential look and feel of a corporate accountant. He headed up the firm's tax practice and frequently acted as a foil between McCabe and Willis. He could have passed for a clone of Wally Cox, and McCabe liked him because Appleton knew where every penny of revenue was and where it eventually ended up.

"Guys, why don't we move to the agenda," Appleton offered, trying valiantly to be a stabilizing force in the soon-to-be acrid debate. "There are three names on the list. All of the candidates have been vetted by their sponsoring partner, their performance ratings and billing histories are all in each file."

McCabe knew that the litigation arm of the firm brought in nearly 35 percent of the firm's revenues, so it was important not to go too far with Willis. Even so, he did enjoy the saber-rattling.

"You're right, Peter. My apologies, Robert. I came across as an old arrogant ass."

"Al, you are an old arrogant ass," Willis said, trying to bait his nemesis by completely ignoring McCabe's apology. "Have you read the three submissions?" Willis asked.

"I have. I've read them with great care, Robert," McCabe said.

"Good. So, where are you on all three?"

"Well, I'm sure my assessment won't be a surprise to you, but let's go down the list. Leopold Carlson's an ass kisser who's been here for seven years. His billings are up to speed, and he seems to be well liked but he hasn't gone anywhere on client development. He's a mule. He's not a stallion. Besides, he wants to be a partner too much. So, he's a no. Justin Thomas—he did very well with the IBM case. Been here eight years, does anything you ask of him, but he's only brought in one significant piece of work. But I have to say, he's like a hockey player, he puts a lot of shots on goal. Plus, he's a sharp dresser. He asked me where I get my suits tailored."

"That's important," Willis quipped.

McCabe ignored the insult. "I'll vote yes on him as a non-equity partner with a $25,000 salary kicker and one level on his bonus and he can come back next year, and we'll see. That's my take on Thomas. So, on the first two partner candidates are we in agreement?"

"I am," Appleton said.

"Bob, what do you say," McCabe said.

"Agreed. What about Elizabeth?" Willis asked."

"I have to admit I'm curious about her. But she's a woman, Bob."

"No shit, Al, I never would have guessed. What's your point?"

"My point is I'm intrigued by your girl Elizabeth. So, if she's your proposal make out a case for her as an equity partner, Bob. If she's admitted she'll be taking money out of your pocket, not just mine."

"And mine," Appleton chimed in.

"To start, she's not my girl."

"Oh, my, you're testy this morning, Bob. Have a scone, won't you? You'll feel more relaxed."

"Cut the crap, Al. Just sit back and listen for a change."

"Elizabeth Natale has been with the firm for ten years. She came by way of Holland and Ritter, where she spent nine years."

"Did I know that?" McCabe asked, suddenly focusing on the topic. "I thought we stopped hiring all the lateral senior associates."

"We did, but you were down with that mitral valve repair, and I didn't bother telling you. To be perfectly blunt, I didn't want to hear any of your shit. I knew she would be a good fit in my section, so I made the decision. As it's turned out, her billings more than speak for themselves. She's getting the gross revenues of two lawyers and carries the least expense for her support staff in the entire litigation group."

"So, if she's one of your trial lawyers, why do I see her name on the Cisco acquisition of Calpana?"

"Because she can do both and the client likes to play golf with her."

"Is he fucking her? I mean she's a good-looking woman..."

"Al, do you work at being a misogynistic asshole or do you come by that naturally?"

"No, I'm pretty sure it's a natural talent, Robert. So, why does Jameson want to play golf with her?"

"Because he's a three handicap and has a weed up his ass because he can't beat her. She played college golf at Penn. She's a member at Merion in Philly and tinkered with possibly turning pro but decided to go to law school."

"Okay, Bob, you've established she plays golf well and she's not your girl. How did the clerkship with Justice O'Connor come about?" Appleton asked.

"According to Elizabeth, she got a call out of the blue from the Justice herself. O'Connor had read a law review piece from Penn where Elizabeth argued very cogently that there should be a recognizable cause of action for an individual parental consortium claim flowing from emotional injuries suffered by their child."

"That tort shit is such crap. I'm surprised O'Connor was even interested," McCabe interrupted.

"Can I answer your question, Al?"

"Of course, Robert. I'm sorry. Please continue."

"So, Justice O'Connor asked her to send in her resume. Apparently, all they talked about was golf. O'Connor's an avid golfer. Three weeks later she got a letter from the Court offering her the clerkship."

"So, why haven't I seen her around much?" McCabe asked.

"She's a bit of a loner. She does her work and then some, she brought in the Calpana Cisco deal. She runs in the morning, actually she qualified for the Boston Marathon twice and ran both in under four hours. She's at her desk usually by seven-thirty. She's a grinder, perfect billing machine and she's not afraid to try a case. She's been out now twenty years and she thinks she has earned an equity position in the firm."

"Why does she think that, Bob? With salary and performance bonuses she pushed $650,000 last year. Where else is a single woman going to make that kind of money as a non-equity partner? Christ, first string call girls don't make that kind of money."

"You speaking from experience, Al, or from your intimate knowledge of the sex trade industry?" Willis shot back.

McCabe was caught flat-footed. There was a reason Willis was known to be one of the best trial lawyers in the country and McCabe had just experienced verbal checkmate.

"Point taken, Bob, but what do we really know about her? Her credentials are all in order, but it looks like she has no life. Where did she grow up?"

"She was raised in D.C," Willis said, paging through the submission. "Let's see, father died when she was young, I think she was pretty close to him. Apparently, the father and the grandfather were some big deal stone carvers at the Catholic Shrine in the city. I met her brother; he's a priest in D.C. He's a little weird, but a helluva piano player."

"Damn, Bob, I need to get this info to the Cardinal at next Tuesday's Red Mass. Are you going?"

"Hardly. I'll leave it to the Irish Catholics to represent the firm."

"One of our lawyers' brother is a Catholic priest, Bob. Jesus, that's a calling card with the Cardinal. You might be singing a different song if I get the Archdiocese as a client. The Archdiocese owns all the ground underneath the Palace Hotel and with Leona Helmsley getting convicted of tax evasion the whole property is screwed up. It's going to be a real cluster fuck, which means a litigation bonanza. If we can get in on the land lease side of the deal or with the bond holders' takeover of the hotel it could be a good entree for more work."

"Knock yourself out, Al. Let's get back to Elizabeth."

"Fine. Is she a lesbian?"

"Jesus, Al, what's that got to do with anything? I have no idea. Why the fuck would I know that or even care?"

"Bob, spare me your liberal bullshit."

"Al, just be careful with what you say," Appleton said, losing his patience. "You say it here and it could slip out somewhere else. In case you haven't noticed, we've become a pretty big target."

"Alright, alright. Relax, Peter, don't get your dick in a knot! I get it."

"So, Bob, your girl—excuse me, your colleague, comes out near top of her class at Penn, she was law review, clerked with O'Connor, has a brother who is a priest, she runs marathons, plays golf better than most men, earns big money for the firm, good looking, not married, might be gay but that doesn't bother you, but as you say she's a bit of a loner. So, we got some kind of fucking wonder-woman in our midst."

"Basically," Willis said dryly. "Elizabeth would make a good partner here."

"What are you missing, Bob?" McCabe taunted.

"I don't understand, Al. What do you mean?"

"I mean there's something missing. The big gorilla in the room is why she left the Holland firm. How did she get here?"

"I represented her."

"Really," McCabe said, genuinely surprised. "For what?"

"A personal matter involving her prior firm."

McCabe leaned back in his chair and started to laugh. "What kind of bullshit answer is that, Robert?"

"She was a client. The case was settled under a very strict

confidentiality agreement, so I can't really share that information with you."

"Well, you better find a fucking way to share it with me or this conversation is over."

Willis slid a file folder toward McCabe.

"What's that?"

"It's a confidentiality agreement to disclose the underlying facts of her case and an attorney client agreement with Elizabeth for both of you. Peter has already signed."

"You're fucking kidding me, right?" McCabe said, pushing his chair back from the conference room table.

"C'mon, Al, don't be an ass, Bobby is doing exactly what he should be doing."

McCabe grabbed the agreement from Willis, studied it for a full minute, scrawled his signature on it and shoved it to Appleton.

"There, you happy now?" Not waiting for an answer, McCabe thrust his hands in his trouser pockets. "Now what the fuck is the story?"

"You would have done the same thing, Al," Willis said, collecting the paperwork. "Old man Holland was hitting on her for the better part of a year. For about three months before she left the firm, she recorded some really vile shit on one of those tiny Norelco tape recorders when she was in his office. Then when they were out of town in San Francisco on a deposition for an expert, she was in her room, and he came to the door. He wanted to get in, but she had the security lock on it. She thought it was going to be the same verbal crap, so she told him to wait a second. She went to the desk and turned on the tape and as soon as she went back and unlatched the door, and he jumped her. He told her if she wanted to make partner, she had to fuck him. He started groping her then they struggled for a bit, and he tried to get her clothes off. He tripped and fell, but when he got up, she hit him in the face."

"Hit him in the face with what?" McCabe asked.

"Her fist. She knocked a tooth out and when he saw the blood coming out of his mouth he freaked and ran out of the room."

"She punched Eddie Holland in the face with her fist?" McCabe howled.

"Yes."

"And she had a tape of all that?"

"Yes. All of it."

"Old fool, that's the funniest fucking thing I've heard in a while. He could have cratered his entire firm over a piece of ass. So, then what did you do? I mean this is a great fucking story," McCabe laughed.

"I went to see him. Let him listen to the tape. Told him I wanted a check for $750,000 and personal letter of recommendation signed by him and that we would enter into a confidentiality agreement that provided for liquidated damages if Elizabeth breached and he had twenty-four hours to decide."

"Where's the tape?"

"I turned it over to him."

"And all the copies?"

"Like I said, I turned the original over to him."

McCabe studied Willis carefully, knowing full well the wrong decision could push the course of the firm into a different direction or worse, McCabe Willis & Houghton could become the victim of a messy and embarrassing break-up. Willis was not affected by all the embellishments of the firm. His section could merge with any number of big law competitors or stand on its own for that matter, so McCabe chose his words carefully.

"Robert, I agree with your assessment of Natale, on one condition and with one caveat."

"What's the condition?" Willis asked.

"If she's going to be my partner who shares in the equity of the firm, she needs to close the Calpana Cisco deal. That represents

$2 million in fees to the firm and a $3 million performance fee for us. That's real money."

"And the caveat—" Willis said.

"The caveat is more for you, Robert."

"What's that supposed to mean, Al?" Willis asked.

McCabe turned his back on Willis and calmly looked out the window to the spires of St. Patrick's Cathedral.

Willis turned to Appleton. "Are you on board with this proposal, Peter?"

Without hesitating, Appleton voiced his unqualified assent. "I am, Bob. Elizabeth's a money machine. With her work ethic and productivity, she's more than I could ask for in a partner."

McCabe turned to Willis with a wry smile on his face. "You know, Bob, I'm a bit of a film buff."

"I know that, Al."

"Do you know who Joey Zaza is?"

"Who?" Willis asked, somewhat dumbfounded. "Is he a client?"

McCabe laughed. "No, no, he's a character in Godfather III. He's moving up in the crime syndicate so he's talking to Michael Corleone about a beef he has with Michael's nephew Vincent Mancini, Sonny Corleone's bastard son," McCabe explained.

"I know who Sonny was, Al. I was unaware you were such a film student. Is this going somewhere?"

"Of course. I'm sorry, Robert. So, Joey Zaza says to Michael, 'I've got a stone in my shoe.' I'd never heard that saying before and it stuck with me. I've got a stone in my shoe with this Natale woman. Actually, it's more a nagging outlier feeling. Can't put my finger on it, but something's there. You said she was a loner and despite her being here for eight years, I don't think we really *know* her. At least I don't. All I'm saying is be careful what you wish for."

"Well, maybe you should spend more time with her."

"Maybe I will, Robert, maybe I will," McCabe said.

MEASURE TWICE, CUT ONCE

Elizabeth decided to walk from her office to the offices of McCracken & Dunn. In a borough of over a million and a half people, Elizabeth found surprising comfort in the anonymity of the streets of Manhattan. On the days when she hated being in her own skin, walking the sidewalks of the city provided a temporary respite from her self-loathing.

The McCracken law firm was housed in a stately building in the heart of midtown at 437 Madison Avenue. Built in 1967 with a phenomenal rooftop terrace on the fifteenth floor, it was home to many of the national law firms servicing the glut of corporate takeovers and mergers. Ben McCracken had set up three conference rooms, one each for the buyer and seller and a more elaborate main conference room for the next day's closing.

"Good afternoon, Elizabeth, I want to send up coffee and tea service and anything else you will need. How many will you be today?"

"Thanks, Ben, that's very kind. It'll be me, two associates and two legal assistants, so we're five today."

"Is there anything pressing now that you want to talk about?" McCracken asked.

"Actually, I want to make sure Cisco's and Calpana's HR departments are in synch on which payments to my clients are to be treated as compensation for withholding tax purposes and, of course, the amounts we agreed to on the term sheet and the MOU."

"That's fine, anything else for me now?'" McCracken asked.

"Yes, I think it would be wise to create a new exhibit identifying the board members and members of Calpana's operating committee who will remain following the closing."

"Okay, prepare the exhibit and send it down. I'm sure it'll be fine."

"Thank you, Ben, and thank you for your hospitality."

Elizabeth made her way through the labyrinth of meeting rooms and offices to her assigned space. She was relieved to find her entire team set up and ready to work. Chris Allen was Elizabeth's lead associate on the deal. He was supported by Andrea Watson, a three-year lawyer out of Georgetown, Margi Kowalski, her legal assistant who had moved with her from the Holland firm, and Margi's assistant Carol Eaton. The table was covered with spreadsheets and files.

"Okay, let's start at the top. What, if anything, are we missing?"

For the next seven hours, the team went through the entire transaction from the original term sheet to every due diligence memo on every issue identified on several transaction spreadsheets.

"Chris, do you completely understand this entire transaction?"

Allen studied the spreadsheet and the checklist chronology Margi had been preparing as each issue was put to bed. "I do. We're ready for tomorrow, Elizabeth," he said with authority.

"Good, I concur. Okay, gather each file that corresponds to each element on the spreadsheet, inventory them and seal them up with our firm's tape for tomorrow morning. We close at ten. I'll be here at eight-thirty, so everyone plan accordingly."

"Liz, I'll take the face sheets home, for sure, but are you worried about something in particular?"

"That's the problem, Chris, I'm not worried about anything. It's something I heard my grandfather say when I was growing up. 'Measure twice and cut once.' He said he worked paranoid. It's even more true in the law." Elizabeth began to feel a familiar darkness approach, first settling into her stomach and then moving to a pulsating pain at the base of her neck. She knew she needed to recharge herself in private so she could function in the morning.

"Chris, Willis has been blowing up my pager all afternoon so I'm going to step out, call him and go for a run. See you in the morning."

As Elizabeth went to the lobby, she found an empty private telephone carrel and dialed Willis' number.

"Hello, Willis here."

"Hey Bob, it's Liz."

"Jesus, Liz, where the hell have you been? I must have sent you twenty pages."

"I know," she said as she slipped off her high heels, replacing them with her favorite Asics Gel Kayano's for the walk to her apartment.

"You know? Why the hell didn't you pick up the phone and call me?" Willis demanded, annoyed by the slight.

"Bob, don't be angry, you know how I get just before kick-off. I was going through the deal from start to finish."

"You mean you were torturing your team is more like it. Your group is going to start asking for hazardous duty pay before long."

"They probably deserve it," Elizabeth chuckled.

"Well, the reason I called was to tell you McCabe and Appleton agreed with my sponsoring you as an equity partner—you're in!"

Willis waited several seconds for Elizabeth to respond. "Are you still there?" Willis asked. "I thought you'd be ecstatic."

"Yes, I'm still here," Elizabeth answered weakly, fighting to keep her breathing and the shake in her voice even as she felt her heart rate increase. "Thank you, Bob. We'll celebrate later, I'm actually not feeling well and was on my way out to get some fresh air."

"Are you sick?" Willis asked, suddenly worried.

"No, I'm fine. I'll call you later. Thank you, Bob, really, thank you. I'm very excited." Elizabeth didn't wait for him to respond and hung up the phone.

Willis was flabbergasted by Elizabeth's ability to ice people out, even him. His anger started to ripen as he remembered McCabe's story about Joey Zaza.

On the elevator ride down to the street level, Elizabeth's breath began to normalize, and she cursed herself for not being more gracious to her mentor and friend. Out on the street, Elizabeth relished the warmth of the late afternoon October sun, relieved there was enough light left to get to her apartment and go for a run through Central Park. She knew if she did not beat back the darkness of her childhood secrets she would be in trouble for the next day. Second-guesses and imagined "what ifs" began to fill her head as she walked north, mentally jousting with the enveloping depression and self-loathing.

At the corner of East 50th and Madison Avenue, she looked across the street and saw four men and two women quietly holding signs reading, "Priests That Rape Kids Should Be In Prison Not Parishes." Elizabeth blanched at the word "Rape" as her eyes began to blur and refocus on each sign, noticing that several signs had the word "SNAP" on them.

The demonstrators walked quietly under the menacing eyes of two burly New York City policemen perched on the first step of 452 Madison Avenue, the home of Cardinal Archibald Hurley. The Cardinal's residence was long regarded as the city's preeminent example of a perfectly executed Gothic revival residence.

Elizabeth waited through three cycles of the traffic light, frozen by the cascade of memories that had just been unleashed in her mind. The push of the throng of office workers walking north on Madison Avenue to their respective commuter hubs broke Elizabeth's trance as she leaned against the corner brownstone of the historic Villard Mansion. There did not appear to be any commotion as the protesters kept to their tight knit oval, careful not to block the sidewalk. The green patina of the copper clad roof over St. Patrick's Lady's Chapel was striped by the late afternoon sunset as it marched between the Westside towers of Manhattan. Elizabeth gingerly crossed Madison Avenue as if a magnet were drawing her to one particular placard that had a picture of a little brown-haired girl. Getting closer, she heard the gruff directive of the Patrol Sergeant.

"You have fifteen more minutes before your permit expires, Miss Blaine, then you and your group have to pack up and leave. We clear?"

The soft green eyes of the young girl in the picture wearing a white scalloped dress with a delicate crucifix around her neck bored through Elizabeth like a laser. Standing on the corner, Elizabeth was out of breath and shaking. Staring at the picture, she was unable to move, overwhelmed by the vision of her small hands grabbing the sides of the sacristy mirror with Dolan thrusting into her.

"Are you alright, miss?" a woman protester asked.

Elizabeth did not acknowledge her, continuing to stare at the picture. "What is that little girl's name?" Elizabeth asked as she continued to stare at the photograph on the placard.

"Her name is Barbara and it's a picture of me at the age when I was abused by a priest. Can I give you a flyer about our organization?"

"No. Why are you here?" Elizabeth barked.

"We're protesting the Archdiocese of New York and the cover-up of priests sexually abusing children. Are you sure I can't give you a flyer about our organization?" Blaine repeated, noticing Elizabeth's distress.

"I told you no," Elizabeth said. "Now leave me alone."

"That's okay," Blaine said calmly, "but if you ever want to talk, here's a card. My number is on the back."

Without looking at the card, Elizabeth slipped it into her jacket.

Blaine was skilled at recognizing abuse survivors. An abuse survivor herself, she had founded SNAP, a grassroots organization made up wholly of victims of clergy sexual abuse. SNAP's aim was to provide self-help, support and information to survivors, equipping them with tools to politically challenge the Church on its tolerance of sexual crimes committed by priests against children.

With boundless energy, Barbara had become the face of the survivor movement. "Relentless in the cause of justice," was how she was described in the media, raising her unfiltered voice to chronicle every deception offered by the Church hierarchy. Her small frame and soft voice belied the grit of a warrior.

Elizabeth felt unsteady on her feet and reached for the trash receptacle on the corner to keep her balance.

"How old were you in that picture?" Elizabeth asked, not looking at Blaine.

"I was twelve at the time. Father Chet Warren abused me," Blaine said. "What's your name?" Blaine asked.

"My name is Nancy," Elizabeth lied. "I'm sorry, I have to go."

Within seconds, Elizabeth disappeared into the crowded sidewalk. She broke into a jog up Madison Avenue to 58th Street heading for the Oak Bar at the Plaza Hotel. Finally reaching the Grand Army Plaza, Elizabeth found an empty stone bench directly in front of the New York landmark hotel. She fumbled with her shoelaces as she switched back into her high heels. The darkness began to envelope her, and Elizabeth noticed her hands trembling as a torrent of memories and images took hold of her brain. She hurried through the lobby and took a seat on a green leather barstool at the end of the bar, knowing that a double dry vodka martini would be the tonic to dull the intensity of the flashbacks.

"Hey, Miss Natale, good to see you. You're all red in the face, did you run here?" joked Teddy Harrison, the longtime Oak Room bartender. "Long day?" he asked.

"Long life," Elizabeth said blankly.

"Your usual, Miss Natale?" Teddy asked.

"Yes. Dry martini up, two olives," Elizabeth said, staring straight ahead. "And Teddy, I'm not here tonight, okay?"

"You got it, Miss Natale."

"And Teddy, keep them coming."

Elizabeth stared at Everett Shinn's mural of the dimly lit Pulitzer Fountain behind the bar. Painted in 1944, it portrayed an iconic scene just outside the Plaza Hotel in the very early years of the twentieth century. Elizabeth studied the glistening texture of each painted water droplet as it edged off the lip of the fountain as a way to push the darkness of her physical sensations out of her mind. The black box of abuse memories that quite literally was up on the top shelf of her closet had come spilling out onto the sidewalk in front of the Cardinal's mansion.

As she sipped her third martini, the alcohol finally taking hold, she felt the heaviness of her memories relenting.

"Teddy, could you get me a check?"

"I can, but the gentleman at the end of the bar in the grey suit sent this over," he said as he placed yet another dry Blue Label martini in front of her.

"Did you tell him my name?"

"Of course not, you're a regular here."

"Thanks, Teddy, send it back and get me my check. Better yet just put it on my house account and the fifty is for you."

"Let me get you a cab."

"I'll be fine. I'm going to walk."

Elizabeth got up, feeling dizzier than she expected. As she was gingerly passing the man in the grey suit he got up from his stool and faced her.

"Miss, please accept my apologies. It wasn't my intent to offend you. Please, have a good evening."

"Well, you did offend me, so let's leave it at that," Elizabeth said acidly as she moved toward the exit and into the lobby. As she subtly stopped at a pillar to gather her bearings and her balance, she was struck by the gentleman's tone. He actually sounded sincere in his apology. She waited a moment then reentered the Oak Bar. The gentleman was seated where she had left him, nursing the martini she had declined. Elizabeth took the seat next to his.

"I thought you bought that martini for me."

"I did, but I think I insulted you and that wasn't my intention. I'm here at the Plaza for one night and simply was looking for end of day conversation in this glorious venue with an attractive woman."

Elizabeth's memories and self-loathing began to compete with her growing intoxication. She knew where this was headed.

"I should have been more gracious. I was rude and I apologize," Elizabeth offered. "Let's start over. My name is Nancy."

"I'm Frank Weatherly. It's a pleasure to meet you, Nancy."

ARE WE GOING TO DO THIS IN THE HALLWAY?

It was 9:00 A.M. the next day, and both settlement teams had assembled for the Cisco Calpana settlement. Elizabeth's senior associate, Chris Allen, had been trying to reach her since the previous evening after the pre-closing dinner at the Four Seasons. With the closing scheduled to commence at nine-thirty, he began to panic. Allen decided to call Willis for instructions.

"Mr. Willis, this is Chris Allen. I'm over at the McCracken firm and I haven't heard from Elizabeth since yesterday afternoon and the Calpana closing is scheduled to start in thirty minutes. There's no answer at her apartment and I've sent her over a dozen pages."

"Is the deal in shape and ready to go?"

"Yes, sir, but McCracken is looking for her to be here."

"I'll be right over. Don't do anything; just tell McCracken I'll be there in ten minutes, something non-deal related has come up."

Sprinting out of the elevator, he got to the main conference room of McCracken & Dunn in under ten minutes. Willis walked into the conference room talking, not waiting for any questions.

"Ladies and gentlemen, let's proceed. Elizabeth sends her apologies; she had an extremely pressing and urgent family crisis involving her mother and left for Washington last night. But she briefed me on the entire acquisition and Chris has been on this since the beginning, so we're ready to go."

Willis turned to Allen and whispered, "Don't fuck it up, Chris."

Chris Allen knew the Washington story was complete bullshit. Elizabeth called him an average of three or four times a night after work. Something was wrong; she was never out of touch.

It took until 6:00 P.M. to close, but it was done and signed off. Willis was sure that his pager would go off at any minute, but not a single word came from Elizabeth. He went back to his office to check his messages. Nothing.

"Margi, call our service and have a car meet me downstairs."

"Where should I tell them they're going?"

"Tell them I'll let them know when I get in the car." Willis hustled out of the elevator. The firm's Town Car was waiting as he exited the building.

"Hey, Mr. Willis, where we headed?" asked Charles Matthews, the perennially cheerful driver who had been with the firm for twenty years.

"Thanks, Charlie, take me to 279 Central Park West."

The drive took a full thirty minutes with Willis trying to reach Elizabeth the entire time. He was worried about what he would find at her apartment. Any scenario seemed bleak.

A twenty-dollar tip to the attendant at the desk got Willis on the owner's elevator without calling ahead to Elizabeth. Willis had no idea what he was walking into. *Nothing good can come out of the next thirty minutes,* he thought as he took the elevator to her floor.

As his protégé, Willis had witnessed Elizabeth's meteoric rise in the law firm, and he needed her vote as a partner on firm matters. Willis also needed her revenue to keep the wolves away from his door. Although Elizabeth was admired in the firm because of the results she achieved, she was not particularly well liked. Willis and his wife, Audrey, saw a much different side of her. When she got out of the city and came to their Jersey shore house, she talked about her father and how much she missed him and more recently about how much she admired him. She actually laughed at times. But inevitably, something would snap and her mood would darken, and she would become detached. Audrey would try reaching her, but Elizabeth would deflect. She was very good at that.

Willis held his breath as his hand reached for the doorbell. No answer. He knocked. Still no answer. He knocked again.

"Elizabeth, it's Bob. Are you in there?"

Nothing.

Then Willis heard what sounded like someone shuffling towards the door.

"Who's there?" Elizabeth said, her voice hoarse from the bruises on her neck from the night before.

"Elizabeth... It's Bob. Are you okay?"

"How did you get up here? I'm fine, I'll call you in the morning."

Willis had had enough.

"You will not call me in the morning! Please open the door and let me see you're okay, then I'll leave."

Willis had no intention of leaving. He heard the deadbolt turn over. Elizabeth opened the door but kept the safety latch engaged, yielding only about a three-inch view. She showed her face and what Willis saw shocked him.

"I'm fine, see?"

"Yeah, right, Liz, and I'm a fucking alien from the planet Zoltar. You should see your face."

"I ran into a door."

"Are we going to do this in the hallway or are you going to let me in?"

Elizabeth slammed the door shut, released the latch and opened the door with such force it put Willis on his heels. Elizabeth was a mess. The imprint of Weatherley's fingers was still visible on her neck. Her face was terribly swollen, her eyes bloodshot. Her hair was soaked, and she was shivering, her body wrapped tightly in a heavy bathrobe.

"Jesus, Bob, what do you want?" Elizabeth demanded.

He had seen her angry before and knew better than to press her.

"What's the matter, cat got your tongue? Or are you not liking what you see? Your rising star, your new partner, your protégé, do I look like your protégé?"

"How about some answers, Liz? That'd be a good start," Willis said calmly.

"What do you want to know, Bob? What?" Elizabeth screamed. "Where I've been? Okay, I've been here! Why didn't I show up? I'm fucking drunk, that's why! My eye? You want to know about my eye? Some asshole slapped the shit out of me and wanted to choke me when I was fucking him. So, now you have the story. Will you please leave me alone? I'll be in the office tomorrow."

Willis was determined not to provoke. "So, other than all of that, how are you doing?"

In a matter of seconds, rage, resignation then uncontrollable sobbing coalesced, causing Elizabeth to tremble and then collapse in Willis' arms. He held her for several minutes as she struggled for air. He sensed that her body would give up and cry itself out. He gently let her sit back on the couch.

"Just hold on, let me get you some water and some tissues."

"There's none left."

"No water?"

"No, you asshole, no tissues!"

"No worries; a towel will work."

Elizabeth broke into a tearful laugh. "Jesus God, this is fucking insane," she blurted out.

She looked worse than a rain drenched mutt, still drunk and half-dressed in a bathrobe with her senior partner fetching a towel from the kitchen to wipe her face. Elizabeth panicked when she heard Willis talking on the phone.

"Bob, who are you talking to?"

"It's Audrey, don't worry."

"Bob, please, I'll be fine in the morning."

"Okay, leave right now and call when you're five minutes away," Willis said into the phone.

He turned back to Elizabeth. "Now listen, Liz, it's been a very long day and I'm worried about you. So, I'm either going to call the police, call an ambulance or you're going to get dressed, get some clothes and come home with Audrey and me and we can sort this out. She has already left and should be here in thirty minutes."

Elizabeth was spent. She decided it might be a good thing to get out of the city, if for no other reason than to get a break from her self-destructive routine.

"I have some coffee made. Make yourself a cup and I'll get some things. Just a couple of days, Bob. I have a lot going on and I'll need to get back."

"For what it's worth, Liz, I talked to Chris and he said you're in good shape for next week."

"Chris is a pompous little shit; he would tell you anything to get your vote at the next partnership meeting."

"Don't be such a dick, Liz. He did a great job today. And for the record, you're still a partner at the firm. McCabe said the Calpana deal had to close; he didn't say you had to close it. You have any milk?"

"In the fridge."

As Willis talked from the kitchen, he looked at a sheaf of Lexis printouts of newspaper stories spread out on the kitchen table with yellow highlighting all over them. Each article revolved around priest sexual abuse incidents from throughout the country. Willis moved away from the table to the counter and window overlooking Central Park.

"So, what are you working on?"

"What do you mean? You know what I'm working on," Elizabeth responded, annoyed.

Willis walked back into the living room.

"Why did you ask what I'm working on?"

"Well, I couldn't help but notice the printouts on the kitchen table..."

"Is that a question, Bob? Tell me, what are your questions?" Elizabeth asked, flashing her characteristic anger. "What, Bob? Go ahead, ask your fucking questions."

"Christ, Liz, does everything have to be a war with you," Willis said, his feelings genuinely hurt.

Elizabeth took a deep breath. "I'm sorry, Bob, but listen to me – it's private, it's complicated and I'm not ready to talk about it. I may not ever be ready to talk about it, so I'm asking you please... just leave it alone. It doesn't concern you."

"Fair enough. Finish getting your things together and let's go downstairs. Tell the doorman you ran into a door."

"That's an original thought."

"Come on, Liz, stop fucking with me. Audrey should be here in a little bit."

Bob and Audrey Willis lived in Hoboken, New Jersey in a huge four-thousand-square-foot condo that was converted from three single units in the old Lipton Tea factory. The home had a direct view of the Empire State building as well as the entire Manhattan skyline. Each room had a view of the Hudson.

Willis' home gave Elizabeth a sense of familiarity, that even though she was in New Jersey she was still in the city, and that helped her blunt her constant need to run. After thanking Audrey profusely for opening her home, she went to the guest room, opened the curtains so she could see Manhattan and slept for the next twelve hours.

Morning came with a harsh reality. For a long time, anonymous sex had been a currency for her physical release and a way to cope with her demons. She felt dirty and she could not get clean.

Elizabeth lay in bed looking out the window, mesmerized by the barge traffic plying the Hudson River. Her head was pounding but she could smell bacon frying and realized she hadn't eaten in over twenty-four hours and was starving.

Seeing the swelling of her cheek out of the corner of her eye, Elizabeth avoided looking at herself in the mirror. Last night had been her first real brush with danger and she realized she had been lucky to get out of Weatherby's room alive. She began to feel that this was a day of reckoning. She reached for her purse and unzipped a side compartment, removing the boss stone her grandfather had given to her right after her father died. As she rubbed the stone with her thumb, she realized she had no desire to run that morning.

The black box in her closet was open and she could not get it closed. She had been running since she was a little girl. Anger was her fuel, distrust her best friend and depression her constant companion. Elizabeth inventoried the overwhelming feeling of hopelessness and knew she had to leave New York, but where to go was the question.

Her mind quickly assessed that Elizabeth Natale grew up a fractured and damaged kid running from horrible, intrusive memories of being raped by an agent of God. Her powerlessness over this was the ignition point of her daily rage. It was a rage that not only isolated her but had also poisoned her personality. She was a hopeless cause, serving a life sentence in the penitentiary of her memories.

Audrey gently knocked on her bedroom door, temporarily interrupting Elizabeth's downward spiral.

"I made some breakfast, Liz. Are you hungry?"

"I'll be right out, Audrey. I'm starving. Give me five minutes to shower."

The two women sat alone at the breakfast table overlooking the skyline of Manhattan making small talk. Audrey tried to break the ice.

"Can I do anything for you, Liz?"

"I doubt it, Audrey, but I appreciate the offer. I just have to find my way, but right now I'm going in circles and things are out of control. I do know one thing: I'm done with the firm, and I'm done with New York."

"Have you told Bob?" Audrey asked.

"No, but I don't think he'll be surprised. He'll be pissed but not surprised."

Willis walked down the steps from their upstairs bedroom dressed for the office. "You feel any better?" he asked.

"A little. It was a rough forty-eight hours," Elizabeth said, trying to make light of a very awkward situation.

"I'd say. Listen, my first client isn't until eleven-thirty, can we talk for a bit now?" Willis asked meekly.

"Sure. What do you want to talk about," Elizabeth said, trying to get Bob on the defensive.

"I don't know, you making partner. Life after today, the stuff on your kitchen table."

"I said that was private," Elizabeth snapped.

"I know what you said, and I respect that."

"Really," Elizabeth said. "That's the second time you've brought it up in twenty-four hours."

"Let's be fair, Elizabeth. You blow off a $210 million closing on some drunken bender with a guy who knocked the shit out of you the day after you make partner on my nomination. Your associate and yours truly cover the closing and I find you in your apartment after trying to reach you for a full day, surveying the literature on priest sexual abuse of children. I mean really, what the fuck, Liz? Don't you think you owe me a little more of an explanation?"

"Not really, Bob. I'm really not concerned with you right now. I need to find out if this is the way it's going to be for me. Whether there's any hope for me. Whether I can control the demons, or they control me, and what I found out yesterday."

"What did you find out?"

"That stupid saying about making the same mistake over and over and expecting something different to happen has a ring of truth to it."

"Liz, what about some therapy?" Willis gingerly suggested.

"Oh, God, Bob, spare me. They're whores who have as much interest in prolonging your agony as they do seeing you get well."

"I don't think that's accurate. I mean what are you basing that on?"

"It's just my impression. It doesn't matter. My therapy is running and hitting balls on the driving range."

"Gee, Liz, how's that working out so far," Willis said pointedly.

"Being a smartass doesn't become you, Bob. Listen, I just can't do this anymore.

I'm leaving the firm, Bob, as soon as I can get things in order."

"Don't you think that's over-reacting just a bit? Look at what you've accomplished. What we've done together. You just made partner and you're a woman. You can't just walk away from all of that."

"Do you say that to the guys that make partner?" Elizabeth asked.

"Say what," Willis responded, missing the point.

"You just made partner and you're a man?" Elizabeth queried.

"Goddamn, Liz, you can be a real pain in the ass."

"Really, Bob? Did you personally benefit from my productivity? Did your stature in the firm increase because our section was responsible for nearly 40 percent of the gross revenues? And not to put too sharp a point on it, how about the fact that I can try a big case to verdict and do a complicated transaction and increase our value to the firm's clients? Does that have anything to do with me being a woman?"

Audrey had been listening from the kitchen and had enough. "Robert, you owe Elizabeth an apology. This isn't about you. You're trying to make Liz feel guilty. She has to make decisions that are in her best interest, not yours, and certainly not in the interest of Alistair McCabe, that pompous Irish asshole."

"Liz, this is a major decision. Are you sure you don't want to sit on this for a bit? Your stock will vest in thirty days," Willis said, trying to shift the argument.

"I'm not going to wait around so my stock can vest and then have you guys buy it back. I know I can be an asshole but I'm not a prick."

Willis laughed. "Okay, if you're dead set on leaving, what about this? Get your cases reassigned internally, and we'll give you a year's salary and benefits and you tender back your stock to the firm. The Calpana deal brought in a hefty performance bonus so I'm sure Al will go along with that. I'd also like you to do some interviews for one or two associates to replace you in our section."

"I'll do the interviews. The tender exchange for salary and benefits is fine, but I want my bonus as if I didn't make partner since I'll be tendering back the option."

"Jesus, Liz, that could bring the package to over a million. Christ, you're fucked up in the head, but something seems to be working upstairs. What about a leave of absence and we freeze everything until you come back?"

"I want a clean break, Bob. You would have paid the bonus anyway if I didn't make partner," Elizabeth countered.

Willis processed how his conversation would go with McCabe. "Okay. Give me a day or two, but I'll make it happen. Can I tell McCabe if he doesn't agree you won't tender your stock?"

"Bob, you can tell him whatever you want, but if he doesn't agree, I won't tender and you'll be stuck with buying me out."

"I thought you said you weren't going to be a prick about it."

"Well, like you said, I can be a real pain in the ass. Anyway, it doesn't matter. McCabe will jump on this because he never wanted another female partner to begin with," Elizabeth said flatly. "And, Bob, one more thing…"

"Christ, Liz, what?" Willis said, exasperated.

"Thank you. From the very bottom of my fucked-up heart, you have been a great friend and a tremendous mentor." Elizabeth threw her arms around him and hugged him tightly.

MOMMA, IT'S ELIZABETH

Over the next two weeks, Elizabeth listed her condo for sale and went about the business of extricating herself from her law practice. She produced thirty-four multi-part memos on the status of each of her files along with her best thoughts on value and a detailed methodology for successfully concluding each matter. Virtually everything in her apartment had been packed to go into storage. When she signed the contract, she checked the box "undetermined" for the length of time. Except for her running gear and a week's worth of clothes she was ready to start her odyssey back to her roots, for better or for worse.

By the time her last day came around, she sat in her office with nothing to do but look out the window and watch the crowds.

Willis popped his head into her office. "We still on for tonight?"

"Yeah, but it's just you and Audrey, right?"

"Yep, just the three of us. Seven o'clock sharp."

"Where are we going?"

"Your favorite spot, The Four Seasons."

"The pool room?"

"Yes, Liz, the pool room. Christ, you're picky for someone out of a job."

"Who's buying, because I'm on a budget, Robert," Elizabeth cracked.

Willis smiled and shook his head. "I'll see you there."

Elizabeth got to the Seagram building early and was greeted by Kathy Zietel. It was a perfect night, the beneficiary of a beautiful late summer day with no humidity and a rising moon over the East River. Street light and moonlight filtered in through the cavernous double height windows of the restaurant, casting a willowy effervescence on Picasso's steel braided curtain hanging magnificently between the Grill Room and the Pool Room.

"Hey, Kathy, good evening. I'm waiting for Bob and Audrey."

"Would you like to be seated? Mr. Willis would not leave me alone until I guaranteed him a poolside table. Must be a special celebration on a big case."

"No, just a celebration of sorts. If you don't mind, I'd like to take a good look at all the artwork in the restaurant."

"Wonderful," Zietel said. "If you have any questions let me know, and when Mr. Willis gets here, I'll find you. Enjoy your evening, Ms. Natale."

Willis and Audrey arrived twenty minutes later, and they settled into the lap of Chef Albin's culinary masterpieces.

"So, Miss Natale, do you have a plan?"

"Go back to D.C. After that I don't know. Look for a house or apartment."

"Do you think you'll work?"

"Not right away. I have to get a driver's license and a car."

"You don't drive?" Willis asked, shocked.

"Never had to, and being in New York for the last twenty years never had time."

"And after you get your driver's license?"

"I may go back to school."

"Really, what for?" Willis asked.

"I've been talking to a woman in the Midwest. She's an abuse survivor and after she realized I was a civil lawyer, she mentioned she had a friend who had graduated from the school of Canon Law at Catholic University."

"Don't you have to be a priest to get in there?" Audrey asked.

"Nope, but I think they've had only a few women go through the degree. It's just a thought. I'm going to take my time to sort this all out."

Dinner was an international tour of taste, texture and subtlety, leaving little energy for substantive conversation. Aromatic fresh foie gras burnished with ripe papaya and caviar with roasted potato skins and chopped egg were passed around for appetizers. Whole baked sea bass, a saddle of roasted baby lamb with the famous bar slaw and Elizabeth's favorite, crisp skin roasted duckling, rounded out the entrees. Chocolate, raspberry and cappuccino soufflés finished the decadent meal, which was topped by a bottle of vintage 1967 Chateau d' Yquem.

"What a treat this has been, Robert. Thank you both for all of your kindness. I know it's not what you wanted."

"Robert wants what's best for you, Liz. He'll bitch and moan but in the end we're on your side."

"Audrey's right, I'll bitch and moan, but whatever you need— call me. When are you actually leaving, Liz?"

"I think tomorrow. I'll be at the Willard for a week because I'd like to find something downtown," she said as they moved down the steps onto the street.

"Well, stay in touch. You're always welcome here. Can we give you a lift uptown?"

"No, that's not necessary, Bob. I'll take a cab. Let's not prolong this. Besides, I don't want to start crying again."

Elizabeth kissed Audrey goodbye and turned to Willis. "I'll stay in touch."

"You do that," Willis said. He shoved a business card into Elizabeth's hand as he kissed her on the cheek.

"Who is this?" Elizabeth asked, looking at the card.

"He's an old friend, college roommate, just a great guy. If you get stuck look him up."

Elizabeth stared at the card blankly and slid it into her purse. "Until that time," Elizabeth said with a smile and walked up 52nd Street to the cabstand.

The cab pushed its way up Park Avenue in heavy traffic. Suddenly, Elizabeth thought she had just made a huge mistake. She was about to undo her entire life.

And for what? she pondered. She reached into her purse and pulled out the business card.

SOLOMON REICH
CLINICAL PSYCHOLOGY
WASHINGTON D.C. (202) 967-8320

At forty-six years old, Elizabeth felt like it was time to start over. She had no idea where she would land or how to start. All she knew is that it started in Washington, a town to which she swore she would never return.

Twenty-four hours later, Elizabeth arrived in Washington, D.C., aboard Amtrak Train 127 on one of those awful, rainy forty-degree nights. She went straight to a pay phone in the main terminal and dialed her old number on Shepherd Street.

"Momma, it's Elizabeth."

"Elizabeth? Where are you?" Lucy asked, alarmed.

"I'm in Union Station."

The phone went quiet.

"Are you still there, Momma?"

"Yes, it's just I haven't heard from you in months, so you surprised me."

"I know, I'm sorry, I've been busy at work, but that's about to change."

"You're always busy at work."

Elizabeth felt the chill through the phone. "Would another time be better?"

"No, no, of course not. Come on over. The Bishop just left and your grandmother and I were cleaning up. Did you eat?"

"No, but I'm starving. Did you say the Bishop?"

"Yes, Bishop Ryan. I'll tell you about it when you get here. I have some leftover pasta and chicken parm, I'll heat it up."

"Okay, I'll grab a cab and should be there in twenty minutes."

The ride over felt like an eternity. She wanted to tell the cabbie to turn around and take her back to Union Station. Nothing seemed right about this. She had not talked to her mother in months, had not seen her in over two years, and tonight she was going over for leftover pasta and chicken. Elizabeth remembered that Francis had mentioned years ago that Ryan had been to the house more than a few times and did not know what to make of it.

So, why was he there tonight? she wondered. The rain hitting the glass on the side window of the cab transfixed Elizabeth. She watched the drops hold for a second on the glass until gravity forced them to wiggle down to the bottom of the window. She realized the cab was not moving.

"You gonna get out, lady? We're here."

"Yes, of course. I'm sorry, but I need you to wait."

"Lady, I can't wait, I lose money waiting."

"Will $100 cover it?"

"Damn, miss, I can wait for that. Just take your time, I'll be right here at the corner."

Anna was out on the porch waiting. "Elizabeth!" she called out. "Come on, child, get out of the rain."

Elizabeth entered through the foyer and the familiar smell of the house and paneling took her immediately back. Nothing much had changed, but it seemed smaller to her. There was Poppa's chair, seemingly untouched since the day he died. She went to sit in it but immediately began to feel uncomfortable as memories started to come.

Lucy yelled upstairs to Rosemary. "Rose, come down! Elizabeth is here!"

"Elizabeth who? The Elizabeth who never calls or writes her Aunt Rose, that Elizabeth?"

"Thanks, Aunt Rose, I can always count on you to bolster my cause."

"Enough!" Anna said.

Both Lucy and Rosemary knew that Anna would side with Elizabeth.

"Come in the kitchen, the food's ready. Elizabeth, you want wine?"

"No. Water will be fine, Momma."

"Go ahead, *mangia*," Lucy said.

After catching up on the family news, the conversation turned to why she was there. Elizabeth told them about her pending move. She did not share that intrusive memories had become her daily companion. It was not uncommon for Elizabeth to act impulsively. She came home to find out more about the demons that haunted her sleep, ruined her days and tortured her nights.

Elizabeth no longer went to church. She was furious with God but missed the certainty of the rule-based Catholic dogma and ritual. She missed being a person of faith but had not a clue as to how to recapture her beliefs. She believed, (but did not share), that her shattered life might have some purpose if she made an effort to find out why this had happened to her and to the others she was reading about in the news.

She was a lawyer, and a skilled one at that. She slowly laid out her plan to apply to the Canon Law School at Catholic University. Elizabeth knew she was capable of going into the belly of the beast to look for answers and change the system from within. It was naive but consistent with her stubbornness and her drive to overcome. It would be a new way of coping with the flashbacks that were frequent visitors and, for the most part, controlled her life.

"So, let me understand this," Rosemary chimed in, "you quit your job as a partner in one of the most prestigious firms in the country and sold your condo overlooking Central Park to move to Washington to go to Catholic school?" Rosemary asked incredulously.

"The short answer is yes in answer to your question."

"That's the dumbest thing I've ever heard from you. You hit change of life early?"

"Jesus, Aunt Rose, come on!"

"Where is this all coming from?" Rosemary asked. "This isn't making sense to me."

"I'll tell you exactly where," Elizabeth said, determined to get part of her reasoning on the table. "I met a woman named Barbara Blaine. She's an activist and an advocate for sexual abuse survivors who have been sexually assaulted by priests."

"Jesus Mary and Joseph, can somebody pour me a glass of wine," Anna said, her voice trembling.

"I'm a lawyer. I've made some decent money and I can help. With a Canon Law degree, I'll be taken seriously and perhaps I can help remove these bad priests from ministry."

"I thought you were a lawyer already."

"No, Grandmom, this is different. It's Church law. The laws of the Church."

"Then what?" Lucy said, starting to get shrill.

"Maybe I'll apply to work in the Archdiocese."

"Where?"

"Here, here in D.C."

"You've got to be kidding. You, Liz, to do what?" Lucy screamed.

"To be a voice, to be an advocate for sexual abuse victims. To help the Church see the damage sexual abuse by priests has done to the children and to the Church."

Lucy flew into a rage. "You! You, help the Church? You want to work for the Archdiocese? My God, Liz, how good of you to come to the Church's rescue. You don't even go to church anymore for God sakes! Do you even remember church, Liz?" Lucy asked, mocking her daughter. "Going to Mass, receiving the sacraments, it's part of the discipline, it's the least you can do for the Son of God giving up his life for you."

"Oh, Christ, Mom, will you stop with that holier than thou crap? Have you read the papers or turned on the news? Every week there's someone new coming forward saying they were sexually assaulted by a priest. And why the hell was this Ryan guy here for dinner in the first place?"

"You knew him as Monsignor Ryan. He's the auxiliary Bishop for the Archdiocese of Washington and it's Bishop Ryan to you. And another thing... these people saying they were abused; they're vermin looking for money! Telling lies about priests! Your brother is a priest. When was the last time you talked to him? Have you told him what you plan to do? Do you know what happens to people who tell lies about priests?" Lucy screamed. "I'll tell you! They go to hell, that's where they go! You're a lawyer, worked at the Supreme Court for that O'Connor woman. You believe everything you read in the papers? And for your information I will invite whoever I damn well please over for dinner, including the Bishop!"

Elizabeth had had enough. "Lies—are you serious, Mother? Do you really believe these victims, what did you call them, vermin, are coming forward for money?" Elizabeth screamed.

"Yes, I do, and I'm ashamed that a daughter of mine would be a part of this attack against the Church. I'll tell you one thing, Elizabeth Natale, you're putting your soul in jeopardy."

"Mother, my soul is already in jeopardy." Elizabeth pushed herself from the table and went to get her coat, not saying a word.

She walked to the door and Anna, now crying, grabbed her before she got off the porch.

"Lizzie, I love you with all of my heart." Anna pulled Elizabeth's head to her lips and whispered, "You do what you think you need to. Your father would be proud of you."

"Grandmom, I love you, too, with all of my heart."

Rosemary followed Anna out onto the porch. "Lizzie, give your mother a few days, she'll come around, and I'm sorry I ran off at the mouth. I think that's what got her cranked up," Rosemary said, trying to salvage something from the argument.

"Forget about it, Aunt Rose, I knew better than to come here. My old boss said you can never go back. He was right. So, what's going on with Momma and Ryan? Is she sleeping with him?" Elizabeth asked.

Anna went inside, not wanting to be around that conversation.

"Liz, that's a long story for a different day. Your mother will have to handle that one."

"What the hell, Aunt Rose. So, she is sleeping with him," Elizabeth said.

"I didn't say that, and I don't know that. Leave it for now, Liz. Get settled with where you're living and figure out what you want to do. If you want to talk, call me at work." Rosemary didn't wait for a response. She kissed Elizabeth goodnight and went back inside.

The only thing that could make this horrible visit worse would be Elizabeth's cab leaving. Elizabeth exhaled deeply, seeing her cab at the corner.

"Where to, miss?"

"I'm staying at the Willard downtown, but I want to go to the National Shrine first," Elizabeth said, her voice shaking.

"Yo, lady, I'm not a tour guide."

"How much do you make on a good night?"

275

"Couple of hundred."

"Here's another hundred. Go to the Shrine, park in the lot on the east side and shut the fuck up. I'll only be a few minutes, then drop me at the Willard and you'll have had a good night. Do not leave me. Do you understand?"

"Yes, ma'am, I got it."

It was only a five-minute drive to the Shrine from the Shepherd Street house, but Elizabeth felt like she was starting to unravel. Her heart was racing, and she wanted to lash out, cry, run… anything to keep the darkness from taking her over.

As soon as the cab rolled into the east portico lot of the National Shrine, Elizabeth raced up the stairs to the statuary next to the three massive oak entry doors to the side church and pushed her face into the wet Indiana limestone. Elizabeth looked at the carvings, remembering how proud Joseph was of the work. She had to get close to her father, her rock. She had to channel his strength into her body. She traced her fingers over the coarse limestone, rubbing the grit on the tips of her fingers then rubbed the boss stone she took out of her purse.

"Poppa, I can feel your touch," Elizabeth whispered as she rolled her hands over the niches and florets of the columns. Elizabeth moved around the corner where her grandfather took her right after Joseph died. She looked up and started to cry.

"Poppa, please help me. Please, Poppa, give me your strength," Elizabeth sobbed into the limestone wall. As she pressed her lips even closer to the stone, Elizabeth could feel her breath bouncing back on her face. "Poppa, stay with me. I need you." She stepped back with her father's boss stone in her hand and started to catch her breath. She went back to the car and flopped into the back seat. "Okay we're done; take me to the Willard."

The cabbie took a right out of the lot to get on Michigan Avenue and headed toward North Capitol Street. Elizabeth noticed her fingers were tingling. She felt threatened and vulnerable.

"How much longer?"

"Ten to fifteen minutes, depending on traffic."

Elizabeth started to feel nauseated. She could feel sweat forming on her scalp. She was sliding into the darkness. She needed to escape the pain, the memories, the smells of the sacristy at Aquinas Hall. It was all coming back.

The cab had barely come to a stop and Elizabeth was out the door. She breezed past the doorman and checked in at the front desk. After having her luggage sent up to her room, she headed straight to the Round Robin bar, which was just a few steps off the main lobby. The posh mahogany venue, a favorite Washington haunt, was literally in the round with huge windows overlooking Pennsylvania Avenue. It was the place where Henry Clay introduced the Capitol City to the mint julep and where lobbyists and diplomats honed their skills.

"What'll it be, miss?" the bartender asked.

"Double eighteen-year-old McCallum, if you have it."

"Yes, ma'am, perfect drink for a cold rainy night."

Elizabeth brought the glass to her mouth and effortlessly downed the scotch in one fluid motion. She knew what would happen next. The darkness was upon her. Lobbyists at this particular Washington watering hole were like soldiers in uniform, they stood out like tulips in the spring. She got up to move her seat next to an unattended thirty-something at the bar, checking to see if he had a wedding band or had recently removed one.

"Hi, can I buy you a drink?"

"Sure," Elizabeth said. The barkeep had seen this scene play out hundreds of times.

"What's your name?"

"Nancy."

"Nancy what?"

"Just Nancy."

"What's yours?"

"Tom. Nice to meet you, Nancy."

"Nice to meet you, Tom."

"Same thing, ma'am?" the barkeeper asked.

"Yeah, sure, why not."

As the liquor began to process into her blood, Elizabeth's purse slipped from her lap and spilled onto the floor. Pushing her bar stool back, she bent down to pick up the entire contents of her purse. Tom, of course, was there to help. Then she saw it, perhaps the only thing that could derail her self-destructive spiral. The card Bob Willis gave her leaving the Four Seasons was laying on the floor face up:

SOLOMON REICH

CLINICAL PSYCHOLOGY

Elizabeth felt a surge of adrenaline hit her body.

"Thanks for the drink, Tom, but I'm feeling a bit under the weather."

"Allow me to walk you to your room."

"I'm not staying here."

"Would you like me to call a cab for you?"

"No. No thank you. They're always out front." Elizabeth grabbed her coat and purse and went to the front lobby. Tom followed close behind. She was glad she had not lost her bearings as Tom was being persistent, hoping against hope. The doorman whistled a waiting cab and she got in, leaving Tom on the curb.

"Perhaps another time, Tom," she said as she slammed the door to the cab. "Go."

"Where to, Miss?"

"Just drive for twenty minutes but end up at the entrance on F Street."

"You know you could have gotten there by walking through the lobby," the cabbie said, annoyed.

"I know that, but I wanted you to take me."

Elizabeth got to her room using the hotel's back elevator, locked the door behind her and sat on the bed. She was shaking like a cornered animal waiting to be attacked. Elizabeth felt an uncontrollable urge to take a shower to wash the darkness off her. She reached in her purse and got three Valium and chased them with half a bottle of wine from the welcome basket in her suite. She stripped off her clothes and let the near scalding water pelt her body into submission. After thirty minutes, exhausted, she dried herself and put the "Do Not Disturb" sign on the door. She had cheated the darkness for the first time.

CHAPTER SEVEN

You Need to Kill It

AWAKENING

A ribbon of daylight hit Elizabeth's face through a small opening in the pulled drapes of her suite. Sleep slowly gave way to semi-consciousness. Alcohol laced with Valium was the elixir for escaping the enveloping darkness of childhood memories. Like so many times before, Elizabeth now had to deal with the morning after.

First came an almost ritualistic self-loathing as anger began to prickle the nerve endings on her bare skin. Elizabeth closed her eyes and tried to remember how she got to her bed and whether she had fucked the young man who bought her a drink at the Round Robin Bar. Lying on her stomach, her bloodshot eyes began to focus on her clothes on the floor. A path of underwear and high heels led to the bathroom, still lit from the previous night.

Elizabeth had played this scene out many times before and she knew exactly what came next. She would simply slide off the bed into the bathroom, gathering her clothes and shoes as she went, and would be dressed and out of the room in under three minutes. It was much easier to face the awkwardness of an anonymous tryst fully clothed in a lobby, rather than naked in a bed. As she lay there, her pulse started to quicken, listening for any sound of someone else on the other side of the bed. Turning gingerly off her stomach, she reached her arm and gently touched the other side of the king bed. She was shocked to find she was alone. Turning on her back and exhaling loudly, she felt the adrenaline subside from her system.

Elizabeth wrapped herself in a sheet, walked to the phone and picked up the receiver, which automatically dialed room service.

"Good morning, Ms. Natale. How may I assist you?"

Elizabeth tried to keep her tone civil. The faceless, nameless attendant had no idea who she was talking to but for the name that flashed on her switchboard in the kitchen.

"Good morning. Could you send up some black coffee to Room 820, please?" Elizabeth said, reminding herself that the woman was just doing her job.

Catching a glimpse of herself in the mirror, Elizabeth looked away. But for the happenstance of Sol Reich's business card falling from her purse, she would not have been alone in her bedroom. Turning back to her reflection, she glared at the mirror. "You're nothing but a fucking slut," she hissed. Within seconds, she was transported back to Shepherd Street as a little girl.

Grabbing a sports bra, a pair of long running tights, and a zip-up shell from her suitcase, Elizabeth dressed quickly, retreating into her go-to scenario to escape the incoming tide of madness. As she finished tying up her shoes, her coffee finally arrived.

Elizabeth pulled an oversized chair and ottoman in front of the full height window and threw open the long drapes, taking in the view of Pennsylvania Avenue. While she waited for the caffeine to do its magic, her left foot yo-yoed back and forth as tension consumed her body. The Washington Monument and the west lawn of the White House was to her right, the District Building to the left, and the Department of Commerce directly in front of her window.

Taking in the expanse, Elizabeth was transported back in time. She remembered how, as a little girl, her entire family would trek down to Ellipse for the Peace Pageant every Christmas. At the corner of 15th and E Street NW, Elizabeth would race ahead, gravitating towards the live animals and Yule log fire pit where anxious parents dodged the fluttering embers raining down on the delighted children. After what seemed only like a minute or two, Lucy would find her and pull her toward the crèche, where they would spend a ridiculous amount of time simply staring at the nativity scene.

Elizabeth swallowed hard, remembering the loneliness she felt during the Christmas season as the memories of Father Dolan bubbled into her consciousness. No one would ever be able to understand how different she was from everyone else in the world. She quickly opened the mini bar, found two miniature bottles of vodka and downed them both to settle the darkness. She needed to get out on the street.

Elizabeth quickly breezed through the lobby and headed south on 14th Street. Instead of stretching, she warmed up at a slow pace, trying to relax the tension in her upper body. Her pounding headache was made worse by the jackhammering of the sidewalks at the construction site of the Ronald Reagan building. The weather was perfect for running. Windless, in the mid-fifties, the brilliant sun warmed Elizabeth's face.

Putting her head down, she powered through the long block to Constitution Avenue, crossing the street to the Smithsonian Museum of American History. Elizabeth began to formulate a to-do list as her cadence picked up to a "leisurely" seven-minute mile along the bridle path on Madison Drive.

First, she needed to talk to Francis. It had been two years since they last spoke and through her ebbing mental fog, she recalled that their last conversation went poorly. Housing and a car would come easily, as money was all that was required to secure an adequate place to live and reliable transportation. Elizabeth increased her pace to make the light across the 12th Street overpass to continue her route up Madison Drive toward the Capitol. Then there was the matter of Sol Reich and Barbara Blaine. Elizabeth felt a spurt of vodka-tinged reflux seep into her esophagus. She had become an expert in beating back the emotional and physical pain during her runs, but the thought of unpacking her childhood memories, especially those involving Dolan, overwhelmed her. She reached for a water bottle on her fanny pack to dislodge the bile in her throat. She wanted to find Dolan, she wanted to face him, and she wanted to hurt him like he hurt her.

Dolan had robbed the little girl who lived on Shepherd Street of her childhood, leaving her lost in a wasteland of emotional blackness, addiction and self-loathing. Her fists clenched as she imagined her hand on the gun in her father's nightstand. She pictured Dolan's head exploding as the bullet crashed into his skull spewing bone, flesh and tissue. Her pace picked up to competition level, each foot making a perfect strike on the gravel path. She powered past the National Gallery, the East Annex for modern art and across 3rd Street to East Capitol Circle, taking a serpentine path toward the Supreme Court and the Library of Congress then turning west on Independence Avenue toward the Lincoln Memorial. Elizabeth focused on taking in long draws of oxygen through her nose. Her legs were now absorbing the punishing blows of a full racing stride, fueled only by a dwindling supply of glycogen and an overwhelming sense of loss and anger. Wallowing in the exquisite details of her homicidal fantasy, Elizabeth let loose a full-throated "The mother-fucker raped me," startling several tourists walking in the opposite direction.

Ignoring the stunned faces of the people around her, Elizabeth turned onto Independence Avenue past the Canon Office Building, reserved mostly for junior Members of Congress. She crossed against the light at Independence Avenue and 1st Street, ignoring a shrill whistle from a Capitol Police Officer standing on the opposite corner, incredulous at how helpless she was to control the cascade of terrible memories.

Elizabeth's face contorted with rage as she remembered that first time Dolan had assaulted her. It was as if she were looking at a video recording. There she was standing in front of the vestment mirror, her small hands grabbing the side of the frame, her back to Dolan with her dress pushed up to her waist, her white underpants around her ankles. It was afternoon when she had gotten home. She felt a pressure and a burning sensation in her vagina and dampness in her underpants. Francis was not home but both her mother and grandmother were in the kitchen preparing dinner. They wanted her to talk about her day, but Elizabeth told them she had to go "number two" and rushed upstairs to the bathroom, the only private refuge available in the small house. She remembered them both giggling, telling her to use spray.

Elizabeth's brain was saturated with details of the past as she headed downhill toward the U.S. Botanical Gardens Building.

Sitting on the toilet, she stared at Joseph's shaving kit arranged neatly on the counter and the magnetic plastic Jesus planted neatly on the metal cup holder grouted into the checkerboard of pink and green tile on the wall. Lucy had suggested that she keep it next to the sink to remind the family to say their prayers before bed, but Elizabeth sat there trying to process the incongruity of being sexually assaulted by the very priest who awarded her the plastic Jesus prize for the third grader who raised the most money for the rescue of "pagan babies" during Lent. "Who the fuck were those pagan babies anyway?" she blurted out in full stride.

Elizabeth felt her heart pounding in her chest as she relived the memories of that first afternoon of being alone in her bathroom. She was still amazed that Dolan got her to stay silent.

As her legs pounded the pavement, she felt tears running down her cheeks.

Was anyone in the hallway? Could anyone hear her? What would she do with her blood-stained underpants? Would her mother notice she was walking funny? How could she hide them without her mother finding out? Elizabeth recalled in vivid detail breaking her trance-like gaze of the plastic Jesus and looking down to her underpants stretched wide by her legs. She was disgusted by what she saw but decided to put them back on and sneak out of the house after dinner and put them down the sewer outside when no one was looking. If somehow she were missed for the few minutes she would be gone she would say she wanted to look at the night sky.

Suddenly, a knock at the door made her jump.

"What?" Elizabeth snarled through the door.

"You gonna be in there all day?" Francis answered.

"Frannie, I'm going number two. Do you mind?"

"Don't stink it up, jerk face."

"You're a jerk face. Now shut up, Frannie, and go downstairs and wait."

She was riddled with shame and guilt because she made a priest sin. The crisis passed, as she heard Francis going down the steps. Elizabeth clambered on top of the toilet seat to look at herself in the mirror, making sure there was no blood on the back of her legs. All through dinner she was terrified that the bleeding would start again, and questions would come that she could not answer. She wished God would take her right on the spot so it would be all over. She vowed to never tell a soul what had happened. Not her parents, not a doctor, not her teachers. No one.

The haunting memories from her childhood and the physical punishment of the cement had taken their toll. Elizabeth's legs began to cramp with lactic acid, forcing her into a grotesque limp. She hobbled toward the restroom in the southeast corner of the lower lobby of the Lincoln Memorial for water and a piece of fruit from a street vendor.

Trying to catch her breath, Elizabeth refilled her water bottle. Stretching her legs out on the edge of the sink the cramps slowly subsided. She took the elevator to the main chamber and mixed with the tourists marveling at Daniel French's masterpiece. She could not help but notice the contemplative yet determined look on Lincoln's face as he rested a closed left hand on the pedestal and an open hand on the right.

That was a guy who knew his course, she thought as she gathered herself for the long walk back to the Willard Hotel. Elizabeth looked at her watch. It was time to get to work. She had a score to settle.

I WANT TO EXPLAIN SOME THINGS

The "Do Not Disturb" sign was hung from Elizabeth's door. After a long shower and two large glasses of chocolate milk ordered up from room service, she reviewed the notes on her yellow legal pad, waiting for her body to fully recover. She wrote out a list of priorities, and with a deep breath she began to execute. First, she owed her brother Francis an apology. Elizabeth picked up the phone and tucked it under her chin so she could steady her hand to dial the number.

"Good morning, St. Stephen's Rectory. How may I help you?" came the cheerful voice on the other end of the line.

Elizabeth closed her eyes. "Good morning, this is Elizabeth Natale, Father Natale's sister. Is he available by any chance?"

"Oh, Miss Natale, of course; let me see if I can find him," the office secretary said. "Can you hold for a minute?"

"Yes, I can wait," Elizabeth said, her gut churning as she fidgeted in her chair. Staring at the two empty Smirnoff miniatures in the wastebasket next to her desk, she nervously tapped her pad with her pen as she waited for the call to be connected.

"Hello."

The tone was flat. Elizabeth was hoping for something less intimidating from her brother.

"Hey, Frannie, it's Liz."

"I know that," Francis said curtly. "Mrs. Howard, our secretary, told me you were on the phone."

"Okay, listen, I realize you are still angry with me…"

"You're damn right, Elizabeth, I'm still really angry with you. I've reached out to you a dozen or more times. Nothing. Momma has called you—nothing. You didn't come to my ordination. You've never seen me say Mass. I've been to maybe a dozen chamber music recitals in New York over the years, I invited you to each one and you never even gave me the courtesy of a response. So, yes, Elizabeth, I'm pissed off. Perhaps we can conclude this before I say any more," Francis fumed.

"No, please, don't, Frannie; please don't hang up on me. I know I've been an asshole; I want to apologize; I want to see you. I want to explain some things you may not know about. Let me take you out to dinner. Frannie, you're my brother. I know we can't go back but I want at least to try and make things right, or at least make things civil between us. Let me take you out to dinner. I'm in the city. Please, Frannie," she begged, pushing the phone even closer to her mouth.

"Does this have anything to do with you quitting your job in New York," responded Francis, trying to tease more information out of the call.

"Why, have you been talking to Momma?" Elizabeth asked bluntly.

"Of course I talk to our mother. I talk to her every week, usually about you."

"Frannie, please, give me a couple of hours of your time and if you think I'm full of shit you don't ever have to talk to me again."

"Don't be ridiculous, Liz. I do think you're full of shit but you're still my sister."

"Where and when?" Francis added in a formal tone.

"How about Tiberio's on K Street at seven, tomorrow night? It has great Italian food," Elizabeth offered.

"I know that place. My extra money goes to people in need. I can't afford Tiberio's, and I have confessions on Tuesday night in any event."

"Well, I'm buying. What about Wednesday?" Elizabeth persisted.

"I can do it Wednesday, it's my day off. Did you say seven o'clock?"

"Yes, seven. By the way, Frannie, do you remember Tommy Atkinson, the kid I wanted to go to the prom with?" Elizabeth asked.

Francis was well aware of Atkinson. For the last ten years Atkinson had been a pariah in the eyes of the Catholic hierarchy and Francis had secretly cheered him on.

"Vaguely, Liz, why do you ask?"

"I had a terrible crush on him in high school and I always wondered if he actually became a priest. Do you remember Tommy? He asked me to go to his senior prom at Gonzaga High School and then Sister Angela wouldn't let me go because I was a sophomore and Momma went along with her. I was so pissed off. I don't think I talked to anybody for a week."

"It was weeks, Liz," Francis laughed. "Do you remember I went and talked to Tommy?" he asked.

"I do," Elizabeth said with a smile. "And I also remember he didn't want to go to the prom without me and instead we went to Gusti's. He did that for me. I'll never forget it. Anyway, he somehow got tickets to the Carter Baron Amphitheater to see Herb Alpert and the Tijuana Brass, and we had our own prom."

"To be honest, Liz, I'm not sure if he entered the priesthood. I know all the priests in this Archdiocese and he's not a priest here."

NO ONE WANTS TO HEAR ABOUT THIS

Francis hung up the phone, pounding his fist on the desktop. Lucy had called Francis to share Elizabeth's recent outburst about the sex abuse scandal during her brief visit. During the call, Francis deflected the conversation, distracted by the traumatic memory of Lucy's grief-stricken wail when Monsignor Ryan told her that her husband was dead.

The subject made him feel uncomfortable and isolated. The arc of his entire life had been built on secrets to preserve the status quo. Francis knew it was just a matter of time before Elizabeth would connect the dots and his story would unravel, harvesting a well-deserved punishment from God.

Francis had the number for the direct private line to Bishop Ryan's desk. He had been told to hang up if Ryan did not personally answer by the second ring. Ryan answered on the first ring.

"Bishop Ryan here."

"Good morning, Bishop, this is Francis."

"Good morning, Brother Daniel, it's good to hear your voice from the mid-continent. Are you well?"

Francis was impressed with how nimble Ryan had become as people must have been in his office. "I am, Bishop, thank you for asking. I got a call from my sister Elizabeth. Would you like me to call back?" Francis inquired.

"Just hold on." Ryan turned to his visitor and apologized for the unexpected interruption. "My dear Father Long, would you please give me a moment? I need to speak privately with a brother bishop in the Midwest," Ryan said as if the call had been scripted days before.

Francis heard Ryan's heavy oak door close just as he came back to the receiver.

"Are you still there?" Ryan asked.

"Yes, I'm here, Bishop."

"Now what's this business about a call from your sister?" Ryan asked in a tone that mixed harshness with curiosity.

"We have been somewhat estranged for several years but this morning she called me out of the blue. She said she wanted to explain some things from the past. I presume she believes this explanation will make her behavior more understandable. And she wants to meet for dinner."

"Francis, I'm at a loss as to what the urgency here is."

"Well, the urgency here is that right after you left my mother's house two weeks ago, my sister came in from New York. She announced to my mother and Aunt she had just quit her job and was contemplating applying to Canon Law School at Catholic University. This morning during our call she wanted to know if Tommy Atkinson ever became a priest. You would know 'Tommy' as the Reverend Thomas Patrick Atkinson, formerly secretary to the Papal Nuncio Pio Laghi, and now a powerful advocate for abuse survivors."

Ryan exhaled deeply into the phone. "Good God, how in the hell does she know Atkinson?"

"I think he was her first love in high school," Francis said, stabbing a pencil onto his notepad, breaking the lead.

Francis recalled his own memories of being sexually abused by Dolan and how he had participated in what could only be described as a cover-up. He was a victim of Dolan but because of his own selfishness and shame he had become complicit in a decades long secret. He had thrown his own sister into a toxic cauldron to fend for herself and had ceded power over his life to Cletus Ryan. When his conscience bothered him, he would remind himself of the fear he felt as a teenager and the very real threats Dolan made to guarantee his silence. That rationale did not hold up as an adult, and still he said nothing.

"You said she quit her job in New York. What did she do?" Ryan pressed.

"She was a lawyer who had just made partner at McCabe, Willis & Houghton and quit."

"Jesus, Francis, did I know that?"

"With respect, Bishop, I don't know what you know. I know I didn't tell you because, quite frankly, it never entered my mind to advise you of my sister's work history."

"Listen to me, Father Natale. You pursued your vocation in a manner that took advantage of your musical talent. Did I not support you in that endeavor?" Ryan hissed into the phone.

"You did, Bishop."

"Did I pressure you to tell your mother what really happened the night your father died?"

"No, you didn't, Bishop," Francis said, trying to keep his tone respectful.

"As a priest, didn't you choose to protect our Archdiocese from scandal? Didn't you agree that Mother Church was more important than your own individual needs?"

"It's true, Bishop, I did at the time," Francis said.

"At the time?" Ryan thundered. "Let me suggest to you that right now is the time for you to support me!"

"I am supporting you, Bishop," Francis protested. "I called you as soon as I got off the phone with Elizabeth."

"That's not enough, Natale," Ryan growled. "You need to kill it. You need to make sure your sister doesn't have some goddamn epiphany with her old flame and create problems for this Archdiocese, not to mention the other dioceses that had Dolan before he came to us."

"And how would you like me to, as you say, 'kill it'?" Francis replied.

Ryan exploded. "No one wants to hear about this, Francis. Parents don't want to go to the police. They don't want to tell their friends or family. They don't want to be embarrassed in their own parishes. What they want is for the scourge of sexual abuse and the assholes that do this to simply go away. They want someone like me to assure them that they're doing the right thing by their family and that it will never happen again. That's the drill, Francis. Good Catholics do not want to see their Church attacked by scandal. And the last thing anybody wants is a bunch of greedy lawyers trying to make us look bad to the people in the pews. Did you forget that the people in the pews pay all of our bills?"

"And again, Bishop, I'm not arguing with you, but how would you precisely want me to kill it?"

"That's your problem. She's your sister. I'll handle Atkinson. You convince your sister that she's fine and needs to go back to New York and practice law."

"With respect, Bishop, telling my sister to do anything is quite impossible."

"I don't want to hear that, Father Natale. I want to hear you'll handle it. Listen to me, when you finally told your father what Dolan did to your sister, what did he do, Francis?" Ryan whispered into the phone.

"He put me in the car and we came to see you, Bishop."

"And what did your father say?" Ryan asked, turning his back to the door so he could not be overheard.

"He said you would know what to do," Francis said, choking down his rage.

"Exactly!" Ryan wailed. "I knew what to do then and I know what to do now. The reputation of the Church is bigger than any of us. The kids will get over it with some time, and with that time we'll figure out what to do with these priests. The passage of time is what makes this two-thousand-year-old institution tick, Francis. Time is the lifeblood of the Church's longevity. Eternal Salvation, Francis, that's our stock in trade, that's the bargain for loyalty and faith in the institution. That's what the faithful want and that's what we must deliver. The Church has weathered many severe attacks over the centuries, and, with time, this nuisance will pass as well. We both have a lot to lose here. Keep that in mind, Francis. You found a home in the priesthood for your lifestyle and your music. You told your father about Dolan, and you watched him have a heart attack in my rectory. I kept your secret, Father Francis Natale, all of your secrets! Remember, Francis, all of your secrets. Now, after you have dinner with your sister, I want you to call me. I want to be kept informed."

"So, you want me to spy on Elizabeth," Francis said, rising out of his chair in indignation.

"Don't get cute with me, Father. If we aren't clear, you could find yourself playing your precious piano at an old age retirement home for priests and nuns in the middle of bum-fuck nowhere, not that cushy rectory in Bethesda that you're calling me from. It would be a big change for you, Father Natale. So, again, are we clear?"

"Yes, Bishop, I'm clear." Francis flinched at the sound of the phones disconnecting and felt his face contort with anger. Stunned by Ryan equating the sexual assault of children to a historical nuisance, he could only hope that Elizabeth would be up to the task.

BIG BEN'S IS RIGHT BEHIND YOU

A half-eaten turkey club sandwich and a tossed salad crowded the small desk in Elizabeth's suite. By mid-afternoon, Elizabeth had made progress on her list. She found a spacious one-bedroom apartment for rent at Harvard Hall and faxed over her application. It was in the Adams Morgan district overlooking Rock Creek Park and the west entrance of the National Zoo.

The hotel's concierge secured dinner reservations for two on Wednesday evening at Tiberio's. The business of the car was crossed off in red; getting a driver's license in the District of Columbia was more complicated than it was worth. Elizabeth could not see herself taking a Driver's Ed course when parallel parking, a requirement of the driver's test, appeared to be dramatically outside of her wheelhouse. Cabs, trains, planes and buses would have to do for now.

Elizabeth took a deep breath as she stared at Barbara Blaine's name on her list. Getting up from her desk, she paced the room back and forth. Elizabeth had never shared the contents of her black box of memories with anyone. She hated having no control over her self-loathing. She hated that she did not stand up for herself when she was a little girl. And she hated that Dolan convinced her that God wanted her to keep his sick secret.

She began to flush as her scalp tingled with nervous energy and fear. Emptying her lungs of air, Elizabeth violently shook her arms and legs as if she were about to insert herself into racing blocks. She flopped into a chair and dialed Blaine's number in Chicago. But before the number connected, she hung up.

Elizabeth cursed herself as she stared at the phone. "You're such an asshole," she muttered into the mirror over the desk. She dialed the number again and waited for the call to connect.

Blaine answered the phone on the first ring. "Hello, this is Barbara."

Elizabeth was silent. She recognized the voice. It sounded warm, almost inviting.

"Hello, this is Barbara, is anyone there?"

Finally, Elizabeth stammered an awkward yes into the phone. "Yes, yes, I'm here, this is Elizabeth, Elizabeth Natale. I saw you on the street in front of the Cardinal's residence some months back. You gave me a business card with the name Barbara Blaine and this number. Is this Barbara Blaine?" Elizabeth asked.

"It is and I'm glad you called, Elizabeth," Blaine said, searching her memory for a connection to Elizabeth's name.

"I'm sure you don't remember me. I told you my name was Nancy when we met on the street in New York. You were protesting."

"Nancy!" Blaine shrieked into the phone, "I do remember you. You had a beautiful black wool pants suit, white blouse and a matching black coat with these insane yellow and green running shoes. New

York high fashion in running shoes, I don't think I could ever forget that," Blaine added, causing them both to erupt in laughter.

"Whew," Elizabeth said, "I haven't laughed in a while."

Of course you haven't laughed in a while, Blaine told herself as she braced for one more of the dozens of painful phone calls she received each month.

"How can I help you, Elizabeth?" Blaine asked.

"I don't know. Actually, I don't know where to start. I've always felt alone," Elizabeth said. "Ever since it happened, I've felt different from everybody else."

"Elizabeth, I know how you feel. I was abused by Chet Warren, an Oblate priest, when I was thirteen years old. He made me promise not to tell anyone because if I did, he would go to jail and no longer be a priest. He knew I wanted to be a nun so he told me we would be engaged as a couple on earth and then get married when we were in heaven. From that day on I thought of myself as an evil temptress. I had sinned and I had made a priest sin. I was a cheap dirty sinner. From there I went down a rabbit hole. Shame, guilt, seething anger…but then I came out on the other side."

"That happened to me. But I haven't come out on the other side," Elizabeth said.

"Don't get me wrong, I have scar tissue, for sure, but I knew I had done nothing wrong. I'm telling you this because I want you to know you're not alone, and I don't want you to hang up."

"Barbara, I have to go," Elizabeth choked through tears.

"Elizabeth, please, don't," Blaine pleaded. "At least give me your number. It's normal to feel overwhelmed."

"I just don't see myself coming out of that rabbit hole. For me, it just doesn't seem possible. I just think that this is it. This is my life and someday it will kill me," Elizabeth sobbed.

Blaine, concerned for Elizabeth's safety, drilled down on the call with all her experience. "That's how you feel now but believe me there will be other days when you don't feel this way. I needed help also, lots of it. But there is life, rich rewarding life, after abuse. You've just got to believe that. That's not to say memories ever leave, they're part of you, but there are other parts of you to focus on."

"Barbara, I really have to go. Thank you."

"Wait, please. You need something to help you unravel all the shit you've been through. There's a book that was just published that will act like a road map."

Elizabeth was silent.

"Are you still there?" Blaine asked again.

"I'm here. So, what's this roadmap you speak of?" Elizabeth asked dryly.

"It's Jason Berry's book *Lead Us Not Into Temptation*. It's not an easy read. It will piss you off, probably make you cry, but it will chart out how this abuse scandal unfolded over the last ten years and more or less chronicle why it all happened. It's really a stunning expose. I'm just saying, it'll help give some context to what you're going through."

Elizabeth jotted down the title. "Barbara, thanks for all but I really have to go," Elizabeth said, getting impatient.

"I know, just one more thing. Father Tom Atkinson is giving our keynote speech at our annual meeting. He's the guy on the inside that blew the whistle on all of the Bishops that have swept this under the rug."

Elizabeth didn't hear anything past the name Atkinson. "Barbara, did you say a priest named Atkinson?" she asked.

"Yes, Atkinson. Tom Atkinson."

A jolt of electricity surged through Elizabeth's body.

"Why? Do you know him?"

"Well, I knew a Tommy Atkinson way back in high school. He told me he was going to be a priest, but it couldn't possibly be the same person."

"Well, Elizabeth, all I know is that he's one tough guy. He has the bishops on their heels. He's basically been fired from the Church, so now he's an Air Force Chaplain. But he has kept the pressure on the bishops by helping the plaintiff lawyers bring these cases. He decodes the bishops' Church-speak and helps them find all of the skeletons. And he's not shy about it," Blaine said, laughing. "Plus, he's a Canon Lawyer. He worked at the Vatican Embassy for five years. He's helped me a ton. He's a Dominican priest from Washington, D.C. Does that sound like him?"

"I don't know, Barbara, I lost track of him during college." Elizabeth's head was spinning. *How could all of this be happening?* "Do you have his address so maybe I could write him?" Elizabeth asked.

"I have his number. You could call him to see if it's the same person you're talking about. I talk to him a few times a month," Blaine said. "Here's his number. He's in Washington State at McChord Air Force Base."

Elizabeth's hand was shaking as she scribbled the number on her pad. "Barbara, I really can't talk about this anymore. It's making me really crazy."

"I know, and I understand. Just be careful; go slow on all of this. Will you call me again?"

"I will," Elizabeth said as she pushed the switch hook down with her finger to disconnect the call. As soon as she got a dial tone, she called the concierge desk.

"Hello, this is the concierge."

"Good afternoon. This is Miss Natale in Room 820, I'm looking for some help finding a bookstore within walking distance of the hotel."

"Of course; give me a moment."

"I remember the name of the store had the word 'prose' in it," Elizabeth added.

"Ah, I know it well. I go there myself. It's called 'Politics and Prose,' it's on Connecticut Avenue. They close at five, but if you take a cab you'll have plenty of time."

"Thank you so much."

Reaching down to open the mini bar, a stabbing pain coursed through the back of Elizabeth's head to just above her eyes, causing her to slip out of her chair. Scrambling to her feet and putting pressure on the back of her head, she threw on a jacket over her tracksuit, grabbed her sunglasses and the rest of the miniature bottles from the bar and stuffed them into her purse. It was nearly four o'clock and she needed to get uptown quickly.

Traffic was miserable as the cab weaved its way up Connecticut Avenue.

"I'm just picking up a book at this address. Will you wait and then take me back?" Elizabeth piped through the hole in the Plexiglas barrier.

"I can wait with the meter running," the cabbie quipped.

"I have one more stop after that, is that okay?"

"Lady, if the meter is running, we can stop and go all night."

"Got it," Elizabeth said tersely. She opened her purse and downed two of the miniatures, then realized the cab had pulled to the curb.

"Why are you stopping?" Elizabeth screamed.

"No drinking in my cab. Please leave. I'm Muslim."

"What? Are you fucking kidding me?"

"Please leave."

"Jesus Christ! Okay, I won't drink in your cab. See, look—there are no more left. Look in my purse if you like," Elizabeth pleaded, holding her opened purse up to the barrier.

"No drinking," the cabbie warned as he pulled away from the curb.

Elizabeth purchased the last two copies of *Lead Us Not Into Temptation* and settled back into the cab. She wondered whether she dared ask the Muslim driver to stop at Big Ben's Liquor store at the corner of North Capitol Street and New York Avenue.

"I'm sorry I offended you. I didn't know you were Muslim."

The cabbie simply nodded his head.

"Do you know Big Ben's on North Capitol Street?" she ventured.

"I know it."

"Would it be okay if I made a quick stop there? I understand no drinking in your cab."

After a long pause, the cabbie finally answered. "We can stop."

Elizabeth reached into the bag and removed one of the copies. Squinting her eyes behind her sunglasses, she rubbed her hand over the soft texture of the dust jacket. Her pulse quickened as she mouthed the words of the subtitle: Catholic Priests and the Sexual Abuse of Children. That said it all. As her grandmother Anna used to say to her when she was a little girl, it was the "nut in the nutshell." What Elizabeth was not prepared for was the description of the scandal on the back of the dust cover. The bluntness of the bullet points appealed to her as a lawyer, but the substance of those bullet points enraged her.

Over the last ten years, more than four hundred priests had been reported to the authorities for sexually assaulting children. Mostly boys, she read. *But why the fuck did that matter?* she brooded. Her small hands on the vestment mirror were all she could see behind her sunglasses. Thousands of affected children, "often struggling with alcoholism, drug addiction, molestation of others and suicide… a billion dollars in payouts by century's end."

"How is this even possible?" she asked herself in a soft voice. She sunk into the seat, cradling her head in both hands. "Can you fucking stand it? There's a book on this fucking shit," Elizabeth muttered.

The cabbie interrupted her thoughts. "We're here, but I can't stop at the corner. Big Ben is right behind you. Don't forget the meter is running."

Elizabeth reached for her purse but hesitated getting out of the cab. A battle raged in her mind between the enveloping darkness and the embarrassment she was feeling by her public lust for alcohol, intensified by the obvious disgust coming from the front seat.

"I'll be right back," Elizabeth said, giving in to the familiar habit.

It was nearly noon the next day when Elizabeth was roused by the sound of doors opening and closing and the muffled voices of the maids doing their floor rounds. An entire legal pad of notes, along with a marked-up copy of Jason Berry's book, was still perched on her stomach. Her hair was matted against her head and her running clothes felt moist against her body.

She looked for her Valium on the bedside table but saw only an unopened bottle of vodka and an empty glass. Groggy, she reached for the legal pad and rifled through the pages to see if it was her own handwriting. Elizabeth inhaled sharply through her nose as the distinct feeling of being chased crowded her psyche. She flung herself out of bed. She had no idea what had happened and needed to get out on the street and run this new darkness to the ground. She opened the bottle of vodka on the table, took a long pull and left.

Instead of heading toward the Capitol, she ran toward the Lincoln Memorial. She passed the west lawn of the White House and continued up Constitution Avenue to the Vietnam Memorial. As Elizabeth increased her pace, she realized that Blaine was right. Berry's book was a roadmap. But now her brain was at war, waging a battle between fear and self-loathing on one side and intellect and anger on the other.

She slapped the top of her head to halt the onslaught of emotion, using a technique her marathon coach had taught her. Elizabeth focused on an image of a cylinder of white, semi-transparent fluid drilling through the top of her skull, releasing a river of energy to her entire body. As she ran, she lowered her arms out straight and let the white light cascade into her entire body and out her fingertips. Feeling a rush of clarity, Elizabeth began to process what filled an entire legal pad from the night before.

YOU REALLY LOOK GREAT

Elizabeth reached into her purse and ran her fingers over the cover of Jason Berry's book as she exited her cab in front 1915 K Street in northwest Washington. The last time she had visited Tiberio's was when she was courting the CEO of Calpana, after a tech journal posted a note that Calpana was an attractive takeover target for Cisco. Whether or not the uniformed doorman actually recognized her, Elizabeth felt good that he acted as if he had. She spotted Francis seated at the small bar sipping a Campari and soda.

Elizabeth squeezed through the crowded bar to stand directly behind her brother. In a voice loud enough for the patron next to him to hear, Elizabeth announced herself.

"You going to be my date tonight, you handsome devil?"

Francis turned around, his face flushed with embarrassment. He smiled and hugged his sister. "Did you think you were going to catch me in my clerics?" Francis mused.

"Actually I did, Frannie, and you spoiled it," Elizabeth laughed. "Look at you. You really look great in that suit."

The dining room, a favorite haunt for all of Washington's power brokers, was a long room with a four and six-top center section framed by a long line of two and four-tops along each exterior wall. Each table was adorned with a small silver vase of pink roses. The taupe draped walls and carpeted floors trapped much of the serving noise, forcing conversations to occur in low and muted tones. Indirect lighting set the mood for a serene culinary experience, facilitating the work of lobbyists, influence peddlers, lawyers and politicians. Much of the country's political and economic business was transacted over Barolo and the signature Vitello Tiberio, a cholesterol-laden dish of veal scallops, prosciutto, mushrooms, and black truffles glazed in a light cream sauce.

"So, Frannie, you've never been here?" Elizabeth asked as the dining room captain settled them into their table and handed them wine and food menus.

Elizabeth wanted the night to be special. She ordered two vintage bottles of Brunello reserve from the Poggio-Rubino winery in Montelcino.

"Liz, have you looked at the prices on that wine?" Francis asked, wide-eyed. "Those two bottles are more than my monthly stipend as a Music Director."

"Frannie, this is my treat. Besides, I told you I wanted to apologize to you for being such a shit over the years. So, tell me, what have you been up to?"

Francis relaxed into his chair. "You know, not much—parish work. It's a big parish. The pastor is not, how would you say, a workaholic, so a lot falls on to me. I still do music direction and programs at the Shrine along with a couple of Catholic high schools, so I'm really busy. I did a Sacred Music chamber recital at St. Patrick's in New York last July, which I invited you to and never even heard back…"

"I know, I feel really bad about that," Elizabeth said.

"You should, Liz. That really hurt my feelings. Momma kept making excuses for you, but it stung. It just seems like when Poppa died so did our relationship."

"I don't think that's true," Elizabeth protested. "I admit it was different, but I don't think it died. Jesus, Frannie, don't you think that's a little overstated? I mean, you're here, you didn't stand me up for dinner."

"Of course I didn't stand you up for dinner, Liz. I've missed you. I'm pissed off at you, but I've missed you."

"That's kinda why I wanted to see you. For the last twenty-five years I've been in a rat race, and so far the rats are winning. It's just been one big black hole of shit."

"What are you talking about, Liz? You're beautiful. From everything I hear, you've been phenomenally successful. You have a big place in New York, you clerked at the Supreme Court. I mean, what are you talking about?"

"I've done some things I'm not very proud of, Frannie. I feel like I've been running away from my roots all my life. Ever since Poppa died."

Francis felt a nervous pit in his stomach forming as he sipped from a glass of water on the table.

Fortunately for Francis, they were interrupted by the wine service. The sommelier presented the reserve bottle to Francis to taste as the hair on the back of Elizabeth's neck stood on end.

"No, let the wine connoisseur taste, please," Francis said, motioning toward Elizabeth.

"My apologies, Signora," the steward said, trying to deflect Elizabeth's indignant stare.

Elizabeth swirled then tasted the aromatics in the tiny portion, noting the long legs in the glass. "It's fine," she announced crisply.

"Here's to tonight, Francis," Elizabeth said, raising her glass. I sincerely hope you accept my apology."

With that, the waiter appeared. "May I get you something to start with?"

"Yes, you can," Elizabeth said. "Frannie, you still like ravioli?"

"How do you stop liking ravioli?" Francis asked, mocking his sister.

Elizabeth arched her eyebrows from across the table. She ordered two orders of the fresh spinach stuffed agnolotti and said, "We'll split an order of prosciutto and melon as a second course. I know I want the Veal Tiberio for my main course. Frannie, do you know what you want?"

"Yes, I'll have the Dover Sole."

"Excellent," replied the waiter.

"And a few minutes between second course and entrées," said Elizabeth, handing the menus back to the waiter.

"My pleasure, Signora."

Francis touched his glass to hers. "There's no need to apologize to me, Liz. We each more or less charted our own way. I'd say we did the best we could."

"Maybe for you, but for me I'm not so sure," Elizabeth said. "So, what's going on with Momma and Bishop Ryan?"

Francis took a deep breath, surprised by the pole vault in conversation. "Well, they've known each other forever, actually before Poppa passed as I recall. I know they're friends. Momma has shared with me what a wonderful man he is. They discuss the influence of Aristotelian philosophy on the writings of Thomas Aquinas."

"Oh, my God, I want to puke. The writing of Thomas Aquinas and Aristotelian philosophy," Elizabeth repeated in disgust.

"I think he goes to the house quite frequently," Francis continued.

"I asked Aunt Rose about it, and she clammed up and said I'd need to ask Momma," Elizabeth recounted.

"So, did you ask Momma?" Francis asked.

"Well, sort of. She bit my head off when I raised the issue, but it was all in the same pot that I quit my job, am a fallen Catholic and was thinking about enrolling in Canon Law School. There was a lot of yelling."

"Canon Law School, what the hell for?" Francis asked, trying to act surprised.

"Forty–eight hours ago I had the notion that I might have something to contribute to the survivor movement to help stop this insanity with abusive priests. But then I read something that really changed my mind. I'll get to that in a minute. Do you think Momma's sleeping with Ryan?"

"Elizabeth, keep your voice down. I have no idea. Christ, you're talking about our mother."

"Yeah, and what do you think Poppa would think about Momma spending all this time with a priest?"

"Liz, I just can't go there. Momma's an old woman…"

"She's only seventy-two, Frannie, and she still looks great. I hope to hell that I look that good in my early seventies," Elizabeth said as she took a quick glance at the age spots starting to show on her hands.

"Poppa has been dead for decades. Whatever they may or may not be doing when they're together is their business."

"That's bullshit, Francis. Momma's still a good catch and I think Ryan's taking advantage of her. You think these guys want to eat rectory oatmeal the rest of their lives and not be in the company of women? Momma's a great cook, she's still a beautiful woman, and she's a true believer."

"And you aren't," Francis noted.

"No, I'm not. Strike that. I don't know what I believe in. I do know when a man is sucking up trying to get a woman's pants down," Elizabeth said, gritting her teeth. "He's supposed to be celibate."

"I can't believe we're having this discussion. Is this what you wanted to talk to me about?" Francis demanded.

"Actually, no, but it's been on my mind, and I wanted to ask."

"So, let's drop it, shall we," Francis said.

"Fine. We'll drop it… for now," Elizabeth said, signaling that it was far from a closed topic.

"So, do you like the agnolotti?" Elizabeth asked, changing the subject.

Francis was wilted by the exchange and momentarily closed his eyes.

"I'm sorry I upset you," Elizabeth offered.

"I'm fine, Liz, and yes the agnolotti are spectacular with the parmesan and cream sauce. It just feels like I'm inside a tornado when I'm talking to you."

"Do you remember Catania's bakery?"

"Sure," Francis said hoping for a respite in the conversation. "Momma would go down there every week for bread and bullshit. Boy, that brings back some memories," Francis said, shifting position in his seat to get his bearings.

"They provide the bread here," Elizabeth said matter-of-factly.

"How do you know that?" Francis asked.

"One of the waiters told me the last time I was here. I just happened to remember it. That's kinda what I wanted to talk to you about. I've been having these memories."

"What kind of memories? You mean about the bread, Liz?" Francis asked, trying to keep his tone level.

"Don't be a smart-ass, Frannie. Not about the bread but about that same time period," Elizabeth said, smiling.

"I know, I was breaking your stones."

"Like you always do, Francis Natale. No, seriously. Do you remember Father Dolan?" Elizabeth asked.

Francis put his fork down and looked directly at his sister. "Liz, c'mon, why are you asking me that? How could I forget that asshole? He was my piano teacher for three years. You know that. He was also the biggest prick I ever met."

"Wow. I wasn't expecting that."

"Why, because I'm a priest? Liz..."

"No, because I thought you liked him. Wasn't he why you went into the priesthood?" Elizabeth chided Francis.

"No, it wasn't. We all have our demons, Liz. I'm no different. I'm a priest. I'm not a saint, contrary to what our mother may think. I called him a prick because of the way he treated me. Nothing was ever quite good enough for him. And for the record, as you lawyers say, I handle things differently than you. You escape by running; my escape is music. No one on this planet can take that from me," Francis said in a tone that bordered on defiance.

Elizabeth was genuinely surprised. "Gee, I thought he was kind of a mentor to you.

"I hated him," Francis said sternly.

"Is he still a priest?" Elizabeth persisted.

"Have no idea. I lost track of him after high school," Francis said, reaching for his water. He took a long drink, trying to settle his nerves.

"How can you find out if he's still a priest?" Elizabeth persisted.

"Liz, what's with all these questions about Dolan? What's going on?" Francis asked.

Elizabeth took a sip of wine and reached for her purse underneath their table. She handed Jason Berry's book to Francis. Francis looked down at the cover. The gold-colored subtitle announcing the scandal triggered a rush of adrenaline in Francis. He turned to the back cover and read for nearly a full minute, focusing on a quote by Father Andrew M. Greeley: "Jason Berry has uncovered what may be the greatest scandal in the history of religion in America and perhaps the most serious crisis Catholicism has faced since the Reformation."

Finally, Francis looked up and met his sister's eyes.

"Are you saying that Dolan…"

"Yes, you're the first person I've told and put a name to it."

"Shit, Liz, I don't know what to say. I mean I feel awful that happened to you."

"Do you know if Poppa knew?" Elizabeth asked.

"Knew what? That this happened to you? Why would Poppa know if I was the first person you ever told?" Francis countered as a knot formed in his chest.

"I remember hearing the adults talking, I think I heard something from you about telling Poppa about going to seminary or something like that. Poppa got really mad and then you two went to see Monsignor Ryan and then he died."

"That's what happened, Liz. I know you still blame me for Poppa dying," Francis said defensively.

"Don't be an idiot, Frannie. Poppa died because of a spontaneous coronary artery dissection. It could have happened at the Shrine when he was carving stone or at the dinner table."

Furious, Francis dug his thumb into his fist. "Well, it didn't happen at the dinner table or at the Shrine. It happened when I was with him at St. Francis' rectory, and he was mad as a hornet. And how the hell do you know what Poppa died from?"

"Because I forged Momma's name on a release and requested the autopsy report from the hospital on my firm letterhead. That's how. I'm just thinking that somehow Momma found out about Dolan and told Poppa."

"That's absurd. She would have raised holy hell. Why don't you ask her, Liz, if you truly think she may have known," Francis said, no longer worried about the possibility of a public argument with his sister.

"Really, Francis? Did you really ask me that question, Momma being the way she is about the Church? I'm just convinced she somehow knew, and she was embarrassed to let anyone find out."

"Liz, I'm confused. You told me this why? You want me to report him?"

"No, goddammit, I'm more than capable of reporting him if that's what I choose to do. Besides, I think there were other girls in my class that he did this to."

"Do you know that for a fact?"

"No, Francis, I don't know for a fact, because I never asked them. But looking back, I have a strong suspicion. Did you read the back of the book? Over four hundred priests reported, a billion dollars in damages and a cover-up by the bishops of this entire shitstorm. So, I don't know exactly everything about Dolan. But I know what I just read.

With a blank expression, Francis feigned ignorance. "Elizabeth, what the hell are you talking about?" Francis asked.

"Listen to me, Frannie, there's another part to this. I met Barbara Blaine on the street during a protest in front of the Cardinal's residence in New York City."

"Who in the hell is Barbara Blaine?" Francis sputtered.

"She formed the Survivors Network of those Abused by Priests. She told me about a priest named Thomas Atkinson who blew the whistle on all of this. I'm telling you it's Tommy Atkinson, the boy I was asking you about when I talked to you on the phone the other day. Father Thomas Patrick Atkinson. He worked at the Vatican Embassy for some Cardinal and saw all the complaints going over to Rome, so he started talking to lawyers and anyone else who would listen. That's our Tommy from Gonzaga, I know it! Barbara Blaine gave me his telephone number. Tomorrow, if I still have the courage, I'm going to call him and ask."

"Good Lord, Elizabeth, you were protesting in front of the Cardinal's residence in New York?" Francis asked, shocked at the thought.

"I didn't join the protest, but I watched it from across the street and that's how I met Barbara. And what if I did join the protest? Do you have a problem with that, Frannie?" Elizabeth said with a marked edge in her voice.

"Jesus, Liz, if what happened to you is true…"

Elizabeth leaned in across the table. "What the fuck is that supposed to mean?" she whispered through her clenched teeth. "There's no goddamn *if* here, Francis. This did happen to me, and it happened more times than I would like to remember," Elizabeth said on the verge of tears.

"Take a breath, Liz, that's not what I meant at all. I don't doubt for a second that what you just told me is true," Francis said as the floor captain and the table waiter suddenly appeared at the table. In perfect synchrony, they theatrically removed the silver cloches to reveal the Dover Sole and the Veal Tiberio.

"Thank you. It looks delicious," Francis said, hoping the arrival of their dinners would momentarily distract Elizabeth.

"Will there be anything else, Signor, Signora?" the captain asked professionally, ignoring the obvious tension at the table.

"Nope. It all looks excellent," Elizabeth stammered, her face now a crimson red.

"*Bene. Buon appetito,*" the captain said, taking his leave.

"You okay?" Francis asked.

"I'm fine, Francis," Elizabeth snapped, taking a sip of wine and dabbing at the corner of her eyes with her napkin.

"What I meant was that if this happened, which I believe it did, then you'll have more credibility with the Church if you don't associate yourself with this Atkinson fellow or the SNAP people. They're not well liked."

"By whom?" Elizabeth fumed. "By the asshole bishops that let this happen?"

"It's more complicated than that," Francis protested.

"No, this scandal is not complicated at all. I'll tell you what's complicated: me. That's what's complicated, Frannie," Elizabeth said as she slammed the butt of her knife onto the table. "I'm forty-six years old. I'm not married, never even close to being married, I'm too old to have any kids, I drink too much, take too many sedatives, and I can't cope with these fucking flashbacks; they force me to run myself to exhaustion so I literally won't kill myself. I'm unemployed, but basically, I was fired. Plus, there's other shit that I'm absolutely not going to talk about with my brother, but I can assure you it's off the charts ugly. Then I read this crap has been going on for decades,

311

maybe centuries for Christ sakes. You say this scandal is complicated, I say that's bullshit. What happened to me, and probably thousands of kids like me, that's what's complicated, Francis."

"Liz, what do you want from me? I mean really, what can I do to help you?" Francis asked, trying to calm the situation.

"Promise me you'll read Jason Berry's book and answer this question."

"I'll read the book, I promise. What's the question?"

"Do you believe me?" Elizabeth whispered.

"Of course I do, Liz, and the fact that it was a brother priest makes it even worse."

"Don't call Dolan a brother priest, Francis. He's a sexual predator."

"You're right, Liz. Dolan and the predators like him high-jacked the priesthood."

"Well, maybe they high-jacked the priesthood, but the bishops high-jacked a religion and the lives of thousands of kids. You need to think about that," Elizabeth said.

"When will I see you next, Liz, now that you're in D.C?"

"I should be settled in my apartment in a week or so. I'll call you and we can meet somewhere, or maybe you can come over to my apartment. It's up by the zoo on Harvard Street."

"That's close to my parish. Maybe next time pizza."

"You didn't like it here?" asked Elizabeth.

"I loved it here. It's just I have a hard time sitting down to a meal that costs more than I make in a month."

"I get it. Next time, beer and pizza."

"Listen, Liz, whatever you decide to do about this, I'll support you. But if you decide to go to the Church, call me first. I'll give you some tips to get your message across so that it's heard. I want to leave you with one thing. I don't believe for a second that Momma knew, not one second. She loved you then and loves you now."

"I wish I could believe that." Elizabeth hesitated for several seconds and started to speak but stopped.

"What were you going to say?" Francis asked.

"What I was going to say is that I'd like to get a gun and put a bullet in Dolan's skull and splatter his brains on a wall."

Francis looked across the table in shock. "Elizabeth, stop it. I mean it, just stop it."

Seeing that she had crossed a line, Elizabeth backtracked. "I was just kidding, Frannie, relax. C'mon, forget I said it. Do you want to share a dessert? The profiteroles are fabulous with the chocolate sauce. I'm done talking about that asshole Dolan."

"Notwithstanding the topics, I'm glad we got together. I do accept your apology," Francis said, looking into Elizabeth's eyes.

"And I'm sorry I upset you, Frannie. I really am. But I've started on this journey, and I have to finish. I have to find out what's next for me. I want my sanity back. I do love you, more than you know," Elizabeth said, tears rimming her eyes. "Do you believe me, Frannie?"

"I do, Liz, and I love you too."

Francis' mind raced ahead, knowing that Ryan would be expecting an update on the discussion with Elizabeth. At some level, he wished Ryan could have heard the entire conversation. If so, he would have realized that "handling" Elizabeth was a laughable proposition.

MAYBE WE SHOULD START OVER
The morning broke to a beautiful day in Washington. Free from the grip of humidity, a light northerly breeze inspired Elizabeth to throw open the drapes and crack both windows in her corner suite.

Elizabeth nursed the remaining half bottle of vodka and stared out the window from her corner perch as she replayed her dinner conversation with Francis. She looked down and marveled at the firmness of purpose displayed by the National Park Service landscaping team, which kept the sunken contours of Pershing Park meticulously groomed and swept clean. After repeatedly dialing six of the seven digits of Lucy's phone number and hanging up, Elizabeth let the call connect. Putting her glass down and sitting up straight in her chair, she waited for her mother to answer the phone.

"Hello, Momma, it's Elizabeth. How are you?" Elizabeth asked.

"I'm well," Lucy answered in a measured tone. "Where are you, Elizabeth?" Lucy asked.

"I'm still at the Willard. Momma, I called to apologize for the other night. I was way out of line, and I was upset about how I left New York. I shouldn't have raised my voice to you. I wanted to call you and say I was sorry."

"Maybe we should start over, Liz. You should come over for dinner. Have you found an apartment yet?"

"Actually, Momma, I just got word that my application was accepted. So, I'll be able to get my stuff from New York and move in next week."

"So, do you want to stay here for the week?" Lucy asked, hoping to spend some time with her daughter and find out why she was so angry.

"Actually, Momma, I have a job interview with a law firm here in D.C., but the hiring partner is in Chicago so I'm going out there tomorrow or the next day. I'll be back by the weekend, but if you don't mind, I'd like to crash in my old room tonight if you still have a bed in there."

"Liz, your room's just the way you left it."

"Really," Elizabeth said, shocked. "Momma, I've been gone from the house since before law school."

"I know, but after Poppa died and you and Frannie left, I was alone in the house. So, I would sleep in your room some nights, then in Frannie's room, and I would feel better."

"What about Aunt Rose?" Elizabeth said. "She was there with you."

"Aunt Rose!" Lucy screeched. "She's in her own world; I never know when she's coming or going. All she does is work and when she's not working, she goes out with her friends. That's it. When are you leaving the hotel?" Lucy asked.

"I can check out anytime."

"I have to go to Catania's. That's close to your hotel, so why don't you meet me there? We'll get our bread, have some coffee and visit with Gianna, and then come home."

"Who's Gianna?" Elizabeth asked.

"Do you remember the Formica's, Alonzo and Connie?" Lucy asked.

"Of course."

"Gianna's their granddaughter. She went to the Culinary Institute in New York and came back to run the bakery. She's done a great job expanding. They're selling all kinds of sweet pastries now, but she still makes Alonzo's bread just like in the old days. Let's say we meet there in an hour."

"That sounds great, Momma. I'll see you in an hour." Waves of anger, shame and self-loathing washed over Elizabeth as she hung up the phone. Very little of what she discussed with Lucy was sincere or even true. She was going to spend the night on Shepherd Street for one reason and one reason only.

LOOKS LIKE WE HAVE A NEW BOSS

Francis surveyed the meager breakfast buffet the rectory cooks had prepared for the priests. His Pastor, who typically ignored Francis, looked up from reading the Catholic Standard in the dining room and greeted him warmly.

"Looks like we have a new boss, Francis."

"Really? How do you mean, Monsignor?"

"Seems like the Roman Curia have been up late. They announced that Archbishop McIntyre will be made a Cardinal for St. Louis. And our Holy Father has tapped Bishop Cletus Ryan as the next Archbishop of Washington, D.C."

"You're serious?" Francis asked, dumbfounded.

"Why are you so surprised, Father Natale?" the Monsignor said indignantly. "Ryan has been our auxiliary bishop for several years. In my opinion he's a good choice."

"I'm of course happy for him, it's just a shock that someone I've known since I was a boy is now a sitting archbishop," stammered Francis. "I suspect after a few years he'll be a newly minted prince of the Church who will actually cast a ballot in the next Papal election. That's just amazing to me."

"Do you have any idea why he would be calling you?" the Monsignor said tersely.

"Who called me, Monsignor?" Francis asked, confused.

"Our new archbishop. There's a message from last night in your box."

"I have no idea. Excuse me, Monsignor, I suspect I should return our new archbishop's call at once."

"If it's anything to do with our parish, please let me know."

"Of course, Monsignor." Francis turned and trudged back up to his room.

Before he got to the second-floor landing, Mrs. Howard called out to him. "Father, our new archbishop is on the phone. He said he would like to discuss some music selections for his installation."

"Of course he did," Francis huffed to himself. *The asshole even has cover stories for the parish secretaries.* "I'll take it in my room. Thank you, Mrs. Howard." Francis took a deep breath, turned his pocket recorder on and picked up the receiver. "Good morning, Bishop. Or should I say good morning, Your Excellency," Francis said in a solemn voice.

"Thank you, Father. I haven't knocked on the door of the Cathedral yet, a traditional part of an archbishop's investiture, so 'Your Excellency' is a bit premature, but thank you for bringing it up."

"Well, my sincerest congratulations, Bishop, I wish you well."

"Thank you again. My call is of course about your meeting with your sister. It seems we have a bit of a problem on our hands. I suspect that Cardinal Hurley of New York will want to speak to us both."

"What problem, Bishop?"

"Well, there have been some more incidents in New York and we thought Dolan was on ice in treatment in Canada. We figured he could stay there for six months and get a good recommendation."

Francis allowed his anger to seep into his voice. "You mean the bastard is still at it!"

"Apparently," Ryan said, not reacting to Francis. "He got a furlough without notice to anyone for a Boys Choir performance in Brooklyn and managed to get his dumb ass arrested with two choir members in a rental car. The problem is, he got caught giving the kid oral sex in the car by a beat cop. The kid's friend was in the back seat and of course the parents are involved. There's a chance that Bishop Warner in Brooklyn may be able to handle this if the parents drop the charges. The prosecutor will have to go along but with the right inducements I think it can get handled. But it would be helpful if I could brief him on your sister."

"Inducements, what do mean by inducements, Bishop?"

"Listen, neither the cops nor the prosecutors want to deal with our dirty laundry. That's a fact. Dolan was never a priest in Brooklyn; he was there pretty much on a lark. Brooklyn didn't know about it and the Archdiocese of New York thought he was in treatment in Canada. So, if we assure the authorities that he'll stay out of the City, and the parents go along with it, we may be able to dodge the bullet."

"Why would the parents and law enforcement go along with that, Bishop?"

"Excuse me, Father, what did you say?"

"Why would they go along? I mean it just seems…"

"Because they're goddamn good Catholics, Father Natale, that's why!" Ryan screamed into the phone. "Did your father run to the police? No, he came to me!" Ryan said, furious at the question. "Now, today at a time of your choosing I want you to come to my residence. If anyone asks, it's to discuss my investiture at the Cathedral. I want a full brief on last night's dinner in person. I made some discrete inquiries about your sister, and it appears she has quite a reputation in the legal community as a ball breaker."

"You have no idea, Bishop."

"What do you mean by that, Father Natale?"

"What I mean, Bishop, is when she locks her mind on something she's relentless. At the moment I'd say she's locked onto Dolan and the bishops she read about in Jason Berry's book *Lead Us Not Into Temptation*. Have you read it, Bishop?" Francis asked.

"Should I?" Ryan asked, his curiosity piqued.

"I would if I were you, Bishop. Elizabeth certainly has, she's already been in contact with the founder of SNAP, Barbara Blaine, and got Atkinson's number from her. I know you expected me to 'kill it,' but any thought that my sister was going to back off and go back to practicing law in New York City is a pipe dream."

"Shit," Ryan said, settling into his chair to absorb the information. "Can you be here within the hour?"

"I can, Bishop." Francis clicked off the recorder and removed the tape.

THERE ARE THREE BOXES MARKED "JOSEPH"

"Do you know Catania's Bakery on North Capitol?" Elizabeth asked, sliding into the back seat of her cab.

"I sure do, ma'am. That where we headed?"

"Yes."

Elizabeth sat in the back of the cab, sinking into the darkness. Everything was moving forward as planned, but she felt little relief from the constant flashbacks of the abuse and what she had become. Her conversation with her mother had only added to that self-loathing. *How do you make nice with a parent that abandoned you to the Church?* she wondered. She knew what the issues were; you can never go back and reclaim what was lost. *So, why call Sol Reich?* she reasoned. There was no measure of healing for her, but she could exact her revenge.

"Now ma'am, this isn't the best neighborhood, you sure you're okay with that big suitcase and all?"

"I'll be fine. Thank you."

Lucy saw Elizabeth struggling with her suitcase on the sidewalk outside Catania's and went out to help.

"Oh, hey, Momma, let me get this beast inside so I can give you a proper hug."

"Maybe we'll take a cab home. I don't think we could lift that suitcase onto the bus," Lucy laughed.

"There," Elizabeth said, pushing her suitcase behind the front door.

"Don't worry, Gianna, Liz isn't moving in."

"We can use all the help we can get, Lucy. You must be Elizabeth. I'm Gianna Formica. Your mother talks about you constantly. I'm so happy we finally meet."

"Does she now," Elizabeth said with a wry smile.

"Come sit. I'll get some coffee and I just filled some cannoli. Lucy, you want a cannoli?" Gianna asked.

"Sure, let me pick out the loaves I want, and I'll be right over."

In the span of fifteen minutes, the three women covered the gamut of the state of food in the District's restaurants, Newt

Gingrich's Contract with America and the parish's upcoming Christmas bizarre. It was a distraction for Elizabeth that temporarily eased the pain, but it did not last for long.

"We should go, Liz. I want to help Mom with dinner. She's really slowed down but she's insisting that she cook for you, but Gio needs her to be around. He has dementia. I think it's Alzheimer's so it's not a happy place. I told her he belongs in a home, but Anna won't even consider it. She told me as long as she can take care of him, he stays in his house. He takes his meals with just your grandmother so she's fretting about not having dinner with you. Would you mind sitting with him after dinner? All he does is listen to music, but Anna would love it if you spent a bit of time with him."

"Of course, Momma. I'd like that. Let me call a cab."

"No, no, no," Gianna interrupted. "One of the guys will give you a lift. Mario, get my car out front and load that big suitcase in the back, and put it in the house where Lucy tells you."

"That's so sweet," Elizabeth said hugging Gianna. "You take care and don't be a stranger."

"I'll be back, for sure."

Anna started to cry when she saw Elizabeth walk in the front door. "So, what's with the tears, Grandmom?" Elizabeth said, embracing Anna.

"I'm just happy to see you. Tonight, we have a beautiful dinner just the four of us. I'll sit with Gio when he has his dinner and then I'll come over and we can catch up. Is that okay with you, Lizzie?" Anna asked.

"Of course, Grandmom."

"Rose is coming home early from work, so we'll be all together."

"When I see her walk through the door then I'll believe it, Mom," Lucy hollered from the kitchen.

"Momma, do you still have the old photo albums that Poppa and I used to go through with all the pictures from the old country?" Elizabeth asked.

"Of course I do, but they were hard for me to look at after he was gone. So, I put them with the rest of his things upstairs in the attic."

"What are you going to do with it all?" Elizabeth asked.

Lucy looked surprised. "Well, nothing, Liz. They're just there. I go up sometimes and just sit and think about him and what a pain in ass he must be in heaven."

"You really believe that's where Poppa is, don't you, Momma?"

"I do, Elizabeth. It's called faith. It's what I believe and how I was raised."

"I was wondering, do you think I could take one or two of the albums for my new apartment?"

"Sure you can. When you get to top of the stairs in the attic, there are three boxes marked 'Joseph.' They're in one of those boxes. Dinner's in about forty minutes so be down in time to set the table."

"I can do that, Momma."

Nervous tension gripped Elizabeth's body as she climbed the steps to her room. She was startled that the house smelled the same as what she remembered. The plastic Jesus was still standing in the cup holder as her mind replayed that awful afternoon when she sat on the toilet. She was forced back in time to a period that she never wanted to relive but here it was, right in her face. She grabbed a sweater from her suitcase and headed upstairs to the attic.

The large boxes were exactly where Lucy said they would be. There was a footstool next to the boxes. On top of the stool was a half a pack of cigarettes and a book of matches next to her father's tin ashtray that she remembered was always on the back porch. Next to her father's name, Lucy had drawn a tiny red heart. Elizabeth felt ashamed that she had questioned her mother about Bishop Ryan. She opened the first box and started to shake. Reaching in, Elizabeth removed several shirts and held them up to her face. The smell of Old Spice still clung to the checkered wool work shirt that she remembered was one of his favorites.

She carefully opened each box. There was a fine layer of stone dust on several pairs of work pants and Joseph's tool apron from his last days at work. Shoes, a canvas belt, bandanas, and underwear were neatly arranged as if they would be used the next day. The other two boxes held the rest of the tangible evidence of her father's life: pictures, notebooks, some small tools, newspaper clippings of the Shrine dedication and all his winter work clothes and coats. Elizabeth ran her hands over each item, cementing in her brain a tactile connection to her father. At the bottom of the third box, wrapped in a felt cloth inside a manila envelope, was the item she had come for.

Elizabeth remembered the day that she found her father's gun. She had been looking for loose change to take to the corner store for candy and when she opened his nightstand, there it was. She opened the folder and gently wrapped her hand around the small pistol. Elizabeth made a mental note of the engraving on the barrel. It was a Smith & Wesson Model 10 handgun. She ran her fingers over the worn wood grip and fumbled with the thumb latch until it released the cylinder. She removed the six bullets and wrapped the two-inch snub-nosed revolver up in her sweater. Closing the boxes, she carefully repacked everything as she found it and went to the landing to listen for anyone on the second floor.

Back in her old room, Elizabeth hid the revolver and bullets in the bottom of her suitcase. She would get the gun out of the house in the morning.

DO YOU REMEMBER WHEN YOU GAVE THIS TO ME?
"Bowls or plates, Momma?" Elizabeth asked as she started to remove tableware from the cupboard in the dining room.

"We'll use both tonight. Did you find the album?" Lucy asked from the kitchen.

"I did. The one I wanted to put in my apartment has the pictures of Poppa and me when he took us for the pony rides and all the pictures of him as a boy in Italy with Grandpop. Where was that, Momma?" Elizabeth asked.

"Italy or the pony rides?" Lucy asked.

"Both," said Elizabeth.

"Well, the pony rides were at a stable just off New York Avenue at Bladensburg Road, but now it's a hotel on a big four lane highway. The pictures from Italy were all taken in Viggiu where Poppa was from."

"Also, there was a framed picture of me and Poppa with the bishop by the steps of the Crypt Church. If it's okay, I wanted to take that as well."

"Absolutely, your father always liked that picture."

"And a shirt, Momma. I took one of Poppa's shirts. It still smelled like him," Elizabeth said, her voice shaking with emotion.

Hearing Elizabeth was upset, Lucy rushed out of the kitchen, went to Elizabeth and hugged her.

"We all miss him, Liz. Every day I miss him. No one knows this but I still sleep with his pajama top. I never washed it."

For a few moments Elizabeth's body shook under Lucy's embrace.

"Go wash your face and I'll finish the table."

"Okay, Elizabeth said, "I'm going next door to see Grandpop. Do you think he has finished his dinner?"

"I'm sure he has. Anna took it over a bit ago."

Elizabeth looked at her watch. "Okay, I'm going to go sit with him for a little and I'll be back for dinner."

"Honey, don't be upset if he doesn't recognize you," Lucy said, concerned that seeing him would be a shock.

"I'll be fine, Momma." Elizabeth slid over the bannister between the two front porches and went in the front door.

"Lizzie, I'm glad you came over, he's all finished with his dinner," Anna said, kissing her. I'll be next door with your Momma.

When you're ready to leave call me. I'll get him settled and then we'll have dinner. Just like the old times."

Elizabeth entered the living room and stood behind Giovanni, watching him sway slightly to music. Bending over the top of his chair, she kissed him on the head. "How are you, Grandpop? It's Lizzie," she said.

"Lizzie, you home from school early. How was your day? Did you learn something?"

Elizabeth was shocked to hear her grandfather use her name. "I had a good day, Grandpop. That music's so pretty, what is it?" Elizabeth asked.

"Francisco know the name. He'll play for me after dinner."

"Does he play every night?" Elizabeth asked.

"Every night. You want to sit with me when he plays?"

"That would be fun, Grandpop," Elizabeth said as she knelt down in front of him to grasp his hand."

"See, it's me, Grandpop. It's Elizabeth... Lizzie. I'm all grown up."

Giovanni looked confused but not upset.

"I want to show you something," Elizabeth said, taking the boss stone she had carried for thirty years from her pocket and putting it in Giovanni's hand. "Do you remember when you gave this to me on the scaffold?" Elizabeth asked.

Giovanni held the stone for several minutes, turning it over and over in the palm of his hand.

"Do you remember giving this to me, Grandpop?"

"Can you change the record when you leave?" Gio said. "And ask Lizzie to come sit with me. She lost her stone and I give it back. I have to get ready to meet Poppa at the quarry, we work the violino tomorrow."

"Where's the quarry?" Elizabeth asked.

"Ah," Giovanni said laughing, "You try to trick me. It's right at the end of the street next to Poppa's house."

"Do you want me to give Elizabeth the stone?" Elizabeth asked.

Giovanni stared at the stone then placed it in Elizabeth's hand. "You a nice lady."

Elizabeth got up and kissed him on the cheek and started to the back porch.

"*Salut d'Amore*," Giovanni said.

"What did you say, Grandpop?" Elizabeth asked, surprised.

"*Salut d'Amore*. The lady ask me the name, it's *Salut d'Amore* by Elgar."

"Okay, Grandpop, I'll get the lady to change the music."

Elizabeth got to the back door as Anna returned with a dish of Gio's favorite fruit cookies. Elizabeth broke into tears.

"You okay?" Anna asked.

"It's hard, Grandmom, to see him like that, it's like he has bits and pieces but can't put it all together. But I have to say he does enjoy his music."

"It's hard. But what can you do, Liz? The good thing is at least now I don't think he realizes he only has bits and pieces of his memory. Francis brought all of his recordings over and he listens to them over and over. This is our life now, Lizzie. Tell your Momma I'll be there as soon as he gets his cookies down and he's settled."

Slinging her leg over the bannister between the houses, Elizabeth thought that the morning could not possibly come too soon. Finding Tom Atkinson was the only thing on her mind.

CHAPTER EIGHT

Running into The Darkness

BARBARA BLAINE GAVE ME YOUR NUMBER

Elizabeth pushed her canvas briefcase under the seat in front of her and stared out the window as United Flight 326 began its final descent into Seattle Tacoma International Airport. The familiar and comforting thump of the landing gear locking into place helped focus her mind.

The flight path for Runway 16 Left drew her gaze directly over the Rainer Golf and Country Club. The verdant, manicured fairways reminded her of how as a junior league player she had used golf to escape her madness. It was a game that did not supplant her ego to a team, a place where her darkness could be aggressively channeled into the singular nature of the sport without worry that her fury would somehow reveal her disgusting secrets.

Despite the irrational hue, a cross country trip to make a cold call to a man Elizabeth had not seen nor talked to for nearly thirty years seemed not at all cringeworthy. Upon reflection, her excursion seemed to be a perfectly rational response to her emerging feelings surrounding Andrew Dolan. Besides, who better to talk to than the man at the center of the Church's ugly cover-up?

Elizabeth believed, despite the passage of time, that she knew Father Thomas Aquinas Atkinson through his press clippings and interview transcripts Barbara Blaine had sent to her. That sweet caring teenager, who had been her first love, was now a warrior for the truth in a firestorm of political and moral scandal.

High stakes litigation suited Elizabeth's personality. But her professional judgement was clouded by the debilitating impact of childhood sexual abuse. The sting of Lucy mocking her desire to be a voice for the survivor movement served only to heighten Elizabeth's sense of self-doubt and abandonment by her mother. She was vulnerable and she knew it.

With her satchel of notes and yellow pads under her arm, Elizabeth grew impatient as she moved slowly up the jet-way with the rest of the passengers and into Concourse B of the Seattle-Tacoma International Airport. Grabbing a cup of coffee from a kiosk vendor, Elizabeth settled into a semi-private bank of pay phones away from the din of baggage claim and disembarking flights. Taking a deep breath, she punched in her AT&T credit card number and the number Barbara Blaine had given her. With her eyes shut tightly, Elizabeth coiled her torso and legs into a Gordian knot of tension, waiting for the call to connect.

With military precision, her call was picked up on the first ring. "Good afternoon, Base Chaplain's Office, Sergeant Porter speaking. How may I help you?"

"Good afternoon, Sergeant, this is Elizabeth Natale. I'm an old friend of Father Atkinson. By any chance is he available?" Elizabeth asked in a chatty tone. She pressed the receiver to her shoulder as she downed one of the miniature vodkas she had stockpiled from the plane.

"Hold on, ma'am, I'll check to see if he's available."

Her heart started to pound as she listened to the automated hold message detailing the base's religious schedule for the variety of faiths practiced at the sprawling facility.

On hearing the name of the caller, Atkinson immediately picked up the receiver.

"Is this Lizzie from Notre Dame Academy in D.C.?" Atkinson asked, ignoring the more formal etiquette reserved for an Air Force Captain.

The warmth of the still familiar voice slowed Elizabeth's shaking. She opened her eyes and placed her pen on her pad as a broad smile covered her face. Elizabeth straightened her body and sat taller in her stool. "It is," Elizabeth said in a cheeky tone as she fought to keep her composure. "I'm sorry to call you out of the blue, Tommy – oh excuse me – is it okay to call you Tommy," Elizabeth said, catching herself.

"Of course it is, Liz, the Air Force is kinda loose on stuff like that around here. So, how the hell are you?" Atkinson asked warmly.

Elizabeth hesitated, unsure as to how to open a conversation with a man she had not seen for decades. She took a deep breath and dove headlong into the conversation. "Barbara Blaine gave me your number and sent me to a bookstore to get a copy of Jason Berry's book," she blurted into the phone.

Tom Atkinson knew what that meant. Since he had been fired from his post as a Canon lawyer and secretary to Cardinal Pio Laghi, the Vatican ambassador in Washington, D.C., he had fielded hundreds of similar calls over the last eight years.

Atkinson picked up the cradle for the phone and walked around his small desk, closing the door behind him. "Holy shit, Liz, I wasn't expecting that," he said in a hushed tone. "Where are you, it sounds like you're at an airport."

"I am, and I'm sorry for all the noise," Elizabeth apologized, furious with herself for being so forward. She scrawled the word *asshole* on her notepad and underlined it. "I shouldn't have just put that out there on the phone, Tommy, I'm really sorry. After reading Jason Berry's book I just wanted to reach out and talk to you and I didn't know where to start," Elizabeth said, her voice cracking.

"No worries, Liz, really," Atkinson said, calming Elizabeth's impending sense of panic.

Atkinson had seen how quickly these calls could get out of hand and if he wasn't careful, he could easily be on the phone for hours.

"We need to talk, Liz, but you caught me literally getting ready to adios the State of Washington. I'm leaving tomorrow for the East Coast. Let me finish packing my truck and I'll call you tonight on my way out of town. You're three hours ahead so how about seven your time, does that work for you?"

"Sure," Elizabeth said, sounding deflated. "But I'm not three hours ahead."

"Where exactly are you, Liz?" Atkinson asked, surprised by Elizabeth's comment.

"I'm not three hours ahead on the East Coast because I'm at SeaTac," Elizabeth said, unwinding her legs and standing up from her stool.

Atkinson's mind raced to the memory of the beautiful dark-haired beauty on the night of his prom at Gonzaga, remembering that she could be a handful and more than a bit complicated.

"So, let me understand," Atkinson chuckled. "You've been talking to Barbara, she gave you my number, you read Jason's book and you hopped on a plane to run me down?"

"Actually, I read it three times," Elizabeth said, interrupting Atkinson in mid-sentence. "But the short answer is yes."

"So, I guess I really shouldn't be surprised you're in Seattle, thirty miles away from me," Atkinson said causing them both to share a laugh and breaking the tension in Elizabeth's body.

"I know, I'm sorry for being so forward," Elizabeth said, biting her lip.

"You're not being forward at all," Atkinson said, trying to stay calm but more than a little annoyed.

330

"You never were a good liar, Thomas Atkinson. But I do appreciate you trying to make me feel a little better," Elizabeth said, a tone of embarrassment creeping into her voice.

Atkinson had been looking forward to a singular cross-country journey as an opportunity to come to grips with his own crisis of isolation. He was questioning everything about the priesthood. Scorned by the very men he had looked up to as a young priest, he found himself disconnected from all he thought he had wanted as a man. His only recourse at this stage was to use this trip to figure out what he wanted to do with the rest of his life and why he became a priest in the first place. Slowly he began to think that Elizabeth may be a good sounding board for what he was trying to accomplish on the long road back, not to mention that as he remembered her from college, she was pretty damn easy on the eyes.

"Lizzie, I have a proposition for you."

"That's interesting, coming from a Catholic priest," Elizabeth said playfully.

Grateful that he was alone at his desk, Atkinson's face flushed as long dormant memories of Elizabeth flooded his mind.

"Okay, Lizzie, point for the Natale team. But seriously, I have an idea. Please don't take this the wrong way, but what are you doing for the next ten days?"

Elizabeth was confused by the question, as she fingered the cap of an unopened miniature of vodka. "What do you mean?" she asked.

"Well, like I said you caught me leaving town, but I'm going by way of a cross country road trip to my next duty station. I only have Boomer as my co-pilot-"

"Who's Boomer?" Elizabeth interrupted.

"He's my dog. Why don't you come along, and we can talk along the way and more or less unpack all the crap that got you on a plane. I've got some unpacking to do myself. How does that sound?" Atkinson asked.

Elizabeth was shaken by the offer. Her heart rate increased as she felt a familiar darkness pushing into the conversation. She opened her last bottle of vodka and downed it in one pass. Ten days alone with the man at the center of an international shitstorm was a terrifying thought and at the same time an exhilarating prospect.

The pause in the conversation stretched to an awkward length. Atkinson finally broke the silence. "It's okay if you don't want to come but if you still want to chat about why you called me, it'll have to wait until I'm off the road and settled so we can have a meaningful conversation."

Elizabeth tried to think of something sensible to say. She felt awkward, embarrassed and vulnerable. "Do you think it's okay, me riding with you and you being a priest and all?"

Atkinson let out a howl of laughter. "Jesus, Lizzie, it's not like there's a bumper sticker on my truck saying, 'priest and married woman on board.'"

"Who said I'm married," Elizabeth said, her vintage sass reminding Atkinson of her as a teenager.

"I'm sorry, I just assumed," Atkinson said, flustered.

"Nope, never married, no kids and no pets. So far just work," Elizabeth said, tapping the eraser of her pencil on the counter of the pay phone. She silently lamented the mess her life had become and what she was about to lay onto a friend who was offering so much of his time.

"I think two old school friends getting reacquainted while I'm between jobs will not be a problem for me, unless it's a problem for you. Besides, it might be good for you to get out on the road and sort things out."

"Well...I'm not sure. I mean how will it work?" Elizabeth asked, not wanting to raise the issue of sleeping arrangements and her inherent distrust of all men. "I mean what happens at night?"

"Out here on the West Coast it usually gets dark," Atkinson said, amused at her shyness. "Of course, you'll have to pay for your own room, and a little gas money since you're taking Boomer's seat."

Elizabeth let Atkinson's words sink in as she surveyed the blank faces of a seemingly endless ant stream of passengers in the terminal. Her eyes narrowed to her hand trembling above her notepad and felt a rush of excitement. "Then I'm in. What do I need? All I have is some jeans and my winter running stuff in an overnight bag."

"Excellent. Keep it that size; I'm packed to the gills. Maybe we'll pick up some hiking boots along the way."

"Hiking boots!" Elizabeth exclaimed. "What the hell, Tommy, are we walking to Maine?"

Atkinson laughed. "Okay just bring some comfortable shoes as there are a couple of trails along the way that have overlooks that I want to see."

"I have running shoes with me," Elizabeth said, eyeing her carry-on.

"They'll be fine. Okay, so here's the deal, what terminal are you in?" Atkinson asked.

Elizabeth scanned the overhead signage trying to figure out where she was. "Okay, there it is. I'm in Terminal 3, Tommy."

"All right, I know exactly where that is. You hang out at the airport for a couple of hours. Just outside at Terminal 3 baggage claim there's an overhead sign that says 'passenger pick up.' I'll be there at three o'clock sharp."

"That sounds perfect," Elizabeth said, stuffing her yellow pad and empty bottles into her canvas briefcase. "I'll have a bright red running hat on."

"Elizabeth, one more thing," Atkinson said, his suddenly serious tone causing a flutter in Elizabeth's stomach. "I'm really sorry we have reconnected under these circumstances but I'm really glad we have."

Relieved by the sincerity in his voice, Elizabeth added, "I am too, Tommy, and thank you for saying that. This has been a little awkward for me and you've been really sweet about me just dropping out of the sky and showing up on your doorstep."

Elizabeth closed her eyes as she hung up the phone. She clasped her hand to her mouth and tried to slow her breathing. She had no idea what would happen next, but she sensed that whatever happened, she would be safe with her old friend. Elizabeth watched the time and waited in the United Club room. Her feelings of excitement were tempered by the reality of why she had traveled across the country to meet with the whistleblower of the entire Church scandal. Several vodka and tonics and trips to the ladies room to adjust her hair and makeup assuaged the nervous tension that filled her body.

She replayed the night she was going to tell Atkinson her secret. It was the same night she had fallen in love with him. They were meeting because they both had news to share. Elizabeth wondered how different her life may have been had she not insisted that Tommy go first with his news. Atkinson told Elizabeth he was entering the seminary, and Elizabeth, trying to disguise the gut punch she had just taken, demurred on her secret and instead told him that Villanova was recruiting her for track. That was the instant that Elizabeth concluded she was alone in the world.

YOU DON'T LOOK SO BAD YOURSELF

A few minutes before 3:00 P.M., Elizabeth stood under a sign for passenger pick-up waiting for a priest in a white truck who would take her on a journey to bare her soul. The irony was thick with sadness.

Elizabeth used her compact mirror for one last check, adjusting her ponytail out the back of her red ball cap when the deep rhythmic bellow of a hundred-pound, flop-eared boxer echoed though the underground lane for cars picking up passengers.

Atkinson's diesel truck grumbled to a loud idle right in front of Elizabeth. Nearly half of Boomer's torso was hanging out the rear of the cab. His tail was wagging furiously, his jowls flapping with each bark.

Elizabeth smiled at the spectacle, her feet still planted on the curb.

Atkinson slammed the gearshift into park and jumped out of the truck, his face beaming with excitement. "I'm sorry, Liz, he can be really embarrassing sometimes, but he'll settle down. God, Liz, you look great, I mean look at you," Atkinson gushed as they hugged at the rear tailgate of his truck. "You don't look a day over thirty."

"Ha, well we both know that's not true," Elizabeth exclaimed with a nervous laugh.

Elizabeth did a quick inventory of Atkinson. She had wondered what he would look like after so many years and here he was. She expected some kind of uniform or priest type clothes, maybe even a bit of a paunch, but Atkinson was dressed in jeans, a flannel shirt and a waxed leather vest. He was gorgeous. Lean and close to six feet, Atkinson was clean-shaven with sandy brown hair and a weathered complexion set off by tortoise-shell glasses. When they hugged, she could feel the hardness of his shoulders and back. *This is a tough guy, just like Barbara said*, she thought. Nothing at all like the men she had known.

"You don't look so bad yourself, Thomas Atkinson," Elizabeth said warmly as she lifted her carry-on toward the back of the truck.

"Let me get that for you." Atkinson grabbed her suitcase and put it into the last space available in the bed of his truck. "So, are you hungry?" he asked.

"I'm starved," Elizabeth said, gathering her purse and waiting to see if she should get in the truck.

"Don't worry, Liz, he's friendly."

"He's so big, Tommy, you sure it's okay?"

"You'll be fine, Elizabeth." Atkinson made direct eye contact with his dog. "Boomer, down," Atkinson said crisply.

Elizabeth peeked her head through the front passenger window as Boomer obeyed the command.

"Oh, wow, that was impressive," Elizabeth said, surprised at the dog's response based on his wild yodeling as Atkinson pulled in.

"Sometimes I have to help him find his off switch, but generally he's a real sweetheart. Liz, I take it you're not a dog person."

"Well, I've never had a dog, but I wouldn't say I'm not a dog person. At least not yet."

"Fair enough, you'll know by the end of the trip whether you are or you're not," Atkinson laughed.

"You ready to go, Elizabeth?" Atkinson asked, formally extending his hand across the front seat to Elizabeth.

"I am," Elizabeth said, excited by the prospect of such an impromptu journey.

Atkinson motioned to his backpack in the front seat. "There are a few Triple A books and an Atlas in my pack, get them out and I'll show you where we're headed. There are some nuts and pretzels in the glove box to hold you over until we get to Ray's," Atkinson said as he pulled onto the northbound lanes of Interstate 5 for the thirty-minute drive to Everett, Washington, where Route 2 begins its trans-continental journey.

"What's Ray's?"

"It's a burger joint that's been around since 1952. They do plain road food very well. If you like fish and chips, it's the real deal. Jimmy Doleshel, the owner's son, hand cuts and batters fresh Alaskan cod and deep-fries it with the potatoes. Add some malt vinegar and it's a feast."

"That sounds great. I'm getting hungry all over again," said Elizabeth as she got the maps out of Atkinson's pack. "Will Boomer be okay if I open the pretzels?" Elizabeth asked as she turned in her seat to eye her four-legged road companion.

"He'll be fine until you give him the first one," Atkinson said with a twinkle in his eye. There was no good way to open an unpleasant conversation, so Atkinson plunged in. He put the truck on cruise control and adjusted his seat. "So, Elizabeth Natale, what got you on a plane to come out here unannounced?"

Elizabeth did not know why, but she was surprised at the directness of the question. "Jesus, Tommy, I don't even know where to start," Elizabeth said, staring out the passenger window.

"Start with what you want to tell me," Atkinson said as he merged into the right lane.

Elizabeth exhaled loudly as her leg started to bounce against the truck's floorboard. "I met Barbara in New York. Actually, I ran into one of her demonstrations coming out of my office. It was in front of the Cardinal's residence, and I was drawn to the picture of her as a girl when she was being abused by a priest."

"I see. You said you were coming out of your office, what do you do?" Atkinson asked.

"I'm a lawyer."

"You don't say, Liz. I've been dealing with a lot of lawyers lately. So, you saw Barb's picture as a young girl, then what?"

"Long story short, it kind of threw me into a tailspin," Elizabeth said, resting her chin in her palm and avoiding Atkinson's gaze. "It's been with me since I was little and over the last week it made me deal with the fact that what happened to Barbara happened to me when I was little. I know one thing, Tommy."

"What's that?" Atkinson asked.

"I didn't feel as alone after talking to her," Elizabeth said, tapping her fingers against the armrest on the door.

"Does your perpetrator have a name?"

Elizabeth seethed as she spoke the name of the man who sexually assaulted her. "Yeah, Tommy, he has a name alright, it's fucking Andrew Dolan and I'd like to kill the son-of-a-bitch."

Atkinson waited for the rawness in Elizabeth's voice to settle. "I'm not surprised. As I remember, Dolan was the only priest that was in regular contact with your family. Am I right about that?"

"Yes," Elizabeth said tersely. "He gave my brother piano lessons for years and he was always over at Campus School," Elizabeth said, trying to keep her foot still.

Atkinson kept his eyes on the road. "First things first, Liz. I want to apologize for what a Catholic priest did to you. I know it doesn't mean much to you under the circumstances, but with everything I've seen, I believe it's something that needs to be said."

"It means a lot coming from you, Tommy, but truthfully it should have come long ago from someone in the Church," Elizabeth said as the first tears streaked her cheeks. "Shit, that didn't take long," Elizabeth said, wiping her face with the sleeve of her shirt.

"There's a box of tissues under your seat."

"Thanks, I'll be fine," said Elizabeth as she dabbed her eyes with the cuffs of her shirt, trying to keep her eyeliner from running down her face.

Elizabeth turned in her seat to face Atkinson and to change the subject, as she was not comfortable having Atkinson see her so upset. "So, what do you think, Tommy? Do my wardrobe choices fit the trip?"

Atkinson did not press the issue any further. "They do, Lizzie. You got the sweater and the jeans thing going. An insulated parka, ball cap, I'd say you're road warrior worthy. Cocked, locked and ready to rock."

Valiantly trying to keep her anxiety at bay, Elizabeth fidgeted with the atlas in her lap, exhaling a loud nervous laugh. "Well, we'll see about that, Tommy."

Ray's Drive-In, from all outward appearances, looked a little shaky to Elizabeth. It was a plain, one-story white box with red and blue trim around the windows but based on the number of cars in the parking lot you would have thought they were giving food away.

"So, we eat in the car?" Elizabeth asked, her left eyebrow fully arched.

"Oh, good God, no. That would put Boomer over the edge. Jimmy will cook him a plain hamburger and I'll mix it with some kibble when we're finished."

"So, he waits in the car?" Elizabeth asked as she grabbed her purse from the floor.

"That's the plan, unless you want to take him for a short walk while we wait for the food."

"I would like that. How do you do that? I mean, is there a protocol?"

Atkinson looked over the fender of the car toward Elizabeth, pulling his glasses to the tip of his nose. "Did you just ask me if there was a protocol on how to walk?"

"Don't be a smart-ass, Tommy, you know what I mean."

"I know, I know," Atkinson laughed. "All right, here's the drill. He has a collar and a choker chain collar. When you walk him around roads or in cities, use the choker chain collar. If anyone asks, he's been fixed."

"Tommy, I'm not a dog person. Fixed with what?" Elizabeth asked as she attached the leash to the choker.

"You know, fixed."

Elizabeth looked at Atkinson with a blank stare on her face.

"Lizzie, Boomer is fixed," Atkinson bellowed. "You know, neutered, castrated."

"Oh, good God, Boomer, you poor thing," Elizabeth cooed. "Tommy, why on earth would you do such a thing to the beast?"

Atkinson looked at Elizabeth, a faint smile coming to his face. "Maybe on day five we'll go through that. I'm going to order the food. Cheeseburger or fish and chips?"

"Fish."

Atkinson reached into his pocket and pulled out a blue plastic bag and handed it to Elizabeth. "You may need this."

"For what?" Elizabeth asked, genuinely confused.

"Boomer may poop, so you put your hand in the bag, like a glove, pick up the poop and turn it inside and out and you're done."

"Really, Tommy," Elizabeth said. "I don't think so." Elizabeth bent down and looked directly into Boomer eyes. "Now, Boomer, don't you poop."

"That's good, Liz, Boomer will add that to his list of protocols and get right on that for you," Atkinson said as he turned to order their food.

After they finished their meal, Atkinson and Elizabeth sat alone in the tiny table section at the front of the building.

"So, what do you think? Were they the best fish and chips you ever had?"

"Tommy, they actually were," Elizabeth said, draining the last bit of her milkshake. "My compliments to the chef."

Atkinson pushed his chair away from the table. "So, Liz, I saw you through the window while you were walking Boomer."

"Okay, I didn't pick up his poop. I'm sorry. I mean, Tommy, it was gigantic."

"That's not what I was talking about," Atkinson said as he doodled on the paper placemat on the table.

"Then what?" Elizabeth asked.

Atkinson stared across the table until Elizabeth finally spoke.

"Oh, that," Elizabeth said meekly.

"Yep, Liz, that. I've been there. I'm an alcoholic. I drank my way through 1983 to 1988. I went through the whole gig. Drinking alone, hiding my bottles, a DUI, a night in jail, rehab, the meetings, relapses, more meetings, the whole shit box. So, when I see you pounding miniatures on the edge of the parking lot, I see a problem. Do you see a problem with that, Liz?"

"No, I don't see a problem, I have a problem," Elizabeth said, pulling her chair closer to the table. "I'm pissed off and I'm not sure what to do about it. But one thing I can do is to try to drink it away. And you know what else," Elizabeth added in a tortured whisper.

"No, what," Atkinson said, unmoved.

"It works for me. It's good enough to get me through the day."

"Really, now? How's that working for you, Liz?"

Elizabeth's face flared with anger. "It's not, goddammit, and I don't need you to tell me that."

"I'm not telling you anything, Liz, I'm asking."

Elizabeth jammed her straw into the empty milkshake glass, staring down at an empty plastic basket. "I'm sorry, Tom, I didn't mean to snap like that."

Atkinson reached into his shirt pocket and pulled out a tiny leather-bound notebook and handed it to Elizabeth.

"What's this?" she asked.

"Go to the last page that has any writing on it and look at the number on the top right-hand corner. What does it say?"

"One thousand, eight hundred and twenty-five."

"That's the number of days since my last drink."

Elizabeth stared at the number as her eyes began to fill with tears.

"Have you ever detoxed?" Atkinson asked.

"Yes, once by myself at home."

"Why did you decide to detox?"

"I missed a court date."

"How did it go?" Atkinson asked, pulling closer to the table.

"It was a disaster."

"How long did you last?"

Elizabeth, expecting a disapproving look from her friend, emptied her lungs through her cheeks as she grasped the back of her head with both hands. "Five, maybe six hours."

"Geez Liz, that's great. When I first tried, I only made it two hours. Listen, Lizzie, I'm not a therapist and maybe we can revisit the detox stuff later, but I'm not drinking with you."

"I get it, Tommy. I'm not asking you to drink with me and I promise I won't drink in front of you."

"Or Boomer?" Atkinson asked warmly.

"Or Boomer. I won't set a bad example for him either," Elizabeth said, smiling.

"Seriously, Liz, we can surely talk along the way, but I'm not sure I have all the answers you're looking for. I'm a priest with more than a few issues myself, and I'm in the middle of a war with the hierarchy of the entire Roman Catholic Church. It's like a giant swirling cesspool that doesn't have a bottom."

Elizabeth was embarrassed. Half of her wanted to get out of the truck and go back home and half of her wanted to stay. She folded her hands on the table and looked squarely into Tom Atkinson's eyes. "I'm an unemployed lawyer. A single woman who's been running, hiding and drinking most of her life and I don't see any end in sight. Tommy, I have no idea where all of this is going but I'd say we're the perfect couple."

Atkinson slammed his hand on the table and laughed. "Agreed, Counselor. Let's get on the road. Maybe we'll get lucky and sort it all out."

Atkinson pulled his truck onto Broadway and headed south to Hewett Street. "Okay, Lizzie, it's coming up. You see the I5 overpass ahead just past Maple Street?"

"I do."

"My camera's in the glove box. Get it out, I want to get a picture. Do you know how to use it?" Atkinson asked.

"Christ, Tommy, it's an Instamatic, of course I know how to use it. You click the shutter, and it takes a picture," Elizabeth said, feigning intellectual insult.

"Excellent. Take a picture as we go under," Atkinson said excitedly. "That's the western terminus to Route 2. We're headed toward the town of Wenatchee, only 2,500 miles to Houlton, Maine!" Atkinson cackled.

Passing through the Victorian town of Snohomish and the tiny mining town of Gold Bar, Elizabeth's mood seemed to lighten.

"These mountains are beautiful. It's so different from the East Coast. You open a window and you can actually smell the pine," Elizabeth said marveling at the view.

The miles clicked off effortlessly, punctuated only by the hypnotic tapping of the tires running over each expansion joint in the road. Elizabeth reached between the seat and rubbed Boomer's head and behind his ears as he drifted off to sleep.

"Can I ask you some questions, Tommy?" Elizabeth asked as she stared out at the endless expanse of Douglas fir covering the western foothills of the Cascade Mountain Range.

"Shoot, Liz, we got nothing but time."

"So, when I left my job in New York, I told you about meeting Barbara and reading Jason Berry's book and I came to the conclusion that I would be better served if I went back to school and became a Canon Lawyer and worked on this issue from the inside. I had been thinking about it for a while, and I was collecting articles that appeared in the newspapers. I'm a victim of this type of abuse, who better to inform than the bishops," Elizabeth reasoned.

"So, the reason you want to be a Canon Lawyer is to inform the bishops of their lapse of judgment and total disregard for the safety and welfare of God's children," Atkinson said, scoffing at the suggestion.

"Jesus, Tommy, don't get pissy. But yeah, that's exactly why."

"Liz, I'm a Canon Lawyer. I worked in the Vatican's diplomatic mission in Washington for five years. I saw all of these complaints going over to Rome. I worked for a Cardinal who votes on who's gonna be the next Pope. I watched them hide these assholes in plain sight. I saw the inside of an international cover-up. I saw how the bishops exploited the cops and judges to make all this crap go away and if that didn't work, they would threaten the parents. You said you talked to Barbara, so give me a grade on a scale of one to ten on how I did getting the bishops to deal with Catholic priests sexually molesting kids."

Elizabeth sat silently in her seat staring out the passenger window.

Atkinson persisted. "Really, Liz, I'm serious, how would you say it's working out for me? I co-wrote a goddamn report to the bishops going through the whole friggin' history, gave them hard facts on incidence and a solid prediction as to what was financially and morally at stake for the Church. Gave them an overview as to what modern therapy techniques could work for the treatment and retention of perpetrators. The report was shit canned. The topic was shit canned, and I was shit canned. At the rate they're paying out now I wouldn't be surprised that our billion-dollar estimate swells to four, possibly five billion. That's real money, Counselor."

"So, I guess you're thinking it's a bad idea," Elizabeth said meekly.

"Well, I didn't think you wanted me to blow smoke up your ass," he said, accelerating on a miles long ribbon of asphalt.

"I don't want anything up my ass," Elizabeth said tartly. "I just want some answers."

"I'm sorry, Liz. To what questions?" Atkinson pressed.

"Okay, here's something that makes no sense to me: How do you reconcile the Church's position on birth control and right to life with the cover-up of sexual crimes committed by priests against children?"

"Ha! Spoken like a true lawyer. The answer is you can't reconcile those two positions. The better question: What's the rationale of each position, which would explain why they're treated so wildly differently by the Church hierarchy."

"There shouldn't be any difference," Elizabeth countered, sitting upright in her seat.

"Don't get the dog nervous, Liz. Look at his eyes; you're making him nervous."

"It's okay, Boomie, we're just talking." Elizabeth reached down and stroked the boxer's ears.

The conversation was didactic, but Atkinson found it cathartic in dealing with his own conflict. It was forcing him to examine why he was even attracted to the priesthood in the first place.

"Let me answer that," Atkinson said, fully engaged. "Elizabeth, let's just suppose your mother walked in on Dolan abusing you, to the point that she wouldn't be able to deny that it happened."

"That's disgusting. Now you're making me nervous."

"Just stay with me, Liz. Knowing your mother as you do, think about these scenarios. Would she want to believe that the bishops had no way to predict or anticipate Dolan's sexual crimes committed against her daughter?"

"In my mother's case, absolutely," Elizabeth said, reaching for her notepad.

"Would your mother not want any of this to be broadcast within the parish?"

"For sure."

"Would she want to believe that Dolan would never be in a position to abuse another child and that the bishops knew best, with guidance from God, how to handle this?"

"Big yes on that."

"That if she reported this to the authorities, it would bring public scandal to her beloved Church and her entire family?"

"Yes. Jesus, Tommy, you're killing me."

"Now one last question: Would your mother be susceptible to the argument that public exposure of a priest committing a sexual crime against her child is in the end an attack on the Church that would put her quest for eternal salvation in jeopardy with God?"

"Yes, she would. Tom, could you pull over, I need some air," Elizabeth said as she hugged Boomer around his massive neck.

"Of course, Liz. Steven's Pass is right around this next curve and there's a nice turn-out."

Before Atkinson had put the truck in park, Elizabeth got Boomer's leash on and was out of the truck.

"You want any company?" Atkinson yelled after her.

"Nope, just give me a few minutes."

"Okay, but stay on the trail and take this," Atkinson said as he tossed a bear bell to Elizabeth. "Snap that on his collar."

"Got it."

As soon as Elizabeth was out of sight, she raced to the nearest tree to steady herself and vomited up her fish and chips. Elizabeth bent over and heaved until there was nothing left in her stomach. Her head started to throb. She was shocked at how Atkinson's recitation had caused an almost immediate physical reaction.

Twenty minutes had gone by, and Atkinson was worried. He locked up his truck and started out on the summit trail but within a minute he heard Boomer's bell and got back in the truck. Elizabeth opened the passenger side and Boomer bounded in.

"You have a good walk, Boom?" he asked as the boxer settled into the back seat. Noticing Elizabeth was pale and perspiring, he asked, "You okay, Liz?"

"No, but I'll be fine. How long are we going to drive today?"

"I was hoping to get to Spokane. It's about four to five hours. If that's too long, we can stop. Your call."

"Nope, that's fine," Elizabeth said as she pulled hard on the waist hem of her down parka.

"You pissed off at me or something, Liz?"

"No, I'm not, but I'd like to get going."

"Roger that."

Atkinson put his truck in reverse and backed out of the parking space and eased down from the crest of Steven's Summit. There were 228 miles to go to Spokane, so he slipped Stan Getz's *Desafinado* into his CD player in hopes of mellowing things out with Elizabeth. Traffic was light as the strains of bass, percussion, guitar and saxophone lightly filled the cab of his truck. His sense was that the lawyer was processing information based on the number of pages she was filling in her legal pad, leaving him in his own quandary. If the reason he wanted to be a priest was to be closer to God, how could that even be possible if the organization turned a blind eye to the children who were abused?

The stunning views down the Wenatchee Valley coming into Leavenworth, a surreal Bavarian enclave nestled into the eastern foothills of the Cascades, barely got a glance from Elizabeth.

After two hours of silence and furious writing, Elizabeth exploded. "You know what I'm pissed off about?"

"I'm not sure I want to know, but go ahead," Atkinson said with a wry look on his face.

"I'm pissed off about everything you said a hundred miles back that made me puke my guts out. And I'm pissed off at my brother Francis."

"Why is that, Liz? I mean he isn't involved in any of this, is he?"

"No, but before I came out to find you, I took him to dinner and basically gave him the story on that fucker Dolan. No details, just the headlines. He said if I decided to report Dolan it would be better for me to not be associated with you or Barbara, that I would lose credibility with the bishops. He said it was complicated."

"How did you handle that, Liz?" Atkinson asked, mildly amused.

"I about took his head off. If we hadn't been out in public I would have smacked him."

"Liz, I just think he's looking out for you and maybe himself a little bit. My name is toxic with the hierarchy. What diocese is Frannie in?"

347

"I don't know. What's it matter? He lives just outside D.C. in a parish."

"The clerical grapevine has Cletus Ryan being named Archbishop of Washington. So, I don't want to aggravate you anymore, but your brother is simply drinking his boss's Kool-Aid."

"Did you say Cletus Ryan?" Elizabeth asked, gripping her pen.

"Yes, why?"

"He was just over at my mother's house for dinner. I got into a huge argument with my mother as to what he was even doing there. I think there's something going on between them."

"Whoa, whoa now, hold on there, Counselor. It certainly wouldn't be the first bishop to carnally 'know' a parishioner, but do you know, or do you suspect?"

"I suspect. I said I 'think' there's something going on between them, because I asked my grandmother and my Aunt Rose who lives with Momma and they were all buttoned up, and told me I would have to talk to her myself."

"Did you?"

"Of course not. What am I supposed to say? 'Hey, Mom, you screwing the local bishop?' Don't be ridiculous, Tommy," Elizabeth fumed.

Atkinson smiled.

"What are you smiling about?"

"It's just the way you talk, Liz," Atkinson said.

"Well, when you work in New York most of your life, you learn to be blunt."

Atkinson put the truck on cruise control, slowly moving his head to the beat of the music.

"Say something, Tom!"

"I'm thinking."

Frustrated and out of vodka, Elizabeth reached into her purse and pulled out a bottle of Valium. Without any water, she popped two tablets.

"What you got there, Liz?"

"I thought you were thinking," she shot back.

Atkinson looked straight down the roadway.

"I'm sorry, Tommy, that was uncalled for. I'm really itching for some vodka, and I'm so pissed off at Frannie I can't see straight."

"Do you want to stop and get some?" Atkinson said, glancing at Elizabeth.

"Are you okay with that, I mean I thought…"

"No, I'm not okay with it, but I'm not here to stop you from drinking. You had your last drink about four hours ago. We can go into Spokane, have a nice dinner with plenty of vegetables and protein and as much water as you can pour down your gullet, then we can take a little detour and go over to Gonzaga University's library and do some work on Dolan."

"What kind of work?" Elizabeth asked.

"I want to show you how to use the Official Catholic Directory to track Dolan's assignments. After we do that, I'll tell you what I was thinking about a bit ago."

Putting her yellow legal pad back into her pack, Elizabeth asked, "What's the Official Catholic Directory?"

"It's published every year, diocese by diocese, parish by parish, and included in that are all the other Catholic institutions, schools and hospitals in a specific area."

Elizabeth did not respond. Instead, she climbed over the front seat and cuddled next to Boomer. Atkinson, smiling, eyed the spectacle through the rear-view mirror as Boomer began his happy groan.

Elizabeth looked at Atkinson in the mirror and Boomer groaned in delight as Elizabeth rubbed his chest. Let's get to Spokane before I change my mind. I'll pass on the vodka – for now."

"You sure?" Atkinson said to Elizabeth in the mirror.

"At this moment, I'm sure. I can't tell you I'll be sure in two hours," Elizabeth said as she held Boomer's head in both of her hands.

Ripples Restaurant and Lounge was a favorite of Atkinson's when he needed to do research at Gonzaga's Foley Library. A Jesuit Institution founded in 1887, Gonzaga had extensive theological holdings and one of the few complete sets of the directory dating back to 1817 on the West Coast.

The weather was warm for early spring in the foothills of the Cascades, so Atkinson and Elizabeth opted for a table on the outside terrace overlooking the Spokane River. As a bonus for Boomer, the restaurant was dog friendly.

"You know, Liz, the key to detoxing is water. There are other things that are going on, but water is critical. Now listen to me, this can be dangerous. Everyone detoxes differently. The fact that you're in decent shape will help."

"Did you say decent shape? Tommy, I'm forty-six and I run between fifty and sixty miles a week."

"Now how would I have known that if you hadn't told me? Okay, so you're in great shape."

"I am in great shape, right Boomer?" Elizabeth asked as she reached under the table to rub Boomer's head.

"The point is, Liz, we're not in a hospital or treatment setting. I don't have any drugs to reduce cravings and if this goes bad I'm going to take you to a hospital. You on board with that?" Atkinson thrust his hand across the table.

"Deal," Elizabeth said, extending her hand to meet his.

"Now keep pounding the water and we'll get some food into you," Atkinson said in a reassuring tone.

"I just lost all the food from lunch. I can't think of food right now."

Atkinson looked directly at Elizabeth and put his hand on top of hers. "Well, Counselor, unless you want to fold your tent and go to a liquor store, you're going to have to."

ACT OF FAITH

THESE RECORDS ARE PREPARED EVERY YEAR
The stacks in the Foley were spread out, well-lit and airy, totally different than most East Coast libraries. Atkinson purchased $20 in ten-cent tokens and picked a table in between the copier and the Official Catholic Directory collection.

"Okay let's pull one to see if we can find him," said Atkinson as he strolled through the rows of brown and burgundy volumes.

"How do you know which one to start with?"

"I don't, my dear," Atkinson said, giving Elizabeth his best Groucho Marx double clutch eyebrow impression.

"That was actually really funny," Elizabeth laughed.

"Laughing is a good thing, Liz. Grab 1984, I'll get 1994, and meet me back at our table."

Elizabeth was impressed with the weight of the nearly four-inch-thick volume and thumped it on the reading table.

"Sit down a minute, Liz, I want to give you some context for what's in front of you. First, never in their wildest dreams did any of the American Catholic Bishops think that plaintiff attorneys would read these books line by line."

"How so?" Elizabeth asked, her lawyerly curiosity now piqued.

"It's got everything you need to build a case. It's like the view from ten thousand feet. The entire organization is graphed out. The physical geography of each diocese, all the population demographics, all the schools, names of principals, addresses, telephone numbers and the assignment history of each ordained Catholic priest in the entire country. Basically, it's a who, where, and what you are doing guide for the entire Catholic priesthood throughout the country."

"Get the hell out of here! Are you serious," Elizabeth said, grabbing the 1994 volume.

"Look for yourself. Go to the tab in the back marked alphabetical lists of priests and find Dolan."

Elizabeth pulled her chair to the desk and thumbed through the back pages of the OCD until she reached the alpha list and Dolan's name. Her face grew dark as she moved her finger down the list. "There's the asshole, *Andrew X. Dolan,*" Elizabeth hissed.

"Now look, the two-digit number next to his name is the year he was ordained."

"Okay, I follow, it says fifty-eight," Elizabeth said, making a note on a clean sheet in her legal pad.

Hovering over Elizabeth, Atkinson closed his eyes for an instant, distracted by a rich aromatic scent from her ponytail tumbling out of her cap.

"So, what's the SY mean next to the year?" Elizabeth asked, looking back at Atkinson. "What's wrong, Tom?"

"Nothing, something just flew into my eye," Atkinson said gamely, trying to hide his embarrassment. "The SY means he's incardinated to the Diocese of Syracuse, New York."

"What's incardination mean?" Elizabeth asked.

"It's the physical location of the priests, or in this case the bishop or archbishop, of a diocese. It's a Church mechanism that legally, physically and canonically attaches a priest to his ecclesiastical supervisor, in this case a bishop or archbishop in a specific diocese. Now do you see that capital letter in parentheses?"

"Yes, it says V."

"Okay, so go to the Diocese of Syracuse and look under the heading '*Institutions Located in the Diocese.*' Go to the listing under the letter 'V' and you'll find his name."

Elizabeth rifled through the pages for the Diocese then stopped and looked up at Atkinson.

"I'll be damned. This is insane. So, you go back to 1958 and repeat the process year by year, diocese by diocese, and you have each priest's assignment history?" Elizabeth asked incredulously.

"That's the ticket. You'll get a ton of information that'll give you 90 percent of the perpetrator's personnel history, his supervisors, whether a school was attached to his parish, his general physical location, potential witnesses, his supervisors... it's really a roadmap," Atkinson said.

"That's a fucking gold mine for a litigator," Elizabeth said, recognizing the implications of the material. "Do all the lawyers handling these cases do this?" she asked.

"Some do, some don't, unfortunately."

Elizabeth flashed with anger. "Why the hell if you were representing a client would you not do this?"

"You want the blunt answer, Liz?"

"Shit, any answer would do at this point."

"In the early days, bishops were just throwing money at the lawyers. They would write a letter and the bishops would pay. They would enter into a confidentiality agreement, and it would be over. Now that the evidence of conspiracy has been leaking out and people are getting their heads around how widespread the incidence is, some of the lawyers that have consulted with me are doing the work and getting all the pieces in place. They still have the statute of limitations to contend with, so the negotiations resemble a game of chicken. You know the game, Liz?" Atkinson asked.

"I know the game, Tommy," Elizabeth grunted.

Elizabeth raced back to the stacks, and Atkinson followed with an available rolling cart. She pulled all the late fifties through 1963 to start. Back at the table, they divided the years and marked each page that they wanted to copy.

Elizabeth was perched on her knees in the library chair, tabbing each page and making notes. "Tommy, there's no entry for 1958, what's up with that?"

"I'm not surprised; they're published usually a year behind actual events. Go to 1959."

"Got it," Elizabeth said as she burrowed back into the single space fine print of the volume.

Atkinson had gone through this same exercise dozens of times before, so much so he could take a book to the copy machine and copy the relevant pages as he went. Elizabeth found Atkinson at the copier. "Hey, Dolan is in the index in 1960 but it says California not Syracuse."

"Let's see, that could be important," Atkinson said, taking the book from her and carefully looking at Dolan's listing. "What this means is that Syracuse wanted to transfer him to Los Angeles, and they accepted."

"Accepted what? I don't understand," Elizabeth said, looking confused.

"It's like a trade in major league baseball. The bishops know which other bishops to talk to when they have a problem priest that they want to tuck away somewhere."

"How fucked up is that," Elizabeth said as she flipped her pen on the desk. "That's just disgusting, Tommy."

Atkinson could see Elizabeth's face begin to contort with anger. She looked like she wanted to explode. Atkinson moved his chair to face her and grabbed both of her hands into his, so they were face to face.

"Hey, listen to me. We can leave right now."

Elizabeth broke free from his grasp. "No! I don't want to leave. I want to fucking finish, Tom," Elizabeth said, seething with fury.

"Liz, give me your hand."

"No! Let's get back to it," Elizabeth said coldly.

"Elizabeth! Stop it and listen to me," Atkinson ordered. His tone caught her by surprise. "Elizabeth. Will you please give me your hands?" Atkinson asked in a more conciliatory tone.

Elizabeth put her pen and legal pad on the table and faced Atkinson, putting her hands in her lap. Atkinson slid his hands under Elizabeth's and waited for her to clasp his. He noticed the softness of her fingers and her meticulous manicure. He was impressed by her willingness to stay in the ring and absorb the pain of actually looking at Dolan's history.

Elizabeth did not look up but gradually clasped Atkinson's hands.

"I didn't mean to sound like I was ordering you around."

"Well, that's what it sounded like to me," Elizabeth interrupted him.

Atkinson bent down in his chair to catch Elizabeth's gaze. "Will you look at me, Liz?" Atkinson pleaded.

Elizabeth snapped her head up, squeezing Atkinson hands so hard that he began to get uncomfortable. "What do you want from me, Tom?" Elizabeth said, boring her green eyes into his.

"You can start by letting me out of that vice grip."

Elizabeth looked at her knuckles, which had turned white and released the pressure.

"All I wanted to tell you is I've been where you are. It's a lot like a fifteen-round prizefight. There are stages. You're a fighter but you also have vulnerabilities."

"Yeah. I'm fucked up, Tommy."

"Maybe, but you can change things. You just have to pace yourself. You run, right?" Atkinson asked.

Elizabeth shrugged yes.

"What you're doing now is processing this shit pile of new information and at the same time trying to make sense of your life. How maybe it could have been different. So, it's all about pace. Then there's the booze and how you feel and whether you feel like you are going crazy because you're not drinking. I've been there, that's all I'm saying. You're going to win some rounds and lose some. The trick is to be there at the end, upright – you know what I'm saying." Elizabeth's hands started to tremble as Atkinson gently applied some pressure. "Liz, have you ever tried any therapy from a professional?" he asked, trying to break the ice.

"Before today?" Elizabeth said, smiling as she took a deep breath and gathered her notes and papers.

"You want to keep working or go and get some air?" Atkinson asked.

"Let's keep going. I feel better. Should we check on Boomer?"

Atkinson glanced at his watch. "No, he's fine for a little longer. Okay, here's what I was about to show you," Atkinson said as he stood up and positioned the 1961 volume in front of Elizabeth. "Give me a second, let me find it again."

Elizabeth stood close to Atkinson, hovering over his hands as he scrolled down the listing. Suddenly, Atkinson turned to her. "Here it is, Liz, you just hit pay dirt."

"What do you mean, why?"

"C'mon back to the table."

Elizabeth gathered her notes and followed Atkinson.

"So, these records are prepared every year on forms submitted by the publisher. Sometimes folks who didn't know there was a massive conspiracy to hide sexual perpetrators inside the Church filled these forms out and sent them back to the publisher. So, in 1961, some Diocesan lackey filled out Dolan's form out and said where he was."

"Where was he?" Elizabeth demanded.

"Via Coeli."

"Via what? What is that?" Elizabeth asked.

"Via Coeli is in Jemez Springs, New Mexico. It's run by the Servants of the Paraclete. They're a religious order that has taken in sexually abusive priests for treatment."

"So, are they part of the problem or the solution?"

"Actually, both. They identified sexual predators and made recommendations for removal. But in most cases those recommendations were ignored, and priests found a way to get back into ministry, just like Dolan did. The one thing they didn't do was call the police. So, follow this... Dolan's incardinated in L.A. You were assaulted in Washington and now he's in Syracuse. The bishops all knew he was a problem because someone sent him to treatment early on. He could be the cover boy for this conspiracy."

Elizabeth flopped into her chair, deflated. She stared at the open book. "I want to go check on Boomer."

Atkinson fished out his truck keys from his pack. "Hey, I know this is upsetting. I can finish this up quickly. Why don't you get Boomer and take him down by the river walk? You okay?" Atkinson asked.

"So, they knew about him before he came to Washington," Elizabeth said, disturbed by their discovery.

"They did. Liz, you're almost at eight hours since your last drink. Take this water bottle. Drink the whole bottle."

Elizabeth took the bottle and ran out of the library, fighting back a flood of tears.

Atkinson left the library an hour later armed with three inches of copies that tracked Dolan from 1958 to 1994. As he walked to the car he listened for Boomer's bell. A building anxiety blossomed into a panic when neither Elizabeth nor Boomer was at the truck. He sprinted toward the river, scanning left and right for a woman and a large boxer. As he crested the riverbank, he finally spotted them. Elizabeth was lying flat on her back, her head resting on her pack, and Boomer was curled up asleep next to her. Atkinson gave a whistle, causing Boomer to wake up and stand next to Elizabeth.

"Hey down there, you coming or are we sleeping outside tonight?"

Elizabeth rolled over and gathered her things, following Boomer up to Atkinson.

"You okay, Liz?"

"Yeah, I actually took a nap." Elizabeth opened her backpack. "Here's your bottle. It's empty."

"Damn, Lizzie, you're rocking."

"Really, Tommy? Then why do I feel like I've been stoned by an angry mob?"

"C'mon, you're doing fine," Atkinson said as he pulled her up the bank and walked to his truck. "No more talk about this stuff today. Tomorrow will be glorious. You ever gone through Glacier National Park?"

"Never been anywhere out in this section of the country, so this is all new," Elizabeth said.

"Tommy, you used the word conspiracy back in the library. That's a legal conclusion that covers a lot of territory."

"I thought we were leaving that for tonight," Atkinson said as he checked his atlas and the mileage to the Idaho border.

"You said that. I didn't say that."

"Liz, did you ever think that it was possible that I was tired of talking about all of this shit?"

Elizabeth turned her back on Atkinson and started to walk back down to the riverbank.

Atkinson ran ahead of her. "Liz, listen, we will have time for all of this, I promise. You have a lot on your plate right now. Just trust me on this. Please."

Elizabeth stared at Atkinson, her eyes ready to fight, then lowered her gaze as Boomer nudged her leg. "Okay, let's get to where we're sleeping tonight, I'm tired and want to go to sleep."

"C'mon it's forty miles up the road. It's a cute little one-story motel that takes pets."

"So, it's not the Ritz?"

"It is definitely not the Ritz. It's the Newport Antler. Triple A says it's no frills, but it is clean."

"That means it's a dump. If it's a dump, I'll sleep in the back of the truck with Boomer," Elizabeth said.

"That's a deal, but it should be fine," Atkinson laughed.

"Would you mind if Boomer sleeps with me tonight?" Elizabeth asked as they pulled into the gravel parking lot.

"Not at all, Liz, but he snores, and he farts," Atkinson chuckled.

"How romantic," Elizabeth quipped. "If it's too bad I'll bring him back."

It took about an hour to drive forty miles of single-lane highway to the Newport Antler. Atkinson opened the screen door to the office and found himself in a warm and comforting roadside inn. The walls were knotty pine, and the wide plank flooring was worn but clean. A small wood stove crackled in the corner, emitting a pleasant pine aroma from the pewter spice pot sitting on the corner of the stove. Two, large bulletin boards were covered with upcoming events in and around Newport, Washington, used items for sale and dozens of help wanted ads. On the other wall was a huge set of moose antlers with a plaque and a picture of the trophy kill. Susan St. James greeted Atkinson warmly from behind her desk and in ten minutes imparted most of her life story and that of her husband. Theirs was a simple life without pretense or agenda. Atkinson was envious. His life was anything but.

Atkinson took the room keys and walked out of the office toward his truck.

"Your wife is delightful," Atkinson said as he walked past Richard St. James who was leveling out the gravel in the parking lot.

"Yeah, the Newport philosopher. I'll bet she talked your ear off," Richard mused.

Atkinson was fascinated by the elegant simplicity of the St. James' lifestyle. There was no shroud of piety or pretense that they hid behind. They were part of a community for all things big and small. That stood in stark contrast to the isolation Atkinson felt in his position as a vocal outlier in a two-thousand-year-old institution.

Atkinson's life and career was in shambles. He moved from one crisis to another. The only constant was the survivors; they kept coming and calling with no apparent end in sight. Then there was the matter of Elizabeth. It was hard to deny that he had feelings for her and that in many respects she had captivated him.

"So, what kind of adjustment does a Catholic priest make with that?" he muttered to himself. His dream of leading a diocese was gone, replaced by the role of a truth teller. Hundreds of years of corruption weighed on his spirit. Boomer's barking seemed to break the grip of his melancholy.

"What took you so long?" Elizabeth asked. "Boomer is going nuts with that dog across the street."

"Sorry, Liz, got to talking with the owners. Great couple. Here's the key for your room. Take Boomer with you and get settled in. I'm going to run across the street and get some fruit and hopefully some yoghurt and crackers."

"Tommy, I can't eat another thing."

"You have to, Liz, and you have to keep pounding the water. If you wake up in the middle of the night, I want you to eat something and drink more water. It's important, Liz. We're not in a detox center."

"Okay, okay, I get it," Elizabeth said, slamming the door.

Atkinson was back in fifteen minutes and knocked on Elizabeth's door.

"Come in. I think Boomer likes it in here with me."

"I'm sure he does," Atkinson deadpanned. "Here is some yoghurt, a spoon, a protein bar and some bananas and an apple. Take one of these multivitamins tonight and one in the morning."

"Yes, Mother," Elizabeth snorted.

"C'mon, Liz, this is serious. I want you to eat most of this before you go to sleep and drink at least one liter of water. The nearest ER is in Kalispell and so far you're doing great. How are you feeling now?"

"I want a drink, but I'm not crazy. I'm getting some rushes, and I need a shower. I've been sweating like a pig."

Elizabeth had changed out of her jeans and was barefoot, wearing a cut-off sweatshirt and running shorts. Her legs rippled with long, well developed muscles from years of running. She had been on Atkinson's mind all day but now the beautiful woman was front and center.

Atkinson replayed the night he told Elizabeth he was entering the seminary. His news had caught her by surprise, and he had said something stupid to the effect that he could still love a girl but not in the way a real couple would. Elizabeth had gotten so angry she spun him around by his shoulders, grabbed his head with both of her hands and passionately kissed him on the lips. When she was done, she said, "Thomas Atkinson, I hope you remember that," and turned and left him on his parent's front porch.

Atkinson felt the heat behind his ears and tried to regain his bearings. It was clear to him it was time to go. "Liz, I'm right next door. Bang on the wall or knock on my door if you need anything. Did you check in?"

"I did. She's a nice woman. We traded old war stories of growing up on the East Coast."

"So, you're good?"

"I'm fine. I'll come and get you if I have a problem."

"Okay. Good night, Liz."

"Night, Tommy. And Tommy, thanks for everything you're doing. I know I can be a pain in the ass."

"You're not a pain in the ass, Liz. Far from it. Lock the door behind me." Atkinson waited until he heard the deadbolt click into place and then went to his truck, lit a cigar and put in a tape to settle his nerves.

IT'S BEAUTIFUL OUT HERE

The Cabinet and Salish Mountains on Route 2 from Newport to West Glacier, Montana, captivated Elizabeth. The weather was chilly but clear with little ground fog. Dolan was not mentioned during the four-hour drive until they stopped at the Logan Pass Visitor Center in Glacier National Park.

Atkinson put the truck in park and was pleasantly surprised to see so few cars. "How are you feeling, Liz?" he asked, trying to keep the mood light.

"Not so hot. I keep getting these rushes and increased heart rate."

"What about that small tremor in your left hand I've been noticing all morning?"

"Well, that, too. Can we take a walk anywhere around here?"

"Sure. Hidden Lake trail is 2.7 miles, round trip. It has a great overlook, and it starts just behind the visitor center. You up for that?"

"Can Boomer come?"

"Sure, but he needs to be on his choker. Keep him close. If you let him get a head of steam up with all these mountain goats around, he'll rip your arm out of its socket."

"Got it."

The Hidden Lake trail was on an elevated plateau, making the trek relatively flat. It was wide enough for Atkinson and Elizabeth to walk side by side with Boomer in the middle.

Elizabeth zipped her parka and pulled a wool cap over her ears while taking in the view down the Salish Valley. "After we left the library at Gonzaga, you never told me what you had been thinking about in the truck when we first started talking about Dolan."

"Hmm," Atkinson mumbled.

"That all I get, a hmm?"

"Watch your step here, Liz, it's slippery. Can I ask you some questions first?"

"Sure."

"Tell me about how you met Dolan."

"Well, I never really met him; it just seemed like he was always around the house on holidays and Sunday afternoons. He spent time in the music room at school and me and a few other girls helped the nuns get the altar ready for Mass at Aquinas Hall. He was also Frannie's music teacher. He spent a ridiculous amount of time with him. Frannie was good on the piano. Actually, he was great on the piano; he probably would have had a much happier life not being a priest."

"There's a lot of that going around," Atkinson said as he stopped to take in the towering rock formations and lush meadows.

Elizabeth smiled. "It's beautiful out here, Tom, thank you for showing me this. But it's so weird seeing all this beauty and talking about all this crap. I remember Frannie said something else that really surprised me."

"What was that?"

"He said Dolan was a prick. Actually, Frannie kinda flipped out on me at the restaurant. He was going on about never being able to please him and some nonsense about Dolan never being able to take his music away."

"How you doing, Liz?"

"Stop asking me how I'm doing. I'm okay; I run six or seven half marathons a year, so I think I can walk two and a half miles, for Christ's sake. Damn, Tom, why do you keep changing the subject?" Elizabeth snapped.

"It's pretty damn simple, Liz. I've spent a lot of time with survivors and unpacking thirty years of shit with you while self-detoxing on a cross-country road trip with an over-indulged boxer is no joke."

"I know," Elizabeth said as she reached in her jacket pocket and tossed Atkinson two unopened miniatures of vodka that had ended up in her suitcase.

STEPHEN RUBINO

"You had these last night, Liz?" Atkinson asked, catching both bottles in his hands.

"I did, Boomer and I slept with them on the night table. I'm not a lightweight, Thomas, so don't try to manage me. I appreciate your help and I really appreciate you being here, but when I get in trouble, I'll let you know. I'm on the edge but I need to get back from the edge by myself."

"I got it, Liz," Atkinson said, opening both bottles and pouring them on the ground. "Where were we?"

"We were talking about Dolan and my brother."

Atkinson put the empty bottles in his pocket. The scent of spilled alcohol hung in the air. "Dolan was assigned to St Francis de Sales in the early sixties, right?"

"I know that, Tommy, and Monsignor Ryan was the Pastor."

"Yes, but Monsignor Ryan was later the Vicar General for the Archdiocese. As Vicar, he would have been privy to all of Dolan's records and all of the records that would end up in the Secret Archive, like his treatment records at Via Coeli, and now the soon to be consecrated archbishop."

"What the hell is a Secret Archive?" Elizabeth asked.

"The Church maintains an archive of sensitive or confidential documents that only the Bishop has access to. Dolan was excardinated from Los Angeles and into the Archdiocese of Washington, and now he's in Syracuse, right?"

"Yes, but..."

"Liz, I remember you telling me at your dad's funeral something about your dad dying at the St. Francis rectory while Frannie was there."

"He did die there. What are you saying, Tommy?"

"I'm not sure, it's just something doesn't make sense to me. I can't put my finger on it. Was Frannie friends with any of the girls who did the altar work for Dolan's Masses?"

364

"Not that I know of. Wait, there was a Christine. I forget her last name, I think it was Green, but she took my place when I didn't go over to Aquinas Hall."

"What about any other girls? Did you get a hint from any of your friends that Dolan was abusing them?"

"No. If they were like me, no one was telling anyone about anything. It sounds absolutely stupid, but I really thought God wanted me to keep it secret," Elizabeth said, shaking her head in disgust.

"It's not stupid at all, Liz; it's the perpetrator's weapon of choice. There's a reason they call these guys sexual predators. They prey on the weak and vulnerable."

"Well, that was me at eleven," Elizabeth said.

"Exactly. Look how long you kept your secret."

"A long time, Tommy."

"Liz, most survivors are secret keepers. Many take it to their grave. You gotta stop beating yourself up for this. All I'm saying is that it may be a coincidence that Bishop Ryan struck up a friendship with your mom after your dad passed or it could be more. If he doesn't know the full story on Dolan, he can surely find out in his position."

"I did ask Frannie if he thought Momma had found out and had told Poppa."

"What did he say?"

"He was emphatic, absolutely not, there was no way." The conversation was starting to take a physical toll on Elizabeth. "I can't do this anymore, Tom. Can we go back? I want to get on the road and try to get my head around all of this." Elizabeth walked ahead and by the time Atkinson and Boomer got to the truck she was in the passenger seat holding her head.

"You ready?" Atkinson asked.

"Yes, let's go." Elizabeth buried her face in her knees and slowly rocked her body back and forth in her seat.

Atkinson gently laid a bottle of water and a banana on Elizabeth's leg. Without looking up, she gathered both in her lap.

"Just so you know, we're headed back to Route 2 and eventually Wolf Point where we'll stay tonight. It'll probably be dark."

Elizabeth kept her head down and simply gave Atkinson a thumbs up.

Atkinson settled himself in his seat and let the road unfold in front of him: beautiful, stark, and empty, just as he had imagined. This is why he wanted to take this way back East. The miles of open plains, swaying wheat fields and blue-sky traversing through the Blackfeet Indian Reservation energized him. He understood why all the travel books called it Big Sky Country. A strip of blacktop thirty-five feet wide stretching to the horizon was the perfect place to organize his thoughts about leaving the priesthood.

VODKA AND VALIUM

The next morning, Atkinson woke early and bolted out of the room in search of coffee. Scrawled on his windshield was a note, *"out running with Boomer."* It was barely light, and Wolf Point was a town full of natural gas and crude oil roughnecks, but since Boomer was with her, he decided to simply wait for Elizabeth to show up.

Propped up on his tailgate with his coffee and a local paper, Atkinson heard Boomer's bell before he saw him. Thirty yards away, with Boomer tugging at his leash, Elizabeth let him go.

"Go get him, Boomer. There's Tommy; go get him," Elizabeth wailed across the parking lot. About ten feet away from Atkinson's perch, Boomer hurled his entire body into the back of the truck, crashing into the neatly arranged boxes, Atkinson, his coffee and newspaper.

With Boomer licking his face and his shirt soaked with coffee, Atkinson struggled to roll him off the tailgate.

"Not very funny, Natale! Payback's a bitch, you know!"

"I'm really sorry, Tommy," Elizabeth said, doubled over convulsing in laughter. "But that was hilarious."

"Yeah, I can tell you're sorry," Atkinson said, annoyed.

"Let me have your shirt. I'm going to grab a quick shower and I'll rinse it out, then we can go. C'mon, let me have it."

"We'll do it tonight. I have another one in my room. I want to get going."

"You're mad at me, aren't you?" Elizabeth asked, drawing close to him.

"Go get your shower, Liz."

Elizabeth was showered and in the truck before Atkinson came back out. Sitting in the front seat with most of Boomer on her lap, she hummed some of the melody from Desafinado that Atkinson had played the day before. The crisp fragrance from her shampooed hair filled the cabin.

Atkinson felt a flood of emotions, but anger wasn't one of them. "I should be angry, but it's good to hear you laugh so hard, even if was at my expense."

"Where are we headed today?" Elizabeth asked with an air of excitement.

"Maybe to Grand Forks. That's right at the border of North Dakota and Minnesota."

"How far is that?" Elizabeth asked.

"About 420 miles. That'll get us out of Montana and most of the way across North Dakota."

"I don't mean to be rude, Liz, but you're awful cheery this morning. What's up?" Atkinson asked as he pulled out of the lot heading east on Route 2.

"A lot, Tommy. I've been running away from this shit all my life. I've been a slave to something I call the darkness. It just comes over me. I get completely isolated. I get scared and it affects everything I'm doing and everyone I'm with. I have to run to the point of exhaustion to beat it back. Vodka and Valium just get me through the day. It paralyzes me and I get all fucked up. It's actually a *thing*. I call it the darkness, but I can actually see it."

"What do you see?" Atkinson prodded.

"It's like I'm standing on a narrow wooden deck and at the end of the deck there's this, like this large space that goes from the ceiling to the floor and it's black as pitch. I cannot stop myself from moving into it. It started this morning when I was waking up, so I took Boomer out for a run. Then I remembered that beautiful church, St. Aloysius, by the Foley Library in Spokane."

"What about it?" Atkinson asked, not seeing the point.

"You remember showing me row after row of Official Catholic Directories in the library and me wondering why the Church would go to the trouble of putting out all this information year after year? The physical location of every single Catholic entity in the United States?"

"I do."

"Well, this morning I had this urge to run *into* the darkness. It was the first time I ever felt that way. It was like I had to embrace it. Get it on me, kinda wallow in it and then it started to fade. I could see everything around me and then it hit me like a ton of bricks."

"I'm just not following you, Liz," Atkinson said impatiently, tapping the steering wheel.

"It's the fucking real estate!" Elizabeth chortled, startling Boomer in the back seat. "The Church needs to lay out all of their brick-and-mortar activities every year to protect their non-profit tax exemption with the Government. They probably have $1 trillion of market value in their real estate holdings that appreciates in value, tax free, year after year. What do you think St. Patrick's Cathedral or the National Shrine is worth? All their artwork, investment portfolio," Elizabeth rattled off, not waiting for an answer. "They pay zero fucking dollars in taxes and that's why the Official Catholic Directory is published every year."

"Damn, woman, you were busy this morning."

"I was, but just hold onto that for a bit. I want to talk to you about something else."

"Shoot," Atkinson said.

"Talk to me about this celibacy crap," Elizabeth said bluntly. "I read in Berry's book this mandatory celibacy stuff started with Pope Gregory way back when," Elizabeth said as she opened her pack and took out her pen and yellow pad.

"Basically yes, but it's more complicated than just a time marker."

"What do you mean?" Elizabeth asked as she drew a vertical line down the center of her yellow pad.

"Much like what you concluded this morning about the Church's real estate holdings, Pope Gregory was obsessed with not losing ecclesiastical property to the children and wives of then married priests. So, that's the rationale as to why it happened."

"Sounds like a 'but' is in there somewhere," Elizabeth said, taking notes.

"It's actually a big 'but.' The Church spun the mandatory celibacy rule in such a way as to elevate the priests above the laity. I have done a lot of work on this. I call it clericalism. They put the celibate priesthood on a glorified pedestal. It was a tactical calculation on the part of Pope Gregory. The so called 'grace of purity' set priests apart from everyone else, solidifying their power and prestige. As God's earthly representatives, the priests were the chosen ones.

"I mean Jesus, Tommy, you have to give up..." Elizabeth stopped in mid-sentence, realizing she was in dangerous territory.

"What?" Atkinson asked. "What were you going to say?"

"No, I don't want to pry."

"You're not prying, I'll let you know if you're prying. Now what?"

Elizabeth sat silent for several seconds rubbing Boomers ears. "Sex. I was going to say you have to give up sex." Flustered,

Elizabeth tried to terminate the conversation. "Forget I even mentioned it, Tommy. Really, I'm sorry."

"That was the deal I made in order to be closer to God, Liz."

"So, you never… Christ, I can't believe we're talking about this. So, you've never been with someone," Elizabeth stuttered.

"I didn't say that, Liz," Atkinson said.

"But what about that 'grace of purity' stuff?" Suddenly Elizabeth flushed with fear and excitement. "So, you have…"

"Listen Liz, I'm far from perfect. It was when I was overseas. She was a nurse. We were attracted to each other, and it just happened. We spent three months together and she rotated out of the unit."

"Then what? Did you ever see her?" Elizabeth asked.

"We talked a few times but we both had our other life, and we just went our separate ways."

Atkinson felt tremendous relief. It was if he had gone to confession. He was glad that Elizabeth knew the part of his past that he had struggled with. His relationship with God was evolving and he wanted Elizabeth to be a part of it, but there was so much in the way.

Elizabeth wished she was anywhere but in the cab of Atkinson's truck. She could hardly believe that her only true love was sitting right next to her, and she was damaged most likely beyond repair. It was if she had lost him for the second time and she had no one else to blame but herself and her addictions. Her only recourse was to go to work.

"You okay, Liz?" Atkinson asked.

"I'm fine, Tommy. Can we go back to the theoretical?" Elizabeth asked.

"Probably not a bad idea," Atkinson mused. "The faithful's belief in the celibate clerics allowed the priesthood to cast an air of superiority over us mere mortals. It locked in their power base. Look at it this way, Liz, did you see the movie The Lion King?"

"No, it's one of the Disney movies isn't it?"

"It is, and it's actually pretty good. I took my nieces to see it. Anyway, there's a song in the movie called the Circle of Life. Priests are involved in every significant stage of a Catholic's life. When your parents are married, a priest officiates the ceremony and endows the couple with the grace of the sacrament in the eyes of God. They're encouraged to go forth and multiply, you know that whole shtick, and it's the same for you when you're baptized. You become a formal member of the club at your First Holy Communion, and then you get turbo charged with the Holy Spirit at confirmation to practice your faith even more fervently. They bring in the heavy artillery for that because a bishop usually officiates. The priest privately relieves you of the burdens of your sins in confession and when you die, they bury you and send you off to heaven. For the believers, all of this is powerful juju. The only ones that can deliver such godly service to the faithful are those select celibate men called to the priesthood by God himself. It's the circle of life and the priest is at the center, beginning and end of each Catholic's life, wielding power and influence over Catholic kids and their faithful families."

"Wow, Tommy, that's pretty depressing coming from a Catholic priest," Elizabeth said.

"I've had my eyes opened since the time I was a young priest, Liz. I drank the Kool-Aid myself. Now I'm simply looking at facts."

"Tommy, this is crazy. It's nothing but a house of cards. But I want to get back to the relationship between the Church's assets and celibacy. So, let me understand, do we agree that mandatory celibacy does not cause a perpetrator to sexually act out with kids?"

"I agree with that," Atkinson said.

"So, the rule itself creates the environment for sexual abuse to flourish."

"Well said, Counselor, with one caveat."

"What's that?" Elizabeth asked.

371

"That the Church's obsession with secrecy when combined with mandatory celibacy creates an environment for sexual abuse of minors to flourish."

"So, what exactly do you mean about obsession with secrecy?"

"Let me explain it this way. Let's assume a heterosexual priest is involved in an entirely consensual sexual relationship with a woman. And let's further assume a homosexual priest is engaged in an entirely consensual sexual relationship with a man. Now, finally, assume that a priest is having criminal sexual contact with either a male or a female. One of those three acts is a crime, the other two are simply breaches of their commitment to remain chaste. Unfortunately, bishops view them *all* as equally scandalous. In effect, no one's ox would be gored without disclosing other secrets that would be scandalous to the faithful. The Church's bizarre view of sex in general has allowed thousands of sexual predators to hide in their midst."

"To what end? To what possible end, Tom?" Elizabeth asked, putting her pen down.

"That's easy, Liz. To maintain power over the faithful, and to protect the true believers from scandal. The bishops need to know that they'll be able to continue to fill the pews and those are the same people who will be the financial life blood of the organization. The faithful need to believe that their local priest is special, and their belief is that if they follow the dogma as laid out for them, they'll get in the gates of heaven. The bishops know that people who have faith are vulnerable to that way of thinking and that by continuing to exploit their fears the circle is complete."

"And thousands of innocent children get lost in the shuffle," Elizabeth said, repeatedly stabbing her pen into her yellow notepad.

"You're missing the point, Liz. It's easy to call the cover-up of these crimes by bishops criminal acts. They very well may be. Some day in the future some Federal prosecutor may have the balls to indict them all, but not today. But you really have to understand

372

this, the bishops didn't think about it that way. No one wants to believe that a sitting bishop would knowingly put an innocent child in the sights of a dangerous sexual predator. Better to suggest, if they are absolutely forced to, that a few bad apples committed these isolated incidents."

"What a crock of shit," Elizabeth said, staring out on the vast landscape.

"Well, you may call it a crock of shit but if you're going to do anything about this you better understand how they think."

"Okay, Father Atkinson, I'll play along. How do they justify the cover-up?" Elizabeth said with all the snarkiness she could muster.

"They don't see it as a cover-up at all. The bishops see the sexual abuse of minors as an attack on the clerical state. They see the faithful being exposed to scandal, which puts their very soul in jeopardy. The bishops believe that if they acknowledge the cover-up as a criminal act, the word of God will be compromised, the prestige of the Church will be tarnished and, here's the key, Liz: They're morally bound not to let that happen on their watch. The bishops believe that the greater good for the faithful trumps any individual slight by one of its clerics, even if it's the sexual assault of a child. In effect, the bishops use religious duress against their own folks to keep them toeing the line."

"Well, Tommy, maybe it's time we change that," Elizabeth said, drawing a line across the bottom of her notes.

LIKE AS IN A COUPLE?

For the next three days, Thomas Atkinson and Elizabeth Natale were road trip tourists. Neither seemed interested in exploring the topic that brought them together, save the intermittent furious note taking by Elizabeth. Atkinson decided to leave her to her own devices and wait for her to share when she was ready. They had a good laugh "walking across" the Mississippi River headwaters at the Lake Itasca State Park in Minnesota, touring the outdoor sculpture garden at the Lake Park in downtown Duluth and enjoying road food in places not particularly attractive but that had a lot of local license plates in parking lots.

"Can I ask you something?" Elizabeth asked as she sized up a huge Cobb salad at Grandma's Saloon and Grill in downtown Duluth, a local favorite since 1976.

"Sure, what's going on in that head of yours?" Atkinson asked.

"Tommy, have you ever thought about leaving the priesthood?" As soon as Elizabeth heard the words come out of her mouth, she wished she had not asked. "I'm sorry, Tommy, that's way too personal. Forget I said anything."

Atkinson ignored her comment. "Actually, Liz, I've thought about it a lot. It's about all I have thought of the last three days. Why do you ask," Atkinson said.

"Well, do you remember when I kissed you when we met during winter break in college?"

"Really, Elizabeth," Atkinson said, blushing.

"I was pissed that you stole my thunder," Elizabeth said, not willing to give an inch.

"Christ, Liz, you told me to go first. And you chose not to say anything about Dolan."

"Wow, that was harsh," Elizabeth said, putting her fork down.

Atkinson pushed his half-eaten pastrami sandwich to the side. "You're right it was harsh but it's the truth."

Elizabeth looked up and smiled. "It is the truth. So, we're even. Let's start this conversation over. Why don't you finish your sandwich? Here is what I was getting at... Do you think our lives would be different if I had told you what had happened to me and that I was in love with you?"

Atkinson squirmed in his seat. "Liz, I don't have a lot of experience with these types of conversations."

"What kind of conversation?" Elizabeth asked, oblivious to Atkinson's distress.

"The kind that opens the door for a reexamination of just about every decision I've made in my adult life. The kind that plays out against the backdrop of a beautiful woman and an international scandal. Those kinds of conversations," Atkinson said, pushing his sandwich with his fork.

"Jesus, don't get huffy. Thank you for the compliment, but we're just talking, Tommy."

"Liz, do you remember how you described what you called the darkness?"

"I certainly do," Elizabeth said, leaning into the table.

"I have something similar. It's called a black hole for me, and my black hole is alcohol. For the first time in almost five years, I was thinking about having a drink. You remember the other day, when I said I wanted to take a walk?"

"Yeah, why?" Elizabeth asked.

"I went and found a meeting. I needed some support from people who know that you stay sober one day at a time."

"You mean an AA meeting?"

"Yes, and I felt guilty for not inviting you."

"You shouldn't have, I wouldn't have gone. I don't do the group thing well."

"I'm not going to touch that, Liz. I'll just say that without the group I doubt I would have survived."

"And I don't want to argue with you about my drinking or your sobriety," Liz said. "I haven't had a drink in almost a week. I'm not taking pills. Besides, I have you taking care of me."

"And when I'm not around? What then, Liz?"

Elizabeth looked away.

"I told you earlier I wasn't a therapist," Atkinson said.

Furious, Elizabeth put her fork down again and waited for

Atkinson to look at her. "So, what, Tom? So fucking what," Elizabeth hissed. "Does it really matter if you're not a therapist or does stringing together days where I'm not barking at the moon for a drink or popping pills matter? Isn't that what matters? And for the record, when you're not around I'll figure it out. And one more thing… while we're talking, my darkness is right next to me. The second I'm not doing something it slithers its way into my head, and it's a fight just to stay upright."

Atkinson was flummoxed. His desire for the company of a woman was running headlong into his vocation as a Catholic priest, all over a Cobb salad and a pastrami sandwich. He leaned back in his chair, crossed his legs and ordered a cup of coffee. He looked at Elizabeth as he fiddled with the check the waitress had put on the table, wondering where all this was going.

"You asked me a question and I want to answer it. I think I remember it," Atkinson said, choosing his words carefully. "You asked whether I think our lives would be different if you had told me about Dolan and that you were in love with me. Do I have it right?" Atkinson asked Elizabeth.

"You do."

"My answer is that it doesn't matter, because I can't go back any more than you can. Any other answer would be influenced by what I know now and what I feel now. And right now, looking back, I could have just as easily fallen in love with you. But we can't go back, can we, Liz?"

A faint smile spread across Elizabeth's face. "We can't go back, but it's nice to know it was a possibility even if it's in hindsight. Do you want to talk about it anymore?"

"Not really, Liz. Not now."

"Okay, but are we still a team of road warriors?" Elizabeth asked awkwardly.

"Indeed we are, Elizabeth, a team of misfits and that includes your buddy Boomer."

"So, where to next, Tommy?" Elizabeth asked, hoping the transition was not too obvious.

"You have to see Mackinac Island. I was there as a kid, but you take a ferry from Mackinac City, and there are some nifty places to eat and up on the hill there is a huge, kinda old world hotel called the Grand. It's really spectacular at sunset."

"Are we staying there? That sounds interesting," Elizabeth said.

"They don't take pets, I looked before. Besides, it would break the budget."

"Well, if Boomer isn't welcome, I wouldn't want to stay there either," Elizabeth said, reaching back to grab her jacket on the back of the chair.

"Liz, wait a minute. I want to ask you one question before we leave."

Elizabeth was already standing at the table waiting for Atkinson to get up. "Should I sit?" A sense of worry tugged at her as she wrapped herself in her jacket and sat back at the table.

"Yeah, just for a minute," Atkinson said, unsure if there was a right way to ask his question. "So, when you asked me about what my feelings were about you when we were in college..." Atkinson hesitated in mid-sentence as Elizabeth waited for him to speak. "I'm sorry, Liz, I'm not very good at this stuff."

"That's not a question, Tommy," Elizabeth said.

"I know it's not a question, Liz. Jesus, give me a second." Atkinson was in uncharted territory, so he just said what was on his mind to clear the air and to get the rock off his chest. "How do you feel about me now?"

"I don't understand, Tommy. How do you mean? Like what you're doing with the bishops?"

"No, no, not that."

Elizabeth processed the look on Atkinson's face as an alarm went off in her head. "Oh, I wasn't expecting that. You mean us, like as in a couple."

Atkinson's sympathetic nervous system was at full throttle, relieved and embarrassed that he didn't have to explain his question any further. "Yes, like a couple," Atkinson said weakly as his blood vessels opened wide, turning his face crimson red.

Elizabeth felt a jolt of adrenaline course through her body. She knew that what she now needed to share would be the end of the subject. Suddenly she felt the death rattle of her familiar darkness began to stir.

"You know when we were talking about therapy," Elizabeth started.

"Yeah," Atkinson said, looking down at the table.

"Tommy, look at me," Elizabeth commanded. "Remember when I said I hadn't gone to any therapy until our trip?"

"Yes."

"Here's what I didn't tell you. I don't know how to be in a relationship with a man. I've never had one. Never learned it. If I wasn't having one-night stands, I was drinking, working, or running, or all three until I was hollowed out." Elizabeth shuddered as she heard the words tumble out. "As much as I want something different intellectually, I feel powerless to change. I'm damaged goods and I have no one to blame but myself."

"Liz, let me say something."

"No, Tommy, I need to get this out. Before I came out here, I went to my mother's house, and I got a gun my father had when he died."

Atkinson looked up, concerned about what he had unleashed. "Where is it now, Liz?"

"It's in the National Airport in a locker. My plan was to talk to you, come home and then track the motherfucker down and kill him."

"Were you worried you would get caught?" Atkinson asked.

"I had no plans of getting caught, Tommy. That's my darkness," Elizabeth said, her voice starting to crack.

"We both have baggage, Liz," Atkinson said.

"And, Tommy, no matter how much either of us wants it to be different, that baggage will always be there. How do I feel about you?" Elizabeth posited. "I think you're the best thing that's ever happened to me."

"And this business about Dolan and the gun?"

"No, I'm not going to kill him. He's a piece of shit. Maybe someone else will kill him but it's not going to be me."

Atkinson got up and walked behind her chair to pull it out for her. He put his hands on her shoulders and bent down to her ear. "How do you lawyer types say it, for the record…"

"Yes, that's the phase," Elizabeth said, smiling.

"For the record, you're the best thing that has ever happened to me too."

SO, WHAT'S NEXT FOR YOU?

Knowing that their time together was drawing to a close, Atkinson intentionally took two days to drive the 420 miles from Duluth to Mackinac Island, Michigan. They arrived at the ferry terminal just before noon the next day. Atkinson and Elizabeth settled in their seats with Boomer in between them for the forty-minute ride to Mackinac Island.

"So, what's next for you, Liz?"

"Haven't got that far, Tommy."

"You know there may be someone in D.C. who you might like to meet. I called back to my office at the base and this guy left three messages, and with his firm being in D.C. I thought it might be interesting to you. I thought maybe we could meet him together."

"Well, who is it?" Elizabeth asked.

"His name is Paul Weinstein, he's a lawyer with a big firm down there and with you having that eureka moment about the Church asset thing, it might be fun to exchange notes."

"Has he sued the Church before?" Elizabeth asked.

"From the gist of the message, I don't think so. He has signed up a number of cases and he was talking about a possible class action and that he wanted to talk to me. That's all I know right now. Apparently, he's read Jason Berry's book too, but that tax exemption stuff you were talking about is something I don't think anyone has ever thought about."

"Well, there's more to it than that," Elizabeth said, stroking Boomer's head. "Have you ever heard of the civil RICO laws?"

"I don't think I have. What is it?" Atkinson asked.

"It's a statutory scheme that permits you to sue a corrupt organization for damages and other relief if certain conditions are met. RICO stands for Racketeer Influenced and Corrupt Practices Act."

"You mean like Al Capone?"

"Well, yes, but it's not limited to organized crime. It could apply to any organization. It's a little convoluted but just stay with me. You mentioned that the Church hierarchy has been engaged in cover-up, right?"

"Yes," Atkinson answered firmly.

"And they were covering up sexual crimes committed against minors and then transferring priests around to different churches and some even out of state to go back into parishes."

"Yes, all the time."

"So, this business of clericalism you explained and the suppression of scandal to the faithful, that was their motive to continue the cover-up. Am I right about that?"

"Absolutely, Liz. I see where you're going."

"Now here's where it gets tricky. If the Diocese knew they had sexual predators in their ranks and continued to facilitate the assaults by leaving them in parishes, that's what's called a predicate act, in this specific case it's fraud. But it has to cause an injury to business or property. It's a jurisdictional requirement. You still with me?"

"Just like I'm going to school, Counselor," Atkinson quipped, enthralled by Elizabeth's logical progression in explaining her argument.

"The injury to business or property is the suppression of the lawsuit. A lawsuit is a right of property, the law review geeks call it a 'chose in action.' It's how you explained the hierarchy's motivation for the cover–up. A lawsuit against the Church by a Catholic would in and of itself be scandalous to the faithful."

"Whoa. I just fell off the turnip truck. I didn't follow that."

"Okay, listen. Didn't you tell me that the bishops didn't look at this as a cover-up?"

"Yes."

"And that's because, whether they believed it or not, they acted as if any revelation about sexual predators would be an attack on the Church, which would be scandal to the faithful, knocking them cleanly off their self-made pedestal onto their fat fucking asses."

"Now I see where you're going. At the heart of their mission statement was the preservation of the money flow."

"Exactly, Tommy, with one monumental caveat. They intended to preserve their tax-free money flow at any cost, even at the expense of children. So, aside from punitive damages, my theory would be that the only way to prevent this from happening again is to revoke their IRS tax free status based on their predicate act crimes against children under the equitable relief section of the statute."

"Jesus, Liz, is this really possible?" Atkinson asked, awestruck at Elizabeth's recitation.

"Yes, it's possible. Whether it's probable, that's a completely different story."

"Why do you say that?" Atkinson asked, intrigued.

"Well, the first problem is you need the right client willing to go through the shit storm of litigation. Then you need a kick ass law firm willing to put their reputation on the line for something that has never been done before. Then there's the parade of horribles, law firm overhead when you start losing institutional clients because you're calling the princes of the Church racketeers. Then, whoever's in charge, they would have to find really smart lawyers who are willing to tank their careers if they end up on the wrong side of this turd. Then there's this messy business of freedom of religion as it relates to the separation between Church and State. The Church lawyers will bang on this as long as the judges allow them. It's a total bullshit argument and they'll keep making it, hoping to break the financial back of the plaintiff's lawyers. Finally, not to put too sharp a point on it, you won't only be fighting the other side's lawyers, you will be fighting the judges who won't want to go anywhere near this pile of shit."

Elizabeth was surprised at the pressure she felt in her stomach. Listening to herself going through the "what if" scenarios created a dark, toxic knot in her gut. She could not imagine what it would be like going through it for real.

As they neared the Mackinac Island dock through the confluence of Lake Michigan and Lake Huron, the clouds above the horizon became a mix of cobalt blue and pink as sunset approached. Boomer was more than ready to get off the ship, seemingly unnerved by the engine vibrations coming up through his feet through the deck plates.

The walk up from the docks on Astor Street was crowded with sidewalk vendors and a variety of tourist traps and horse smells, which put Boomer on alert. The flavor of the island as a summer colony for the wealthy was on full display as they strolled past the large homes on Market Street and B&Bs from the early twentieth century. The patio at the Gate House was equipped with overhead heaters and dog bowls for "friendly critters," as long as they were tethered to the wrought iron fence surrounding the outside deck. Elizabeth ordered toast and a pot of tea.

"Don't mind me, eat something if you're hungry. I'm fine, my stomach is just a bit off. I get upset talking about all that bullshit."

"It sounded as you had it pretty well sorted out to me."

"Really, Tommy? Well, I've learned a couple of things along the way practicing law."

"And pray tell what's that," Atkinson said, playfully mocking Elizabeth.

"A great plan without the ability to execute is just a pipe dream. It was a theory, unproven and untested. That's all it was, Tommy."

"Then why did you get so upset?" Atkinson asked.

"Because it puts me back into the shit pile and the shit pile is right next door to the darkness. I'm tired of it, Tom. I can't seem to control it. You know, do you ever get just fucking tired of it all?" Elizabeth said, pointing her spoon at him.

"Of course I do, but here's what I've learned along the way, as you say. You have to keep banging on that door. Just keep getting up and getting into the goo and one day when you least expect it, the darkness won't have as much power over you. Susan St. James says you just wake up and see what life dishes out and you adjust."

"Who the hell is Susan St. James," Elizabeth stuttered.

"She owns the Newport Antler. Remember back in Washington, the coffee, Boomer crashing into me…"

"Oh, now I remember," Elizabeth said, laughing.

"What about that morning when you were on your run, and you told me about your feeling of running into the darkness?" Atkinson asked. "I think you said embracing the darkness."

"Jesus, are you writing down everything I say?"

"No, but I remember the important stuff. Liz, let me just throw something out. If you think I'm full of shit, I'll drop it and we'll go along our merry way to Houlton, Maine. Agreed?"

"Go ahead, Tommy, it's your dime in the jukebox."

"Ever hear of the word synchronicity?"

"Sure, what about it?" Elizabeth asked.

Here's my point, Liz. All of what has happened over the last week are meaningful coincidences that when looked at alone would have little or no significance. Your story of abuse and how it has shaped you, how Barbara Blaine got you to me, the growing survivor movement at SNAP, my story of being on the inside of the scandal, your theories on tax exemption and RICO, Paul Weinstein's thought about a class action, Jason Berry's book being published and the media coverage it has generated. All of the dots are getting connected. You see that, right?"

"I see what you're saying, but it doesn't mean it'll be successful. But I have to admit, I'm curious."

"Liz, listen, I realize that any one of these facts alone couldn't move the ball. But because we're at this particular time, in this particular place, with these particular people, the improbable become possible. That's synchronicity!"

Elizabeth pressed her tea bag against her spoon, allowing the liquid to drain into her cup. "When were you going to meet this Weinstein lawyer?"

"He left it open. I just need to give him a day or two notice."

"How long a drive to D.C.?"

"From here or from Houlton, Maine?"

"From here, Tommy, unless you really want to go to Maine and have time before you have to go to Florida."

"If we leave from here, I'll be stuck in D.C. because my base housing isn't available for another ten days. I could see if I'm still welcome at the Dominican House across from the Shrine."

"You can stay at my place, and the building allows tenants to have pets so Boomer wouldn't be a problem. I can stay at my mother's. Besides, I need to spend some time with Frannie. I've got a major fucking bone to pick with him."

Atkinson pushed some cold French fries around his plate.

"You're disappointed we're not going to Maine?"

"Not really, Route 2 isn't going anywhere."

"Then what's the matter?"

"Nothing really. I just think that this may end up being a big deal with a life of its own."

"Maybe it will. Bobby Willis was my mentor at my old firm. He had a saying for these situations."

"What was it?"

"Go big or go home."

Atkinson laughed. "I like him, and I don't even know him."

"You may not like him if you knew him. He can be a real ball breaker in a courtroom."

"Well, today I like him. We'll leave for D.C. in the morning, and I'll call Weinstein back and tell him we'll meet him on Monday. You good with that, Liz?"

"I am, Tom. This should be interesting."

PART THREE
DELIVERANCE

CHAPTER NINE

Trust No One

ARE YOU A MAN OF RELIGIOUS FAITH?

Alistair McCabe had a spring in his step as he walked up 51st Street toward Cardinal Archibald Hurley's residence on Madison Avenue. He thought of the stories his father loved to recount at the dinner table about his Irish grandparents crossing the Atlantic in steerage, "Broke, hungry and on the balls of their skinny Irish asses." Both his grandfather and father sold vegetables out of a 1915 Model T Ford Huckster in the spring and summer and coal and kerosene in the winter. His grandmother had been a maid at the Pierre Hotel and his beloved mother worked for forty years as a seamstress in the garment district making custom shirts. Alistair would wear the seconds that his mother brought home, forging his lifelong love of fashion, fine clothing and the accoutrements of success.

McCabe glanced at his reflection in the glass storefronts as he walked, smiling at the thought that his suit was worth more than what his father made in a year. Cocktail conversation and discrete judicial referrals had perfectly positioned his firm to pick up the gauntlet of defending the Church against an incoming tide of abuse cases.

The firm had successfully closed a lucrative land lease deal for the Palace Hotel earlier in the month and word through the legal grapevine was that the Archdiocese wanted to decisively crush what Cardinal Hurley described as "an unfortunate nuisance that would quickly pass like all the other attacks on the Church."

Now the Cardinal Archbishop of New York needed McCabe's services to smooth over a crisis involving two minors. McCabe's only regret was that he was late to the party. Priest sex abuse cases were breaking all over the country and he had already missed out on several years of fees.

At 9:00 A.M. sharp, acknowledging the two burly security guards stationed at each side of the arched entrance, McCabe climbed the seven steps to 452 Madison Avenue. He cheerfully presented himself to the closed-circuit camera in the limestone alcove of the Cardinal's residence and waited to be buzzed in.

"Alistair McCabe to see Cardinal Hurley. His Eminence is expecting me."

His announcement was acknowledged by the electronic deadbolt releasing the polished bronze door, permitting him entrance to the main foyer.

"Good morning, Mr. McCabe, my name is Father Patrick Stanton, I'm one of His Eminence's secretaries. I'll escort you to His Eminence's office. If you would follow me…"

"Thank you, Father Stanton, that would be excellent," McCabe said crisply to the Cardinal's adjutant.

The foyer was framed by a gleaming inlaid marble floor, a Spanish cedar ceiling and a two-story mahogany staircase. He paused to admire the intricately carved newel post and balusters on the staircase as well as the finely executed life-sized portraits of the previous Cardinals who had resided in the building since 1880. The Cardinal's office was on the second floor at the end of a long hallway overlooking the sacristy and west transept of the Lady Chapel at the rear of St. Patrick's Cathedral. Father Stanton knocked once on the heavy oak raised paneled door and entered the Cardinal's office.

"Good morning, Mr. McCabe. So good of you to come on such short notice," Cardinal Hurley said as he got up and walked around his desk.

McCabe was relieved that the Cardinal did not offer his ring to kiss, but instead moved to the coffee service on a sideboard next to his desk.

"I've been looking forward to our meeting, Your Eminence."

"I have as well, Mr. McCabe. May I serve you some coffee, Mr. McCabe? It's freshly brewed."

"If it's not a bother, that would be delightful. Thank you for your personal letter last week on the closing of the land lease for the Palace Hotel. It'll be a wonderful keepsake."

"Well, you did a superb job at a critical time for the Archdiocese and their faithful. How do you take your coffee?"

"Black, please, Your Eminence."

"Easy enough," Hurley said as he placed the cup of steaming coffee on a slate coaster on the side table next to McCabe.

McCabe felt it odd that the Cardinal was serving him coffee and wondered if it were somehow tactical on his part. McCabe took inventory of the man in front of him. Taller than McCabe would have preferred, the Cardinal's refined features and mannerisms were characteristic of the aristocracy. His perfectly tailored full-length cashmere cassock, the scarlet silk sash around his waist and matching zucchetto all revealed to McCabe a man totally at ease with his position and political power. Hurley's soft blue eyes, offset by his styled sandy hair and ready smile, were the public mask of the steady erudite shepherd of two million Catholics in the New York metropolitan area.

Beneath that charming façade, though, the Cardinal was every bit the part of a seasoned Fortune 500 CEO. He was a trained lawyer with the demeanor of a poker player and the manicure of an elegant patrician whose sole focus was the financial bottom line of his archdiocese. The sexual and financial excesses of the eighties did not appear to deter Hurley's rigid adherence to Catholic dogma. Even in the scrum of New York liberal politics, Hurley's ability to leverage the diverse weight of the Catholic laity, the unions and, of course, the judiciary, ensured he would remain a potent political force that could not be ignored.

"Please sit, Mr. McCabe, and bring me up to date on this Dolan matter. Father, would you mind excusing us? And let everyone know that I don't wish to be disturbed."

"Of course, Your Grace," Father Stanton said as he gathered several files from the corner of Hurley's desk and took his leave.

McCabe noticed a flash of indignation on Stanton's face and made a mental note about potential palace intrigue that he may have to manage in the future. McCabe waited for the door to close before he spoke.

"I couldn't help but notice that Father Stanton would have preferred to remain," McCabe said as he sipped his coffee.

"That shouldn't come as a surprise to someone like yourself, Mr. McCabe."

"How so?"

"Well, we have a difficult situation to deal with in this Dolan matter. You're an outsider, so to speak, so naturally my staff would have a tendency to be somewhat guarded. They're very loyal to our mission and to me."

"I understand, Your Eminence. But to be blunt, I'm not exactly sure what you're going to tell me that might be adverse to your interest. So, at the outset I worry about potential witnesses, notwithstanding your belief that your advisers are loyal to you and the Church."

"I see, McCabe, so you're saying trust no one."

"It certainly is not a bad rule, Your Eminence."

Hurley turned from the window and faced McCabe. "Does that include you, Mr. McCabe?" the Cardinal asked as he fingered the gold and scarlet braided cord and pectoral cross that hung around his neck.

"I'll let my performance guide you to that conclusion, Your Eminence, but allow me to suggest that your staff has no clue as how to protect you, your mission, or the Church under these circumstances."

"And you of course you do, Mr. McCabe," Hurley said with just enough sarcasm to annoy McCabe.

"Your Eminence, I believe my firm was recommended to you... " McCabe started.

"Highly, I might add, Counselor," Hurley interrupted.

"So, let me lay out what I can bring to the table."

"Please do, Mr. McCabe, that would be helpful."

McCabe took another sip of coffee and very deliberately laid the china cup into the saucer. "In a word, Your Eminence, it is resistance. I cannot tell you whether Dolan is the tip of the iceberg or an aberrant isolated event. My suspicion is that it's the former not the latter."

"And you base that on what, Mr. McCabe?" Hurley asked.

"Before I came here, I asked three of my associates to do a literature search on the topic of Catholic clergy sexual abuse. I like to see what's ahead of me, who my adversaries are, in a way to get the pulse of public opinion as shaped by the media. They assembled and summarized over a thousand pages of articles from the New York Times, Washington Post, The Cleveland Plain Dealer, National Catholic Reporter, Dallas Morning News, the Pittsburgh Post Gazette, all on Roman Catholic Clergy sexual abuse. They gave me books to read by Richard Sipe, Elinor Burkett, Guy Bruni and Jason Berry. I talked to Ray Mouton, who defended Gilbert Gauthe, and it seems this Thomas Atkinson fellow has become quite the thorn in your collective sides. Shall I continue, Your Eminence?"

"I think not, Mr. McCabe. I see your point."

"I mean no offense, Cardinal Hurley, but I would be remiss if I didn't clearly advise you that you have a tidal wave headed for you over these priests. I can resist, I can raise defenses, I can intimidate, but in the end, I cannot make a thousand-year-old problem go away."

"And do share with me, Mr. McCabe, what you perceive to be our thousand-year problem," Hurley said, thinly disguising his disdain.

"Whoever was in charge when they came up with your system underestimated nature. Nature always finds a way, Your Eminence, even in the face of Church law to the contrary. Men are sexual entities and sexual acting out comes in all different flavors. Most are legal, at least in the eyes of prosecutors, but one is very decidedly illegal. Once the Church becomes aware that a particular priest had sexual contact with a minor and that same priest goes about re-offending, then you're really stuck with him, and any jury will punish you."

Hurley crossed his legs and reached for his coffee, letting McCabe's words sink in. "You said you can resist. What exactly do you mean by that, Mr. McCabe?" Hurley asked as he went to his desk.

McCabe paused for a moment and walked to the window to gather his thoughts to give Hurley his best answer.

"We'll wear some plaintiffs and prosecutors out, and quite possibly we can influence others to simply stand down because of their religious faith. We can gin up negative public opinion about the accusers and their greedy lawyers through our media contacts. We'll also be able to buy out many cases in the coming months or years in the ten to $50,000 range and keep them contractually confidential."

"How so, Mr. McCabe?" Hurley asked.

"If we let the plaintiffs' bar know we intend to avail ourselves of every conceivable defense while at the same time make it very hard on the accuser, they'll think twice about pushing a decades old claim. They'll settle at a discount. There may well be situations that allow you to use the statute of limitations to convince the claimants to go away as their duty as good Catholics with a few dollars for therapy. But in the end, Your Eminence, after all I've read, some, maybe many, will get through. When that happens, you won't want juries deciding your fate. My sense is that if there are cases out there not subject to the statute of limitations and there's any kind of reasonable notice, we'll be talking real money."

Hurley looked up, surprised. "Many, Mr. McCabe?"

"Possibly, Your Eminence. Several states are pushing for an expansion of the statute of limitations. Some legislatures, like New Jersey, are implementing a discovery rule by statute, so as they say, this will be a marathon not a sprint. I've even heard some rumors about convening statewide grand juries. You have defenses, Cardinal Hurley. Your priests have defenses. The criminal statute for most of these incidents has run. So, generally, there's no interest in the police opening a criminal investigation. That's why this Dolan matter has to be nipped in the bud. You have statutes of limitation for civil claims that are very problematic for the plaintiffs. There's the First Amendment as it relates to the separation of Church and State. In some jurisdictions, like New Jersey, there's Charitable Immunity. The Newark Archdiocese dodged a huge bullet on that one. The kid was a boy scout and was assaulted by his Franciscan troop leader. The boy ultimately committed suicide, and New Jersey's statute immunized the Archdiocese from negligence."

"Is that available in New York?" Hurley asked.

"Unfortunately not, Your Eminence."

"But resistance, as you say, will lessen the impact of these cases. Am I correct in that assumption?" Hurley persisted.

"It will, but at a price."

"What do you mean, Mr. McCabe?"

"Well, for starters you'll pay my firm an obscene amount of money with no guarantee that you'll get the results you want. There will be plenty of bad publicity from the outset that will need to be managed, and if any of these cases get through to discovery it could prove embarrassing and expensive. If blood gets in the water, we could be playing wack-a-mole with the plaintiff's bar."

Hurley got up from his desk and walked to the oversized print of St. Patrick's Cathedral during construction that hung in his office opposite his desk.

"You paint a fairly bleak picture, Mr. McCabe."

"I trust you prefer to have an accurate picture, bleak or otherwise, Your Eminence."

"You're correct, Mr. McCabe. I must say I'm curious as to why you haven't asked what we knew about Dolan's misguided affection toward children."

McCabe stiffened in his chair. It sounded like a test to him. Hurley was the Cardinal, but he was also an attorney. Now it seemed he liked chess. McCabe needed to keep the playing field level.

"Your Eminence, of course I'm curious, but curiosity as they say could kill the cat. At the moment, no one has sued you about what, if anything, you knew about Dolan. I'm working under the presumption that you know nothing of Father Dolan's behavior other than what was reported to you after the fact. When and if someone shows me otherwise then we'll deal with that reality."

"I see, Mr. McCabe." Hurley slowly paced between the window and his desk, appearing somewhat detached from the conversation. "Is that how you manage all of your clients, Mr. McCabe?" Hurley asked.

McCabe wanted to choose his words carefully. He knew he was verging on arrogance, which would have been off-putting to Hurley, but he knew that CEO clients also wanted exclusivity.

"Your Eminence, I don't manage my clients. They manage me. As the facts become clearer, I'll tell you what your exposure is and then you'll make the decision as to how you want to handle it, and what you're willing to pay for it. My only requirement is that you don't talk to anyone about Father Dolan without talking to me first."

"Under the circumstances, that's fair, Mr. McCabe," Hurley said. "Do you have an initial sense as to the Archdiocese's exposure as it relates to Dolan's recent arrest?"

"Based on the fact that these two boys are minors, there's potentially significant exposure, Your Eminence. A minor's case, with notice to the Archdiocese of prior bad acts, worked up properly by the plaintiff's lawyer, could easily return a verdict in excess of $1 million."

"Are you a man of religious faith, Mr. McCabe?"

"Perhaps in this circumstance, I should be, Your Eminence, but in truth, I'm not. There's little room in the courthouse for religious faith."

Hurley laughed at McCabe's confident bluntness. "I was counseled by my Board of Consultors to hire a well-known Catholic who would act as lead counsel to manage our response."

McCabe smiled at Hurley. "Well, that would not be me, Your Eminence."

"No, that would not be you, Mr. McCabe. I chose you on the strength of your recommendations and the fact that your faith, or in this case your lack of faith, would not cloud your judgment."

"I think we'll be a good fit, Your Eminence. Can we move onto Father Dolan's criminal matter?" McCabe asked.

"Of course," Hurley said.

McCabe removed a pad from his leather-clad folio. "I received confirmation that Dolan's lawyer was paid by a lay friend of the Archdiocese. Arrangements have been made for Father Dolan to plead guilty to two misdemeanor indecency charges. He'll appear tomorrow morning at 9:45 A.M., fifteen minutes before the criminal arraignments begin. Dolan won't be in clerics and he will appear on the docket simply as Andrew Dolan."

"And the prosecutors, how did this lawyer get them to agree to downgrading these charges?"

"Cardinal Hurley, with all due respect I don't believe you need to be aware of those details other than it was perfectly legal. I think your interest would be better served when the criminal plea is entered on the docket, to allow me to facilitate a meeting with the parents. Tell them you're sorry and offer a small but not insulting offer for future educational costs in exchange for confidentiality and a full release admitting no wrongdoing on your part or the Archdiocese. I would call it a pastoral offer of assistance. Nothing more."

Hurley leaned back in his desk chair and took a deep breath. "Do you mind if I smoke, Mr. McCabe?"

"Not at all, Your Eminence."

Hurley reached into his top desk drawer and removed a silver case. "It's a filthy habit, but it helps me think," he said as he lit his cigarette. "I don't like this incremental set of factoids. I'm much more comfortable with the big picture."

McCabe chuckled as he looked up from his notepad. "As a lawyer I fully understand your sentiment, but I'm not in that role. You're the client, Your Eminence, and someday you may have to sit in a deposition and testify as to what you knew and when you knew it."

"All I know was that the woman detective was removed from the case. The Seal of Confession would prevent me from discussing this any further, Mr. McCabe."

McCabe was furious that Hurley used this bizarre form of religious redaction to keep him in the dark. McCabe channeled his anger at Hurley's arrogance into a mask of calm. "Your Eminence, that's a possible land mine that you should avoid stepping on. If there is a rogue detective with some pang of conscience, it could come back to explode in your lap."

"I understand completely, Mr. McCabe." Hurley exhaled a huge cloud of purple smoke and stamped out an unfiltered Lucky Strike cigarette in the ashtray. "And your job, Mr. McCabe, is to make sure that my deposition never happens."

"I understand, Your Eminence."

INTERSTATE 76, SOUTH OF PITTSBURGH, PENNSYLVANIA

Coursing through the Allegheny foothills on the perennially busy Pennsylvania Turnpike, Atkinson pondered the mountain of work that lay ahead of him. There were dozens of phone messages from lawyers, abuse survivors, family and friends wanting his new contact information. His Dominican Superior and the bishop who supervised the Catholic Chaplain Corps in the military both wanted to speak to him before he left for Hurlburt Field, home of the Air Force's Special Operations Wing.

Elizabeth was busy drafting long pages of notes that seemed more like a frenzied rant by the number of scrawled underlines and loud punctuated periods dotted on her notepad. The slight tremor in Elizabeth's hand seemed to be getting worse, which only highlighted Atkinson's desire to just collect Elizabeth up and take her to a real treatment center. In sum, he was in a foul mood.

"You gonna get that checked out when you get back to D.C.?" Atkinson asked, keeping his eyes and both hands on the steering wheel.

"Was that a question, Tommy?" Elizabeth said, noticing Atkinson's tone. "You seem cranky this morning."

"Do I? Maybe the end of trip reality is setting in. I'm getting slammed with pager messages each time we stop, and I'm more than a little worried about you."

"I'll get it checked out. Does that make you feel better?"

Atkinson lost his temper. "It does, goddammit, but I shouldn't be the one to nag you about it. Shaking means you're still detoxing, or you're agitated about something, making the tremors worse."

"Really, Tom. Now what in the world could I possibly be agitated about?" Elizabeth said sarcastically as she put her legal pad into her backpack.

"That's my point, Liz. We both have a lot going on and you're just starting on a road to recovery, and it gets chunky along the way. Ten days on a road trip isn't going to fix all the shit you went through. You need backup, support and a community that's engaged in the same journey."

"Why are we arguing, Tommy, I mean really, why are we arguing!" Elizabeth shouted over the Peterbilt tractor trailer roaring past Atkinson's truck.

"Well, one, because I care about you and two..."

Elizabeth interrupted him, not wanting to hear anymore. "If you care about me, let me find my way through all of this, unless you're telling me I can't talk to you after we get to D.C."

"I'm not telling you any such thing, of course we can talk."

"Every day?" Elizabeth asked, turning to him and grabbing his hand.

"Every day, Liz. Whatever it takes."

Elizabeth kissed his hand and pressed it to her cheek. "I don't want to argue with you. I promise I'll see a doctor about my hand. Now can we stop talking about me?"

"We can," Atkinson said, sounding defeated.

"Can we make a stop as we go into the city?" Elizabeth asked, changing the subject.

"We can, for what?"

"I know it's a bit out of the way, but I'd like to stop at National Airport," Elizabeth said.

"You know, I was going to ask you about that. You're done with that killing Dolan business?" Atkinson asked.

"I told you yes before, Thomas," Elizabeth snapped.

"After you get it what are you going to do with it, Liz?"

"I'm going to put it back, Thomas. If you don't want to take me there, it's fine, I'll take a cab tomorrow and do it myself."

Atkinson let all the air out of his lungs through his mouth and cheeks. "Nope, we'll swing by and pick it up."

"It's right inside the main door to the terminal. I'll be in and out in a couple of minutes."

"We'll make it work, Liz. I'll just be glad when the gun is back where it's supposed to be."

"I know. Listen, I can't tell you how much I appreciate this trip. Aside from the beautiful scenery, I think I'm starting to process all this shit in a healthier way. I have my to-do list and I'm going to take them one at a time."

"What's first on your list?" Atkinson asked as they entered the Tuscarora Mountain Tunnel.

"Frannie. Frannie's first on the list."

"That poor soul," Atkinson mused. "By the way, I picked up a message from Paul Weinstein. He said he can meet us Friday at his office."

"I thought we were meeting Monday," Elizabeth said, annoyed at the change of plans.

"All I know is he said something came up and we have to meet Friday."

Elizabeth tapped the end of her pen on the pad that was in her lap. "Are you okay with that, Tom?"

"Well, it's cutting me pretty thin, but I can get some things done between now and Friday."

Atkinson noticed Elizabeth looking out her window, seemingly impressed by rolling fields of new crops that dotted the Pennsylvania Turnpike.

Elizabeth stayed silent for several seconds. "I need to tell my mother what happened with Dolan. I should have done it thirty years ago. It's time."

401

"Wow, did you just decide that? Do you want me to come with you?"

"No, I don't think so. I think it would be better if I did it alone. I've been thinking about it for a couple of days. It's time, and it's time I stop holding that fucker's secret."

A BRILLIANT JEWEL UNDIMINISHED

Seven years after he left, Washington traffic was just as awful as Atkinson remembered it when he worked at the Vatican Embassy.

"You know what?" Atkinson asked as he exited the Capital Beltway at the George Washington Parkway and headed south to National Airport. "I think you're smart not to drive. It's Sunday and it's a parking lot out here."

Elizabeth laughed. "I'd go straight back on the GW Parkway and pick up Rock Creek Parkway and get off right at Harvard Street. There are some one-way streets coming in that way but that's the fastest way to get to my place."

"Okay, I know exactly where you are. That whole area, Adams-Morgan and Woodley Park used to be my old stomping grounds when I was at the Embassy."

"Really?" asked Elizabeth.

"You could actually walk to the Embassy from your apartment."

"I didn't know that. Do you want to drive by?" Elizabeth asked, seeing a look of melancholy on Atkinson's face.

"I don't think so, Liz. I'll be here for a week, and I want to get Boomer settled and do some laundry. Maybe later. We can take a walk by."

"You miss it, don't you?"

"Miss what?" Atkinson said.

"The action."

Atkinson stared ahead at a line of cars stopped at the entrance to the George Washington Parkway.

"I'm sorry, Tommy. I didn't mean to pry."

"You're not prying. I do miss it. But it's not the action, I miss having a course to move on. I thought my life was laid out. I was comfortable with it; I really did enjoy helping people find spiritual nourishment in the Church. I felt close to God. I believed I was doing God's work."

"And you liked the thought that someday you might be in charge of your own diocese," Elizabeth said, trying to not be confrontational.

Atkinson turned to Elizabeth and smiled.

"I did, Liz. That was true back then but not now. Now I'm an outsider in my own organization. Look at the birth control debate. It split parishes in two. Priests have left in droves over Pope Paul VI's mandatory celibacy encyclical of 1968. We treat women as second-class citizens, the hierarchy rails against homosexuality but in 1968 the Pope denied 'scandalous rumors' about himself."

"Wow, was the Pope gay?" Elizabeth asked, surprised.

"I have no idea. Actually, I couldn't care less," Atkinson fumed. "We've all been ordained under the mandatory celibacy rules, but the idiots forgot to look ahead to the twentieth century. Celibacy was just a power grab rooted in money. In the face of this scandal our moral authority is in the shit house. We're sexual beings and any Catholic teaching that denies the reality of that fact under the rubric of a brilliant jewel is just asinine."

"What do you mean about a brilliant jewel?" Elizabeth asked.

"Pope Paul VI, in his encyclical, described the Church's golden law of sacred celibacy as a brilliant jewel undiminished in value over the centuries. It's total bullshit," Atkinson huffed. "And the laity is on to us."

"So, why don't you just leave?"

"Elizabeth, I've asked myself that question a thousand times. I don't know why I don't leave. I'm in the Air force now as a Chaplain and I'm doing my thing."

"That's pretty lame. I think you're in the Air Force hiding, Thomas Atkinson."

"You know, Liz, ten days ago if you had said that to me, I would have put your butt right out on the curb."

"Then I'm really glad I didn't open my big mouth earlier in our trip," Elizabeth laughed. "I can tell you one thing I got out of the last ten days."

"Now, I'm interested in hearing that," Atkinson said.

"I learned not to be afraid of being sober. It doesn't work every day, but I've had some days when I wasn't afraid."

"And today, are you afraid?" Atkinson asked, looking over at Elizabeth.

"I am. It's not crazy out of control, but knowing I'm going to see my mother and Frannie has got me going a bit."

"Liz, I'll go over there with you."

"I know. You're sweet to offer but I want to do this alone. We didn't make it to Houlton Maine, but I have to say it was a helluva trip. Thank you, Tommy."

"It was a helluva trip, Liz," Atkinson said smiling. "Now we need to take care of this gun thing."

"Okay, Tommy, go slow, we're almost there. Just past that next driveway there's a pull in for dropping passengers. The lockers are right inside the main door. I'll be in and out in a flash."

"Do you have your key?" Atkinson asked.

"Yes, of course I have it."

"Okay, take it out."

Atkinson reached under his seat, feeling for a grease bead on the steel guide rail of his seat. He held up his index finger with a dollop of purple grease on the tip of his finger. "We use these lockers in the military all the time and the keys are notorious for getting jammed in the lock after they have been out and about."

"My word aren't you the handy one," Elizabeth said.

"C'mon, Liz, this is serious. When you come out put the bag in the back of the truck with the luggage. Is it loaded?" Atkinson asked.

"Of course it's loaded. I was going to kill the son-of-a-bitch."

"Christ Almighty, Liz." Atkinson jammed the truck into park annoyed at Elizabeth's arrogance and naiveté. He grabbed the key from Elizabeth's hand. "I'll be right back."

Atkinson rubbed the grease on his finger along the blade of the key, noting the embossed number and crossed the island curb on a trot. Once inside, he quickly found the locker. The key slid in and unbolted the lock. Atkinson did not look around but reached into the locker to feel the outline of the pistol. Unzipping the small pack, he opened the cylinder, released all the bullets and zipped up the bag and left. He hurried to the back of his truck and opened the bed, depositing the black case behind the suitcases. He got in the truck and slowly pulled into traffic, heading for the exit.

"Now, Elizabeth, we're done with the guns, right?" Atkinson said sternly.

"Yes. I'm sorry, Tom. I told you I would have done it myself."

Atkinson was furious. "Yeah, I heard that, but walking around with a loaded unregistered firearm in the District or in Virginia is a felony. You could lose your law license and a judge could sentence you to prison. All for what, Liz? That asshole Dolan?" Atkinson screamed. "So, when you take it to your mother's house, make sure it's in a suitcase and not your purse. We clear?"

Elizabeth realized it was a stupid decision that could have blown up in her face. She reached over, took Atkinson's hand into hers and held it tight. "I'm clear, Tommy."

Atkinson and Elizabeth rode in silence until they were out of the airport and near the turn for Harvard Street.

"There's a horseshoe drive in front of the apartment. We can unload there and then look for a place to park on the street. I'm expecting some mail that the concierge is holding for me. I'll be right back to help you." Elizabeth hoped that the material she had paid for had arrived but hoped there would be no need for her to use it.

YOU SAID YOU WERE GOING TO CALL

Atkinson moved the last piece of luggage into the foyer of Elizabeth's one-bedroom apartment.

"So, what do you think?" Elizabeth asked from the galley kitchen.

"I love it," Atkinson said. "It's a big improvement over my military quarters and if I stayed at the Dominican House of Studies, they probably would have put me in a broom closet. How did you get everything furnished so quickly?" Atkinson asked.

"Oh, this is all my stuff from my New York apartment. Do you like it?" Elizabeth cooed.

"I do, Liz. It's very warm and at the same time New York edgy. Did you take all these black and white pictures?"

"Oh, no, they were done by a landscape photographer friend of mine in New York."

"They're stunning images, but..."

"But what?" Elizabeth asked.

"Well, they're stark, Liz; there's no people in them."

"Gee, I never thought about it that way. Are you diagnosing me with some dreadful mental defect?" Elizabeth quipped. "Did you notice the one of me and my father when I was little?" she asked.

"I should have known that was you. It's a great picture of you and your dad and no, I was not diagnosing you with any type of defect," Atkinson said, smiling.

"Good, I don't think I could handle that coming from you. Give me a second, Tommy, I want to call my mother."

"Do you want some privacy? Boomer and I can take a walk."

"Don't be ridiculous. After the last ten days, what could be private? There's some diet soda or some bottled water if you prefer in the fridge. Make yourself at home," Elizabeth said as she went into the bedroom.

She sat on the bed and noticed that her heart was beating uncomfortably as she flipped through the surveillance photographs from an investigative agency in Washington. As she dialed her old number and waited for the call to connect, Elizabeth wondered whether the horrible spirals of pain in her gut would ever end.

"Momma, it's Elizabeth, I'm back in D.C." Elizabeth tapped her leg furiously and her eyes squinted, waiting to hear the tone in her mother's voice.

"Elizabeth, you said you were going to call," Lucy said. "I had no idea you got to California safe, no way to reach you, nothing. Now you call me to say you're back. Is that fair? Your grandmother was worried sick."

"It's not fair, Mother, but I can explain when I see you."

"Well, come on over then. I suppose you will want to eat?" Lucy's sarcasm had the expected effect on Elizabeth.

"Is that an invitation, Momma, because if it's too much trouble I can make other plans."

"Well, it's just us, Rose, and your grandmother. We eat at five-thirty."

"I'll see you then, Momma. Bye." Elizabeth stood up from her bed, her whole body shaking with rage. She picked the receiver back up and banged it repeatedly into the cradle. "What a fucking insufferable bitch!" she shouted. "How are you, Elizabeth, did you have a good trip, Elizabeth, do you want to come over, Elizabeth, and have dinner, Elizabeth, are you settled in your new apartment, Elizabeth?" Elizabeth fumed as she paced from the bathroom to her bed.

Atkinson leaned against the doorjamb of her bedroom. "So, it went well."

Elizabeth looked at him, dumbfounded, as Atkinson smiled back at her with his arms crossed on his chest.

"Yeah, right, Tommy. It actually went just as I expected."

"So, I'll ask you again: Are you sure you don't want me to go with you?"

"Listen, Tom, it's not that I would not like you to be with me, it's just something I should have done for myself thirty years ago. I can't undo the damage, but I can get some self-respect back and then start to move on. She has to know. What she does about it is her business, but she has to know."

WHAT DO YOU WANT FROM ME?

With traffic in the city, it took about forty-five minutes to transit from the upper northwest quadrant of the city down to the southern side of the northeast quadrant. Elizabeth turned in her seat and reached back to give Boomer a kiss on his head.

"Thanks for the ride, Tommy."

"Listen, there's a parking lot at the top of the hill right across the street from the Monastery," Atkinson said. "I'll hang out there for two hours and if it goes south on you, walk up the hill and I'll give you a ride back to your place."

"I'll be fine, Tommy. I'll call you tomorrow." Elizabeth patted Boomer on the head and was out of the car with the small black duffel bag under her arm. Climbing the steps to the porch, she could see Anna and her Aunt Rose waiting behind the glass front door.

"How are you, Grandmom?" she asked as she gave Anna a hug and kissed Rosemary. "Grandmom, I'm sorry you were worried, I should have called."

Anna held her close. "It's not a problem, Lizzie. Your Momma was making a big deal over nothing," she whispered. "I'm glad you're safe and home."

Her old house had a familiar aroma that on any other occasion would have been comforting, but the secret she came to reveal to her family was gaining power over her. She was once again overtaken by memories of Dolan, but this time no amount of shame, guilt or fear of not being believed was going to deter her from sharing her story.

Rosemary slid behind her. "Who's the guy in the truck, Liz?" she needled.

"I'll tell you about it later. Where's Momma?" Elizabeth asked, surprised she was not at the door. Anna locked arms with her granddaughter and walked towards the kitchen.

The sound of Lucy's voice from the kitchen did not offer a welcoming note. "I'm in the kitchen making dinner," she called.

Elizabeth walked into the kitchen but Lucy continued her work at the counter.

"Momma, it's obvious that you're angry with me but I'd like to explain some things."

"We'll talk after dinner, I'm busy right now. Go clean-up for dinner."

"Why are you being so bitchy, Momma?" Elizabeth said, deciding to meet her mother's passive aggression with the real thing.

Lucy slid a tray of tiny meatballs into the boiling stock. "Elizabeth, it may come as a shock to you but there are other people in the world. You drop in and out of here expecting everything else to stop. I have no idea when you're coming; God knows what you're doing. So, for the second time, after we eat there will be plenty of time to talk. Now if you want to do something help your grandmother set the table."

Elizabeth broke free from Anna's grasp and stormed out of the kitchen.

Rosemary was waiting for her in the dining room. "Play it out, Liz, I don't know what you're going to tell her but if you came here to talk, don't leave because of this pissing contest over making dinner. Your mother's just as stubborn as you. C'mon, settle down, let me make you a drink."

"Let me get some air on the porch, Aunt Rose. I'll have some ice water."

"Ice water," Rosemary said, surprised. "You sure you don't want a drink? I'm sure going to have one."

Elizabeth was on the edge of losing control. She knew alcohol would help her get through the next hour. She took a deep breath and thought of Tommy waiting for her on the hill and the last ten days of sobriety.

"Aunt Rose, I would love a drink, but not now."

Anna came out on the porch. "Are you okay, Lizzie?" She put her arm around Elizabeth's waist. "Child, you're shaking, what's the matter with you?" Anna asked, alarmed.

"I'm fine, Grandmom. I just have a lot on my mind. Don't you worry about me," she said as she wiped the tears from her cheek with her sleeve. "How's Grandpop, is he next door?"

"Oh, yes, just sitting in his chair listening to music. I still have to help him with his food and going to the bathroom. There's a nurse that comes every second day and he helps him getting a bath. He screams at him to leave him alone, so except for that we're taking it a day at a time."

"Is it time to maybe look into a home for Grandpop so it's not so stressful on you?" Elizabeth asked.

"Oh, no, he made a promise to stay, so I stay with him. That's the way it works. He just sits in his chair, and we walk out to the porch a few times a day and I play some records on the phonograph. Lizzie, your Momma made some chicken pastina with some egg and cheese. You eat that and you'll feel better."

Elizabeth laughed. "Grandmom, is there anything you can't fix with chicken soup?"

"Everything can be fixed with chicken soup, child," Anna said, kissing her on the forehead.

Rosemary and Anna made small talk over dinner. The weather, family news, and Aunt Rose's pending retirement and purchase of a small beach house on the Delaware Shore filled an awkward silence.

"Thank you, Momma, that soup was delicious," Elizabeth said trying to open a conversation with Lucy.

"You didn't eat any of the pasta, Elizabeth," Lucy said curtly.

"Momma, I had a little, I'm just not hungry. I didn't come over to eat, I came over to talk."

"See, I told you the soup would be good for you, don't you feel better?" Anna said, trying to keep things light.

Elizabeth chuckled. "I do, Grandmom." She pushed away from the table. "Let me clear the table."

"No, no, Anna and I will clear," Rosemary chimed in. "You and your mother get whatever you need to get sorted out, sorted out."

"I want you all here to hear this," Elizabeth said, clear eyed. "This is my family and I want you to hear this as a family."

"What about your brother, Elizabeth? He's family too."

"I've already talked to Francis, Mother."

Lucy knew something bad was about to happen, but it did not lessen her anger at her daughter.

Rosemary returned from the kitchen with perked coffee and cups and saucers. "Who's having coffee?" she asked.

"Just pour four cups, Rose, and stop making a fuss," Lucy snapped.

Elizabeth retrieved her backpack and came back into the dining room. Joseph's place at the table was always set and had been that way for decades.

"Momma, may I sit in Poppa's place?"

"Why? No one has sat in that chair since he passed."

"Because it would make me feel closer to him while I share what I have to tell you."

"Fine, take his seat and let's get on with this, Elizabeth."

Elizabeth pushed her father's place setting toward the center of the table and placed her backpack in front of her. "A friend of mine took the bullets out of Poppa's gun. He said Father Dolan wasn't worth a bullet," Elizabeth said, laying the weapon on the table.

Lucy stood up at her place, enraged. "When did you take that gun out of my house?" she screamed at Elizabeth.

"The same day you gave me the picture of me and Poppa at the Shrine with the Bishop."

"Jesus, Mary and Joseph, Lizzie, why would you want a gun, do you want to hurt yourself?" Anna wailed.

"No, no Grandmom, the gun was not for me," Elizabeth said, trying to calm Anna.

Lucy walked around the table and retrieved the gun, placing it on the floor next to her seat.

"I had no intentions of hurting myself, Grandmom," Elizabeth said. A priest named Andrew Dolan raped me when I was eleven years old in Aquinas Hall at Campus School. It wasn't just one time; it was several times. I'm sure there were others. I know every parish where he was assigned. I know he was sent away to New Mexico for treatment before he got to D.C. and now he's in a parish in New York. He told me when I was a little girl it was okay with God to do this and that I was special. Then he threatened me to stay quiet because no one was going to believe me, and I did. I did keep quiet for thirty years, but no more. The gun was for him, Grandmom. The morning I left the house for the West Coast, I fully intended to track him down and kill him. Not from afar—up close so he would know it was me and what he did to me." Elizabeth was shivering, rubbing the boss stone that Giovanni had given her in her hand under the table. "I'm an alcoholic. Most days I hate myself. I'm unmarried, have no children and have a problem with men. I use sex as an escape or a weapon, depending on the circumstance. The only thing I'm actually good at is work, and I quit my job." Elizabeth, breathing hard as if she were running, looked down at the table. The only sound was Lucy putting her cup into a saucer.

412

"What do you want from me?" Lucy finally asked.

Elizabeth could feel the chill in her question. "I don't want anything from you, Momma. I thought you would want to know."

"That you were raped, you say, by a man of God? That he did it more than once, in a church?" Lucy seethed.

"It was in the sacristy, Mother."

"Okay, in the sacristy, and that neither your father or your mother knew anything about it? You didn't tell us, and now years later you expect me to believe this craziness to explain what a mess you've made out of your life? Maybe you should think about going to confession, asking God to absolve you of your sins and asking for forgiveness for making such a charge. He's a priest for Christ sakes! Did you hear yourself saying those things? Do you realize how this could hurt your brother?" Lucy demanded.

Elizabeth felt a strange sense of calm surround her. Her mother's attack left her with a feeling of liberation. "I told you because it happened. There was no 'you say' in what I just told you. You know, Mother, I've told two priests this same story and they both believed me. Francis was one of them. Neither suggested I go to confession. But I do think, since you and your boyfriend believe in all this religious mumbo jumbo, you might consider going to confession to ask God to forgive *you*."

"What in the hell is that supposed to mean?" Lucy said, looking directly at Elizabeth.

Elizabeth reached into her backpack, pulled out a manila folder and tossed it toward her mother at the end of the table. "Two Fridays ago, a private investigator followed you to the Stevensville Motel just past the Bay Bridge. Do you remember that, Mother?"

Lucy's face began to flush as Elizabeth's eyes locked in on her.

"You had dinner in the corner table overlooking the fishing boats, you took a short walk out on the pier, you held hands and you retired to the same room with Washington's newest Archbishop, Cletus

Ryan. You left in separate cars the next morning. Really, Mother, you both should consider being a little more discreet based on his position. You can share them with Ryan, I have plenty of copies."

"Lucy, didn't you tell me you were going to Hershey, Pennsylvania on a bus trip with the sodality two Fridays ago?" Anna asked.

"Anna, this is between Lucy and Elizabeth. I think you should stay out of it," Rosemary said.

"I will not, and I don't care what you think, Rose. Elizabeth is my son's child!" Anna screamed, shaking her finger at Rosemary and Lucy.

Lucy got up from her chair, wrapped the gun up in a dish towel and put the manila folder under her arm. "I'm going to bed. Elizabeth, I expect you to leave. We really don't have anything to talk about."

Anna and Rosemary hovered over Elizabeth as she gathered her backpack and purse.

"You can stay with me and your grandfather, we have plenty of room," Anna said.

"Grandmom, I really didn't want you to get upset, but I wanted you to hear it."

"Lizzie, you didn't upset me, your mother did. She's blinded by all this Catholic stuff. She's out of her head."

"At least I know where she stands," Elizabeth said with a tone of finality.

"No, you don't. She'll come out of this. It's like the devil got in her. She's been under a spell since your father died. She knows how to be a mother, just give her some time."

"I don't have any time left, Grandmom. I've lost thirty years on this crap, and I'm going back to work." Elizabeth looked at her watch. It was 7:25 P.M. "I may have a ride back to my place if I can get up the hill in five minutes. Could you give me a lift, Rose?" Elizabeth asked.

"Absolutely, my car's out front."

Elizabeth gave Anna a kiss goodbye and clambered down the steps into Rosemary's car. "Grandmom, I'll come back and sit with Grandpop. I just need to get settled."

"Jesus, Liz, I feel like I'm in some Broadway play. What a fucking bombshell. Are you okay and who's waiting for you?" Rosemary asked.

"The fellow who dropped me off."

"Really, Liz, I figured that out on my own. What's his name?"

"Well, no, I'm not okay and his name is Tom, and he's a priest. He's just a friend that I've been hanging out with."

"That's been going around a lot in this family," Rosemary deadpanned.

"He happens to be the guy who broke this priest sex abuse scandal out into the mainstream. He worked for the Vatican, he saw what was going on from the inside and blew the whistle. I just drove across the country with him and his dog. I was supposed to go to his prom at Gonzaga and mother wouldn't allow it."

"What the hell, Liz? I mean that sounds so romantic. Are you guys like some kind of number?"

"A number, did you just ask if we were a number? We're not back in the forties, Rose, and no we're definitely not a number. We knew each other in high school and college."

"Well, it's been a strange night, so that's the only reason I ask. When you told your mother about Dolan, I was going to tell her I was gay since all hell was breaking loose. Seemed like the perfect time to slide that in."

Elizabeth howled with laughter. "What a pisser you are, Aunt Rose. So, what's the deal? What's her name?" Elizabeth asked.

"It was Janis. Unfortunately, Liz, there's not much to talk about," Rosemary said ruefully.

"Was?"

"Yes... *was*. We broke up last month," Rosemary said.

"I'm sorry, Aunt Rose."

"I'm not. It was getting complicated, and it wasn't like I was ready to invite her to Christmas dinner on Shepherd Street."

Elizabeth laughed and reached to hug her aunt.

"I really do love you, Aunt Rose. I'll talk to you later about the holidays. I'll call you in a couple of days," Elizabeth said as she kissed her on the cheek.

Elizabeth reached into her backpack and pulled out Jason Berry's book. "Here, read this alone, it's my only copy and you'll understand what all the Church shit is about. All the underlines are mine. I'll call you later."

Atkinson watched Elizabeth come around the truck and get in. "I saw you laughing in the car with your mother. So, it went well?" he asked.

"It went horribly. That was my aunt. She just told me she's gay. She was going to jump on my train, but my mother was such an asshole she decided just to tell me."

"Shit, that could have been an episode in 'All in the Family.'"

"Yeah, the Italian mother from hell attacks gay sister and daughter while Grandmom talks meatballs," Elizabeth groused.

"Are you okay to be alone in your apartment tonight?" Atkinson asked.

"Why would I be alone?"

"Well, the Dominican House is five minutes away. I was going to crash there tonight."

"Absolutely not. We have a meeting on Friday. You can stay at my place. You take the bed and I'll sleep on the couch. And don't argue with me. I fit on the couch and you don't. Besides, I'd miss Boomer."

"Well, then, I guess it's settled. So, what's next for you?" Atkinson asked.

"Tommy, I've got to get back to work and I don't have a job. I need to run, and I'm thinking about vodka a lot. A whole lot."

"Have you had anything to drink since we left SeaTac?"

"No, goddammit!" Elizabeth exploded.

"I'm just asking, Liz. Don't get angry with me. Tell me what happened back there."

Elizabeth took a deep breath. "I basically gave her the whole story. I told her about the gun. I told her what Dolan did to me. I told her how it impacted me."

"And..." Atkinson prompted.

"She didn't believe me, Tom," Elizabeth said bursting into tears banging her fists into the dashboard. "She said it was crazy talk and I was trying to explain away why I had made a mess of my life and that I should go to confession."

"Jesus, are you kidding me! Your mother is a true believer. What did you say, Liz?" Atkinson asked.

"I got really pissed off and I gave her some surveillance photos of her and Bishop Ryan during a little tryst on the Eastern Shore of Maryland two weeks ago."

"Holy shit...holy shit, I can't believe I just heard that. How in the world did you get them?"

"Thomas, I worked at two major law firms in New York City. What do you think, we play patty cake up there? It wasn't cheap, but all it took was a phone call to a firm I've used in other cases, an address and description of my mother, and a photograph of Cletus Ryan that's on the back page of the parish bulletin. Then I sat back and waited. That's the package I picked up from the concierge when we got to the apartment this afternoon."

"Well, Miss Natale, I have some big news for you to round out your day."

"What's that?" Elizabeth asked.

"Dolan was arrested in New York City."

"Are you fucking kidding me? How do you know?"

"Well, it's pretty convoluted but here's what I know so far. Two months ago, he was arrested in Brooklyn. The Archdiocese was able to keep it under wraps. No publicity, nothing. The police arrested him for felony sexual assault against two minors."

"Did you say minors, Tommy?" Elizabeth shrieked. "Who told you this?"

"Barbara left a message on my base phone and I called her back, and there's much more. Seems this Detective in New York has a real weed up her ass because after the arrest she was reassigned, and Dolan was given a sweetheart deal to plea to two misdemeanors. Somehow, 'wink,' she got a hold of Barbara and three days later she got an unredacted copy of the arresting officer's report and the boy's statements in the mail with no return address."

"This is huge. C'mon, let's get back to my place, I want to make some notes. Do you think Barbara would talk to me about this?" Elizabeth asked.

"Why wouldn't she," Atkinson said as he pulled out of the parking lot heading west toward Michigan Avenue.

"I don't know, I mean I called the woman for help as a survivor and now I want to talk to her about a potential client. I don't know, it's just weird."

"Potential client for who, Liz?" Atkinson asked.

"I don't know, for Weinstein maybe or someone else who's doing this work."

"What about you? You're a lawyer licensed in New York."

"Me? Don't be ridiculous. I don't even have a job, no office, no secretary, no malpractice insurance, nothing."

"Perfect. You can tell the family all of that and then sign them up."

"You're talking stupid now, what do you mean sign them up?"

"Barbara got the parents of one of the boys on the phone with me. They have a meeting scheduled with Cardinal Hurley of New York next Monday. Barbara convinced them that before they go and meet the Cardinal, they should at least talk to me. I told them I could come up Thursday with the lawyer that knows more about Dolan than anyone else in the country."

"Now you pissed me off. Why would you say such a thing?"

"Because it's true. You have his entire assignment history. You were one of his victims, you experienced how he groomed kids, how he kept them silent. You probably know others who had the same thing happen."

"You should have talked to me first before you said anything. I'm too close to this! What don't you understand about that, goddammit?"

"Well, I didn't and I don't, Elizabeth!" Atkinson yelled.

"You have no idea what it's like to be in my shoes."

"I'll never be in your shoes, Elizabeth, but here's what I know. If you don't stop running from these demons, they will literally kill you," Atkinson said as he made a sharp right-hand turn into the lot for the basketball courts at Turkey Thicket Park.

"What are you doing? Why are you stopping, Tom?"

Atkinson got out of the front seat with Boomer's leash and slammed the door. Opening the back door, he hooked up the dog. "Boomer needs a walk and I need some air, Elizabeth," he said, walking away.

WELL IT'S NOT TIBERIO'S

Father Francis Natale, in his priest clerics, walked into Ben's Chili Bowl on U Street in the northwest section of the city and was immediately spotted by Ben Ali, the Trinidadian proprietor of one of Washington's most popular institutions. Ben's was a neighborhood haunt visited and loved by the entire social milieu of Washington.

It had survived the violent spasms of the King riots fueled by Martin Luther King Jr.'s assassination and the de facto segregation that still persisted in the city's housing and education. People came to Ben's because it had always been there, and of course for the perfectly grilled half smokes smothered in Ben's wife Virginia's chili.

"Father, so good to see you, how have you been?" Ali asked.

"Ben, I'm fine. I'm meeting my sister here in a few minutes. Can we grab that empty table in the corner?"

"Of course, help yourself. Mondays are always a little slow. I'll get two menus for you."

"We'll only need one, Ben, I already know what I want," Francis said as Ben nodded his approval.

Elizabeth walked through the front door and immediately spotted Francis. She made her way back to the corner table where Francis was kibitzing with the kitchen staff.

"So, I see they know you here, Frannie?"

"They do, I've been coming here for years. Actually, I came here the first time with Poppa and Grandpop. They had done some work downtown at the Commerce Building on a Saturday and took me along, and we came here for lunch. It's not Tiberio's, but if you like a grilled half smoke you'll love it here, and I can afford to buy you lunch."

"Well, it's not Tiberio's, but I'm really happy you picked a place that Poppa went to.

"Hey Ben," Francis called out to Ali, who was sitting at the end of the counter.

"You ready to order, Father?"

"We'll have two half smokes with chili, fries and some mustard and sauerkraut on the side."

"What do you want to drink?"

"A Coke is fine," Elizabeth said.

"And two Cokes, Ben."

"So, what's got a bee in your bonnet that we had to talk today?"

Elizabeth allowed a faint smile to cross her face. "Andrew Dolan was arrested in New York a couple of months ago and he pled guilty to two indecency charges involving two minors. They're misdemeanors, but he pled guilty and no one knows anything about it. Never made the news, but it will. I think he got some bullshit sweetheart deal from the DA in Brooklyn. What's wrong, Frannie?" Elizabeth asked, realizing his expression hadn't changed. "I would have thought you would have been ecstatic; I mean didn't you call him a big prick when we were at Tiberio's?"

"I did call him a prick."

"Oh, I get it; you talked to Momma," Elizabeth said, her temper flaring.

"About what? What are you talking about?"

"Momma didn't call you last night?" Elizabeth demanded.

Before Francis could answer, Ben walked over with their tray of food.

"Here you go, Father, two half smokes, fries and two Cokes. I'll bring the mustard and kraut right over."

"Thanks, Ben." Francis leaned across the table, close to Elizabeth. "I haven't talked to Momma in a week," he whispered.

"So, she didn't tell you I came over for dinner last night?"

"No. What happened?" Francis asked.

"Well, I told her the whole story."

"Then what happened?" Francis asked.

"Basically, she called me a liar and said that I was using that as an excuse for what a mess I had made out of my life."

"So, she didn't believe you. How did it end?" he asked.

"I got pissed off and gave her some surveillance photos of her and Bishop Ryan down at a motel and restaurant in Stevensville, Maryland."

"Jesus Mary and Joseph, Liz! What do they show?" Francis asked, alarmed.

"They were having dinner, walking out on a pier holding hands, kissing on the dock and staying in the same room overnight. I held back the one kissing. You're the only person who knows besides the investigator."

421

"Liz, I have to talk to you privately. Are you going to eat?" Francis asked.

"I kind of lost my appetite."

Francis walked over to where Ben was sitting. "Hey, Ben, listen. I'm really sorry, but I just got a page from the hospital and I have to go immediately for someone who wants Last Rites," Francis said as Ben made a sign of the cross.

"Of course, do you want me to box your lunch up?"

"That would be great, Ben. You're the best."

Elizabeth was still sitting at the table.

"Liz, here's twenty bucks, pay the bill and leave the rest for a tip. I'll go get my car and meet you out front."

Francis drove several blocks without saying anything. After a ten-minute drive across town, he pulled into the visitor parking lot of the Bishop's Garden at the National Cathedral.

"Frannie, you look terrible, what's wrong? I mean there's no color in your face. I thought you'd be happy about Dolan finally getting caught. Are you pissed I had Momma followed?"

"I'm pissed that our mother is carrying on with Ryan, who happens to be my boss and the fucking Archbishop of Washington."

"Who cares whether he's your boss? And Momma's an adult. If she wants to fuck up the family how would you stop her?"

"She's our mother for Christ sakes, Liz. Do you have any idea what will come down on our heads if this comes out?"

"I really don't give a shit, Frannie," Elizabeth said, outraged. "Yeah, she's our mother, so what? I'm going to spend my time on Dolan, Frannie. A couple of days ago I was afraid. Well, I'm not afraid anymore. I'm going to run him to the ground. I'm going to nail the son of a bitch and all the assholes that protected him," Elizabeth said as she banged her hand on the closed passenger side window. "You need to get the hell out of this bullshit, Frannie. You're an accomplished musician, you have options. Just leave. I can give you some money to get an apartment. Just get away from these people. They're fucked up."

Francis felt he was watching a slow-motion train wreck. His entire life was disassembling right in front of him. He alternated between the image of Joseph lying dead at the foot of Mrs. McGinty's desk and Ryan's cross examination of him in the confessional. Face to face with his sister, Francis doubled down on his lifetime of lies.

"Liz, it's not that simple," Francis said.

"That's bullshit, Frannie. Ever since you were a little boy you've wanted to overthink shit and make it more complicated than it is," Elizabeth said, getting frustrated.

"Elizabeth, I don't want to argue with you today."

"I don't want to argue with you either. I want you to listen to me!" Francis could hear her breathing as she clenched her fists. "Look at me, Liz."

"I'm sorry to go off like that, Frannie."

"Liz, look at me."

Elizabeth turned toward her brother. "What is it, Frannie?"

"I can't get away from them. I need them. I have AIDS."

Elizabeth froze in her seat, unable to talk.

"Based on my T-cells, I'm holding my own. I haven't lost much weight and my lungs are clear."

Elizabeth cleared her throat. "You have AIDS, Frannie? I mean, are you sure?" Elizabeth stammered.

"I'm very sure, Liz. Listen, I knew I was gay from about eighth grade. So, where was I going to go, coming from a family like ours? Dolan had gay musician friends, they were really nice to me and I just kind of fell into a lifestyle that had to stay in the closet. The priesthood was a perfect place to hide. No pun intended."

"Don't joke about this, Frannie. It's not funny."

"I'm not joking, Liz. That's what happened. Right after I was ordained, I met a cellist from the National Symphony. We fell madly

423

in love. We did several recordings together. We traveled together. He was my soul mate. It was the happiest time of my life. I became a priest because I felt responsible for Poppa's death."

"Stop, Frannie."

"Yeah, I know, Liz, Pop died of a heart attack, but I wasn't believing any of that at the time. I went into the priesthood because I felt I had to hide my sexuality, but I had the security of my music. I was ready to leave and be with him and one day he called me to meet him at the Dubliner Restaurant for lunch right across from Union Station."

"What was his name, Frannie?" Elizabeth asked.

"Danny. His name was Danny," Francis said, wiping tears off his cheeks.

"What happened?"

"I met him at the Dubliner. We sat down, ordered lunch, then he told me he was married, his wife was pregnant and that he could never see me again and that he loved me. We cried and that was it."

"Then what happened?"

"Nothing. I never saw him again. My life spiraled out of control. I was drinking a lot, having unprotected sex and basically living a double life. Priest and musician by day, fuck up by night."

"And after, that's when you got AIDS?" Elizabeth asked.

"After Danny is when I got AIDS, Elizabeth," Francis said.

"Is that why you work at the AIDS mission?"

"Yes, and because they accept me there. But the real reason is that I love it. It's the only thing that makes me feel alive as a priest."

"Did they tell you how long?" she asked as she broke down crying. "Does Momma know?"

"She does not and I'm asking you to keep this confidential. I have a lot on my plate right now and I don't need Momma freaking out. Hey, listen Liz, I'm sorry to have laid this on you."

424

"Don't be stupid. I'm your sister and I love you. Can I do anything for you? What about your treatment?" Elizabeth asked. "Who's paying for that?"

"The priest fund has been helping and I have insurance with the Archdiocese but I'm going to have to talk to Ryan and let him know. Probably soon."

"Why does that shit need to know anything?" Elizabeth raged.

"He's my bishop, and I don't expect you to understand. I have to handle this in my own way. Please, Liz, I don't need any more pressure than is already on me."

"Who else knows, Frannie?"

"Just a couple of priest friends for now."

"Frannie, why did you tell me this today?"

"I have no idea. I certainly wasn't planning to when you called me for lunch. I guess when you told me about your and Momma's blowout, Dolan's arrest and the Ryan crap, I just thought I should tell you."

"I'm so sorry, Frannie." Elizabeth flopped her head hard against Francis' shoulder. "Could you drive me to my apartment? I have to wrap my head around all of this."

"Sure, Liz, and thanks for not asking a bunch of questions."

"Francis, promise me we'll talk about this again."

"I promise, Elizabeth."

When they reached her apartment, Elizabeth reached into her purse, pulled out the boss stone and put it into Francis' hand, closing his hand around it. "Here, keep this. I know you always liked this one better. You keep it until you get better."

WHERE IN THE HELL IS EVERYONE RUSHING TO?

Elizabeth woke with a horrible pain in the back of her head. It was a few minutes past 4:00 A.M., and she knew she had to get out of her apartment for a run. Slipping on her running gear in the dark, she walked past Boomer sleeping by the bed and was out on the street by four-thirty.

She brutalized herself at a competition pace for ten miles. Physically spent, she hobbled back to her apartment, showered and totally transformed herself. Elizabeth needed to detach her mind from the last twenty-four hours—Francis, Ryan, Rose, her mother—everything. It was the only way she could function without alcohol. The day before had been unbearable and in a few hours, she needed to be on her game to meet the parents of one of Dolan's abuse victims.

The Northeast Corridor Metroliner crept out of Union Station at exactly 8:00 A.M. Both Atkinson and Elizabeth settled back in their seats with bagels and coffee. If all went well, they would pull into Penn Station at 10:54 A.M. and be in Murray Hill in time to meet with Barbara Blaine.

"Is Barbara coming in just for this meeting?" Elizabeth asked, sipping her coffee.

"I believe so. I think the parents asked her to be with them when we meet."

"Where are we meeting her, Tommy?" Elizabeth asked.

"There's a little gyro deli across the street from the parent's apartment. We'll have a bite there and go over the papers that Barbara's bringing with her."

"What papers?"

"Apparently, the father sent Barbara the police report of the arresting officer and the interviews of the two boys the night Dolan was arrested."

"How did he find Barbara?" Elizabeth asked, taking notes.

"I don't think he did. The mom did, as I understand it. I got the feeling there's a lot of tension between the parents…"

"You mean they're not on the same page as to how to handle this," Elizabeth said.

"That's my assumption, Liz, but we'll see."

Elizabeth felt a jolt of excitement as Train 232 pulled into Penn Station. The mad rush to exit encapsulated everything Atkinson hated about New York and everything that she loved.

The underground platform was acrid, dirty and hot. People walked stone faced through the double doors and up a narrow-gauge escalator to be deposited into a sea of commuters moving in all directions.

"Hard to believe this is the same country. Where in the hell is everyone rushing to, Liz?" Atkinson huffed.

"God, Tommy, you sound like an old man, stop whining. It's the city, just stay behind me. We'll go out on 7th Avenue and get a cab."

Four hundred one East 34th Street was only a mile and a half from Penn Station, but with traffic Elizabeth realized it would take at least a half hour to push through the midday rush. The queue for a taxi was even worse.

"Why don't we walk, Tommy," Elizabeth said, stopping at the half wall in front of Madison Square Garden to change from her three-inch heels into her Asics running shoes.

"That works for me," Atkinson said. "So, it's like this every day?"

"Every day, don't you just love it?" Elizabeth asked.

"Actually, Liz, I don't. And after the last ten days, I'm not sure why you do, but here we are."

SO EXACTLY WHAT ARE YOU PROPOSING?
Barbara Blaine was seated in the corner of the small dining room of the Gyro Shop reading the want ads from the Chicago Tribune. Elizabeth could barely contain herself as she rushed through the door and gave her a warm hug.

"My God, Barbara, it's so good to see you."

"It's good to see you too, Elizabeth. Tom has been saying lots of good things about you," Barbara said as Elizabeth looked at Atkinson.

"Has he now," Elizabeth laughed. "Well, we just spent ten days driving across the country and we haven't killed each other yet," she joked.

"Would both of you stop talking about me like I'm not here," Atkinson piped in.

"He's been grouchy all morning," Elizabeth said.

"I give up with you women, what's everyone having for lunch? I'll order."

Elizabeth answered first. "I'll have a chicken gyro with lettuce, tomatoes and onion and extra tzatziki sauce and a bottle of water."

"I'll have the same. But, Tom, it's not very private here," Blaine said. Before you got here, I found a park just up the street with outdoor tables. Why don't we go there? I want you and Liz to read what the dad sent me before we meet."

"Okay then, why don't you and Liz go there and get a table or a bench and I'll get the food," Atkinson said.

Barbara and Elizabeth walked arm in arm up First Avenue to the park.

"You look like a different person than the one I met in front of Cardinal Hurley's house. How are you doing, Liz?"

"Honestly, it's been a roller coaster. I told Tom some days I feel like I've been stoned by an angry mob."

"He told me he thought you were doing great and that with your background you could be a huge asset to the movement. There are a lot of lawyers out there, but there's only a handful that move the ball down the field."

"Barbara, I'm unemployed. I don't even have a desk!"

"Those are minor details. You need to think about it, Liz. We need good people in the fight."

"So, what did the boy's father send you?" Elizabeth asked, trying to change the subject.

"Are you ignoring me, Elizabeth?" Barbara joked.

"I've had no success in ignoring Tom and I suspect the same will be true for you," Elizabeth laughed. "I hear you, Barb, we can talk about it after we meet the family."

The trio sat silently on the bench as both Atkinson and Elizabeth read then traded the arrest report and statements from the boys.

Elizabeth looked up, her face flushed with anger. "This son-of-a-bitch has been doing this to kids for thirty years and nothing has happened."

"That's probably true for 95 percent of the offenders," Barbara said. "Between the criminal statute of limitation and the Church working its magic on the cover-up, most of them have gotten passes."

"That's such bullshit. The only reason he got caught was because he got reckless. Christ, the beat cop caught him in the act," Elizabeth railed. "The report has the search warrant box checked off. Do you know anything about the affidavit or the return inventory?"

"What's a return inventory? I've never heard that before," Barbara said.

"Well, there's an implication that a search warrant was either going to be obtained or they had one. In order to get one, the arresting officer has to file an affidavit of probable cause with a judge and if they execute a search warrant, they have to state in writing with the court what they found. That's the return inventory."

"I don't know."

"And I assume you don't know who sent you this stuff?" Elizabeth asked.

"I'm sure it was the detective but there's no way to prove it," Blaine said.

"What do you know about the parents, Barb?" Atkinson asked.

"Not much. My main contact is with the mom. She's a nurse at NYU Medical Center. The father sounds like a handful. He's pissed and wants to do something. He retired from the Navy as a Chief

Petty Officer in the Seabees and now he's a crane operator in the city with the local operating engineers."

"He sounds like a tough guy," Atkinson said.

"And the boy? What do you know about the boy?" Elizabeth asked.

"Just what the mom said, which wasn't much, Liz," Barbara said. "He sang in the City Boys Choir. Dolan was the Music Director there up until last year, according to their website."

"Well, in my opinion, no one should be doing anything without the boy fully on board. Christ, Barb, what's his name? I don't like calling him the boy," Elizabeth said, raising her voice.

"It's Robert, I think the parents call him Bobby," Barbara said. "You're right, my mistake."

"Robert has to decide what he wants to do. It's not the father's case. It sounds like the Chief Petty Officer has had his ego bruised and he wants to lash out."

"That's a pretty common reaction of a lot of parents, Liz. I wouldn't be too put off by that."

"I'm not put off, it's just selfish in my opinion. This happened to Robert, not his father."

"Elizabeth, this happened to the entire family. Just look at your own experience. I can say the same thing for my abuse from Chet Warren, it affected everyone in my family."

"I know, Barb, it's just I get riled up when I think about this shit. Let's go up. Are they expecting us at one?" Elizabeth asked.

"Yes, let's go, it's a two-minute walk from here," Blaine said.

Delores and Robert Tompkins lived at 401 East 34th Street across the street from NYU Tisch Medical Center and ten blocks south of the United Nations Headquarters. The soaring, two-story atrium that served as the complex's lobby was in effect a microcosm of the city, with dozens of different nationalities mixing together in a twenty-four/seven pool of frenetic coming and going. In the middle of the fray stood a slight woman with a closely cropped shock of salt and pepper hair. Looking to be in her early forties, the woman tentatively approached Barbara.

"Excuse me," she said, barely audible over the echoes in the lobby. "Are you Miss Blaine?"

"I am. Are you Mrs. Tompkins?"

"I am, I recognized you from your picture in the paper. Thank you for coming all this way," Delores said, starting to sob as Barbara put both arms around her for a long embrace.

Barbara could feel her shaking in her arms. "Mrs. Tompkins, listen to me, we'll get through this. I brought friends with me," Barbara whispered into her ear. "C'mon, wipe your tears. This is Father Thomas Atkinson, he's the priest I told you about who worked in the Vatican Embassy."

"Please, Delores, call me Tom."

"I will if you call me Delores," she said, smiling.

"And this is Elizabeth Natale, she's a lawyer who used to work right here in Manhattan but has since relocated to Washington, D.C. Elizabeth and Tom grew up together in Washington."

"I'm very pleased to meet you both. Let's go upstairs so we can get some quiet. Bob Sr. is up there, and Bobby will be home in an hour. My husband's a blunt person and all of this has affected him badly. I'm not making excuses for him because I'm angry as well, but he can come across pretty strong."

"We totally understand, Delores," Atkinson said. "It's not a problem."

The Tompkins home was modestly furnished, but had a warm, lived-in vibe that put the group at ease. After the introductions with Bob Sr. were finished, the group settled around the Tompkins' dining room table in an awkward silence.

Robert Tompkins broke the silence. "I'm not sure why you folks came all this way, but my wife asked me to talk to you before I meet with the Cardinal on Monday afternoon. I talked to the father of the other boy, and he met with Cardinal Hurley and they offered him $100,000 to offset his boy's education. That's not pocket change for this family. You folks understand that, right?"

Elizabeth immediately knew what Mr. Tompkins was getting at. Why would he put his family through a meat grinder when $100,000 tax-free dollars was on the table? She wanted to reach across the table and slap him and tell him what sexual abuse of a child looks from the inside. She bit her tongue and waited for someone else to speak.

Barbara Blaine spoke first. "Mr. Tompkins, of course we do, and I want to thank you for meeting with us. When Delores called me we talked for a long while and no parent, let alone child, should have to go through this. Father Atkinson can give you some history on the abuse scandal in the Church, he's been there from the beginning. I'm a survivor and the founder of SNAP. It's an organization that supports survivors coming forward, highlights the systemic problem in the Church as it relates to the cover-up of sex abuse by priests and advocates for transparency and accountability."

Robert Tompkins looked directly at Elizabeth. "So, I know why the Father is here, and why Miss Blaine is here. What do you do, Miss Natale?"

"That's a good question, Mr. Tompkins. I asked that same question myself on the train coming up."

"I don't understand. I thought you were the lawyer. Delores said you folks are against parents going down to the Archdiocese alone and I should bring a lawyer with me to meet the Cardinal."

"Actually, I said that to Delores, Mr. Tompkins," Barbara said.

"Mr. Tompkins, I'm not entirely sure you should meet the Cardinal at all, but yes, I'm a lawyer," Elizabeth said. I've worked in Manhattan for the better part of the last twenty years, but I quit my job and moved back to Washington, where I'm from." Elizabeth felt a building pressure in her chest. The adrenaline and the prickle

ACT OF FAITH

on her skin were old warning signs that foretold a visit from the
darkness. "Delores, could I have that glass of water?" Elizabeth
asked, trying to maintain her composure.

"Of course, I'll bring some for everyone."

"Mr. Tompkins, about two months ago I had a major meltdown
after meeting Barbara on the street in front of Cardinal Hurley's
residence. When I was a little girl, Andrew Dolan raped me in the
vestment room of a chapel where I went to school. He did it more
than once and for thirty years I kept it secret. I can say with almost
100 percent accuracy that your son and his friend are on a long list
of many, many others. I kept this bastard's secret because I was
convinced as a little girl that that's what God wanted me to do. I've
been carrying this shame and guilt with me all of my life. Many days
it has gotten the best of me. It all but destroyed me and I'm far from
out of the woods, but these two people sitting next to me have
helped me turn a corner. You say you're angry. Well, I'm angry, too,
Mr. Tompkins."

Atkinson could see Elizabeth was building a head of steam.

"Mr. Tompkins, let me give you some history and context so
that if and when you meet with the Cardinal it may make more
sense to you."

For the next twenty minutes, Atkinson went through his own
personal history and the history of the scandal and how the Church
hierarchy tried to manage the crisis that emerged from the Gilbert
Gauthe case in Louisiana.

"But, Father, let me ask you one question," Tompkins said.

"Certainly."

"I met with Monsignor Bell at our parish and I asked him
straight up, did they know about this asshole—excuse me, ladies—
and he said this is the first they had any inclination of this behavior."

Elizabeth jumped in. "Now, everyone here remembers Watergate
and the term plausible deniability."

"That's exactly right, Liz," Atkinson said. "First they tell you that this scandalous behavior cannot be publicized to the faithful because it will shake the confidence the Catholic laity has placed in the Church."

"He did say that Father, and I told him I didn't give a rat's ass about the feelings of the Catholic laity and that all I cared about was my son."

"How did Monsignor Bell react to that?" Atkinson asked.

"He said he understood, but that I needed to think about my son. That there could be rumors that he may be homosexual. He said he of course didn't think that but that people in the parish sometimes talk. Bell said there would be some people who will never believe a priest is capable of that type of conduct and conclude these allegations are an attack on their faith and that my family's standing in the parish would be forever changed. He said God wanted me to be a loyal Catholic. When I met with the prosecutor a week before Dolan pled guilty, he said almost the same thing. He said Dolan had got a lawyer, he said he was a real asshole."

Elizabeth laughed. "And what did you say?" she asked Tompkins.

"I said I didn't know there was any other kind."

Atkinson and Blaine let out a howl of laughter.

"You certainly walked into that one, Liz."

Elizabeth smiled at Robert Tompkins. "I did, didn't I."

"Yes, ma'am, you sure did, but seriously, Monsignor Bell suggested there was a possibility that the lawyer was going to suggest that my boy consented to that shit. That it could get very ugly and embarrassing for Bobby and the family. He said it didn't matter that Bobby couldn't legally consent, that the lawyer could place doubt in the jury's mind. He said it was a big risk for my family. He also said that the Church promised Dolan was going to be sent away for treatment. And just so you all know, my son is not a fag."

434

"Unbelievable," Elizabeth said, slumping into her chair. She reached into her briefcase. "Mr. Tompkins, I recently took a long trip with Father Atkinson and got quite an education. Let me show you something." Elizabeth pulled a heavily highlighted sheaf of papers from her file folder and turned to the 1965 entry for Andrew Dolan. "Do you see the highlighted entry next to Dolan's name?" Elizabeth asked.

"I do, it says, Via…"

"The name is Via Coeli," Atkinson interrupted.

"Tommy, would you tell Mr. and Mrs. Tompkins what Via Coeli is?" Elizabeth asked.

Atkinson explained the entire history of the Servants of the Paraclete and the founding of their treatment center in Jemez Springs, New Mexico in 1947 by Father Gerald Fitzgerald.

"Now, Mr. Tompkins, based on the history of Dolan that Elizabeth and I have pieced together, it's my opinion that the only reason he was sent to Via Coeli nearly thirty, that's three-zero, years ago was his sexual abuse of minors. There's been a lot of litigation handled by a lawyer named Bruce Pasternak out in New Mexico, but he basically described Via Coeli as ground zero for the priest pedophilia cases."

"What's that word you used, Father Atkinson?" Robert asked. "Pedophilia?"

"Yes, that's the word. I've never heard that word," Robert said.

"It's when an adult is sexually attracted to a child."

"That's disgusting. How could the Church tolerate so much of this crap?" Robert pushed his chair away from the table and stood up. "What do they think, we're stupid?" he said, forcefully thrusting his hands into his trouser pockets. "This is really pissing me off."

"Robert, please calm down," Delores said.

"I'm not calm. Bell lied to me, Delores! They knew about this before it happened to Bobby, and they want to give him $100,000. For what?" Robert screamed.

Delores heard the keys in the lock of the front door. "Robert, stop it, Bobby just got home and I want him to meet everyone. Now, please, sit down, we're here to discuss options, not listen to you rant."

Robert ignored the comment and left the dining room. "I'm going to make myself some coffee."

"Mr. Tompkins, do you mind if I join you?" Elizabeth asked as she quickly excused herself from the table. Atkinson nervously watched her follow Robert into the kitchen.

"Suit yourself." Robert went into the cupboard to retrieve the percolator.

"Where do you keep the coffee, Mr. Tompkins?" Elizabeth asked.

"It's in the refrigerator in a silver canister."

Elizabeth got the coffee and handed it to Tompkins. "You seemed to want to make a point that your son was not... What did you say? A fag?"

"Yeah, that's what I said, Miss Natale. Do you have a problem with that?"

"Well, I might if I was gay man, but that's beside the point." Elizabeth walked to the end of the counter and gave the swinging panel door to the kitchen a gentle push so it would close. "Mr. Tompkins, I'm told you're retired Navy."

"Yes, ma'am. That's right."

"And you retired as a Chief Petty Officer?"

"Yes, ma'am. Mustered out as an E8 from the Navy in '84."

"So, blunt talk doesn't bother you."

"No, Miss Natale, blunt talk doesn't offend me in the least."

"Good, so listen up. You say your son isn't gay or, as you say, a fag. Great, but what if he is or thinks he might be? What if this abuse has made him question his own sexuality? What if he's completely confused as to what the hell was happening between him and Dolan and he's really a heterosexual? What if Dolan said to Bobby 'God is okay with this.' That other people wouldn't understand. That Bobby was chosen because he was special in the eyes of God. Do you think that when his father announces, 'my son is not a fag' that in your goddamn misguided homophobic opinion you are somehow helping the situation?" Elizabeth said.

Robert kept his back to Elizabeth as he clicked the percolator top shut and plugged it in.

"Bobby's your flesh and blood. I just told my own mother what happened to me. She didn't believe me. Said I was making it all up to explain away how fucked up my life was. I can tell you that her words will stay with me the rest of my life. All I'm saying to you is, don't be that guy. And I take my coffee with a little milk. I'll see you back in the dining room."

When Robert turned around Elizabeth had left the kitchen. He was relieved because he had started to cry.

"You must be Bobby," Elizabeth said as she walked back into dining room. "I'm Elizabeth Natale."

"Hi," Bobby said without looking up.

"Everything okay in the kitchen, Liz?" Atkinson asked nervously.

"Oh, for sure. I was just helping out. He's upset but I think he's okay."

"Bobby, look at Miss Natale when she speaks to you," Delores said, sending a clear message to her son that he was being rude.

"Bobby, it's fine. I want to show you something." Elizabeth got an unmarked folder from her briefcase and removed a picture and handed it to Bobby. "Tell me what you see."

Bobby took the picture and studied it.

"Do you see the little girl next to the boy?" Elizabeth asked.

"Uh-huh," Bobby muttered.

"That's me about six months before Father Andrew Dolan raped me in a Church sacristy."

Bobby drew the picture closer and stared at it for over a minute. "That's really you?" Bobby asked.

"It's really me, Bobby. Dolan abused me just like he abused you."

Bobby continued to stare at the picture. "Who's the boy next to you?" he asked.

"He's my brother."

"What happened to him?" Bobby asked.

"Nothing, Dolan was his piano teacher, and then he went off and became a priest. He's a priest in a parish in Washington, D.C. Bobby, you're not alone and you're not the only one who this has happened to. Barbara, you and I are all survivors of sexual abuse by people we trusted. So, when I say I know exactly how you feel, I know exactly how you feel."

Robert pushed the kitchen door open with his back and carried in two mugs of coffee. "Is that dark enough for you, Miss Natale?" Tompkins asked.

"It's perfect, thank you."

"How was school, Bobby?" Tompkins asked.

"It was okay, Pop. Just a regular day."

"I know Mom talked to you about Father Atkinson and Barbara Blaine and Miss Natale coming over and we've been talking. So what if you just hang out with us and let them lay out our options, then we can talk later just the three of us?"

"Okay Pop," Bobby said nervously.

Atkinson spoke first. "Bobby, first of all, as a Catholic priest I want to apologize to you. It never should have happened and I'm sorry."

Bobby looked at Atkinson and nodded.

"Elizabeth here's a lawyer and she's also a survivor, as is Barbara. We're all here as resources for you when you want to talk. Liz, would you explain to the family what you were talking to me about when we were coming back East?"

"Sure. So, like so many other big corporations, you have to follow the money to understand their reluctance for this sex abuse scandal to see much daylight. That's why when somebody like Bobby comes around, they have to settle quickly and forever. It's a gross oversimplification, but what I see now is that the Archdioceses of Los Angeles, Washington and New York all knew about Dolan. These kids, now adults, could be anywhere in the country. The Church has pressured parents into not filing lawsuits to protect their brand."

"So, exactly what are you proposing?" Robert asked Elizabeth.

"I wouldn't meet with the Cardinal. I would put it off. At a bare minimum, just about any lawyer will get you more money than what they're offering with Bobby being a minor."

"So, you're taking Bobby's case?" Delores asked.

"No, no," Elizabeth said, shocked at the suggestion. "I'm not in any position to handle such a big case as this. You need a major firm willing to do battle with the Church. Because Bobby's a minor and their chief defense is gone, this could get very big very fast. That's not me. I don't even have a desk or an office. As I told you, I'm unemployed. Besides, it's really weird being a victim of the same priest and a lawyer working on the case. Now what I can do is help you find the right firm to do this and get the ball rolling."

"Is something being weird a legal conflict?" Atkinson asked.

Elizabeth flashed an angry glance toward Atkinson.

"I'm just asking, Liz."

"No, it's not a conflict, but for me it would feel like one."

"Would you do it if I asked you?" Bobby asked.

"I'd have to think about it, Bobby," Elizabeth said.

"Will you think about it and let me know?" Bobby asked.

"I will."

"Or you could sign the family up as New York counsel and then associate with a firm big enough to handle a case like this," Barbara said, looking down at her notes on the dining room table.

Elizabeth sighed loudly. "Why don't we table this until we hear from the family as to what they want to do. There's some truth to the point that this could get ugly, Mr. Tompkins. You have to consider that as it relates to Bobby." Elizabeth got up first, making clear the meeting was over for her. "Bobby, it was great meeting you even under these circumstances. Here's my card. I don't work at this office any longer, but my pager number is on the back. If you want to call me for any reason just dial the number on the back and I'll call you right back."

As the group moved toward the front of the apartment, Robert Tompkins stopped Elizabeth and pulled her aside. "So, in your opinion, Bobby has a case?"

"Mr. Tompkins, Bobby has a big case, that's why it needs the right firm with the right resources."

"Okay, I got it. And by the way, thanks for your advice in the kitchen. I can be an asshole sometimes. I saw what was going on in the dining room; so now let me give you some advice. Don't be that gal."

"And what did you see going on at the dining room table?" Elizabeth asked, looking Robert in the eye.

"That you're the best lawyer to handle Bobby's case and you're afraid."

Elizabeth looked at Tompkins, turned and left without saying a word.

Elizabeth was in front in the elevator car. Atkinson thought the ride in silence would never end. As soon as the elevator opened, she charged through the atrium and out through the opened doors of the lobby onto the street. Near the curb, she turned and waited for Barbara and Atkinson.

"What the fuck do you both think you were doing up there?"

"Now, Liz, don't go off half-cocked."

"Tommy, just shut the fuck up, I don't want to hear it! No one's going to pressure me into taking a case. No one!" Elizabeth screamed at them both. She reached into her purse and shoved her keys into

Atkinson's chest. "I'm staying in New York tonight," she said as she stepped into a waiting cab.

"What about the four o'clock with Paul Weinstein tomorrow?" Atkinson yelled into the cab.

"What about it," Elizabeth said as she slammed the door and left, heading west on 34th Street.

"Jesus, when she goes off it's an event. I'd ask you to go for a drink but you don't drink anymore," Barbara said.

"Yeah, that's unfortunate, but she'll come around."

"Tom, if you're not drinking anymore you've taken up drugs. She's not coming around. Listen, I got to go. My plane leaves in an hour and a half out of LaGuardia. Call me when you know something. This is an important case. If this is going to go, I want to make sure the PR is handled. As always, it's been real," she said as she leaned over and kissed Atkinson on the cheek and took the next cab in the queue.

YOU ON THE WAGON?

Traffic was miserable. The entire city seemed to be under construction. For most of her adult life, Elizabeth had lived and thrived on the vibe of the city. For the first time, she realized she did not like it anymore. Elizabeth leaned over the front seat of the cab and asked the driver to drop her at corner of 59th and 5th Avenues.

"Do you know the Sherry Netherland?" she asked the driver.

"Yes, ma'am, is that where you're going?"

"Yes, anywhere around 59th and 5th."

Elizabeth had been in the cab for a full thirty minutes and she needed to get out and walk. She tossed a twenty-dollar bill over the front seat and got out on 63rd Street and 5th, which was in gridlock.

It had been a while, but she realized she was not alone. The events of the day allowed the darkness to follow her as she walked. Her black box of abuse memories was open, and the heaviness of the blackness centered in her gut and around her face. Beard stubble prickled the back of her neck. It smelled of English Leather and incense and she instinctively rubbed her hands over her arms and neck to get it off her. Nerve endings fired in her rectum and belly as she began to jog toward the same stone bench she had sat on in front of the Plaza Hotel the day she met Barbara Blaine.

She closed her eyes and imagined the lush grass prairies of eastern Montana, letting each reed of grass touch her skin until the blackness left. Slowly, Elizabeth's brain opened to the sound of the Pulitzer Fountain. Sitting on the stone bench, she waited for the sound of the water to wash her mind of the sights and smells of the past. When the lid closed and the clasp locked, she felt safe to stand up and walk into the Oak Bar at the Plaza Hotel.

"Well, look who's here," Teddy exclaimed as Elizabeth walked into her familiar haunt. "Where the hell have you been, Miss Natale?"

"I don't know, Teddy, life. Sometimes life just gets in the way. It's really good to see you."

"It's good to be seen, Miss Natale. Can I get you your usual?"

"Not today, Teddy, but you know those Transfusions you make…"

"Sure do. Is that what you want?"

"Yes but make it a virgin."

"Oh, wow, Miss Natale, you on the wagon?" Teddy joked.

"Actually, I am, Teddy. Some days, like today, I could use a seatbelt, but so far so good. You know, one day at a time."

"Hey, Miss Natale, I was just kidding, I didn't mean anything by that," Teddy said with a distressed look on his face. "We've all been there."

"Don't be silly, Teddy, you've been my therapist for years, I could never be mad at you."

"I'm really glad to hear that, Miss Natale. You know your pager is blinking."

Elizabeth looked down at her purse where she had clipped her pager and saw that it was a New York number. She reached in her purse for her notepad and realized that someone at the Tompkins' home was calling her.

"Do you need to use the house phone, Miss Natale?" Teddy asked.

"Do you mind, Teddy? It's a local number."

"Of course not."

Elizabeth moved away from the other patrons and dialed the Tompkins' number. The call connected on the first ring.

"Hello, this is Elizabeth Natale, I had a page that someone called."

"Yes, it's me, Robert. Are you already on your way back?" Tompkins asked.

"No, actually I'm still in New York."

"Oh, because something came up that I want to clear up."

"What's that, Robert?"

"You remember you gave Bobby your card?"

"Yes, of course."

"Well, Monsignor Bell called and asked if I would be okay with Cardinal Hurley's lawyer being present for our meeting on Monday if any questions came up."

"That's actually not a surprise. Is that your question?" Elizabeth asked.

"No, what confused me was that you said you don't work at the firm on the card anymore."

"Yes, that's right. I left the firm two months ago. Why are you asking?" Elizabeth said, now curious.

"Because the lawyer that Cardinal Hurley wants at our meeting is a fellow named Alistair McCabe and the firm name is the same name on your card."

A jolt of electricity shot through Elizabeth's body. Whatever fears or demons that plagued her were now front and center.

"Miss Natale, I don't know how these things work but can you represent Bobby if you worked at the same firm?" Robert asked.

"Robert, you're sure the Monsignor said Alistair McCabe?" Elizabeth asked.

"Yes. I remember it because the name is so unusual," Robert said.

"What you're talking about is a potential conflict. But I left my old firm before they started to work for the Archdiocese, and I'm 100 percent sure of that. So, to answer your question specifically, I can represent Bobby. If I had worked on any Archdiocese file it would be a problem, but I didn't."

"Excellent. Then we want you to do it, Miss Natale. Will you represent Bobby?" Robert asked.

Elizabeth was seated at the very end of the Oak Room bar. Teddy was busy mixing cocktails. There was a curious order in the room except for the fact that she was not drinking. She looked down at her trembling right hand. Without any more thought, she plunged ahead.

"Okay, I'll represent your son, but you must understand, I'll have to associate a firm that has the same resources as the McCabe firm. But as far as your family is concerned there will only be one fee and I'll be his lawyer."

"Okay, I understand. Bobby wanted to ask you something."

"Sure, put him on."

"Hey, Miss Natale."

"Hey, Bobby, you doing okay with all this?"

"Yeah, I'm okay, I think. So, will you be with me the whole time?" Bobby asked.

"Bobby, I literally will be right next to you. We'll do this together and in a couple of weeks I'll get back to New York and we can spend some more time together to go over everything and I'll explain how everything works. You good with that?" Elizabeth asked.

"Okay, that sounds good and thanks for coming up. Here's my Pop."

"Hi, Robert. This changes things a little. What I'd like to do is get a retainer agreement put together and meet you after dinner. I'll go over the whole thing with you and Delores, and then I'll head back to D.C. early tomorrow and meet with Paul Weinstein and check out his firm. I'd like you to call Monsignor Bell back and tell him you'd like to bring your lawyer with you. Don't give him my name unless he asks. Then we'll see what happens. Call me on this same pager number this weekend and I'll call you back. If the meeting doesn't get cancelled, I'll take the train up Sunday or early Monday. And please, call me Elizabeth."

"All that sounds good. I'll call you when I'm ready to come over. Talk soon."

Elizabeth hung up the phone and handed it back to Teddy.

"The gentleman at the end of the bar would like to buy you a drink," Teddy said.

Elizabeth looked at him and smiled.

"I didn't tell him you were drinking ice water."

Elizabeth chuckled and smiled toward the gentleman. "Tell him thank you but no thank you. I have a prior engagement."

Elizabeth surveyed the room. Everything looked the same. The green leather bar stools, the Shinn paintings and the décor, all the same. The clink of glasses mixed with the vibrations of muffled conversations and for the very first time in over thirty years she could identify a purpose for her work that wasn't chasing money or running away from the darkness.

CHAPTER TEN

It's Always About the Money

BRING THE FIRE

Elizabeth left the Tompkins home a few minutes after 11:00 P.M. She grabbed a cab and headed across town. The New Yorker Hotel, built in 1930, was across the street from Madison Square Garden and the Amtrak station. The hotel's original art deco opulence was in decline, but for this night it served a purpose.

Elizabeth sat in her darkened hotel room waiting for her train and the morning light. She stayed in her clothes, dozing off and on and watching the clock. Far from the elegant confines of the Oak Bar and the Plaza Hotel, she let the nonstop rumble of trucks, sirens and endless stream of people on 8th Avenue keep her company through the night. It was the first morning in nearly two weeks she did not awaken with Atkinson and Boomer nearby, and she did not like it.

At 7:30 A.M., Elizabeth descended the cramped escalator tube to Amtrak's underground platform for the 8:10 train to Washington's Union Station. The foul-smelling exhaust from the diesel locomotives mixed with the chilly air temperature to create a harsh microclimate that matched Elizabeth's mood. A profound sense of gloom overwhelmed Elizabeth as she waited to board her train. There was no way to undo her outburst on the street from the day before with

447

Atkinson and Blaine, nor did she want to, but she recognized there would be consequences.

The mash of Elizabeth's emotions helped her ignore the four messages she had received on her pager from Atkinson. She settled into a seat, hoping that the three-hour ride, softened by the river views around the Upper Chesapeake Bay and the Delaware River, would blunt her angst and give her the words to apologize to Tommy and Barbara. Finding out that Alistair McCabe was representing the Archdiocese had changed everything. It was a seminal event out of nowhere—a noble fight, a war to the death. This was her path to sanity. What she had learned out on the curb was that she did not have the tools to deal with conflict when it dealt with her memories.

As her cab from Union Station traveled north on 16th Street and past Meridian Park, Elizabeth remembered that the park was the home of Paul Dubois' sculpture of the equestrian Joan of Arc, the martyred patron saint of France, burned at the stake by the English for religious heresy. For a lapsed Catholic about to organize a racketeering lawsuit against the Archdiocese, it was a laughable irony. Spotting Atkinson's truck parked on a side street, Elizabeth wondered if she would have the right words. Standing at her door, she listened as Boomer sniffed at the sill plate, picking up the presence of a visitor.

"Boomer, it's me," Elizabeth whispered into the crack of the door. The dog wildly forced air through the bottom threshold of the door as Elizabeth knocked twice on her apartment door.

"Get back!" Atkinson scolded Boomer as Elizabeth stood straight to face him.

She heard Atkinson unlatch and open the door. "I'm a jerk," she announced, making no movement to come into her apartment.

Atkinson hesitated a moment, leaning against the open door. "Okay, is 'I'm a jerk' an apology or is 'I'm a jerk' just a statement of fact?"

"I'm a jerk and I'm sorry, and I'm a jerk is a statement of fact so it's both," Elizabeth said, a tiny smile forming on her lips. "I felt you were trying to bully me into taking Bobby's case and I went ape-shit on you."

"To be honest, Liz, I just thought you were the right person for the job. That's all I was saying."

"I know that now," Elizabeth said.

"Well, then, we're good. Come on into your apartment. Boomer has missed you. Where did you stay last night?" Atkinson asked.

Boomer leaned his entire body weight against Elizabeth, furiously wagging his tail as she glanced at all the "new resident" mail on her counter. Turning toward Atkinson, she said, "Are you really asking me if I had anything to drink or where I stayed?"

"I thought my question was pretty simple, Liz. I figured if you did have anything to drink you would tell me."

Elizabeth smiled as she bent down to give Boomer a kiss on his head. "I would have told you, Tommy, and thank you for not asking. I stayed at the New Yorker across the street from Penn Station."

"Sweet," Atkinson said, delighted. "I was just going to take Boomer out to do his business, do you want to come?"

"I'd love to, but I want to get cleaned up and get over to Georgetown's law library and do a little research on Paul Weinstein's firm. That's why I took an early train."

"What do you mean?" Atkinson said, stopping short in the hallway and walking back into the kitchen.

"What I mean is that I have some news," Elizabeth said, pacing back and forth in the small galley kitchen.

"Can it wait until we get back?" Atkinson asked, amused by Elizabeth's excitement.

"No, I have to get ready. But the top line is Bobby's dad called me after we left. The lawyer on the other side for the Archdiocese of New York is a prick named Alistair McCabe. He's the managing partner of my old firm!" Elizabeth exclaimed, slapping her hand on the counter.

"So, that's good news?" Atkinson asked, confused.

"It's great news, Tommy. I worked there for eight years. I know how they think. I know what to expect, I know what they're like in a trial," Elizabeth said through gritted teeth.

"Wouldn't they know the same thing about you, Liz?"

Elizabeth stared at Atkinson, walked within inches of his face and then smiled. "Exactly, Tommy. They'll know exactly what to expect from me. That's why I decided to stay in New York last night. Bobby's dad called me and told me about my old firm representing the Archdiocese and we met for dinner last night and I had the family sign a retainer agreement with me with an understanding that I would associate with a much larger firm with resources to match up with McCabe & Willis."

"Wow, Liz, that is big news. So, are you going to the meeting at four today?" Atkinson asked.

"I am, but I have to get two weeks of road dirt off me and get over to the library. So, do you want to meet me downtown at four?" Elizabeth asked, walking through the living room toward her bedroom. Suddenly she turned around and rushed back to Atkinson and kissed him on the cheek. "Thank you, Tommy... for everything."

Atkinson called out before her bedroom door slammed shut. "That sounds good. I'll take care of Boomer, make some calls and meet with my Dominican Superior."

Elizabeth stopped and turned to Atkinson. "Is everything all right?" she asked, concerned.

"Probably not. I think he got a few letters from some bishops who are pissed off at me for helping the survivors and their lawyers. Some of my more intemperate remarks have gotten into the press."

"That's a funny word. That sounds like a priest word."

"I'm a priest, Liz, and in my position calling the bishops 'clueless' on the issue of clergy sexual abuse could be considered intemperate, even to the Jesuits."

"I don't know, Tommy, that sounds pretty tame after what I read in Berry's book. Now, if you were quoted in the Washington Post calling the bishops fucking assholes, now that would in my mind sound intemperate."

Atkinson chuckled. "What can they do, fire me again? Besides, my military boss is cool so as long as they don't take my canonical endorsement away, I'll have a job," Atkinson said, opening the door for Boomer. "I'm glad you're going to the meeting, Liz."

"Me too, Tommy."

Standing against her bedroom door, Elizabeth took an inventory of her emotions, knowing full well there was no return if she started this journey. She wondered if she was up for the fight. But for her entire career, she always worried whether or not she was up for the fight. Those familiar butterflies in her stomach seemed to stabilize the shaking in her hand. She stripped off her clothes and turned on the hot water in the shower. A light fog began to cover the full-length mirror on the back of the door. She looked at herself. Leaning even closer into the mirror, she traced with her finger "Bring the Fire."

Atkinson returned with Boomer a little more than an hour later, hoping to see Elizabeth before she left. Boomer raced into the apartment, but it was too late. Her perfume lingered in the air as Boomer went room to room looking for her.

"She's gone, Boom," Atkinson said as Boomer settled in at the foot of Elizabeth's bed to pout and wait. Atkinson felt uncomfortable in Elizabeth's apartment. Her perfume triggered an all too familiar angst, an emotional tug of war between his service to the priesthood and the intimate warmth of being close to another human being. Her clothes, undergarments and shoes strewn from one end of the bedroom to the other did not help matters.

451

Peering into Elizabeth's bedroom, Atkinson saw life on display—no pretense, no agenda, just the rawness of action. For Atkinson, it became painfully apparent that the celibate lifestyle to be unburdened by such a powerful connection would in the long run frustrate the very goals of the consecrated priesthood. The inability to live a full life with the full range of human experience and emotion precluded any meaningful connection to the very people who sought him out for spiritual solace. The centuries old and rigidly honed clericalism of the past did indeed separate the laity from the priesthood, but at a frightful and counter-productive cost.

He had it all wrong, but he needed to keep his job, and he needed to get out of Elizabeth's apartment.

I DIDN'T SEE THAT COMING
Elizabeth took the elevator to the eighth floor of the Hawthorn Building to the law firm of Courso, MacDonald, Peters & Weinstein. Her research on the firm showed highly regarded peer reviews for virtually every lawyer in the firm, particularly Paul Weinstein.

The main lobby of the reception area for the firm was dominated by an unadorned glass wall that looked into the conference room, highlighting a perfect view of Lafayette Park and the White House beyond. Elizabeth arrived a full hour early for the four o'clock meeting with Paul Weinstein and Father Atkinson, telling the receptionist that she was happy to wait.

Getting comfortable in a plush wing chair, she took out her day planner and notebook to observe and be observed. She counted thirty calls into the switchboard in the first twenty minutes of waiting. That was a good sign. She noticed a gentleman looking directly toward her through the glass wall in the conference room on the phone. He hung up the phone and walked out of the conference room. Elizabeth looked up and smiled as the gentleman approached.

"Excuse me miss, Mrs. Natale?" he gently asked.

"It's Miss, and please, it's Elizabeth," she said as she extended her hand.

"I'm Tony Courso. Paul Weinstein's secretary let me know you were here. Why don't you get settled in the conference room where we'll meet and I can give you a tour of the firm, if you'd like."

"I'm sure you're busy, Mr. Courso. I know I'm early and I have plenty to work on."

"It's not a bother at all. I just finished up and I have nothing on the calendar until four."

Elizabeth gathered her things and moved toward the conference room. "In that case, I would enjoy that very much," she said, relishing the opportunity to soak in the vibe of the law firm.

"Paul said that Father Atkinson will be here at four and he asked me and Frank Peters, our managing partner, to sit in with him. Paul knows the politics of the firm and it seems that some of these abuse cases can be tricky."

"How do you mean, Mr. Courso?" Elizabeth asked as she walked toward a center chair of the cherry and ebony inlaid conference table, surprised Courso would be so candid with someone he just met.

"Good God, Elizabeth, I'm seventy-two years old, I don't need to be reminded of my age. Please call me Tony," he said as he removed his suit jacket.

Elizabeth was amused at Courso's attempt to be self-deprecating. He looked far less than his stated age. He was fit and wore it well in his impeccably tailored Canali suit. Topped off by a contrast collar custom shirt, self-tipped Milano tie and Gordon Gekko-esque pinstripe suspenders, Courso belied anything but the man in charge of the firm. As the two lawyers settled around the huge custom table, Elizabeth was intrigued as to why the founder and the firm's managing partner were going to attend what she assumed was a simple meet and greet with Weinstein.

"Tony, your offices and this view of the White House are magnificent," Elizabeth said, trying to keep the conversation light.

"Actually, I have my grandfather and father to thank for that. My dad's pop bought this entire block at the turn of the century, and it has stayed in the family. Hopefully my son, who just finished law school at Georgetown, will come here, learn the ropes and the legacy will continue," Courso said wistfully.

"That's quite a legacy," Elizabeth said, impressed by Courso's momentary foray into sentiment.

"So, tell me, Elizabeth, what brings you to our firm?" Courso asked, putting Elizabeth on the spot.

"That's actually a bit of a work in progress. I'm an old college friend of Father Atkinson and I was shocked to find out that he was the whistle blower in this Catholic sex abuse scandal, and I wanted to learn more. So, I looked him up, tracked him down and hitched a ride with him from Everett, Washington. He gave me a weeklong primer on the cover-up by the bishops and here I am. I understand that Paul Weinstein wanted to meet with Father Atkinson as he has some cases that he wanted to go over with him."

"Fascinating. Paul tells me that you're a lawyer from New York. The only Elizabeth Natale from New York that I could find works in Alistair McCabe's firm."

"*Worked* in Alistair McCabe's firm," Elizabeth said, coldly emphasizing the past tense.

"Unpleasant parting?" Courso asked as he grabbed at a few jellybeans from a crystal vase on the side table, popping one into his mouth. "At sixty-eight I had to quit smoking and my wife bought me this goddamn vase and a potato sack full of jellybeans for my birthday."

Elizabeth knew she was being probed. "So, how's it working out for you?"

"The jellybeans?" Courso asked.

454

"No, the smoking," Elizabeth said as she picked some jellybeans out of the vase.

"Like shit," Courso laughed. "I still want to smoke."

Elizabeth chuckled. "I get it, Tony. We pay dearly for our vices."

"Indeed we do, Elizabeth," Courso agreed.

"But in answer to your question, leaving McCabe was not unpleasant. I'd say it was more complicated than unpleasant," Elizabeth said as Courso cleared his throat.

"Can you share, Elizabeth?" Courso gushed. "I'm a total sucker for New York legal gossip."

"Perhaps another time," Elizabeth demurred. She found the gentle inquisition enjoyable but remained curious as to why so many senior lawyers were going to meet with Atkinson. "Tony, you said earlier these abuse cases were tricky. What did you mean by that?" Elizabeth asked, trying to move the conversation away from her.

"Well, Elizabeth, that's complicated," Courso said as they both laughed. "Walk with me to my office and I'll explain."

"Can I leave my things here?" Elizabeth asked.

"Absolutely," Courso said as Elizabeth picked up a single legal pad and pen to take with her.

The long hallway down to Courso's corner office was flanked on both sides by taupe-colored cubicles in neatly organized pods with room for eight secretaries and legal assistants in each pod. The attorney offices were steps away, boasting floor to ceiling windows on either the H Street side facing the White House for the partners and junior partners or the 16th Street side for associates and non-equity partners.

Courso's office was a surprise. It was small, with a round table with room for four seats, and a sitting area facing the windows. A couch and four oversized leather chairs, side tables and reading lamps at each corner of the coffee table filled the opposite side of the room. It looked more like an elegant living room than a founding partner's law office. Several Charles Bragg bronze sculptures were strategically placed on black lacquered pedestals. Courso took great pride in one of Bragg's original castings for "Out of Court Settlement" that featured two bulbous litigants in a furious wrestling match with one gentleman in an intractable headlock while the other waited for capitulation.

The heavily tinted glass windows and backlighting through small portals in the deeply coffered ceiling created a palatial but sophisticated tone. It was a room with only one purpose in mind. Major clients felt more comfortable in plush surroundings and, despite the obscene rent the firm paid to the family trust, the trappings proved to be a major business producer. Institutional clients and their fees allowed the personal injury side of the firm to take on larger and more complex national cases and class actions. It was in this area that Paul Weinstein had come into his own as an attorney.

The walls were adorned with family photos and Dali originals. Behind the circular table were dozens of framed restaurant menus from around the world. Elizabeth surveyed the wall of bookcases and stood there staring for a moment. She took several steps down the wall, looking at each of the shelves and noting the titles. She turned to Courso with a quizzical look on her face.

"I know, it's an odd assortment," Courso said as he flipped a switch on the wall for the motorized sunshades to decrease the glare of the late afternoon sun.

"It's not an assortment at all, Tony, they're all cookbooks," Elizabeth replied, settling into one of the leather side chairs.

"I know, it's a sickness, but they go back to the early 1800s," Courso said as if he had been caught doing something wrong by his first-grade teacher. "Madeline, my wife, thinks I've lost my mind, but I assure you there's a method to my madness," Courso added proudly.

Elizabeth arched her eyebrow and turned her attention to the framed picture sitting on the credenza. "Is that your wife, Tony?" Elizabeth asked.

"Yes, that's my Irish rose," Courso said with genuine pride. "We've been married forty-three years. Maddie is hell fire on wheels, can't cook worth a lick, but I love her to bits."

"That's really great, Tony, forty-three years." Elizabeth began to feel a wave of sadness and melancholy. She was forty-six years old, and this was a part of life that she had never known. She instinctively changed the subject. "So, what's the deal with all the cookbooks, Tony?" Elizabeth asked.

"It's an important collection that has become very valuable," Courso said firmly.

"You don't say," Elizabeth said, amused. "I don't cook either."

"What, you have an Italian last name, and you don't cook?" Courso said in mock disgust.

"Tony, I fall in line with Madeline on that one, not a lick," Elizabeth laughed.

"So, these abuse cases, like I said, they can get tricky," Courso said, putting his feet up on the corner of the coffee table.

"Yes, I'm interested in what you mean by that," Elizabeth said, pushing herself back into the chair.

"Paul has had a couple of these cases settle with the Archdiocese of Baltimore. They were for adults, but they settled for significant money. And get this, Elizabeth, the files were a quarter inch thick."

"What do you mean?"

"What I mean is that the Archdiocese paid $700,000 on the first case and $850,000 on the second case on the strength of a five-page letter, a draft complaint and a few phone calls. Both were barred by the statute of limitations. Who the fuck, oh excuse me, Elizabeth," Courso said, checking himself.

"No worries, Tony, I've heard worse. Paul never filed a lawsuit?" Elizabeth asked.

"Nope, they just paid. Who the fuck pays that kind of money on a statute barred case?" Courso said, raising his voice and thrusting both of his hands in the air, much like Elizabeth's grandfather did at the dinner table on Shepherd Street.

"Someone who has a lot to hide," Elizabeth said quietly. "Someone who has a lot to hide, someone who realizes that this is the tip of the iceberg and someone who will do just about anything to keep this crap under wraps. I suppose there was a confidentiality agreement?" Elizabeth asked.

"Ironclad and detailed. It has provisions for liquidated damages and attorney fees in the event of a breach, the works," Courso said, rubbing his eyes from the glare of the sun.

"That's part of the problem, Tony," Elizabeth said, bracing herself for a backlash.

"So, in a statute barred case that goes away on a three-page motion to dismiss, the Archdiocese puts $700,000 cash money in front of *your* client, so you tell the client what, Elizabeth?" Courso fumed. "I'll tell you what you do," Courso said, not waiting for her to answer. "You take the money or notify your malpractice carrier."

"Don't get your knickers in a knot, Tony. You misunderstood what I meant. Of course you take the money. What I meant was that the confidentiality agreements are becoming the institutional safe for keeping the secrets. Not every adult survivor is going to get that type of deal. It's only where the risk of not paying is worse for the Archdiocese do they decide to pay that kind of money. That's when they pay the big money. The vast majority of these cases are statute barred across the country and they'll settle for peanuts," Elizabeth countered.

Courso nodded. "Well, in any event the partners were not enthused with Paul taking these cases, but they were far enough away from D.C. for our Catholic partners and of course they did like the money."

"Of course," Elizabeth said dryly. "It's always about the money."

"But now he has twelve adults with the Archdiocese of Washington. Paul is a brilliant trial lawyer. He has absolutely no fear, but Frank and I are concerned and of course all these new cases came in after news of the settlements with the Archdiocese of Baltimore leaked out."

"How did that happen?" Elizabeth asked with a smirk on her face.

"If I knew, I wouldn't say," Courso chuckled. "You know, Elizabeth, or you seem to know, that the Archdiocese isn't your run of the mill corporate defendant. So, when I heard Paul was going to meet with Father Atkinson and you were coming along, I thought some of the adults in the room should attend. Don't get me wrong, I love Paul. I brought him into the firm. He's the best natural trial lawyer I've ever seen, it's just sometimes his judgment is like that of a kid who's had too much sugar and chocolate before school."

Elizabeth let out a belly laugh. She really liked this man.

"But Paul went ahead and reached out to Father Atkinson. He's been talking to some lawyer in Minnesota..."

"Jeff Anderson?" Elizabeth interrupted.

"That's him," Courso said, surprised. "How did you know?"

"I was referred to a book by a woman I met in New York. Her name is Barbara Blaine, and the name of the book is *Lead Us Not Into Temptation* by Jason Berry. Berry wrote about some of Anderson's early cases and the whole Gilbert Gauthe mess in Louisiana."

"Jesus Christ, Weinstein talked to that Blaine woman two weeks ago! Is this some kind of coffee klatch cabal?" Courso fretted.

"Did you read Berry's book?" Elizabeth asked, glancing at her watch.

"No," Courso said, his voice starting to get hoarse.

"Well, you should. I'm finding out it's a small universe of firms willing to tackle a two-thousand-year-old boys club that's selling eternal salvation," Elizabeth said. "It's almost four, Tony." She got up from her chair. "Let me go out front and see if Father Atkinson is here yet."

Elizabeth walked up the hallway toward the main lobby. Atkinson was sitting in the corner of the room with his head down, scribbling into a notepad. Elizabeth's heels clicked efficiently across the marble floor to where Atkinson was sitting.

"Hey, good-looking, do I know you?" Elizabeth chortled loud enough for the receptionist to giggle and embarrass Atkinson.

Atkinson scrambled to his feet and began to blush when he saw her. Elizabeth's road jeans and flannel shirt had been replaced by high heels, a stunning blue knit dress and a St. John's felted wool and cashmere three-quarter jacket. Her chestnut hair, which fell to her shoulders, framed a shining complexion with just a hint of makeup and lipstick. A simple black pearl pendant necklace radiated off her translucent skin. Atkinson was mesmerized by the transformation.

"Jesus, Liz, you're all dressed up. I'm glad I had a set of clean clerics."

"This is my work uniform, Tommy. I'd much rather be wearing jeans."

"I don't think so, Liz, you look pretty good in that uniform."

"As do you, Father Atkinson," Liz said, smiling. "C'mon, they're in the conference room. I've already met the senior partner, Tony Courso. Interesting guy. Where's Boomer?" Elizabeth asked.

"He's fine, Liz. He's with a friend at the Dominican House. We'll pick him up on the way back."

"Does your friend like dogs? I mean is he like a dog person who loves dogs?"

"He's happy as a clam, Liz. Don't worry."

Atkinson held the door for Elizabeth as both Frank Peters and Tony Courso stood up as she entered the room. After everyone made the rounds of introductions, they settled toward the center of the conference room table on opposite sides.

Peters was a confidant of Tony Courso. A tall, unassuming man, prone to wearing brightly colored bowties, Peters had the persona of a dignified professor. Courso hated and was not particularly good at dealing with personnel matters, so it fell to Peters to keep all the players in check. Peters never shied away from embarrassing Paul for his constant lack of courtesy, but at the same time was one of his biggest champions inside the executive committee. Whether it changed any behavior going forward was a different matter.

Peters was aggressive, fair, and always in control. As managing partner, he worked tirelessly, cajoling and stroking the egos that made up a high-powered law firm. What separated Peters from most of his contemporaries was that at age fifty-eight he had increased the number of cases he tried himself during the last ten years. He was considered by many a methodical genius, laying traps for recalcitrant witnesses' hours, sometime days before he pounced on a significant inconsistency in testimony. His proudest achievement was that there had not been a single partner defection since 1980.

Peters used his experience and non-confrontational manner to discipline and reward this group of egocentric lawyers. His wife Laura called it his own personal animal house. A partner at Courso, MacDonald, Peters & Weinstein, Peters knew that the long-term interests of the firm were paramount over any individual lawyer, and that included Paul Weinstein. For whatever reason, Peters was able to convince the partners that their personal goals could be achieved from within, as members of the firm.

Paul Weinstein was an enigma to his partners and in particular to Peters. He had been under Peters' wing for some time and Peters worried that Weinstein never seemed to care about people's feelings, despite the fact that his entire caseload was personal injury litigation. Money was not Weinstein's motivation; in fact, he had spent a fortune via an inheritance before his thirty-fifth birthday. It was apparent that what turned Weinstein's fancy was combat. The higher the stakes and the more ruthless his adversary the better he performed. For Weinstein, trial work was living theater. The courtroom was his stage, but the story was always the same in his mind: good versus evil. Weinstein viewed himself as the tip of the spear, a vehicle of sorts, which allowed society to vent its collective rage against corporate malfeasance and skullduggery through jury verdicts. For many, he was over the top, but his partners tolerated him for no other reason than his productivity.

While the group waited, Frank Peters set the stage for the discussion.

"Is it okay if I call you Tom, Father?" Peters asked awkwardly.

"Please," Atkinson said.

"My job here is to try and keep this high-strung group of people more or less moving in the same direction. Anything I'm going to tell you now, I've told to Paul Weinstein in person or in writing. He's looking at some cases against our local Archdiocese that aren't only difficult but are politically dangerous. He reached out to you, Tom, and I think that's great. My job is to direct resources where we can do the most good. To be blunt, getting into a years-long struggle with the Church where there are structural vulnerabilities with the cases isn't the best use of our resources no matter how just the cause. I'm sure Paul will see it differently and to be honest that's why he's been successful, but a drug or car manufacturer is a lot different than picking a fight with a religion."

"Okay, I think I'm getting the picture," Atkinson said, smiling.

Elizabeth looked directly at Peters. "So, you're afraid of these cases?" Elizabeth asked in a tone that could send the meeting sideways but for Peters' experience.

"I am, Elizabeth, but not for the reasons you may think. I had a chance to speak to one of Paul's Baltimore clients and the pain this man was still in from events that happened decades ago was something I had never observed in all my years' experience. It was humbling," Peters said.

"Why did you find it humbling?" Elizabeth asked, interrupting Peters.

"Everyone in this room has represented clients. But from my view, when you take on these cases, you're not just representing a client in a dispute. You're representing a life that has been essentially turned upside down. What I saw in these guys was a hurt so bad that even a healthy sum of money could not touch."

Elizabeth felt an instant pain in her belly. Adrenaline flooded her body as she tried to keep her composure.

"Does Paul Weinstein agree with that sentiment?" Elizabeth asked, trying to settle herself.

"I'm not sure. Perhaps you can ask him when he gets here."

"I will, Frank," Elizabeth said.

"And the politics, Frank, what about the politics of doing these cases?" Courso inquired.

"I think you have to expect some blowback, Tony."

Elizabeth watched Courso closely.

"We've gotten blowback before. I'm not too worried about that. But a client who we cannot serve well who goes back, if you pardon the expression, back into the shit house. That's a different story. That's what I'm worried about."

At 4:20 P.M., the conference room door burst open and Weinstein rushed in, apologizing in advance for being late.

"On time and dressed for the occasion," Peters cracked as Weinstein flopped his pile of books and files at the end of the conference room table.

On top of the stack was Jason Berry's book. Weinstein was dressed in blue jeans, a black tee shirt, and a houndstooth jacket with a red wool ball cap. Totally unconcerned about his tardiness, he worked the room like an emcee at an awards show. He rushed over to Atkinson from the opposite side of the table.

"Hi, I'm Paul. Even a Jew could tell you're the only priest in the room. Welcome, Father, it's a pleasure to finally meet you," Weinstein said, laughing.

Courso and Peters both rolled their eyes.

Weinstein turned next to Elizabeth. "I don't believe we've ever had a clerk of a Supreme Court Justice in this building. I'm truly honored to meet you, Mademoiselle Natale." He bowed, exaggerating his welcome as if he were meeting the Queen of England. "Mademoiselle Natale, I like that," Weinstein complimented himself. "It just rolls off your tongue like butter." This, of course, had the desired effect of reducing everyone to laughter and lessening the tension coming from Courso and Peters.

Elizabeth turned to both Courso and Peters across the table. "Is it like this every day?" Elizabeth asked, chuckling.

Courso shook his head in mock disgust. "Every day, Elizabeth. Paul, come sit between Frank and me so we can get started."

Weinstein looked at Atkinson and smiled. "I'm being disciplined now, Father."

"Let's begin," Courso said in a tone that gaveled the banter to a close. "Father Atkinson, the floor is yours."

For the next two hours, Atkinson reviewed the crisis decade by decade. It was a tale of cover-up, intrigue and callousness. At the root of the malevolence was something very familiar to the lawyers who litigated corporate misbehavior that injured or killed consumers – institutional self-preservation.

Both Courso and Peters had dozens of questions about the uniformity of the Secret Archives across the 256 dioceses throughout the country. Atkinson assured them that while each diocese may have different mechanics for document storage, the bishops rarely, if ever, had the courage to go outside the parameters of Church Law and freelance.

"I want to be clear," Atkinson said. "The bishops are more than willing to ignore the spirit and in some cases the letter of the civil law."

Atkinson felt a twinge of embarrassment. This was the organization he had dedicated his life to. Dressed in his black clerics, he felt dirty and cheap as a visual representation of all that was evil.

"Could you give me an example, Tom, of this kind of behavior?" Frank Peters asked.

"Sure, the easiest example is what they do when they get an actual report of abuse.

This would usually come in from a parent. First thing they would do is to distance themselves from the report of abuse."

"Don't you just love this shit," Weinstein spewed, interrupting Atkinson's flow.

"Tom, please continue," Courso said, trying to maintain order.

"The bishop or the priest getting the report would routinely suggest that this was an extraordinary event. That they had no knowledge of prior bad acts on the part of this or any other priest."

"What you are saying is they lie," Peters stated.

"Exactly," Atkinson said.

"As I was saying, the bishops would suggest that the story is so extraordinary that it strains credulity. Parents would be cautioned as to severe consequences of a priest being falsely accused. The bishops would subtly suggest how the family and the victim could suffer extreme embarrassment and isolation from the faithful community because, as everyone knows, it's highly unlikely that priests are even capable of such deviant behavior. They would sow doubt by asking if anything else is going on in the home that would cause the child to invent a story to seek attention. If that does not achieve the desired effect, they break out the sixteen-inch guns. They say that the report itself is an attack on

God." Atkinson was talking faster than the group could take notes. "Should I slow down?" Atkinson asked. "I can see the looks on your faces."

"No, no, we're with you, keep going," Courso said.

"Okay, so here's how they sell it. If a parent brings a claim, any claim, God and the faithful will view it as an attack on the Church, threatening the existence of their very souls. There would be no recovery from excommunication and eternal salvation will be lost for them forever."

"This is craziness," Courso lamented as Atkinson took a sip of water and continued for another thirty minutes.

Elizabeth was feeling sick by the ugly reliving of her own abuse that Atkinson's recitation roiled up inside her. Atkinson could see she was fading and was happy she spoke up.

"Would anyone mind if we took a ten-minute bathroom break?" Elizabeth asked.

"Not at all," Courso said. "After that monologue I think everyone could use a bit of air.

Elizabeth left immediately for the ladies room. Weinstein followed Atkinson to the men's room. Standing at the urinal next to Atkinson, Weinstein struck up a conversation, apparently oblivious to the most basic of social protocols.

"Father, thanks again for coming. By the way, do you know if Elizabeth is married?" Weinstein asked.

The question shocked Atkinson into silence until the business at hand was concluded. Safely in front of the lavatory and hand soap dispenser, he responded to the question, amazed by how defensive he was feeling.

"Well, I've known her since high school, but no she's not married. I think the law business is her first love."

"Seems like a waste," Weinstein said, straightening his sport coat and admiring his looks in the mirror.

"You've known her a long time, Tom, do you think if I asked her out she would be pissed?"

"Being a priest, I try to stay in my lane on those matters. Are you married, Paul?"

"Nope, there's no room in my life for a wife now," Weinstein said as he pushed closer to the mirror and vanity, swishing a half cup of mouthwash into the basin.

"Interesting, that's one of the pillars of mandatory celibacy in the Church. To be unburdened with the demands of intimate relations. Perhaps you have a vocation, Paul."

Weinstein looked at Atkinson in the mirror, perplexed by the comment.

"I'm just fooling with you, Paul. Let's get back and I can wrap up my spiel. I want you and your group to hear Elizabeth out on this. She has some idea as to how to proceed that I think you'll find interesting."

"I'll be all ears, Tom," Weinstein said.

Atkinson noticed that Elizabeth was not back in the conference room or on the patio, so he decided to wait in the lobby for her to return. He worked hard on stifling his anger at Weinstein's inquiries about Elizabeth. It was not logical for him to be offended by the question. She was single and Weinstein was single, and it was normal for attractions to occur. Atkinson tried to convince himself that it did not matter how Elizabeth chose to live her life, but after the last two weeks, it mattered in every way.

Elizabeth tapped him on the shoulder from behind, startling him.

"You ready to go back in?" she asked.

"If you are. You seemed to be upset when you asked for a break."

"Well, of course I was. It's never far from the surface, Tommy, even now. And with Bobby signed up I'm feeling the pressure. But I'll be fine. I just needed a few minutes to gather myself."

Atkinson frowned, looking at the floor.

"What's wrong, Tommy?" Elizabeth asked.

"Nothing, let's go back in."

"Well, something's wrong. What is it?" Elizabeth asked with more force than Atkinson would have preferred.

"When we get back to the apartment, I'll tell you then."

"No, you'll tell me now," Elizabeth said as Atkinson noticed that the lawyers were coming back to the conference room. "Tell me what's wrong, they can wait."

"I was in the men's room and Weinstein asked if you were married."

"And what did you say?" Elizabeth asked, sizing up the situation.

"I told him you weren't, and he said it was a waste, and that pissed me off. Then I asked him if he was married, and he said as a lawyer he didn't have room for a wife in his life. Then I told him it's the same for priests and that maybe he had a vocation."

"You didn't," Elizabeth said, covering her mouth so her laughter would not be overheard in the lobby. "That's hilarious."

"What? What's so damn funny?" Atkinson huffed.

"You're jealous, Tommy, and I think it's cute. C'mon, let's go back in."

"I won't even dignify that with a comment," Atkinson said walking back into the conference room, wondering why he did not share Paul's desire to ask Elizabeth out.

Atkinson riffed through several methods bishops used to transfer perpetrators and shield them from criminal prosecution. He covered one Bishop's secretly recorded remarks suggesting to other bishops how the use of Diplomatic Immunity could shield incriminating documents from discovery prior to a subpoena being issued. He gave an abbreviated lesson on the Official Catholic Directory, much like he gave Elizabeth at Gonzaga University. As he moved through the minutiae of what could only be described as a massive criminal conspiracy, his anger at Weinstein lingered.

ACT OF FAITH

"Just so you understand the gravity of what you're dealing with, consider this," Atkinson said in a tone akin to a scientific lecture. "Tony, is that a white board behind that drapery?"

"It is- please feel free," Courso said, walking around the table so he could see.

"Number One. They will lie under oath using the doctrine of mental reservation to rationalize that any scandal involving the Church is an attack on the very foundation of the religion that must be resisted. Number Two. They will attack the lawyers as money hungry anti-Catholics and will mobilize as much nasty public sentiment as possible against you. Once that train leaves the station, the next one will try to break you financially and to make it so uncomfortable for the clients that you give up or go away."

"Jesus, Tom, they should do it like the Mafia," Peters commented.

"I'm sorry to interrupt, Tom," Courso said.

"That's okay, Tony, go ahead."

"Will they actually try a case?" Courso asked.

"They rarely do. When they do, I think Anderson has had two, and I'm sure there's more, then they get hammered. Actually, Tony, you hit on their weakness," Atkinson said.

"I'll shut up. Go ahead, Tom," Courso said, pouring himself a cup of coffee.

Atkinson went back to the white board. "Number Three. They will use the First Amendment and the separation of Church and State to hide their written documentation and, more importantly, their prior knowledge of known sexual predators of children and teenagers.

Number Four. They will send perpetrators out of the jurisdiction for 'treatment' then ignore recommendations from the therapists that the offenders be closely monitored or removed from ministry. Number Five. The hierarchy of the Catholic Church, as a seminal part of their culture of governance over the laity, believe with every fiber in their being that they are better than us. That they know more than we do, and most importantly, that they alone know what's best for us. Number Six. They will invent a special language to deny sexual crimes: For example: *unnatural affection, misguided attraction, unintended physical contact, unnatural involvements, and the best one: misguided judgments due to emotional and psychological underdevelopment.*"

"What a crock of shit," Weinstein chimed in. "I'm surprised these assholes aren't in jail."

"Paul, you have to understand. Very few people and fewer prosecutors have ever seen any of this stuff. That's why this remained under the radar until the Gauthe case," Atkinson said. "Number Seven. A confidentiality agreement and agreements not to report to police in exchange for help with therapy costs reign supreme. Over the decades, hundreds, if not thousands of cases have been settled under this protocol. Number Eight. If you think that bishops and cardinals don't have their own sexual indiscretions to keep out of the public eye, think again. They do. So, long story short, you're dealing with the largest criminal conspiracy to cover up the sexual assault of children in United States history. They act like thugs because they are thugs."

The room fell quiet. The only noise was the muted traffic.

"Are there any questions?" Atkinson asked the group.

"Actually, I do have one," Weinstein said. "If this were as serious as you suggest, and I'm not doubting you, why would the Church let this go on for so many decades?"

Atkinson took his place at the table. "Because, their worldview is over centuries, not years. Each diocese and archdiocese is a separate legal and canonical entity, and they'll pay these claims out with other people's money. Their reservoir of funds is faith. People will still believe, they'll still contribute, and they'll ignore the fact that the bishops enabled this crisis with the full cooperation of the Pope for fear that their shot at eternal salvation is *kaput.*"

"Tom, it really doesn't matter about the Pope. He's a sovereign leader so we couldn't sue him, but why do you say he fully cooperated?" Courso asked.

"Because, Tony, the Vatican and Cardinal Ratzinger have seen all of these reports."

"Cardinal who?" Weinstein asked.

"Cardinal Joseph Ratzinger. He was in charge of all the cases being sent to the Vatican about priests sexually acting out with kids. They knew what was going on. I sent many of them myself when I was working at the Embassy. By making it so difficult to get these priests out of ministry they have sided with the priests against the children, in my opinion."

The sun had slipped behind the Washington Monument and the Tidal basin. Tony Courso wanted the conversation to continue but it was approaching the dinner hour.

"Before Elizabeth starts, let me make a suggestion. There's a wonderful restaurant on the first floor and they will bring our meals up here. I can have menus sent up, we can order, then we can eat here so we can make use of our time together. How does that sound to everyone?" Courso asked.

"What about Boomer?" Elizabeth asked Atkinson, hoping that he would take the cue. She had wanted to make it an early night and the business with Weinstein in the men's room had gotten under her skin.

"Oh, he'll be fine. I left food with Brother Gerald, but I'll call just to make sure," Atkinson said. "That sounds great, Tony."

"Elizabeth, why don't you start," Courso urged.

Elizabeth got up from her chair and walked to the whiteboard. As she was erasing most of Atkinson's shorthand notations, she spoke directly to Weinstein. "Tom said you were thinking about a class action of sorts, is that right?" she asked.

"Yes and no," Weinstein said. "There are some very straightforward common questions on liability that surround the cover-up that Tom briefed us on and..."

Elizabeth cut him off in mid-sentence. "It falls apart on causation and besides there are no common elements of damages with sexual assault. You'll never get a class certified and it'll be a waste of time and money."

"That's good to hear on the front end," Peters quipped to Weinstein who was annoyed at being man-handled by a woman in front of his partners.

"But I think there is an option."

"Well, I'm all ears, Elizabeth," Weinstein said. He removed his ball cap and tossed it on the table, unhappy that Elizabeth appeared to be lecturing him.

"Have you given any thought to using the RICO statute?" Elizabeth asked.

"Are you serious, Elizabeth?" Courso asked, somewhat alarmed. "Isn't that like jumping out of the frying pan into a volcano when these claimants are adults? Christ, suing the Archdiocese as Mafiosi racketeers is..." Courso paused long enough for Weinstein to jump in.

"Listen, Elizabeth, I'm very familiar with the RICO statute," Weinstein said. "I'll grant you this, you have a hierarchical enterprise running the show, and you have a pattern of covering up a conspiracy with criminal intent. You probably have a choice of the predicate acts between mail fraud, wire fraud or obstruction of justice engaged in or affecting commerce to satisfy the pleading requirements, but you're going to run into a problem that all of their bad acts have to injure the plaintiff's business or property. Even if you could artfully get around that in a pleading that would survive to trial, you'll never get past the statute of limitations. It's a four-year statute and the twelve people who have contacted me are all adults. So, in answer to your question, I very briefly considered RICO and have concluded it's just not available and not worth the risk, but I do think I can get these cases settled."

Peters quietly leaned over to Courso and whispered, "Never thought I'd hear Paul talking like a businessman," as Courso leaned back in his conference chair and smiled.

Elizabeth walked away from the whiteboard to her seat across from Weinstein. Atkinson noticed the crimson flush on Elizabeth's neck and thought she was about to rip into him.

"Paul, before I get to the statute of limitations question, let me answer the injury to business or property required under the statute." Elizabeth remained calm and focused, which shocked Atkinson, being only two days removed from her violent outburst in New York.

"Are you familiar with the abortion clinic cases in Pennsylvania and Illinois where the RICO statute was greatly expanded to activities way beyond what people typically understand as organized crime type activity?"

"That's a clear-cut business that was being economically and violently targeted by the destruction of their medical equipment, Elizabeth," Weinstein said, objecting to the analogy.

"Will you just hear me out?" Elizabeth asked, raising her voice an octave.

"Go ahead," Weinstein said as Elizabeth ignored the hint of condescension that had crept into his voice.

"What is a chose in action, Paul?" Elizabeth asked.

"What do you mean, like in the abstract?" Weinstein hedged.

"No, not in the abstract," Elizabeth said, her words boring into Weinstein. "In the real world! We can prove there's an ongoing conspiracy to suppress or bribe the claimants from filing lawsuits. The right to file a lawsuit is, by definition, a personal property right."

"But isn't the lawsuit derivative of an action for personal injuries, which is the opposite of injuries to property?" Peters asked Elizabeth.

"That's what the Archdiocese will argue, but look at it this way," Elizabeth said, walking back to the white board. "There are zero cases that say it's not an injury to business or property. The Supreme Court just removed the need for us to prove the Archdiocese had a profit generating purpose by their bad acts so it's a case of first impression. The Courts have expanded the reach of the RICO statute the last three times it has been in the appellate court. With these facts they could easily do the same in the priest cases," Elizabeth said.

"In what decade, Elizabeth?" Weinstein asked sarcastically. "We could be in the appeal courts for years."

"Right, Paul, it's like the kids who carry these scars for the rest of their lives," Elizabeth said. "What side of that timeline do you want to be on, Paul? What side?" Elizabeth yelled.

"Okay, okay, settle down," Peters said. "We're here to try and figure this out, not take sides."

"I see the argument, Elizabeth. Actually, it's a good one. It's good enough to keep us out of any frivolous claim crap, but at the end of the day we would be filing a RICO case in our home jurisdiction for twelve adults way past the four-year statute of limitation."

"Just so we're clear, this law firm is not doing that," Courso said, asserting his ultimate authority, not to mention his majority equity in the firm.

"You won't have to," Elizabeth said, opening her briefcase and removing two files. "Here is a signed retainer by the parents of a fourteen-year-old. Father Andrew Dolan was arrested two months ago in New York City on two counts of oral copulation of a minor. He has abused minors in Los Angeles, Washington and New York dating back to the late fifties. Behind the retainer agreement is a copy of the police report and a statement from the arresting officer."

"How the hell do you know he abused kids in Los Angeles and here in D.C.?" Weinstein asked, dumbfounded.

Elizabeth opened the second file. "Tom walked me through a series of books called the *Official Catholic Directory*. Here's his entire personnel history," she said as she slid a one-inch stack of stapled sheets across the table to Paul Weinstein. "The page that's flagged with the blue sticky from 1971 is an entry that indicates he's at Via Coeli. Via Coeli is a treatment center for sexual offenders run by the Church."

"Jesus, that's amazing," Courso said, walking to where Weinstein was seated to look at the file himself.

"And in D.C., how do we know he offended anyone here? Father Dolan wasn't mentioned by any of the twelve clients I've interviewed," Weinstein said, still looking at the directory pages.

Elizabeth stood up from her seat and returned to the white board and printed Andrew Dolan's name in large capital letters. "Because he raped me when I was eleven years old at Aquinas Hall, which is about a fifteen-minute drive from here, and I'm sure there are others. We just have to find them."

"Holy shit, I didn't see that coming," Courso said as both he and Atkinson approached Elizabeth, who was becoming visibly upset.

"I'm fine," Elizabeth said. "Believe it or not it gets easier every time I say it." She glanced at her watch and turned to Courso. "Are we still eating together?" she asked.

"We are if you want to continue," Courso said as he picked up his notepad from the table.

"Fine, let me splash some water on my face and we can continue."

Courso watched Weinstein eye Elizabeth from head to toe as she left the room.

"Paul, before you go down, could I see you for a moment in my office?" Courso said as he headed for the conference room door.

"Sure, Tony, let me drop my stuff in my office and I'll be right there."

Courso was standing at his office window. He looked down at the tourists milling about Lafayette Park enjoying the pale amber light from the sunset that bathed the west façade of the White House. Weinstein knocked once on Courso's door that was left ajar.

"What's up, Tony?" Weinstein asked.

"How long have you been with the firm?" Courso asked.

"Geez, Tony," Weinstein pondered. "Counting the two summers I clerked here when I was in law school...sixteen years."

"Are you happy here?" Courso prodded Weinstein.

"With the exception of that Irish asshole partner of yours, Jerry MacDonald, yes I'd say I'm happy."

"He's your partner too, Paul," Courso snapped.

"What's your point, Tony?" Weinstein asked, annoyed.

"My point is that you may think I'm some seventy-year-old grizzled prick who's lost his instincts, but this could be the biggest case of your life and the biggest case in the history of this firm."

"I know that, but it's far from a slam dunk," Weinstein said.

"And you think that fact has been lost on me, Paul?"

"Like I said, Tony, what's your point?"

"My point, Mr. Weinstein, is that you're the firm's top trial lawyer. You're also by far the least considerate. You're a workaholic and a maniacal taskmaster with virtually no family. You don't have a steady girlfriend, but I highly doubt you're celibate. You're the firm's resident pain in the ass. You've gone through six secretaries and countless paralegals over the last five years while still averaging $4 million in net fees per year over all salaries and costs."

"It's been seven secretaries, Tony."

"Don't get cute with me, Paul," Courso chafed.

"Where's this going, Tony," Weinstein said, flopping into one of Courso's side chairs.

"I'll tell you where it's going, Paul. So, when I see you eyeballing Elizabeth as she's walking out of the room, that sends up a big red flag for me. She's obviously got a lot on the ball, she's beautiful and unattached, but in the last sixteen years you haven't demonstrated that you give a rat's ass about anyone but yourself and trying cases. So, word to the wise, Paul, keep it in your pants."

"We done, Tony?" Weinstein said, trying to keep his tone civil.

"Yep, I said what I had to say. I'll see you back in the conference room."

DO YOU PLAY NICE IN THE SANDBOX?

Paul and Elizabeth walked back into the conference room at the same time. An oblong table was laden with family style servings of hot and cold hors d'oeuvres, panzanella, gazpacho, and carafes of sparkling and flat water.

"Ah, Elizabeth, you asked me about all the cookbooks in my office?"

"Yes," Elizabeth said not knowing what to expect.

"I have this theory that just about any problem can get to resolution over great food and wine. Adversaries don't change their stripes when eating but personal connections are made when you share a meal. Often, intractable problems get resolved over a meal, because eating food well prepared is a shared experience that can be built on."

Elizabeth was intrigued. "So, would you rather be in a law practice or an upscale restaurant?" she mused.

"Well, Elizabeth, my family is my love, but food culture is my mistress."

"And the law practice you've built?" Elizabeth asked, now genuinely curious.

"Well, Elizabeth, the law practice just makes everything else work," Courso laughed, taking a sip of a vintage Chianti Classico Reserve that had been poured for the side table as they walked in.

"The entrees you ordered will be ready in twenty minutes."

"May I pour you a glass of Chianti, Elizabeth?" Courso asked.

Elizabeth glanced across the table to Atkinson. "No thank you, Tony. I prefer sparkling water when I'm working."

"How about you, Tom?" Courso said, turning to Atkinson.

"Thanks, Tony, but I'm a recovering alcoholic and seven years sober. Water is fine for me," Atkinson said, smiling at Elizabeth.

"I have some questions on logistics, Elizabeth, if we can talk through those over dinner."

"That's fine, Tony, but let me make one more point on the RICO discussion," Elizabeth said as she picked at her panzanella salad.

"Sure, go ahead," Courso said.

"Each diocese or archdiocese is tax exempt. They do that through a group tax exemption request to the IRS. When they file their request, which happens every year, they submit about a five-inch-thick hardbound book that details every name and address of every church, parish, school, convent or any other Catholic institution for 198 dioceses and archdioceses. That amounts to billions of dollars in tax exemptions. So, if the Church is guilty of an unlawful conspiracy that facilitated the criminal sexual abuse of minors, why should they be entitled to hold billions of dollars in assets free from any governmental tax?"

"They shouldn't," Weinstein said as he settled into a chair at the dinner table. "It's total horseshit what they have gotten away with."

"I agree," Elizabeth said. "Now, the only religious organization that had its tax-exempt status revoked was Bob Jones University because its admissions policy was racially discriminatory."

"Was that a Supreme Court case?" Peters asked.

"Yes."

"Who brought the claim against Bob Jones University, was it the IRS or a private party?" Courso asked, slicing a healthy piece of Pecorino cheese from a wedge on the table.

Elizabeth was pleased that Courso seemed to be on the right track. "No individual claimant can bring a cause of action to revoke the tax-exempt status of a nonprofit. The Bob Jones case was initiated by the Internal Revenue Service," she said.

"So, what are you saying, Elizabeth?" Weinstein asked.

"What I am saying is if we're successful, the Court in a RICO case can fashion any just and reasonable remedy to deter any future illegal conduct and revoke their tax-exempt status based on their prior bad acts."

"What you're really saying is that if we put that in the complaint and hold a press conference, we can shake a lot of trees in the Justice Department and the IRS because they're not in the business of giving tax exemptions to criminal enterprises."

"Exactly, Paul. Imagine being the lawyer for the Church when the Cardinal asks, 'can the result in the Bob Jones case happen to us?'" Elizabeth said, raising her voice to make the point.

"That would certainly raise some eyebrows at the Vatican," Atkinson said.

"That's more than a little intriguing, but let's not get ahead of ourselves. So, can I ask my questions? If anyone else has some, please, jump in," Courso said.

"Absolutely," Elizabeth said as she slipped the broad blade of her fish knife under the skin to reveal the long filet of a fish.

"So, as I understand, you have a retained minor client with a case against Dolan and perhaps some or all of the archdioceses that employed him, correct?" Courso asked.

"Yes."

"Any other lawyers involved?"

"Not at this time," Elizabeth smiled.

"So, do you have a proposal?" Courso asked.

"Yes, I want to associate with your firm and bring the action against all three archdioceses under the RICO statute."

"Do you want just local counsel to file the suit, or do you want to collaborate on the lawsuit as co-counsel?" Weinstein asked.

Elizabeth hesitated.

Courso saw the quandary in Elizabeth's eyes. "If you simply want local counsel to file the suit we wouldn't be interested. Can

I speak for both of you?" Courso said, turning to Peters and Weinstein.

"Yes," they answered in unison.

"So, Elizabeth, what are you thinking?" Courso asked.

"To be honest, I've run my own practice group at McCabe for several years even as a senior associate. So, my concern is strategy and decision making, basically who is driving the bus."

"I thought the client drove the bus, Elizabeth."

"You know what I mean," Elizabeth said, annoyed.

"So, if I hear you correctly, you want to manage the client and be the ultimate decision maker," Courso said, taking a moment to cut into his veal chop to check for doneness. Looking back up to Elizabeth, he smiled. "With whose money, Elizabeth?" Courso asked.

"I'm prepared to front the expenses on the case, Tony," Elizabeth said as she stole a glance toward Weinstein to see how he was reacting to the conversation.

"How much?" Weinstein asked as he split open the side of a dinner roll.

"With a say in how and when it's spent, $500,000," Elizabeth said.

"I guess my only question would be is do you play nice in the sandbox?" Weinstein said, smiling and leaning back in his chair.

"I guess that depends on who's in the sandbox with me," Elizabeth said.

"That's a fair point, but for all intents and purposes it would be me," Weinstein said.

"And do you come with a $500,000 match for costs?" Elizabeth asked.

Before Weinstein could answer, Courso cut in. "Absolutely not. We're putting up all the bodies and infrastructure it will take to run this case, Elizabeth. If McCabe is actually going to defend, he'll organize an army between the defendants to keep us busy. Not to mention he will personally bill the shit out of the file."

Elizabeth put her fork down and stared directly at Courso. "You haven't asked me about the fee split, Tony," Elizabeth said.

"I know that Elizabeth. We haven't gotten past the expense issue," Courso said, swirling his wine with the stem of his glass. "But I assumed it would be half if you're putting up the five hundred and working the file."

"If there's a recovery, I want my money back before any fees are taken, plus 6 percent interest, but I do not want a fee."

"Whoa, what did you say?" Peters asked.

"I said I don't want to take a fee," Elizabeth said, pushing her chair back from the table.

"I thought that's what I heard. May I ask why?" Peters said.

"Frank, as a victim of this priest and now representing a victim who's a minor, it just doesn't feel right. So, here's my deal, we each put up $500,000; I want someplace to work and a secretary. I want my money back with interest and you take the fee."

"Tony, that sounds good to me," Weinstein said.

"Of course it does, Paul, that's why you and I have different offices. But before you get all pissed off, it sounds good to me as well. But there are a few items I'll need to button up, Elizabeth, before we can commit."

"Such as?" Elizabeth said.

"The first thing would be the briefing on the RICO statute. I want to see it laid out in writing and I also want to make sure we aren't running afoul of any frivolous litigation rules in state or federal court. The second thing is a conflict check because I have to let my other partners know. I want them on board. It'll be a decision that will impact the entire firm. Last," Courso said, looking at Atkinson, "I need to know whether you can commit to being our Church law expert."

"I can do that, Tony. I've been qualified as an expert."

"When do you present the case to your partners?" Elizabeth asked.

"We meet every Wednesday morning at 7:00 A.M., so I'll have an answer for you next Wednesday."

"So, if you get all that buttoned up, as you say, do we have a deal?" Elizabeth asked.

"Assuming the client is on board, yes of course. I'll confirm it in writing."

"That sounds perfect, Tony, and by the way, the branzino was excellent."

"See, now aren't you glad you came here to work this out?" Courso howled in delight.

Elizabeth smiled.

"Well, I know I am," Atkinson said. "The dinner was just fantastic. I do have one request."

"What is it, Tom?" Courso asked.

"If you guys accept this case, I suspect Elizabeth will be spending a fair amount of time here in the office."

Elizabeth turned to Atkinson, wondering what he was getting at.

"So," Atkinson continued, "I just found out today my permanent base housing won't be ready for ninety days and I'm moving into a dorm for non-commissioned officers that will be very problematic for Boomer."

"Who's Boomer?" Weinstein asked.

"Boomer's my dog, who in the past two weeks has become very attached to Elizabeth. So, would he be able to come to the office with her? He's very well behaved, but she would need a ride to and from the office as taxis in this city don't take dogs."

"Tony, we have a no dog policy for the tenants," Peters reminded Courso.

"Frank, it's my building, for Christ sakes. Elizabeth, if we do this, just make sure he doesn't become a nuisance," Courso said. "If he does, he'll have to go. You don't drive?"

Elizabeth blushed. "Never had to, Tony."

"You should put it on a to-do list, Elizabeth."

"So I've been told," Elizabeth laughed, seeing the grin on Atkinson's face.

"What kind of dog is Boomer?" Weinstein asked.

"He's a magnificent, regal Boxer," Elizabeth said proudly.

"That drools here and there," Atkinson added. An audible groan escaped from Courso as he leaned back in his chair.

Elizabeth beamed across the table at Tom and mouthed, "Thank you."

Dinner closed with espresso, freshly chilled panna cotta and dessert wine.

Atkinson glanced over at Elizabeth and Weinstein, in animated conversation in the corner of the conference room.

"I'm scheduled to meet with McCabe on Monday," Elizabeth said to Weinstein. "The client was invited to meet with the Cardinal, and they said to bring a lawyer if they wanted. The other boy in the car settled for $100,000, so they think they're going to make the same type of offer to Bobby's parents."

"You sure you have control over the client, Elizabeth? It wouldn't be the first time a client caves when the money's actually on the table."

"The client's rock solid," Elizabeth said. "The dad is retired Navy and after listening to Tom he's pissed."

Frank Peters methodically placed all of his notes into a manila folder, then turned to Weinstein. "Paul, I'll draft up a memo on all of this and circulate it to you and Tony for comment and then, Elizabeth, I'll send you a copy. It was a pleasure meeting you." Peters said. He handed Elizabeth his business card and walked to the door to leave. "If all this works out, the partners will need you to be covered under our malpractice insurance, so I'm thinking we'll just add you to the letterhead as counsel to the firm. Would that be okay with you?" Peters asked.

"Good catch, Frank," Weinstein said to Peters.

"That would be fine," Elizabeth said. "Good night, Frank, it was nice meeting you as well."

DO YOU WANT ME TO DROP YOU AT THE DOOR?

Atkinson guided his truck out of the underground parking lot and headed east on H Street, weaving his way through the northwest quadrant of the city toward Michigan Avenue, the Dominican House of Studies, and Boomer. Fifteen minutes later, he arrived at Dominican House, where he studied as a seminarian.

"I'll be right back," Atkinson said to Elizabeth, pulling into the visitors' parking lot.

"Can I come with you and meet Brother Gerald?" Elizabeth asked, oblivious to the appearance of Atkinson visiting the headquarters of his Order with an attractive woman dressed to the nines in tow.

Atkinson simply looked at Elizabeth until the lunacy of her request sunk in.

"Oh," she chuckled. "You're already in the dog house so I wouldn't help your cause by meeting Brother Gerald."

"I'm glad you figured that out, Liz," Atkinson said, closing the driver's side door.

Elizabeth stared out the windshield at the massive façade of the Shrine directly across the street from the Dominican House of Studies. She remembered all the times she had gone to this exact place for strength and to be close to her father and to keep the darkness at bay. She started to shiver and leaned over to turn the ignition switch to turn on the heat.

Boomer was excited to see Elizabeth, pushing his way from the back into the front seat between them.

"He's going to slobber all over your dress, Liz," Atkinson said as he pulled out of the lot.

"I'll get it cleaned, Tommy, he's fine."

"So, I saw you and that Weinstein fellow in what seemed an intense conversation after dinner, is there a problem?" Atkinson asked as he waited for the light to turn green at the corner of Fourth Street and Michigan Avenue.

"No, not at all, we were just discussing tactics and the media angle to cases against the Church. And actually, we were talking about you. How I met you, how canon law implicates general negligence, you know, lawyer stuff. I told him about meeting with McCabe and the clients on Monday. He said he would like to go just to get a feel for McCabe and the Cardinal."

"I thought Tony said it wouldn't be until Wednesday before they would let you know."

"Paul said he would keep it very low key and only tell McCabe the case was under consideration by his firm."

Atkinson grunted as he stared at the red light.

"Oh, now I see why you're pouting," Elizabeth said.

"I'm not pouting. Don't be ridiculous, Elizabeth," Atkinson huffed.

"You're pouting, Thomas, you're still pissed off about Paul's comment in the restroom, aren't you?" Elizabeth asked, holding Boomer around the neck. "Look, Boomer, for the very first time I have a guardian angel for my virtue," Elizabeth exclaimed.

"Now you're making fun. Forget I said anything, Liz, it's really none of my business."

"It isn't any of your business but it's so sweet you're concerned," she said as she reached over to touch Atkinson's hand for a slight squeeze.

485

Elizabeth looked at the Shrine as the truck approached Michigan Avenue. Frozen in thought, she replayed the images of when she was with her father and grandfather at the church as a little girl.

"Did you want to stop before we head uptown? I remember you said your Pop used to work here when it was being built."

"Nope. That's the past, Tommy. Nothing I can do about that now. But for the first time I see a future and I have you to thank for it," Elizabeth said.

"Just keep doing what you're doing, Liz, and it'll all fall into place for you."

The ride from the Dominican House to Elizabeth's Harvard Street apartment only took twenty minutes. A light drizzle started to paint Atkinson's windshield. With only a few cars on the road, the mercury vapor streetlights cast a veil-like amber glow on the blacktop, causing Atkinson's headlamps to emit ropes of white light from his headlamps, making the actual road hard to see.

"I'm glad we don't have to go far in this fog. The lights make it creepy," Elizabeth said, unnerved by the unusual mix of weather and light.

"Do you want me to drop you at the door?" Atkinson asked.

"No, no, find a place to park and I'll walk with you and Boomer. Doesn't he have to do his business before he goes in for the night?"

"He does, but he'll be quick. Brother Gerald took him for a long walk."

"I want to thank you for letting Boomer stay with me. I have to say, your timing on asking if he can come to work with me was impeccable."

"Well, I think the damn dog likes you better than me anyway."

"Well, I'm glad he'll be with me for the next ninety days. Tommy, on second thought I'm going to pass on the walk. These shoes are killing me," Elizabeth said, kicking both shoes off in the lobby elevator. I'll meet you upstairs. I'm going to grab a shower, do you need the bathroom?" Elizabeth asked.

"No, go ahead. I'll get Boomer settled, it's been a long day," Atkinson said as the elevator door closed behind Elizabeth. Boomer sat at the door, thinking Elizabeth was behind it.

"You're a traitor," Atkinson said to the dog. Boomer looked at Atkinson and wrinkled his brow, then yawned.

It took Elizabeth less than ten minutes to shower, remove her makeup, and change into running shorts and a tee shirt. Her hair was pulled tight in a ponytail and her face was pink from the hot water scrub. She was barefoot and carried with her two legal pads and a pencil. She settled into the couch in the living room.

On his return to the apartment, Atkinson found Elizabeth deep into pages of notes that covered the kitchen table.

"I know, I'm just finishing. I wanted to make a few notes before I go to bed."

"Liz, don't forget it's a marathon not a sprint. Don't flame out before you start," Atkinson said.

"Yes, Father Atkinson," Elizabeth said, playfully mocking him.

"Liz, let me take the couch tonight and you sleep in your own bed."

"Don't be ridiculous, I fit on the couch and you don't. It's not a problem," she said as she flopped on the couch and pulled a blanket around her. "I'll see you in the morning. Tommy, leave the door ajar in case Boomer wants to get on the bed."

"Like I said, spoiled rotten. Good night, Liz," Atkinson said as he moved toward Elizabeth's bedroom.

"You could do one thing for me," Elizabeth said.

"Sure, what do you need?" Atkinson asked.

"I've been in high heels all day and my feet are killing me, would you rub my feet? Do you mind?" Elizabeth asked.

"Of course not," Atkinson stammered.

"You think it's weird, don't you?" Elizabeth asked sheepishly.

"I do not, Liz. Not at all."

"Here, come sit at the end of the couch," Elizabeth said as she laid out straight on the couch and raised her legs to make room for Atkinson.

Atkinson sat there with Elizabeth's feet in his lap, desperately trying to convince himself that this was somehow normal.

"Right below the ball of each foot, that's where it really hurts," Elizabeth said as she closed her eyes.

Atkinson lightly held the top of Elizabeth's right foot and placed his thumb just behind the ball of her foot, adding pressure into her arch with his other hand.

"Oh, my God, that feels incredible," Elizabeth gasped.

Atkinson alternated for several minutes between each foot, noticing the care that she had put into her pedicure. Each nail was perfectly cut and polished a deep crimson red. Her skin was supple and soft, allowing his fingers to glide effortlessly across the top and bottom of each foot and between her polished toes. The fact that what he was doing was so ordinary in every respect, clashed violently with this new experience of intimacy with a woman.

As he pushed on the bottom of her foot toward her shin to stretch her Achilles tendon, he heard a slow rhythmic expulsion of air from her nose and realized she was sound asleep, her hands gently folded on top of the legal pads perched on her chest. Atkinson waited a few minutes as he relished looking at her, relaxed and at peace, a short respite from the demons that lay just below the surface. He slowly lifted both of her feet so that he could slide off the couch, covered her with another blanket and turned off the lights.

I CAN THINK OF AT LEAST ONE THING

A gasp of conscious panic tore Elizabeth out of her nightmare. Seconds before, she had been falling into a deep black mine shaft, unable to move either her arms or legs, screaming for help but unable to make a sound. Rolling off the couch and onto her knees, she pushed the beads of sweat off of her forehead into her hair. Night-light from the street guided her into the darkened kitchen for a glass of water. Standing at the sink, she began to feel the adrenaline pushing her into a heightened sense of awareness, allowing her to figure out exactly what was bothering her.

She hadn't been alone for nearly a month. For the first time in her adult life, she felt she had a backstop. Tom had become her safety net in recovery, and he was leaving for his Air Force assignment Monday morning. She shuddered that the same woman who had deftly negotiated the exact deal she wanted with Tony Courso several hours earlier was in her kitchen, petrified of being left alone in her own apartment.

The nightlight in the hall just outside her bedroom door helped her see the outline of Boomer at the foot of the bed. She pushed the door open to see if Atkinson was awake. Boomer lifted his head, sniffed the air and returned to the bolstered pillow Elizabeth had laid out for him. Elizabeth went to the opposite side of the bed where Atkinson was sleeping on and slid under the blankets behind him. Elizabeth pushed closer to him as Atkinson turned to look over his shoulder.

"What's wrong, Liz?" Atkinson asked, still half asleep.

"I had a nightmare," Elizabeth sobbed.

"Okay, I'll take the couch," Atkinson said.

"No," Elizabeth whispered. "Can I stay here with you? I don't want to be alone right now."

Atkinson was still on his side as he reached for Elizabeth's forearm and tucked it into his chest. "You'll be okay, Liz, it was just a dream."

Elizabeth pushed even closer into Atkinson's back, her breath warming the back of his neck. He could feel the softness of her breasts on his back through her tee shirt, her bare legs folding neatly into the back of his. He was grateful he had gone to bed with at least his boxer shorts on. The smell from her hair and skin was electrifying. His brief excursion into a moment of sexual longing gave way to worry about whether this was some perverse experiment with his emotions. Elizabeth ran hot and cold, hard and vulnerable. Sweetness and talent mixed with promiscuity and the toxic impact of depraved sexual abuse by an authority figure.

It was hard to see the future, let alone know what he wanted in his future, so he tried to stay in the moment. He could feel the tension in her body release as she fell back asleep. He rolled over on his back, allowing Elizabeth's head to fall neatly between his jaw and upper chest, her outstretched arm gathered around his torso. Wondering why anyone would give up this bliss, he soaked in every moment of being physically close to someone he loved.

Atkinson was ushered out of bed by the light of a clear sunrise and into the kitchen for some coffee. The emerging daylight had stolen his intimacy with Elizabeth. She had rolled onto her stomach and was still asleep. Boomer had taken up residence at the front door as a cue that he needed to go out.

"C'mon, goofball, let's get some air," Atkinson muttered to Boomer as he pulled on a coat and took the stairs to the ground floor. Atkinson unhooked Boomer from his leash as he walked the tree line in the park. He pulled his tee shirt up from the neck and put it to his nose. He could still smell Elizabeth's perfume. How could he have been so wrong about the life he chose? How was it possible that with all he had been through the only thing that mattered to him was being with Elizabeth? He was amazed at how his priorities had changed. Everything fell behind the woman whose bed he had just left. After a lifetime of cultivating God's existence in the world and the very essence of religious life, he was adrift, sent away by the callousness of power-hungry men who sacrificed the actual lives of children in order to protect their image.

ACT OF FAITH

It was just past seven and the whining of a concrete saw making pedestrian curb cuts pushed Elizabeth into consciousness. She called out for Atkinson and Boomer, but she quickly realized she was alone. Her heart started to beat faster as she looked for any of Atkinson's things, trying to make sure he had not left her. Seeing his keys on the side table calmed her down. She hoped nothing was said or done during the night that would further exacerbate an awkward situation. Putting on a robe, she walked towards the smell of perked coffee and sat at the table to wait for Tom and Boomer to come back. On her second cup, she heard the key in her door and Boomer scurry up the hall and into her lap.

"In the kitchen," Elizabeth called out. Elizabeth waited for Atkinson to appear, making an effort to untangle her hair from a ponytail that had gone awry.

"So, you doing okay?" Atkinson asked, seeing Elizabeth seated at the kitchen table.

"Hey, Tommy, I'm so sorry for barging in on you last night. I just got frightened. Did I say anything stupid?" Elizabeth asked, wincing.

"Like what?" Atkinson asked.

"You know like, forward or weird, like anything inappropriate?" Elizabeth blushed.

"Oh, like that," Atkinson said, smiling. "Nope. All good, Liz. But you do snore."

"I do not snore, Thomas," Elizabeth said, shocked at the suggestion.

"Now, Elizabeth, how would you know if you snored or not?" Atkinson said, making an effort to appeal to her logic.

"Maybe you were dreaming that I was snoring, did you ever think about that?" Elizabeth said in mock defiance. "Tommy, do I really snore?" Elizabeth asked, deflated.

"Yes, you do, Liz."

"So, I kept you up?" Elizabeth asked, embarrassed.

491

"You didn't keep me up, I stayed up. I was sleeping with a woman and quite enjoyed it."

"Jesus Christ," Elizabeth exclaimed, standing up from her chair. "Did we…" Elizabeth stuttered, covering her face.

"No, no nothing happened, Liz, relax. Like I said you went to sleep."

Elizabeth sat back in her chair and put her head in her hands, running her tangled, thick hair through the fingers of both hands and pulling it off her face.

"Tommy, I'm in love with you and I don't want you to go. There, I said it. I mean it. I know it's complicated you being a priest and all, and I'm being forward, you know, weird, but that's the way it is," Elizabeth said, moving to face Atkinson who was leaning on the kitchen counter. She slid her hands under Atkinson's crossed arms, putting her head just under his chin.

"Well, there is one thing I've been meaning to mention."

Startled, Elizabeth pulled her head off his chest. "What. What is it?"

"I'm in love with you too, Elizabeth. I've been in love with you ever since high school, and yes, it's very complicated. For the moment, there's nothing we can do about it."

Elizabeth smiled at Atkinson. "I can think of at least one thing we can do about it," Elizabeth said, pushing her face to his lips.

Atkinson could feel the heat from her body as he held her tight in his arms. Elizabeth kissed him on the lips. He remembered the first time Elizabeth had kissed him in high school, but this time it was different. Atkinson kissed her back.

"Listen to me, Elizabeth. Nothing would make me happier, but we both have to finish things up. We both have work to do and when that's done, the decks will be clear for us."

"Does this have something to do with logic and impulse control?" Elizabeth said as she burrowed her head into his chest.

"Yeah, impulse control and delayed gratification about covers it," Atkinson said, laughing. "For both of us, Liz."

"Tommy, do you really love me? I mean do you really love me, warts and all?" Elizabeth asked, pulling away from him and looking at Atkinson in the eyes.

"Warts and all, Liz."

"But you don't think I have a lot of warts do you, Tommy?" Elizabeth asked.

"Shhh," Atkinson whispered as he held her tight in his arms. "I love you, that's all that matters.

I'M VERY SURPRISED TO SEE YOU

As Elizabeth looked out the window of her cab, she realized she was looking forward to her meeting with Alistair McCabe. Elizabeth Ann Natale would be the last person McCabe would think he was meeting with over Andrew Dolan's sex abuse case.

Paul Weinstein waited just outside the Metro Club, a lounge reserved for first class passengers inside Union Station. Elizabeth spotted him from across the main hall and waved. Their outward appearance was that of a refined power couple. Weinstein wore a narrow chalk stripe navy suit, pale blue shirt and a gold and blue Zenga silk necktie. Elizabeth arrived in a three-quarter chestnut colored cashmere coat with matching sash over a simple pale yellow print dress, with a weathered, over the shoulder leather satchel from Venice that doubled as a purse and a briefcase.

"Well, good morning, Elizabeth, you're looking like a bad-ass midtown lawyer," Weinstein joked. "How was your weekend?"

Elizabeth enjoyed the compliment. "Actually, it was very busy. Father Atkinson got all his stuff packed up and is on his way to Florida and Boomer and I are getting used to apartment living."

"Oh, really. How's that going?"

"It's fine, but he does like going places, so today he's with a friend of Tom's where he studied in seminary. Are you a dog person?" Elizabeth asked.

493

"Not really, I don't have any time for pets."

"I was the same way when I was practicing. You might want to revisit that."

"Duly noted," Weinstein said. "So, tell me about McCabe," Weinstein said as they took a private elevator down to the tracks.

"He's a wealthy, talented prick who will stop at nothing to prevail in a case. Plus, he's a control freak."

"So, I gather your parting was stormy."

"Not at all, it was mutual. Paul, let's start off on the right track. You're here, more than likely without the firm's blessing, at least that's what I presume. I agreed to you coming because I think your firm would be stupid for letting this case go to someone else. Plus, it would be a good opportunity for the client to meet you. Second, I'm not interested in being interviewed. I know you heard what I said happened to me as a young girl, so I apologize in advance if I appear or sound crusty, but it's just who I am. I'm not looking for a job or a partnership or, as you recall, a fee. My plan is to work my ass off, conclude this case and move on with my life. Are you okay with all that?" Elizabeth asked they walked to the first-class car.

This was a new experience for Weinstein, served up in equal measures of hubris and annoyance by Elizabeth. "Has anyone ever accused you of being arrogant?" he calmly asked.

"Actually, the people who know me say I'm a lovable cupcake," Elizabeth smiled.

"Like who, your mother?" Weinstein said, trying to get anything on the board with this challenging woman.

"Definitely not my mother," Elizabeth said emphatically, stepping over the gap and onto the waiting car.

Yanking on the knot of his tie, Weinstein took a controlled, deep breath and followed.

They grabbed a cab on 7th Street for the ride uptown.

"Where are we meeting?" Weinstein asked.

"My old offices, 345 Park," Elizabeth said, checking her pager for messages.

"High rent district," Weinstein quipped.

"Nothing but the best for Alistair," Elizabeth mused.

Traffic was horrible as the cabbie danced from lane to lane, first on West 31st Street, then onto West 27th trying to get to Park Avenue.

Weinstein looked at his watch. "We may be a few minutes late. Have you talked to the client?"

"Of course I have, and I know we may be late."

"You should really break down and try a cell phone instead of that clunky pager you keep checking."

"Do you have one with you?" she asked.

"Actually, I do. You can use it if you ask nicely," Weinstein jabbed.

"I'm sorry. I'm a little on edge seeing that prick again, especially under these circumstances," Elizabeth said as Weinstein handed her a Nokia 1011 GSM phone.

"Somehow, Elizabeth, I'm sure you'll find the right words," Weinstein said. "Just put the area code in and dial like you normally would."

"Gee, this is a whole lot smaller than the door stop I've seen guys walking around with lately. So, it's not true that D.C. lawyers are a bunch of southern hillbillies," Elizabeth said.

"Cute, Elizabeth."

Elizabeth and Weinstein got to the lobby ten minutes after the meeting was supposed to start.

"Jesus, somebody blew their brains out decorating this place," Weinstein said as he surveyed the palatial lobby.

"I think you just made McCabe's point, Paul," Elizabeth said as she smiled and walked to meet Delores and Robert Tompkins.

"How are you?" Elizabeth asked, giving Delores a warm hug.

"We're good, Bobby wanted to come but I'm glad you told him that he needed to go to school. He needs a schedule, but I have to

495

say he's doing better in school since the criminal case is over. Elizabeth, do most firms look like this? I don't think we've ever been to a place like this."

Elizabeth laughed. "It's a little gaudy for my taste but no, most firms don't look like this. I don't imagine we'll be here too many times. Robert, are you well?" Elizabeth asked.

"So far, Elizabeth," Robert said, struggling in an uncomfortable suit and tie.

"Robert, Delores, this is Paul Weinstein. He's a partner in the firm I talked to you about last Saturday."

"It's a pleasure to meet you both," Weinstein said warmly.

"Okay, I'll let the receptionist know we're all here. By the way, has anyone tried to engage you in any conversation?" Elizabeth asked.

Weinstein made a mental note of approval of Elizabeth's attention to detail.

"No, the receptionist just told us to make ourselves comfortable," Robert said.

"Excellent. I'll be right back." Elizabeth could see McCabe at the conference room table and two other gentlemen dressed in black, one of whom she assumed was Cardinal Hurley. She let her high heels hit heavily on the floor, hoping to get the attention of McCabe.

McCabe looked up, expressionless, his eyes moving up and down Elizabeth's visage. He walked to the window behind the reception desk. Without acknowledging her, he closed the shade to the conference room.

Game on, Elizabeth thought.

Elizabeth walked over to Weinstein. "The guy who closed the shades was McCabe," she whispered.

"He didn't seem very happy to see you," Weinstein said.

"That's a good thing, Paul."

The group waited in the lobby another twenty minutes. Weinstein was getting agitated. He pulled Elizabeth aside.

"This is horseshit, Elizabeth. He's just breaking balls."

"I know, it's what he does. I think I know what he's doing."

"Tell me," Weinstein said.

"He's checking to see if he can conflict me out of the case," Elizabeth said.

"Good stuff, Elizabeth. Should be fun in there," Weinstein quipped.

"C'mon, they're ready for us. Remember you're thinking about taking the case, Paul, and don't call him Al, he hates it."

"I won't, just don't give them too much information, Elizabeth."

"This isn't my first rodeo, Paul. I got it," Elizabeth said, bending down to get her shoulder bag.

The Tompkins family walked in first, followed by Elizabeth and Weinstein. Both Cardinal Hurley and Father Stanton stood as the group came into the room for the cursory introductions. McCabe remained seated at the head of the table, ostensibly drafting something on a yellow sheet of paper. Tearing it from his pad, he gave it to the associate with a directive to take care of it.

"Forgive me," McCabe said as he stood. "Something came up that required my attention. Mr. and Mrs. Tompkins, it's a pleasure to meet you, notwithstanding the circumstances that bring us together." Turning to Elizabeth, McCabe extended his hand. "I must say I'm very surprised to see you here but as a former member of this firm you're always welcome."

"It's good to see you as well, Alistair, but I could have saved you some time while we waited."

McCabe acted surprised. "Really? How so, Elizabeth?"

"I left the firm before you handled the Archdiocese ground lease for the Palace Hotel, so there's no conflict with me representing the Tompkins."

"Hmm," McCabe grunted. "I'm sure you're not offended I checked."

"Not at all, Alistair, I'm just saying you could have asked."

Weinstein was enjoying the back and forth. It was like he had landed in the middle of a Bobby Fisher grudge match with Boris Spasky. At the moment, he would put his money on Elizabeth.

"And, Mr. Weinstein, you're here because?" McCabe said, jotting a note on the paper in front of the family.

"I would think that's obvious, Mr. McCabe," Weinstein said, without any expression on his face.

"I see. Elizabeth, I want to make you aware that Cardinal Hurley came here today over my objections to try and resolve this matter," McCabe said.

"Why on earth would you object?" Elizabeth asked, angered by the unnecessary comment.

Weinstein twitched under the table, understanding that Elizabeth had made a big mistake.

"It's a mistake to throw money at this now," McCabe said calmly.

"Did you mean to say, 'at this,' Alistair?" Elizabeth asked, moving further into the trap. "This has a name, Alistair. It's Bobby Tompkins!"

Weinstein groaned under his breath. He was well aware that Elizabeth was exposing Delores and Robert to naked intimidation conducted by a master.

McCabe did not provoke. "Of course I did. Think about it, Elizabeth, Father Dolan pled guilty to a misdemeanor with a reservation of rights that his plea could not be used in a civil proceeding." Directing his gaze to Bobby's parents, McCabe dug deeper. "We haven't talked to your son, Mr. Tompkins, as to exactly what happened, how it happened and what, if any, prior contact with the boy that may have confused Father Dolan as young Tompkins' intent on agreeing to meet with him that evening. My goodness, I could think of a hundred questions that would shed light on the true impact to Bobby as a result of his meeting with Father Dolan on the evening in question. The answers to these questions could be difficult for a young boy still in high school when the setting is in a public forum." Turning back to Elizabeth, McCabe knew she was on the defensive. "You know how mean kids can be don't you, Elizabeth? So, here we are. Notwithstanding my objections, the Archdiocese is prepared to offer $100,000 to resolve this matter amicably today, with, of course, the standard confidentiality agreements. Then all of this unpleasantness will be behind your family, Mr. and Mrs. Tompkins."

Robert Tompkins looked at McCabe, stone faced, ignoring that Delores had welled up and was about to cry.

"May we have a minute with our clients, Mr. McCabe?" Weinstein interrupted to stop the bleeding.

"Of course. Cardinal Hurley, why don't you and Father Stanton join me in my office for a cup of coffee. Mr. Weinstein, just let the girl outside know when you're ready to resume."

Weinstein waited for the door to close and McCabe to be down the hall.

"Elizabeth..."

"Paul, please don't speak, I know I messed up. Delores, I should have never taken his vile bait. Robert and Delores, I'm sorry you had to listen to that diatribe. I didn't ask you to come here and have him make you cry."

"I'm not crying because I'm upset, Elizabeth. I'm crying because I'm angry," Delores said, gritting her teeth.

"Elizabeth, listen, he's just yanking your chain because you let him. It happens to everyone. Forget about it, he knows he's got exposure," Weinstein said.

"Well, I think he's a pompous little asshole who needs a good old-fashioned ass whupping," Robert said, tapping his fingers on the conference room table.

Weinstein started to laugh and looked at Elizabeth, who started to laugh herself.

"Can I say something?" Delores asked.

"Of course you can, Delores, you're our client," Elizabeth smiled.

"When we came down here, Robert and I agreed we would make our decision on how they treated us. No one said they were sorry this happened to Bobby. Cardinal Hurley sat there like a sphinx and let this McCabe fellow try to threaten our family. We're not stupid people. We may not have a lot, but we're not stupid. We know our son, he's a good boy. And when you called him out that Bobby has a name, I made up my mind. Isn't that right, Robert?" Delores said, turning to her husband.

"Yes, it was disgusting what I heard in this room and for a Cardinal of the Church to stand by and say nothing told me everything I needed to know. Whatever you folks think best we will do."

Elizabeth worked hard to keep her composure. This was not just a negligence case where a young boy was injured; it was a case where the entire family was being attacked. It was one thing to know the theory of the lengths the Archdiocese would go to defend itself against these claims, it was quite another to be sitting next to the victims taking the venomous body blows coming from the Church.

Weinstein listened to Delores and Robert speak. As a mass tort litigator, he had been removed from the visceral impact cases like these had on actual people. It was like when he got out of law school: a single client taken advantage of with absolutely no recourse except a young energetic lawyer to take up his claim and pursue justice on his behalf. One of the great rewards in the law was watching the powerless realize that the playing field was level because a lawyer was willing to take up their cause. Weinstein had been away from that for far too long.

"I have an idea as to how to proceed, if anyone would like to hear it," Weinstein said.

"I would," Elizabeth said, still agitated by her lapse of battlefield tactics.

"So, you and I go back and decline their offer, without Delores and Robert. I think you both should go to that little corner deli right to the left of where we came in. We'll tell them that you folks were going to decide on their offer based on how they were treated, that the only thing they saw coming from the Church was disrespect, so they have left it in our hands. Then we'll have some lox and bagels for lunch, and we'll go to work."

"Works for us," Robert said, looking at Delores.

"I'm fine with it too, Delores," Elizabeth said. "Barbara Blaine warned me that something like this might happen. Are you both still willing to sit with us and some of the SNAP people at a press conference at some point soon?" Elizabeth asked.

"If we're up there with you, absolutely."

Elizabeth broke out into a wide grin and went to hug both Robert and Delores.

"Give us fifteen minutes and we'll meet you at the deli," Weinstein said.

Weinstein waited in the conference room as Elizabeth walked the Tompkins to the bank of elevators. Weinstein remained silent as the Cardinal, McCabe and Father Stanton filed back into the conference room, followed by Elizabeth. Weinstein and Elizabeth sat directly opposite McCabe, who was flanked by the two priests.

"Shall we wait for Mr. and Mrs. Tompkins?" McCabe asked.

"That will not be necessary under the circumstances."

"Wait a second, what circumstances," McCabe said, annoyed. "Who's speaking for your client here, you or Elizabeth?"

"We both are. My firm has accepted Elizabeth's referral, she's joining us as counsel to the firm. So, you get two lawyers for the price of one."

"So, you're not accepting the Archdiocese's offer?" McCabe asked in a shrill voice.

"We are not, Mr. McCabe."

McCabe's face contorted with barely contained anger. "Then it is withdrawn, counsel, and I'll confirm that in writing as soon as you leave. Is there anything else?" McCabe said.

"I understand," Weinstein said. "I don't have anything else, do you, Elizabeth?"

"I do not, Paul," she said as she gathered her notes in front of her and stuffed them into her satchel.

"I would like to ask a question before we leave."

McCabe was shocked that Cardinal Hurley had ignored his instructions to say absolutely nothing of substance at this meeting.

"Perhaps we could meet privately, Cardinal, for a minute," McCabe quickly offered.

"What's the matter, Al? It's just us, there's nothing admissible here." Weinstein hoped by using a name McCabe hated he could get him to say something he would regret in front of his client. "Cardinal Hurley," Weinstein started. "I'm a Jew and I got a lecture before I came up here from my Irish Catholic partner about what to call you. He suggested 'Your Eminence' but Mr. McCabe refers to you as Cardinal Hurley. Which is appropriate here?" Weinstein asked.

"I appreciate the courtesy, Mr. Weinstein. Cardinal Hurley is perfectly acceptable."

"Fine. Cardinal Hurley, our clients came here with an open mind. One hundred thousand dollars is significant, but they thought, based upon Mr. McCabe's comments, that he was trying to frighten them as to the unpredictability and rigors of litigation. No one said they were sorry that this had happened to their son, and with all due respect, you sat silent and allowed them to be re-victimized by Al here. Long story short, they weren't shown any respect."

"What a bunch of horse poo," McCabe ranted. "Weinstein, you listen here, it's always about the money, and the people like you that want to profit off the Church."

"People like me," Weinstein bristled. "Didn't you really mean Jewish lawyers like me, Al," Weinstein said, not giving an inch to the aging patrician.

"You said it, Weinstein, not me."

"So, Al, we're going to leave in a minute. But when you go back, ask your lawyers what a Federal Racketeering lawsuit will look like naming Los Angeles, Washington and New York in a conspiracy to obstruct justice where the predicate acts are mail and wire fraud and the injury to business or property is the suppression of lawsuits. Then ask them, if a minor is driving the case and you don't have the statute of limitation defense, how much pre-trial discovery we would get on other offenders that'll blow this up across the country. This goes all the way back to when LA sent Dolan to Via Coeli," Weinstein said, looking directly at Hurley. "When you have done all that, ask your troops if there may be a risk that the IRS would revoke the Archdiocese's tax exemption as a nonprofit charity if we generate enough bad publicity, again, Cardinal Hurley, with all due respect."

"Okay, we're done, here," Elizabeth said as Weinstein gathered his things to leave. "Cardinal Hurley, Father Stanton, thank you for coming."

"Elizabeth, do you have a lawsuit prepared?" McCabe asked.

"We do."

"I'll accept service on behalf of the New York Archdiocese, and I can get the names of defense counsel for both Washington and Los Angeles."

"That's not how this case is going to work, Alistair. Cardinal Hurley and the Archbishops of D.C. and Los Angeles will be served personally, preferably in some public forum. The newspapers will run with the filing of a lawsuit and after service you will get a chance to look at it and respond. I believe the rules say we have ninety days to serve it to your client. That's ninety days of the media poking and prodding around Los Angeles, Washington, and New York. Good day, Al." Elizabeth said as they left the room.

Cardinal Hurley stood and walked to the window, taking in the view of lower Manhattan, the twin towers and the Empire State Building. He waited for the conference room door to close before he spoke. "Mr. McCabe, I have another meeting, but I'm curious as to whether this is typical."

"Is what typical, Your Eminence?" McCabe responded, still distracted by Weinstein's comments about the IRS.

"What I just witnessed, Mr. McCabe. I would say it went rather poorly."

McCabe got up and walked to the credenza for a bottle of Perrier. "Well, the case didn't settle, but I wouldn't go so far as to say it went poorly. The Natale woman is for some reason personally invested in this and I will find out why. There's something there and when I find out what it is, I'll break her back with it and she'll get reasonable. It's the Weinstein fellow that I'm concerned with. What's this Via something he mentioned in Los Angeles?" McCabe asked.

"Via Coeli. It is a treatment center in New Mexico for priests accused of sexual misconduct."

"Well, damn. That's not good. Did you know about it, Your Eminence?"

"Not until I asked about Dolan last week," Hurley said.

"Asked whom, Cardinal?" McCabe demanded.

"Archbishop Ryan of Washington," Hurley said.

"I see. Cardinal, it's now time that these potential co-defendants get a heads up so that they can retain their own counsel. If I have your consent, I'll reach out to them."

"Go ahead, Mr. McCabe. It doesn't sound like this is going to go away quickly."

"I highly doubt it. By the way, do you have any insight as to how they know Dolan went to Via Coeli?" McCabe asked.

"I don't, Mr. McCabe, but I'll look into it."

"Please let me know as soon as you find out anything. I'm worried about a mole," McCabe said as he excused himself.

IS THIS SOME SICK JOKE?

The famous macadamia nut sticky buns from Baldwin's bakery on Monroe Street were a welcome treat for the 7:00 A.M. weekly meeting to open new business for the firm. Every Wednesday, whether the partners met or not, one hundred individually wrapped pastries were delivered to the firm for the partner's meeting and the staff at large.

This assembled group was growing impatient waiting for Weinstein. The grousing was led by Jerry MacDonald, a middle-aged Irish Catholic who was steeped in the rules of procedure, defenses cases and, above all, decorum—when it suited him, as Paul Weinstein would frequently note. MacDonald's John Houseman persona, embodied in aristocratic Old English phrasing, a rumpled bowtie perched high above a noticeable paunch, with wisps of misdirected red hair dotting his freckled head, was a rich target for Weinstein's antics.

Thirty minutes after the meeting was to start, Weinstein finally walked in.

Frank Peters was the first to pounce. "Ah, Mr. Weinstein, we're all so happy you could join us. I know it must be very difficult for you to manage your law firm obligations with your very busy schedule."

"Frank, I'm really sorry. There was a water main break on M Street. I promise, next week I'll open the place at six-thirty."

"Sure, Paul. Gentleman, let's get started."

Paul Weinstein had his share of enemies in the legal community, but his Achilles heel was dealing with MacDonald's latent anti-

Semitism. Twenty-five years Weinstein's senior, MacDonald identified well with the patrician elements of the Washington bar. Formal, unctuous, meticulous in his speech and mannerisms, he found Weinstein's style of practice reprehensible and Weinstein himself offensive. Weinstein found his perfectly elocuted monologues on the issues of the day unnecessarily long and boring. Ignoring Weinstein's fee productivity, MacDonald on several occasions had lobbied Peters and Courso, the majority owners of the firm, to fire Weinstein.

On Sunday night, the day before his meeting with Alistair McCabe, Weinstein had called Frank Peters' secretary to add on a case for Wednesday's meeting.

MacDonald's defense practice generated sizable fees and both Courso and Peters showed him deference. Most of the cases on the agenda were routine, save one and it was the only one MacDonald wanted to talk about.

"This last add-on, Paul, it says RICO with a question mark, 'Archdiocese of Washington et al.' Is this a car wreck or something?"

Weinstein gave an impressive and detailed summary of Jason Berry's book and the national implications for more sex abuse cases against a defendant that could pay.

"Jerry, this could end up being our bread and butter. Children and young teenagers being sexually assaulted across the country." Weinstein saw MacDonald blanch. "Jerry, I'm not suggesting every priest is an offender, far from it, but according to the estimates somewhere around 5 percent out of $40,000. That's a shit-pot full."

Weinstein summarized both his meetings with Courso, Peters and Elizabeth as well as his meeting with Alistair McCabe and why the Federal RICO statute was applicable. He finished by emphasizing that the client was a minor so if the RICO case didn't work they still had a negligence case that was not statute barred.

Jerry MacDonald cleared his throat, seemingly unfazed about what he had just heard.

"Paul, I have one question. You said 'client.' You haven't committed the firm to this case, have you?"

"I did."

"Christ sakes, Frank, this is a precise example of my problem with Paul, and it should be a problem for everybody in this firm. We're supposed to have procedures, we need to do conflict checks. I for one would not take this case even if it were perfect and we all know there's no such thing as a perfect case." MacDonald slammed his fist on the table. "We shouldn't be involved suing the Archdiocese, the Archbishop and the home of 300,000 Catholics in our own fucking backyard! It's just plain stupid and dangerous for the firm. It's shitting where we eat!"

"Right, Mac, I guess we should just kick the can down the road. What about the kids? Does it matter to you that this crap has been going on for decades and two, possibly three bishops knew about it? We can make a difference here!" Weinstein fired back.

"We're not here to fix every problem that walks into the firm, kid. Grow the fuck up, will you? I know it may come as a shock to you, but this law firm isn't your personal playground!" MacDonald shouted back.

The meeting exploded with everyone talking at the same time trying to get his point of view on the table.

MacDonald thundered over the scrum. "I can't believe you guys are even considering such a dangerous case!"

Courso jumped in the fray. "Listen, Paul, you know I've supported you on just about everything but Christ, both Frank and I said Elizabeth's case needed to go before the firm. It impacts all of us. You just don't willy-nilly file a Federal Racketeering lawsuit against an archdiocese without everyone being on board."

MacDonald refused to relent. "Tony, how many times have we sat here and turned down good cases listening to some jingoistic nonsense from you about trying to make an ugly duck into a swan, or making chicken salad out of chicken shit? This case may, and I mean may, have some upside for the family, but it has no upside for the long-term interests of the firm." MacDonald leaned over the conference table. "Listen to him, Paul. Tony's your mentor, your great protector!"

Weinstein snapped and got right in MacDonald's patrician grill. "Jerry, Jesus lighten up, no, no wait a minute, I have a better thought... Jerry, go fuck yourself."

At that very moment the conference room door opened, and the kitchen staff rolled in a coffee and beverage service.

"Not now, get out!" Courso screamed at the ashen faced service staff as they scampered out of the room.

Peters banged on the table, shouting for order. "Enough! Now everybody, and I mean everybody, just stand down!" Peters stared everyone into silence. "Paul, you have to admit this situation is far from routine and you shouldn't have agreed to take this case on especially since you knew it had to come to this meeting."

Weinstein sat at the table with his arms crossed.

Peters turned to MacDonald. "Jerry, listen to me, we've had high profile cases before. Paul isn't the enemy here and these cases do have national implications."

MacDonald would not be silenced. "Frank, don't patronize me with these national implications crap. Each case is different, and you know as well as I do that, win or lose, everyone in this room could be blackballed in this city. What if we can't prove our case, what do we say to the Archbishop? What, Frank? What do we say?" MacDonald spewed in a full-throated caterwaul that could be heard outside the room. "Do we take him downstairs and have Tony and Carlo cook him a nice Italian dinner and say 'Sorry, we fucked up?' Think that will work, Frank?"

Weinstein pushed his chair away from the conference table so hard it bounced off the wall.

"Paul, where the hell are you going?" Peters demanded.

"Let me know what you decide, and then I'll give you the answer to your question." Weinstein left the office and called Elizabeth from his cell phone.

Courso chased after Weinstein, only a few minutes behind, and went straight to his empty office.

"Where is he, Bonnie?" Courso asked Weinstein's secretary.

"I don't know, Mr. Courso, he blew out of here and said he'd call me in a couple of days. I don't know what's going on except I know he was angry."

"Shit," Courso said as he headed back to the main conference room.

"Mr. Courso," Bonnie called out, "You may try Draper's."

Courso turned around and smiled. "Thanks, Bonnie. That's the cigar place a couple blocks away, right?" Courso asked.

"Yes. But don't say I told you, Mr. Courso."

"Got it, Bonnie," Courso said, moving up the hall toward the partner's meeting.

Courso entered the room with Peters sitting at the table, looking at spreadsheets and making notes on each page while MacDonald had his feet up on an empty chair, holding court with several of the minority shareholders.

"Ah, Tony, I'm glad you didn't waste any more time on this bullshit."

"You mean on Paul, Jerry?" Courso asked.

"Yes, exactly. He's just a classic case of the tail wagging the dog and it's time we actually do something about it. This law firm has significant standing around the country and I'm tired of watching that shit-head treating the firm like it's his own personal playground."

Courso glanced over to Peters, who still had his head down on his paperwork.

"Jerry, would you agree that at least 90 percent of the problems you see with this firm should be laid at Paul's doorstep?" Courso asked as he took his seat at the head of the table.

"My God, Tony, I've waited seven years to hear you say that. I'm tickled you've come to your senses," MacDonald said, his feet landing heavily on the floor.

"And that your defense practice generates 20 percent of the gross revenue of this law firm," Courso added, scribbling a note on the pad in front of him.

"Actually, 18.7 percent, Tony," Frank Peters said, looking up from his spreadsheets.

"Well, Tony, my estimates for next year look like about 21 percent," MacDonald said.

"Jerry, I sincerely hope you're right," Courso said as Peters, recognizing the tone, turned his chair to face Courso.

"Have you told Weinstein, Tony?" MacDonald asked.

"Told him what," Courso said, expressionless.

"Told him he's out of the law firm," MacDonald sputtered.

Courso took measure of MacDonald and Frank Peters as Peters closed the file folder in front of him.

"I didn't tell Paul, because it's time this firm separates from you and your practice, not from Paul."

The room fell silent as all eyes went to Tony Courso at the head of the table.

"Is this some sick joke, Tony? Frank, are you on board with this? Tony cannot do this without you," MacDonald demanded as he rose from his seat.

"Jerry, it's time. There's been a clash of cultures here for too long, and I agree with Tony," Peters said.

MacDonald exploded. "This is such bullshit, Tony. Twenty years has come down to this?"

"Jerry, I've looked at our buyout agreement."

"I'll bet you have, Tony, three times net revenues over five years. What a crock, Tony. That was to keep everyone here, that's not fair compensation for building a defense practice here in this building for the last twenty years."

"I didn't hear that complaint when we were paying out retained earnings bonuses based on Paul's jury verdicts, Jerry," Peters said.

"Jerry, please sit down and hear me out," Courso said.

"What, Tony, you want to kick me out and you still want to be friends?" MacDonald asked, taking a chair and mocking Courso.

"Actually, I don't want to be friends with you, Jerry, but I agree with you that under the circumstances the agreement that you signed may not be fair since we want you out. Take the defense practice as it sits right now. You take the core associates, doing defense files. You agree not to solicit or announce your departure to any existing client other than defense clients you have now or have had in the past. You provide monthly audited billing statements for three years..."

"In return for what, Tony," MacDonald said, interrupting Courso.

"For a 10 percent origination fee back to the firm, 90 percent goes to you."

"What about the unbilled time that's sitting in files now?"

"Jerry, that should have been billed already," Peters noted, never falling too far astray from his accounting background.

"Bill it out, Jerry. We'll split it fifty-fifty, but this firm will do the collections," Courso said.

"Tony, that's extremely generous," Peters said, pulling his eyeglasses to the tip of his nose.

"I'm aware of that, Frank. Jerry, I just want audited billings, and I want your client list and who you're sending your announcement letter to before you send it. That's the offer on the table. You good with that, Frank?" Courso asked, looking at Peters.

"I'd like the current billings to be a different number, but I can live with that, Tony."

511

MacDonald rose from his chair. "Tony, let me think about it overnight."

"Well, okay, but the deal tomorrow is the agreement you signed, not what I just outlined."

"So, you want an answer right now," MacDonald railed, spittle forming in the corners of his mouth.

"I do, Jerry," Courso said.

"Deep down, Tony, I always knew you were a prick." MacDonald stared out the conference room toward the White House and the Washington Monument. The side of his face pulsed as he gritted his teeth, breathing heavily through his nose. "I accept your offer," he said as he tossed his meeting notes on the table.

"Deep down, Jerry, I always knew that's what you thought of me. Before you leave, just be aware the current agreement you signed is still in full force and effect until you sign our new offer. Agreed?"

"Yes, Mr. Courso. Agreed," MacDonald seethed.

"Gentlemen, this meeting is adjourned. We'll get back together in a day or so after Jerry signs the agreement. Everybody just go back to work and relax. It's all good. Frank, would you join me downstairs in the lobby in say, five minutes?"

YOU SOUND LIKE MY GRANDFATHER

Courso and Peters jaywalked across H Street and hurried through Lafayette Park toward the Main Treasury building.

"Where the hell are we going, Tony?"

"I want to find Paul before he does something stupid."

"So, like I said, where are we going?" Peters asked as they turned the corner on Pennsylvania Avenue heading toward Draper's on 14th Street, Washington's oldest cigar store.

"I think he might be having a cigar to settle down. He's either there or drinking scotch at the bar at Old Ebbitt Grill."

"Tony, we just passed Ebbitt Grill," Peters said, trying to keep up with Courso's pace.

"I know, I think he's at Draper's."

"Did you try calling him on his cell?"

"I did, he isn't picking up," Courso said as they rounded the corner to the outdoor vestibule of Draper's. A blue cloud of premium cigar smoke hung in the open area, escaping with each patron coming or going from the store.

"Jesus, Tony, if he's in there let's get him outside before we all choke."

Weinstein was at the cashier with a lit cigar, paying for half a box of Fuente Opus X Double Coronas.

"You coming or going? You left in a bit of a rush," Courso said from the doorway, trying to gauge Weinstein's state of mind. Weinstein recognized Courso's voice and turned around.

"What's up, fellas, I just talked to Elizabeth and she said all hell is breaking loose in the firm."

"Where is she?" Courso asked, surprised.

"She's in the law library working on the memos for the RICO case," Weinstein said, taking his credit card from the cashier.

"What did she say?" Peters asked.

"She said Jerry was running around ordering all the secretaries to pull all the defense files and bring them into the main conference room."

Courso laughed and turned to Peters. "There may be more unbilled time in those files then we thought, Frank. "I think you're slipping in your old age," Courso teased.

"Don't start with me, Tony. You were out there without a net a little bit ago with Jerry and I just went along and said yes," Peters said as both men broke out into laughter.

"What's going on, guys, because I just asked Elizabeth to form a new LLC."

"First thing, we have to leave here because the smoke is killing us. Call Elizabeth and ask her to stop the nonsense on the LLC and meet us for lunch at the Occidental in twenty minutes. Frank and I kicked Jerry out of the firm, and he has reluctantly accepted our terms. I'll fill you in on all the details at lunch."

Weinstein hesitated long enough for it to become awkward.

"Of course, if you're okay with that," Peters said.

Weinstein looked at Courso. "I'm fine with that, Tony. What's the equity look like?"

"Full partners. Each of us gets a third, but the long-term lease for the old firm is assumed by the new firm." Weinstein looked at Peters.

"I'm fine with it, Paul, but you're twenty years younger than I am, so in the long run it'll be your rock to pull behind you," Peters said.

Weinstein nodded his head. "Got it, Frank," he said as he extended his hand to both Tony and Peters. "I'll get Elizabeth and meet you at the Occidental in twenty minutes."

The Occidental was a chic Washington eatery where people went to see and be seen. The main dining room and the luxurious booths were under the watchful gaze of portraits and caricatures of virtually every notable statesman, member of congress or elite personality. Weinstein and Elizabeth walked in and looked for Courso and Peters who were already in their booth nursing dirty Grey Goose martinis. While waiting, Peters gave Weinstein and Elizabeth a blow by blow of MacDonald's departure.

Toasting the firm of Courso, Peters and Weinstein, Elizabeth felt uneasy by not at least having a glass of wine to celebrate, but she was convinced that one drink of anything would send her into the darkness. Weinstein curiously noticed her discomfort but did not pry.

"Paul, I'd like to get a letter to the client over both your and Elizabeth's signatures confirming the joint representation. Elizabeth, can you get Frank and me your memos by early next week?"

"I can and maybe even earlier," Elizabeth said, taking out a small Moleskine notebook from her purse.

"I'd rather you not rush it. I just want it drilled down on the law and if we're arguing for extension of existing case law, I want that clearly delineated, and I want Father Atkinson buttoned up as our expert."

"I understand," Elizabeth said, feeling a flush of excitement.

"Paul, who do we know in the media that we trust?" Courso asked as if he were going down a mental checklist.

"I don't know that I trust any of them but there are some that will keep a bargain."

"Anyone at the Post?" Courso asked.

"There's one woman at the Post who wrote some scathing articles about James Porter and the Fall River Diocese in Massachusetts. Actually, Father Atkinson told me about her. I think she used him on background for research."

"What's her name?" Peters asked.

"Margo St. Claire."

"That's apt," cracked Courso. "Is she Catholic?"

"With a name like that, I'd bet anything she's Catholic. If she's pissed about all this stuff and she's been railing against the Fall River Diocese, she's most likely a retired Catholic like me," Elizabeth joked.

"I know her, Tony," Weinstein said, pushing aside his appetizer. I gave her some stuff on background in the Dalkon Shield cases and all the stuff we did on exploding gas tank cases.

"What exactly are you looking for?" Elizabeth asked.

"I want to soften these guys up. We have a police report out of New York where a known offender got some crazy sweetheart deal. No one in the prosecutor's office is going to want to talk about this and then the leaks will start flowing. I've seen it before. Somebody's pissed off that this guy got the deal of the century. I mean really, how do you read that police report and walk out of court with a misdemeanor and no jail time?"

"McCabe's a legendary fixer in New York, Tony. That's what he does," Elizabeth said.

Weinstein scooted his bench seat closer to the table. "Here's what you do. Copy all of Dolan's Official Catholic Directory records, which I would note are in the public domain, put a nice goddamn bow around them and give her a copy. That'll give her a lot to chew on right off the bat. If you embargo our RICO complaint and give her a two-day exclusive to write the story, the New York Times will drill themselves into the ceiling and start digging. Then we'll have two nationals going after this. They'll have all the parishes this asshole was assigned to from California to New York and they'll do their thing."

"Damn, Paul, how long have you been thinking about this?" Elizabeth asked with a chuckle.

"Well, between that asshole McCabe and that asshole MacDonald they pissed me off. Now it's time to get in the dirt."

Courso smiled as he gave the sommelier the wine order. It had been a while since he had been rolling in the dirt on a big stakes case.

"Don't forget Barbara Blaine and SNAP," Elizabeth said.

"I'm glad you mentioned that Elizabeth. What's up with these folks?" Courso asked.

"Barbara's a survivor and she's been keeping this issue in the news. She's an activist. SNAP gives survivors a forum to come together and they stay in the Church's face on this crap, especially the cover-up. She's a total warrior. I talked to her last night and they're ready to do anything they can to help."

"Like how?" Courso asked.

"Once a perpetrator has been identified they beat the bushes."

"Spell it out, Elizabeth, that's Tony's deer in the headlights look," Weinstein said, spooning a fork full of jumbo lump crab meat into his mouth.

"Very funny, Paul," Courso said as he tasted the first bottle of Haut Brion.

"Beautiful," Courso said to the sommelier, ignoring Weinstein's needle.

Elizabeth leaned into the table so as not to be overheard. "SNAP will picket the parishes Dolan was in and leave leaflets on all the cars in the parking lot at Sunday Masses," she explained. "Each chapter will go to where Dolan was stationed and leave information on his arrest and phone numbers to SNAP offices, basically to invite any interested people to join the party, so to speak. If anyone wants to pursue a case, she'll give them our number or names and other lawyers who are working in this field near to them. According to Father Atkinson, there's a guy who works with Barbara, David Clohessy, who's brilliant with public relations."

"Jesus, the Church must hate that. What does she want?" Courso asked.

"The Church does hate that, and Barbara doesn't want anything," Elizabeth said.

"There's no quid pro quo?" Courso persisted.

"Zero. SNAP's mission is to get the Church to confront this issue and remove the people who committed sexual crimes against children and the bishops who hid them."

"Then cut both of them the hell loose at a press conference!" Courso directed. "What I'd like to see is a headline that says *Former D.C. Priest Arrested in New York for Sex Abuse* here in the Post. Float that with your contact that he got a sweetheart deal and where he was from LA to New York. Then, hopefully between SNAP and the other outlets we'll start hearing from as many people as possible. The Times in Los Angeles will pick it up, then we follow with the lawsuit and press conference and sit back and wait and let the chickens come home to roost."

"Why wait, Tony? Let's just serve the assholes and jump into discovery, we have a minor so all they really have is a First Amendment argument," Weinstein said.

Courso looked at Elizabeth. "Do you know why?"

"I do, Tony. It builds pressure, gives us free discovery with people coming out of the woodwork and the Church has to sit there and take it until we formally serve them with the complaint. I do have some concerns though."

"What do you think, Frank, about filing the complaint and jumping into discovery straight away?" Weinstein asked Peters, interrupting Elizabeth.

"At first I agreed with you but let me ask Tony something. Let's say we hang out the full ninety days before we serve them, the media pounds away at them from Los Angeles to New York; aren't most of the clients out there that are victims going to be in other jurisdictions and also be adults outside of the statute? I mean Christ, we would be in a massive conflict with the minor in New York."

"Maybe," Courso said.

"Maybe," Weinstein and Elizabeth said simultaneously, loud enough to make the people at the table next to them look up.

"That's what I was going to say a minute ago. It's a major concern," Elizabeth said. "Stay with me, guys. Bobby Tompkins' case has inherent value, based on what happened to him, how it affected him and some reasonable amount for punitive damages, forgetting for a moment the RICO claim which, in my opinion, is an appeal no matter what happens, win or lose. Do we all agree about that?"

Three simultaneous yeses came back.

"Okay, so we set a reasonable value for Bobby's case and use it as a floor. We then bundle up the rest of the cases against Dolan and set a reasonable value on the basis of what happened to them, how it impacted them, et cetera. Then discount them for being outside of the statute of limitation."

"Tony, that's insane, we cannot do that as the attorneys for all the clients," Weinstein said as both Elizabeth and Peters nodded their agreement.

"There's a way. First, the parents of the minor client have to agree. The family has to be the type that understands the greater good, and they have to believe they will be treated fairly based on the fact that their case is driving all the others. We get them truly independent counsel to advise them of their rights so that if they agree we have it in writing. Then we present a settlement matrix for the adults that would be administered by a third party with a floor and a ceiling. They get a floor same as Bobby but obviously much lower. Everything is done above board; our ethics counsel has to sign off and all the clients must agree in writing. Then we can negotiate a pot for everyone and use the kid and RICO as leverage."

"That sounds like we're scared to try this case, Tony. Alistair will sniff that out in a second," Elizabeth said.

"I agree with her, Tony. We try cases here. That's what we do."

"Well, let me ask you both a question. Why does Elizabeth not want to be a plaintiff in this matter?" Courso said, challenging both of them. "She's a victim of Dolan, she's pissed off at the Church, and she wants them punished, perhaps even revenge is on her mind." Courso paused. "Elizabeth, am I right?" Courso asked, breaking a piece of crusty peasant bread and dipping it into a slurry of grated cheese and olive oil.

"You sound like my grandfather, Tony," Elizabeth said quietly. "But I'm telling you, McCabe has a sixth sense for weakness. It's a bad strategy."

"Not if we spend the money and act like the only thing we want is a trial. I'll tell you what," Courso said, sipping some wine. "I give you my word, if a trial in this matter is what we have to do, we'll do it. But give me some credit for my experience. I'm not some old fool ruminating out in the woods talking to owls."

519

Elizabeth started to giggle.

"What the hell are you laughing about, Elizabeth?" Courso demanded.

"It's just a funny picture. You ruminating in the woods talking to owls. I'm sorry, Tony, don't mind me," Elizabeth said, continuing to giggle.

Courso furrowed his brow. "If we play this right on the front end, we'll get a settlement for the clients that'll be the best they'll ever do, and we'll avoid all the crap that Elizabeth herself wants to avoid. That, in my opinion, is doing the job we were hired for. And for you, Paul, you'll have a war chest to beat the drum again, if everything you say about the Berry fellow's book is true."

"We'll all have skin in this game. Can we agree that we'll all have to agree to whatever we decide to do?" Weinstein proposed to the group. "That means, Tony, that your share of the firm isn't the ultimate decision maker. The four people sitting here have to be one voice."

Courso looked up from the table and pulled his chair in closer. "On this case and this case only, I'll go with a three to one vote. Not unanimous."

Weinstein looked at Elizabeth. "It's your money, Liz, what do you want to do?"

"I'm okay with that," Elizabeth said. "I actually like it."

FATHER, I DID SOMETHING TERRIBLE

For the next two weeks, the newly constituted law firm was the scene of frenetic activity. Pleadings were drafted and redrafted after some of the best minds in the firm added comments and questions. Discovery documents went through the same process with a goal of getting them finely tuned and narrowed. Margo St. Claire met with Elizabeth and Atkinson by phone on background, while the Brooklyn's District Attorney's office was still not commenting on the Dolan file.

ACT OF FAITH

Both Peters and Courso encouraged Elizabeth to take whatever time she needed to help with her brother's diagnosis of AIDS. Her routine was centered around a daily visit to her brother's rectory usually no later than 7:00 A.M. with Boomer in tow. On days with good weather, Francis would walk and meet Elizabeth and Boomer in Pierce Park, which was only a half-mile from her apartment. Monsignor Barton, who was the pastor, was aware that Francis had AIDS and that his sister spent extended periods of time in Francis' room, which ordinarily would have been a total breach of protocol risking severe punishment. When he was up to it, Francis would play classical music on his boyhood piano that had been moved from Shepherd Street to his rectory in Bethesda. Barton would drink his red wine and they would simply talk about their lives and the priesthood; what it had become and what was needed for it to advance into the twentieth century. These daily excursions from the pressure of his parish responsibilities had become a huge comfort to both men.

Elizabeth kept a written diary of his visits to the Whitman Walker Clinic and his T-cell count and helped with getting his prescriptions of AZT and Bactrim filled to ward off the opportunistic infections that plagued victims of the disease.

It was a sun-drenched morning and the walk to Pierce Park with Boomer was exhilarating, but it was still a surprise to see Francis sitting on a bench well past their regular meeting place. Elizabeth let Boomer off his leash and he ran directly to Francis.

"I know, Boomer, I'm happy to see you too," Francis said as the dog whirled himself around in a circle, waiting for Francis to reach down and pet him.

"What are you doing here?" Elizabeth asked as she calmed Boomer.

"Well, you weren't at your normal spot, so I kept walking. Now I'm a little tired."

"Are you okay? Do you want me to get a car for you?" Elizabeth asked.

"No, no, I'll be fine. I just need to rest here for a bit."

"What's wrong, Francis?" Elizabeth said, noticing the blank look on his face. "Did your T-cells come back lower?" Elizabeth asked.

"Actually, they're the same as last week, which I guess is good," Francis said as he got up from the bench.

"Then what is it?" Elizabeth asked, showing no interest in moving until she found out what was wrong.

"Do you remember Mrs. McGinty?"

"No, who is she?" Elizabeth said, exasperated and still concerned about how her brother looked.

Francis organized in his mind the bizarre events of the last twenty-four hours. It had been over thirty years since Francis had seen Gwendolyn McGinty. His memory of the pretentious woman with the prickly personality conflicted wildly with the frail nonagenarian who had come to visit him. Hunched over from unrelenting osteoporosis, McGinty's faded blue eyes and facial expression bore the imprint of guilt. Gone was the condescending tone of Monsignor Cletus Ryan's gatekeeper. She had come to visit Francis to unburden herself from her own complicity of silence.

"I'm surprised you forgot her. She was the parish secretary back at St. Francis de Sales when we were kids."

"Oh, my God, I do remember. She was the bitch that said I looked like a Maria and implied my science project was done by someone else. Wasn't she at the rectory when Poppa died?"

"She was."

"She came to my rectory yesterday."

"She did *what*, Francis? What are you saying?" Elizabeth demanded.

"Her granddaughter called me last night. Apparently, she's in a nursing home up in Bethesda but she's still very sharp.

She's been reading the newspapers about Dolan being arrested in New York."

"Jesus, how old is she?" Elizabeth asked.

"Old, like ninety-one years old."

"Now that I know who you're talking about, I'm surprised she hasn't died of meanness. Momma couldn't stand her. So, what happened with the old bat?"

"The granddaughter brought her to the rectory yesterday afternoon. She said Mrs. McGinty had something to tell me, but she wanted me to hear her confession."

"Christ, Frannie, this is too weird. What the hell does a ninety-one-year-old have to confess to?"

"Never mind what she said in confession, but after that her granddaughter came back into my office with a file folder of copies of pictures from Dolan's room. They're all of kids being abused in his car," Francis said.

"Oh, my God." Elizabeth took a few seconds to register what Francis had just said. "Okay, Frannie, let's just back up. First of all, how did she get them and are they pictures or copies of pictures?" Elizabeth asked, trying to organize the flow of information coming from her brother.

"The first thing that came out of her mouth was 'Father, I did something terrible.' Here, see for yourself," he said as he placed the file in her lap.

Elizabeth flinched as she placed her hand over the closed file.

"That sick fuck took a picture of me jerking him off in his car," Francis said. "Go ahead and look. It's the first one."

Elizabeth gingerly slid the top sheet out of the folder. "Frannie, all I see is a small hand around an erect penis in what looks like a car."

"It's a picture of me because I remember him taking it. And that line in the picture just behind my thumb... Remember I had an operation when I fell out of the tree in the backyard?" Francis blustered in a state of near panic.

"Yes," Elizabeth said. "Why?"

Francis tugged on his sleeve, revealing the keloid scar on his wrist. "Because I still have it."

Elizabeth was dazed, realizing exactly what Francis was telling her.

"So, we were both abused by the same priest?" Elizabeth asked in a shocked monotone. She sat on the bench, tapping her fingers on the closed file, trying to process the revelation. Finally, her mind kicked into gear. "Did she say how she got them?"

"She admitted she didn't much care for Dolan, and she was angry that Monsignor Ryan thought she was a bit of a busybody, but when everyone was out of the building she went into Dolan's room and snooped around, and she found these."

"Sounds like she was a busy body," Elizabeth said.

"Liz, I'm just telling you what she said, okay?"

"I'm sorry, go ahead," Elizabeth said.

"She said she didn't know what to do with them, so she made copies of them on the rectory's copier. She even had the model and serial number; it was a Xerox 914. Afterwards, she put them back where she got them. A few days later she said there was this big argument. Apparently, Dolan thought a nun had found them but then she thought she heard something like a fistfight, a 'helluva racket,' she said, and she heard Dolan say he was glad that the Bishop had the pictures."

"How did the Bishop get the pictures?"

"Because she overheard Monsignor Ryan tell him that he gave them to Bishop Guilfoyle."

"I guess Mother knows nothing about this," Elizabeth said with little emotion.

"No," Francis said nervously.

"Frannie, I just don't understand why you didn't say anything about this when we were at Tiberio's."

"I couldn't tell you about my abuse without telling you something I was going to take to my grave."

"Take to your grave? What are you talking about?" Elizabeth asked.

Francis took a deep breath. "I saw what happened to you at Aquinas Hall."

Elizabeth stood up from the bench and started to tremble. "What exactly did you see, Francis?" Elizabeth asked as she put her head into her hands.

"I was at the end of the hallway where we put on our vestments. The sacristy door was slightly opened, and I crept up to see who was in there."

"I asked you what did you fucking see, Francis?" she growled through her hands that were still covering her face.

"I saw your back with your dress over your waist and I saw Dolan humping you and his pants were down to his knees. I saw your hands holding onto the vesting mirror. I saw him wipe some blood off the back of your legs. After you left, I went to hide but he caught me. Then he threatened me with the worst stuff, that God would strike down Poppa or Momma, it was awful, and I thought for sure you were going to say something. Remember when you said to me, I killed Poppa? You were right. I told him what happened, and he tore out of the house with me by the arm and we went to see Ryan. He died right in front of Mrs. McGinty desk."

Elizabeth was doubled over sobbing uncontrollably. As she tried to get up from the bench she fell to the ground. Francis rushed to help her up.

"Don't touch me. Stay away from me!" she screamed, pushing away from him with her heels digging into the gravel path. "Just stay the fuck away from me," she cried as she grabbed Boomer and sprinted back to her apartment.

WE HAVE TO FIND YOUR SISTER

Paul Weinstein settled in with a tuna fish and provolone sandwich at his desk. All morning he had been reading Elizabeth legal memorandum on the applicability of the federal and District of Columbia racketeering statute. He was envious of the clarity of her arguments and her ability to translate them to the written word. It was obvious she had a vast arsenal of talent honed both at the Supreme Court as a clerk to Justice O'Connor and fifteen years of private practice in some of the best law firms in the country.

Carol Holmes, a stout, no-nonsense secretary, pushed open his office door and stood there with her hand on her hip.

"What do you want, Carol?" Weinstein asked coarsely.

"What I want is for you to pick up your intercom if you're sitting right next to it, so I don't have to walk over hell's half acre to look for you thinking you're not in your office. That's what I want." Carol Holmes was the longest serving secretary in the firm and Tony Courso was determined to put an end to Weinstein's horrible reputation among the staff. Carol was Courso's first secretary and Weinstein knew that she was untouchable, but that didn't seem to slow the bickering back and forth.

"I apologize, Carol, I've been calling Elizabeth all morning and she hasn't returned any of my calls."

"Then you'll be interested to know that a Catholic priest is out in the lobby. He says his name is Francis Natale, Elizabeth's brother."

Weinstein jumped from his desk chair. "Get the hell out of here, are you serious? What's he doing here?" he asked Carol.

"I have no idea, but he said he'd like to talk to you."

Weinstein put on a suit jacket and took the steps down to the lobby floor. Francis was standing in the corner near the window, taking in the view of downtown Washington. Weinstein walked to him and greeted him warmly, extending his hand. Francis' face was drawn but his eyes sparkled when the two men shook hands.

"Thank you for that, Mr. Weinstein. I looked at myself in the mirror this morning and I'm not sure I would have been so gracious. May I speak to you?" Francis asked.

"That may be problematic. I want to make sure who you're speaking for."

"I'm not sure I understand, Mr. Weinstein."

"Well, you're an employee of an entity we may be suing shortly."

"Please, Mr. Weinstein, I came here to speak on my own behalf. Elizabeth has shared with me generally what's afoot and I would like to share with you what I know."

"Have you told Elizabeth?" Weinstein asked.

"That's actually what I wanted to talk to you about."

"Father, come with me, let's take the elevator to my office."

The two men walked down the hallway to Weinstein's office, and both settled into the two chairs facing his desk.

"First of all, Father, have you seen Elizabeth?"

"Not for a couple of days," Francis said. "We've had a difficult event that has come between us."

"What happened, Father?" Weinstein asked, concerned.

"I saw Andrew Dolan raping Elizabeth in a vestment room near where we both went to school. I knew what happened to her and I kept it a secret. I told my father eventually, but he never got a chance to confront Cletus Ryan or Dolan. He had a massive heart attack in the rectory when we both went to Ryan to tell him. After that, life just went on. I was afraid to tell anyone about what Dolan did to Elizabeth because I was convinced someone that I cared for would die. When I figured out I was just being manipulated, I still stayed quiet. I was a gay Catholic priest in the closet. I was ashamed I didn't speak up at the time and I just hated myself. Two days ago, a woman named Mrs. McGinty brought me these." Francis placed a folder in front of Weinstein. "One of them is a picture of me."

"Doing what, Father?" Weinstein asked.

"Dolan's making me hold his erect penis in his car."

"Jesus, Father. Elizabeth knows all of this?" Weinstein asked, incredulous.

"Yes, I told her two days ago. I want to tell the truth about what happened, and I want to do it in public so people can see how destructive this crap is and do something about it. Plus, I'm dying of AIDS, and I don't want to die with this on my conscience."

"Father, please, just slow down. What are you saying?" Weinstein asked.

"I want to sue my Archdiocese. I want to lend my voice to this. I owe it to my sister."

"Does she know about you coming here today, Father?"

"No. I didn't get a chance to tell her. She was very angry when she left, I doubt she'll ever forgive me, but this is something I have to do."

"I'm not sure you really understand what you're saying, Father. This will get really ugly for you."

"Mr. Weinstein, I'm a Catholic priest with AIDS because of some really bad choices I've made and facing my own mortality—that's ugly. Telling the truth after all these years will be a breath of fresh air."

For the next hour, Weinstein listened to the agony pour out of Francis Natale. Weinstein's practice had hardened him to terrible facts but to be this close to the depraved madness of a centuries old cover-up of priests sexually acting out on children shook him to his core.

Weinstein opened the file in front of him and winced as he paged through the images of the children. "And which one is you?" he asked.

"The one on top, Mr. Weinstein."

"And you got these from whom?" Weinstein asked, taking a long deep breath.

"A former parish secretary. She found them, made copies and put them back. Apparently, Archbishop Ryan and Dolan had a fight in the upstairs bedroom, and she overheard Ryan admitting he found the pictures in Dolan's room and took them to Bishop Guilfoyle, who's dead now, but he was Bishop at the time."

"And this is the same Ryan who's the Archbishop of Washington?" Weinstein asked, shaking his head.

"Yes."

"Do you know how to reach this Mrs. McGinty, Father?" Weinstein asked.

"Yes, I have her number at Rossmoor in Bethesda, that's where she's living. It's an assisted living place about thirty minutes from here."

"Do you think if I send a car up for her, she would come down? You said assisted living, is she handicapped?"

"Not that I could tell. She's old but..."

"How old?" Weinstein interrupted as he raced around to his desk to get a yellow pad.

"She's ninety-two."

"Shit," Weinstein mumbled, which was followed by an ear-piercing bellow loud enough for the entire floor to hear. "Carol! Father, can you stick around for a bit today, you can stay here in my office and make yourself comfortable."

"Sure."

Carol appeared at the door, her face crimson red. "Excuse me, Father Natale. Mr. Weinstein, I'm not some cow you holler for like you're outside on a farm. I'm twenty feet away."

"You can be mad at me later, Carol. I want you to get a videographer and a court reporter down here and keep them here until we're ready. Call this number," he said as he handed her a note page with the numbers. "And find Mrs. McGinty. Tell her Father Natale is with us at the firm right now, and we'd like for her to come down and tell her story. I want you to go with the driver and pick her up, keep her comfortable and get her here. Do you have all of Father Atkinson's numbers?" Weinstein asked.

"Yes," Carol answered. "Find him and ask him to call me, and tell the switchboard to find me when he calls in."

"Mr. Weinstein, I would also call the granddaughter and give her a heads up," Francis said, writing her number down and giving it to him.

"Carol, if she wants to come go get her, too. I want the woman in the building today before I take custody of this file. Finally, when you get back, prepare a retainer agreement for Father Francis Natale. You got all that?" Weinstein asked as Carol closed her steno pad.

"I do."

"Make it happen," Weinstein ordered as he left his office. "Father, if you need anything I'll be down the hall in Tony Courso's office. We have to find your sister."

Weinstein hurried down to Courso's office, ignoring protocol by walking into his office.

Courso glared at him. "I guess the closed door while I'm dictating isn't a clue for you, Paul."

"I'm sorry, Tony, but something has come up involving Elizabeth and her brother. I've been trying to reach her for two days."

"What the fuck are you talking about? I just saw her downstairs an hour ago going into the law library with a tray of food and the goddamn dog."

"I can't believe it, what a bitch," Weinstein said, immediately turning to leave.

"What the hell is going on, Weinstein?" Courso yelled at him.

"I'll tell you later," Weinstein yelled back over his shoulder.

The law library occupied half of the entire fourth floor on the H Street side of the building. Weinstein scanned the main reading section and saw no sign of Elizabeth.

"Have you seen Miss Natale, Marjorie?" he asked the reference librarian. "You know, the lady with the dog?"

"Oh, of course, Boomer. Try one of the cubicles on the back wall. She usually uses one of those. Can I ask you a question, Mr. Weinstein?" the librarian asked.

"What is it, Marjorie?"

"Is the dog staying?"

"Has he been a problem?" Weinstein said, ready to take that up with Elizabeth as well.

"On the contrary, Boomer is so well behaved that he seems to keep everyone calm down here, kinda like meditation music on four legs, plus he takes his treats like a gentleman," Marjorie giggled.

"That's wonderful, Marjorie, I'll be sure to let the partners know at our next meeting," Weinstein said, trying his best to keep his tone civil.

Weinstein walked to the only cubical that had a light on. The walls in each room were coated with neutral colored sound proofing fabric and corkboard to maintain privacy and aid in concentration. A comfortable desk chair, plush carpet, office supplies and a full-length glass door made long hours of tedious research bearable in what otherwise would trigger a full tilt bout of claustrophobia.

Elizabeth was surrounded by dozens of volumes of recent Federal cases, Xerox copies of opinions and reams of handwritten notes. Boomer was lying at her feet, curled into a muscular ball of fur through the glass window in the door.

Weinstein knocked and opened the door a few inches. Boomer was mildly curious and raised his head to look at Weinstein.

"Is it safe to come in? He doesn't look happy."

"You would know if he wasn't happy," Elizabeth said.

"C'mon, Liz, stop fucking with me. Something big has come up and I need to talk to you. I've been trying to reach you for two days."

"He gets nervous when people raise their voices," Elizabeth cautioned.

"I didn't raise my voice, Elizabeth," Weinstein protested.

"You were about to. I was just giving you a heads up, Paul."

"Can I come in or not?" he asked in a whisper.

"Sure, I'll sit on the floor with Boomer, you sit in the chair. Just don't raise your voice, there's no place to hide in here."

"Very funny, Elizabeth." Weinstein took Elizabeth's seat, making sure to step over Boomer's long tail.

"So, what's got a bee in your bonnet, Paul? I sent you and Tony a draft of the complaint that incorporated all your thoughts," Elizabeth said as she tossed one of Boomer's chew toys between his legs.

"Your brother Francis is sitting in my office. I just spent an hour with him. He wants to go public with the whole story. He told me about your blow up at the park."

"You said my brother Francis is in your office right now?"

"Yes."

Elizabeth sprung to her feet and bolted out of the room, leaving Weinstein and Boomer tethered to his leash in the twelve-foot square cubical. Weinstein gingerly grabbed the end of the leash. Boomer made no effort to move and sat there looking at Weinstein. He was relieved to see the knock on the door was from Marjorie.

"Would you like me to take him to the reference desk for you, Mr. Weinstein?" Marjorie asked.

"You're a saint, Marjorie. I don't think the dog likes me."

"That's odd, he seems to like everyone. Maybe you should work on that, Mr. Weinstein," Marjorie said as she led Boomer between the stacks and up to the reference desk where he promptly put his nose on the drawer that held the box of Milk Bones.

Weinstein approached Courso's office cautiously and when he knew he was alone, he sat down and briefed Courso on the afternoon's developments. Both men realized that a priest with AIDS as a plaintiff in a Federal Racketeering case would be explosive. They needed to get Mrs. McGinty on the record and under oath. A deposition without notice to an adverse party was problematic, but at ninety-two they both concluded it was worth the risk. At least they would be able to establish a chain of custody for the photos, assuming Francis was not dead from AIDS.

Courso and Weinstein had kept an eye on Weinstein's office door, which had remained closed for over two hours.

"Any explosions?" Courso asked Carol.

"None that I've heard, Mr. Courso."

"Paul, I don't want Mrs. McGinty to wait here too long. Have you briefed her as to how it will go?" Courso asked.

"Yes, she's ready to go."

"Okay, go ahead and start and get each photograph authenticated that she copied and make sure you cover the backstory of what she overheard and how she copied them. I'll wait for Elizabeth and Father Natale."

"I'm on it, Tony."

Thirty minutes later, Weinstein's door opened. When Elizabeth saw Courso waiting in the hall she walked back in and sat next to Francis.

"I was starting to worry about you two," Courso said.

Elizabeth's eyes were bloodshot and swollen.

"We're doing okay, Mr. Courso, just a lot of years to process," Francis said.

"Frannie, do you still want to go to Momma's tonight?" Elizabeth asked. "We could always do it tomorrow."

"No, I'm going to need to rest tomorrow and decide whether I'm going to tell Archbishop Ryan what's going on or let him read about it."

"What are you guys talking about?" Courso asked Elizabeth.

"Frannie told me Paul was trying to get Mrs. McGinty down here, so I assumed we were moving up filing the complaint," Elizabeth said as she spotted Boomer trolling the hallway. "Come

533

here, Boomie," Elizabeth cooed to the dog. "Do you mind if he comes in, Tony?" Elizabeth asked.

"What the hell? After today, having this beast prowl the halls seems perfectly normal."

Boomer padded into the room, placing his gigantic head in Elizabeth's lap.

"I do want to move up the complaint," Courso said. "Father, you're absolutely sure this is what you want to do?"

"One hundred percent, Mr. Courso. My time is probably short, so I want to leave on my own terms," Francis said as he reached out for his sister's hand.

"We just can't file it until I let my mother know, and Frannie says he wants to go over tonight, so I'll be back in the office tomorrow and we can lay out the logistics. So, you want to go now, Frannie?"

"Yes," Francis said firmly. "Tonight."

"Okay, let me call Brother Gerald and see if he can take Boomer for the night. Tony, is the car service available this late?" Elizabeth asked.

"It will be if I call," Courso said with a grin.

The black Lincoln Town car pulled out of the Dominican House lot, traveling directly to Michigan Avenue. Elizabeth stared out the passenger window behind the driver.

"I can't get over how pretty the front of the Shrine is. Every time I see it, it just amazes me," Elizabeth said, almost daydreaming.

"It wouldn't have anything to do with the fact that Poppa and Grandpop had a lot to do with the stonework, would it?" Francis asked, smiling.

"It does, but how do you reconcile that it's built on the back of lies and crimes? We were kids, Frannie," Elizabeth said as a light mist turned to a steady drizzle.

"I know, Liz, that's not how most people look at it. God's presence in that magnificent structure requires an act of faith. People want to believe that. For them it's a natural extension of why they're here on the planet."

"Do you believe in God, Frannie?" Elizabeth asked, turning in her seat to face her brother.

"At this very instant, Elizabeth? Is that what you're asking me?"

"Yes. This very instant, Frannie."

"To be totally honest, Liz, I don't know what I believe any longer. I do know this: it takes just as much of an act of faith to believe in God as it does to not believe in God. Let me put it another way. Whether I die believing or not believing, it will not change how I live out the rest of my life."

Elizabeth helped Francis out of the back seat and up the stairs to the house on Shepherd Street. Francis knocked on the door. Anna opened the door on the opposite of Lucy's house with a frightened look on her face.

"Who died?" she asked Francis.

"No one, Grandmom," Elizabeth said as she leaned over the porch rail to give her a kiss. "We came to talk to Momma."

"Okay. She's home. Frannie, come by after you finish and I'll give you some food to take back. I don't think they're feeding you over there at your parish."

"I will, Grandmom."

Anna grabbed Elizabeth. "Let me kiss you again. Where have you been?" Anna asked.

"Work, Grandmom, just work."

"You need a man."

"Is that what I need, Grandmom?" Elizabeth teased.

"Yes, a man and a vacation. And make sure your brother gets more to eat."

Lucy opened the door and saw her two children. "What's wrong, Frannie?" she asked.

"Nothing, Momma, we just came to talk."

"At eight-thirty at night?"

"I know it's late, Momma, but it's important."

"Does this have anything to do with the last time your sister was here," Lucy said, walking back to the kitchen, ignoring Elizabeth.

"You mean your daughter Elizabeth who's standing right next to me?"

"Yes," Lucy said defiantly.

"It does to some extent. I wasn't here when you last spoke but neither one of you had the whole story. I do, and you need to hear it. I'm not here to judge you, Momma."

"That's refreshing," Lucy snorted.

"Mother, please don't talk. Just listen. Elizabeth told you what happened to her at the hands of Andrew Dolan. It happened. I saw it with my own eyes. I thought Dolan didn't hear me, but he caught me. He threatened me that if I told anyone, horrible things would happen to me and everyone else in the family. I knew for sure that Liz would say something when she got home. She didn't, because he threatened Elizabeth just like he threatened me."

Lucy swallowed hard. She got a cigarette from the counter drawer and took a seat at the kitchen table.

"A few weeks later, Poppa got it out of me," Francis continued, "because I was being sexually abused by Dolan as well."

"What are you saying, Francis?" Lucy asked, starting to cry.

"Momma, please just let me get this out. My whole world came crashing down. But I didn't tell Poppa about what Dolan did to me. I was afraid. I just told him about Elizabeth. That's my sin, Momma. Poppa got so angry he went straight to the rectory and took me with him. He said Monsignor Ryan would know what to do. He never got to tell him. That's when he died of a massive heart attack. Cletus Ryan has used you for thirty years. I know he knows what happened because I told him in confession. He told me I bore some of the responsibility for Poppa's death and I believed him. That's why I decided to become a priest. I went into the priesthood to hide from my sin and myself. I'm gay, Momma, and through a lot of denial and very bad choices I ended up contracting AIDS. My doctors say I have six months, a year if I'm lucky."

Lucy put her cigarette down and closed her eyes tightly as she dug her fingers into her scalp. She let out a long howl, staggered to the sink and vomited. Elizabeth watched her mother retch into the sink then got behind her and held her upright by the waist and turned the water on.

"Frannie, go upstairs and get some towels," Elizabeth said.

Francis turned to leave the kitchen and saw Rosemary at the threshold holding a towel and washcloth.

"Did you hear all of that, Aunt Rose?" Francis asked.

"Yes. Every word, Francis. We can talk later," she said as she went to her sister. "Keep the water running, Liz," Rosemary said as she flipped the switch for the garbage disposal. The high-pitched whine of the motor was a surreal addition to the tension in the room. As Rosemary wiped her sister's face and hair with water, Lucy let out chilling wails of grief and anger.

"Liz, get a chair behind her before she falls," Rosemary ordered. Lucy's body went limp in the chair. "She's in shock, Liz, help me get her into bed. Lucy, look at me!" Rosemary screamed at her sister. She reached into her robe pocket and pushed a Valium into Lucy's mouth. "Drink some water with this, Lucy, it'll help you settle down and go to sleep," Rosemary said as she and Elizabeth helped Lucy out of the chair and into her bedroom.

Rosemary and Elizabeth got Lucy out of her robe and into bed. Rosemary climbed on the bed and laid next to her sister, smoothing her hair off her face with a warm compress.

"Do you still know how to say the rosary, Aunt Rose?" Elizabeth asked as she waited at Lucy's bedroom door.

"Yes, why?"

"When I was upset, that's how Momma put me to sleep when I was little," Elizabeth said.

"Wait for me downstairs, Liz, I want to talk to you both before you leave."

Elizabeth walked downstairs and found Francis in the kitchen in front of a glass of whiskey.

"Are you allowed to drink with the medicine you're taking?" Elizabeth asked, alarmed.

"Not supposed to, but tonight I'm making an exception. Do you want one?"

"I'm an alcoholic, Frannie, and yes I want some," she said as she reached into her purse and pulled out the Moleskine pocket notebook and pen.

"What's that?" Francis asked.

"You see this number in the corner?" Elizabeth asked as she leaned over the table and opened the book.

"Yes, it says forty-three."

"Right, and today is the forty-fourth day I haven't had a drink. The problem is, I still want one. So, I'm smoking more," Elizabeth said as she walked to the cupboard where Lucy hid her cigarettes. She lit the cigarette on the stove and took a long deep drag of nicotine into her lungs.

"Is that good for your running?" Francis asked as Elizabeth broke into laughter.

"Not really, so I'd say we're even tonight. Aunt Rose wanted us to wait before we leave.

Rosemary held onto the banister as she descended the staircase, still trying to process everything she had overheard. "Is there any more of that whiskey, Frannie?" she asked.

"Yes, Aunt Rose."

"Pour me a shot," she said as she sat at the table and pulled the curlers that littered the top of her head out of her hair. "So, I heard everything you said but there was no 'why.'"

"Why what?" Francis asked.

"Why, on a Tuesday night, did you come over to tell your mother this parade of horribles?"

Elizabeth took another deep drag.

"I can answer that, Aunt Rose," she said, pulling up a chair at the kitchen table. "Three months ago, Andrew Dolan was arrested in New York on a sexual assault charge involving a minor. One of the boys is now a client of mine. To make a very long story short, the Church knew about Dolan for years, but they just kept him in the priesthood and bounced him from Diocese to Diocese. I've associated with a big D.C. firm and within a week we're going to file a Federal Racketeering lawsuit against the Archdioceses of Los Angeles, Washington, and New York. Francis is going to be one of the plaintiffs and is going to appear in a press conference and speak when the lawsuit is announced."

"Well, goddamn, that might make the papers. When is this happening?" Rosemary asked, tapping her finger on the side of her glass of whiskey.

"Most likely in a week. Maybe sooner if we get everything in place."

"Have you told your doctors, Frannie?"

"No, and I probably won't until it's over."

"Who's taking care of you?"

"I am," Elizabeth said. "Frannie can stay at my place. I've been taking him every morning to the clinic at Whitman Walker."

"And when you're working?" Rosemary asked, annoyed. "When Frannie's really sick, then what? Listen, Liz, I don't want to start an argument, but this isn't about you and your mother. It's about who can deliver the best care to Frannie, and what he wants." Rosemary turned to Francis and took a sip of whiskey. "Does the Archbishop know?"

"No, whether I tell him in person, or he hears about it through the press conference, I'll be suspended and most likely be sent to a convent or monastery."

"Once your mother gets over the shock, I know her, she'll want you to stay here so she can take care of you."

"And what about her lover Cletus Ryan?" Elizabeth snarled.

"Liz, I don't know what to say about that. I expect that once she realizes she's been used she'll get a head of steam up, much like your father, and do something about it. I don't know. I warned her nothing good was going to come of it. That whole situation never made any sense to me."

"So, you knew," Elizabeth said, glaring at Rosemary.

Rosemary got up and went to the sink to run some warm water. "Think about it, Elizabeth," she said as she wiped cold cream from her forehead with a clean washcloth, then tossed it into the sink. "Both you kids were abused when you were little. You both lived in this house, which was a cathedral to Catholic orthodoxy. I'm a closeted lesbian. Francis is a gay priest who's going to tell the world, at a press conference announcing a lawsuit against the Church, that he was abused and has AIDS. You're an alcoholic struggling with your own demons and my sister's having an affair with the local Archbishop. I mean really, what the fuck? All this started by one asshole. You can't make this shit up. So, you guys can do what you want, but since no one here can go back and make things right, I think we should cut each other as much slack as everyone needs to get through this crap." Rosemary shook her fingers through her hair and downed the rest of her whiskey.

"Come here, both of you, and give me a kiss goodnight," she said as the three of them huddled in front of the sink. "Call me tomorrow, Elizabeth, and check in, please. I'll have to figure out what to do with Anna."

"I will, Aunt Rose."

NOTHING COULD PREPARE ME FOR THIS DAY

Elizabeth sat on the edge of her bed and looked at the time. Boomer was nestled in his bed, the very tip of his tail flickering in the shadows to acknowledge the movement above him.

"Hey, sweetie," Elizabeth said to Boomer as he wrinkled his brow to the sound of her voice. "Go back to sleep."

Boomer laid his head back on the pillow and pushed a large volume of air through his nose and mouth, causing his oversized lips to comically flap.

"You're such a goof," Elizabeth said, rubbing his ears and dialing Atkinson's number.

He picked up on the first ring. "Yes, this is Father Atkinson."

"You up, Tommy? It's me," Elizabeth said, bobbing her crossed leg off the side of the bed.

"I am now. It's still dark here, what time is it?"

"It's four-thirty, I'm sorry for calling so early, I just needed to hear your voice. It's gotten really crazy up here."

"What going on, Liz?"

"It's too long a story but we're moving up filing the lawsuit and my brother Francis is going to be one of the plaintiffs. He's dying of AIDS and was abused by Dolan as well. He wants to go public with this before he can't," Elizabeth said, choking out the words.

"My God, if he's in this lawsuit as a priest with AIDS it'll be heard all the way to the Vatican. Is Francis aware of what's going to come down on him?" Atkinson asked.

"He wants to do this, Tommy, so I'm going to do everything I can to make it happen. Tony wanted me to ask you if you could come up. We're trying to get Barbara Blaine here with David tomorrow or the next day."

"When did you want me to come?" Atkinson asked, grabbing his calendar. "I'd have to talk to my boss, Liz, but a same day ticket from Pensacola to National would cost a fortune."

"Oh, no, the firm would pay. You just have to let me know if you can come."

"Okay, I'll check and let you know as soon as I go into work. How's Boomer?"

"Oh, God, Tommy, he's a peach. Everybody loves him at the firm, well almost everyone. He's sleeping right next to my bed. Do you want to say hello?" Elizabeth asked.

"No, don't be ridiculous," Atkinson said as Elizabeth giggled into the phone.

"Oh, you're such a killjoy. But seriously, I want to ask you something. I was at my mother's house last night and Frannie went through the whole story and afterwards he poured himself a glass of whisky. I wanted it so badly. I literally stared at it."

"What did you do?"

"I got my book out and wrote forty-four in the corner. But I still wanted to drink, and with all this shit going on, I'm afraid."

"But you didn't, right? That's the point, Elizabeth. You just need more time. You may relapse but you start over. You have to keep moving forward until you own your sobriety."

"Do you still want to drink when you see whiskey?" she asked.

"I don't see whiskey. I see a hot stove with my hand just above it. I know it'll kill me if I get near it, and it'll be a painful death."

"How long did it take?" Elizabeth asked, noticing her heart rate increase.

"A long time, Liz. Keep doing it a day at a time and I'll call you at nine when I see my boss. If you run into any trouble tonight, call me. I'm here."

Elizabeth stared at her Moleskine notebook on her nightstand. She picked it up and, in the corner, wrote a question mark next to forty-five.

Two days later, at 6:00 P.M., Tony Courso called the law firm meeting to order. The filed and stamped copy of the complaint, along with the exhibits, were stacked in the middle of the conference room table. Thirty minutes before the meeting started and after the Clerk's office was closed, Paul Weinstein handed Margo St. Claire of the Washington Post an embargoed copy of the filed complaint. As agreed, all of his comments were on the record but within the four corners of the complaint.

The angle of the early evening sun had created a warm glow in the main conference room. A stack of embossed legal pads and sharpened pencils were left on the credenza under the main window along with a hot and cold beverage service.

"Let me start by saying thank you for dropping everything on such short notice to get here. Before I start, does anyone have any questions?" Courso asked.

"I do," David Clohessy said. "Barbara and I can speak to SNAP's mission and exactly what we're doing in the individual parishes, but when the media gets to the press conference tomorrow, they're going to be pissed out of their minds about the Post exclusive. So, if it's okay with you, instead of SNAP issuing the notice for the press conference tonight, can it be done on your firm letterhead? Then we won't have to listen to a bunch of guff from the reporters that we have relationships with," David said.

"Absolutely. Blame it all on Weinstein if any questions come up. He's got big shoulders," Courso said as the group had a good laugh at Weinstein's predicament.

"You're a real sport, Tony, thanks."

"Okay. Paul, Elizabeth and I have everyone's talking points. Are there any additions or corrections before we make copies? They're really well done, I have to say."

"Tony, I checked with the Tompkins and Francis, they're both good," Elizabeth added. "They understand they're not taking questions and obviously you'll be there to make sure it doesn't happen."

"Do they know that after the press conference it'll be a shit storm? Do they clearly understand they are not to make any statements?"

"They do, but I'll emphasize again."

"Then we're set. Paul, can you get your assistant to lock these copies up in our vault until tomorrow morning?" Courso asked.

"I'll make sure that happens, Tony."

"If it'll help, we have some SNAP members who are happy to attend to support Father Natale and the Tompkins family," Barbara said.

"I'll have some staff downstairs in the morning to help with circulating the copies," Weinstein said.

"That would be great. Thanks, Paul," Courso said. "So, ladies and gentlemen, I believe we're set."

"Paul, get the notice out to the press for tomorrow at 11:00 A.M. on our letterhead. Okay then, everyone's invited downstairs. Chef Carlo is waiting for us. Be sure to tell Frank and the staff who are working late to join us. Elizabeth, when will Father Atkinson get here?"

"He should be here by eight."

"Excellent. Does he have a place to stay?" Courso asked.

"He said Brother Gerald at the Dominican House has room for him for a night or two."

"And the Tompkins?" Courso asked, going through a mental checklist.

"They're in the lobby. We have them staying at the Marriott on 14th Street so they can walk here for tomorrow morning."

"Excellent," Courso said as he got up to meet the Tompkins.

"Spend some time with them, Tony," Elizabeth said. "They're really nervous."

"I will. Make sure they sit next to me at dinner. How is Francis feeling?"

"He's a little tired but he's resting at my place."

"He knows he's invited here, right?"

"Of course he does, and you're sweet. It means so much to him, Tony," Elizabeth said as she hugged him and kissed him on the cheek.

"Just make sure he knows he's welcome here any time. The man's got AIDS, it doesn't make him radioactive."

The next morning at 4:00 A.M., Margo St. Claire posted her story on the Post's fledgling digital service and teletype and within forty-five minutes the major wire services were detailing the first case to ever file Federal Racketeering charges against the Catholic Church in a civil lawsuit.

A two-column, inch tall headline above the fold announced to the world that the Catholic Church abuse crisis had reached a boiling point. By 7:00 A.M., the switchboard at Courso, Peters and Weinstein had received over 150 media inquiries seeking comment. By nine-thirty, the entire first floor lobby of the building was crawling with reporters and camera men from all the major print, cable and network media outlets. At 11:00 A.M. sharp, Anthony Courso introduced all the participants.

Two dozen members of several East Coast Chapters of SNAP stood silently around the perimeter of the room holding pictures of themselves at the age they were abused. A flurry of shouted questions concerning the timing of the Post story were batted down and referred to Weinstein at the conclusion of the press conference. David Clohessy knew that if the complaint was widely available at the conference it would sooth the angst and egos of the reporters who were overlooked for the exclusive.

Courso moved through the agenda, referring all questions to specific sections in the complaint or the exhibits. At precisely 11:30 A.M., he introduced Father Francis Natale to the assembled reporters. For those who had not read the first page of the complaint, the image of a priest in his black clerics was a shock.

545

Francis stood erect at the podium. There was a slight tremble in his hands as he held his written statement.

"Good morning, everyone. My name is Francis Joseph Natale, and I am a Roman Catholic priest assigned to a parish in the Archdiocese of Washington, D.C. My voice is a little hoarse, so please bear with me," Francis said, eyeing the crowd in front of him. "Nothing could prepare me for this day. The reason I say that is because I was one of the young boys described in the lawsuit. As a youngster and musical student, Father Andrew Dolan repeatedly sexually assaulted me, beginning when I was thirteen years old."

Hearing the collective sound of dozens of reporters ruffling the pages of their notebooks momentarily distracted Francis. He paused in reading his statement in order to get his bearings. "Andrew Dolan is a former priest of this Archdiocese, and is now a priest in the Archdiocese of New York," Francis continued. "What is written about me in the complaint is true; it's what is not written about me in the complaint that I want to share with you. I kept Andrew Dolan's perverted secrets out of fear and self-preservation. After I told my father some of what happened, he took me to see our parish priest believing he would know what to do. As he waited in the rectory he had a massive heart attack. I watched him die of a broken heart trying to protect me. Andrew Dolan told me that if I ever told anyone about the abuse God would strike down that person. I foolishly believed him. Now the proof was before my very eyes. Andrew Dolan and the current Archbishop of Washington, Cletus Ryan, then a Monsignor at my parish St. Francis de Sales, convinced me that I was partially to blame for my own father's death. He told me that I had turned my face away from God when Dolan was abusing me. He told me that my family would be isolated and that if I revealed this secret, it would be considered an attack on the Church. From that day on, I decided to live a lie, until this past week. I believed that I could hide my secrets and my homosexuality in the priesthood."

Francis' voice was shaking, and he paused to collect himself and take a sip of water.

"I let my family down, I let the scores of victims down that came before and after me. I knew what was the right thing to do; I was simply too frightened and ashamed to speak the truth. I let my brother priests down who have, with great difficulty, maintained their promise of chastity, and I let myself down. Thousands of effective and caring ministers to the faithful have left the priesthood because they were unwilling to live a lie. They are the brave ones. My very first sexual experience was at the hands of a Catholic priest. I was a boy, a student of classical music; he was a grown man whose day was ordered by an insatiable drive to gain access to children. So, I embarked on a life-long journey of hiding the truth. It turns out I wasn't hiding at all, because through a series of horrible choices, which included violating my promise to live a chaste and celibate life, driven primarily by my own self-loathing, I have contracted Acquired Immune Deficiency Syndrome, otherwise known as AIDS."

There was an audible gasp in the room, as many present had no idea that such an explosive disclosure would be the centerpiece of the press conference.

"My prognosis is poor; I am told I have perhaps a year to live. I believe it's important to set the record straight today, in my own words. Priests are people. We have flaws just like everyone else. The hard truth is we serve the faithful; we are not better than the faithful. The Church's inability to effectively deal with sexual realities inside the priesthood, both homosexual and heterosexual, has driven the bishops to keep secrets and put children at risk, sheltering sexual predators from exposure. As long as our sexual realities are kept in the closet, the hierarchy embraces us. I can be a homosexual in the abstract without recrimination from the Church, but if I announce that fact or, God forbid, act on those realities in a loving relationship, I'm a sinner and am cast aside from serving. So be it. I do not ask for anyone's sympathy. I do ask for forgiveness from the people I have hurt. Thank you."

The expected unruliness at the conclusion of a press conference was muted by the visceral incongruity of what had just happened.

"As I said before, our clients are not taking questions," Frank Peters announced as he ushered Francis out of the lobby.

"But Mr. Weinstein is available to speak to you," Courso hollered over the shouted questions as he left the podium.

Elizabeth had spotted her mother in the far corner of the room but had not made eye contact. By the time she waded through the scrum of reporters to the back of the room, Lucy was already gone.

Elizabeth walked Francis to a service elevator that would take him back to her office. When the doors closed, he leaned into the heavily padded walls and forcibly pushed all the air out of his lungs.

"How did I do?" Francis asked.

"I thought you were magnificent. You stood up to them, Frannie. It was big, really big. Did you see Momma in the back of the room?" Elizabeth asked.

"No, I didn't. Was she there?" Francis asked, shocked.

"She was. She heard your whole statement. I tried to get to her, but she had already left. Frannie, this is going to take on a life of its own."

"I got a sense of that this morning. It's kind of hard to fathom I won't be around to see how it ends."

"Jesus, Frannie, don't say that. You don't know," Elizabeth said as the elevator door opened to the back-office area.

"Liz, I want to go home. I don't want to go to the hospital. If I'm going to die, I want to die in my own house where I grew up. My T-cells took a dive. I got the count yesterday afternoon and to be honest, Liz, I don't want to be alone."

"What kind of dive?" Elizabeth asked, concerned.

"They dropped by thirty. I'm at sixty-two now. So, that puts me in a very dangerous range for opportunistic infections."

"In one week? Jesus, Frannie, you're doing everything right. Have you heard from the clinical trial at Hopkins?" Elizabeth asked.

"Not yet. If I get in, I'm still going to have to leave the parish and get to Baltimore three times a week. Besides, even if I get into the study, you don't know whether you're getting the drug or the placebo." Francis hesitated and looked down at the scuffed linoleum floor of the elevator car. "Do you think I'm an asshole for wanting to go home?"

"Don't be stupid, Frannie. Let's get you home to my place and I'll set it up with Momma. Do you want Boomer to stay with you?" Elizabeth asked.

"That'd be great, Liz, thanks."

Elizabeth got Francis settled in the small windowless office the firm had given her to do her research. "Wait here, and I'll let Tom know about Boomer. He's upstairs meeting with Tony."

For the next sixty days, a dark routine enveloped the lawyers and staff working on Andrew Dolan's case. The media plan had worked perfectly. Both local and national outlets had picked up the story. The only comment from the Church was that child sexual abuse was abhorrent and occurs throughout all of society. But because the matter was now in litigation they gave no further comment, making a point that they had not been officially served with the complaint.

Francis, after a few days of rest and care from Lucy, had been able to make a short appearance on Larry King Live along with Weinstein and Courso.

The Church had wheeled out every law professor they could get on cable news to subvert the applicability of the RICO statute. Several parishioners from Dolan's New York parish came to his support but the cover-up seemed to dominate each news cycle.

As Weinstein waited for the ninety-day period to serve the complaint, Elizabeth vetted twenty-one abuse survivors, all adults, with the aid of Dolan's assignment record, school records from the clients, contemporaneous pictures and credible accounts of abuse that had striking similarities, based on the fact that the victims had never disclosed to anyone the facts of their abuse.

The most helpful instrument was a lengthy questionnaire that, when compiled, presented a chilling profile of a serial sexual predator shuttled from one archdiocese to the next. Most galling was the near identical recitation of how Dolan used music instruction to gain access to his victims.

For the two and a half months after the press conference, Weinstein arranged to have videographers visit each family and survivor to get what happened recorded in the survivor's own words. Without those individual impact statements, there was a substantial risk of creating a homogeneous reaction to the individual reports of abuse.

The one bright spot was the dozens of priests who visited the Natale home on Shepherd Street. It was a shock for both the family and the lawyers. Francis was a different face in the AIDS crisis. Priests who had been routinely spurned into forced isolation were left in many cases to fend for themselves. Most bishops were either indifferent or simply ill-suited to deal with the reality of priests having AIDS. To embrace them as priests in the ministry was a political and religious impossibility, so they were reduced to a netherworld of loneliness and death, attended to only by heroic hospice volunteers and their brother priests.

MOMMA, THAT'S A MUCH LONGER TOPIC OF CONVERSATION
As the deadline for filing the racketeering complaint against the Church drew closer, Elizabeth noticed her runs were getting longer and more painful. Her abuse memories were being triggered by her frequent visits to Francis. Both Lucy and Elizabeth avoided any conversation other than Francis' health and care, despite several of Rosemary's attempts to touch on the

chasm in their relationship in conversation. Lucy refused to allow Boomer in the house so Elizabeth had to leave him with Brother Gerald on the days when Francis could not bundle up in his wheelchair and sit on the porch. She started to feel she was being stalked by the darkness.

The tease of an early spring in Washington was replaced by a cold, thirty-four-degree mixed sleet and rain event that fouled moods and traffic throughout the city.

Brother Gerald was waiting by the back service door of the Dominican House of Studies.

"I'll be a few minutes, Johnny," Elizabeth said to one of the law firm's drivers.

"Shall I bring Boomer around for you, Miss Natale?"

"Nope, he's staying with me today. I won't be long, Johnny."

Brother Gerald was a mainstay in the running of the Dominican House. Much like a Master Supply Sergeant in the military, he made the building work. Every system and operation had his imprint on it, from the food supply to air-conditioning to maid service. Everyone from the Superior General to the newest aspirant knew to hold Brother Gerald in the highest regard.

His cherubic face beamed as he opened the door and met Elizabeth halfway from her car with an umbrella.

"Brother Gerald, you didn't have to do that," Elizabeth said as she scurried under the shelter of a large golf umbrella.

"Now aren't you glad I did," Brother Gerald chuckled.

"I am," Elizabeth said, pounding the rain off of her shoes just inside the doorway.

"Where's my boyfriend today? I thought you needed me to watch him."

"I did, but my brother seems to do better when he's around so I'm going to keep him today. I wanted to come in and thank you for pitching in. You've been a godsend."

"Tommy and I go back a long way. There aren't too many guys like him floating around. How's he doing with all the hubbub?"

"What hubbub?" Elizabeth asked.

"You know, with Bishop Clark."

"No, I don't, Brother Gerald. Who's Bishop Clark?"

"He's the head of the Military Vicariate. He fired Tommy."

"I didn't know anything about it. How can he be fired? He's a chaplain in the Air Force," Elizabeth said, surprised.

"Clark pulled Tom's endorsement, in effect putting him out of a job. Tom's ruffled a lot of feathers in all the abuse work he's been doing."

"So, are they kicking him out of the priesthood?"

"Certainly not," Brother Gerald said. "He's a Dominican priest, a member of our Order. Tom's a legend here. He's getting our highest honor in the Order next month. It's called the Catholic Courage Award, for everything he's done for abuse victims. This Bishop Clark stuff is a lot of baloney. Here's a guy really doing God's work and he gets canned. As soon as he went public, they started gunning for him."

"So, what's he doing? I can't believe he didn't say anything about this."

"The Air Force is like us, they love him. Tommy told me his colonel is going to find him something to do. I know he's a certified alcohol counselor, I think that's what he'll end up doing in the Air Force."

"Is he now? You don't say," Elizabeth said, smiling.

"Tommy's a truth teller, Elizabeth," Brother Gerald said. "Someday the world will thank him," he chuckled. "Tommy's letting the world see all of the dirty laundry. He's shining light on what happens in private. Now the Church is going to have to deal with it."

"Maybe someday soon, Brother Gerald," Elizabeth mused.

"Here, take this umbrella to get to your car. Give it back next time," Brother Gerald said.

Elizabeth hooked Boomer's leash before he got out of the car so he wouldn't be tempted to go wander in the rain before they went into Lucy's house. Elizabeth dried Boomer off on the porch and took a deep breath.

She had barely gotten into the house when Lucy boomed from the kitchen, "Elizabeth, I told you I don't want that dog in the house."

"Mother, let me fill you in on something. My brother and your son is dying upstairs. If Boomer lessens his burden, then that's how it's going to go. You can go next door and stay with Grandmom if this is such a nuisance."

Lucy tore off her apron, grabbed her cigarettes and went outside on the back porch, slamming the door behind her. Elizabeth picked up one of the throw rugs from the parlor and took Boomer upstairs. Francis was in his mother's room because of the extra space. Elizabeth peered in to see if he was sleeping.

"Are you awake?"

"Of course I'm awake, Liz. All of Shepherd Street is awake when the two of you lock horns. You know, I could never do that with Momma. You really do amaze me sometimes."

"She can be such a mule sometimes," Elizabeth said as Boomer curled up at the foot of the bed.

"Thanks for bringing him over."

"Frannie, I've been thinking. Remember at the press conference you said that bishops embrace homosexuality in the abstract until it becomes public?"

"Yes. It's true and the height of hypocrisy."

"Brother Gerald said something similar when I was talking to him today. So, based on everything you know, the bishops don't care so much about what's done in private, it's when it becomes a public embarrassment that gets their attention?"

"Yes, that's exactly what Atkinson's talking about when he uses the word 'clericalism.' Anything that knocks the Church off its pedestal, that interrupts the potential flow of money: that's when the sword of Damocles falls."

"I got it," Elizabeth said as she bent down and gave Francis a kiss. "Boomer has been fed and walked so he's good for four or five hours. I'm going down to talk to Momma then go to the office. I'll be back around dinnertime."

"Do you guys need a referee?" Francis asked.

"Maybe," Elizabeth grinned.

Elizabeth went to the back door. Lucy was huddled in a parka sitting on a beat-up fruit box. Based on the ashtray, she appeared to be on her fifth Camel.

"Momma, come inside, I want to talk to you."

"Is that another one of your orders or are you asking me," Lucy snapped.

Elizabeth had the sudden urge to grab her mother by the hair and drag her inside but fought hard to keep her tone calm. "I'm asking, Momma. I think it's important for Francis."

Lucy stamped out her cigarette and walked past Elizabeth, throwing her parka off onto the floor and taking a seat at the kitchen table.

"What do you want to say to me, Elizabeth?" Lucy asked defiantly.

Elizabeth was struck that the kitchen table that had been the focal point of so many family celebrations had now become a frequent battlefield.

"I want to have a civil conversation with you about Francis. We can have a knock down drag out fight if that's what you want, but truth be told right now I'm the hammer and you're the nail."

"How dare you be so disrespectful to me."

Elizabeth did not bite. "Like I said, I want to have a civil conversation with you."

Lucy, breathing hard, was silent for several seconds. "What about Francis?" she asked.

"I saw you at the press conference. Did you stay for the whole event?" Elizabeth asked.

"Yes."

"What did you think of what he said?" Elizabeth prodded.

"I was embarrassed, but then I thought that your father would've been very proud of him."

"Did you tell Francis that Poppa would have been proud of him?" Elizabeth asked.

"He knows you were there. Don't you think it would make him feel better, Momma?"

"Elizabeth, what do you want from me? I've been ostracized by my own Church, I'm the mother of 'that priest,' I'm like…"

"And what about Ryan," Elizabeth said, cutting her mother off. "Has he been isolated or spurned by his peers?" Elizabeth pressed.

"Of course not, he's a big shot Archbishop. Just last week he was on the cover of the Catholic Standard all puffed out like a rooster. Mark my words, Elizabeth, give it some time, they'll sweep this under the rug and life will go on. You think they're afraid of you? Let me tell you, they are not."

"What if I told you that you could change that for Francis' sake? Make them pay, make them acknowledge what they've done, say they're sorry."

"That's ridiculous, Elizabeth, you're in a fantasy."

Elizabeth bored in. "Mother, did you show Ryan any of the pictures I gave you?"

"Of course not. I burned them."

"That's exactly why I kept the originals. Did you have sex with him, Mother?"

Lucy glared at her daughter. "Yes!"

"Did you have sex with him the night those photos were taken in Stevensville, Maryland?" Elizabeth said, slapping her hand on the table.

"God forgive me, yes," Lucy said in an explosion of tears.

Elizabeth got up and went to the powder room for a box of Kleenex and glass of water. "Momma, you were used by Ryan. He knew about Dolan. He knew about Francis and me, and he sat back and left us out to fend for ourselves. Then he cultivated a relationship with you because he knew you would never say anything. Look at this logically, you burned the pictures to protect him and the Church. He doesn't even know about them, for God sakes."

Lucy wiped her face and blew her nose. "We talked about theology and philosophy and the Saints. We went to concerts and Tanglewood in the summers and then one night he kissed me and I kissed him back, and the rest, well you know the rest," Lucy moaned as she pulled her hair off her face. "What's this got to do with Francis?" Lucy asked.

"I have a plan to force a settlement for Francis and the rest of the clients. Francis wants to give any money he gets to the priest's medical fund for anyone suffering from AIDS who doesn't have a support system."

"He wants to do that?" Lucy asked.

"That's what he told me, Momma."

"If you think for one second I'm going to stand up in front of a bunch of reporters you're out of your mind," Lucy said.

"You wouldn't have to do anything like that."

"So, what are you saying? What do I have to do, then?" Lucy asked.

"Nothing. You don't have to speak or give testimony or anything like that. All you have to do is go to New York with me and sit in a lobby. That's it. You don't have to speak to a soul."

"Then what?"

"If it works out, Francis can die knowing he left a legacy."

"My God," Lucy said, resting her head on her hand. "How did we get here, Elizabeth?"

"Momma, that's a much longer topic of conversation. Maybe someday we can unpack that, but I have to get back to work and try and pull this together. I'll be back in a few hours." Elizabeth got her coat and looked outside to make sure Johnny was still there.

"You still don't drive?"

"Nope."

"Maybe you should learn," Lucy said dryly.

"Maybe I will."

"What's the dog's name?" Lucy asked as Elizabeth turned around at the door and smiled.

"His name is Boomer, Momma," she said as Lucy crossed her arms across her chest.

"Hmm. Elizabeth?"

"What, Momma, I really have to go."

"The sex was miserable. He was a putz, nothing like your father."

"Mother! I don't need any of that information!" Elizabeth said, choking back a laugh.

"I just wanted you to know."

"Okay, Momma, now I know," Elizabeth said as she walked back and gave Lucy a kiss on the cheek. "We'll talk later."

CAN WE SPEAK?

Lucy waited for twenty minutes then crept upstairs to look in on Francis. He was sound asleep. As she looked at him from the door left ajar, Boomer opened one eye and yawned. The house was silent.

Lucy stretched the long cord on the telephone in the kitchen under the porch door and closed it. She had not spoken to Ryan since the lawsuit had been filed. Lucy dialed Ryan's number, let it ring once and hung up. She waited one minute and called again. This was their code, a procedure they had used successfully for decades.

The phone was answered but no one spoke. Finally, Lucy broke the silence.

"It's Lucy. Can we speak?" she asked. The ambient sounds of the neighborhood from Lucy's back porch and the soft tones of classical music coming from Ryan's desk radio that Lucy had given him for Christmas were all that could be heard on the open line.

Ryan was alone in his office. He looked at the first-class ticket from JFK to Rome's Fiumicino airport scheduled for the weekend. His audience with the Pope was set for Monday. He remembered the first time he had taken Dolan over to the Natale home for dinner with their family. He remembered the perfume Lucy had on and Giovanni's 'toast to the dogs.'

Lucy waited. Still, no one spoke on the line.

"Cletus, if you do not intend to speak to me about what has happened between us and what's happened to my family, hang up and I will leave you to your own conscience."

Lucy pressed the phone to her ear. She heard the faint rasp of Ryan's breathing and then the click of the receiver quietly being placed on the cradle.

YOU'LL MAKE A FINE COUPLE

Elizabeth got back to the office just as Paul Weinstein was finishing up a deposition.

"Hey, can we talk?"

"Sure. Your office or mine, Liz?"

"Really, Paul? Have you seen the closet you guys put me in?" Elizabeth said in disgust.

"Right, let me get a cup of coffee and I'll be right in. Does Tony need to be here?"

"If he's around that would be good," Elizabeth said.

Elizabeth strolled around Weinstein's large office. There were plenty of pictures but only of him getting some award or honor.

"Liz, before I get Tony, can I ask you a question?"

"Sure. What is it, Paul?"

"When this is all over, do you think we could perhaps see each other socially?" Weinstein asked.

"Socially," Elizabeth said. "Like alone, socially?" Elizabeth stammered.

"Yeah, like dating."

"Paul, you're sweet to ask me properly but as you can imagine I have a fair amount of retooling to do to get to old age in one piece."

Weinstein laughed. "That's an interesting way to put it. So, let me ask another way. If and when you would like some company during your retooling process, I'd be pleased to join you."

"Paul Weinstein, you do have some romance in the deep recesses of that prickly personality," Elizabeth laughed. She directed her gaze to the floor and started to blush.

"I detect a 'but,' Elizabeth," he said, watching her.

Elizabeth drew in her bottom lip and nodded her head.

"Tom?" Weinstein asked.

"Yes."

Weinstein walked back from his doorway and stood in front of Elizabeth. "You'll make a fine couple," he said, smiling as he bent over and kissed Elizabeth on the cheek. "How do you take your coffee, Miss Natale?"

Elizabeth smiled back at him. "Black."

Tony Courso walked into Weinstein's office.

"Liz, why does the goddamn dog always stand up when I'm around?" Courso asked, eyeing Boomer.

"Because he knows you don't like him, Tony."

"What's going on, Liz?" Courso asked. "I have a full calendar this afternoon."

"I want you and Paul to go with me to New York and take a shot at settling the case."

"That's nuts. They won't settle now, McCabe hasn't earned enough money," Courso said.

"I thought you were all jacked up to try these cases, Elizabeth," Weinstein said. "What's changed?"

"Nothing has changed and I'm happy to try these cases, but I just spent two months vetting twenty-one really good cases that are all statute barred. If we file any of these, with maybe the exception of my brother, they'll just pick them off one at a time."

"That's a given, Elizabeth. I think everyone knows that. We added your brother to the Tompkins case because he wasn't only a witness, he was a victim, and he has a great equitable argument that may get a judge to rule that Francis' statute was tolled because of religious duress. Either way, we have the minor's case, Mrs. McGinty and your brother, assuming he's around for a deposition, and I don't mean that harshly."

"I know you don't, Tony," Elizabeth said. "You've been nothing but great to Francis. What if I have evidence that the Archdiocese's newly minted Archbishop was having sex with the mother of two of Dolan's victims the night his appointment was announced?"

"Then I think you should put in a call to McCabe, and we should get our butts up to New York. When do you want to go?" Courso asked, rubbing his hands together.

"I'll need a few days. I'm going to have to work this through Bobby Willis, McCabe's partner. He's the big brain in the outfit."

"I assume you'll grace Paul and me with a few more details before we go?" Courso asked.

"I promise," Elizabeth said, rushing out of her office.

THIS ISN'T A GROCERY STORE

Bob Willis was the first to greet Elizabeth as she, Courso and Weinstein walked into the lobby of McCabe, Willis & Houghton.

"Jesus, how the hell are you, Liz? It's so good to see you," Willis said as he grabbed her hand and pulled her in for a hug.

"It's great to see you, Bobby, is Audrey well?"

"She's great. She sends her regards."

"Hey, thanks for putting this together, Bobby."

"Well, I damn near had to beat Al over the head, so I hope you have something that'll move the needle. He's itching to get started."

"I get it. Please give her a kiss. Bobby, this is Tony Courso and Paul Weinstein."

"Gentlemen, pleased to meet you. Let me make sure everything is ready for you in the conference room."

Elizabeth was surprised to see McCabe talking to Father Stanton, Cardinal Hurley's secretary, but his presence signaled an opening.

"Folks, we're ready, come on in," Willis said from the conference room door.

Courso fell in behind Elizabeth as they walked across the room.

"Isn't that the woman in the pictures you showed us last week?" Courso asked.

"Yes," Elizabeth said.

"What's her name, Liz?"

"Lucy, and she's my mother."

"Jesus Christ, Liz, you left that part out last week," Courso said.

"Elizabeth, gentlemen, good to see you again. There's coffee, juice, water, some scones for those of you with a sweet tooth, just make yourself at home. If it's okay, Father Stanton's going to join us for a bit and if the Cardinal is needed, we can reach him. Is that agreeable?" McCabe asked.

"Of course," Courso said.

"Elizabeth, you've made quite a splash with this case," McCabe said. "But you know there are always two sides to a story."

"Of course, Alistair, that's why there are lawyers," she said as everyone joined in a nervous laugh. "Lawyers spend years trying to read the tea leaves of an adversary's opening gambit."

"So, what's on your mind, and who's doing the talking," McCabe said, irritating Courso right off the bat.

"All of us, Alistair. This has been a collaborative effort in my office and right now Elizabeth has the floor," Courso said, trying to blunt the advantage that McCabe had from being on his own turf.

"Alright, Elizabeth has the floor. And this probably doesn't need to be said but are we all agreed this is off the record?"

"Agreed," Courso said as he moved to the beverage service. He squeezed a lemon into a large glass of sparkling water.

"So, Elizabeth, what's on your mind?" McCabe bristled.

Elizabeth opened her briefcase, removed a stack of papers and passed stapled copies of several pages of the Official Catholic Directory around the table.

"The first page you see in the folder is a note that Father Andrew Dolan resides at Via Coeli, and we all know what that's about. But here's the interesting part... Between the time he was at Via Coeli and the time he was transferred to Washington he had four different assignments in various California parishes. The bishop who would have overseen those assignments is deceased. We can assume there were problems because I have vetted credible claims from three of the four parishes."

"You meant to say, credible as deemed by you," Willis snapped.

"That's correct, Bob, but take comfort that I'm going to leave you with VHSs of the survivors impact statements, and you can judge for yourself. May I continue?" Elizabeth snapped back.

"Please," McCabe said.

"The same pattern occurred in Washington. The bishop in charge during three different postings in Washington is also deceased."

"Am I permitted to ask a question?" Stanton asked McCabe.

"Sure. Go ahead, Father."

"Miss Natale, can I assume you've also heard from individuals from those parishes as well?" Father Stanton asked.

"Yes, Father. In those assignments, we've heard from individuals in each one of Dolan's parishes. The same pattern was found in New York. Cardinal Hurley's investiture occurred well after Andrew Dolan's last posting. The only living people who knew what was happening were Archbishop Cletus Ryan and Cardinal Hurley."

"Elizabeth, c'mon, how would you know that?" McCabe asked.

"I'm interested in that as well," Father Stanton chimed in.

"Well, we know that because we were given copies of Polaroid pictures that Dolan took when he was abusing kids. Here are photographs of the copies," Elizabeth said as she gave them each a file of the pictures.

"Who gave them to you, Liz?" Willis asked.

"A woman named Gwendolyn McGinty, she's ninety-two and she was the parish secretary for Cletus Ryan when he was the pastor at St. Francis de Sales. She overheard a physical altercation between Dolan and Ryan and Ryan's admission that he gave them to Bishop Guilfoyle who, as you will recall, is long dead. Her recall is pretty remarkable. Paul took the deposition, and he has a transcript and copy of the video for you."

"What deposition are you talking about, Elizabeth?" McCabe wailed. "We never got any notice. Christ, you won't even serve us with the complaint."

"Al, I took the deposition," Weinstein said. "I didn't give you a notice, and I'm happy to do it over, but I wasn't going to allow a ninety-two-year-old woman to walk out of the office after what she told me. And to be blunt, I wasn't going to get dicked around—excuse me, Father—trying to schedule three defendants, none of whom have been served with the complaint."

"Can you leave the VHS of the deposition, Elizabeth?" Willis asked.

"I had planned to, Bob," Elizabeth said.

"Okay, is that all that you want to share, because while we haven't been extended the courtesy of being served so we can respond to these allegations, I'm pleased to get this preview of your version of the case," McCabe snarled.

Willis had tried dozens of cases and he knew when someone overplayed his hand or, in McCabe's case, was talking out of his ass.

Anthony Courso was furious. "Mr. McCabe, allow me to suggest that we came here not to indulge you in 'free discovery.' We came here to give you a preview of how fucking awful this can get for your client and how the Pope and the Cardinal Archbishop of New York may, just may, take a rather dim view of an opportunity lost. The minor client is Elizabeth's client and we're going to follow her instructions."

"With all due respect," McCabe intoned.

Robert Willis cut him off. "Alistair, stop. I'll be trying this case. Elizabeth, what else did you want to share?" Willis asked.

"The woman sitting in the lobby is the paramour of Archbishop Cletus Ryan. Proof of a decades long sexual relationship, these pictures were taken the night his appointment was announced as the new Archbishop of Washington, D.C."

"Do you have copies?"

"No."

"Will you provide copies, Elizabeth?"

"No. You can look at them, you can call Cardinal Hurley to look at them, but after today you'll only see them with a court order or a protective order with an amended complaint."

"What's her name?" McCabe growled.

"My only suggestion to you is to call Archbishop Ryan and ask him. I'm not giving you her name. If you like, you can come behind me and I'll go through all the photographs."

Father Stanton was first to move behind Elizabeth, followed by Robert Willis. Elizabeth spread out both the pictures of Dolan abusing children and the photographs of Ryan and Lucy in two separate columns.

"Mother of God," Stanton said, walking away. "Mr. McCabe, could you direct me to a phone?"

"Father, my office is right through that door. In fact, can we take a break for ten minutes?" McCabe said.

Willis guided Elizabeth to a quiet corner as the group broke up. "Elizabeth, I assume you came with an offer."

"I did, Bobby, just keep McCabe from pissing Tony off. They're cut out of the same cloth. I'll work with you."

"Of course you'll work with me, you're holding all the cards at the moment."

Elizabeth walked over to Weinstein and Courso, who were huddled in the opposite corner of where Lucy was sitting.

"What did Willis have to say?" Weinstein asked.

"I told him we had an offer and I told him to keep McCabe and Tony from mixing it up because they were cut out of the same cloth."

"I like that, Elizabeth, very elegant job of splitting us up," Courso beamed.

"Don't kid yourself, Tony. He comes off all sweet and reasonable; you know what his nickname here is?"

"No, what?" Courso asked, excited.

"The Prince of Fucking Darkness."

Courso's face erupted in a wide grin. "Now, I ask you, where else can you get this type of entertainment? I love this shit. Okay, I'll be right back. Don't start without me, I gotta pee."

Willis walked out to the lobby. "Folks, why don't you wait in the conference room where there's more privacy? Father Stanton called Cardinal Hurley and he's on the phone with Cardinal Burke of Los Angeles, but he would like to come over in a half an hour. Is that okay?"

"Thank you, that will be fine," Courso said as the group moved into the conference room.

"Hey, Tony, you're a student of classical mythology, right?" Weinstein asked.

"Yeah, yeah, Laocoön, the Trojan Horse, beware of Greeks bearing gifts, I got it."

Forty-five minutes had stretched to an hour when Willis popped his head in. "Stanton called again. The Cardinal's coming but as you can imagine the call to California is delicate. Would you gentlemen mind if I chat with Elizabeth?"

Elizabeth looked at her partners. "We're in this together, you tell me."

"Go ahead, Liz." Courso said. "Paul, you good with that?"

"Yep, I can make some calls while we wait."

Willis chuckled as they walked down the hall to an outside terrace. "You got them pretty riled up in there, Liz."

"That was the plan, Bobby."

"So, what's the deal, Liz?" Willis asked as he took out a legal pad.

"I want the records from Via Coeli and the associated correspondence and who they went to from California to New York."

"What about Dolan's privacy rights?"

"He waived his privacy rights by virtue of the requirement to share his treatment plan with his bishop. But if it makes you happy or gives you cover, make the agreement with me. Give Dolan notice and make a proffer to the court, let him object if he's around and we'll let a judge decide. But you agree you have no standing to object on his behalf."

"What else?"

"No confidentiality."

"That's going to be hard, Liz."

"No, it's not; just agree to it because Bobby Tompkins is a minor. If you don't, it's a deal breaker and we go back to our corners and flail away at each other."

"Go ahead, how much?"

"Twenty-five million."

"Jesus fucking Christ, where did that come from?"

"There are twenty-one cases, plus my brother and the minor and the boy's parents. Do the math. You want to put a number on the punitive damages with a big city jury?" Elizabeth asked. "I think it's a deal."

"Of course you do. In what decade do you think you'll collect on a jury award, Liz?"

"Bobby, I'm all in. Of all the people in this firm you should know what that means. Can we go inside? I'm getting cold out here," she said as the pair moved down the hallway from her old office.

"What about the conflicts, Liz?"

"All waived with independent counsel, plus the clients have all agreed to a settlement mediator in an agreed upon pot. But that's none of your concern if I give you a release."

"Just so I'm clear, is the window closed on Dolan's cases?" Willis asked.

"It's open until you agree. If more people come in with credible claims, you can add them to the list and the price goes up. If they come in after, it'll be an adult case at square one. You have all your defenses, we have the documents and we have the prior clients as habit and pattern witnesses. It'll be game on."

"Okay, I understand where you are."

"There's one more thing, Bobby."

"Christ, Liz, this isn't a supermarket."

"My mother's going to bury her son. I would like to have Father Thomas Atkinson say the Funeral Mass and homily in his home parish."

"If that's a demand and a deal killer, you'll be disbarred. You know damn well I cannot negotiate who can do what in a Catholic Church."

"I know, but you can ask."

"I'll ask."

"That's it. Can I read your notes?" Elizabeth asked.

"Sure."

"And make a copy?"

"All of a sudden you don't trust me?"

"I trust you, Bobby, I'm just doing what I learned here, from you." Elizabeth hurried back to the conference room where Weinstein and Courso were waiting.

"Wow, Liz, you were with him a long time," Weinstein said, now agitated he was out of the loop.

"Don't get pissy. I made him copy his notes for you."

"Too many bulls in the same corral," Courso muttered.

Weinstein worked down the list of handwritten notes. "Liz, this is for $5 million more than we talked about."

"That's not a complaint is it, Paul?" Courso asked.

"It's not a complaint, I just think we should have talked about it."

"Paul, did you forget you agreed to me talking to Willis? I know my way around this firm. I know how they think and that little arrow pointing down on the $25 million is their fee. More than likely $1 million."

"So, he wants to save the client's fee in front of the Cardinal?" Courso asked.

"That's what I would do if I were him."

"Okay, let's see what they come back with."

"He's got something up his sleeve, I can feel it," Elizabeth said.

"Well, Elizabeth, I think you may be right. The Cardinal is chatting your mother up in the lobby."

"Those fucks," Elizabeth said as she stormed out of the room and across the lobby. "Can I help you, Cardinal Hurley?" Elizabeth asked in a less than friendly tone.

"I'm sorry if I offended some protocol, Miss Natale. I just told your mother that she has our thoughts and prayers in this difficult time with Father Natale. Good day, Mrs. Natale. I think Mr. McCabe is waiting for me."

Lucy was flushed from embarrassment. "I thought you said I wouldn't have to speak," Lucy said, upset with her daughter. "He came right up to me and knew my name."

Elizabeth knelt on the floor directly in front of Lucy. "Momma, just relax," she said in a whisper. "They must have called Ryan, because I told them I wouldn't tell them your name. That's all. Just relax. Let's see what happens. If you're not comfortable, we'll go home."

Lucy looked over her shoulder.

"Elizabeth, we're ready to reconvene," Courso called out.

"Coming, Tony." Elizabeth looked at her mother. "Momma, you'll be fine."

Willis spoke first. "I've had a few minutes to review your settlement demand with the Cardinal and by phone with the Archbishop of Los Angeles. They understand the significance of being the successors to individuals who may have, in hindsight, exercised less than optimal judgment, and appreciate your analysis. That said, even if we agree to the non-monetary aspects of your demand, the amount you're requesting at this time is exorbitant and beyond our means without cooperation from insurance and possibly Rome."

"So, if I'm reading this correctly," Elizabeth said, interrupting Willis, "Rome needs some additional motivation to settle, notwithstanding the complicity of Archbishop Guilfoyle's and Cardinal Riordan's covering up Father Dolan's crimes. Are you saying Cardinal Hurley wants to hear from my mother?" Elizabeth snapped.

"Mr. McCabe, may I?" Cardinal Hurley said.

"By all means, Your Eminence."

"Precisely, Miss Natale. This, of course, is not your problem. But believe it or not, His Holiness does not have the power to, how would you say, fire Archbishop Ryan. The Archdiocese of Washington is a separate canonical entity and while certain pressures can be brought to bear, in the end it'll be Archbishop Ryan's decision to resign and be recalled to Rome for further disposition of his ministry. He has some very particular rights under Canon Law that even the Pope has to live with. As you can imagine, he feels somewhat under attack."

Paul Weinstein was visibly agitated by Cardinal Hurley's semantic gymnastics. "Or we can agree to disagree, button up and get this case into a courtroom," Weinstein said, tapping the end of his pen on the granite topped table.

"Yes, we can," Willis shot back.

The room fell silent as Elizabeth detected a subtle nod from Courso.

"What, precisely, do you want to hear, Cardinal Hurley?"

Hurley fingered the gold crucifix that hung from his neck. "Miss Natale, today I have been requested to be the eyes and ears of His Holiness the Pope. I want to see and hear what your mother wants to share with me."

Elizabeth turned to Willis and McCabe. "What are the ground rules?" Elizabeth asked.

"What would you expect, Elizabeth?" Willis said.

"That's why I'm asking," Elizabeth said, annoyed.

"We're in a settlement conference, nothing said by either party is admissible," Willis said.

"I want to talk to Tony and Paul, can you give us a few minutes?"

"Sure, you folks stay, we'll leave, just knock on the door when you're ready," Willis said.

Elizabeth waited for the door to close. "I told her she didn't have to say a word. So, I'm not going to ask her to talk to Cardinal Hurley about a sexual relationship she had with Ryan. She'll have a goddamn heart attack."

Weinstein was livid as he paced the floor. "I think they're just stalling and want to get a preview of your mother's testimony. I've tried more cases than both of you and I'm telling you, we should tell that pompous prick to go shit in his red yarmulke."

"I don't think it's a yarmulke, Paul," Elizabeth smiled.

"Whatever, that's my take on where we are."

"Don't think I'm not listening, Paul," Courso said. "Liz, can I talk to your mother alone?"

"Why?" Elizabeth said defensively.

"Because we're the same age, and I think I'd like to give her my view on how to best proceed."

"I want to tell her again she doesn't have to do anything, and she can go home."

"Agreed," Courso said.

Elizabeth walked over to her mother and extended her hand to help her out of the leather club chair.

"Where are we going?" Lucy asked.

"In the conference room where it's more private." Elizabeth and Lucy walked arm in arm into the conference room.

"Here, Momma, sit here."

Lucy sank into the large chair.

"Momma, Tony wants to talk to you privately and tell you what has happened. I promised you that you didn't have to say anything today."

Elizabeth could see tiny beads of perspiration on Lucy's forehead. "Is that changing?" Lucy asked, looking up to Elizabeth.

"No, it's not. After Tony talks to you and you want to go home, we can grab a cab and go to Penn Station and be on our way. Are you okay with that?" Elizabeth asked.

"Yes."

Courso moved from across the table to sit next to Lucy. As soon as Weinstein and Elizabeth left, Lucy spoke first.

"Mr. Courso, I'm not part of your world. I've cooked and cleaned all my life, raised my kids as best I can and taken care of my sister and in-laws. The Catholic faith has been as important to me as my family and that's probably how I got here. That's been my life. Now my life is upside down. You are Italian, yes?" Lucy asked.

"Yes, Mrs. Natale."

"Both sides?" Lucy asked.

"Yes."

"Then you understand that when the family nest has been fouled nothing is right in the world. You *capisce*?" Lucy asked.

"I understand."

"So, what is that you want to talk to me about?" Lucy asked.

"Mrs. Natale, over your lifetime how many holiday meals have you cooked?" Courso asked.

"Pardon me?" Lucy said as she shifted her position in her seat.

"Hundreds, maybe?" Courso asked.

"At least," Lucy said.

"So, when the gravy is off a little bit you know exactly what to add, and when you stuff a chicken breast…"

"You take out the rib first," Lucy chuckled.

"Exactly," Courso bellowed as both of them started to laugh. "What about your meatballs, Mrs. Natale? How much beef do you use?" he asked.

"That's your first mistake, Mr. Courso. No beef, just pork and veal. Forty years ago, my mother-in-law told me how to do it. You should try it. You would not be the first *molto grosso* that's come around," she said as laughter filtered out of the conference room.

Elizabeth watched what was going on through the glass wall in the lobby. "What the hell are they doing in there?" Elizabeth said, shocked. "They look like they're having a party."

"I don't know, Elizabeth, Tony gets weird sometimes," Weinstein said.

Lucy sighed and settled back into her chair. "But you didn't ask to speak to me so we could compare notes on meatballs, did you, Mr. Courso?"

"No, I did not, Mrs. Natale. They're deciding whether to settle or not. My belief is that they want Archbishop Ryan recalled but they want him to resign first, most likely due to health reasons or some such crap. Cardinal Hurley has said that on this case and business with Archbishop Ryan, he has been asked to be the eyes and ears of the Pope. So, if you want to tell the Pope how he should be making meatballs and gravy, now's your chance."

Lucy looked down and folded her hands. "He actually said the eyes and ears of the Pope?" she asked.

"Those were his exact words, Mrs. Natale."

"Then I will speak to the Cardinal."

"Okay, I'll let the others know."

"On one condition, Mr. Courso."

"What's that, Mrs. Natale?"

"He says that he's the eyes and ears of the Pope. Then I'll speak to him in private, or I go home."

"Whoa, that's a twist. I can't agree without talking to the others."

"That's fine, but that's the only way I'll do it, or I go home."

"Okay, wait here. Do you want to talk to Elizabeth before?"

"No need. I can talk to her on the way home," Lucy said.

"Wait here, Mrs. Natale. I'll be right back."

Courso assembled Weinstein and Elizabeth and went to McCabe's office.

"Mrs. Natale is willing to speak to Cardinal Hurley. Alone, without any of us present."

"I don't think I like that," Willis said.

"I concur," McCabe said.

"We finally can agree on something," Weinstein snorted.

Cardinal Hurley stared at the carpet then looked up to Elizabeth. "I am happy to accept your mother's invitation."

"Cardinal Hurley, may I have a word?" McCabe said.

"If it's an objection to my sitting down with Mrs. Natale, it's duly noted. Is there anything else?" Hurley asked.

No one spoke.

Cardinal Hurley knocked on the conference room door and entered. Lucy stood when she saw the Cardinal enter.

"Please sit, Mrs. Natale; this isn't a day for formality, and thank you for agreeing to speak with me," Hurley said as he took a seat on her side of the table.

"Cardinal Hurley, I wanted to speak to you alone because this is my private business, and I was told that you were acting as the eyes and ears of our Holy Father. Is that true?" Lucy asked.

"I spoke to his Holiness earlier this afternoon. Yes, it's true."

"Then here's what I want the Holy Father to know. You have sinned. You have abandoned the faithful with lies and deceit to protect your reputation. You have done the opposite of Jesus' teachings. You haven't protected the children you're responsible for. You have allowed them to be sexually violated by your very own. Who does such things?" Lucy said, raising her finger to the Cardinal.

All of the lawyers were way out of their comfort zone watching through the glass wall.

"Shit, Liz, I guess your mom's okay; she just pointed her finger at the Cardinal."

"He has no idea what he's in for," Elizabeth said.

Lucy pushed herself back into the conference room chair and took a deep breath. "Who stands by and allows these priests in the name of God to prey on innocents? Is it possible that His Holiness thinks parents are better off not knowing their children have been sexually abused by a priest? That somehow it's better for these children to suffer in silence and be afraid to tell what happened to them? Who leaves these children alone with this horrible secret, so they can be isolated from the very people who brought them into the world? What tools did you give them to try and understand why their first sexual experience was with a Catholic priest? You have no reputation with the faithful to protect, Cardinal Hurley. You threw that away when you chose not to protect the children of God."

"Mrs. Natale, may I say something in our defense?" Hurley asked, folding his hands in his lap.

"No, you may not, because you have no defense."

Lucy got up from her chair, walked to the credenza and poured herself a glass of water.

"My son, a Catholic priest, is in the bed where my husband and I conceived him, the bed I nursed him in as an infant. He's dying from AIDS. He said to the world he hated himself so much that he made horrible decisions in the hope of finding love to extinguish the hate he had for himself. He was convinced by an evil so black that he was somehow responsible for his own father's death, my husband!" Lucy shrieked. "Francis was a loving child, a brilliant pianist. You knew about this monster before Francis was born. You, and the bishops that came before you, let it happen for your own twisted purposes. I have my own sins, Cardinal Hurley. When I look at my beautiful daughter, I see no path for her to forgive me, nor should there be. There are some sins that are unforgivable. As a loyal Catholic it was inconceivable to me she was telling the truth. What mother does not believe her grown child when she speaks the truth, knowing full well I have shared a bed with a prince of the Church? Cletus undertook this relationship with me on his own accord. My husband was gone. My children were gone, and I was lonely. We had common interests, a shared love of philosophy and theology, of music and the arts. He was curious about sex and marriage. He wanted to have intimate relations. He wrote about it in countless letters professing his conflicted love for me. We had sexual relations dozens of times. I was with him when he got word of his appointment as Archbishop. He manipulated me because he saw my loneliness, and I foolishly tried to rationalize my actions as something special while he oversaw the destruction of my family. He knew what happened to my children and he knew I would never hear from my husband Joseph what my beloved son saw happen to his sister. These are my sins, Cardinal Hurley. This is what I will be held to account for until I draw my last breath."

"Cletus spoke of you frequently," Lucy said, causing a reflexive arch in Hurley's eyebrow. "He said you were ambitious and a skilled politician, 'deft in the ways of the Roman Curia,' he used to say. He said if America was going to have a Pope in the next conclave it would be you. So, if that's true, I could be talking directly to the next Pope. Here is my message, Cardinal Hurley. Nothing you say or do will matter, unless everyone who had a hand in these crimes committed against children is openly and publicly held to account for their sins."

Lucy started to cry. Her hands trembled slightly as she fumbled with the clasp of her purse. Hurley reached into his breast pocket and offered a pressed linen handkerchief. Lucy stood up and caught the tears that had formed in her eyes and returned the handkerchief to Hurley.

"That's all I have to say, Cardinal Hurley."

Hurley's hands were trembling, his face flushed with emotion. He felt dirty and exposed, taking a deep breath to gather himself. "Before you sleep tonight, His Holiness will hear your words, Mrs. Natale. On my own accord you are not the only one who has sinned."

Lucy turned and walked to the door.

"Mrs. Natale, would you wait a moment?"

"Yes, what is it," Lucy said curtly, turning back to face Hurley.

Hurley removed his scarlet zucchetto from his head and walked to Lucy. He went down on both knees and bowed his head to the floor, kissing the top of her shoe. "On behalf of one of Our Lord's Servants, I humbly ask for your family's forgiveness, in the name of the Father, Son and Holy Spirit, Amen."

Lucy stared down at the top of Hurley's head and felt an emptiness that she had never felt before. Elizabeth was waiting for her at the door to the conference room, surrounded by the stunned gaze of the lawyers.

"Take me home, Elizabeth, I'm very tired now."

THEN LET'S GO UP THE ROAD, TOMMY

Atkinson boarded the Washington Metro at National Airport, bound for the Catholic University Station in Brookland. He was already a half hour late and walked right past Elizabeth, who was sitting on a stone bench outside the Mullen Library.

"Hey! Where you going, stranger?" Elizabeth called out.

Atkinson turned to the familiar voice, but something was out of place.

"It's me Liz," she said to Atkinson.

His eyes grew wide. "What did you do to your hair? I didn't even recognize you," Atkinson said with a grin.

"You don't like it?"

"It's just so different. I mean it was so brown and full, now it's so… short," Atkinson stuttered.

"You don't like it. It's okay; my mother thinks it makes me look stupid."

"Wow, that's harsh. It doesn't make you look stupid."

"But you don't like it."

"I didn't say that," Atkinson said, getting more uncomfortable by the second. "Do you like it? That's all that matters, Liz."

"I hate it."

"Now that's a problem, Elizabeth. C'mon, what's the big deal, it'll grow back. So, what's up with you? Your message said it was urgent. I'm up here a day early so I'm all yours. By the way, where's Boomer?"

"Brother Gerald's keeping an eye on him until we get over there. Hmm, let's see, what's up with me? Well, it took a month of Paul and me going nonstop to close out the Dolan case and get the clients all squared away. I'm getting my apartment ready to sublet so I can be closer to your post."

"That's a good thing," Tom said warmly.

"Let's see. Tony's actually practicing law and he and Paul are both going full tilt on abuse cases. I'll bet it's a good ten-year run."

"I'd bet twenty. I'm sure your clients were really happy with the result in Dolan's case."

"I think they were surprised to see all that money in one spot, but they all had the look on their face, like now what do I do? It kinda blew me away a bit," Elizabeth said. "Oh, you'll like this."

"What?"

"I learned how to drive."

"You're kidding! That's great. Who taught you how to drive?"

"Brother Gerald, he was great."

"Oh, that's such a hoot. I'm proud of you, Liz. Do you have a car?" Atkinson asked.

"I have a vehicle," Elizabeth said coyly.

"What's that mean?"

"You'll see it when we walk over, but Boomer loves it."

"And you and your mom, how's that going?"

"I'd say that's a work in progress. Right after Frannie's funeral we were spending a lot of time just doing things. Getting all his stuff together, thank you cards, hospital bills. Momma's doing AIDS volunteer work, so that's pretty neat. She's still talking about your homily at Frannie's Mass."

"I still can't believe they let me do it," Atkinson said.

"The Natale women can be very persuasive, Father Atkinson," Elizabeth said, laughing. "But Momma and I are really different; I just don't know that we can get past all the bullshit. I think we need some space. I know I need some space. Tony did form Frannie's foundation, so that took time because we were getting contributions."

"That was a beautiful thing your brother did."

"He was a beautiful guy, Tommy," she said, wiping the tears off her cheeks with her sleeve. "What else? Oh, I forgot. You'll love this one," Elizabeth chuckled. "Aunt Rose brought her girlfriend to Sunday dinner. So, here's the picture: me, my mother, my ninety-four-year-old grandmother, my aunt and her girlfriend, eating meatballs, eggplant and pasta. It was right out of a *Seinfeld* episode," Elizabeth said, her laugh fading to a distant gaze across the Mullen Library quad. "Let's go get Boomer. I want to show you my ride."

The pair walked between Gibbons and O'Connell Hall toward Michigan Avenue and the Dominican House. Elizabeth looked down as Atkinson grabbed her hand for the walk over to the Dominican House.

"Don't you think you're in enough trouble, Father Atkinson?" Elizabeth said.

"I'm over twenty-one," Atkinson said, smiling.

As they rounded the corner, Atkinson spotted Boomer sitting in the driver's seat of a new Ford Crew Cab F-250 Super Duty pickup truck.

"You've got to be kidding me! That's a kick ass work truck. Do you really drive this beast?" Atkinson gushed.

"I do, but not for long. Do you really like it, Tommy?" Elizabeth asked as Atkinson slid behind the driver's wheel.

"Are you kidding me, it's beautiful! Look at the room in here," he said as Boomer licked the side of his face.

"Good, because it's for you," Elizabeth said, reaching into her satchel and pulling out the title to show him.

Atkinson stared at the title in disbelief.

"See? It's got your name on it, Tommy."

"Oh, my God, Elizabeth, you're unbelievable. I can't believe you did all this. Thank you. This is unbelievable."

"Get in and start it up," Elizabeth said, her voice starting to crack.

As Atkinson started up the engine to check the motorized side view mirror, he noticed Elizabeth was crying.

"What's wrong? Why are you crying, Liz?" Atkinson asked. Perplexed, he turned off the engine.

"I relapsed, Tommy."

"Shit, Liz, why didn't you call?"

"I was afraid."

"Afraid of what?"

"I don't know. I was embarrassed. I was afraid you would be mad at me. I was just afraid," Elizabeth sobbed.

"Did something happen, Liz?"

"No, it wasn't one thing. It was everything—the case, Frannie, the funeral, my mother, going to the cemetery every day."

"Are you sober now?" Atkinson asked.

"More or less."

"So, how many days were you drinking?"

"For about the last two weeks. I'd get Boomer and pack some food and water for him, and we'd walk to the liquor store and then to the park and I would drink a fifth of vodka."

"So, why did you stop?"

"I fell asleep in the park and Boomer wandered off, and when I woke up, I saw he was gone and I panicked," Elizabeth said sobbing.

"So, how did you get him back?" Atkinson asked.

"I stayed at the park twenty-four/seven for three days asking everyone I saw and giving out pictures. Then a police officer told me he found him and sent him to the pound on New York Avenue."

"You were lucky you got him back."

"I know," Elizabeth wailed, falling into his arms. "I'm so sorry."

"Liz, you got him back. That's all that matters. He's right here in the truck.

"You trusted me with him, and I fucked up!" Elizabeth shouted, folding over in the passenger seat.

"Okay, I got it. So, what's the plan?" Atkinson said as he rubbed her back.

Elizabeth slowly started to catch her breath between spasms of painful hiccups. "I called a guy whose card I kept, Sol Reich. He's a clinical psychologist. We talked for about four hours, and he referred me to an inpatient hospital. I called them and I talked to their intake people, and they have a bed if I come before eight tonight. It's in Havre de Grace, Maryland."

"Father Martins Ashley," Atkinson smiled.

"How did you know?" Elizabeth asked.

"Well, I was a patient there ten years ago and I've given several talks there since as an alumnus. That's a six-month program, you know that, right? It's very intense, but if you do the work, you'll be on your way," Atkinson said.

"I know, I wanted you to come up here to ask you to be my sponsor, that's why I said it was urgent. I have no right to ask, but I wanted to know if you would wait for me to get out," Elizabeth said.

"That's interesting, Liz, because I've been thinking about what I was actually going to say to you."

"Is there a problem, Tommy?"

"It could be a problem."

"You're scaring me, Tommy."

"There's nothing to be scared about. Now listen to me. In the last talk I gave at Father Martins Ashley, I noticed a curious intersection of the words of Albert Camus, Teddy Roosevelt and Willian Henley. Liz, life truly is the sum of our choices. You really have entered Roosevelt's arena. Your face will be marred with sweat, blood and tears in pursuit of a worthy cause to end up as Henley did, in the face of adversity-"

Elizabeth interrupted Atkinson to finish the quote. "The captain of your fate and the master of your soul."

"Precisely," Atkinson said, smiling.

"I get it, Tommy, and I also get we will never be together unless I can stay sober."

"Elizabeth, just engage with whatever is in front of you. Nothing else will matter. Remember this. Greatness is not reserved for the few or the privileged. Greatness is found everywhere where there are individuals trying to find it. You got to believe that." Atkinson reached behind him, got his briefcase and took out his pocket notebook.

"Where's your notebook?" he asked.

"In the back in my pack."

"Could you get it out?"

Atkinson went to the last numbered page, tore it out and handed it to Elizabeth. "Keep it with you, Liz, it'll help you keep your focus. Here's my book. You take mine and put that page in it. I'll take yours and in six months we'll trade."

Elizabeth fell into his arms, her body heaving with emotion. She buried her head into his chest for several minutes. Seeing her distress, Boomer started to nose whistle.

"So, we going up the road? Boomer's getting worried," Atkinson said.

Elizabeth pulled her head off his chest, wiping the tears off her face.

"Will you be my sponsor?" Elizabeth asked. "And will you bring Boomer when I can have visitors?"

Atkinson smiled at Elizabeth and grabbed her hand. "Elizabeth Natale, have I ever said no to you?" he answered as he turned on the radio and moved into traffic.

"Then let's go up the road, Tommy. Because after I'm done with this, I've got a lot of work to do."

Epilogue

It will take decades, perhaps longer, for historians to write the full accounting of the sex abuse crisis in the Catholic Church. Secrecy and fear of scandal still exist. Unnamed Bishops, Cardinals and priests have yet to be publicly identified as to their complicity in the furtherance of the conspiracy. Grand Jury investigators continue to wade through the "hide-the-ball" mentality of the hierarchal Church.

In fact, an entire vocabulary was instituted to facilitate the cover-up. Words like "immaturity" described sexual contact with minors. "Mistakes in judgment" described incidents of rape. "Scandal," a canonical entity, was used to describe the preservation of a criminal enterprise, the object of which was the protection of serial sexual predators and the reputation of the hierarchal power structure.

The prevalence and cover-up of sexual crimes committed against children, which has shredded the reputation of the institutional Church, has been a study in juxtaposition. How is it possible that in the early 1980s mainstream America was unaware of the incidence of priests and other religious sexually assaulting children, when the 1917 Code of Canon Law not only discusses the matter but has an internal criminal process to prosecute the clerical offender? Likewise, the pro-life movement is both a political and religious force of nature for the protection of the unborn, but the safety and well-being of children already here on the planet is an afterthought, leaving them

583

and their families to fend for themselves against the horrors of sexual abuse. Then, of course, there is the money. It is quite an easy task to raise significant funding for the rights of the unborn—much harder to raise funds for the Catholic hierarchy to facilitate and conceal a conspiracy of silence for centuries.

Throughout the muck of the last forty years, serious effort has been made by Catholic apologists to shift attention from the "Catholic scandal" to the incidence of sexual abuse in society at large. The Boy Scouts were frequently used as a diversion by the Church, which was quick to point out that other institutions had their own problems with sexual predators. Other Christian denominations were highlighted for their failures. Rabbinical "Beth din, or "Bet din" tribunals, which privately dispensed "justice" were also targets. Yes, yes, and yes. All true. All have had issues with sexual predators. Aside from being an irrelevant rationalization, (we are talking about serious felonies committed against children), the chief difference is that Catholic leaders thought they knew better. Their cultural elitism, hubris and belief that the hierarchy is subject to a different moral standard than the rest of us was, in the end, the beginning of their undoing. In the past, I have likened it to a transaction. If, by theological design, you become the oracle of eternal salvation and you have believers, any scandal that would diminish your moral currency severely weakens your ability to maintain control of the faithful. A scandal, which implicates Church leadership, involving the sexual abuse of children would also severely impact your ability to raise money for the enterprise. Coupled with an absurd clerical structure that positions the laity as an inferior subset of humanity, the alchemy of the crisis became self-perpetuating.

It is equally difficult to reconcile the rush to canonize Pope John Paul II on April 27, 2014, as a saint, with the protection he and other Vatican insiders offered former Cardinal Theodore McCarrick and Marcial Maciel Degollado, founder of the Legionnaires of Christ.

Both men were widely acknowledged to be sexual predators, and both were contributing substantial funds to Vatican operatives. After reports of prior settlements and new claims against McCarrick surfaced, a Vatican Tribunal convened in 2018. The Vatican tribunal found that there was credible evidence to return Cardinal Theodore Edgar McCarrick to the lay state, and strip him of all priestly faculties and status. In effect, McCarrick was exiled. But a lingering question remained. How was it possible that a sexual predator, in this case a high-ranking prince of the Church and prolific fundraiser, avoided detection for so long? The short answer was—he did not. The long answer is revealed by an exhaustive factual record uncovered by Jeffrey Lena. Lena was not a Vatican plutocrat. He was a lawyer from Los Angeles; a third party, not a priest, and not an insider. Lena was given carte blanch investigative power on behalf of Pope Francis himself to document how it happened. In the doorstop sized report, which is now widely available on the internet, Lena lays out, in excruciating detail, the evidence of the "Holy See's Institutional Knowledge and Decision-Making Related to Former Cardinal Theodore Edgar McCarrick." After being questioned by Lena several times in October and November 2020 on a case I handled against McCarrick, I not so subtlety cajoled him to label the conduct he was uncovering. Unfortunately, he declined, indicating that it was not his mandate. Lena's mandate aside the document itself is an important contribution to the history of the scandal. Its voice is in clear unembellished prose, and it's not pretty. I would urge anyone who wants to take a deep dive into how internal decisions at the highest levels are made, or in this case not made, to read the McCarrick report. It offers a rare and historic window into hierarchal thinking. Suffice it to say that money, power, and fear of scandal trumped truth and the protection of sexual abuse survivors. Clearly, history has documented John Paul II's accomplishments, and rightly so. However, his blind spot on the clerical sexual abuse scandal raises significant questions on the timing of the current Pope's actions in moving John Paul II to sainthood. The evidence in the Lena report supports the argument that the clumsy attempt to change the narrative should not have happened. On July 29, 2021, McCarrick was criminally charged with three counts of indecent sexual assault of a minor over fourteen years old in Dedham, Massachusetts. McCarrick was arraigned on the charges on September 3, 2021. He is the first US Cardinal to be criminally charged with sexual assault of a minor.

While Act of Faith ends in 1994, the sordid legacy of the cover-up has fueled on-going criminal Grand Jury reports, investigative panels, trials, settlements, Diocesan bankruptcies and criminal prosecutions, and has prompted numerous state legislatures to reopen Statutes of Limitations. Just this past May 2021, prosecutor Anthony Gulluni of Hampden, Massachusetts announced he was prepared to issue arrest warrants against former priest Richard Lavigne for the murder of then thirteen-year-old Danny Croteau in 1972. Long considered the prime suspect in the murder, Lavigne died the very day of Gulluni's announcement.

Costs to the institutional church have surpassed $4 billion. The damage to its reputation cannot be quantified. What has not happened is the full disgorgement of the institutional evidence of the cover-up and the incidence of sexual abuse. The documents of the conspiracy need to see the light of day. Long lists of those "credibly accused" simply will not do. In simplistic terms, history requires the names of people who knew, what they knew and when they knew it. Perhaps the most stunning example of historical juxtaposition is that despite centuries of cover-up of the sexual crimes committed against children, the institutional church has been permitted to maintain its tax-exempt status as a charitable religious entity. The scandal is far from over. More states will open windows for Statutes of Limitations to be revived, more Dioceses will seek shelter in bankruptcy courts and more history will be made by the facts that are uncovered.

It seems clear that the people who actually set this horrible scandal in motion did not view children as one of their constituencies. That should give everyone pause. Notwithstanding what the Bible says about children, the men of the hierarchy were not parents, or those who were believed that the repercussions of scandal trumped the well-being of their own children. They did not hold their infants for the first time and experience the raw, emotional realization that they would willingly sacrifice their own lives to save the lives of their children. Can that bond prove to be a useful litmus test as to whether the life of a child is more important than the reputation of an institution? If it is, the men of the Church have failed that test. Perhaps in the future, knowing now what is at stake, the life of a child will be the Church's first priority. We'll see.

Andover, Vermont, September 2021

Acknowledgments

It may sound odd, but the dozens of rejections from literary agents, publishers and publicists proved to be invaluable. A few provided their reasons: "it's too long," "maybe a trilogy," "looks more like a screenplay," "the pandemic has thrown the industry on its head," and my favorite, "readers today do not have the attention span to get through your book." And then there was this one from a very prestigious agency: "Lot to like here, great characters, but the field has been ploughed." They all said they liked it. (I was skeptical). They all wished me luck, and some apologized for their months late response assuming I was already represented. (I was not).

My training as a trial lawyer helped with the rejections. Judges, adversaries, corporations, and juries say no all the time. Finishing became the goal, with a story that put the reader in the space and time of the unfolding crisis. So, after applying copious amounts of salve to a wounded ego, I am truly grateful. Something I knew was reinforced in real time. Don't quit.

Tom Doyle, the prime mover and whistle blower in the early days of the crisis and the resident historian of the last thirty-five years, proved to be invaluable for reading and re-reading the manuscript for the accuracy of the period ambience I was attempting to re-create. I also want to thank him for sharing his life with me. He is a true friend, and valued colleague. For a comprehensive list of source material see his bibliography at the following Bishops Accountability link. https://www.bishop-accountability.org/Doyle-Bibliography/

If you have gotten this far in the book, you realize I made Jason Berry's book, *Lead Us Not Into Temptation,* a character in *Act of Faith.* I knew Jason long before we actually met. Throughout the 1990s, I sat with hundreds of clients, siblings and parents trying to make sense of how and why we were brought together. So many were shocked to find out that "their experience" was not out of the norm. Thousands of people were suffering, and they were far from alone. I purchased many copies to give to clients, as I saw Jason's book become an anchor in the same way a therapist provides a structure and context for an individual's experience. Over the years, a friendship developed. *Lead Us Not Into Temptation* did not undo the clients' pain, but it did provide some emotional side boards, providing clarity as to how the century's old Catholic clergy sex abuse scandal evolved. Along the way, Jason provided expert advice and critical suggestions for character development in this manuscript. Every successful writer understands and embraces the concept of "kill your darlings." When I first heard the phase I thought it was heresy. "How is it possible that elegant paragraphs would be unceremoniously slashed out of the manuscript by the ugly blue pen?" It was painful, but I finally got with the program. Earning his journalistic chops as a reporter, Jason has excelled as a historical narrative writer and has published several well-received books and documentary films. I cannot thank him enough.

Barbara Blaine was instrumental in the effort to get all this down on paper. She would frequently call and chide me with the fact I was not getting any younger. She was one of the earliest clients that I represented, and our friendship grew as she became an international advocate for the rights and safety of abuse survivors through her work at SNAP (Survivors Network of Those Abused by Priests) and the fledgling The Accountability Project. I owe her much as she was the first person to read the abuse scenes in *Act of Faith*. They had to pass though her lens and speak credibly to those feelings only survivors know. She was my sounding board. Her unexpected passing in 2017 was a blow to everyone who knew and loved her.

The manuscript was sent to many colleagues and friends. Several must be noted for their willingness to provide critical feedback on the flow of the story. Miles and Elaine Alexander from Atlanta provided texture on both "big law" and several of the personalities depicted. John DeDakis is a superb writing coach, author and lecturer and was an early reviewer of the entire manuscript. His critical feedback drove all of the early revisions. Anne Barrett-Doyle, Terry McKiernan, Richard Sipe, Marianne Sipe, M.D., Alan and Susan Klien, Annette Swanson, Robert and Teri DiMedio, Joelle Casteix, David Clohessy, Susan Leader, Barbara Dorris, Patricia Keelin, Michael Buric, lent their time and real-world experiences to critically comment on the way the material resonated with the reader. I knew what the history was, but their assistance helped me choose the right words to convey that history. After all, at the intersection of the sacred and the profane is the dissonance created by the scandal as facilitated by the so-called "men of God." To that end, to visually create that image, I am indebted to Kalli O'Malley, a first-rate attorney in her own right, for the original concept sketch of the cover artwork.

I have leaned on William E. Foote PhD for years. Bill is a world class clinical psychologist, expert witness, author and friend. He always took my calls and always kept me straight when talking about pathologies. Lucille Marchisello, a first-rate pianist and teacher parsed through all of the music scenes for accuracy and mood.

In order for anyone to complete a project as complex as a multi-generational novel chronicling the characters' place in the chaos of a worldwide scandal, the infrastructure that supports the writer is key. Ida Mae Specker edited the entire manuscript. She was a one-stop shop in that her talents spanned both music as a performing artist and teacher, as well as writer, producer and editor. The most important attribute was her honest response to my almost daily question – "does this make sense to you?"

Another key source of support were the lawyers. Lisa Pearson of Kilpatrick Townsend graciously gave her time and wise counsel. Geoff Budden, from St. John's Newfoundland, Paul Mones, Terry Giles and Katherine Freberg, the best law partners anyone could ask for, Jeff Anderson, Ed Ross, my deceased former partner, Slade McLaughlin, Lewis Bornstein, David Carter, James Stang, Hon. Charles (Tim) McCoy Jr. (ret), Hon. Peter D. Litchman (ret.), Michael Dowd, Irwin Zalkin, Anthony DeMarco, Ray Boucher, Tim Hale, Richard Serbin and Marci Hamilton. These individuals, and quite honestly many more, answered my questions and pushed me along. Others helped me remember details of years past that greatly contributed to the sound and feel of *Act of Faith*. And to the defense bar, for those who were willing to talk to me but preferred not to be named, you know who you are. Thank you.

A special debt of gratitude is owed to Carol Kwoka, my legal assistant for nearly twenty-five years. Carol passed away on May 30, 2007. Without compromise, she would translate the fragmented stories of unspeakable memories into a cohesive narrative that focused each survivor, providing me the tools to take up their cause.

As every case concluded, the file would end up in Carol's office. She would prepare the file for storage, returning original documents to clients, indexing the file and paying any remaining costs. What I found out later, shortly before her death, was that Carol had been, for years, stripping the files of any notes I had made, labeling each one as to its source. So, but for Carol, I'm not certain I would have been able "to gather in one place, thousands of notes, names and cryptic phrases written on calendars, journals and other bits of ephemera that I had carted around with me for decades," that, is the rest of the story.

Never having heard the term beta-readers before 2016, I did know that there was core group of people whom I wanted to involve in the very first of many iterations of the material. I had confidence that that they would not hold anything back, and they didn't. The first of course was my wife Helen, my two older brothers Lou and John, and their spouses Catherine and Ronnie. You all have been unwavering in your support, and generous in the time you have given me. At our age, time is a precious gift.

Finally, to all of my former clients. Without you and your courage nothing would have been possible.

Author's Notes

The Annunciation tympanum on the south front of the Basilica of the National Shrine of the Immaculate Conception, which plays a vital role in the early chapters of *Act of Faith*, was indeed designed by John Angel. The carving of the design as is indicated on the credit panel of the actual sculpture was executed by J.A. Campo. The National Shrine was designated a minor Basilica on October 12, 1990.

Much of the inspiration for the Natale stone carving family came from my youth. I grew up in the northeast section of Little Rome and had an almost daily view of how stone carvers transformed limestone into art. I caught the public architecture bug early. As an altar server at Campus School and at the National Shrine of the Immaculate Conception in the late 1950s and early 1960s, I had a front row seat of how the iconography evolved. My Uncle Joe Cuozzo, who lived next door, worked on the Iwo Jima Memorial in Arlington, Virginia, while my Uncle Jerry (Gerardo) Rubino was a stone mason at the National Shrine and many other places. I remember the limestone dust in their hair and their canvas tool bags filled with hammers, chisels, hand drills and pitches when they would come home from work. I remember them relaxing with a beer on late summer afternoons in the backyard. They worked hard. I wish I had asked more questions.

As a teenager, I would frequently hang out in the quad adjacent to the Mullen Library and the parking lot behind the carver's shed at the Washington National Cathedral to watch how the buildings were artistically transformed. Further inspiration was drawn from the field notes and technical descriptions and interviews conducted by Marjorie Hunt that are contained in her magnificent book *The Stone Carvers*, Smithsonian Press, 1999. There she takes the reader into the art form of stone carving through the lens of the people who created the masterpiece of Washington's National Cathedral.

Barbara Blaine appears as herself.

David Clohessy appears as himself.

Jeff Anderson appears as himself.

Lead Us Not Into Temptation, a critically acclaimed book, was written by Jason Berry in 1994 and remains one of the seminal texts on the history of the Catholic Clergy sex abuse scandal.

Cover Art: Carlos Oviedo,
"The Cardinal's Sin" Puerto Vallarta, JAL Mexico
Cover Art Concept Sketch, Kalli O'Malley